Also by Sandra Brown

Unspeakable
White Hot
Chill Factor
The Alibi
Standoff

About the author

Sandra Brown is the author of more than sixty books, of which over fifty were *New York Times* bestsellers, including *Unspeakable*, *The Crush*, *Envy*, *The Switch*, *Standoff*, *French Silk*, *Fat Tuesday*, *Exclusive*, *The Witness*, *Charade*, *Where There's Smoke*, and *Hello, Darkness*. Her novels have been published in more than thirty languages. She and her husband divide their time between homes in Texas and South Carolina.

SANDRA BROWN

The Crush

Hello, Darkness

HODDER

The Crush Copyright © 2002 by Sandra Brown
Hello, Darkness Copyright © 2003 by Sandra Brown

The Crush first published in Great Britain in 2002
by Hodder and Stoughton
Hello, Darkness first published in Great Britain in 2003
by Hodder and Stoughton
This omnibus edition first published in 2006 by Hodder and Stoughton
A division of Hodder Headline

A Hodder paperback

2

A CIP catalogue record for this title
is available from the British Library

ISBN 0 340 92217 6

Printed and bound in Great Britain by
Clays Ltd, St Ives plc

Hodder Headline's policy is to use papers that are natural,
renewable and recyclable products and made from wood grown
in sustainable forests. The logging and manufacturing processes
are expected to conform to the environmental regulations
of the country of origin

Hodder and Stoughton Ltd
A division of Hodder Headline
338 Euston Road
London NW1 3BH

THE CRUSH

Prologue

Dr. Lee Howell's home telephone rang at 2:07 A.M.

His wife, Myrna, who was sleeping beside him, grumbled into her pillow. "Who's that? You're not on call tonight."

The Howells had been in bed barely an hour. Their poolside party had broken up around midnight. By the time they'd gathered up the debris and empty margarita glasses, stored the perishable leftovers in the fridge, and visited their sleeping son's room to give him a good-night kiss, it was nearing one o'clock.

As they undressed they had congratulated themselves on hosting a successful get-together. The grilled steaks had been only a little tough, and the new electric mosquito zapper had sizzled all evening, keeping the insect population to a minimum. All things considered, a good party.

The Howells had felt mellow but agreed that they were too exhausted even to think about having sex, so they'd kissed each other good night, then turned to their respective sides of the bed and gone to sleep.

Despite the shortness of time Dr. Howell had been asleep, his slumber, assisted by several margaritas, had been deep and dreamless. Yet when the telephone rang he was instantly awake, alert, and responsive, as years of conditioning had trained him to be. He reached for the phone. "Sorry, hon. A patient may have taken a bad turn."

She nodded grudging assent into her pillow. Her husband's reputation as an excellent surgeon wasn't based solely on his operating-room skills. He was dedicated to his patients and interested in their well-being before, during, and after their surgeries.

Although it was unusual for him to be telephoned at home in the middle of the night when he wasn't the doctor on call, it wasn't altogether rare. This inconvenience was one of the small prices Mrs. Howell was willing to pay for the privilege of being married to the man she loved who also happened to be in demand and well respected in his field.

"Hello?"

He listened for several moments, then kicked off the covers and swung his feet to the floor. "How many?" Then, "Jesus. Okay, all right. I'm on my way." He hung up and left the bed.

"What?"

"I've gotta go." He didn't turn on the lamp as he moved toward the chair where he'd left the pair of Dockers he'd been wearing earlier in the evening. "Everybody on staff has been called in."

Mrs. Howell came up on one elbow. "What's happened?"

Serving a busy metropolitan area, Tarrant General

Hospital was constantly on alert to handle major disasters. The staff had been trained to provide immediate emergency treatment to victims of airplane crashes, tornadoes, terrorist attacks. By comparison this night's emergency was mundane.

"Big pileup in the mix-master. Several vehicles involved." Howell shoved his bare feet into a pair of Dock-Sides, which he loved and his missus despised. He had owned those shoes for as long as she had known him and refused to part with them, saying the leather was just now molding to his feet and becoming comfortable.

"A real mess. A tanker trailer overturned and it's burning," he said as he pulled his golf shirt over his head. "Dozens of casualties, and most are being sent to our emergency room."

He strapped on his wristwatch and clipped his pager to the waistband of his slacks, then leaned down to kiss her. Missing her mouth, he caught her between nose and cheek. "If I'm still there at breakfast time, I'll call and update you. Go back to sleep."

As her head resettled into the pillow, she murmured, "Be careful."

"Always am."

Before he got downstairs, she had already fallen back to sleep.

Malcomb Lutey finished reading Chapter 3 of his newest science-fiction thriller. It was about an airborne virus that within hours of being inhaled turned the internal organs of human beings into a black, oily goo.

As he read about the unaware yet doomed blond Parisian hooker, he picked at the pimple on his cheek, which his mother had admonished him to leave alone.

"That only makes it worse, Malcomb. Until you start picking at it, it's not even noticeable."

Yeah, right. The pimple was way beyond "noticeable." It was the current peak on the ever-evolving, knobby red mountain range that comprised his face. This severe, scar-producing acne had ushered in Malcomb's adolescence and for the past fifteen years had defied every treatment, topical or oral, either prescribed or purchased over the counter.

His mother blamed this chronic condition on poor diet, poor hygiene, and poor sleep habits. On more than one occasion she had hinted that masturbation might be the cause. Whatever her current hypothesis, it invariably suggested that Malcomb was somehow responsible.

The frustrated dermatologist who had valiantly but unsuccessfully treated him had offered up different, but as many, theories on why Malcomb was cursed with the facial topography of a Halloween mask. Bottom line: Nobody knew.

As if the acne weren't enough to keep his self-esteem at gutter level, Malcomb's physique was another misfortune. He was pencil thin. Supermodels who were paid to look undernourished would envy his metabolism, which seemed to have a profound aversion to calories.

Last but no less genetically dire was his kinky, carrot-colored hair. The fiery thatch had the density and texture of steel wool and had been the bane of his existence long before the onset of acute acne.

Malcomb's odd appearance, and the shyness it had bred, made him feel a misfit.

Except at his job. It was night work. And it was solitary. Darkness and solitude were his two favorite things. Darkness dulled his vibrant coloring to a more normal hue and helped to obscure his acne. Solitude was part and parcel of being a security guard.

His mother didn't approve of his career choice. She constantly nagged him to consider making a change. "Out there all by yourself night after night," she often said, tsking and shaking her head. "If you work alone, how're you ever going to meet anybody?"

Duh, Mother. That's the point. This was Malcomb's standard comeback—although he lacked the courage to say it out loud.

Working the graveyard shift meant fewer times he had to conduct a conversation with someone who was trying hard not to stare at his face. Working through the night also allowed him to sleep during most of the hated daylight hours when his hair took on the brilliance of a Day-Glo orange Magic Marker. He dreaded the two nights a week he was off, when he had to endure his mother's harping about his being his own worst enemy. The recurring theme of her lectures was that if he were more open to people he would have more friends.

"You've got a lot to offer, Malcomb. Why don't you go out like other people your age? If you were friendlier, you might even meet a nice young lady."

Sure he would.

Mother scoffed at him for reading science fiction but *she* was the one living in a dream world.

His post at Tarrant General Hospital was the doctors' parking lot. To the other guards it was the least desirable post, but Malcomb preferred it. There wasn't a lot of activity at night. Business didn't pick up, so to speak, until early morning when the doctors began to trickle in. Most hadn't even arrived when he clocked out at seven in the morning.

However, this being a Friday night, there were more cars in the lot than on a weeknight. Invariably the weekend increased the traffic in the emergency room, so doctors came and went at all hours. Just a few minutes ago Dr. Howell had driven up to the gate and disengaged the arm with the transmitter he kept clipped to his sun visor.

Dr. Howell was okay. He never looked past Malcomb as though he weren't there, and sometimes he even waved at him as he passed the guard shack. Howell didn't get all bent out of shape if the arm failed to disengage and Malcomb had to release it manually from inside the shack. Dr. Howell seemed like a regular guy, not snotty at all. Not like some of those rich assholes who acted so hoity-toity as they drummed their fingers on their padded steering wheels, impatiently waiting for the arm of the gate to rise so they could speed through as though they had someplace to be and something to do that was real important.

Malcomb read the first page of Chapter 4. As expected, the Parisian blond hooker succumbed mid-coitus. She died in the throes of agony and grotesque vomiting, but Malcomb's sympathies were with her hapless customer. Talk about a major bummer.

He turned the book facedown on the counter, straightened and stretched his spine, and sought a more comfortable position on his stool. As he did, he happened to catch his reflection in the window glass. The pimple was growing by the second. Already it was a monument of pus. Disgusted by his image, he focused his eyes on the parking lot beyond.

Mercury-vapor lights were strategically spaced so that most of the lot was well lighted. The shadows were deep only beneath the landscaping that formed its perimeter. Nothing had changed since the last time Malcomb had looked out, except for the addition of Dr. Howell's silver Beemer—third row, second car. He could see the gleaming roof of it. Dr. Howell kept his car in showroom condition. Malcomb would too if he could afford a set of wheels like that.

He returned to his novel but had only read a couple of paragraphs when something odd occurred to him. He looked toward Dr. Howell's Beemer again. His pale eyebrows furrowed with puzzlement. How had he missed Dr. Howell when he had walked past the shack?

In order to reach the sidewalk that led to the nearest employee entrance, one had to come within yards of the shack. It had become second nature for Malcomb to note when someone came past, either heading toward the building or returning to his car. There was a correlation. One either left the building and then shortly drove away in his car, or drove into the parking lot and then shortly passed the shack on his way into the building. Malcomb subconsciously kept track.

Curious, he marked his page and set the book beneath the counter next to the sack lunch his mother had packed for him. He tugged the brim of his uniform hat a little lower. If he were forced to talk to someone, even someone as easygoing as Dr. Howell, he didn't want to subject him to his unsightly face any more than necessary. The brim of his hat provided an extra layer of concealing shadow.

As he stepped from the shack's air-conditioned interior he didn't notice any decrease in the outdoor temperature since making his last rounds. August in Texas. Almost as hot in the wee hours as at high noon. Heat from the asphalt came up through the rubber soles of his shoes, which made virtually no sound as he walked past the first row of cars, then the second. At the end of the third row, he paused.

For the first time since taking this job almost five years ago, he felt a prickle of apprehension. Nothing untoward had ever taken place on his shift. A couple months ago a guard in the main building had had to subdue a man who was threatening a nurse with a butcher knife. Last New Year's Eve a guard had been summoned to break up a fist-fight between fathers over which of their newborns had been the first baby of the new year and therefore winner of several prizes.

Thankfully, Malcomb hadn't been involved in either incident. Reportedly they had drawn crowds. He would have been mortified by the attention. The only crisis he'd ever experienced while on duty was a dressing-down from a neurosurgeon who had returned to his Jag to discover that it had a flat tire. For reasons still unknown to Mal-comb, the surgeon had held him responsible.

So far, his shifts had been luckily uneventful. He couldn't account for his uneasiness now. Suddenly his good friend Darkness no longer seemed as benevolent. He glanced around warily, even looking back behind him the way he'd just come.

The parking lot was as silent and still as a tomb—which at the moment wasn't a comforting analogy. Nothing moved, not even the leaves on the surrounding trees. Nothing appeared out of the ordinary.

Nevertheless, Malcomb's voice quavered slightly as he called out, "Dr. Howell?"

He didn't want to sneak up on the man. In a well-lighted room crowded with people, his face was startling to the point of being downright scary. If he were to come upon someone unexpectedly in the dark the poor guy might die of fright.

"Dr. Howell? Are you there?"

Receiving no answer, Malcomb figured it was safe to step around the first car in the row and check out Dr. Howell's Beemer, just to put his own mind at ease. He had missed him; it was as simple as that. When the doctor walked past he must've been concentrating a little too hard on what the blond hooker was doing to her john before she went into paroxysms of pain and started puking black gunk all over the guy. Or maybe he'd been distracted by the newest volcanic formation on his cheek. Or maybe Dr. Howell hadn't taken the paved path and instead had slipped through the shrubbery. He was a tall but slight fellow. He was slender enough to have squeezed through the hedge without creating much of a disturbance.

Whatever, Dr. Howell had slipped past him in the dark, is all.

Before rounding the first car in the row, just for good measure, Malcomb switched on his flashlight.

It was discovered later beneath the first car in the row where it had come to rest after rolling several feet. The glass was shattered, the casing dented. But the batteries would have done that annoying pink bunny proud. The bulb was still burning.

What was spotlighted in the beam of Malcomb's flashlight had frightened him more than anything he'd ever read in a science-fiction thriller. It wasn't as grotesque, bloody, or bizarre. But it was real.

Chapter 1

N ice place you've got here."

"I like it." Ignoring the snide and trite remark, Wick dumped the pot of boiled shrimp into a colander that had never seen the inside of a Williams-Sonoma store. It was white plastic, stained brown. He didn't remember how he'd come by it, but he figured it had been left behind by a previous occupant of the rental house, which his friend obviously found lacking.

After the hot water had drained through, he set the colander in the center of the table, grabbed a roll of paper towels, and offered his guest another beer. He uncapped two bottles of Red Stripe, straddled the chair across the table from Oren Wesley, and said, "Dig in."

Oren conscientiously ripped a paper towel from the roll and spread it over his lap. Wick was on his third shrimp before Oren got around to selecting one. They peeled and ate in silence, sharing a bowl of cocktail sauce for dipping. Oren was careful not to get his white French cuffs in the horseradish-laced red stuff. Wick slurped carelessly and licked his fingers, fully aware that his sloppy table manners annoyed his fastidious friend.

They dropped the shrimp shells onto the newspaper that Wick had spread over the table, not to protect its hopelessly scarred surface but to keep cleanup to a minimum. The ceiling fan fluttered the corners of this makeshift tablecloth and stirred the spicy aroma of the shrimp boil into the sultry coastal air.

After a time, Oren remarked, "Pretty good."

Wick shrugged. "A no-brainer."

"Local shrimp?"

"Buy it fresh off the boat soon as it docks. The skipper gives me a discount."

"Decent of him."

"Not at all. We made a deal."

"What's your end of it?"

"To stay away from his sister."

Wick noshed into another plump shrimp and tossed the shell onto the growing heap. He grinned across at Oren, knowing that his friend was trying to decide whether or not he was telling the truth. He was a bullshit artist of renown, and even his best friend couldn't always distinguish his truth from his fiction.

He tore a paper towel from the roll and wiped his hands and mouth. "Is that all you can think of to talk about, Oren? The price of shrimp? You drove all the way down here for that?"

Oren avoided looking at him as he belched silently behind his fist. "Let me help you clean up."

"Leave it. Bring your beer."

A dirty table wasn't going to make much difference to the condition of Wick's house—which barely qualified as such. It was a three-room shack that looked like it would succumb to any Gulf breeze above five knots. It was shelter from the elements—barely. The roof leaked when it rained. The air conditioner was a window unit that was so insufficient Wick rarely bothered turning it on. He rented the place by the week, paid in advance. So far he'd written the slum lord sixty-one checks.

The screen door squeaked on its corroded hinges as they moved through it onto the rear deck. Nothing fancy—the plank surface was rough, wide enough only to accommodate two metal lawn chairs of vintage fifties style. Salt air had eaten through numerous coats of paint, the last being a sickly pea green. Wick took the glider. Oren looked dubiously at the rusty seat of the stationary chair.

"It won't bite," Wick said. "Might stain your suit britches, but I promise that the view'll be worth a dry-cleaning bill."

Oren sat down gingerly, and in a few minutes Wick's promise was fulfilled. The western horizon became striated with vivid color ranging from bloodred to brilliant orange. Purple thunderheads on the horizon looked like rolling hills rimmed with gold.

"Something, isn't it?" Wick said. "Now tell me who's crazy."

"I never thought you were crazy, Wick."

"Just a little nutty for shucking it all and moving down here."

"Not even nutty. Irresponsible, maybe."

Wick's easy smile congealed.

Noticing, Oren said, "Go ahead and get pissed. I don't care. You need to hear it."

"Well, fine. Thank you. Now I've heard it. How're Grace and the girls?"

"Steph made cheerleader. Laura started her periods."

"Congratulations or condolences?"

"For which?"

"Both."

Oren smiled. "I'll accept either. Grace said to give you a kiss from her." Looking at Wick's stubble, he added, "I'll pass if you don't mind."

"I'd rather you did. But give her a kiss from me."

"Happy to oblige."

For several minutes they sipped their beers and watched the colors of the sunset deepen. Neither broke the silence, yet each was mindful of it, mindful of all that was going unsaid.

Eventually Oren spoke. "Wick . . ."

"Not interested."

"How do you know until you've heard me out?"

"Why would you want to ruin a perfectly beautiful sunset? To say nothing of a good Jamaican beer."

Wick's lunge from the glider caused it to rock crazily and noisily before it resettled. Standing at the edge of the weathered deck, tanned toes curling over the edge of it, he tilted back his beer and finished it in one long swallow, then tossed the empty bottle into the fifty-gallon oil drum that served as his garbage can. The clatter spooked a couple of gulls who'd been scavenging on the hard-packed sand. Wick envied their ability to take flight.

He and Oren had a history that dated back many years, to even before Wick had joined the Fort Worth Police Department. Oren was older by several years, and Wick conceded that he was definitely the wiser. He had a stable temperament, which often had defused Wick's more volatile one. Oren's approach was methodical. Wick's was impulsive. Oren was devoted to his wife and children. Wick was a bachelor who Oren claimed had the sexual proclivities of an alley cat.

In spite of these differences, and possibly because of them, Wick Threadgill and Oren Wesley had made excellent partners. They had been one of the few biracial partnerships on the FWPD. Together they had shared dangerous situations, countless laughs, a few triumphs, several disappointments—and a heartache from which neither would ever fully recover.

When Oren had called last night after months of separation, Wick was glad to hear from him. He had hoped that Oren was coming to talk over old times, better times. That hope was dashed the moment Oren arrived and got out of his car. It was a polished pair of wing tips, not flip-flops or sneakers, that had made deep impressions in the Galveston sand. Oren wasn't dressed for fishing or beach-combing, not even for kicking back here on the deck with an Astros game on the radio and cold beer in the fridge.

He had arrived dressed for business. Buttoned down and belted up, bureaucracy personified. Even as they shook hands Wick had recognized his friend's game face and knew with certainty and disappointment that this was not a social visit .

He was equally certain that whatever it was that Oren had come to say, he didn't want to hear it.

"You weren't fired, Wick."

"No, I'm taking an 'indefinite leave of absence.' "

"That was your choice."

"Under duress."

"You needed time to cool off and get it together."

"Why didn't the suits just fire me? Make it easier on everybody?"

"They're smarter than you are."

Wick came around. "Is that right?"

"They know, everybody who knows you knows, that you were born for this kinda work."

"This kinda work?" He snorted. "Shoveling shit, you mean? If I cleaned out stables for a living, I wouldn't have to do as much of it as I did in the FWPD."

"Most of that shit you brought on yourself."

Wick snapped the rubber band he habitually wore around his wrist. He disliked being reminded of that time and of the case that had caused him to criticize his superiors vociferously about the inefficiency of the justice system in general and the FWPD in particular. "They let that gangbanger cop a plea."

"Because they couldn't get him for murder, Wick. They knew it and the DA knew it. He's in for six."

"He'll be out in less than two. And he'll do it again. Somebody else will die. You can count on it. And all because our department and the DA's office went limp-dick when it came to a violation of the little shit's rights."

"Because you used brute force when you arrested him." Lowering his voice, Oren added, "But your problem with the department wasn't about that case and you know it."

"Oren," Wick said threateningly.

"The mistake that—"

"Fuck this," Wick muttered. He crossed the deck in two long strides. The screen door slapped shut behind him.

Oren followed him back into the kitchen. "I didn't come to rehash all that."

"Could've fooled me."

"Will you stop stomping around for a minute and let me talk to you? You'll want to see this."

"Wrong. What I want is another beer." He removed one from the refrigerator and pried off the top with a bottle opener. He left the metal cap where it landed on the wavy linoleum floor.

Oren retrieved a folder he'd brought with him and extended it to Wick, who ignored it. But his retreat out the back door was halted when his bare foot came down hard on the sharp teeth of the bottle cap. Cursing, he kicked the offender across the floor and dropped down into one of the chrome-legged dining chairs. The shrimp shells were beginning to stink.

He propped his foot on his opposite knee and appraised the damage. There was a deep impression of the bottle cap on the ball of his foot, but it hadn't broken the skin.

Showing no sympathy whatsoever, Oren sat down across from him. "Officially I'm not here. Understood? This is a complex situation. It has to be handled delicately."

"Something wrong with your hearing, Oren?"

"I know you'll be as intrigued as I am."

"Don't forget to pick up your jacket on your way out."

Oren removed several eight-by-ten black-and-white photographs from the folder. He held one up so that Wick couldn't avoid looking at it. After a moment, he showed him another.

Wick stared at the photo, then met Oren's eyes above it. "Did they get any shots of her with her clothes on?"

"You know Thigpen. He took these for grins."

Wick snorted acknowledgment of the mentioned detective.

"In Thigpen's defense, our stakeout house gives us a clear view into her bedroom."

"Still no excuse for these. Unless she's an exhibitionist and knew she was being watched."

"She isn't and she doesn't."

"What's her story?"

Oren grinned. "You're dying to know, aren't you?"

When Wick had surrendered his badge a little more than a year earlier, he had turned his back not only on his police career, but on the whole criminal justice system. To him it was like a cumbersome vehicle stuck in the mud. It spun its big wheels and made a lot of aggressive noise— freedom, justice, and the American way—but it got nowhere.

Law enforcement personnel had been robbed of their motivation by bureaucrats and politicians who quaked at the thought of public disapproval. Consequently the whole concept of justice was mired in futility.

And if you were the poor dumb schmuck who believed in it, who got behind it, put your shoulder to it, and pushed with all your might to set the gears in motion, to catch the bad guys and see them punished for their crimes, all you got in return was mud slung in your face.

But, in spite of himself, Wick's natural curiosity kicked in. Oren hadn't shown him these pictures for prurient purposes. Oren wasn't a Neanderthal like Thigpen and had better things to do with his time than to gawk at pho- tographs of half-naked women. Besides, Grace would throttle him if he did.

No, Oren had a reason for driving all the way from Fort Worth to Galveston and, in spite of himself, Wick wanted to know what it was. He was intrigued, just as Oren—damn him—had guessed he would be.

He reached for the remainder of the photographs and shuffled through them quickly, then more slowly, studying each one. The woman had been photographed in the driver's seat of a late-model Jeep wagon; walking across what appeared to be a large parking lot; inside her kitchen and her bedroom, blissfully unaware that her privacy was being invaded by binoculars and telephoto lenses in the hands of a slob like Thigpen.

Most of the bedroom shots were grainy and slightly out of focus. But clear enough. "What's her alleged crime? Interstate transportation of stolen Victoria's Secret merchandise?"

"Uh-huh," Oren said, shaking his head. "That's all you get until you agree to go back with me."

Wick tossed the photographs in Oren's general direction. "Then you made the drive for nothing." He tugged again at the rubber band on his wrist, painfully popping it against his skin.

"You'll want to be in on this one, Wick."

"Not a chance in hell."

"I'm not asking for a long-term commitment, or a return to the department. Just this one case."

"Still no."

"I need your help."

"Sorry."

"Is that your final answer?"

Wick picked up his fresh beer, took a large swallow, then belched loudly.

Despite the smelly shrimp shells, Oren leaned forward across the table. "It's a murder case. Made the news."

"I don't watch the news or read the papers."

"Must not. Because if you had, you'd have sped straight to Fort Worth and saved me this trip."

Wick couldn't stop himself from asking "Why's that?"

"Popular doctor gets popped in the parking lot of Tarrant General."

"Catchy, Oren. Are you quoting the headline?"

"Nope. I'm giving you the sum total of what we know about this homicide. The crime is five days old and that's all we've got."

"Not my problem."

"The perp did the killing within yards of a potential eyewitness but wasn't seen. Wasn't heard. As silent as vapor. Invisible. And he didn't leave a trace, Wick." Oren lowered his voice to a whisper. "Not a fucking trace."

Wick searched his former partner's dark eyes. The hair on the back of his neck stood on end. "Lozada?"

Settling back in his chair, Oren smiled complacently.

Chapter 2

■■■■■■■■■■■

Dr. Rennie Newton stepped off the elevator and approached the central nurses' station. The nurse at the desk, who was usually talkative, was noticeably subdued. "Good evening, Dr. Newton."

"Hello."

The nurse took in the black dress under Rennie's lab coat. "The funeral today?"

Rennie nodded. "I didn't take time to change afterward."

"Was it a nice service?"

"Well, as funerals go, yes. There was a large turnout."

"Dr. Howell was so well liked. And he'd just gotten that promotion. It's too awful."

"I agree. Awful."

The nurse's eyes filled with tears. "We—everybody on this floor—we saw him nearly every day. We can't believe it."

Nor could Rennie. Five days ago her colleague Lee

Howell had died. Given his age, a sudden death from cardiac arrest or an accident would have been hard to accept. But Lee had been murdered in cold blood. Everyone who knew him was still reeling from the shock of his death as well as from the violent way he'd died. She almost expected him to pop out from behind a door and cry "Just kidding!"

But his murder wasn't one of the lousy practical jokes for which Lee Howell was famous. She had seen his sealed, flower-banked coffin at the church altar this morning. She had heard the emotional eulogies delivered by family members and friends. She had seen Myrna and his son weeping inconsolably in the front pew, making his death and the permanence of it jarringly real and even more difficult to accept.

"It will take time for all of us to absorb the shock," Rennie said in a tone both quiet and conclusive.

But the nurse wasn't ready to let the subject drop. "I heard the police had questioned everybody who was at Dr. Howell's party that night."

Rennie studied the patient charts that had been passed to her during the conversation and didn't address the implied question underlying the nurse's statement.

"Dr. Howell was always joking, wasn't he?" The nurse giggled as though remembering something funny. "And you and he fought like cats and dogs."

"We didn't fight," Rennie said, correcting her. "Occasionally we quarreled. There's a difference."

"I remember some of those quarrels getting pretty rowdy."

"We made good sparring partners," she said, smiling sadly.

She had performed two operations that morning before the funeral. Considering the circumstances, she could have justified rescheduling today's surgeries and closing her office this afternoon. But she was already in a time crunch due to a recent, unavoidable ten-day absence from the hospital, which had proved to be an awful inconvenience to her and her patients.

Taking another day off so soon after her return would have been unfair to those patients whose surgeries had been postponed once already. It would have placed her further behind and created yet another logjam in her scrupulously organized calendar. So she had elected to perform the operations and keep the appointments in her office. Lee would have understood.

Seeing the post-op patients was her last official duty of this long, emotionally draining, exhausting day, and she was ready to put an end to it. Closing the topic of her colleague's demise and funeral, she inquired about Mr. Tolar, whose esophageal hernia she had repaired that morning.

"Still groggy, but he's doing very well."

Taking the charts with her, Rennie entered the surgical recovery room. Mrs. Tolar was taking advantage of the five-minute visitation period that was permitted a family member once each hour. Rennie joined her at the patient's bedside. "Hello, Mrs. Tolar. I hear he's still sleepy."

"During my last visit he came awake long enough to ask me the time."

"A common question. The light in here never changes. It's disorienting."

The woman touched her husband's cheek. "He's sleeping through this visit."

"That's the best thing for him. No surprises on his chart," Rennie told her as she scanned the information. "Blood pressure is good." She closed the metal cover on the chart. "In a couple of weeks he'll feel like a new man. No more sleeping at a slant."

She noticed how dubiously the woman was gazing at her husband and added, "He's doing great, Mrs. Tolar. Everyone looks a little ragged fresh out of surgery. He'll look a thousand percent better tomorrow, although he'll be so grumpy and sore you'll wish he was anesthetized again."

"Grumpiness I can take, so long as he's not suffering anymore." Turning to Rennie, she lowered her voice to a confidential pitch. "I guess it's okay to tell you this now."

Rennie tilted her head inquisitively.

"He was skeptical when his internist referred him to you. He didn't know what to make of a lady surgeon."

Rennie laughed softly. "I hope I earned his confidence."

"Oh, you did. On the very first visit to your office you had him convinced you knew your stuff."

"I'm pleased to hear that."

"Although he said you were too pretty to be hiding behind a surgeon's mask."

"When he wakes up, I must remember to thank him."

The two women exchanged smiles, then Mrs. Tolar's expression turned somber. "I heard about Dr. Howell. Did you know him well?"

"Very well. We'd been colleagues for several years. I considered him a friend."

"I'm so sorry."

"Thank you. He'll be missed." Not wishing to have another conversation about the funeral, she returned the topic to the patient. "He's so out of it he won't really know whether or not you're here tonight, Mrs. Tolar. Try to get some rest while you can. Save your energy for when you take him home."

"One more visit, then I'll be leaving."

"I'll see you tomorrow."

Rennie moved to her next patient. No one was standing vigil at her bedside. The elderly woman was a charity case. She resided in a state-funded nursing facility. According to her patient history she had no family beyond one brother who lived in Alaska. The septuagenarian was doing well, but even after reviewing her vitals Rennie stayed with her.

She believed that charity went beyond waiving her fee. In fact, waiving her fee was the least of it. She held the woman's hand and stroked her forehead, hoping that on a subconscious level her elderly patient was comforted by her presence, her touch. Eventually, convinced that the small amount of time she'd given the woman would make a difference, she left her to the nurses' care.

"I'm not on call tonight," she told the nurse at the desk as she returned the charts. "But page me if either of these patients takes a downward turn."

"Certainly, Dr. Newton. Have you had dinner?"

"Why?"

"Pardon me for saying so, but you look done in."

She smiled wanly. "It's been a long day. And a very sad one."

"I recommend a cheeseburger, double fries, a glass of wine, and a bubble bath."

"If I can keep my eyes open that long."

She said her good night and made her way toward the elevator. As she waited for it, she ground both fists into the small of her back and stretched. Being away, and for a reason not of her own making, had cost her more than time and inconvenience. Her pacing was still off. She wasn't yet back into the rhythm of the hospital. It wasn't always a regular rhythm, but at least it was a familiar one.

And just as she was beginning to get back into the swing of things, Lee Howell had been murdered on the parking lot she traversed each time she came to the hospital.

While she was still stunned from that blow, more unpleasantness had followed. Along with everyone who'd been at the Howells' house that night, she had been questioned by the police. It had been a routine interrogation, textbook in nature. Nevertheless, it had left her shaken.

Today she had seen Lee Howell buried. She would never quarrel with him again over something as important as OR scheduling or something as petty as whole milk versus skim. She would never laugh at one of his stupid jokes.

Taking all that had happened into account, it was an understatement to say that the past three weeks had amounted to a major upheaval in her routine.

This was no small thing. Dr. Rennie Newton adhered to rhythms and routine with fanatical self-discipline.

Her house was a ten-minute drive from the hospital. Most young professionals lived in newer, more fashionable neighborhoods of Fort Worth. Rennie could have afforded to live anywhere, but she preferred this older, well-established neighborhood.

Not only was its location convenient to the hospital, but she liked the narrow, tree-lined brick streets, which had been laid decades ago and remained a quaint feature of the neighborhood. The mature landscaping didn't look as though it had been installed yesterday. Most of the houses had been built prior to World War II, giving them an aura of permanence and solidity that she favored. Her house had been quaintly described as a bungalow. Having only five rooms, it was perfect for a single, which she was, and which she would remain.

The house had been renovated twice, and she had put it through a third remodeling and modernization before she moved in. The stucco exterior was dove gray with white trim. The front door was cranberry red with a shiny brass knocker and kick plate. In the flower beds, white and red impatiens bloomed beneath shrubbery with dark, waxy foliage. Sprawling trees shaded the lawn against even the harshest sun. She paid dearly for a professional service to keep the yard meticulously groomed and maintained.

She turned into the driveway and used her automatic garage-door opener, one of her innovations. She closed the garage door behind her and let herself in through the connecting kitchen door. It wasn't quite dusk yet, so the small room was bathed in the golden light of a setting sun that filtered through the large sycamore trees in her backyard.

She had forgone the suggested cheeseburger and fries, but since she wasn't on call tonight she poured herself a glass of Chardonnay and carried it with her into the living room—where she almost dropped it.

A crystal vase of red roses stood on her living-room coffee table.

Five dozen perfect buds on the brink of blossoming open. They looked velvety to the touch. Fragrant. Expensive. The cut crystal vase was also extraordinarily beautiful. Its myriad facets sparkled as only pricey crystal can and splashed miniature rainbows onto the walls.

When Rennie had recovered from her initial shock, she set her wineglass on the coffee table and searched among the roses and greenery for an enclosure card. She didn't find one.

"What the hell?"

It wasn't her birthday, and even if it were, no one would know it. She didn't celebrate an anniversary of any kind with anyone. Were the roses meant to convey condolence? She had worked with Lee Howell every day for years, but receiving flowers on the day of his funeral was hardly warranted or even appropriate given their professional relationship.

A grateful patient? Possibly, but unlikely. Who among them would know her home address? Her office address was the one listed in the telephone directory. If a patient had been so moved by gratitude, the roses would have gone either there or to the hospital.

Only a handful of friends knew where she lived. She never entertained at home. She returned social obligations by hosting dinner or Sunday brunch in a restaurant. She had many colleagues and acquaintances, but no friendships close enough to merit an extravagant bouquet of roses. No family. No boyfriend. No ex- or wanna-be boyfriends.

Who would be sending her flowers? An even more unsettling question was how the bouquet had come to be inside her house.

Before calling her next-door neighbor, she took a fortifying sip of wine.

The chatty widower had tried to become a chummy confidant soon after Rennie moved in, but as tactfully as possible she had discouraged his unannounced drop-overs until he finally got the message. They remained friendly, however, and the older gentleman was always pleased when Rennie took a moment to visit with him across their shared azalea hedge.

Probably because he was lonely and bored, he kept his finger on the pulse of the neighborhood and made everyone's business his own. If you wanted to know anything about anyone, Mr. Williams was your man.

"Hi, it's Rennie."

"Hey, Rennie, good to hear from you. How was the funeral?"

A few days ago he had waylaid her when she went out to get her newspaper. He had plied her with questions regarding the murder and seemed disappointed when she didn't impart the gory details. "It was a very moving service." In the hope of preventing more questions, she barely took a breath between sentences. "Mr. Williams, the reason I called—"

"Are the police any closer to catching the killer?"

"I wouldn't know."

"Weren't you questioned?"

"Everyone who was at Dr. Howell's house that night was asked for possible leads. To the best of my knowledge nobody had anything to offer." Instead of relaxing her, the wine was giving her a headache. "Mr. Williams, did I receive a delivery today?"

"Not that I know of. Were you expecting one?"

He was the only neighbor who had a key to her house. She had been reluctant to give him one, and it wasn't because of mistrust. The notion of someone coming into her home when she wasn't there was repugnant. As with rhythms and routine, she was a stickler for privacy.

But she had felt that someone should have a spare key in case of an emergency or to let in repairmen when necessary. Mr. Williams had been the logical choice because of his proximity. To Rennie's knowledge he had never abused the privilege.

"I was on the lookout for a package," she lied. "I thought it might have been delivered to you since I wasn't at home."

"Was there a notice on your door? A yellow sticker?"

"No, but I thought the driver might have forgotten to leave one. You didn't see a delivery truck parked at my curb today?"

"No, nothing."

"Hmm, well, these things never arrive when you're looking for them, do they?" she said breezily. "Thanks anyway, Mr. Williams. Sorry to have bothered you."

"Did you hear about the Bradys' new litter of puppies?"

Damn! She hadn't hung up fast enough. "Can't say that I have. As you know I've been out of pocket for a couple of weeks and—"

"Beagles. Six of them. Cutest little things you ever saw. They're giving them away. You should speak for one."

"I don't have time for pets."

"You should make the time, Rennie," he advised with the remonstrative tone of a parent.

"My horses—"

"Not the same. They don't live with you. You need a pet at home. One can make all the difference in a person's outlook. People with pets live longer, did you know that? I couldn't do without Oscar," he said of his poodle. "A dog or cat is best, but even a goldfish or a parakeet can ward off loneliness."

"I'm not lonely, Mr. Williams. Just very busy. Nice talking to you. Bye."

She hung up immediately, and not just to curtail a lecture on the benefits of pet ownership. She was alarmed.

She wasn't imagining the roses, and they hadn't simply materialized on her coffee table. Someone had been here and left them.

She quickly checked the front door. It was locked, just as it had been that morning when she'd left for the hospital. She dashed down the hallway into her bedroom and checked under the bed and in the closet. All the windows were firmly shut and locked. The window above her bathtub was too small for even a child to crawl through. Next she checked the second bedroom, which she used as a study. Same there: nothing. She knew that nothing in the kitchen had been disturbed.

Actually, she would have been relieved to find a broken window or a jimmied lock. At least that element of this mystery would have been solved. Returning to the living room, she sat down on the sofa. She had lost all appetite for the wine, but she took another drink of it anyway in the hope it would steady her nerves. It didn't. When the telephone rang on the end table, she jumped.

She, Rennie Newton, who at fourteen had climbed the narrow ladder to the very top of her hometown water tower, who had put herself in peril by visiting practically every danger spot on the globe, who loved a challenge and never backed down from a dare, who wasn't afraid of the Devil, as her mother used to tell her, and who daily performed surgeries that required nerves of steel and rock-steady hands, nearly came out of her skin when her telephone rang.

Shaking spilled wine off her hand, she reached for the cordless phone. Most of her calls were work related, so she answered in her normally brisk and efficient manner.

"This is Dr. Newton."

"It's Detective Wesley, Dr. Newton. I spoke with you the other day."

The reminder was unnecessary. She remembered him as a physically fit and imposing black man. Receding hairline. Stern visage. All business. "Yes?"

"I got your number from the hospital. I hope you don't mind me calling you at home."

She did. Very much. "What can I do for you, Detective?"

"I'd like to meet with you tomorrow. Say ten o'clock?"

"Meet with me?"

"To talk about Dr. Howell's murder."

"I don't know anything about his murder. I told you that . . . was it the day before yesterday?"

"You didn't tell me that you and he were vying for the same position at the hospital. You left that out."

Her heart bumped against her ribs. "It wasn't relevant."

"Ten o'clock, Dr. Newton. Homicide's on the third floor. Ask anybody. You'll find me."

"I'm sorry, but I've scheduled the operating room for three surgeries tomorrow morning. To reschedule would inconvenience other surgeons and hospital personnel, to say nothing of my patients and their families."

"Then when would be a convenient time?" He asked this in a tone that suggested he wasn't really interested in going out of his way to accommodate her.

"Two or three o'clock tomorrow afternoon."

"Two o'clock. See you then."

He disconnected before Rennie could. She returned the telephone to the end table. She closed her eyes and took deep breaths through her nose, exhaling through her mouth.

Lee Howell's appointment to chief of surgery had

been a major blow. Since the retirement of the predecessor, she and Lee had been the leading contenders for the position. After months of extensive interviews and performance assessments, the hospital board of directors had finally announced their decision last week—while she had been conveniently away, a move she had thought ultra-cowardly.

However, when word of Lee's appointment reached her, she was glad she was away. The hospital grapevine would be circulating the news with the speed of fiber optics. By the time she had returned to work, the buzz had died down and she wasn't subjected to well-meaning but unwelcome commiserations.

But she hadn't escaped them entirely. A comprehensive write-up about his appointment had appeared in the *Star-Telegram*. The article had extolled Dr. Lee Howell's surgical skills, his dedication to healing, his distinguished record, and his contributions to the hospital and the community at large. As a consequence of the glowing article, Rennie had been on the receiving end of many sympathetic glances, which she had deplored and tried to ignore.

Basically, being chief of any department involved reams of additional paperwork, constant crises with personnel, and haggles with hospital board members for a larger share of the budget. Nevertheless, it was a coveted title and she had coveted it.

Then three days after the newspaper profile, Lee had made headlines again by being slain in the hospital parking lot. Looking at it from Detective Wesley's standpoint, the timing would be uncanny and worthy of further investigation. His job was to explore every avenue. Naturally, one of the first people he would suspect would be Lee's competitor. The meeting tomorrow amounted to nothing more than a vigilant follow-up by a thorough detective.

She wouldn't worry about it. She simply wouldn't. She had nothing to contribute to Wesley's investigation. She would answer his questions truthfully and to the best of her knowledge and that would be the end of it. There was no cause to worry.

The roses, on the other hand, were worrisome.

She stared at them as though intimidation might cause them to surrender the sender's identity. She stared at them so long that her vision doubled, then quadrupled, before she suddenly pulled it back into sharp focus—on the white envelope.

Tucked deeply into the foliage, it had escaped detection until now. Being careful of thorns, she reached into the arrangement and removed the card from the envelope, which had been attached to a stem by a slender satin ribbon.

The hand with which she had established a reputation as an exceptionally talented surgeon trembled slightly as she brought the card closer. On it was a single typewritten line:

I've got a crush on you.

Chapter 3

∎∎∎∎∎∎∎∎∎∎∎∎∎∎

Uncle Wick!"

"Uncle Wick!"

The two girls rushed him like linemen intent on sacking the quarterback. Officially adolescents, they still had the exuberance of children when it came to showing affection, especially for their adored Uncle Wick.

"It's been ages and ages, Uncle Wick. I've missed you."

"I've missed y'all, too. Look at you. Will you please stop growing? You're going to get as tall as me."

"Nobody's as tall as you, Uncle Wick."

"Michael Jordan."

"Nobody who doesn't play basketball, I mean."

The younger, Laura, announced, "Mom finally let me get my ears pierced," and she proudly showed them off.

"No nose rings, I hope."

"Dad would have a cow."

"I'd have two."

"Do you think braces are ugly on girls, Uncle Wick? 'Cause I may have to get them."

"Are you kidding? Braces are a major turn-on."

"Seriously?"

"Seriously."

"Your hair's blonder, Uncle Wick."

"I've been on the beach a lot. The sun bleaches it out. And if I don't start using sunscreen I'm going to get as dark as you."

They thought that was hilarious.

"I made cheerleader."

"So I heard." He high-fived Stephanie. "Save a seat for me at one of the games this fall."

"Our outfits are kinda dorky."

"They are," her younger sister solemnly agreed. "Totally dorky."

"But Mom says guess again about making them shorter."

"That's right, I did." Grace Wesley joined them at the front door. Moving her daughters aside, she hugged Wick tightly.

When he released her, he whined, "Grace, why won't you run away with me?"

"Because I'm a one-woman-man kind of woman."

"I'll change. For you I'd change. Cross my heart I would."

"Sorry, still can't."

"Why not?"

"Because Oren would hunt you down and shoot you dead."

"Oh, yeah," he grumbled. "*Him.*"

The girls shrieked with laughter. Over their protests, Grace shooed them upstairs, where chores awaited them, and ushered Wick into the living room. "How's Galveston?"

"Hot. Sticky. Sandy."

"Are you liking it?"

"I'm loving being a beach bum. Where's your old man?"

"On the phone, but he shouldn't be much longer. Have you eaten?"

"Stopped at Angelo's and scarfed a plate of brisket. Didn't realize how much I'd missed that barbecue till I took my first bite."

"There's chocolate pudding in the fridge."

"I'd settle for a glass of your iced tea."

"Sweetened?"

"Is there any other kind?"

"Coming up. Make yourself comfortable." Before leaving the room, she turned back and said meaningfully, "Sure is good to have you back."

"Thanks."

He didn't correct her. He wasn't *back* yet and didn't know if he was coming back. He had only consented to think about it. Oren had an interesting case cooking. He had asked for Wick's professional opinion. He was here to help out his friend. That was all.

He'd yet to darken the door of PD headquarters, and he didn't intend to. He hadn't even driven past it or felt a nostalgic yearning to do so. He was here as a favor to Oren. Period.

"Hey, Wick." Oren bustled in. He was dressed for home in knee-length shorts, sneakers, and a University of Texas T-shirt, but he was still all cop; a case binder was tucked beneath his arm. His pager was clipped to his waistband. "How was your drive up from Galveston?"

"Long."

"Don't I know it." Oren had made the round trip the day before. "Get checked into the motel all right?"

"Is that rat-hole the best the FWPD can afford?"

"Oh, and you left such luxurious accommodations in Galveston."

Wick laughed good-naturedly.

"Grace take care of you?"

"In the process." She came in with two tall glasses of tea and set them on coasters on the coffee table. "The girls said for Wick not to dare leave without saying good-bye."

"I promise I won't. I'll even tell them a bedtime story."

"A clean one, I hope," Grace said.

He shot her his most wicked grin. "I can edit as I go."

"Thanks for the tea," Oren said. "Close the door behind you, please."

This was a familiar scene. Before moving to the coast, Wick had often spent evenings at the Wesleys' house. It was a happy house because Grace and Oren's happiness with each other permeated the place.

They'd met in college and married upon graduation. Grace was a student counselor and vice-principal at a public junior high school. With each year her responsibilities increased and became more complicated, but she never failed to have a hot evening meal for her family and mandated that everyone be there for it.

Their home was noisy and active with the girls and their friends trooping up and down the stairs, in and out of the kitchen. Neighbors stopped by with or without an invitation, knowing they'd be welcome. The house was as clean as a U.S. Navy vessel but cluttered with the trappings of a busy family. When Grace was at home, chances were very good that the washing machine would be chugging.

Reminder notes and snapshots were stuck to the refrigerator with magnets. There were always cookies in the cookie jar.

Wick had been a guest so often he was considered one of the family and pitched in when it came time to do the dishes or take out the garbage. He teased Grace about doing her best to domesticate him. The joke wasn't far off the mark.

Following dinner and cleanup, it had been his and Oren's habit to seclude themselves in the living room to discuss troublesome cases. Tonight was no exception.

"I've got a video I want you to see." Oren inserted a tape into the VCR, then carried the remote control back to the sofa and sat at the opposite end from Wick. "Recorded this afternoon."

"Of?"

"Dr. Rennie Newton."

The video picture came on the screen. It was a wide shot of an interrogation room. Wick had watched a hundred such video recordings. The camera, he knew, had been mounted on a tripod situated behind Oren. It was aimed at the chair occupied by the individual being questioned. In this case it was the woman in the photos Oren had shown him yesterday.

Wick was surprised. "She's a doctor?"

"Surgeon."

"No shit?"

"I called her after leaving your place. She came in for questioning today."

"In connection with the Howell homicide?" Once he had agreed to come to Fort Worth, Oren had given him the basic facts of the case, scarce though they were.

"She agreed to being videotaped, but she also brought along her attorney."

"She's no fool."

"No. In fact she was . . . well, you'll see."

Dr. Newton's lawyer was standard issue. Height, average. Weight, average. Hair, white. Suit, gray pinstripe. Eyes, wary and cunning. It took only one glance for Wick to assess him.

He then directed his attention to Dr. Rennie Newton, who didn't come even close to standard issue. In fact if someone had ordered him to conjure a mental picture of a surgeon, the woman on the tape would not have been it. Not in a million years.

Nor was she typical of someone being questioned about a felony offense. She wasn't sweating, nervously jiggling her legs, drumming her fingers, biting her nails, or fidgeting in her seat. Instead she sat perfectly still, her legs decorously crossed, arms folded at her waist, eyes straight ahead and steady, a portrait of composure.

She was dressed in a cream-colored two-piece suit with slacks, high heels in a tan reptile skin, matching handbag. She wore no jewelry except for a pair of stud earrings and a large, no-nonsense wristwatch. No rings on either hand. Her long hair was pulled into a neat ponytail. He knew from the surveillance photos that when it was down, it reached the middle of her back. Pale blond, which looked as genuine as the diamonds in her earlobes.

Oren stopped the tape. "What do you think so far? As a connoisseur of the fairer sex, your first impression."

Wick shrugged and took a sip of tea. "Dresses well. Good skin. You couldn't melt an ice cube on her ass."

"Cool."

"We're talking frostbite. But she's a surgeon. She's supposed to be cool under pressure, isn't she?"

"I guess."

Oren restarted the tape and they heard his voice identifying everyone present, including Detective Plum, the second plainclothesman in the room. He provided the date and the case number, and then, for the benefit of the tape, asked Dr. Newton if she had agreed to the interview.

"Yes."

Oren plunged right in. "I'd like to ask you a few questions about the murder of your colleague Dr. Lee Howell."

"I've already told you everything I know, Detective Wesley."

"Well, it never hurts to go over it again, does it?"

"I suppose not. If you've got a lot of spare time on your hands."

Oren stopped the tape. "See? There. That's what I'm talking about. Polite, but with a definite attitude."

"I'd say so, yeah. But that's in character too. She's a doctor. A surgeon. The god complex and all that. She speaks and folks sit up and take notice. She isn't accustomed to being questioned or second-guessed."

"She had better get accustomed to it," Oren mumbled. "I think there's something going on with this lady."

He rewound the tape to listen again to her saying, "If you've got a lot of spare time on your hands."

On the tape, Oren gave Plum a significant glance. Plum raised his eyebrows. Oren continued. "On the night Dr. Howell was murdered, you were at his house, correct?"

"Along with two dozen other people," the attorney chimed in. "Have you questioned them to this extent?"

Ignoring him, Oren asked, "Did you know everyone at the party that night, Dr. Newton?"

"Yes. I've known Lee's wife for almost as long as I've known him. The guests were other doctors with whom I'm acquainted. I'd met their spouses at previous social gatherings."

"You attended the party alone?"

"That's right."

"You were the only single there."

The lawyer leaned forward. "Is that relevant, Detective?"

"Maybe."

"I don't see how. Dr. Newton went to the party alone. Can we move on? She has a busy schedule."

"I'm sure." With a noticeable lack of haste, Oren shuffled through his notes and took his time before asking the next question. "I understand it was a cookout."

"On the Howells' terrace."

"And Dr. Howell manned the grill."

"Do you want the menu, too?" the attorney asked sarcastically.

Oren continued looking hard at Rennie Newton. She said, "Lee fancied himself a gourmet on the charcoal grill. Actually he was a dreadful cook, but nobody had the heart to tell him." She looked down into her lap, smiling sadly. "It was a standing joke among his friends."

"What was the reason for the party?"

"Reason?"

"Was it an ordinary Friday night cookout or a special occasion?"

She shifted slightly in her chair, recrossed her legs. "We were celebrating Lee's promotion to chief of surgery."

"Right, his promotion to head of the department. What did you think of that?"

"I was pleased for him, of course."

Oren tapped a pencil on the tabletop for a full fifteen seconds. Her gaze remained locked with his, never wavering.

"You were also under consideration for that position, weren't you, Dr. Newton?"

"Yes. And I deserved to get it."

Her attorney held up a cautionary hand.

"More than Dr. Howell did?" Oren asked.

"In my opinion, yes," she replied calmly.

"Dr. Newton, I—"

She forestalled her lawyer. "I'm only telling the truth. Besides, Detective Wesley has already guessed how I felt about losing the position to Lee. I'm sure he regards that as a motive for murder." Turning back to Oren, she said, "But I didn't kill him."

"Detectives, may I have a private word with my client?" the lawyer asked stiffly.

Unmindful of the request, Oren said, "I don't believe you killed anyone, Dr. Newton."

"Then what am I doing here wasting my time and yours? Why did you request this"—she gave the walls of the small room a scornful glance—"this interview?"

Oren stopped the tape there and consulted Wick. "Well?"

"What?"

"She denied it before I accused her of it."

"Come on, Oren. She's got more years of schooling than you, me, and Plum there added up. But she didn't need a medical degree to guess what you were getting at. Driving a herd of longhorns through that room would have been more subtle. She got your point. Any dummy would have. And this lady doesn't strike me as a dummy."

"She and Dr. Howell had a history of quarreling."

"So do we," Wick said, laughing.

Oren stubbornly shook his head. "Not like they did. Everybody I've talked to at the hospital says she and Howell respected each other professionally but did not get along."

"Love affair turned sour?"

"Initially I posed that question to everyone I interviewed. I stopped asking."

"How come?"

"I got tired of being laughed at."

Wick turned and quizzically arched his eyebrow.

"Beats me," Oren replied to the silent question. "That's the reaction I got every time I asked. Apparently there were never any romantic fires smoldering between them."

"Just a friendly rivalry."

"I'm not so sure it was all that friendly. On the surface, maybe, but there might have been a lurking animosity that ran deep. They were always at each other's throats for one reason or another. Sometimes over something trivial, sometimes major. Sometimes in jest, and sometimes not. But their disagreements were always lively, often vitriolic, and well known to hospital staff."

As he mentally sorted through this information, Wick absently popped the rubber band against his wrist.

Oren noticed and said, "You were wearing that yesterday. What's it for?"

"What?" Wick looked down at the rubber band circling his wrist as though he'd never seen it before. "Oh, it's . . . nothing. Uh, getting back, was Howell's appointment gender based?"

"I don't think so. Two other department heads at Tarrant General are women. Howell got the promotion Newton felt she deserved and probably thought she had sewn up because of her seniority status. She'd been affiliated with the hospital for two years before Howell joined ranks."

"She would resent the hell out of that."

"Only natural that she would."

"But enough to bump him off?" Staring at the static picture on the TV screen, Wick frowned with a mix of skepticism and concentration. He motioned with his chin for Oren to restart the tape.

On it, Oren asked, "Did you go straight home following the party, Dr. Newton?"

She gave a clipped affirmative.

"Can anyone corroborate that?"

"No."

"You didn't go out again that evening?"

"No. And no one can corroborate that either," she added when she saw that he was about to ask. "But it's the truth. I went home and went to bed."

"When did you hear that Dr. Howell had been killed?"

That question caused her to lower her head and speak softly. "The following morning. On television news. No one had notified me. I was stunned, couldn't believe it." She laced her fingers together tightly. "It was horrible to hear about it that way, without any warning that I was about to receive terrible news."

Wick reached for the remote and paused the video. "It appears to me she was really upset about it."

"Yeah, well . . ." Oren gave a noncommittal harrumph.

"Have you asked the widow about their relationship?"

"She said what everyone does: mutual respect, but they had their differences. She said Howell actually got a kick out of pestering Dr. Newton. He was a jokester. She's all business. She was a good foil."

"Well there you go."

"Maybe Dr. Newton thought his getting that position was one joke on her too many."

Wick stood up and began to pace. "Recap the facts for me."

"On the homicide? According to Mrs. Howell, the party broke up about midnight. They were in bed by one. The house phone rang at two-oh-seven. She's definite on the time because she remembers looking at the clock.

"Dr. Howell answered the phone, talked for several seconds, then hung up and told her he was needed at the hospital, said there'd been a major freeway accident with multiple casualties.

"He dressed and left. His body was found beside his car in the doctors' parking lot at two-twenty-eight. That's when the nine-one-one came in. Which was just long enough for him to make the drive from home. The security guard had seen Howell drive in minutes earlier, so he was popped the moment he got out of his car. His wallet was intact. Nothing taken from or off his car.

"Cause of death was massive hemorrhaging from a stab wound beneath his left arm. The murder weapon was left in the wound. Your average filleting knife. The manufacturer says they haven't produced wood hilts in twelve years, so this knife could've come from anywhere. Grandma's kitchen, flea market, you name it. No prints, of course.

"The blade went through Howell's ribs clean as a whistle and burst his heart like a balloon. Best guess is that he was attacked from behind, probably around the neck. Reflexively he reached up, the assailant stabbed him with his left hand. It happened like that," he said, snapping his fingers. "Whoever did him knew what he was doing."

"Like another doctor?"

Oren shrugged.

"Yesterday you mentioned a potential eyewitness."

"The parking-lot security guard. One . . ." Oren opened the binder and scanned a typed form until he located the name. "Malcomb R. Lutey. Age twenty-seven."

"Did you check him out?"

"Considered and eliminated as a suspect. He called in the nine-one-one. Scared shitless, and he wasn't faking it. Threw up four times while the first officers on the scene were trying to get information out of him.

"Hasn't missed a day of work since he's had the job. Works holidays. Has never caused anybody any trouble. Not even a traffic ticket on record. Yes-sirred and no-sirred everybody. Kind of a geek. Take that back. He's a full-fledged geek."

"He didn't see or hear anything?"

"Like I told you, Wick, nothing. Once this kid stopped hurling chow, he cooperated fully. Nervous as hell, but Mom was responsible for that. Scary old bat. She made me nervous too. Believe me, he's not our man."

"And the freeway accident?"

"No such accident occurred. Everyone on the hospital staff denies calling Howell. Telephone records indicate that the call originated from a cell phone."

"Let me guess. Untraceable."

"You got it."

"Male or female?"

"The caller? We don't know. Dr. Howell was the only one who spoke to him. Or her."

"What does the wife get by way of an estate?"

"Plenty. Howell was insured to the hilt, but the missus

came into the marriage with money of her own and stands to inherit more when her daddy passes."

"Good marriage?"

"By all accounts. They were trying to have another kid. There's one seven-year-old boy. Ideal American family. Churchgoers, flag-wavers. No drug abuse or alcoholism. He made small wagers on his golf games and that was the extent of his gambling. Not even a hint of marital infidelity, and especially not with his colleague Rennie Newton."

Oren rattled the ice in his glass, shook a cube into his mouth, chomped on it noisily. "The doc never had a malpractice suit filed against him. No outstanding debts. No known enemies. Except Rennie Newton. And I've just got a gut feeling about her, Wick."

Wick stopped pacing and looked at Oren, inviting him to elaborate.

"Don't you think it's a bit tidy and damn convenient that her rival gets popped within days after he's appointed to a position she wanted?"

"Wild coincidence?" Wick ventured.

"I could concede that except for the phone call that put Howell in that parking lot in the middle of the night. Besides, I don't believe in coincidences that wild."

"Me neither. I was playing devil's advocate." He sank back into the cushions of the sofa and placed his hands behind his head. He stared into the TV at the surgeon's calm face, which was freeze-framed on the screen. "Stabbing? True, she'd know right where to stick you to make it fatal, but I dunno." He frowned. "Just doesn't seem like something this lady would do."

"I don't think she did it herself. Somebody did it for her."

Wick turned and looked hard at his former partner. "Lozada is into knives."

"On occasion."

"But he once used a flare gun."

Oren made a face. "Jesus, was that a mess."

Body parts of that victim had been discovered floating over several acres of Eagle Mountain Lake. Lozada had also used a tire tool once to bash in a skull. That hadn't been a contract kill, as were most of his murders. That poor bastard had just pissed him off. Of course they could never prove that he had committed any of these crimes. They just knew it.

Wick came off the sofa again and moved to the fireplace. He looked at the pictures of Stephanie and Laura on the mantel. Then he went to the window and peered through the blinds. He ambled back to the mantel before returning to the sofa. "You think this Dr. Newton hired Lozada to eliminate her competition? Or had Lozada kill him out of spite? Is that basically it?"

"It's his kind of kill. Silent. Quick. Leaving the weapon."

"I'm not disputing that, Oren. It's her involvement I have a problem with." He gestured toward the TV. "She's a surgeon with a good reputation and no doubt a six-figure income. She seeks out a scumbag—that we all know Lozada to be no matter how fancy he dresses himself up—and hires him to kill her colleague? No way. Sorry, but I ain't buying it."

"What? She's too educated? Too well dressed? Too clean?"

"No, she's too . . . dispassionate. I don't know," Wick said impatiently. "Is there any evidence of a connection between her and Lozada?"

"We're looking."

"That means no."

"That means we're *looking*," Oren stressed.

Wick expelled a deep breath. "Right. Lozada could be having meetings with the pope and we'd be the last to know. He's slippery as owl shit."

"The doctor could be just as slippery, just as deceptive. She spends the majority of her time at the hospital, but nobody—and I mean no one—seems to know much about her personal life. They say she keeps to herself, keeps her private life private.

"That's why everyone laughed at my question about hanky-panky between her and Howell. If she dates at all, nobody knows about it. She's a loner. An excellent surgeon," he stipulated. "On that everybody agrees. Generally she's very well liked. She's friendly enough. Kindhearted. But she's aloof. Aloof. That's a word I heard a lot."

"You need more," Wick said.

"I agree."

Reaching into the breast pocket of his shirt, Oren withdrew a slip of paper and laid it on the sofa cushion that separated him and Wick.

"What's that?"

"Her address."

Wick knew what that implied, what Oren was asking of him. He shook his head. "Sorry, Oren, but you haven't convinced me. What you've got on her is thin. Way too thin. Speculation at best, and nothing substantive. Certainly nothing concrete. There's no just cause for—"

"You heard about Lozada's most recent trial, right? Or is your head buried too deep in Galveston sand?"

"Sure I heard. Capital murder. Another acquittal," Wick said bitterly. "Same song, tenth verse. What of it?"

Oren leaned forward and spoke in a stage whisper. "The jury that acquitted him . . . ?"

"Yeah?"

"Guess who was forewoman."

Chapter 4

■■■■■■■■■■■■■■

Wick wore running shorts, a tank top, and athletic shoes. If he bumped into a nosy neighbor, he could always pretend to be a jogger who was looking for a place to take a leak. That might not go over well, but it was better than the truth: that he was doing his cop friend a favor by illegally breaking into a suspect's house for the purpose of obtaining information.

To make the guise believable, he ran several laps around the city park a few blocks away from Rennie Newton's house. By the time he vaulted the fence that separated her backyard from the rear alley, he had worked up a plausible sweat.

From several houses down came the hum of a lawn mower. Otherwise the neighborhood was quiet. They'd picked this time of day for him to break in. It was too early for most people to be returning home from work and too hot for stay-at-homers to be doing outdoor chores or activities.

He went up her back steps and unzipped the fanny pack strapped to his waist. From it he removed a pair of latex gloves and slipped them on, which he might have difficulty explaining to a nosy neighbor in the I'm-just-taking-a-leak scenario. But better a neighbor than a judge with an indisputable fingerprint match. Next he took his Master-Card from the zippered pouch. In under three seconds the back door was unlocked.

With Oren's final warning echoing through his mind—"If you get caught I never heard of you"—he slipped inside.

Rarely was Wick stunned into silence and left without a clever comeback. But last night, when Oren had told him about Rennie Newton's recent jury duty it was several moments before he found his tongue, and all it could manage was an ineloquent, "Huh."

Oren had baited him and knew he had him hooked.

Now inside the former juror's house, he paused to listen. They hadn't expected a security system. Oren had checked city records for the required registration. No such registration was on file, and no electronic beep alerted Wick now that a system had been breached.

All that came back to him was the hollow silence of an empty house. For almost a week Dr. Newton had been under police surveillance. They knew she lived alone, and Oren had said you could set your clock by her schedule. She didn't return for the day until after making evening hospital rounds. According to him, there was rarely more than twenty minutes' variance in her ETA.

The back door had placed Wick in the kitchen, which was compact and spotlessly clean. Only two items were in the sink: a coffee cup and the coffeemaker carafe. Each held an inch of soapy water.

In the drawer nearest the stove, cooking utensils were lined up like surgical instruments on a sterile tray. Among her knives was a filleting knife. It had a hilt made of some synthetic material that matched the others in the set.

Inside the bread box was half a loaf of whole wheat, tightly resealed and clamped. Every opened cereal box in the pantry had the tab inserted into the slot. The canned vegetables weren't alphabetized, but the neatness of the rows was almost that extreme.

The contents of the refrigerator indicated that she was a conscientious eater but she wasn't a fanatic weight watcher. There were two half-gallon cartons of ice cream in the freezer. Of course the ice cream could have been for a guest.

He checked the drawer in the small built-in desk and found a laminated list of emergency telephone numbers, a ruled notepad with no doodles or notes, and several Bic pens, all black. Nothing personal or significant.

Through a connecting door he entered the living room. It could have been a catalog layout. Cushions were plumped and evenly spaced along the back of the sofa. Magazines were in neat stacks, the edges lined up like a deck of cards. The TV's remote control was squared up with the corner of the end table.

"Jesus," Wick whispered, thinking about the condition in which he'd left his shack in Galveston. When he'd left his motel room this morning it looked like it had sustained storm damage.

Midway down the short hall was a small room she obviously used for a home study. He hoped it would prove to be a treasure trove of information and insight into this woman. It didn't. The titles of the medical books on the shelves were as dry as dust. There were a number of atlases and travel-guide books, a few novels, mostly literary, nothing racy, certainly nothing to suit his unsophisticated reading taste.

On top of the neat desk her mail had been separated into two metal baskets, one for opened, the other for unopened. He scanned the ho-hum contents of both. In the deeper drawer of the desk he discovered an expandable file of receipts—a labeled compartment for each month. He looked through them but did not find a paid invoice for a contract killer tucked into the accordion folds.

It was in her bedroom that he received his first surprise. He stood on the threshold, giving it one swift survey before assimilating it more slowly. By comparison, this room was messy. This room wasn't occupied by a surgeon. It was lived in by a person. By a woman.

He had expected to find a bed that would meet military standards, one you could bounce a quarter off of. But, oddly, the bed had been left unmade. He moved past it to the window, where he knew Oren and Thigpen could see him from the second-story window of a house two houses down and behind Rennie Newton's. He gave them the finger.

Turning back into the room, he began his search with her bureau drawers. Undies were folded and stacked, panties in one drawer, bras in the one below it. She had divided the non-frilly from the frilly.

When she opened those drawers, he wondered what determined her selection. Daytime, nighttime? Work, play? Did her mood dictate which stack she chose from, or vice versa?

He rifled through the garments, looking underneath for keepsakes, letters, photographs that would give him a hint into the personality of Rennie Newton. Was she a woman who would link up with a noted criminal, as Oren suspected?

His search of the bureau drawers yielded several scented sachets but no clues. Nor did her closet, which was as neatly arranged by category as her lingerie drawers. He found nothing in shoe boxes except shoes.

He moved to her nightstand. A fitness magazine had been left open to an article about exercises one could do throughout the day to relieve neck tension. The cap on a bottle of body lotion hadn't been securely replaced. He picked up the bottle, sniffed. He didn't know one flower from another, but it said Goldleaf and Hydrangea, so he supposed that was what it was. Whatever, it smelled good.

Taking the cordless phone from its stand, he listened to the dial tone. It wasn't the broken tone indicating messages on her voice mail. As long as he was here he wished he had a bug to plant, but Oren had nixed the suggestion.

"We'd need a court order, and no judge is going to give us one until we can show probable cause."

"We could learn a lot by monitoring her calls."

"It's illegal."

Wick had laughed. "So's breaking and entering. We can't ever use anything I find in there."

"Yeah, but it's different."

He failed to see the difference but Oren was adamant, and it was Oren's show. He replaced the telephone in the recharger and opened the nightstand drawer. Inside he found a box of stationery, still wrapped in clear cellophane, unused. There was also a tear sheet from a newspaper. He took it out of the drawer and unfolded it.

It was an obituary page. One of them was for Eleanor Loy Newton. Daughter Rennie was listed as her only survivor. He recognized the name of the town on the masthead. Dalton, Texas. Carefully refolding the sheet, he re-placed it in the drawer.

As he did, he noticed a small white triangle barely visi-ble beneath the box of unused stationery. He picked up the box. Under it lay a small card with only one line typed on it: "I've got a crush on you."

It was unsigned, unaddressed, and undated, making it impossible to know if Rennie Newton had received it or if she had considered sending it before changing her mind. It looked like a gift-enclosure card. Had it accompanied a gift she'd received recently, or was it a keepsake from a high school beau, a former lover, last Saturday's one-night stand? It obviously held some significance for her or it wouldn't be in her nightstand drawer along with her mother's obituary.

Curious, but not criminal.

He replaced the card exactly as he'd found it and went next into the adjoining bathroom. He located a damp towel in the clothes hamper along with a pair of boxer shorts and a ribbed tank top. Her sleeping attire last night? Probably. A recent girlfriend had preferred comfy over sexy. Actually he had thought the comfy was pretty damn sexy.

An array of bath salts and gels was lined up on a shelf above the tub. And they weren't just for show. They'd been used often. The room smelled flowery and feminine. The tub was spanned by a wire rack, a resting place for a scented candle, a sponge, a razor, and a pair of reading glasses. She liked to lounge in the tub. But alone; it wasn't large enough for two.

Inside the mirrored medicine cabinet he found her toothbrush and a glass, a tube of toothpaste rolled up from the bottom—he didn't know anybody who actually did that—and mint-flavored dental floss. There was an assortment of cosmetics and night creams, a bottle of aspirin, and a blister-pack of antacid tablets. No prescriptions. Under the sink were rolls of toilet tissue and a box of tampons.

He stepped back into the bedroom and for a long time stood looking at the unmade bed. The pale yellow sheets were rumpled and the duvet was half on, half off. Unless he was very wrong, Rennie Newton not only bathed alone, she slept alone. At least she had last night.

"Took you long enough," Oren said when Wick rejoined them in the second-story room of the stakeout house.

"Yeah, what were you doing in there all that time, trying on her panties?"

That from Thigpen, whom everyone called Pigpen because that was what he looked like. He was crude and sloppy and, in Wick's opinion, unforgivably stupid.

"No, Pigpen, I stopped on my way back for a blowjob. Your wife says to pick up bread on your way home."

"Asshole. We got pictures of you flipping us the bird. Very professional, Threadgill."

"I stoop to the level of the people I'm with."

"I'm gonna add that photo to my gallery." Thigpen hitched his thumb toward the wall where he had taped the more revealing eight-by-tens of Rennie Newton.

Wick glanced at the pictures of which Thigpen was so proud, then angrily grabbed a bottle of water and twisted off the lid. He drank all of it before taking a breath.

"Well?" Oren asked.

Wick sat down and toed off his running shoes. "In a word?"

"For starters."

"Neat. As a pin. Obsessively clean."

He described the kitchen, living room, and study. Of the bedroom he said, "It wasn't quite as tidy. The bed was unmade but everything was in its place. Maybe she was in a rush this morning before she left for the hospital." He itemized what he'd found in the nightstand drawer.

"Was the card in an envelope?" Thigpen asked.

"I told you, no. It was a plain white card. Small. One typed line."

"She's from Dalton," Oren confirmed when Wick told them about the newspaper obituary. "Grew up there. Her father was some bigwig cattleman and businessman. Community leader. An iron in every fire. She was an only child."

"With no living relatives, apparently. She was listed as her mother's only survivor." Which would explain why she had an unopened box of stationery, Wick thought. Who would she write to?

"Did you find anything to indicate—"

"An alliance with Lozada?" Wick asked, finishing Oren's question for him. "*Nada.* I don't think she has a relationship of any kind with anybody. Not one single photograph in the place, no personal telephone numbers scribbled down. Our lady doctor appears to live a very solitary life."

When he paused, Oren motioned for him to expand. "Definitely no sign of a masculine presence, criminal or otherwise. No men's clothing in her closet or drawers. The only razor in the bathroom was pink. One toothbrush. No birth-control pills or condoms or diaphragm. She's a nun."

"Maybe she's a dyke."

"Maybe you're a cretin," Wick fired back at Thigpen.

Oren looked at him strangely, then turned to the other detective. "Why don't you knock off early today?"

"Don't have to ask me twice." Thigpen stood and hiked up his slipping khakis, which rode well below his belly. Giving Wick a sour look, he grumbled, "What's your problem, anyway?"

"Don't forget the bread."

"Fuck you."

"Thigpen!" Oren looked at him reprovingly. "Report back at seven tomorrow morning."

Thigpen shot Wick another annoyed look, then lumbered down the stairs. Neither Wick nor Oren said anything until they heard the front door of the empty house close, then Oren said, "What *is* your problem?"

"I need a shower."

His answer didn't address the question, but Oren let it go for the time being. "You know where it is."

As bathrooms went, it was sadly lacking. The towels they'd brought in were hardly worth the bother. They were cheap and small and didn't absorb. Wick had contributed soap he'd pilfered from his motel room. There was no hot water. But his bathroom in the Galveston house was no great shakes either. He was accustomed to an unreliable hot-water heater. He barely noticed the absence of amenities.

The vacant house was a perfect location for the department's surveillance of Rennie Newton since it afforded a clear view of both her backyard and the side driveway of her home. The house had been in the process of being remodeled when a dispute arose between the contractor and the non-resident owner. The squabble had turned nasty and was now in litigation.

FWPD had asked both parties if the house could be

used, and both had agreed to it, for a small stipend. Its being a construction site made it easy for them to come and go dressed more or less as tradesmen and craftsmen, and to carry in supplies and equipment without attracting unwanted attention from neighbors who were used to having houses in their neighborhood undergoing renovation.

Wick emerged from the bathroom and rummaged in the duffel bag he'd brought along so he would have a change of clothes. He dressed in a pair of jeans and a souvenir T-shirt from an Eagles concert he had attended in Austin years before. He raked back his wet hair with his fingers.

Oren had taken up Thigpen's post at the window. He gave Wick a critical glance over his shoulder. "Strange uniform for a cop."

"I'm not a cop."

Oren merely grunted.

"I guess beer is against house rules."

"Thigpen would rat us out. There're Cokes in the ice chest."

Wick got one, popped the top, and took a long swallow. "Want one?"

"No thanks."

He kicked his running shoes in the general direction of the duffel bag and dropped into a chair. He took another long pull on the soda can. Oren was regarding him closely, watching every move. Finally Wick said, "*What?*"

"What did you find inside her house?"

"I told you."

"Everything?"

Wick spread his arms and raised his shoulders in an innocent shrug. "Why would I hold out on you?"

"Because of your dick."

"Excuse me?"

"For a white woman the doc's pretty good-looking."

Wick laughed, then said, "Okay. So?"

Oren gave him a look that spoke volumes.

"Do you really think . . . ach." He swatted down Oren's surmise, shook his head, looked away. When he came back to meet Oren's unflinching gaze he said, "Look, if she's in cahoots with Lozada, it doesn't matter to me if she's Helen of fucking Troy. In heat. I want that bastard, Oren. You know I do. I'll use whoever I have to, do whatever it takes to get him."

Far from being reassured, Oren said softly, "Which is the second reason you might withhold information from me."

"I don't follow."

"Don't turn this into a personal vendetta, Wick."

"Who came knocking on whose door?"

Oren raised his voice to match Wick's. "I brought you in because I need a good man. Someone with your instincts. And because I thought you deserved to be in on this after what happened between you and Lozada."

"Is there a point floating around in there somewhere?"

Oren wasn't put off by his surliness. "Don't make me sorry I involved you." He subjected Wick to a stare as stern as his warning. Wick was the first to look away.

Oren always played by the rules. Wick found rules restrictive, and he seldom abided by them. It was that difference that usually caused them to clash. It was also what each admired most about the other. While Oren often chided Wick for his recklessness and casual approach to regulations, he admired his audacity. Wick rebelled against rules, but he respected Oren for upholding them.

Oren went back to watching Rennie Newton's house.

After a short silence, Wick said, "One thing I thought was curious. In her closet. Lots of blue jeans. Not designer shit. Worn ones like mine." He rubbed his hand over the denim that time and a thousand washings had bleached and softened. "Three pair of western boots, too. I didn't expect that."

"She rides."

"Horses?"

"It was in her bio. The *Star-Telegram* had an extensive file on her. I asked them for a copy of everything. Dr. Newton's been in the newspaper numerous times. Charity events. Community involvement. Doctors Without Borders."

"What's that?"

A manila folder was lying on the table. Oren picked it up and dropped it into Wick's lap. "Do your own research. Grace is holding dinner for me."

He got up, stretched, reached for a roll of architectural drawings he was using as props, and headed for the staircase. "We didn't finish the video last night. It's there if you want to watch it, but don't let it distract you from keeping an eye on the house."

"I'd like to see the rest of it. Might pick up something."

Oren nodded. "My pager will be with me. Call if anything out of the ordinary happens."

"Like Lozada showing up?"

"Yeah, like that. I can be here in ten minutes. See you in the morning."

"Is there any food?"

"Sandwiches in the minifridge."

The stairs creaked beneath Oren's weight. After he left, the house fell silent except for the occasional groan of old wood. The empty rooms smelled like the sawdust left over from the uncompleted renovation. Most would consider it an unpleasant place in which to spend a night, but Wick didn't mind. In fact he had volunteered for the night shift. Oren needed to be with his family. Thigpen, too. Although Wick imagined that Mrs. Thigpen would probably prefer him to be away as much as possible.

He picked up the binoculars and checked Rennie Newton's house. She wasn't home yet. He used the opportunity to check the small refrigerator and found two wrapped sandwiches. Tuna salad. Turkey and Swiss. He selected the turkey and carried it back with him to the table near the window. He put the tape into the combo VCR and monitor, then settled back to watch the video as he ate his sandwich.

The recording started playing at the point where Oren had stopped it the night before. On the video Oren said, "Dr. Newton, did you recently serve on the jury that acquitted an accused killer, Mr. Lozada?"

Her lawyer leaned forward. "Where's the relevance, Detective?"

"I'll get to it."

"Please do. Dr. Newton has surgical patients waiting for her."

"It could become necessary for another doctor to take over her responsibilities."

"Is that a threat that I might be detained?" Rennie Newton asked.

Oren sidestepped the direct question by saying, "The sooner you answer my questions, the sooner you can go, Dr. Newton."

She sighed as though finding the proceedings extremely tedious. "Yes, I served on the jury that acquitted

Mr. Lozada. You must know that or you wouldn't have brought it up."

"That's right, I do. In fact I've interviewed all eleven of your fellow jurors."

"Why?"

"Curiosity."

"About what?"

"It struck me that Dr. Howell's murder looked like a contract kill. His killer didn't rob him. We can't isolate any other motive. Fact is, his only known adversary was you."

Taken aback by that statement, she exclaimed, "Lee and I weren't adversaries. We were colleagues. Friendly colleagues."

"Who quarreled constantly."

"We had disagreements, yes. That's hardly—"

"You were a friendly colleague of his who recently let a contract killer back onto the streets."

"Mr. Lozada's crime was *alleged*," the attorney said in typical lawyer fashion. "Which has no bearing on this matter one way or the other. Dr. Newton, I insist you say nothing more."

Wick fast-forwarded through the argument that ensued between the attorney and Oren, who evidently persuaded the lawyer that it would be in his client's best interest to answer the questions. Cooperation with an investigation went a long way with the FWPD, and so forth. Wick knew the drill. He'd used it a thousand times himself.

He restarted the tape in time to hear Oren say, "All the other jurors told me you were for Lozada's acquittal from the get-go."

"That's incorrect," she said with remarkable calmness. "I wasn't *for* acquittal. Not at all. I believe Mr. Lozada was probably guilty. But the prosecuting attorney didn't convince me beyond a reasonable doubt. Because of that, and the charge we received from the judge, I couldn't conscientiously see him convicted."

"So it was a matter of conscience that drove you to persuade the other eleven to vote for acquittal."

She took a deep breath and let it out slowly. "As forewoman, it was my duty to see that every facet of the case was explored. It was a heinous crime, yes, but I encouraged the other jurors not to let their emotions overrule their pledge to uphold the law, even though it may be imperfect. After two days of deliberation each juror voted according to his own conscience."

"I think that sufficiently answers your questions." Once again her lawyer stood up. "That is unless there's another totally unrelated subject you wish to chit-chat about, Detective Wesley."

Oren agreed that at this point he had nothing further to ask, and switched off the recorder, ending the tape.

As it rewound, Wick recalled the last conversation he and Oren had had about the case the night before.

"Lozada seemed to make a . . . a connection with her during the trial," Oren had told him.

"Connection?"

"A lot of people noticed it. I asked the bailiff if there was a juror Lozada had especially played to and he said 'You mean the forewoman?' First thing out of his mouth, and I hadn't even mentioned Dr. Newton. The bailiff said our boy stared at her throughout the trial. Enough to make it noticeable."

"Doesn't mean she stared back."

Oren gave him one of his noncommittal shrugs that paradoxically said a lot.

"I'm not surprised Lozada would single out an attractive woman and stare at her," Wick had continued. "He's a creep."

"He's a creep who looks like a movie star."

"Of *The Godfather* maybe."

"Some women get off on that dangerous type."

"Speaking from experience, Oren? I promise not to tell Grace. Details. I want details. The really juicy ones." He had annoyed his friend further by giving him a lascivious wink.

"Cut it out."

It was then that Grace had joined them. She asked what Wick was laughing about, and when he declined to tell her, she reminded him that the girls wouldn't settle for the night until they got their story. He wove them a tale about a sassy rock star and her handsome, dashing bodyguard whose physical description strongly resembled him. He and Oren had no further conversation before he left.

After removing the videotape from the player, he decided to eat the tuna sandwich too. It tasted fishy and old, but he ate all of it, knowing he'd get nothing more until morning. He was dusting crumbs off his hands when he saw a Jeep wagon swing into Rennie Newton's driveway.

He yanked up the binoculars but barely got a glimpse of her before the car rolled into her garage. Less than thirty seconds later the light in her kitchen came on. The first thing she did was slide the strap of her oversized handbag off her shoulder and lower it to the table. Then she pulled off her suit jacket and tugged her shirttail from the waistband of her slacks.

Crossing to the fridge, she took out a bottle of water, uncapped, and took a drink. Then she twisted the cap back on and stood at the sink, her head down. Wick adjusted the focus on the binoculars. Through the window above the sink, she appeared close enough to touch. A loose strand of hair trailed alongside her cheek and fell onto her chest.

She rolled the cold water bottle back and forth across her forehead. Her expression, her body language, her posture indicated profound weariness. She *should* be tired, he thought. It had been a long day for her. He knew. He had been there when her day began.

Chapter 5

■■■■■■■■■■■■■■■

Rennie leaned against the counter and rolled the bottle of cold water across her forehead. It had been years since deep-breathing exercises were necessary for her to regain her calm. Years, but she hadn't forgotten how terrifying it felt not to be in absolute control.

For the last three weeks her life had been in disarray. The disintegration of her carefully structured life had begun with the jury summons. The day after receiving it through the mail, she and a group, including Lee Howell, had been gathered in the doctors' lounge. When she told them about the summons, they had groaned collectively and commented on her rotten luck.

Someone suggested that she claim to have young children at home.

"But I don't."

"You're the sole caretaker of an elderly parent."

"But I'm not."

"You're a full-time student."

She hadn't even acknowledged that suggestion.

"Throw the damn thing away and ignore it," another advised her. "That's what I did. Figured it would be worth the fine, no matter how steep, if I didn't have to appear."

"What happened?"

"Nothing. They never follow up on those things, Rennie. They run hundreds of people through there each week. You think they're going to take the time and effort to track down one no-show?"

"I would be the exception. They'd throw me in jail. Use me as an example to those who try and dodge their civic responsibility." Thoughtfully, she twirled the straw in her soft drink. "Besides, that's what it is. A civic duty."

"Please." Lee groaned around a mouthful of vending-machine potato chips. "It's a civic duty for people who have nothing better to do. Use your work to get you off."

"Work is not an exemption. That's printed in bold letters on the summons. I'm afraid I'm stuck."

"Don't worry about it," he said. "They won't choose you."

"Wouldn't surprise me if they did," another male colleague had chimed in. "My brother's a trial lawyer. Says he always tries to seat at least one good-looking woman on every jury."

Rennie returned his wink with a scathing glare. "And what if the lawyers are women?"

His smile collapsed. "Didn't think of that."

"You wouldn't."

Lee dusted salt off his hands. "They won't choose you."

"Okay, Lee, why not? You're just itching to tell me why I'd be an unsuitable juror, aren't you?"

He counted off the reasons on his nimble surgeon's

fingers. "You're too analytical. Too opinionated. Too out-spoken. And too bossy. Neither side wants a juror who could sway the others."

That was one argument Rennie would have gladly let Lee win. She had been the second juror picked from forty-eight candidates, and then she'd been voted forewoman. For the following ten business days, while paperwork mounted and her patient load got backlogged, her time had belonged to the State of Texas.

When it ended, her relief was short-lived. Through the media, the verdict had been criticized by the district attorney's office. Nor had it won the approval of the average citizen, Dr. Lee Howell being one.

He had voiced his opinion at that Friday night cookout. "I can't believe you let this joker off, Rennie. He's a career criminal."

"He's never been convicted," she'd argued. "Besides, he wasn't on trial for previous alleged crimes."

"No, he was on trial for executing a prominent banker, one of our fair city's leading citizens. The prosecutor was asking for the death penalty."

"I know, Lee. I was there."

"Here they go," said one of the other guests who'd gathered around to eavesdrop on what was sure to be a heated debate. "The staunch conservative and the bleeding-heart liberal are at it again."

"We jurors were informed going in that the DA was asking for the death penalty. That wasn't the reason we voted to acquit."

"Then how was it that you twelve decided to let this creep walk instead of giving him the needle? How could you believe for a second that he was innocent?"

"None of us believed that he was *innocent*. We voted him *not guilty*. There's a difference."

He shrugged his bony shoulders. "The distinction escapes me."

"The distinction is reasonable doubt."

"If it doesn't fit, you must acquit. That bullshit?"

"That bullshit is the foundation of our judicial system."

"She's on a roll now," someone in the background said.

"The so-called evidence against Mr. Lozada was entirely circumstantial," she said. "He could not be placed at the scene of the crime. And he had an alibi."

"A guy he probably paid to lie for him."

"There were no eyewitnesses. There were—"

"Tell me, Rennie, did all the jurors put this much thought into their decision?"

"What do you mean?"

"I mean that you're Miss Precision. You would've lined up all the facts in a neat little row, and God forbid that you take the human element into account."

"Of course I did."

"Yeah? Then tell me this, when you took that first vote, before you even began deliberation, how many voted guilty and how many not guilty?"

"I won't discuss what happened in that jury room with you."

He glanced around the ring of faces as though to say, "I knew it." "Let me guess, Rennie. You—"

"I deliberated the case once, Lee. I don't want to do so again."

"You were the conscientious objector of the group, weren't you? You led the charge for acquittal." He stacked his hands over his heart. "Our own Dr. Rennie Newton, crusader for the freedom of career criminals."

The argument ended there with their listeners' laughter. It was the last verbal skirmish she and Lee would ever have. As always, they'd parted friends. As she said good night to him and Myrna, he'd given her a quick hug. "You know I was only teasing, don't you? Of all the jurors who ever sat on any trial, you would work the hardest at getting it right."

Yes, she had tried to get it right. Little had she known what an impact that damn jury summons, the trial, and its outcome would have on her personally. She had counted on it being an inconvenience. She hadn't counted on it being catastrophic.

Did Detective Wesley really consider her a suspect?

Her lawyer had dismissed her concerns. He said because the police had absolutely no clues, they had thrown out a wide net and were interrogating everyone with whom Lee Howell had any interaction, from hospital orderlies to his golfing buddies. At this point everyone was suspect. Insinuation and intimidation were standard police methods, the attorney assured her. She shouldn't feel that she'd been singled out.

Rennie had tried to reassure herself that he was right and that she was overreacting. But what her lawyer didn't know was that when it came to being questioned by police, she had a right to be a little jittery.

Wesley's interrogation had been in the forefront of her mind this afternoon when the hospital board of directors invited her to join their weekly meeting and offered her the position tragically vacated by Dr. Lee Howell.

"I appreciate your consideration, but my answer is no thank you. You had months to consider me before, and you chose someone else. If I accepted now, I would always feel as though I were your second choice."

They assured her that Dr. Howell had received only one more vote than she and that none of them thought she was an inferior candidate.

"That's not the only reason I'm declining," she'd told them. "I admired Dr. Howell professionally, but I also regarded him and Myrna as friends. To benefit from his death would feel . . . obscene. Thank you for the offer, but my answer is no."

To her surprise, they refused to accept that answer and pressed her into thinking it over for a day or two more.

While flattered and gratified by their persistence, she was now faced with a difficult decision. She had wanted the position and knew she was qualified, but it would feel wrong to get a career boost from Lee's death.

Wesley was another factor to take into account. Were she to assume the position he considered a motive for murder, his suspicions of her involvement might be heightened. She wasn't afraid of his finding anything that would implicate her. There was nothing, absolutely nothing, connecting her to Lee's murder. But before Wesley determined that, she would be put through a rigorous police investigation. *That* was what she feared and wanted to avoid.

With all this weighing on her mind, her head actually felt heavy. Reaching back, she slid the coated rubber band from her hair and shook out her ponytail, then massaged her scalp, pressing hard with her fingertips.

She had performed four major surgeries before lunch. The waiting room outside the operating room had been filled with anxious friends and family not only of her patients, but of other patients.

Immediately following each operation, she had come

out to speak briefly with the patient's loved ones, to report on the condition of the patient, and to explain the
procedure she'd done. For some she was even able to
show color photographs taken during the surgery. Thankfully all the patients' prognoses had been good, all the
reports positive. She hadn't had to break bad news to
anyone today.

Thanks to her able staff, things had gone smoothly in
her office this afternoon. Rounds at the hospital had taken
a little longer than usual. She had the four post-op patients
to see, and three more to brief before their scheduled
surgeries tomorrow morning. One had to be sweet-talked
into his pre-op enema. The frazzled nursing staff had
given up. After Rennie talked to him, he surrendered
quietly.

Then, just before she left for the day, she had received
the telephone call.

The reminder caused her to shudder. Quickly she
finished the bottle of water and tossed it into the trash
compactor. She rinsed out the soaking carafe of the
coffeemaker, then prepared it for tomorrow morning and
set the timer. She knew she should eat something, but the
thought of food made her nauseous. She was too upset
to eat.

She left her handbag on the table—she didn't think
she had the strength to lift it—and turned off the kitchen
light. Then, as she started toward the living room, she
paused and switched the light back on. She had lived
alone all her adult life, and this was the first time she could
remember ever wanting to leave the lights on.

In her bedroom she switched on the lamp and sat
down on the edge of her unmade bed. Ordinarily it would
have bothered her that she hadn't had time to make her

bed before leaving that morning. Now that seemed a trivial, even silly concern. An unmade bed was hardly worth fretting about.

With dread, she opened the drawer of her nightstand. The card was beneath the box of stationery her receptionist had given her last Christmas. She had never even broken the cellophane wrapping. Pushing the stationery box aside, she stared down at the small white card.

She had been making notations on the charts of her post-op patients when the duty nurse had informed her that she had a call. "Line three."

"Thanks." She cradled the receiver between her cheek and shoulder, leaving her hands free to continue the final task of a very long day. "Dr. Newton."

"Hello, Rennie."

Her writing pen halted mid-signature. Immediately alarmed by the whispery voice, she said, "Who is this?"

"Lozada."

She sucked in a quick breath but tried to keep it inaudible. "Lozada?"

He laughed softly, as though he knew her obtuseness were deliberate. "Come now, Rennie, we're hardly strangers. You couldn't have forgotten me so soon. We spent almost two weeks together in the same room."

No, she hadn't forgotten him. She doubted that anyone with whom this man came into contact would ever forget him. Often during the trial his dark eyes had connected with hers across the courtroom.

Once she had begun to notice it she had avoided looking at him. But each time her gaze happened to land on him, he'd been staring at her in a way that had made her uncomfortable and self-conscious. She was aware that other jurors and people in the courtroom also had noticed his unwelcome interest in her.

"This call is highly inappropriate, Mr. Lozada."

"Why? The trial's over. Sometimes, when there's an acquittal, defendants and jurors get together and have a party to celebrate."

"That kind of celebration is tasteless and insensitive. It's a slap in the face to the family of the murder victim, who still have no closure. In any event, you and I have nothing to celebrate or even to talk about. Good-bye."

"Did you like the roses?"

Her heart skipped several beats, then restarted, pounding double-time.

After dismissing every conceivable possibility, it had occurred to her that he might have been her secret admirer, but she hadn't wanted to acknowledge it even to herself. Now that it had been confirmed, she wanted to pretend that she didn't know what he was talking about.

But of course he would know better. He had placed the roses inside her house, making certain she would receive them, leaving no margin for error. She wanted to ask him how the hell he had gotten inside her home but, as Lee Howell had pointed out to her, Lozada was a career criminal. Breaking and entering would be child's play to a man with his arrest record.

He was incredibly intelligent and resourceful or he couldn't have escaped prosecution for all his misdeeds, including the most recent murder for which he'd been tried and that she fully believed he had committed. It just hadn't been proved.

He said, "Considering the color of your front door I guessed red might be your favorite."

The roses hadn't been the color of her front door.

They'd been the color of the blood in the crime-scene photos entered as evidence and shown to the jury. The victim, whom it was alleged that Lozada had been hired to kill, had been choked to death with a garrote, something very fine yet so strong that it had broken the skin of his throat enough to bleed.

"Don't bother me again, Mr. Lozada."

"Rennie, don't hang up." He said it with just enough menace to prevent her from slamming down the telephone receiver. "Please," he said in a gentler voice. "I want to thank you."

"Thank me?"

"I talked to Mrs. Grissom. Frizzy gray hair. Thick ankles."

Rennie remembered her well. Juror number five. She was married to a plumber and had four children. She seized every opportunity to bore the other eleven jurors with complaints against her lazy husband and ungrateful children. As soon as she learned that Rennie was a physician, she had run down a list of ailments she wanted to discuss with her.

"Mrs. Grissom told me what you did for me," Lozada said.

"I didn't do anything for you."

"Oh, but you did, Rennie. If not for you, I'd be on death row."

"Twelve of us arrived at the verdict. No one was singly responsible for the decision to acquit you."

"But you led the campaign for my acquittal, didn't you?"

"We looked at the case from every angle. We reviewed the points of law until we unanimously agreed on their interpretation and application."

"Perhaps, Rennie," he said with a soft chuckle. "But Mrs. Grissom said you argued my side and that your arguments were inspired and . . . passionate."

He said it as though he were stroking her while he spoke, and the thought of his touching her made her skin crawl. "Don't contact me again." She had slammed down the telephone receiver but continued to grip it until her knuckles turned white.

"Dr. Newton? Is something wrong? Dr. Newton, are you all right?"

Drops of perspiration beaded on her face as though she were performing the most intricate and life-threatening surgery. She thought she might throw up. Taking a deep breath through her mouth, she let go of the telephone receiver and turned to the concerned nurse.

"I'm fine. But I'm not going to take any more calls. I'm trying to wrap up here, so if someone wants me, tell them to have me paged."

"Certainly, Dr. Newton."

She had quickly completed her chart notations and left for home. As she walked across the familiar doctors' parking lot, she glanced over her shoulder several times and was reassured by the presence of the guard on duty. She'd heard that the young man who had discovered Lee's body was taking some time off.

On the drive home, she kept one eye on the road and another in the rearview mirror, half expecting to see Lozada following her. Damn him for making her feel paranoid and afraid! Damn him for complicating her life when she had finally gotten it exactly as she wanted it.

Now as she stared at the hateful little card in her nightstand drawer, her resentment increased. It made her furious that he dared speak to her in sexual overtones and with implied intimacy. But it also frightened her, and that was what she hated most—that she was afraid of him.

Angrily she closed the nightstand drawer. She stood up and removed her blouse and slacks. She wanted a hot shower. Immediately. She felt violated, as though Lozada had touched her with his sibilant voice. She couldn't bear to think about his being here inside her house, invading her private space.

Worse, she felt a presence here still, although she told herself that was just her imagination, that it had been thrust into overdrive. She found herself looking at every object in the room. Was each item exactly as she'd left it this morning? The cap on her body lotion was loose, but she remembered being in a hurry this morning and not replacing it securely. Was that the angle at which the open magazine had been left on the nightstand?

She told herself she was being silly. Nevertheless, she felt exposed, vulnerable, watched.

Suddenly she glanced toward the windows. The slats of the blinds were only partially drawn. Moving quickly, she snapped off the lamp and then went to the windows and pulled the louvers tightly closed.

"Damn him," she whispered into the darkness.

In the bathroom, she showered and prepared for bed. When she turned out the light, she considered leaving it on, but only for an instant before deciding against it. She wouldn't give in to her fear even to that extent.

She had never been a coward. On the contrary, her courage when she was a child had caused her mother to wring her hands with concern. As a teen, her bravery had escalated into deliberate recklessness. In recent years she had traveled to war- and famine-plagued corners of the world. She had defied despots, and raging storms, and armed marauders, and contagious disease in order to provide medical treatment to people in desperate need of it, always with little or no regard for her personal safety.

Now, inside her own bedroom, lying in her own bed, she was afraid. And not just for her safety. Lozada posed more than a physical threat. Detective Wesley had mentioned his trial, had insinuated . . .

"Oh my God."

Gasping, Rennie sat bolt upright. She covered her mouth and heard herself whimper involuntarily. A chill ran through her.

Lozada had tried to impress her with a lavish bouquet of roses in a crystal vase. Personally delivered. What else had he done in an attempt to curry her favor?

The answer to that was too horrible to consider.

But obviously the homicide detective had considered it.

Wick opened another Coke, hoping it would wash away the unpleasant aftertaste of the tuna sandwich. Rennie had retired for the night. It had been thirty-two minutes from the time she got home until she had turned out her bedroom light. Not long. No dinner. No leisure activity. Not even a half hour of TV during which to unwind after a hard day.

She had spent some of that thirty-two minutes at the kitchen sink, appearing to be lost in thought. Wick saw her shake her hair loose and massage her scalp. She'd had the aspect of someone weighted down by a major problem, or suffering a severe headache—or both.

Which didn't surprise him. She'd worked her ass off today. He had arrived at the family waiting room at seven that morning, knowing the day began early in the OR. No-body questioned his being there. It was assumed that he belonged to one of the families who had set up temporary camp with magazines and cups of vending-machine coffee. He chose a chair in the corner, pulled his straw cowboy hat low over his brow, and partially hid behind an edition of *USA Today*.

It was 8:47 before Dr. Newton made her first appearance.

"Mrs. Franklin?"

Mrs. Franklin and her retinue of supporters clustered around the surgeon. Rennie was dressed in green scrubs, the face mask lying open on her chest like a bib. She wore a cap. Paper slippers covered her shoes.

He couldn't hear what she was saying because she kept her voice at a confidential pitch to ensure the family's privacy, but whatever she said made Mrs. Franklin smile, clasp her hand, and press it thankfully. After the brief conference, Rennie excused herself and disappeared through the double swinging doors.

Throughout the long morning she had made three other visits to the waiting room. Each time she gave the anxious family her full attention and answered their questions with admirable patience. Her smiles were reassuring. Her eyes conveyed understanding and compassion. She never seemed to be rushed, although she must have been. She was never brusque or detached.

Wick had found it hard to believe that this was the same guarded, haughty woman on Oren's videotape.

He had stayed in the OR waiting room until his stomach started rumbling so loudly that people began looking at him askance. The crowd had thinned out too, so the tall cowboy sitting all alone in the corner with a newspaper he'd read three times was beginning to attract attention. He had left in search of lunch.

Oren thought he'd been sleeping through the day in his dreary motel room. He hadn't told him about going to the hospital. Nor did he tell him that after grabbing a burger at Kincaid's he had staked out Rennie Newton's private office. It was located near the hospital on a street that had formerly been residential but had been given over largely to medical offices.

The limestone building was new looking and contemporary in design, but not ostentatious. The office had done a brisk business all afternoon, with patients going in and coming out at roughly fifteen-minute intervals. The parking lot was still half full when Wick left to go break into her house.

Yeah, Rennie had put in a full day. To reward herself she'd drunk a bottle of water. That was it. When she moved out of the kitchen, she had switched off the light, then turned it back on almost instantly, which he thought was strange.

She had left that light on when she went into the bedroom, where she sat slumped on the edge of the bed, loose hair falling forward. Her whole aspect had spelled dejection. Or terrible trouble.

Then she'd done another strange thing. She had opened her nightstand drawer and, for the next several minutes, stared into it. Just stared. She didn't take anything out or put anything in—she just stared into it.

What had she been looking at? he wondered. He concluded that it had to be the enclosure card. What fascination could an unopened box of stationery hold for her? Her mother's obituary might be something she would read occasionally, maybe in remembrance of her. But he was putting his money on the card. And that made him damn curious about its origin and significance.

Eventually she had closed the drawer and stood up. She'd unbuttoned her blouse and pulled it off. She was wearing an unadorned bra. Maybe the sheer lacy ones were reserved for the days when she didn't perform four surgeries. Or for the man who had sent her the card.

Next she had removed her slacks.

That was when Wick had realized he was holding his breath and admonished himself to resume breathing normally—if such a thing were possible. Could any heterosexual man breathe normally when he was watching a woman take off her clothes? He didn't think so. He didn't know of one. The question might warrant a scientific study.

Conducting his own test, he had inhaled deeply, then exhaled an even stream of carbon dioxide.

And in that instant, almost as if she had felt his breath against her bare skin, she looked toward the windows with alarm. Immediately the bedside lamp was extinguished. A vague silhouette of her appeared momentarily at the windows, then the slats of the blinds were closed tightly, blocking her from sight.

The light in her bathroom had come on and remained on for ten minutes, long enough for her to bathe using one of the scented gels. She might've used the pink razor, too. She'd probably brushed her teeth and rolled the tube of toothpaste up from the bottom before replacing it in the cabinet above the sink that had not one single water spot.

Then the house had gone dark except for the light in the kitchen. Wick surmised that she had probably gone straight from her bath to bed.

And now, after thirty-two minutes, she was probably

sleeping between the pale yellow sheets, her head sunk deeply into the down pillow.

He remembered that pillow. He had stared at it for a long time before peeling off the latex gloves and lifting it from the bed. He'd held it close to his face. Only for a second, though. Only for as long as any good detective would.

He hadn't told Oren about that, either.

Chapter 6

It was the best Mexican restaurant in Fort Worth, making it, in Lozada's opinion, the best restaurant in Fort Worth.

He came here only for the food and the deferential service he received. He could have done without the trio who strolled among the tables strumming guitars and singing Mexican standards in loud but mediocre voices. The decor looked like the effort of someone who had run amok in a border-town curio shop buying every sombrero and piñata available.

But the food was excellent.

He sat at his customary table in the corner, his back to the wall, sipping an after-dinner tequila. He'd have shot anyone who offered him one of those frozen green concoctions that came out of a Slurpee machine and had the audacity to call itself a margarita.

The fermented juice of the agave plant deserved to be drunk straight. He favored a clear *añejo*, knowing that what made a tequila "gold" was nothing but caramel coloring.

He had dined on the El Ray platter, which consisted of enchiladas con carne, crispy beef tacos, refried beans, Spanish rice, and corn tortillas dripping with butter. The meal was loaded with carbohydrates and fat, but he didn't worry about gaining weight. He'd been genetically gifted with the lean, hard physique that people joined health clubs and sweated gallons of perspiration to acquire. He never broke a sweat. Never. And the one time in his life he had lifted a dumbbell he had brained someone with it.

He finished his drink and left forty dollars cash on the table. That was almost double the amount of his bill, but it guaranteed that his table would be available anytime he came in. He nodded good-bye to the owner and winked at a pretty waitress on his way out.

The restaurant was located in the heart of the historic Stockyards area. Tonight the intersection of Main and Exchange Streets was thronged with tourists. They bought trashy Texas souvenirs like chocolates shaped as cow patties or rattlesnakes preserved in clear acrylic. The more affluent were willing to pay handsomely for handmade boots from the legendary Leddy's.

The tantalizing aroma of mesquite-smoked meat lured them into barbecue joints. Open barroom doorways emitted blasts of cooler air, the smell of beer, and the wail of country ballads.

The streets were congested with every kind of vehicle from mud-spattered pickup trucks to family vans to sleek European imports. Bands of young women and groups of young men prowled the wooden sidewalks in search of one another. Parents had pictures of their children taken sitting atop a bored and probably humiliated longhorn steer.

Occasionally one could spot an authentic cowboy. They were distinguished by the manure caked on their boots and the telltale circle worn into the rear pocket of their Wranglers by the ever-present tin of chaw. They also regarded their counterfeits with an unconcealed and justifiable scorn.

The atmosphere was lightheaded, wholesome, and innocent.

Lozada was none of those.

He retrieved his silver Mercedes convertible from a kid he'd paid twenty dollars to car-sit and drove up Main Street, across the river, and into downtown. In less than ten minutes he left his car with the parking valet, crossed the native-granite lobby of Trinity Tower, and took the elevator up to the top floor.

He had bought the penthouse as soon as the renovated building became available for occupancy. Like most of the buildings in Sundance Square, the exterior had been left as it was to preserve the historic ambience of the area. The interior had been gutted from the foundation up, reinforced to meet current building codes—and, hopefully, to withstand tornadic winds—and reconfigured for high-rise condo living.

After buying the expensive floor space, it had cost Lozada another two million dollars to replicate the apartment he had admired in *Architectural Digest*. This financial setback was earned back in only three jobs.

He let himself in and welcomed the quiet, cool serenity of the condo after the festive confusion of Cowtown. Indirect lighting cast pools of illumination on the glossy hardwood floors that were softened only occasionally with sheepskin area rugs. Every surface was sleek and polished—lacquered wood, slate, and metal. Much of the furniture was built-in, crafted from mahogany. The free-standing pieces were upholstered in either leather or animal pelts.

The main feature of his living room was a large glass tank situated atop a knee-high pedestal of polished marble. The tank was eight feet square and a yard deep. This unusual display was the only deviation from the apartment he'd seen in the magazine. It was a necessary addition. Inside the tank, he had created an ideal habitat for his lovelies.

The temperature and humidity were monitored and controlled. To prevent them from killing each other, he saw to it that they had enough prey on which to feed. Presently the tank contained five, but he had had as many as eight and as few as three.

They didn't have names; that would have been ridiculous, and nobody would ever accuse Lozada of being ridiculous. But he knew each of them individually and intimately and occasionally took them out and played with them.

The two *Centruroides* he had smuggled out of Mexico himself. He'd had them less than a year. The one that had been living with him the longest was a female of the common Arizona species. She hadn't been hard to come by, nor was she valuable, but he was fond of her. She had borne thirty-one young last year, all of which Lozada had killed as soon as they had climbed off her back, thereby declaring their independence from her. The other two in the tank were rarer and deadlier. It was hard not to be partial to them because they had been the most difficult and expensive to obtain.

They were the finest scorpions in the world.

He paused to speak to them, but he didn't amuse himself with them tonight. Ever the businessman, he checked his voice mail for messages. There were none. At the wet bar in the living room, he poured another *añejo* into a Baccarat tumbler and carried it with him to the wall of windows that provided a spectacular evening view of the river, for which the building was named, and the neighboring skyscrapers.

He raised a mock toast to the Tarrant County Justice Center. Then he turned in the opposite direction and raised his glass in a heartfelt salute to the warehouse across the railroad tracks.

These days the building housed a business that customized RVs and vans. But the corrugated-tin structure had been vacant twenty-five years ago when Lozada had committed his first murder there.

Tommy Sullivan had been his pal. He'd had nothing against the kid. They'd never spoken a cross word to one another. Fate had just put Tommy at the wrong place at the wrong time. It was during the hot summertime. They were exploring the empty warehouse for lack of something better to do. Boredom had placed them there and boredom had gotten Tommy killed.

Tommy had been walking several steps ahead of Lozada when it suddenly came to him how easy it would be to grab Tommy from behind, reach around his neck, and jab his pocketknife into his friend's jugular.

He'd done it just to see if he could. Tommy had proved he could.

He'd been smart to attack from behind because Tommy had spouted blood for what seemed like forever. It had been a challenge to keep it off him. But overall, killing Tommy had been incredibly easy. It had been just as easy to get away with it. He'd simply walked to Tommy's house and asked his mom if Tommy was at home. She told him no, but he was welcome to come inside and wait; Tommy was bound to show up sooner or later.

So Lozada had passed the time after killing Tommy playing Tommy's stereo in Tommy's room, in delicious anticipation of the hell that was about to break loose inside Tommy's house.

A knock interrupted Lozada's fond recollections. Out of habit, he approached the door cautiously, a switchblade flattened up against his wrist. He looked through the peephole and, seeing a familiar uniformed woman, released the lock and opened the door.

"Turndown service, Mr. Lozada?"

Living in the building came with perks, including the parking valet, the concierge, and twice-daily maid service. He motioned her inside. She went into his bedroom and set about her chores. Lozada refreshed his drink and returned to a chair near the window, setting his switchblade on the table within reach. He stared down at the movie marquee across the street, but none of the featured film titles registered with him.

His mind was on the telephone conversation he'd had with Rennie Newton earlier that evening. He smiled over her poor attempt at playing hard to get. She truly was adorable.

The maid approached him. "Do you want me to draw the drapes, Mr. Lozada?"

"No, thanks. Did you leave chocolates on the pillow?"

"Two. The kind you like."

"Thank you, Sally."

She smiled down at him and then began undoing the top of her uniform. He had never solicited personal information from her. In fact, he wouldn't even know her name if she hadn't volunteered it. She had been eager to tell him that this housekeeping job was strictly temporary. Her ambition was to become an exotic dancer in a men's club.

She had the tits for it, maybe. But not the ass. Hers was as broad as a barn.

When she began to dawdle playfully over the buttons of her uniform, he said, "Never mind that," and pulled her between his thighs, pushing her to her knees.

"I could give you a lap dance first. I've been practicing in front of a mirror. I'm good, even if I do say so myself."

By way of answer, he unbuckled his belt and unzipped his trousers. She looked disappointed that he didn't want to see her performance, but she applied herself to pleasing him. She unbuttoned his shirt and spread it open. She fingered the tattoo on his chest. A bright blue dagger with a wicked blade appeared to be spearing his nipple. Tattooed drops of blood spattered his ribs. "That gets me so hot." Her tongue, as quick and agile as a snake, flicked the tip of the dagger.

He had gotten the tattoo when he was sixteen. The tattoo artist had suggested he get his nipple pierced at the same time. "With this dagger, a ring through your nipple, that'd look cool, dude."

Lozada remembered the fear in the man's eyes when he had grabbed him by his Adam's apple and lifted him off his stool. "You think I'm a fag?"

The guy's eyes bugged. He'd choked out, "Naw, naw, man. I didn't mean nothin' by it."

Lozada had gradually released him. "You'd better do a fucking good job on those blood drops or it'll be your last tattoo."

By now Sally's avid mouth had worked its way down to his crotch. "Condom," he said.

"I don't mind."

"I do."

He never left DNA evidence. Nail clippings were flushed down the toilet. He shaved his entire body every day. He was as hairless as a newborn, except for his eyebrows. Vanity prohibited him from shaving them. Besides, without the eyebrow, the scar wouldn't be as noticeable, and he wanted that scar to show like a banner.

Thankfully he had a perfectly formed cranium. It was as smooth and spherical as a bowling ball. Add to that his olive complexion and he looked very handsome with a bald head. He used a handheld vacuum on his bed and dressing table twice a day just in case dry skin was sloughed off. He'd had his fingerprints burned off years ago.

From the experience with Tommy, he'd learned that a victim's blood could be troublesome. He had been afraid that someone would ask to see his pocketknife, and he wasn't sure that he'd been able to scrub away all the blood. No one ever considered him a suspect, and eventually he'd gotten rid of the knife, but from there on he tried to leave the weapon at the scene. He used common, ordinary things—nothing exotic, recently purchased, or traceable to him. Sometimes his hands were the only weapon necessary.

He had a social security number. Like a good citizen he paid taxes on the income he earned from a TV repair service. An old rummy who'd been drunk since they invented televisions ran the place for him. It was in a bad neighborhood where few bothered to have a broken TV repaired. They simply went to a good neighborhood and stole a newer one. Nevertheless it was a legitimate, if not very lucrative, business.

His real source of income left no trail an IRS auditor—or officer of the law—could follow.

Sally ripped open the foil packet with her large teeth. "You must be awful rich. Having this place. That sweet Mercedes."

He loved his possessions, even more now than before he had languished for eight months in the Tarrant County jail while awaiting trial. That taught one to appreciate the finer things in life.

Of course those months had also cost him revenue. But he wasn't worried. He had been well paid for the job on the banker.

His money was tucked away in interest-bearing accounts in banks all over the world, places he'd never been or intended to go. He could retire anytime he wanted and live very well for the rest of his life.

But retirement never occurred to him. He didn't do what he did for the money. He could make money any number of ways. He did what he did because he was good at it and liked doing it. He *loved* doing it.

"Those scorpions sorta creep me out, but I love your apartment. You've got awesome stuff. That bedspread is real mink, isn't it?"

Lozada wished she would shut up and just suck him.

"Are you as dangerous as people say?"

He grabbed a handful of her dyed black hair and yanked her head up. "What people?"

"Ouch! That hurts."

He twisted her hair tightly around his fist, pulling it tighter. "What people?"

"Just the other girls who work here in the hotel. We were talking. Your name came up."

He looked into her eyes but could see no signs of treachery. She was too stupid to be a paid informant. "I'm only dangerous to people who talk about me when they shouldn't." He relaxed his hand.

"Jeez, no need to get so touchy. It was just girl talk. I had bragging rights and wanted to brag." She grinned up at him.

If only she knew how repugnant that smile was to him. He despised her for her stupidity and coarseness. He would have liked to hurt her. Instead he pushed her face back into his lap. "Hurry up and finish me."

She was here only because she was convenient. He could always get a woman. Women were easy to come by. Even attractive ones would do anything for a little of his attention and a fifty-dollar tip.

But the easy ones weren't the kind of woman he wanted. He wanted the kind he'd never had before.

In school he'd been a punk who ran with a rough crowd. He was always in trouble either with school officials or the police, or both. His parents weren't interested enough to care. Oh, they complained about his bad behavior but never really did anything to correct it.

His baby brother had been born with a severe birth defect. From the day his parents brought the baby home from the hospital, Lozada might just as well have ceased to exist, because in his parents' hearts and minds he had. They devoted themselves exclusively to his little brother and his special needs. They'd assumed that their handsome, healthy, precocious older son didn't have any needs.

Around age four he had gotten angry over their neglect, and he'd never stopped being angry at them for favoring baby brother over him. He learned that being disobedient won him a little of Mommy and Daddy's attention, so he did every mischievous and mean thing his young mind could devise. He had been a hellion as a boy, and by the time he became a teenager he was already a murderer.

In high school the popular girls didn't date guys like him. He didn't use drugs, but he stole them from the dealers and sold them himself. He went to illegal cock fights rather than the Friday night football games. He was a natural athlete but didn't play team sports because he couldn't play dirty and where was the thrill in playing by the rules? Besides, he would never have sucked up to an asshole with a whistle who called himself Coach.

The popular girls dated guys who proudly wore their letter jackets and would go on to UT or Southern Methodist and major in business or law or medicine, like Daddy. The desired girls went steady with the boys who drove BMWs to the country club for their golf lessons.

The girls who dressed well and participated in all the extracurricular activities, the classy girls who held school offices and were members of academic clubs, avoided him, probably fearing they would be compromised if they so much as looked twice.

Oh, he had turned their heads all right. He'd always been good-looking. And he had that element of danger about him that women couldn't resist. But his raw sexuality scared them. If he looked at one too long, too hard, too suggestively, she got the hell away from him. He could never get near the nice girls.

Nice girls like Rennie Newton.

Now *there* was a classy woman. She was all the women he'd ever wanted wrapped in one beautiful package. Each day of his trial he couldn't wait to get into court to see what she would be wearing and how her hair was styled. Several times he'd detected a light floral scent and knew it must be hers, but he never got close enough to be certain.

Not until he entered her house. It was redolent with the fragrance. Recalling the essences of her contained in the rooms she occupied made him shiver with pleasure.

Mistaking the reason for it, the maid tightened her mouth around him. He closed his eyes and envisioned Rennie Newton. He fantasized that it was she bringing him to climax.

As soon as it was over, he told the girl to go.

"Don't you wanna—"

"No." The sight of her heavy breasts disgusted him. She was a pig. A whore.

Validating his thought, she ran her hands down the front of her body and swayed to silent music. "You're the best-looking guy I've ever been with. Even this is cute." She reached up and touched the scar, still pink, that bisected his left eyebrow. "How'd you get it?"

"It was a gift."

She looked at him stupidly. Then she shrugged. "Okay, don't tell me. It's still sexy."

She stretched upward, and when he realized she was about to kiss his scar, he shoved her away. "Get out of here."

"Well excuse me for breathing."

Before she could get to her feet, he clamped his fingers around her jaw like a vise, holding it so tightly that her lips became scrunched and protruding. "The next time you talk about me with anybody, *anybody*, I'll come find you and cut out your tongue. Do you understand?"

Her eyes were wide with fear. She nodded. He released her. For a large girl she surprised him by how quickly she could move. Maybe she had a future as an exotic dancer after all.

After she was gone, he mentally replayed his telephone

conversation with Rennie. He conjured up the pitch of her voice and the cadence of her speech until he could almost hear it.

The moment he had spoken her name, she had known who was calling. How silly of her to pretend she didn't. She had told him not to call her again, but that, too, was posturing. That was just the surfacing of a nice girl's innate wariness of the bad boy, and he didn't mind that. In fact, he had enjoyed hearing the trace of fear.

His experience with women was vast, but it was also limited in the sense that all had been mindless encounters for the sole purpose of sex. He was tired of that. Picking up women and going home with them could be tedious, especially when they wanted to cling. And he hated whining.

Paid whores came with their own set of nuisances. Meeting them in hotel rooms, no matter how upscale, was a tawdry proposition. It was essentially a business transaction, and inevitably the whore believed she was boss. He'd had to kill only one for insisting that she was in charge; they usually submitted to his superiority before it came to that.

Besides, whores were dangerous and couldn't be trusted. There was always a chance that the police were using one in an entrapment setup.

The time had come for him to have a woman who was of his own caliber. It was the one area of his life that was deficient. He owned the best of everything else. A man of his standing deserved a woman he could show off, one other men would envy him for.

He had found that woman in Rennie Newton.

And she must be attracted to him, or why would she have argued so passionately for his acquittal? If he'd had a mind to, he could already have satisfied their physical longing for each other. He could have waylaid her at any time and, if she had put up some bullshit female resistance, eventually subdued her. After he had fucked her a few times, she would've come to the understanding, as he had, that they were destined to be a couple.

But he'd wanted to take a more subtle approach. She was different from all the others; she should be wooed differently. He wanted to court her as a woman like her would expect to be courted. So even before the trial was over he had set out to learn who this glorious creature was and whether she had any enemies. Through his sly attorney the information had been easily obtained.

Killing that other doctor had been almost too easy. It wasn't a sufficient demonstration of his affection. Before calling Rennie, he had felt the need to follow that up with something that would better convey the depth of his feelings for her. Thus the roses. They had struck the perfect romantic note.

He finished his tequila. Chuckling softly, he thought of Rennie's rebuff. Actually, he was glad she hadn't been swept away by these preliminary overtures. Had she given in too soon and too easily he would have been disappointed in her. Her spirit and air of independence were part of her attraction. To a point, of course.

Eventually she would need to be taught that what Lozada wanted, Lozada would have.

Chapter 7

Wick approached the table where Lozada was having breakfast. "Hey, asshole, the glare reflecting off your head is blinding me."

Lozada's fork halted midway between his plate and his mouth. He looked up with anger-controlling slowness. If he were surprised to see Wick, he gave no indication of it, but rather treated him to an unhurried once-over. "Well, well. Look who's back."

"For about a week now," Wick said cheerfully.

"Is the Fort Worth Police Department so hard up they invited you to rejoin their miserable ranks?"

"Nope. I'm on vacation."

Wick pulled a spare chair from beneath the corner table, turned it around, and straddled it backward. Other customers in the hotel's dining room would think him rude, but he didn't care. He wanted to get under Lozada's skin. If the tick in the other man's cheek was any indication, he was succeeding.

"Say, those pancakes look good." He dipped his finger in the pool of maple syrup on Lozada's plate and licked it off. "Hmm. Right tasty."

"How did you know I was here?"

"I just poked my head out the window and followed the stench."

Actually this hotel coffee shop was known by the department to be one of the killer's favorite breakfast places. The son of a bitch had never kept a low profile. In fact, he jeered at his would-be captors from the driver's seat of his fancy car and the panoramic windows of his penthouse, material luxuries that gave the cops all the more reason to despise him.

"Are you having something, sir?"

Wick turned toward the young waitress who had approached the table. "Fun, darlin'," he said, sweeping off his cowboy hat and placing it over his heart. "Just having a little fun here with my old friend Ricky Roy."

Lozada despised his first two names and hated being addressed by them, so Wick used them whenever an opportunity presented itself. "Have you two met?" He read the waitress's name off the plastic tag pinned to her blouse. "Shelley—pretty name, by the way—meet Ricky Roy. Ricky Roy, this is Shelley."

She blushed to the roots of her hair. "He comes in here a lot. I know his name."

In a stage whisper, Wick asked, "Is he a good tipper?"

"Yes, sir. Very good."

"Well now that's nice to hear. And somewhat surprising. See, actually, Ricky Roy has very few redeeming qualities." He tilted his head thoughtfully. "Come to think of it, being a good tipper might be his only redeeming quality."

The waitress divided a cautious look between them that eventually landed on Wick. "Would you like some coffee?"

"No thanks, Shelley, but you're a sweetheart for asking. If I need anything I'll let you know." He gave her a friendly wink. She blushed again and scuttled away. Coming back around to Lozada, he said, "Now, where were we? Oh, yeah, long time no see. Sorry I missed your trial. Heard you and your lawyer put on quite a show."

"It was a waste of everybody's time."

"Oh, I agree. I surely do. I don't know why they would bother with a trial for a sack of shit like you. If I had my way, they'd skip the folderol and you'd go straight to death row."

"Then lucky for me my fate isn't up to you."

"You never know, Ricky Roy. One day soon it just might be." Wick flashed him a wide grin and the two enemies assessed one another. Eventually Wick said, "Nice suit."

"Thank you." Lozada took in Wick's worn jeans, cowboy boots, and the hat he had set on the table. "I could give you the name of my tailor."

Wick laughed. "I couldn't afford him. Those look like expensive threads. Business must be good." He leaned forward and lowered his voice. "Whacked anybody interesting since that banker fellow? I'm itching to know who hired you for that one. His daddy-in-law maybe? Heard they didn't get along. What'd you use on him, anyway? Piano wire? Guitar string? Fishing line? Why not just the old one-two with your trusty blade?"

"My breakfast is getting cold."

"Oh, sorry. I didn't mean to stay so long. No, I just stopped by to say hello and let you know I was back in town." Wick stood up and reached for his hat. He turned the chair around and pushed it back into place. Then he leaned across the table as far as he could reach and spoke for Lozada's ears alone. "And to let you know that if it's the last thing I do, I'm gonna carve my brother's name on your ass."

"I'm not sure that was a smart move, Wick."

"It did my heart good."

"In fact, I'm certain it was a dumb move."

Wick had miscalculated. Oren hadn't found the account of his meeting with Lozada funny. Not in the slightest. "Why's that?"

"Because now he knows we're watching him."

"Oh, like that's a shocker," Wick said sarcastically. "He knows we're always watching him." He'd been irritable to start with, and Oren's disapproval wasn't helping his mood. He lunged from his chair and began to pace. He snapped the rubber band against his wrist.

"That slick-headed bastard doesn't care if we've got a whole division watching him twenty-four/seven. He's been mooning the police department and the DA's office every day of his career. I wanted him to know that I hadn't forgotten what he did, that I was still after him."

"I can appreciate how you feel, Wick."

"I doubt that."

At that Oren got pissed, but he bit back a retort and remained calm. "You shouldn't have placed your personal feelings above the investigation, Wick. I don't want either Lozada or Rennie Newton to get wind of our surveillance. If they were involved in Howell's murder—"

"He might've been. She wasn't."

"Oh. And you're sure of this how?"

Wick stopped pacing and made an arrow of his arm to point out her house two lawns away. "We've been watching her for a whole friggin' week. She does nothing except work and sleep. She doesn't go out. Nobody comes to visit. She doesn't see anyone but the people she works with and her patients. She's a robot. Wind her up and she does her job. When she runs out of juice, she goes home, goes to sleep, and recharges."

The second-story room of the vacant house was uncomfortably warm. They'd had the electricity turned on so they could operate the central air-conditioning system, but it was antiquated and inefficient against the brutal afternoon heat.

The room seemed to Wick to be shrinking around him, and the schedule was as confining as the room. Couple his claustrophobia with Oren's stodgy adherence to the rule book and it was enough to drive him nuts. The investigation had turned stale. It was tiresome, and boring to boot.

"Just because we haven't seen them together doesn't mean they're not communicating," Oren said. "Both are too smart to do anything publicly. And even if they haven't made contact since Howell's murder, that doesn't mean they didn't conspire."

Wick threw himself back into the chair, his temper momentarily spent. Dammit, Oren was right. Dr. Newton could have hired Lozada to take out her rival before the police got suspicious and started watching her. It would have required only one phone call. "Have her phone records been checked yet?"

"All were numbers she calls regularly. But you wouldn't expect her to use her home phone to arrange an assassination." Oren sat down across from him. "Okay, enough of this BS. Out with it. What's bugging you?"

Wick pushed back his hair, held it off his forehead for

several seconds, then lowered his hands. "I don't know. Nothing." Oren gave him a paternal I-know-better look. "I feel like a goddamn window-peeper."

"Surveillance work like this has never bothered you before. What's making this time different?"

"I'm out of practice."

"Could be. What else? You miss the beach? Salt air? What?"

"I guess."

"Uh-huh. It's more than homesickness for that swell place you have down there in Galveston. You look to me like you're about to claw out of your skin. You're restless and edgy. What's the matter? Is it because this investigation involves Lozada?"

"Isn't that enough?"

"You tell me."

Wick gnawed on the inside of his cheek for several moments, then said, "It's Thigpen. He's a goat."

Oren laughed. "And he speaks so highly of you."

"I'll bet."

"You're right. He thinks you're a jerk."

"Well at least I don't stink. This whole house reeks of those godawful onion sandwiches he brings from home. You can smell them the minute you open the door downstairs. And his butt crack sweats."

Oren's laughter increased. "What?"

"Yeah. Haven't you ever noticed the sweat stains on his pants? It's disgusting. And so are these." Again, he came out of his chair like a circus performer shot from a cannon. He was across the room in three strides, yanking the photographs off Thigpen's "gallery" wall.

He crumpled them and tossed the wadded pictures onto the floor. "How juvenile can you get? He's got the mentality of an adolescent pervert. He's crude and stupid and . . ." Oren was gazing at him with a thoughtful frown. "Shit," he muttered and returned to his chair.

Wick lapsed into a sulky silence and stared out the window at Rennie's house. Earlier she had gone for a run through her neighborhood. As soon as they saw her strike off down the sidewalk, Oren had rushed downstairs and followed her at a discreet distance in his car.

After doing five miles she returned, breathing hard and sweating through her tank top. According to Oren, she had done nothing on the outing except run. "The lady's fit," he'd said.

She hadn't gone out again. Because of the outdoor glare on the windowpanes, it was difficult to see anything inside her house except occasional movement. After nightfall she had started drawing her blinds closed.

Wick sighed. "All right, maybe I shouldn't have approached Lozada. But it was hardly a red alert. He knew I would come after him one day. I swore I would."

Oren was contemplative for another several moments, then said, "I think he did Howell."

"Me too."

He had read the completed report as soon as it was available. The CSU had done its detail work, but the crime scene had been as sterile as the victim's operating room. They had no cause for searching Lozada's condo or car, and even if they did, they would find nothing that connected him to the crime. Experience had taught them that.

"He's a fucking phantom," Wick said. "Never leaves a clue. Nothing. Doesn't even disturb the air when he moves through it."

"We'll get him, Wick."

He gave a curt nod.

"But by the book."

Wick looked at Oren. "Go on and say it."

"What?"

"You know what. What you're thinking."

"Don't put thoughts in my head, okay?"

"You're thinking that if I'd played by the book, we would've had him three years ago. For Joe."

The fact was indisputable, but Oren was too good a friend to say so. Instead, he smiled ruefully. "I still miss him."

"Yeah." Wick sat forward and planted his elbows on his knees. He dragged his hands down his face. "So do I."

"Remember that time—you'd just graduated from the academy. Wet behind both ears. Joe and I were staking out that illegal gambling parlor on the Jacksboro highway. Coldest night of the year, freezing our nuts off. You thought you'd be a good rookie and surprise us with a pizza."

Wick picked up the story from there. "I showed up in a squad car, marked you for damn sure. Joe didn't know whether to horsewhip me for blowing your cover or eat the pizza before it got cold." He shook his head with chagrin. "Y'all never let me live that one down."

Joe and Oren had attended the police academy together and shortly after their graduation had been made partners. Joe had been with Oren when both his daughters were born. He'd waited with Oren through anxious hours when Grace had a cyst in her breast biopsied. He'd traveled with him to Florida to bury his mother. Oren had cried with Joe when the woman he loved broke their engagement and his heart.

They had trusted each other implicitly and entrusted

one another with their lives. Their bond of friendship was almost as strong as the one Wick and Joe had shared as brothers.

When Joe was killed Oren had assumed the role of Wick's big brother, and later his partner, although each acknowledged that no one would ever fill the void that Joe had left in their lives.

Almost a full minute of thoughtful silence elapsed before Oren slapped his thighs and stood up. "If it's all right with you, I'm gonna shove off."

"Sure. Tell Grace thanks for the ham and potato salad. It'll go down good tonight after all those lousy sandwiches. Give the girls hugs."

"Sorry you have to spend your Saturday night here."

"No problem. I—" He stopped, remembered something, glanced at his watch. "What's the date?"

"Uh, the eleventh. Why?"

"Nothing. Just lost track of my days. You'd better move along. Don't want Grace to get pissed at you."

"See you tomorrow."

"Yeah, see ya." Wick slumped down in his chair and stacked his hands on the top of his head, trying to look casual and bored.

He waited until he heard Oren's car pull away, then he scooped up his keys and followed him out. He climbed into his pickup and drove past Rennie's house. No signs of her. No hint of her plans for the evening. What if his hunch was wrong? If it was, and Lozada paid a call to her house tonight, Oren would have his head on a pike by daybreak.

But he was going to gamble that he was right.

*   *   *

He made it to the church with three minutes to spare. He jogged from the parking lot toward the sanctuary and barely made it into a seat in the last row before the steeple bells tolled the hour of seven.

Upon leaving the surveillance house, he'd driven like a madman to the nearest mall, entered the department store at a dead run, and had thrown himself on the mercy of a haberdasher who was looking forward to the end of his long Saturday shift.

"Forgot the damn thing until half an hour ago," Wick explained breathlessly. "There I am at the Rangers game, having a cold beer and a chili dog, and it hits me." He smacked his forehead with his palm. "Left the game, and wouldn't you know it? For once the Rangers were leading."

So far the elaborate lie had moved the haberdasher to do nothing except sniff in boredom. Some embellishment was required. "If I don't go my mom'll never forgive me. Her back went out last Thursday. She's laid up popping muscle relaxers and fretting over missing this thing. So I shot off my big mouth and said, 'Don't worry about it, Mom. If you can't go, I will.' I hate like hell to break a promise."

"How much time do you have?"

Ah! Everybody had a mom. "An hour."

"Hmm, I just don't know. You're awfully tall. We don't keep that many longs in stock."

Wick flipped out his credit card and a fifty-dollar bill. "I'll bet this you can find something."

"A challenge," said the haberdasher as he pocketed the fifty, "but by no means impossible."

With the assistance of a tailor who muttered deprecations in an alien dialect while he marked the needed al-

terations, they outfitted Wick for the occasion, including a
pale blue shirt and matching necktie.

"The monochromatic look is in." Apparently the haberdasher had determined, as Lozada had, that he needed
some fashion guidance.

While the suit pants were being hemmed and the
jacket nipped in at the waist, Wick went into the mall and
had his boots shined. Luckily he'd worn his black ostrich
pair today. Next, he located a men's room and wet his hair.
He combed it back with his fingers. Time didn't allow for
barbering.

Now, as he settled into the pew, he didn't believe anyone would guess that he'd been assembled for the affair in
under sixty minutes.

The ceremony began with the seating of the mothers.
Next came the bridesmaids decked out in dresses the color
of apricots. Everyone stood for the bride's grand entrance.

Wick used the advantage of his height to search as
many faces as he could. He was on the verge of thinking
he'd gone to a hell of a lot of trouble and expense for
nothing when he spotted her about a third of the way
down the sanctuary. Best he could tell, she didn't have an
escort.

He stared at the back of her head for the duration of
the ceremony. When it concluded, he kept her in sight as
the guests filed out of the church and returned to their
cars for the drive to the country club. He was glad to see
that her Jeep wagon joined the processional headed toward the reception.

The wedding invitation had been among her opened
mail the day he'd searched her house. He'd read it, mem-
orized the day, time, and place, thinking that the information might come in handy. When Oren mentioned this

being Saturday night, it had sparked his memory. He had taken a chance on Rennie attending the wedding and had made an instantaneous decision to watch her up close rather than from afar through binoculars.

When he arrived at the country club, he opted to park himself and take his keys with him rather than turning his pickup over to a valet. It was faster, and he wanted to be inside the club ahead of Rennie. The haberdasher had called the bridal department of the store and arranged a wrapped gift for him. He carried it in with him and left it on the table draped in white fabric.

A pretty young woman was attending the guest book. "Don't forget to sign it."

"My wife already did."

"Okay. Have fun. Bar and buffet are already serving."

"Great." And he meant it. He had feared it might be a seated dinner, in which case there would be no place card with his name on it and he would be forced to leave.

But he didn't go to either the bar or the buffet. Instead he took up a position against the wall and tried to remain as inconspicuous as possible. He saw Rennie the moment she entered the ballroom and for the next hour he tracked her every move.

She chatted with anyone who engaged her, but for the most part she stood alone, an observer of the festivities more than a participant. She didn't dance, ate sparingly from the buffet, declined the wedding cake and champagne, preferring instead a glass of clear liquid on the rocks with a lime twist.

Wick gradually made his way toward her, keeping to the fringes of the crowd and avoiding the principals of the bridal party lest one of them introduced himself and asked to whom he belonged.

Rennie was concluding a conversation with a couple, backing away from them with promises of another dinner date soon, when Wick saw his opportunity.

He put himself in her path; she bumped into him.

Coming around quickly, she said, "Oh, I'm so sorry. Please excuse me."

Chapter 8

N o problem." Wick smiled and nodded down at her hand. "You're the one who got wet. Allow me?"

He took her glass from her and signaled a waiter, who not only took away the glass but also provided napkins for her to use to dry her hands. "Thank you," she said to Wick when the waiter moved away.

"You're welcome. Let me get you another drink."

"I'm fine, really."

"My mom would disown me if I didn't." Mom again. "Besides, I was about to get one for myself. Please." He motioned toward the bar.

She hesitated, then gave a guarded nod of assent. "All right. Thank you."

He steered her toward the bar and when they reached it, he said to the bartender, "Two of whatever the lady is having."

"Ice water with lime, please," she told the young man.

Then she glanced up at Wick, who was tugging on his ear and smiling with chagrin.

"And here I thought I was being so suave by letting you order for me."

"You're under no obligation to let the order stand."

"No, no, ice water is just what I wanted. Tall, cold, and refreshing. August weddings are thirsty work." The bartender slid the two glasses toward him. Wick passed one to her and then clinked the glasses together. "Don't drink it too fast or it'll go to your head."

"I promise I won't. Thanks again."

She stepped away so other guests could get to the bar. Wick pretended not to recognize a brush-off line when he heard one and fell into step beside her. "I wonder why January and February aren't the big wedding months?"

She looked at him with misapprehension. He didn't know if she was surprised he hadn't taken the hint and left her alone or if she was confused by the random question.

"What I mean is," he rushed to say, "why do so many couples get married in the summer months when it's so blasted hot?"

"I'm not sure. Tradition?"

"Maybe."

"Convenience? Those are vacation months. That makes it easier for out-of-town guests to attend."

"You?"

"From out of town?" Her hesitation wasn't long, but long enough to be noticeable. "No, I live here."

Although she didn't look all that interested, he told her he also was a local. "Are you here on behalf of the bride or the groom?"

"The groom's father and I are colleagues."

"My mother is second cousin to the bride's mother," he

lied. "Something like that. Mom couldn't come but felt that someone from our branch of the family . . . You know how these things go."

She began moving away from him again. "Have a nice time. Thanks again for the ice water."

"My name's Wick Threadgill."

She stared down at his extended right hand, and for several seconds he believed she wasn't going to take it. But then she reached out and clasped it, firmly, but only for an instant before withdrawing. It didn't give him time to register much except that her hand was colder than his, probably from keeping a death grip on her water glass, which she had done since he handed it to her at the bar.

"Did you say Wick?

"Yes. And I haven't got a speech impediment."

"That's an unusual name. Is it short for something?"

"No. Just Wick. And you?"

"Rennie Newton."

"Is that short for something?"

"*Doctor* Rennie Newton."

He laughed. "Pleased to meet you, Dr. Rennie Newton."

She glanced toward the exit as though locating the nearest escape route should the need for one arise. He got the feeling that at any moment she was going to bolt, and he wanted to keep the conversation going for as long as possible.

Even if she hadn't been the subject of a homicide investigation he would be curious. If they'd met innocently, he would still want to know why a woman who appeared sophisticated was this damned nervous over carrying on a conversation with a stranger in the harmless environment of a wedding reception with hundreds of people around.

"What kind of doctor?" he asked.

"Medical."

"Do you specialize?"

"General surgery."

"Wow. I'm impressed. Do you do trauma surgery? Shootings, stabbings, the kind of stuff you see on TV?" The kind of stuff that landed your rival colleague in the morgue? He watched for telltale signs of guilt in the incredibly green eyes, but if she was an accomplice to that crime her eyes didn't give her away.

"Mostly it's scheduled, routine procedures. I sometimes get a trauma case if I'm on call." She patted her beaded handbag. "Like tonight. I've got my pager."

"Which explains your teetotaling."

"Not even a champagne toast when I'm on call."

"Well, I hope there won't be any emergencies that call you away tonight." His tone of voice, and the manner in which he was looking at her, made his meaning unmistakable. And his unmistakable meaning made her unmistakably uncomfortable.

Her smile faltered. Barriers went up all around her like laser beams around a treasured museum piece. If he ventured too close he would trip them and set off all kinds of alarms.

A drum roll drew their attention to the front of the bandstand, where the bride was preparing to toss her bouquet to a group of eager young women all jostling for the best position. Wick stood slightly behind Rennie and to her right. He had read the reactions of enough women to know that his nearness was unsettling to her. Why? he wondered.

By now most women would have either: (A) flirted back and let him know that she was available for the rest of the evening; (B) informed him of a boyfriend who unfortunately couldn't attend the wedding but to whom she was committed; or (C) told him to get lost.

Rennie was in a category of her own. She sent mixed signals. She was still here, but she'd taken cover behind a do-not-touch, don't-even-think-about-it demeanor that was as daunting as a convent wall.

Wick was curious to know how much pressure he could apply before she cracked. So he inched even closer, close enough to make his presence impossible to ignore without actually touching her.

After the bouquet toss, the groom went down on bended knee to slide a frilly garter off his bride's extended leg while several young men reluctantly shuffled forward to form a tight group, hands in pockets, shoulders hunched.

"Ah, the difference between the sexes clearly demonstrated by this simple wedding tradition." He leaned down and slightly forward in order to speak directly into Rennie's ear. "Notice the men's level of anticipation compared to that of the women."

"The men look like they're going to the gallows."

The groom threw the garter. A young man was forced to catch it when it hit him in the forehead. One of the bridesmaids squealed and rushed out to embrace him. She covered his blushing face with kisses.

"I've got a drawer full of those things," Wick said.

Rennie turned. "That many?"

"I always had the advantage of height."

"Anything to show for them?"

"A drawer full of garters."

"All those garters wasted? Maybe your height was a disadvantage."

"I never thought of it that way."

The band launched into a crowd-pleasing song. Other guests began making their way to the dance floor, but they eddied around Rennie and Wick because neither of them moved.

"*Doctor* Newton, huh?"

"That's right."

"Dang the luck."

"Why?"

"I'm healthy."

She lowered her gaze to the Windsor knot of his monochromatic necktie.

"Are you here with anyone, Dr. Newton?"

"No."

"Me neither."

"Hmm."

"Dance?"

"No thank you."

"Another ice water?"

"No. Thanks."

"Is it a breach of etiquette to leave the reception ahead of the bride and groom?"

She raised her head quickly, met his eyes. "I believe so."

"Rats."

"But I think I've had all the gaiety I can stand."

Grinning, Wick nodded her toward the nearest exit. As they wended their way through the crowd, his hand rode on the small of her back and she made no effort to dislodge it.

The parking valets were lounging against the columns on the wide portico. One sprang forward as soon as he and Rennie came through the door. "I parked your car right over there, Dr. Newton. Easily accessible like you asked."

"Thank you."

She opened her handbag for a tip, but Wick was the faster draw. He pressed a five-dollar bill into the young man's palm. "I'll walk Dr. Newton to her car. No need to bring it up."

"Uh, okay, thank you, sir. Keys are in it."

Her smile for the obliging valet froze into place. She allowed Wick to guide her down the wide brick steps toward the tree-shaded VIP parking lot, but her posture was as rigid as an I-beam. Her lips barely moved when she said "You shouldn't have done that."

Yep, she was pissed. "Done what?"

"I pay my own way."

"Pay your own . . . What? The tip I gave the valet? Getting to walk you to your car was well worth the five bucks."

By now they had reached her Jeep. She opened the driver's door and tossed her handbag inside, then turned to face him. "Walking me to my car is all that five-dollar bill bought you."

"Then I guess going for coffee is out of the question."

"Definitely."

"You don't have to give me an answer right away. Take your time."

"Stop flirting with me."

"I only asked you to have coffee, not—"

"You've been flirting since I apologized for bumping into you. If you expected anything to come of it, you've wasted your time."

He held up his hands in surrender. "All I did was tip a valet for you. I only meant to be gentlemanly."

"Then thank you for being a gentleman. Good night." She got into the car and pulled the door closed.

Wick immediately reopened it and leaned in, putting

his face inches from hers. "Just FYI, Dr. Newton, if I'd been flirting you'd know by now that I think your eyes are sensational, and that I'll probably have a real dirty dream about your mouth. Have a nice night."

He closed the door soundly, then turned and walked away.

From the vantage point of his car, which was parked half a block down and across the street from the country club, Lozada saw Rennie emerge from the wide double-door entry of the club. She was wearing a dress of some lightweight summer fabric that clung to her figure, stirring his desire.

When she stepped out from beneath the second-floor balcony the setting sunlight struck her blond hair and made it shimmer. She looked fantastic. He noticed the grace with which she walked. She would—

". . . the *fuck* is this?"

Lost in his fantasies, he hadn't paid any attention to the man walking alongside Rennie. When he suddenly recognized the rangy physique and realized who her companion was, he could barely restrain himself from leaving his car, crossing the street, and murdering Wick Threadgill then and there.

It was bound to happen eventually. He was going to have to kill that smart-mouthed motherfucking cop, so why not sooner rather than later? Why not right fucking now?

Because it wasn't Lozada's style, that was why. Crimes of passion were for amateurs with no self-control. While he would enjoy having the matter of Wick Threadgill finally and satisfactorily settled, he had better things to do than spend the rest of his days on death row, exhausting appeals until they finally ran out and then having the state put a needle in his vein for killing a cop.

If Wick hadn't screwed up, Lozada probably would be awaiting execution for killing his brother Joe. Lozada knew that that mistake still chafed Wick. It must drive him crazy to know that his brother's murderer was living well in a penthouse, wearing hand-tailored suits, driving expensive cars, eating, drinking, fornicating—living free thanks to him.

Lozada fingered the scar above his eye and snickered. He was too clever to react in the heat of the moment as Wick had. Others made mistakes like that, but not Lozada. Lozada was a pro. A pro without equal. A pro didn't lose his head and act without thinking.

Besides, when he finally got around to killing Wick Threadgill, the anticipation of it would be half the fun. He didn't want to take him out now, quickly, and deny himself the pleasure of planning it.

However, as he watched the cop walking close to the woman he would soon possess, he gripped his car's steering wheel as though he were trying to pry it off its mounting.

What the hell was his Rennie doing with Wick Threadgill?

The initial shock of seeing them together gave way to concern. This was a disturbing turn of events. Threadgill had interrupted his breakfast this morning and he was at a wedding reception with Rennie tonight? Coincidence? Not likely.

What was Wick's interest in Dr. Rennie Newton? The role she'd played in his recent trial? Or was it something to do with the Howell murder case that remained unsolved? Lozada wouldn't have known her plans for this evening if he hadn't seen the wedding invitation the day he went snooping through her house after delivering the roses. How had the cop known where she would be tonight? Had Wick also been snooping in her house?

These were troubling questions.

But the one possibility that really nagged him, that made him see red, that caused heat to rise out of his hairless head, was that Rennie might be in league with the police. Had they somehow discovered his attraction to her? Had Threadgill and company enlisted her help to try to trap him?

Oh now, he would hate that. He really would. Having to kill her for betraying him would be a waste of good woman.

He watched with increasing suspicion as Threadgill leaned down into her car, then straightened up and shut the door. She backed out of her parking space, turned out of the country-club parking lot, and drove right past Lozada without noticing him. Her eyes were on the road straight ahead, and she wasn't smiling. In fact, she looked angry. Threadgill's parting words must've made her mad. He was a wiseass with everyone else, he probably was with women, too.

Lozada started his car and executed a tight U-turn. He followed Rennie home. She went in alone. Parking farther down the block, he watched her house for hours. She didn't leave again. Neither Threadgill nor anyone else showed up there.

It was after midnight before Lozada began to breathe easier. His suspicions about Rennie receded. There was a logical explanation for why she'd been with Threadgill. Perhaps he had been investigating her in connection with the Howell murder. It was well known that she and Howell had had their differences. Fort Worth's finest would have learned that. Being questioned by a cop at a social event would have made her angry, which explained why she'd looked pissed when she drove away from the country club.

Satisfied that he'd reached the correct conclusion, he picked up his cell phone and dialed her number.

Chapter 9

Wick trudged up the stairs in the dark. Carrying his new suit jacket and the department-store shopping bag in one hand, he yanked on his necktie with the other. By the time he reached the stuffy second-floor room his shirt was hanging open and his belt was unbuckled.

From the country club he had trailed Rennie into her neighborhood. He didn't turn down her street, but took another route to the stakeout house, which put him there about the same time she pulled into her garage.

He went straight to the window and looked through the binoculars. He toed off his boots and peeled off his socks.

Rennie passed through her kitchen without stopping and disappeared through the doorway leading into the living room.

Wick shrugged off his shirt.

The light in Rennie's bedroom came on. Like him, she seemed to have found her clothes confining. She stepped

out of her shoes—high-heeled sandals, he remembered—
and then reached behind her neck for the zipper of her
dress.

Wick kicked out of his trousers.

Rennie pulled her dress off her shoulders, worked it
past her hips, then stepped out of it.

Wick stood stock-still.

Sexy undies tonight. Pale lavender. Mere suggestions of
raiment that made her look more naked than nakedness.
Fabric as sheer as breath. Totally inadequate, but damned
effective.

She replaced the sandals on a shelf in the closet and
hung her dress on the rod, then went into the bathroom
and closed the door.

Wick closed his eyes. He leaned against the window-
pane to cool his forehead on the glass. Had he actually
groaned? He was salivating. Jesus, he was becoming Thigpen.

Leaving the binoculars on the table, he took a bottle of
water from the small refrigerator. He didn't come up for
air until he'd drunk it all. Still keeping an eye on her
house, he groped inside the shopping bag until he located
the jeans he'd worn into the department store. He pulled
them on but left his shirt in the bag. It was too damn hot
up here to be fully dressed.

"What's wrong with that freaking air conditioner?" he
complained to the empty darkness.

Seeing Rennie come from the bathroom, he grabbed
the binoculars. She had swapped the fantasy lingerie for a
tank top and boxers, which actually held their own against
the fancier stuff but disabused Wick of the notion that she
might be waiting for a lover to arrive.

For the wedding she had worn her hair pulled back

and wound into a bun at her nape. Now it was hanging long and loose. It was a coin toss which he liked best. Both served their purpose. One looked like a professional woman. One looked like a woman, period.

She rubbed her arms. Chilled? Or nervous? She glanced at the window and when she realized that the blinds were open, she quickly extinguished the light. Definitely nervous.

Wick exchanged the regular binoculars for a pair of night-vision ones. He could now see Rennie standing at the window and peering through the open slats of the blinds. She turned her head from side to side slowly, as though searching all corners of her dark backyard. She tested the lock on the window, then she drew the cord that shut the blinds. A few seconds later she reopened them.

Was that a signal to someone? he wondered.

She stood there for several minutes more. Wick kept the binoculars on her, but occasionally swept the yard with them, looking for movement. Nobody scaled her back fence. Rennie didn't climb out the window. Nothing happened.

Eventually she backed away. Wick refocused the binoculars. He could see her turning down her bed. She lay down and pulled the sheet up as far as her waist. She plumped her pillow beneath her head, lifted her hair to fan out behind her, then rolled onto her side, facing the window. Facing him.

"Good night, Rennie," he whispered.

The phone awakened her. She switched on her nightstand lamp and automatically checked the time. It was nearly one o'clock. She'd been asleep over three hours.

When she was on call she tried to sleep when she could, never knowing when a night would be cut short.

She could almost count on being interrupted on a Saturday night when the emergency room stayed busy trying to patch up the damage that human beings inflicted on one another. When the patients outnumbered the surgical residents, or a case required a surgeon with more experience, the one on call was asked to come in.

She answered ready to respond. "Dr. Newton."

"Hello, Rennie."

Instinctively she clutched the sheet against her chest. "I told you not to bother me again."

"Were you sleeping?"

How had Lozada obtained her home number? She had given it only to a very few acquaintances and the hospital switchboard. But he was a career criminal. He would have ways of finding even an unlisted number. "If you continue to call me—"

"Are you lying on your pale yellow sheets?"

"I could have you arrested for breaking into my house."

"Did you enjoy yourself at the wedding?"

This question silenced her. He was letting her know how close he was. She envisioned him smiling the complacent smile he'd worn throughout his trial. It had made him appear relaxed and unconcerned about the outcome, even a little bored.

On the surface his smile had seemed benign, but to her it signaled an underlying evil. She could imagine him wearing that gloating smirk as his victims breathed their last. Knowing that he had discomfited her, he would be smiling it now.

"I liked the dress you wore," he said. "Very becoming.

The way that silky fabric swished against your body, I doubt anyone was looking at the bride."

Following her wouldn't be difficult for him. He had disarmed a sophisticated security system and choked the banker to death in his home while his wife and children slept upstairs.

"Why are you watching me?"

He laughed softly. "Because you are so watchable. I looked forward to seeing you every day of that dreary trial and missed you at night when I could no longer see you. You were the one bright spot in the courtroom, Rennie. I couldn't take my eyes off you. And don't pretend you were unaware of my attention. I know you felt my eyes on you."

Yes, she had felt him watching her, and not only at the trial. She also had sensed it in the past few days. Maybe knowing that he had been inside her house was making her imagine things, but sometimes the sensation of prying eyes was so strong she couldn't have mistaken it. Since the day she got the roses, she hadn't felt alone in her own home. It was as though someone else were always there.

Like now.

She switched off the lamp and moved swiftly from the bed to the window. Earlier she had decided to leave the blinds open, thinking that if Lozada was out there watching her, she wanted to know it. She wanted to see him, too.

Was he out there now, looking in? Feeling exposed, her arms broke out in gooseflesh, but she forced herself to stand at the window while she searched the dark, neighboring houses and the deep shadows of her own yard, which lately had seemed sinister.

"I wasn't flattered by your constant staring during the trial."

"Oh, I think you were, Rennie. You just don't want to admit it. Yet."

"Listen to me, Mr. Lozada, and listen well," she said angrily. "I disliked your staring. I dislike these telephone calls even more. I don't want to hear from you again. And if I catch you following me, there'll be hell to pay."

"Rennie, Rennie, you don't sound at all grateful."

She swallowed hard. "Grateful? For what?"

After a significant pause, he said, "For the roses, of course."

"I didn't want them."

"Did you think I would let a favor go unreturned? Especially a favor from you."

"I didn't grant you a favor."

"Ah, I know better, Rennie. I know more than you think. I know a lot about you."

That gave her pause. How much did he know? Although she realized she was playing right into his hands, she couldn't stop herself from asking, "Like what?"

"I know that you wear a floral fragrance. And that you're never without a tissue in your handbag. You prefer your right leg to be crossed over your left. I know that your nipples are very sensitive to air-conditioning."

She disconnected and threw the cordless phone across the room. It landed on her bed. Covering her face with both hands, she paced the width of her bedroom and breathed deeply through her mouth, trying to stave off the nausea that threatened.

She could not let this maniac continue to terrorize her. Apparently he had developed a sick infatuation for her and was conceited enough to believe that she would reciprocate it. He wasn't only homicidal, he was delusional.

In medical school she had studied enough required

psychology to know that he was the most dangerous kind of criminal. He believed himself invincible and therefore would dare to do anything.

Reluctant as she was, ever, to be involved with the police, this couldn't continue. She must report it.

She retrieved her phone, but before she could dial 911, it rang. She froze. Then she remembered to check the caller ID, which she had failed to do before. Recognizing the number, she took a stabilizing breath and answered on the third ring.

"Hey, Dr. Newton, this is Dr. Dearborn in Emergency. We've got a car-wreck casualty. Male. Early thirties. We're doing a CAT scan now to check the extent of his head injury, but there's a lake of blood in his abdomen."

"I'll be right there." Just before hanging up, she remembered. "Dr. Dearborn?"

"Yeah?"

"My code number, please?"

"Huh?"

The security measure had been implemented after Lee Howell was called out on a phony emergency. "My code—"

"Oh, right. Uh, seventeen."

"Ten minutes."

The instant Wick's bare, wet foot made contact with the tile floor, someone knocked on his motel-room door. "Shit." He stepped from the shower, reached for a towel, and wrapped it around his hips. He hoped to get to the door and put on the chain lock before the housekeeper used a passkey to let herself in.

As though knowing that he was working a graveyard shift every night, she timed cleaning his room within minutes of his return each morning, when he was ready only for a shower and sleep. He thought she might even be on the lookout for him. One of these dawns he might let her catch him bare-assed. Maybe that would cure her bad timing.

"Come back later," he shouted as he stamped across the room.

"This can't wait."

Wick opened the door. Oren was on the other side of it, a white paper sack in his hand, a manila envelope under his arm. He looked as glum as a bulldog.

"Uh-oh. Another hemorrhoid flare-up?"

Oren thrust the sack at him as he pushed his way into the room. "Doughnut?"

"Krispy Kreme?"

"You particular?" Someone knocked; Oren turned. The punctual maid was at the threshold with her cart. "Go away," he barked and slammed the door.

"Hey, I live here, remember," Wick said.

"You said she was a pest."

"But now she might not come back all day."

"Like you're Mr. Clean."

"Jeez, you're in a foul mood. Take a load off." He motioned Oren into the room's only chair. "I apologized for waking you up last night. You told me to call if anything happened, so when something happened, I called. When I saw Rennie Newton rolling out of her garage, I didn't know she was going to the hospital for an emergency.

"Did my call interrupt something? You and Grace dancing the horizontal tango? She put fresh batteries in the vibrator? What? Or maybe Grace wasn't in the mood. Is that why you're so grumpy this morning?"

"Shut up, Wick. Just shut up." Glowering, Oren took

back the sack and plunged his hand inside, coming up with a doughnut.

Laughing at his ill-tempered friend, Wick dropped his towel and pulled on a pair of boxers. He reached for the sack, got himself a glazed doughnut, took a bite that demolished half of it, and said around the mouthful, "No coffee to go with it?"

"Tell me about last night."

He swallowed. "I already did. The doctor got a call a little after one. She left her house within two minutes of getting the call. I nearly broke my goddamn neck running down those dark stairs while trying to get my boots on. Caught up with her on Camp Bowie three blocks from her house. Followed her straight to the hospital. She was there until five-ten. I followed her home. That's where she was when I turned it over to Thigpen. Who, by the way, showed up fifteen minutes late this morning."

Oren tossed him the manila envelope. He caught it against his bare chest. He finished the doughnut and licked the sugar off his fingers before opening the envelope and sliding out the eight-by-ten photographs.

There were four of them. He studied them one by one, then held one up to Oren. "This one's pretty good of me even though it's not my best side."

Oren snatched back the black-and-whites and threw them on the table beside his chair. "That's all you've got to say?"

"Okay, you caught me. I'm busted. What do you want me to say? Congratulations, Detective. Outstanding police work. Or do you want me to kneel and beg forgiveness? Kiss your ring? Kiss your ass? What?"

"What the hell were you doing, Wick?"

"Undercover investigation of a suspect."

"Bullshit." Oren picked up the most compromising photo. It was a rear shot of Wick and Rennie outside the country club walking toward her car. He was looking down at her and his hand was pressed against the small of her back. "Don't insult me."

Wick stewed under his accusatory glare. Finally he said, "We weren't getting anywhere by watching her house, were we? I've been sitting around for a week doing absolutely nothing. I've trimmed my fingernails three times for lack of anything else to do. I've sat so long my ass is growing as wide as Thigpen's. So I thought that maybe, if I exercised a little initiative, I could do us some good."

"By hitting on a suspect?"

"It wasn't like that."

"No? Then you tell me, Wick, what was it like? What was it like to be up close and personal with Dr. Rennie Newton?"

To avoid Oren's incisive glare, he reached into the bag for a second doughnut. "She's an ice maiden. She takes to being touched no better than a rattlesnake. In fact, she hissed at me."

"You touched her?"

"No. That," he said impatiently, pointing to the telltale photo, "and a handshake were the extent of touching. She showed her fangs when I tipped the parking valet."

"He'll give you back your five."

Wick looked at Oren, shook his head with disbelief, snorted, "He was *ours*? That pimply kid?"

"Rookie. Good with a camera. One of those fountain pen–looking things."

"That explains how you got the photos. How'd you know she was going to the wedding?"

"We didn't until she checked in with the hospital. She

stopped by there on her way to the church. We hustled. By the time she reached the reception we had this guy in place.

"Why didn't you tell me all this?"

"Well, now, see, I tried. I even went back to the house to explain where she was going and to tell you that I had someone else covering her, just in case you wanted to take a break, go out for a good dinner, maybe see a movie. I was feeling bad about you being cooped up on a Saturday night. Imagine my surprise when I discovered the house empty and you nowhere to be found."

"I was buying a suit."

"Conveniently, your cell phone was turned off."

"There was sign at the church asking that cell phones and pagers be turned off before entering the sanctuary."

"It doesn't vibrate?"

"Yeah, but . . . It . . ." For once he couldn't think of a plausible excuse or lie. So he took another tack. "I don't know why you're so upset, Oren. I minded my manners. Didn't have a single drink at the reception. I even took a set of steak knives to the happy couple. Nobody there would've guessed I wasn't invited." He finished his dough-nut then stretched out on his back on the bed and bunched the pillows beneath his head. "No harm was done."

Oren looked at him hard for a few moments. "As I sit here, I'm trying to decide whether to continue this con-versation or get up and walk out and to hell with you or come over there and knock the shit out of you."

"You're that pissed? Because I spent twenty minutes, a half hour tops, with Rennie Newton?"

"No, Wick. I'm upset because I saw you fuck up once. And you fucked up huge. And now you've made me real

scared that you're about to fuck up again. Huger than before."

Wick saw red. "Don't let the door hit you in the ass on
your way out, Oren."

"Oh no, I'm not leaving. You need to be reminded
what that mistake cost you. You think I don't know what
that rubber band around your wrist is for?"

"It's a habit I've taken up."

"Yeah, right." It looked to Wick like he still might hit
him. "For those of us who care about you—God knows
why—it hurt to watch the disintegration you went through
after what happened.

"It's a credit to your stamina that you stayed on the
force another two years before you took leave. Looking
back, I see how dangerous you were to have around and to
be around. Don't you remember all that crap, Wick?"

"How could I forget it with you reminding me of it all
the damn time?"

"I'm reminding you because I don't want you to make
the same kind of mistake again."

"I'm not!"

"The hell you're not!"

Wick jackknifed into a sitting position. "What? Because
I went to a wedding reception and shared a glass of water
and some polite conversation with a suspect? Come on,
Oren."

Wick's anger wasn't directed at his friend so much as it
was at the accuracy of what he was saying. If Wick had followed procedure three years ago, they could have had
Lozada for Joe's murder. He was breaking with procedure
again—blatantly by leaving the surveillance house and approaching Rennie Newton at the wedding reception, and
not so blatantly by failing to tell Oren about the telephone

call she had received last night. The first call, the one that
had upset her.

   At least she had appeared to be upset when she rushed
to her window with phone in hand and peered out into the
darkness as she talked. The call, whatever its nature, had
left her distressed. Was it fear, frustration, or anguish that
had caused her to throw the telephone down onto the
bed, cover her face with her hands, and give every appearance of a woman on the verge of unraveling? After that call
she'd been totally different from the calm, cool, and collected woman who had capably rejected him only a few
hours before.

   Who the hell had called? Friend? Foe? Lover? The person who wrote "I've got a crush on you" on that small white
enclosure card? Whoever it was had rocked her world.
Oren needed to know about it.

   But Oren had barged in here like a fire-breathing evan-
gelical laying out all his transgressions for review, so he
wasn't feeling very obliging toward his friend right now.
Anyhow, that's how he rationalized not sharing everything
he knew. Some of it could wait until both had cooled off.

   While he'd been processing this, Oren had been looking at him as though waiting for an explanation for his behavior. "I'm a free agent on this case, Oren, remember?
You recruited me to help out. So okay, I'm helping out. In
my style."

   "Just make sure your 'style' helps and doesn't hurt my
case."

   "Look, my tan is beginning to fade. I miss the sound of
the surf. I even miss scraping gull shit off my deck. I'd just
as soon return to the beach, hang out, go after that
shrimper's sister, and forget you ever came knocking. So if
you don't want my help anymore, please just say so."

Oren regarded him closely for several moments, then shook his head. "And give you an excellent excuse to go after Lozada alone? Uh-huh. No way." He stood up, gathered the photographs, and extended them down to Wick. "Want these for your scrapbook?"

"No thanks. The encounter was unremarkable."

Oren grunted. "You've never had an unremarkable encounter with a woman." He stuffed the pictures back into the envelope, picked up the sack with what remained of the doughnuts, and on his way out, said, "See you this evening. Have a good sleep."

"Oh, I will."

He had no intention of sleeping.

Chapter 10

■■■■■■■■■■■■

W hat're you havin', hon?"

Wick closed the laminated menu and looked across the lunch counter at the waitress. *They must breed them like this somewhere and ship them all to Texas,* he thought. Bleached hair was stacked into an intricate tower. Eyebrows appeared to have been stenciled on with a black crayon. Fluorescent pink lipstick was bleeding into the smoker's lines radiating from her thin lips, which had formed a wide smile for him.

"What do you recommend?"

"You Baptist or Methodist?"

"I beg your pardon?"

"This is Sunday. The Baptist go back to church tonight, so I don't recommend the Mex'can platter for lunch. Heartburn and gas, ya see. They're better off stickin' to the chicken-fried steak, pork chops, or meat loaf. But the Methodist can skip the evenin' service without fearin' hell-fire and damnation, so they're fine with hot and spicy."

"What about us heathens?"

She gave his arm a playful slap. "Had you pegged for one the minute you sauntered in. I said to myself, nobody that good-lookin' can be a saint." She propped her hand on her hip. "Anything we got and you want, you can have."

Winking at her, he said, "I'll start with the chicken-fried steak."

"Gravy with that?"

"You bet. Extra on the side."

"My kinda man. The Sunday plate lunch comes with your choice of strawberry shortcake or banana pudding."

"Can I let you know?"

"Take all the time you need, sugar." She glanced at the neon wall clock. "It's past noon. How 'bout a beer while that steak's fryin'?"

"Thought you'd never ask."

"If you need anything else, just holler for Crystal. That's me."

The Wagon Wheel Café was typical of small-town Texas. Situated two miles off the interstate highway on the outskirts of Dalton, the restaurant served hearty breakfasts twenty-four hours a day. Truckers from everywhere knew the place by name. The coffee was always hot and fresh, the beer always cold. Almost everything on the menu was deep-fried, but you could get a sixteen-ounce T-bone grilled any degree from still mooing to charred.

The restaurant catered to the after-church crowd on Sundays and to the sinners on Saturday nights. The Rotary and Lions Clubs met in its "banquet" room, and adulterous lovers rendezvoused in its gravel parking lot.

The booths were upholstered in red vinyl and each had a mini jukebox linked to the vintage Wurlitzer in the corner, which was bubbling even on this Lord's day. There was a counter with chrome stools for folks in a hurry or parties of one, like Wick.

Diners seated at the counter had a view into the kitchen—too good a look and it could spoil your appetite. But as the sign outside boasted, "Open Since 1919 . . . And We Ain't Kilt Nobody Yet."

The game schedule for the high school football team was taped to the cash register and the civic baseball team's first-place trophy for '88 stood next to a dusty jar in which contributions were collected for the local SPCA.

Wick's beer tasted good after the hot, three-hour drive from Fort Worth. The miles had put him at a safe distance from his friend's advice against making up his own rules of law enforcement as he went along. To Wick's way of thinking, proper procedure put a crimp in creative flow. Rules for just about anything were kept in his personal "major pain in the butt" file.

Everything Oren had said was right, of course, but he didn't dwell on that.

He did justice to the steak, which was fork-tender beneath the crispy breading. He decided on the banana pudding. Crystal poured him a complimentary cup of coffee to go with it.

"First time in Dalton?"

"Yeah. Just passing through."

"A good place to pass through."

"Looks like a nice town. Lots of civic pride." He used his spoon to point at the posters taped to the front windows announcing upcoming local events.

"Oh, I guess it's as okay as anywhere," Crystal said. "When I was a kid I was bent on leaving soon as I could, but, you know." She shrugged philosophically. "Married this sorry-ass because he looked a little like Elvis. He up and left soon's the third kid came along. Life got in the way of my big plans to seek my fortune somewhere else."

"So you've lived in Dalton your whole life?"

"Ever' fuckin' day of it."

Wick laughed, then took a sip of coffee. "I knew a girl in college who hailed from here. Her name was ... hmm ... something unusual. Regan? No. Ronnie? Hell, that's not it either, but something like that."

"Your age?"

"Thereabout."

"You don't mean Rennie Newton, do you?"

"That was it! Rennie. Yeah, Rennie Newton. Did you know her?"

She snorted with disdain. "Was she a good friend of yours?"

"Knew her by sight, that's all."

"That's a surprise."

"How come?"

"Because Rennie made it her life's ambition to know every man around." One of the oily eyebrows arched eloquently. "You were one of the few men that never *knew* her—if you get my drift."

He did. But he was having trouble reconciling Crystal's drift with what he knew of Dr. Rennie Newton the ice maiden. "She got around?"

"That's a nice way of putting it."

"What's the un-nice way?"

That was all the encouragement Crystal needed. She leaned across the counter and spoke softly. "That girl screwed everything in pants and didn't care who knew it."

Wick stared at her blankly. "Rennie Newton? She put out?"

"And then some, honey."

The grin he forced felt stiff. "Son of a gun."

"The way guys talk among themselves, I would've thought you'd know her reputation."

"Just my rotten luck, I guess."

Crystal patted his arm consolingly. "You were better off. Believe me."

"She was bad news, huh?"

"She was an okay little kid. Then about the ninth grade, about the time she blossomed, you might say, she turned bad. Soon as her woman parts started showing up real good, she learned how to use 'em. She just went hog wild. Tore her mama up, the way she slutted around.

"One day I was standing right here behind this very counter filling the ketchup bottles and heard all this racket outside. Rennie came blazing past in the new red Mustang convertible her daddy had given her. She was honking her horn and waving to one and all—nekkid as a jaybird. On the top anyway.

"Seems her and some friends were out swimming at the reservoir. Their horseplay got a little rowdy. One of the boys stole the top of Rennie's swimsuit and wouldn't give it back, so Rennie said she'd teach him not to mess with her. She told him she was gonna drive straight to his daddy's insurance office and tattle on him, and damned if that's not what she did. Went sashaying in there, walked right past a secretary and into that man's private office. Bold as brass. Wearing nothing but her bikini bottoms and a smile. You ready for more coffee?"

Wick's mouth had gone dry. "I'll take another beer."

Crystal checked on two more customers before bringing him back another long-neck. "Be glad you never got tangled up with that one," she said. "You married?"

"No."

"Ever?"

"Nope."

"Why not? You're sure cute enough."

"Thanks."

"I've always been partial to blue eyes."

"The Elvis look-alike?"

"Hell, yes. Had 'em bright as headlights. Turns out that's about all he had goin' for him." She gave Wick an experienced appraisal. "But you're the whole package, honey. I reckon you have to beat the women off with a stick."

"Naw, I've got a nasty temper."

"I'd take the temper if the baby blues came with it."

He gave her the abashed aw-shucks-ma'am grin she probably expected. After another sip of beer, he said, "I wonder what happened to her."

"Rennie?" Crystal used a damp cloth to swipe some spilled sugar off the counter. "I heard she became a doctor. Can you beat that? Don't know whether to believe it or not. She never came back to Dalton after her folks packed her off to that fancy boarding school up in Dallas. I guess after what happened they wanted to wash their hands of her."

"Why? What happened?"

Crystal didn't catch his question. Instead she smiled at an old man who hobbled up to the counter and took one of the stools near Wick's. He was wearing a plaid cowboy shirt with pearl snap buttons and blue jeans, both starched and ironed as stiff as boards. As he sat down, he removed his straw hat and set it on the counter, crown down—the proper way.

"Hey, Gus. How's life treatin' you?"

"Same as yesterday when you asked me."

"What'chu havin'?"

He looked over at Wick. "Been ordering the same god-damn meal for twenty years and she still asks."

"Okay, okay," Crystal said. "Chili cheeseburger and fries," she called out to the cook, who had been catching a break now that the after-church crowd had thinned.

"And one of those." Gus nodded toward Wick's beer.

"Gus is one of our local celebrities," Crystal told Wick as she uncapped a beer bottle.

"Not so you'd notice," the old man grumbled. He took the bottle from her and tilted it to his tobacco-stained lips.

"Rodeo bull rider," Crystal said proudly. "How many years were you a national champion, Gus?"

"A few, I guess."

She winked at Wick. "He's modest. He's got more of those champeen belt buckles than Carter has liver pills."

"That many broken bones, too." The old man took another long drink of his beer.

"We were talking about Rennie Newton," Crystal said. "Remember her, Gus?"

"I may be all bent and broke near in two, but I ain't brain-dead." He looked over at Wick again. "Who're you?"

Wick extended his right hand across the vacant stools separating them. It was like shaking hands with a cactus. "Wick Threadgill. On my way to Amarillo. Killing some time before hitting the road again. Seems I knew one of your local girls."

Crystal moved down the counter to slap menus in front of two young men who had come in and greeted her by name. When she was out of earshot, Gus turned on his stool toward Wick. "You knew the Newton girl?"

"In college," he said, hoping that Gus wouldn't ask which institute of higher learning they had attended.

"You gonna take offense at straightforward man talk?"

"No."

"Some do these days, you know. Everybody's gotta be politically correct."

"Not me."

The old man nodded, sipped his beer. "That little gal was one of the finest looking two-legged animals I ever clapped eyes on. One of the most spirited, too. 'Course she wouldn't't've looked twice at a mangled old fart like me, but when she was racing, everybody stopped to watch. She got the blood of all the young bucks pumping hot and thick."

"Racing?"

"Barrel racing."

Barrel racing? The Rennie Newton he knew used a ruler to stack up her magazines. He couldn't imagine her competing in a rodeo event. "I didn't know she participated."

"Hell, yeah, son. Every Saturday night April through July, Dalton holds a local rodeo. Ain't much of one on a national scale, but to folks around here it's a pretty big deal. Almost as big as football.

"Anyhow, cowboys would stack up three deep to watch Rennie race. Never showed an ounce of fear. No, sir. I saw her throwed off her horse twice. Both times she got right up, dusted off that saucy butt, climbed right back on.

"The cowboys used to say it was the way she rode that made her thighs so strong." He winked his crinkled eyelid. "Don't know myself, as I never had the pleasure of getting between them, but them that did said they ain't never had it that good."

Wick grinned, but his fingers had formed a death-grip around his beer bottle.

"But that was cowboy talk," Gus said with a shrug.

"We're all big liars, so it's anybody's guess as to who was talking from experience and who was talking out his ass. I figure a lot more tried than actually got to enjoy. All I know is, that little filly kept T. Dan good and riled, and that was fine by me."

"T. Dan?"

The old cowboy fixed a rheumy, wary gaze on him. "You didn't know her at all, did ya?"

"No. Not at all."

"T. Dan was her daddy. A son of a bitch of the worst sort."

"What sort is that?"

"Y'all doing all right?" Crystal had returned after preparing cherry Cokes for the two young men at the end of the counter.

Wick said, "Gus was telling me about T. Dan Newton."

"He hasn't been dead near long enough to suit most people around here," she said with a dry laugh.

"What did he do to piss everybody off?"

"Whatever he damn well felt like," she replied. "Just for example, tell him about your beef with him, Gus."

The old cowboy finished his beer. "T. Dan hired me to break a horse for him. He was a good horse but a mean bastard. I broke him, trained him, but wound up with a busted anklebone. T. Dan wouldn't pay for my doctor bill. Said it was my own fool fault that got me hurt. I'm talking about a lousy seventy-five dollars, which was chicken feed to somebody with T. Dan's bankroll."

"He was good at making money but bad at making and keeping friends," Crystal said.

"It sounds like the whole family was rotten to the core," Wick said.

"If you ask me, the town's well rid of 'em." Gus

scratched his cheek. "Wouldn't mind seeing that gal take another spin around those barrels, though. Just thinking about it has got me horny. You got plans tonight, Crystal?"

"In your dreams, old man."

"What I figured." With what looked like a painful effort, Gus got off his stool and hobbled over to the jukebox.

Wick finished his beer. "Thanks for everything, Crystal. It's been great talking to you. You take credit cards?" Before signing the tab, he added a hefty tip and enough for an extra beer. "Uncap another long-neck for Gus. My compliments."

"He'll appreciate it. Never knew him to turn down a free drink."

Trying to appear nonchalant, he said, "Earlier you said that Rennie's parents had sent her to boarding school. What was the final straw for them? Why did they want to get rid of her?"

"Oh, that." Crystal pushed a slipping bobby pin back into her pile of hair. "She killed a man."

Chapter II

❑❑❑❑❑❑❑❑❑❑❑

"Excuse me?"

"You heard right, Oren. She killed a man."

"Who?"

"I don't know yet."

"When?"

"Don't know that either."

"Where are you?"

"Headed back."

"From?"

"Dalton."

"You went to Dalton? I thought you were going to bed and sleep the day away."

"Do you want to hear this or not?"

"How'd you find out that she killed a man?"

"Crystal told me."

"Am I supposed to know who Crystal is?"

Wick recounted most of his conversation with the waitress in the Wagon Wheel. When he finished, Oren said, "Was she credible, you think?"

"As the FBI. She's lived there all her life, knows everybody in town. The café is the epicenter of the community. Anyway, why would she lie?"

"To impress you?"

"Well, I *was* impressed, but I don't think that's why Crystal told me."

"Then for kicks?"

"I don't think so. She isn't the type who'd lie for recreation."

"Well, she's your friend, not mine. I'll have to take your word for it. Did she know you're a cop?"

"I'm not a cop."

"Jesus," Oren muttered. "Did she know or not?"

"No."

"Then why was she divulging all this information to a total stranger?"

"She thought I was cute."

"Cute?"

"That's what she said. But I don't think Gus was all that keen on me." Wick smiled, imagining Oren silently counting to ten.

Finally he said, "You're going to make me ask, aren't you?"

Wick laughed, then repeated almost word for word his conversation with the retired bull rider. "Rennie Newton fanned his embers, but he hated her old man. According to your research, T. Dan Newton was a successful businessman, right?"

"And community gadabout."

"Even so, he wasn't the town's favorite son. Gus called him a 'son of a bitch of the worst sort,' which, in policemen's vernacular, probably translates to somewhere in the vicinity of cocksucker."

Oren ruminated on all that, finally saying, "Rennie Newton was a wild child? Promiscuous?"

"Both said our Rennie was hot to trot."

"The gossip about her could've been exaggerated. Once a girl's reputation goes bad it only gets worse."

"Gus conceded that," Wick said.

"In any case, it sure as hell doesn't match Dr. Newton's present image."

"Sure as hell doesn't."

"So who is this woman?" Oren asked in frustration. "What's the reality and what's the pose? Will the real Rennie Newton please stand up?"

Wick had nothing to contribute. He was more bumfuzzled than Oren. He'd been subjected to a brush-off that still stung. To get that good at rebuffing a man's attention she must've had lots of practice, which was contradictory to what he'd heard today.

Oren said, "The talkative Crystal didn't give you the lowdown on the murder?"

"What murder?"

"She killed a man, Wick."

"We don't know it was a murder. It could've been a hunting accident, an errant tennis serve, a boating mishap, or—"

"Or maybe she screwed some poor bastard into a coronary. Did you check with the local police?"

"I don't have a badge so I couldn't go waltzing in and start asking questions about a killing when I didn't even know the nature of the crime—if indeed it was a crime. I didn't know the victim's name or when the incident occurred."

"Newspaper files?"

"It's Sunday. A highschool kid was baby-sitting the phone, but the offices were closed. Ditto on government offices and the courthouse."

"Public library?"

"Closed for remodeling. Books could be checked out at the bookmobile parked on Crockett Street, but no research material was available."

Oren sighed with frustration.

"I couldn't press Crystal for more information," Wick continued. "I was still experiencing the concussion from her bombshell when the city's baseball team trooped in. They were fresh from practice, hot, thirsty, demanding beer and burgers. Crystal had her hands full.

"Besides, if I'd continued talking about a girl I was supposed to have had a passing acquaintance with years ago, Crystal might have turned suspicious and clammed up. Gut instinct told me she wouldn't have taken such a shine to me if she'd known I was a cop."

"You're not a cop."

"Right. That's what I meant."

"What about the old man? That Gus. Did he have anything else to impart?"

"He'd started talking to a clone of himself about the good ol' days on the rodeo circuit. I couldn't very well interrupt and ply him with more questions."

"Maybe you didn't want to hear the answers."

"What's that mean?"

"Nothing."

Wick did a ten-count of his own. For the last couple days Oren had been casting out these tidbits of bait. Wick recognized them for what they were and refused to bite. Oren wanted to know whether or not he was attracted to

Rennie Newton, regardless of her possible involvement in a homicide. It wasn't a subject he cared to discuss, or even self-analyze.

"I tried to learn more, Oren. I drove around Dalton to see what I could see, but it was futile. As soon as I get back to Fort Worth I'll go on-line and see what I can find, but I didn't bring my laptop—"

"Got it, got it," Oren said. "You did all you could."

"Thank you."

After a long silence, Oren said, "So what do you think?"

"About what?"

"Her, Wick. Dammit! Who are we talking about?"

"Hell, I don't know what to think. We need to find out what this 'killing' amounted to."

"Except a dead man, you mean."

Wick's patience slipped another notch, but he kept his voice even. "Until we know the facts surrounding that, we shouldn't jump to any conclusions."

"She took a life." Oren said it as though that were enough for him, and it probably was. He had unshakable criteria for right and wrong and didn't assign much importance to mitigating circumstances.

"She saved two this morning," Wick said quietly.

"You trying to make me feel bad?"

"No, I just think that's a more than fair equation. It's at least good enough to give her the benefit of the doubt, isn't it?"

The silence became as strained as the tired muscles in the back of Wick's neck. He was going on twenty-four hours without sleep and five hours of driving, and he was beginning to feel it. "Look, Oren, I need to grab a few zees before my shift tonight. Can you cover the first two hours?"

"If you'll do me a favor first."

"Like what?"

"You're on Interstate Twenty, right? West of Fort Worth?"

"Yeah. Not quite to Weatherford."

"Good. You won't need to backtrack."

"Where am I going?"

Rennie nudged the gelding's flanks and he obediently picked up his gait. She had bought him as a colt three years ago and had spent hours training him to respond to the merest squeeze on the reins, the flexing of a leg muscle, the pressure of her heels. Of the five horses in her stable, he was probably her favorite because he was so intelligent and responsive. When she was riding bareback, like today, they moved virtually as one even without a bit and reins. He made it effortless, which was what she needed this afternoon.

The emergency spleenectomy in the wee hours had been tricky. The injury was severe and had left the organ the consistency of raw hamburger. It literally fell apart in her hands when she tried to remove it.

But she had removed it successfully and repaired the patient's other internal injuries. Since his head wounds hadn't caused any permanent damage, he would live and recover. His frantic wife and parents had wept with gratitude for her saving his life.

The ruptured appendix that followed had been easy by comparison, but it was no less gratifying to give good news to the patient's anxious husband.

In her mailbox at the hospital was a letter from the board of directors putting into writing the offer they had extended to her earlier in the week and reiterating their hope that she would accept the chief of surgery position.

She had also received a note from Myrna Howell thanking her for the floral arrangement she had sent to Lee's funeral. She had concluded by urging Rennie to accept the post made available by her husband's death. "Lee would be pleased," she had said.

Rennie was still conflicted over that decision. The letter from the board and Myrna's note had eliminated her reservation in regard to benefiting from Lee's untimely death, but she couldn't dismiss Detective Wesley's suspicions.

This morning she had done her job well and had prolonged the lives of people who might have died. She was being courted for a position she wished to accept. She should feel exhilarated, able to enjoy a Sunday afternoon temporarily free from pressing responsibilities and serious decisions.

But she found it impossible to relax because of the call she had received last night from Lozada.

His intrusion into her life had upset her sense of order and was affecting a major career decision. How could she possibly accept the board's offer knowing that if she did, Wesley would investigate her more thoroughly? And if the detective ever discovered that Lozada was contacting her . . .

Damn him! He gave her the creeps and made her skin crawl. He had never actually touched her, but his voice had a tactile quality that made her feel as though he were stroking her with every word he spoke.

Why in heaven's name had he chosen her to be the object of his affection? She certainly hadn't encouraged him by look, word, or deed. Quite the opposite. Usually her disdain worked on even the most diehard would-be suitor. Around the hospital and within associated circles, she knew of her reputation for being cold and distant. Spurned men, both married and single, talked about her in unflattering, sometimes ugly, terms. She accepted the nasty gossip as a price she must pay for being left alone.

But Lozada was different. He wasn't going to be easily discouraged.

Angered by the thought, she gave the gelding's flanks another nudge and he surged into a full gallop. He ran as though he had only been biding his time until he received the subtle command. Now that she had given him permission, he applied his powerful muscles to the function they had been created for.

His hooves thundered across the dry ground, creating a trailing cloud of dust. He had always run with heart, but this afternoon he seemed to be galloping with more determination than normal. Her fingers meshed in his mane. The hot wind scoured her cheeks and tore off her hat. She let it go.

Astride a horse running full out was the only time she felt completely free. For a short while she could outdistance the bad memories she could never completely abandon.

Out of the corner of her eye she noticed movement and turned her head to see a pickup truck on the road on the other side of the barbed-wire fence. The driver was keeping the truck even with her. Now she understood the gelding's desire to gallop. He was pitting his own speed and stamina against that of a man-made machine.

She had never raced this horse before. Maybe she should have. Maybe he felt cheated. Maybe he wanted to prove himself to her. Maybe she should prove herself to him.

"Okay, boy. You've earned this."

She bent low over his neck and pressed him with her knees. Immediately she felt a burst of renewed energy. He nosed ahead of the pickup. The truck accelerated. The gelding pushed himself, gained on the truck.

Rennie laughed out loud. It was his race. All she did was hang on, and, God, it felt great.

They ran at a full gallop for at least three minutes, staying nose-to-nose with the sporting pickup. Ahead, Rennie saw her house and barn taking shape. In sixty seconds they would be at the fence. Now she should begin slowing him down gradually so she could pull him to a full stop, dismount, and open the gate.

But she was reluctant to forfeit. Lozada's telephone call had left her feeling afraid and vulnerable. She needed to prove she wasn't afraid of anybody or vulnerable to anything. Never, ever again.

Besides, how could she cheat her horse out of a victory when he'd been trying his hardest to win? "Are you game?" He seemed to understand. He sped up, marginally, but she could feel it in the muscles of her legs. "Okay, then. Let's do it."

Her heart was thudding in rhythm to his hoofbeats. She thrilled to the danger of it. She tightened her grip on the coarse hair of his mane. She sensed the pickup beginning to fall behind, but that didn't deter either her or the gelding. They had already won, but they needed to do this.

"Here we go."

She leaned into him and he went airborne. He cleared the fence with a yard to spare and landed hard but gracefully on the other side. Again, Rennie laughed out loud.

It was the crashing sound that caused her to pull back hard on the mane and bring the gelding around in a tight spin. The pickup had come to rest just beyond her gate. It was enveloped in a dense cloud of dust.

As the dust began to clear, she saw that the driver hadn't allowed for the loose gravel on the road. Probably he had braked too quickly. The lighter rear end had spun around and slammed into the metal gatepost. The post was intact. The damage to the truck remained to be seen. But it was the driver Rennie was concerned about.

She slid off the gelding and ran toward the gate. "Are you all right?" The gate was on a track. She rolled it open and ran to the driver's side of the cab. "Sir?"

His head was lying on the steering wheel and at first she thought he'd been knocked unconscious. But when she touched his shoulder through the open window, he groaned and gradually sat up. He pushed back his cowboy hat and removed his sunglasses. "You are no good for my ego, Dr. Newton."

She actually recoiled in surprise. It was the man from the wedding reception. "What are you doing here?"

"Losing a race." He nodded toward the gelding. "That's some horse." Then he looked at her. "Some rider, too. You lost your hat back there."

"I'm not believing this!" she exclaimed angrily. "How did you get here?"

"Interstate Twenty, then north on the Farm to Market Road."

She gave him a withering look.

"Okay, I nosed around till I found you."

"*Nosed* around?"

"At the hospital. I can't believe you were riding that fleet-footed son of a gun bareback. Do you always do that? Isn't it dangerous?"

"Not as dangerous as being tracked down by a total

stranger. Nobody at the hospital would give out personal information."

He unfastened his seat belt, opened his door, and climbed out. "I'm not a *total* stranger, but you're right. I lied. I got the information off the Internet. You own this place. There're records. Property-tax rolls and such. I called the hospital and when they told me you weren't on duty today, I thought just maybe I'd catch you out here." He shrugged. "I needed a Sunday drive anyway."

As he talked he had walked to the rear of his pickup to assess the damage. He hunkered down and inspected the vertical dent on the rear panel. It was about eight inches long and half an inch deep, and the paint was scratched. The truck seemed to have sustained no more damage than that.

He ran his finger down the dent, then dusted off his hands as he stood up. "They should be able to buff that right out."

"Mr.—"

"Wick."

"I gave you—"

"A snowball's chance in hell."

"So why did you come here?"

"I had nothing to lose."

"Time. You've got time to lose. So let me save you some, Mr. Threadgill." His eyebrows shot up. He was obviously impressed that she remembered his name, and she wondered why she did. "I'm not in the market for . . ."

When she hesitated he leaned forward expectantly.

"Anything," she said. "A date. A . . . Whatever you had in mind, I'm not interested."

"Are you married?"

"No."

"Engaged?"

"I'm nothing and don't want to be."

"Huh. Is this aversion a general thing, or is it me in particular you don't like?"

"What I *like* is my privacy."

"Hey," he said, spreading his arms at his sides. "I can keep a secret. Try me. Tell me a secret and see if I don't carry it to my grave."

"I don't have any secrets."

"Then let me tell you some of mine. I've got some dillies."

He had a slightly crooked front tooth that added to the mischievousness of his smile, which he probably thought was disarming. "Good-bye, Mr. Threadgill." She turned her back on him and started for the gate. After going through, she slid it closed with a decisive clang of metal.

"Hold up. One more second?"

He was good-looking and charming, and he knew it. She'd had to deal with his type before. Cocksure and arrogant, they believed that no one, especially a woman, could resist them.

"Please, Dr. Newton?"

She wasn't nearly as furious as she pretended to be or should have been. In spite of her determination not to turn around, she did. "What?"

"I wanted to apologize for that parting remark last night."

"I don't even remember it," she lied.

"About your mouth and the dirty dream? That was out of line."

That wasn't a cocksure and arrogant thing to say, and the disarming grin had disappeared. At least on surface he seemed sincere. Besides, if she made a big deal of the remark, he might think it had gotten to her. It had. A little. But she couldn't let him know that.

"Apology accepted."

"I was . . . Well, whatever—it was uncalled for."

"Maybe I overreacted to your tipping the valet."

He approached the gate slowly. "Maybe we ought to give it another shot."

"I don't think so."

"What could it hurt?"

She turned her head away and squinted into the distance. To anyone else this wouldn't have been a monumental decision. To her it was equivalent to leaping off the crest of a mountain in an unreliable hang glider.

When her eyes came back to him, he was staring straight at her. And though there was no longer a teasing glint in his eyes, they were unnerving nonetheless.

What could it hurt? Maybe nothing, or only everything. In any case it wasn't worth the risk. Which made it all the more surprising when she heard herself say, "There's an ice-cream parlor on the square."

"In Weatherford?"

"I was thinking of stopping there once I've finished my chores, on my way back. You could meet me there."

"I'll help you with the chores."

"I'm used to doing things for myself."

"I believe that," he said solemnly. Then he turned and set off at a jog down the road.

"Where are you going?"

He called back, "To get your hat."

Chapter 12

It took an hour and a half for her to complete her chores. First she walked the gelding around the paddock to let him cool down, then led him into a barn. The rustic exterior was deceptive. Wick knew little about stables, but this one looked state-of-the-art.

"I've got first-class horses," she said in response to his compliment. "They deserve a first-class home."

He was no expert judge of horseflesh, either, but he didn't have to know a lot to recognize that these were impressive animals. Rennie rubbed down the gelding, slowly and methodically, talking to him lovingly the whole while. Wick stood beside her as she combed the horse's long mane.

"He seems to understand what you're saying to him."

She took umbrage. "Why wouldn't he?"

"I didn't know horses had language skills."

"Mine do." Eyes shining with affection and pride, she

ran her hand over the gelding's smooth coat. "At least with me."

"Then that's probably a talent of yours, not the horse's."

She turned to respond, but apparently felt they were standing too close. Ducking beneath the gelding's head, she moved to the other side. Undeterred, Wick followed. "Does this English-speaking wonder have a name?"

"Beade."

"Unusual. Does it have any significance?"

"I like the sound of it."

"You don't elaborate much, do you?"

"No." Then she looked at him and they laughed. "You ask a lot of questions."

"I have a curious nature. Do you race Beade often?"

"Only when he's challenged by a pickup truck."

She moved away then, but glanced back at him over her shoulder and it was as close as she'd come to flirting. Or maybe she was dead serious and it only looked like flirting because of her tight jeans and the long blond braid that hung down her back from beneath the straw cowboy hat that he'd jogged a mile to retrieve. Maybe it looked like flirting to him because he wanted it to.

After all the feed buckets had been filled and she had said a personal good-bye to each of the horses, she led the way from the barn to the house. She excused herself to go inside.

"You can enjoy the porch swing."

"Exactly what I had in mind." Rather than make an issue of not being invited inside, he sat down in the swing and gave it a push. "Take your time."

"If Toby shows up, tell him I'll be right out."

"Toby?"

But she had disappeared inside and Toby remained a mystery until a few minutes later, when a man drove up in a rattletrap pickup. He climbed out of the cab and paused there to stare at Wick before coming up the front steps onto the porch. Wick wouldn't have been surprised to hear the ring of spurs.

He was tall and barrel-chested. Gray hair curled beneath his sweat-stained cowboy hat. When he removed his sunglasses, his deep-set eyes reminded Wick of the bad-ass lawmen in classic Westerns. He curbed his impulse to say "Howdy, Marshal." Somehow he didn't think Toby would appreciate the humor.

"Where's Rennie?"

Not much of a greeting, was it? "Inside. If you're Toby, she said for you to wait, that she'd be out soon."

He sat down on the porch rail, propped a size-twelve Lucchese boot—no spurs—on his opposite knee, folded his arms over his chest, and made no bones about staring at Wick.

"Nice day," Wick offered.

"If you say so."

Okay, Toby hated him on sight. Why?

After a lengthy silence that was broken only by the squeaking chain of the porch swing, the old man asked, "You live around here?"

"Fort Worth."

He snorted as though Wick had replied "I live in Sodom, just this side of Gomorrah."

"Hello, Toby." Rennie emerged from the house and joined them on the porch.

Toby came to his feet and whipped off his hat. "Rennie."

"How are you?"

"Doin' good. Everything meet with your approval?"

"You ask me that every time I come out, and the answer is always the same. Everything is perfect." The way she smiled at him would've made a jealous man murderous. Wick was afraid to define the spark it kindled in him. "Did you meet Mr. Threadgill?"

"We hadn't got quite that far." Wick stood up, extended his hand, and said his full name.

"Toby Robbins." He seemed reluctant to shake hands, but he did. His hand felt even rougher than Gus's. His palm was spiky with calluses.

"Toby owns the neighboring ranch," Rennie explained. "He looks after the horses for me. Sometimes it's a week or more between my trips out here."

"Then you're a good man to have around."

Toby ignored him and addressed Rennie. "The vet came out this week and gave them all a good goin' over. No problems that he could see."

"I hadn't spotted any, but I wanted to be sure. Thank you for arranging his visit. Will he be mailing me a bill?"

"He left it with me." He removed an envelope from the breast pocket of his shirt and passed it to her.

"Thanks. I'll take care of it tomorrow." She stuffed the envelope into her shoulder bag. "Any more signs of the bobcat?"

"Not since he got that calf a few weeks back. Hopefully we scared him off. I think one of my shots might've wounded him. Maybe he crawled off and died or just moved on to friendlier hunting territory."

Wick wouldn't have thought the man capable of smiling, but he did and Rennie returned it. "I hope you're right."

"He's a big cuss," Toby continued. "Big as I've ever run across, but I think we've seen the last of him."

"Well," Rennie said, "we were just about to leave."

"Don't let me hold you up. House secured?"

"I locked up on my way out."

Toby motioned for her to precede him, and the three of them filed down the porch steps. "Anything special you want me to do this week?" he asked.

"I can't think of anything offhand. If I do I'll call you. Just take good care of the horses for me."

"You bet."

"Say hello to Corinne."

"Will do." He tipped his hat to her and shot Wick a look that made his balls shrivel, then replaced his sunglasses, climbed back into his truck, and drove away.

Rennie gave the house and barn a wistful glance, then announced, "I'm ready."

The ice-cream parlor was doing a summer Sunday afternoon business. When one of the small wrought-iron tables became available, Rennie held it for them while Wick stood in line to place their order for two hot fudge sundaes. As he carried them back to the table he was thinking that between Crystal's banana pudding and this sundae he would probably gain several pounds today.

They were well into the ice-cream confections when Rennie asked, "Do you experience panic attacks?"

Coming out of the blue like that, the question stunned him. "Pardon?"

She gave a quick shrug. "I noticed the rubber band around your wrist. It was there last night, too."

"Oh. That. It's a, uh, just an old habit. Can't remember when I took up wearing it or why."

She nodded, but she was regarding him closely. "Sometimes people who suffer acute anxiety are urged to wear a rubber band around their wrist. If they feel a panic attack coming on, they can pop the rubber band. Sometimes that halts the false signal being sent to their brain that they're in mortal danger. It wards off the panic."

"Huh. I didn't know that."

They finished their sundaes in silence. When she was done, she pulled a napkin from the dispenser in the center of the table and blotted her lips. If one could will the dreams he had, Wick would have willed having a dirty dream about her mouth. That would be something to look forward to.

"What made you think I might own property outside the city?" she asked.

"Last night when I walked you to your car I saw a saddle in the back."

"I could've been a member of a riding club."

"You could've been a Canadian Mountie, too, but I didn't think so."

"You're very clever."

"Thanks. But probably not as clever as I think I am."

"That was going to be my next observation."

Her smiles transformed her face. Unfortunately, she didn't smile very often. All afternoon he'd been looking for evidence of the audacious barrel racer who slept around and had all the studs in Dalton standing three deep to catch a glimpse of her. He hadn't seen any. Other than the attire. The jeans did in fact make her butt look saucy, but that's the only aspect of her that came across as such.

What had happened to that wild, reckless girl? he wondered. And who was this tightly contained woman who'd taken her place? He was interested to know what had caused such a dramatic transformation. Rennie was a puzzle he wanted to solve whether or not she was Lozada's client.

His mystified stare must have made her uneasy, because suddenly she declared, "I need to be going."

"How come?"

"I have things to do."

That was what she said. What her expression telegraphed was *None of your damn business.*

He groped for something else to talk about so she wouldn't bolt. "How many acres do you have out there?"

"Two hundred and twenty."

"Ah, that's nice. A good place to escape from the grind."

"What do you do, Wick?"

Well, he'd made some headway. She was still seated, and she had asked him a question about himself, and she had finally called him by his first name. "Computer software."

"Sales?"

"And design."

"Hmm."

"What?"

"Just an observation."

"What?" he probed.

"I can't see you confined to a desk all day working on computer software."

"Very insightful. My job is boring as hell."

"Then why don't you do something else?"

"I'm in the process of looking. I guess you could say I just haven't found my niche yet."

"You don't know what you want to be when you grow up?"

He laughed. "Something like that." Scooting his empty dish aside, he propped his arms on the table. "You seemed sad when you left today. You must really like being out there on the ranch."

"Very much. I love the house."

From what he could see, he could understand why. She had a pleasing place in Fort Worth, but this house appealed to him more. It was a typical two-story ranch-style home with a native stone and cedar exterior and a deep porch running the length of it. Casual but classic. And a lot of house for one person.

Or was it occupied by only one person? Maybe Toby looked after more than the horses. Wick had assumed the mentioned Corrine was Mrs. Robbins, but she could be an elderly aunt or a wire-haired terrier.

"Have you known Toby and Corrine long?"

"Yes."

"Do they have children?"

"Three. Just had their fifth grandchild."

Good. They were a pair, and it was doubtful that Grandpa Toby was a sleep-over at Rennie's ranch house. "Aren't you afraid to stay out there by yourself?"

"Why would I be afraid?"

He raised a shoulder. "A woman alone. Remote location."

She hastily gathered up her shoulder bag and scooted back her chair. "People are waiting on the table. Anyway, it's time I got back to Fort Worth. Thanks for the sundae."

She made for the exit. Wick nearly mowed down a family of four in his rush to follow her out. By the time he reached her Jeep, she was sliding into the driver's seat.

"Hey, slow down. What'd I say?"

"Nothing."

"Then why the sudden split?"

"I need to get back, that's all."

"Rennie, Olympic sprinters don't move that fast. What's wrong?"

She jammed her key into the ignition, then turned to him, eyes blazing. "Your insinuation that I need protection."

"I insinuated no such thing."

"Were you hoping for an invitation to come out and *protect* me?"

"I was making conversation. You're reading a bunch of crap into an innocent question." They wrestled over control of the door. "Listen, if we're talking about fear, let's talk about mine."

"Yours?"

"Yeah. You scare the hell out of me." She stopped tugging on the door and looked at him for an explanation. "You're richer than me, smarter than me." He glanced down at the door handle. "Nearly as strong as me, and I'm afraid you could probably beat me in a foot race."

She ducked her head and he saw a trace of a smile. He pressed the advantage. "Have dinner with me, Rennie."

"What for?"

"Well, for one thing, as soon as this sundae wears off I'll be hungry."

"The sundae *was* my dinner."

"Okay, we don't have to eat. We could go to a movie. Take a walk. Anything. I'd just like to spend time with you."

She turned the key in the ignition and started the motor. "Good-bye, Wick."

"Wait a minute." He added a soft "Please," which

stopped her from reaching for the door again. "Why are you always rushing away from me?"

"I told you. I'm not—"

"I know, I know, you're not in the market. Do you see somebody?"

"Yes."

Don't let it be Lozada, he thought.

"Patients," she said. "I see patients."

"You have dinner with them every night?" He gave her his best sad-puppy-dog smile, but it didn't earn him even one of her half-smiles.

She turned away and stared through the windshield for several ponderous moments. "You're very engaging, Wick."

"Thanks. But . . . ?"

"But things should have stayed where we left them last night."

"That was nowhere."

"That's right."

"Well, I wasn't content with that."

"You'll have to be. I tried to make it clear then. I'm telling you again now. I can't, I won't, see you again. There would be no point." Turning back to him, she added, "And I won't change my mind."

He searched her eyes for a long time. Finally, he extended his hand toward her face.

She whispered, "Don't."

But he didn't touch her. He lifted a strand of hair from her cheek and tucked it beneath her hat. His fingers lingered there just above her ear for several seconds before he withdrew his hand. Softly he said, "I'll follow you home, see that you get there safely."

"I don't want you to do that."

"I already know where you live."

"You won't be invited in, Wick."

"I'll follow you home."

He backed away and closed her car door. She drove off without even a wave. Nevertheless he kept his promise. He followed her all the way home and when she rolled her car into her garage, he tooted his horn twice as his good-bye.

She called the hospital to check on her post-op patients and was told that the doctors on call had nothing untoward to report. The spleenectomy patient's condition had been upgraded from fair to good. He was doing well.

Following that call, she was officially off duty for the remainder of the night. Ten minutes later she was soaking in a tub of hot bubble bath. She breathed deeply and focused on relaxing, but when she closed her eyes she saw an image of Wick Threadgill and smiled in spite of herself. It was impossible not to like him. She liked him more than she had liked anyone in a very long time.

That was why she would never see him again.

Her capacity for romance had ceased to exist. It had died along with Raymond Collier that fateful afternoon in her father's study. She had killed that part of herself as surely as Raymond had been killed.

Or had it died? Maybe it had only been successfully suppressed.

She had denied common yearnings so effectively and for so long that she had convinced herself those yearnings no longer existed for her. What was natural for most women didn't apply to her. She didn't need love and romance. She didn't need anyone or anything in her life except her work. Work was what she desired, so work was what satisfied her. That had been her mantra, her anthem.

It had begun to ring hollow.

Her resolve never to marry and have a family had seemed courageous in her twenties. Now she wondered. Had she spited only herself when she made that decision? Over the years the line between independence and loneliness had become so fine that there was now little distinction between the two.

This man, this lanky Wick Threadgill with the long legs and unruly blond hair, had stirred longings that she had thought long dead. She hadn't wanted to say good-bye to him this evening. She liked his company but feared what she felt when he looked at her in that certain way.

His kisses were probably as potent as his smiles. Not that she would have allowed a kiss. But it would have been nice, when he replaced that loose strand of hair, to have turned her head ever so slightly and to have rested her cheek against his hand. Just for a moment. Just to—

Her telephone rang.

She sat up, scattering mounds of bubbles across the surface of her bathwater. Maybe it was Wick. He was just arrogant enough, persistent enough, to try again.

But it could also be Lozada.

The caller ID registered no number. She hesitated, then cleared her throat and answered.

"Rennie, are you all right?"

Chapter 13

■■■■■■■■■■■

Lozada thrilled to the sound of her light, rapid breathing. Only fucking or fear caused a woman to breathe like that. He would enjoy it either way with Rennie.

"Why are you calling me again when I specifically told you not to?"

"I was worried about you, Rennie," he said. "I'm calling to make certain that you're all right."

"Why wouldn't I be?"

"Because of the company you keep."

He hadn't been able to believe his eyes when she'd arrived home followed by Threadgill in his pickup truck. He could dismiss their meeting at the wedding reception as a bizarre coincidence. But two days in a row? It stunk to high heaven of police tactics.

Threadgill had given two short honks of his horn as he drove away. The only reason the bastard was still alive was because he hadn't gone inside the house with Rennie. But where had they been? How long had they been together? An hour? All day? What had they been doing?

Lozada had considered several ways he could kill Wick Threadgill. Which method would inflict the most pain? He wanted Threadgill's death to be painful, yes, but it must transcend normal pain. He also wanted the death to be ignominious. He didn't want to leave Wick Threadgill a martyr, a dead hero.

He couldn't repeat what he'd done to brother Joe. That would be unoriginal, and Lozada was known for his creative flair. He would devise something unique, something special. Perhaps he would incorporate one of his scorpions. The fear factor alone would be ingenious.

However it came about, killing Wick Threadgill would be his masterpiece, the benchmark of his career. He must take his time and think about it very carefully.

Of course if Threadgill had gone inside with Rennie, he would have been forced to act immediately, killing them both. Threadgill for his poaching. Rennie for her infidelity.

It had then occurred to him that she might be entirely innocent. What if she were unaware that Threadgill was a cop? Threadgill could be using her in hope of getting to him. That was what he'd wanted to believe. To make certain of it, he'd placed this call.

"I don't know what you're talking about, Mr. Lozada," she said. "Furthermore, I don't care."

"I don't approve of your friends."

"I don't give a damn what you approve or disapprove. For the last time, *leave me alone.*"

"I don't like your keeping company with cops."

Her silence was sudden and total, indicating surprise.

"I especially don't like your spending time with Wick

Threadgill. He's a loser, Rennie. Unworthy of you. Unworthy of us."

A few seconds ticked past. When she spoke, her voice was thin. "Wick . . . ? He's a . . . ?"

Lozada's grin spread wide. He'd been right. She hadn't known. "Poor darling. I thought you knew."

"Then what happened?"

"I've told you. About a dozen times." Wick rubbed his eyes. They were scratchy from lack of sleep.

"Tell me again."

"After we left the barn, she went into her house. I was not invited inside."

"Do you think somebody else was in there?"

"I never saw anyone else. There were no other cars around. I have no reason to believe anyone was inside, but I couldn't swear to it. Okay?"

"Why didn't she invite you in?"

"Common sense would be my guess. She had only met me once. Briefly. And I show up at her place in the country with some half-baked explanation about how I tracked her down? If I were a woman I wouldn't have invited me in."

"Good point. Go on."

"I have a question," Thigpen said. "Did you see any weapons around?"

Wick snapped his fingers. "Now that you mention it, she was packing an Uzi in the pocket of her jeans."

Thigpen muttered a disparagement. Oren gave Wick a retiring look and motioned for him to continue. "I forgot where I left off."

"She went in. You stayed out."

"Right. Then this old man shows up. Toby Robbins.

Big, robust dude." He recounted his and Rennie's conversation with the rancher. "He seemed very protective of her and suspicious of me. Kept looking at me funny."

"You're kinda funny-looking."

Thigpen was making himself hard to ignore, but Wick was determined to ignore him. He had hoped that by the time he arrived Thigpen would have left for the day and that he would have to tell his story only to Oren. No such luck.

He also noticed that the photographs of Rennie he had removed from the wall had been smoothed out and replaced. He didn't acknowledge their return. He refused to give the slob the satisfaction.

"Is the FWPD going to pay for the damage to my truck?" Wick asked, changing the subject. "The cost of having it fixed will be just below my deductible. You watch."

Oren dismissed the dent with a negligent wave. "When I sent you there I asked you to scout out the place. I didn't know it would wind up being a date."

Wick rolled his eyes. "We have differing opinions on what constitutes a date. I didn't know I was going to see her. The race just sorta happened and things progressed from there. I went with the flow. I wasn't into it for fun."

Liar, liar. Pants on fire, Wick thought to himself. He had very much enjoyed watching Rennie attend to her horses. Whatever else she might be, or whatever else she might have done, or whoever else she was involved with, when it came to those animals, it was a mutual love affair. That was the only time Wick had seen her looking completely happy and relaxed.

He hadn't minded the earthy smell of the stable. The merest scent of horse flesh stirred the latent cowboy spirit in every Texan. The hay had been fresh and sweet-smelling. And the sight of Rennie riding bareback hadn't exactly been hardship duty. But he didn't dare expound on that.

He said, "I don't consider grooming a bunch of horses a date."

"You went for ice cream."

"At a place where they play Donny and Marie and wear red-and-white-striped shirts. Hardly candlelight and wine. And still not my idea of a date."

"It's not a date unless he gets laid."

"Thigpen!" Oren rounded on him. "Shut up, okay?"

Wick was on his feet, fists tightly clenched. "At least I *can* get laid, Pigpen. How your wife can find your dick underneath all that flab is a mystery to me. If she even wants to look for it, which I seriously doubt."

"For the love of God, will the two of you cut it out!" Oren barked. "We've got work to do here."

"Not me. I'm outta here."

"Wick, wait!"

"I've been up for hours, Oren. I'm tired."

"I know you're tired. We're all tired. No need to get nasty."

"I passed nasty a long time ago. I haven't slept in . . . Hell, I can't even remember when I last slept. I'm going to my home away from home and sleep till this time tomorrow. See ya."

"He was her father's business partner."

The simple statement halted Wick. It also deflated him. He dropped back into the metal folding chair, flung his head back, closed his eyes. Even though he had a strong intuition about what the answer would be, he asked, "Who was her father's business partner?"

"The guy our lady doctor whacked."

Again disregarding Thigpen, Wick opened his eyes and looked at Oren, who nodded somberly. "I spent a few hours this afternoon in our downtown library. I had to go back several years to find the story, but it made even our newspaper."

"The really juicy ones usually do," Thigpen remarked. "And this one's really juicy."

Oren shot him another warning glance before turning back to Wick. "His name was Raymond Collier. He was shot and killed in T. Dan Newton's home study. Present at the scene was sixteen-year-old Rennie."

Sixteen? Jesus. "And?"

"And what?"

"What were the details?"

"Scarce and sketchy," Oren said. "At least in the *Star-Telegram*. I can't really start researching it until tomorrow. I didn't want to call Dalton PD until I could talk to somebody in a carpeted office. I don't want this to filter out through the rank and file. If word got around that she was under investigation, it could backfire on us." He studied Wick for a moment. "I don't suppose she opened up and talked about any of this with you."

Wick waited for several seconds to see if Oren was serious, and when he determined that he was, he laughed. "Yeah. I think it came up when she was trying to decide between strawberry or hot fudge." Oren frowned his displeasure. Wick said tiredly, "No, she didn't open up and talk about anything that happened when she was sixteen."

"Did she mention Lozada?"

"No, Thigpen, she did not mention Lozada."

"The trial? Her jury duty?"

"No and no."

"You spent hours with her. What'd you talk about all that time?"

"Primates and how some are still evolving. In fact, your name came up."

"Wick," Oren said in a chastening tone.

Wick exploded. "He's a moron. Why would she mention Lozada?"

"Why don't you just tell us what you talked about?"

"Her horses. Her place. How much she likes it out there. My boring job in computer software. Nothing. Chitchat. Stuff. Stuff people talk about when they're getting to know one another."

"But it wasn't a date." Thigpen snorted like the hog he was.

Wick sprang up from his seat again. "I don't need this shit."

Oren shouted over him. "I'm only trying to get your impressions of this suspect."

"All right, you want my impressions? Here's the first. She's not a suspect. I think her association with Lozada stopped the minute the judge banged the gavel to end the trial. And speaking of Lozada, has anybody been watching *him*?"

"His Mercedes was in his building's parking garage all day," Thigpen reported.

"Whatever," Wick said. "Keeping this surveillance on Rennie Newton is a waste of time. It's stupid and pointless. She doesn't look like a murderer. She doesn't act like a person who's just knocked off her colleague. What has she done that's the least bit suspicious? Nothing. Not a damn thing. It's been business as usual since we started watching her.

"Meanwhile, while we've been sitting here playing pocket pool to keep ourselves alert enough to monitor everything she does, whoever did knock off Dr. Howell is laughing up his sleeve at us because he got away with it. You asked for my impressions. Those are them."

"You want Lozada as much—no, *more*—than I do."

"Goddamn right I do," Wick shouted. "But she's got nothing to do with Lozada."

"I'm not ready to concede that."

"That's your problem." He scooped up his hat.

"You're leaving?"

"Good guess."

"For home?"

"Right again."

"To Galveston?"

"Tell Grace and the girls good-bye for me."

"Wick—"

"See ya, Oren."

He turned toward the staircase but was drawn up short. Rennie was standing on the top step.

Oren and Thigpen spotted her at the same time. Thigpen muttered something that Wick couldn't hear for the roaring in his ears. Oren, who ordinarily stood tall and proud, lowered his head like a kid whose mother had caught him with a dirty magazine. The stuffy atmosphere became even more claustrophobic, the stale air too thick to inhale.

Her eyes moved from one of them to the other, landing on Wick.

He took one step toward her. "Rennie—"

"You lying son of a bitch."

He decided that for now silence was his best defense. Besides, he felt they deserved her fury.

She crossed the room and raised the night-vision binoculars to her eyes, looking in the direction of her house. Wick discerned a slight sagging of her shoulders, but it lasted only until she returned the binoculars to the table and came around to face them. That was when she saw the photographs Thigpen had taped to the wall, the ones of her in various stages of undress.

Her lips parted silently and color drained from her face, but again her initial reaction was quickly replaced by righteous outrage. "Which of you has the highest rank? Who is responsible for this?"

"I am," Oren replied. "How did you know we were here?" He looked suspiciously toward Wick.

Wick returned a look that said *You know me better than that.*

Interpreting the exchange, Rennie said, "I assure you that Mr. Threadgill was a master of deceit. You can be very proud of him, Detective Wesley."

"Then how did you know—"

"It's my turn to ask questions," she snapped. "What possible explanation do you have for watching my house?"

"You left us with a lot of unanswered questions about Dr. Howell's homicide."

"And you expected to find answers to those questions by spying on me?"

"We thought we might, yes."

"Did you?"

"No."

"Have you also been eavesdropping on my telephone calls?"

"No."

"Spying on me at work?"

"To some extent," he admitted.

"You have invaded my privacy in the most despicable way. Your superiors will be hearing from my attorney first thing tomorrow morning."

"My superiors approved this surveillance, Dr. Newton."

"This isn't surveillance. This is window-peeping. This is—" She threw a disgusted glance at the photos, then, too angry to continue, headed for the stairs. "You'll be hearing from my lawyer."

She jogged down the stairs.

"Well it's hit the fan now."

Wick wasn't interested in Thigpen's editorial. He rushed down the staircase behind Rennie and caught up with her on the sidewalk in front of the house. He hooked his hand around her biceps to stop her. "Rennie."

"Let go of me."

"I want to explain." She tried to wrest her arm free, but he wouldn't release her. "Listen, I need to say this."

"I'm not interested in anything you have to say."

"Please, Rennie."

"Go to hell."

"I'm not proud of myself."

She stopped struggling and looked up at him. She gave a brittle laugh. "Oh, but you should be, Officer Threadgill. You played the role of the handsome stranger so convincingly. But then I wasn't much of a stranger to you, was I? You knew me from the pictures on your wall in there."

"I don't blame you for being mad at me."

"Don't flatter yourself." She jerked her arm away from him. Her eyes blazed. "I don't care enough about you to be mad at you. You aren't important enough to make me mad. I just wish I had never met you. And I don't want to see you again. Not by accident. Not by design. Never."

Wick didn't try to detain her. He watched her turn and jog away. He continued watching until she disappeared around the corner.

Chapter 14

$\blacksquare\blacksquare\blacksquare\blacksquare\blacksquare\blacksquare\blacksquare\blacksquare\blacksquare\blacksquare\blacksquare$

He felt like getting drunk.

To accomplish this unambitious mission, he'd chosen a bar in Sundance Square. In this popular watering hole, Wick sat hunched over his second or so Wild Turkey.

This bar wouldn't have been his first choice. He would have preferred a seedier tavern where the drinks were stiffer, the music sadder, and the customers unhappier. But this lively hangout was right across the street from Trinity Tower, where Ricky Roy Lozada lived like the fucking millionaire that he'd become by killing for hire.

Lozada's affluence contributed to Wick's misery, and heaping one misery onto another somehow seemed appropriate and warranted tonight.

Because of the proximity of Lozada's luxury digs combined with his overall feeling like shit, Wick estimated that it was going to take a couple more bourbons before he started feeling even a little bit better.

"Hey, cowboy, how come you're drinking alone?"

The young woman who plopped down on the stool beside his had dyed black hair and a red T-shirt with YOU BET YOUR ASS THEY'RE REAL spelled out in letters of silver glitter.

"I'll warn you right now, miss, I'm not good company tonight. That's why I'm drinking alone."

"Try me. I'll bet I can stand your company."

Wick shrugged and signaled the bartender. She ordered a bourbon rocks like his. She thanked him for the drink. "I'm Sally."

"Pleased to meet you, Sally. I'm Wick."

"So, why the long face, Rick? You have a fight with your significant other?"

He didn't correct her on his name. "In a manner of speaking."

"That sucks."

"Tell me."

"What was it over?"

"Our falling out? I did something dumb. Lied by omission. Lost trust. You know."

"Guys do that," she said with the resignation borne of experience. "How come, I wonder."

"Nature of the beast."

"Must be, 'cause you're all the same." She took a big slurp from her drink and tried to lighten the mood with a smile. "Change of subject. What do you do?"

"When?"

"For work, silly."

"Oh. You guessed it. I'm a cowboy."

"Really? I was just joking. You're a gen-u-wine cowboy?"

"Um-huh. Just this afternoon I was working in the stable with horses, hay, currycombs. All that stuff."

In his mind he was comparing the Rennie who had so lovingly groomed her horses to the one who had soundly rebuked a trio of Fort Worth's finest. Dr. Newton could not only skillfully wield a scalpel, she could slash with words just as effectively. He cleared his mind of these images and, playing turnabout, asked Sally what she did for a living.

"I'm an exotic dancer." She gave him a wicked smile and executed a move that caused the shiny letters to shimmy.

Wick wasn't impressed, but he let her believe he was. No sense in two people feeling like shit. "Wow."

Flattered, she giggled.

"Where do you perform?"

Her smile faltered. "Well, see, I'm not actually performing yet. I'm still auditioning. Right now I'm working at this temporary job. Over there. Cleaning condos." She nodded toward the high-rise.

Wick's instincts were stronger than the bourbon. His mind instantly sprang to attention. Trying to keep his sudden curiosity from showing, he smiled at her. "Let me know when you get hired to dance. I'd like to see you sometime."

She laid her hand on his thigh. "Maybe I could give you a private show? On the house."

"Where? Over there?" He hitched his thumb toward the high-rise. "Do you live there?"

"Oh sure." She snorted. "Like I could afford it."

"Man, I've always wanted to go inside that place." He gave the facade of the building a wistful glance. "See if it's as fancy as it looks."

"Oh, it's fancy all right. Only rich people live there."

"Like who?"

She took a wary glance around. "I'm not supposed to talk about the residents. If we're caught talking about the people who live in the building, we get canned, no questions asked."

"Oh, sure. I understand."

"It's a privacy thing."

"Right." He turned toward the TV behind the bar and pretended to have a sudden interest in *The Magnificent Seven*, which was playing silently.

"But you look trustworthy." Sally nudged his knee with hers beneath the bar. Regaining his attention, she leaned close enough for him to hear her whisper and to feel the weight of her breast against his arm. "You know the race-car driver?"

Wick named a NASCAR driver who he knew lived in Fort Worth. Sally nodded vigorously. "Ten-B."

"Honestly? What's he like?"

"Nice. But that wife of his?" She made an ugly face. "A bitch royale."

"Any other celebrities?"

"One of the Cowboys lived there through last season, but he moved after he got traded. And there's some old lady on the fifth floor who used to be on *Dallas*, but I don't know her name or what part she played."

"Hmm." He pretended that his interest had waned again and glanced at the closeup of a stoic Yul Brynner. The breast got heavier against his arm and Sally's hand inched a little closer to his crotch.

"Did you see on the news where that guy just beat a murder rap?"

Wick kept his expression impassive. "Murder rap? I don't think so. How long ago?"

"Couple of weeks. His name is Lozada."

"Oh, yeah, I think I remember seeing something about that. You know him?"

She scooted so far toward him he couldn't imagine
how she was managing to stay seated on her own stool. "Me
and him are . . . close. His condo is on the floor where I
work. The penthouse floor. I'm in his place all the time.
And not just to clean." She raised her eyebrows suggestively.

"You're kidding, right? A murderer?"

"*Shh.*" Again she glanced around nervously. "He got
off, remember?" Then she giggled and added, "Now I get
him off."

"Come on." Wick guffawed.

"I swear."

He lowered his voice to a conspiratorial whisper. "Does
he do it different from, you know, regular guys?"

She considered the question seriously before answering. "Not really. Pretty much the same. We've only balled a
few times. Mostly he just likes for me to blow him. And this
is kinda weird." She moved closer still. "He doesn't have
any hair down there."

"Why, what happened to it?"

"He shaves it."

Wick let his jaw drop. "Get out!"

"I swear."

Wick looked at her with feigned respect and awe. "And
you're this guy's girlfriend?"

"Well, not officially." She cast her eyes down and trailed
a finger along his arm. "I mean, he's crazy about me and
all. He's just not the type that shows his feelings, you
know?"

"Have you ever seen him with any other women?"

"No."

"Any ever come up to his fancy apartment?"

"No."

"Are you sure?"

"Well, yeah. And I would know. I pay attention to detail.
There's never been a trace of another woman in the place
and believe me, I check things out while I'm cleaning. I'm
always on the lookout for one of those damn scorpions. If
one ever got out I would freakin' shit."

"Scorpions?"

Wick knew about Lozada's fascination with them, but it
chilled him anew to hear Sally tell about the climate-
controlled tank. "I keep my eyes open when I'm in there."

"What about his phone?"

"His phone?"

"You ever answer it for him?"

"Are you serious? I'd be fired for sure. Besides, he only
uses a cell."

"Have you ever heard him talking on it?"

"Once, but I didn't hear what he was saying."

"So you don't know if he was talking to a woman?"

She withdrew slightly and gave him an odd look. "Hey,
what is this?"

He smiled and patted the hand still resting on his
thigh. "Just trying to help you out, Sally. Looking for signs
that the guy is seeing someone else. But it sounds to me
like you've got no competition."

She snuggled closer. Both breasts were propped on his
forearm now. "You're cool, Rick. Would you like to go to
my place? I've got booze."

"Hey, I don't want this Lozada character after my ass."

"I see other guys too."

"I thought you liked him."

"I do. He's good-looking and wears the coolest
clothes."

"And he's rich."

"For sure."

"Then what's the problem?"

"Well, he . . . scares me a little."

"He doesn't hit you, does he?"

"No. Well, sorta. I mean, he doesn't actually hit, but like the other night, he warned me not to talk—"

"Wick, what the hell are you doing?"

Wick swiveled around. Oren was standing behind them, glowering.

Sally, glowering back, asked crossly, "Who's this?"

"My partner. Oren, meet Sally."

"Did you say partner?"

"That's right."

"You're a *fag*?"

Her screech drew the attention of nearly everyone in the bar. Even Steve McQueen seemed to do a double-take from the TV screen. Sally dismounted the stool with a hop that caused the breasts, of which she was so proud, to bounce like a pair of water balloons. She stamped away on her platform heels.

"I'd still like to see you dance sometime," Wick called after her.

"Bite me," she hollered back.

Oren grabbed him by the back of his collar and practically dragged him through the exit. Once they were outside, he gave Wick a shove that nearly sent him sprawling. "I've been looking all over town for you."

Wick spun around. "You push me again, Oren, and you'll regret it."

Oren looked ready not only to push him, but to slug him. "I've had every cop on the force on the lookout for your truck."

"What for?"

"Because I didn't trust you not to do something stupid." Oren took several heavy breaths as though forcibly tamping down his anger. "What's the matter with you, Wick?"

"Nothing."

"Nothing my ass. You're sulky, edgy, disagreeable. Argumentative. Defensive. Thigpen was right on when he called you a jerk."

"Then why don't you and Thigpen get together and suck each other's dick. I'm going home."

Oren grabbed him by the shoulder and, heedless of Wick's warning, pushed him backward against the wall. He held him pinned there with one strong forearm across his chest. Oren's first beat had been in a tough neighborhood rife with gangs and drugs, but he was just as tough as the criminal offenders and had come to be respected and feared by the meanest of the mean. He and Joe.

"This time I'm not going to let you get away with copping an attitude. That's too easy. You've got a bee up your butt, and I want to know what it is. If Joe were here—"

"But he isn't," Wick shouted.

"If he were," Oren shouted back, "he'd pound it out of you."

"Leave me the hell alone." Wick pushed him aside, knowing he could do so only because Oren allowed it.

"Is it her?"

Wick turned. "Who?"

Oren shook his head, looked at him with a mix of aggravation and pity. "She's bad news, Wick. A whore dressed up in a doctor suit."

"She's not."

"You heard so yourself. From those people in Dalton. She fucked—"

Wick took the first swing, but the last Wild Turkey had finally kicked in. It hampered his speed and his aim. Oren caught it in the shoulder, which was padded with plenty of muscle. Oren's fist caught Wick on the chin, which wasn't padded with anything. He actually heard his skin split. Felt the blood spurt.

Mercifully, Oren grabbed him by the front of his shirt before his knees gave way. He pulled him close and held him face-to-face. "A few days before he was shot, Raymond Collier's wife filed for divorce. She cited adultery. Guess who was named correspondent."

Before he heaved up the bourbon on a public sidewalk, Wick pushed away from Oren, turned, and headed toward the parking lot where he'd left his pickup, which had apparently been spotted by a tattletale cop. It hadn't been that hard for Oren to find him.

"Wick!"

He stopped, then came around and aimed a threatening finger at Oren. "If you ever talk about her like that again . . ." He was breathing hard. Gasping, in fact. He couldn't deliver the warning with the impetus he wished. He had to get out of there, fast. So he settled on "Just don't, Oren. Just don't."

"You shouldn't be driving, Wick. Let me take you to the motel. Or to my house."

Wick turned away and kept walking.

From the driver's seat of an SUV parked in a metered slot on the street, Lozada watched the scene play out between Wick and Joe Threadgill's former partner, Oren Wesley. He was too far away to hear what they were saying, but the exchange was angry.

To Lozada's delight, they actually swapped punches.

This was better than he ever could have anticipated. Dissension within the ranks. Strife between good friends. Everybody close to Wick Threadgill was pissed at him. Perfect.

Earlier he'd had the pleasure of revealing Wick's profession to Rennie. While she was still trying to assimilate that, he had added the *furthermore*. Furthermore, the FWPD had her under surveillance.

Earlier, after Wick had left her with those two cute blasts of his horn, Lozada had trailed him around the block to a house that was supposedly under reconstruction. Since he had been the object of surveillance himself, he knew the signs: three cars parked out front, including Wick's pickup. Building materials scattered around but no evidence of actual work being done. An empty Dumpster in the front yard. These were stage props, the police department's clumsy attempts to put one over on Lozada. How absurd of them to think they ever could.

"They're watching you from a house on the street behind yours," he had told Rennie.

"You're lying."

"I wish I were, my dear."

"Why would they be watching *me*?"

"I suppose because of your murdered colleague."

Coldly, she said, "I don't believe you."

But she had. Within seconds of hanging up on him she had left her house at a jog and run around the block straight to the other house. She was inside for several minutes before emerging, visibly upset, with Threadgill on her heels.

Neither of them paid any attention to the SUV parked nearby. There were no records of his ownership of this car. The police didn't know to look for it. They followed his

Mercedes, and he tolerated that. But when he didn't want to be followed he drove this SUV.

He had been parked within eavesdropping distance of the conversation during which Rennie told Wick she never wanted to see him again. God, what a sensational sight—his Rennie telling off Wick Threadgill, in terms that even a dimwitted cop like him could understand.

From his observation point Lozada felt the heat waves of anger coming off her. It gave him an erection. If she made love with even a fraction of that heat she was going to be well worth the trouble.

She had returned home. Lozada had wanted nothing more than to join her there and begin phase two of his seduction, but his focus was, of necessity, Threadgill. He had followed him as far as the bar, where he had no doubt gone to drown his sorrows.

Poor Wick, Lozada thought now as he watched him storm away from Wesley. First he'd been put down by Rennie, now by his longtime friend. The cocky bastard didn't look so cocky anymore.

A sudden knocking on the passenger window of his SUV caused him to react reflexively. Less than an eye-blink later, the barrel of a small pistol was aimed at Sally Horton's astonished face.

"Jesus, it's just me," she exclaimed through the window glass. "I thought it was you, but I wasn't sure. What're you doing parked out here?"

Lozada wanted to snuff her right then for drawing attention to him. Wesley was still across the street, talking to one of the policemen who patrolled Sundance on bicycle.

"Get lost."

"Can't I join you?" she whined.

Lozada stretched across the console and opened the

passenger-side door. He would rather have her inside than yelling at him through the window. She climbed in. "Where's your Mercedes? Not that this isn't cool too." She ran her hand over the glove-soft leather upholstery.

Lozada was watching Wesley. She followed his gaze. "He's gay."

He looked at her. "What?"

"He's a fag."

Wesley was a family man. It was Lozada's business to know these things. Wesley had a wife and two daughters. "What makes you think he's gay?"

"This guy I met in the bar? He bought me a drink, and we were getting along pretty good, when that man there comes along. Mad as hell. Turns out they're partners."

She had been talking to Threadgill? He had bought her a drink? "Was the other guy black too?"

Sally shook her head. "Blond and blue-eyed. A cowboy. Tough-looking, but cute."

Threadgill.

"I'm not into being a fag hag, I don't care how cute the guy is." She reached across the console and stroked his fly. "Say, that gun of yours really turns me on. And so does your pistol." She laughed at her own asinine joke.

"What did you talk about?"

"Me and the cowboy? I told him about my dream to become a dancer. And then I told him about this guy I like, who likes me." She winked. "Wonder who?"

Lozada forced himself to smile. "It wouldn't be me, would it?"

She squeezed him playfully. "And he said—"

"The cowboy?"

"Yeah, he said that since there weren't any women coming in and out of your place, that I probably didn't have any competition. What do *you* say?"

Lozada reached across and fingered her nipple through the ridiculous T-shirt. "How did he know there were no women coming in and out of my place? Did he ask?"

"Yeah, but I told him—" Suddenly she stopped, looked at him apprehensively, changed course. "I didn't tell him shit. You asked me not to talk about you, so I didn't. I mean, not by name."

"Good girl." He tweaked her, hard enough to make her wince. "You know, you've got me really hot."

"Hmm, I can tell."

"Let's go somewhere more private."

"We can do it here."

"Not what I have in mind we can't."

Rennie looked at her bedside clock. It was after 3 A.M. and she was still awake. She was due at the hospital at 5:45. She fluffed her pillow, straightened the sheet that had become twisted around her restless legs, and closed her eyes, determined to clear her mind long enough to fall asleep.

A half hour later she gave up. She went into her kitchen, filled her electric kettle with water, and plugged it in. She assembled the fixings for tea, but her coordination was shot, her motions clumsy. She dropped the lid of the tea canister twice before she was able to replace it properly.

"Damn him!"

But exactly which "him" she was referring to, even she wasn't sure. Wick Threadgill or Lozada. Take your pick. They were tied for first place on her shit list. Detective Wesley was a close second.

She had every intention of making good the threat she

had issued. Wesley's superior would be hearing from her attorney. Either he could arrest her or he could leave her alone. But she would not live under a cloud of suspicion for a crime she had neither committed nor knew anything about.

The five dozen roses were the returned "favor" to which Lozada had referred. Anything else was unthinkable.

He frightened her. He was a criminal. He was creepy. He was persistent and, she feared, patient. He would continue the phone calls until she put a stop to them. The problem was, she didn't know how.

Reporting him to the police would be the normal course of action, but she was reluctant to do that now. She had waited too long. Telling Wesley this far after the fact would validate, and could even increase, his suspicion. She would eventually be cleared of any involvement in the crime that had cost Lee his life, but in the meantime . . .

It was that "in the meantime" that she must avoid. The incident in Dalton would be resurrected and—

The kettle screamed. She quickly unplugged it and poured the boiling water over the tea bag. Carrying the steeping cup into her living room, she switched on the television set and sat down in a corner of her sofa, tucking her legs beneath her. She channel surfed, trying to find any programming that would take her mind off her troubles with Lozada and keep her from thinking about Wick.

She had lied about not being mad. She *was* mad. Furious, in fact. But she also had been hurt by him, and that was the most unsettling part of this whole thing—knowing that she still could be hurt. She had believed herself immune to caring that much. Obviously she'd been wrong.

She had discouraged him at every turn, but her rejection hadn't deterred him. She had begun to admire his tenacity, and she was flattered by his obstinate pursuit. In all honesty, she had been glad he turned out to be the driver of the racing pickup. When he pushed back his hat and drawled "You are no good for my ego, Dr. Newton," she'd felt an unmistakable flutter of excitement.

But he wasn't a dogged suitor at all, only a detective hot on the trail of a suspect.

His betrayal had been a wake-up call. Time had eclipsed hurtful memories. Years had dulled the pain of deep emotional wounds. Resolves had begun to diminish in importance. Wick's double-cross had been a cruel reminder of why she had made those resolutions. She was back on track now, more resolute than before. She should thank him for that, she supposed.

But she wasn't grateful for his making her experience feelings and sensations she had long denied herself. She hated him for making her miss them, for making her yearn to explore them. With him.

She set her half-finished tea on the coffee table and settled more deeply into the cushions. When she closed her eyes, she relived how grand it had felt yesterday afternoon being astride Beade. The sun and wind hot against her skin. The exhilaration of speed. The feeling that she could outrun anything. Freedom.

Had she known then that Wick was driving the pickup, she probably would have felt even happier. He made her smile, laugh even. That crooked front tooth—

The telephone awakened her.

Chapter 15

Wick got away from Oren with no time to spare. He climbed into his pickup—it seemed to take an hour for the parking-lot attendant to tally his charge—and drove to the edge of downtown. He parked on a deserted side street and then, for the next few minutes, tried to convince himself that he wasn't about to die.

Repeatedly he popped the rubber band against his wrist, hard, but it didn't stop the false signals of imminent death from whizzing toward his brain. He'd never had much faith that a rubber band could work that kind of miracle. It would be like using a bull whip to halt a runaway freight train. But the doctor had recommended it, so Wick had humored him and started wearing it.

His fingers and toes tingled. Numbness crept up his legs and through his hands into his arms. The first time he experienced that temporary paralysis, he took it as proof positive that he had a brain tumor. He had learned that it was symptomatic of nothing except a shortage of oxygenated blood in his extremities due to hyperventilation.

He opened his glove box and took out the brown-paper lunch sack he carried with him. Within seconds of breathing into it, the tingling abated, the numbness receded, and feeling returned.

But his heart was pumping as though he had come nose-to-nose with a cobra poised and ready to strike. He was drenched with sweat. Although he knew he wasn't dying, it sure as hell felt like he was. For five hellish minutes his reason and his body went to war. His reason told him he was suffering a panic attack. His body told him he was dying. Of the two, his body was the more convincing.

He had been having dinner out with friends when he was seized by his first. Midway through the meal it had slammed into him. He hadn't seen it coming. There was no warning. He didn't just begin to feel bad and then gradually get worse.

One second he was fine, and the next a wave of heat surged through him and left him trembling. Immediately he was dizzy and nauseated. He excused himself from the table, rushed into the men's room, and was stricken with violent diarrhea. He shook like he had a palsy, and his scalp felt like it was crawling off his head. His heart was beating like a son of a bitch, and though he was gasping, he couldn't suck in enough breath.

He had believed wholeheartedly that whatever the hell had made him suddenly sick was going to kill him. There and then. He was going to die on the floor of that public rest room. He had been convinced of that as he'd never been convinced of anything in his life.

Twenty minutes later he was strong enough to stand, to wash his face with cold water, to excuse himself from the group of friends. He felt lucky to be leaving the restaurant alive—as wrung out as a dishcloth, but alive. He'd gone home and slept for twelve hours. The next day he was weak but otherwise fine. He figured he'd been gripped by a vicious strain of flu, or maybe the marinara sauce he'd been eating was toxic.

Forty-eight hours later it had happened again. He woke up in his own bed. No nightmare. Nothing. He'd been sleeping soundly when he abruptly awoke, in abject terror of dying. His heart was hammering. Sweat poured from him. He was gasping for air. Again he'd had the tingling in his extremities, the crawling scalp, and the absolute conviction that his time on earth was ending.

This had taken place shortly after all the shit with Lozada had gone down. The assassin was thumbing his nose at the department in general and at Wick in particular. And now he'd been stricken with a terminal disease. That was his take on the situation when he made an appointment with an internist.

"You mean I'm just crazy?"

After putting him through a battery of tests—neurological, gastrointestinal, cardiological, you name it—the doctor's diagnosis was that he suffered from acute anxiety disorder.

The doctor was quick to tell him he wasn't crazy and to explain the nature of the syndrome.

Wick was relieved to learn that his illness wasn't fatal, but the cause was imprecise and that bothered him. He wanted a quick fix and was disheartened to learn that it usually didn't work that way.

"You may never experience another one," the doctor told him. "Or you may have them periodically for the rest of your life."

Wick studied the subject, researched it, exhausted the material available. While he hated to think of thousands of others suffering as he did, he was comforted to know that his symptoms were common.

For a while, he saw a therapist weekly and took the prophylactic medication that was prescribed. Finally, though, he persuaded both doctors, and himself, that he was cured. "I'm over it," he told the psychologist. "Whatever triggered the attacks—and it was a combination of things—has passed. I'm good to go."

And for the past ten months he had been. That was how long it had been since his last panic attack. He'd been fine. Until tonight. Thank God it wasn't a severe one, that it had been short-lived. He'd recognized it for what it was and had talked himself through it. Maybe the rubber band had helped after all.

He waited five minutes more to be certain it had passed before he began driving again. He took an entrance ramp onto the west freeway and drove with no particular destination in mind. In fact, his mind was empty except for thoughts of Rennie Newton. Surgeon. Equestrian. Lolita. Killer.

His panic attack might have been precipitated by hearing that, at sixteen, she'd been involved with a married man. Her father's business partner no less, probably much older than she. She had been a teenage home wrecker.

That jived with Crystal's description of a teenage hellraiser. A girl who would drive around town bare-breasted would also sleep with her father's partner, destroy his marriage, and probably laugh about it later.

Dalton's moral majority would be outraged by such behavior. Throw into the mix the fatal shooting of her father's business partner and it was little wonder that her parents had said good riddance when they sent her to boarding school.

But all that was incongruous with the woman Wick knew. Granted, he'd been in her company all of two times, but from what he had observed, he believed he had a fair grasp on her character.

Far from a party girl, she had the social life of a monk. Rather than flaunting her sexuality, she shrank from being touched, going so far as to say "Don't" when he would have touched her cheek.

Now, was this the behavior of a femme fatale?

He couldn't reconcile the two Rennie Newtons and it was making him nuts, and for reasons that had nothing to do with the Lozada connection and Howell's murder. His objectivity had flown, and Oren knew it. That's why Oren was monitoring his activities, tracking him like a damn bloodhound.

But he couldn't really be angry at Oren. Okay, he was pissed that he'd hit him so hard, and he was dead wrong about Rennie. But Oren was doing his job. He had re-cruited Wick to help him do it, and instead he had added a complication.

Suddenly he realized that his driving hadn't been as aimless as he had thought. He was on the street where he had grown up. He guessed his subconscious had directed him here. Maybe he needed to touch home base, get grounded again. He pulled the pickup to a stop at the curb in front of his family's house.

He had sold it after Joe was killed. It would have seemed like a sacrilege to live there without Joe. He didn't know if the couple who'd bought it from him still lived here or if it had exchanged hands since then, but the present owners were good trustees. Even in the dark he could tell the place was well kept.

The Saint Augustine was clipped and neatly edged, the shrubbery pruned. The shutters had been painted a different color, but he thought his mother would approve it. Her rose bed on the east side still flourished.

He could hear his father saying "You boys should be ashamed of yourselves."

"Yes, sir."

"Yes, sir."

"Your mother prides herself on those roses, you know."

"It was an accident," Wick mumbled.

"But she had asked you not to play ball near her rose bed, hadn't she?"

Wick had been going out for a pass thrown by his older brother. The football had landed in the rosebushes—and so had Wick. By the time he had thrashed around to extricate himself, he'd broken off the branches of several plants at ground level. His mother had cried when she saw the irreparable damage. When their father got home from work, he had laid into them.

"From now on, play football on that vacant lot down the street."

"There're fire ants on that lot, Dad," Wick had said.

"Will you just shut up," Joe hissed.

"Don't tell me to shut up. You're not my boss. You're no Joe Namath either. If you'd hadn't thrown the damn ball—"

"Wick!"

When their dad used that tone of voice he and Joe knew it was wise not to say anything more. "This weekend the two of you will clean out the garage and scrape out the gutters. No friends can come over, and you can't go anywhere. And if I hear any complaining, quarreling, or cussing," he said, looking directly at Wick, "you'll have it even worse next weekend."

Wick smiled at the memory. Even then Joe had shown self-restraint and had known when to keep his mouth shut, lessons Wick had yet to learn.

Many memories had been made inside that house. His mom had made major events of holidays and birthdays. A variety of cats and dogs, two hamsters, and one injured mockingbird had been their beloved pets. He'd fallen from the pecan tree in the backyard and broken his arm, and his mom had cried and said it could've been his neck. The day Joe got his first car, he had let Wick sit in the driver's seat while he pointed out its features.

Parties had been held for each of their school commencements and then again when they graduated from the police academy. Their parents had been proud of them. Wick figured his dad had bored his Bell Helicopter co-workers with stories of his boys the policemen.

There were some sad memories too. Like the day his parents had told them about his father's cancer. By then he and Joe were living separately in apartments, but they came home frequently for family get-togethers.

They had been gathered around the kitchen table, eating chocolate cake and regaling Mom and Dad with cop stories, which they always edited so as not to cause them too much worry, when their father had turned serious. His mother had become so upset she had had to leave the room, Wick recalled.

Two years into her widowhood, a teenage driver ran a stop sign and hit her broadside. The EMTs said she had died instantly. At the time Wick had railed at the injustice of losing both parents so close together. Later, he was glad his mother hadn't lived to see her firstborn slain. She had thought the sun rose and set in Joe. If that car accident hadn't killed her, having to bury him would have, and it would have been much more painful.

His darkest memory was of the night Joe had been taken from him.

After their mother's death, they had moved back into the house together. That night he had been entertaining a group of friends. It was a boozy, noisy crowd, and he had barely heard the doorbell above the blaring music. He was surprised to see Oren and Grace standing on his threshold.

"Hey, who called the fuzz? Is the music too loud?" He remembered raising his hands in surrender. "We promise to be nice, Officer, just don't haul us off to the poky."

But Oren didn't smile, and Grace's eyes were wet.

A slam-dunk of realization, then "Where's Joe?"

He had known before asking.

Wick sighed, gave the house another poignant look, then let his foot off the brake and drove slowly away. "Enough of Memory Lane for one night, Wick ol' boy."

The city slept. There were few other vehicles on the streets. He wheeled into the motel parking lot, got out, locked his pickup, trudged to his door, and let himself in.

The room smelled musty. Too many cigarettes, too many occupants, too many carry-out meals. Disinfectant couldn't penetrate the layers of odors. He turned on the air conditioner full blast to circulate the stale air. The bed, sad and sagging as it was, looked inviting, but he needed a shower first.

Even at this hour of the morning the hot water ran out before he could work up a sufficient lather, but he didn't rush. He let the cold water stream over his face and head for a long time, washing away the aftereffects of the panic attack. Besides, he was beginning to like cold showers, and just as well. It seemed that he and ample hot water were never going to be roommates.

The moment he switched off the faucets, he heard the noise in the bedroom. "Goddammit," he muttered. That maid must have radar. But this was ridiculous. It was . . . He checked his wristwatch. Four-twenty-three. The manager was going to hear about this.

Angrily he snatched a towel off the bar and wrapped it around his waist, then yanked open the door and barged through.

She was lying on his bed, faceup. The silver letters on her T-shirt glittered in the glare of the nightstand lamp. It also reflected in her open eyes and shone garishly on the two neat holes in her forehead.

He sensed movement behind him but didn't have time to react before an iron forearm was clamped down on his Adam's apple. He was punched hard in the back just above his waist. It caused his ears to ring and the room to tilt.

"You can blame yourself for her, Threadgill. Think about that as you die."

The punch started hurting like hell, but it jump-started his conditioned reflexes. He tried to throw off the arm across his throat. At the same time he jabbed his elbow backward. It connected with ribs, but not with any significant thrust. He repeated the movements and aimed for his assailant's kneecap with his heel. Or thought he did. He wanted to. He tried, wasn't sure he did.

Jesus, he hadn't realized he was so out of shape. Or had the panic attack been worse than he thought? It had left him as weak as a newborn kitten.

"Mr. Threadgill?"

His name echoed out of a hollow distance. It was followed by repeated knocking.

"Fuck!"

The arm across his neck let go. When it did, his knees buckled and he went down, landing hard on the smelly carpet. Pain rocketed through his skull. Jesus Christ that hurt!

Oblivion rolled in like a dense fog. He saw it coming, welcomed it.

Rennie rushed from the doctors' parking lot into the emergency room.

"Number Three, Dr. Newton."

She tossed her shoulder bag to the desk attendant. "Watch this for me, please." She ran down the corridor. There was a lot of activity in Room Three, numerous personnel, all busy. A nurse was standing ready with a paper gown for her. She pushed her arms through the sleeves and pulled on a pair of latex gloves. As she adjusted a pair of clear goggles to cover her eyes, she said, "Tell me."

The ER resident said, "Forty-one-year-old male, stab wound in the back, lower right side. Object still buried to the hilt."

"Kidney?"

"Almost certain."

"Pressure's down to eighty," a nurse said.

Other nurses and an intern called out other vital information. The patient had been intubated. He was being transfused with O-negative blood and was getting Ringer lactate solution through an IV. He'd been rolled onto his side so she could inspect the wound. The handle of what looked like a screwdriver extended from it.

"His abdomen's swelling. He's got a bellyful of blood."

She looked for herself and determined there was no need to do a peritoneal lavage or CAT scan. The patient was bleeding out internally.

"Pressure's dropping, Doctor."

Rennie assimilated the barrage of information within thirty seconds of her arrival. A nurse hung up a wall phone and shouted above the confusion, "OR is ready."

Rennie said, "Let's go."

As she turned away she happened to glance at the patient's face. Her wordless cry momentarily halted everyone surrounding the gurney.

"Dr. Newton?"

"You okay?"

She nodding, saying gruffly, "Let's move." But nobody did. "Stat!" That galvanized them. The gurney was wheeled into the corridor. She ran alongside. The elevator was being held open for them. They had almost reached it when someone shouted her name.

"Wait up!"

She stopped, turned. Detective Wesley was running toward her.

"Not now, Detective. I've got an emergency on my hands."

"You're not operating on Wick."

"Like hell I'm not."

"Not you."

"This is what I do."

"Not on Wick."

The gurney had been rolled inside the elevator. She motioned the emergency team to take it up. "I'll be right there." The elevator doors closed. She turned back to Wesley. "He's in shock and he could die. Soon. Do you understand?"

"Dr. Sugarman is on his way. He'll be here in five minutes."

"Sorry, haven't got it to spare, Detective. Besides, I'm a better surgeon than Sugarman and have more trauma experience. A patient needs me, and I'll be damned before I'll let you stop me from saving his life."

She held his stare for ten seconds before turning away and rushing toward the elevator that had been sent back down for her.

"The girls are all right? You're sure?"

"Oren, you asked me that ten minutes ago. I called the house. They're fine."

He took Grace's hand and rubbed the back of it. "Sorry."

"It's okay." She slipped her arm across his shoulders. "The policewoman you sent over was cooking breakfast for them. Another officer is watching the house. They're fine." She massaged his neck. "I'm not so sure about you."

"I'm okay." He pushed himself off the waiting-room sofa. "What could be taking so long? He's been in surgery for hours."

"That could be a good sign."

"But what—"

"Are you Detective Wesley?"

He spun around. A nurse in green scrubs approached. "Dr. Newton sent me to tell you that she would be out in a few minutes. She asked you to wait."

"What about Wick? The patient? What about him?"

"Dr. Newton will be out soon."

She turned and went back through the double doors. Grace reached for Oren and pulled him back down beside her. He covered his face with his hands. "He's dead or she would have told us something."

"She didn't tell us anything because that's not her job."

"He's dead. I know it."

"He's as strong as an ox, Oren."

"It's Joe all over again."

"No it's not."

"The only difference is that when I found Joe he was already dead."

"It's not Joe. It's not the same."

"I wasn't there for Joe, and I wasn't there for Wick."

"You weren't responsible for what happened to either of them."

"If Wick's dead—"

"He isn't."

"If he is, Grace, I'll have let Joe down. He would've expected me to take care of his brother. Watch over him. Protect him from something like this."

"Oren, stop it! Don't do this to yourself. You can't take the blame for this."

"I *am* to blame. Weren't for me, Wick would still be in Galveston. Safe. Not dying on that fucking motel-room floor." His voice cracked with emotion. "He asked me if that place was the best the police department could do. I told him to stop his bellyaching, that he'd slept in worse, and that it was several rungs up from that dump he'd been living in. Jesus, Grace, I can't take this. I swear I can't."

"Wick is *not* dead."

"How do you know?"

She smiled at him gently. "Because he's too ornery to die."

He wanted to believe it, but Grace was a professional counselor. That was what she did all day, every day. She earned her living from knowing good things to say in bad situations. But even if they were platitudes, he was glad she was here beside him, saying the things he wanted and needed to hear.

It was another twelve minutes before Dr. Newton came through the double doors. The sight of her wasn't encouraging. She looked like a battle-scarred soldier who'd lost the battle.

She had pulled on a lab coat, but it didn't hide the bloodstained tunic of her scrubs. Strands of hair damp with sweat trailed from beneath her cap. Her eyes were ringed with dark circles, and she looked like she could stand a hot meal or two.

She didn't prolong their suspense. As she approached, she said, "He survived the surgery."

Oren expelled a deep breath and hugged Grace tightly. She pressed her face into his chest and whispered a prayer of thanksgiving. They held each other that way for several moments. He finally released Grace and wiped his eyes.

Grace extended her hand to the surgeon. "I'm Grace Wesley."

"Rennie Newton."

"Thank you, Dr. Newton."

After the two women shook hands, Dr. Newton handed Oren a plastic bag containing a bloody Phillips screwdriver. "I'm the only one who touched it."

Then she pushed her hands into the pockets of her lab coat and went straight to business. "The wound was deep. The solid part of his right kidney was penetrated. The organ was repaired and should heal without any adverse effect to his renal system.

"He also suffered some muscle damage. I called in our

orthopedic specialist. He did an outstanding job of repairing the muscle. He'll be available for consultation later
today if you wish."

"He lost a lot of blood," Oren said.

She nodded. "Once I found the main source of the
bleeding—a severed artery—I was able to direct the blood
flow back to the kidney. Fortunately we got to him when we
did. Otherwise, he might have lost the organ or died of
exsanguination."

If they'd waited on Sugarman he might not have survived. That was what she was telling him. Oren asked when
they could see him.

"Right now, if you like. Come with me."

She turned and they followed. Grace must have sensed
the underlying animosity between them. She gave him a
quizzical look and mouthed, "What's going on?"

He shook his head. Later he would explain to her the
intricacies of the situation. Once he did she would understand why his conversation with the doctor was polite but
stilted.

She led them through two sets of automatic sliding
doors into the surgical ICU. "He's still under heavy anes-
thesia, and I should warn you that he doesn't look very
good. Something happened to his face."

"He fell on it." Dr. Newton stopped and looked back at
him, her eyes wide, revealing more feeling then she'd
shown thus far. "He was attacked from behind," he explained. "Apparently when his assailant let go of him, Wick
collapsed and landed hard on the floor facedown. That's
how the paramedics found him." He was too ashamed to
tell them that he was responsible for busting open Wick's
chin.

"The orthopedist X-rayed his face," she said. "His cheekbone wasn't broken, but he's . . . well, you'll see."

She motioned them into one of the units. Grace, who was braver than he, went directly to the bed, took one look at Wick, and began to cry. Oren hung back, but he could see well enough. His first reaction was to curse beneath his breath.

Wick lay on his left side, propped up in that position by a body pillow. The right side of his face, the one visible, was so badly swollen and bruised that he was hardly recognizable. Both eyes were closed but he couldn't have opened his right one if he had wanted to—it was that swollen. A breathing tube was taped to his lips. The cut on his chin seemed inconsequential compared to the other injuries, but that was the one that caused Oren to grimace.

"We're giving him antibiotics through his IV to prevent infection, although there's nothing to indicate that the bowel was punctured, which would have complicated his condition considerably," Dr. Newton explained in a voice that sounded mechanical and detached again. "He has a catheter. There was blood in his urine initially, but it's cleared."

"That's a good sign, right?" Grace asked.

"Definitely. His heart is strong, pulse steady. We're keeping a tight check on his blood pressure. We'll be taking him off the respirator as soon as he regains consciousness. Naturally he'll be sedated for pain. His good physical condition helped him survive and it will help him recover. He'll remain in ICU for several days, and I'll continue to watch him closely, but his prognosis is good."

The three stood and stared at him in silence for a couple more minutes, then Dr. Newton motioned them out. "Is there someone who should be notified? Does he have a family? We didn't know if there were someone we should call."

"Wick isn't married," Grace said, answering before he could. "He has no family."

Dr. Newton's hands disappeared once again into the pockets of her lab coat, delving deep, as though she were trying to push her fists through the bottom seams. "I see."

"Is there anything we can do for him?"

She gave Grace a wan smile. "Presently, no. Once he's released, he'll need someone with him for at least a week. He'll require a lot of bed rest. Until then, our capable nursing staff will take good care of him. By late tomorrow I'll allow him to have visitors, but only on a limited basis."

Oren said, "Unfortunately, Dr. Newton, *I* can't allow him to have visitors. He was the victim of a crime. He's also a key witness."

"To what?"

"Murder."

Chapter 16

██████████████

"A young woman was in the room with Wick when he was attacked," Wesley said. "She was dead at the scene."

Rennie schooled her features not to show any reaction. It wasn't easy. Mistrusting her voice, she only nodded.

"The CSU is going over the room now. The motel housekeeper, who'd been a nuisance until this morning, saved his life. She came into Wick's room with her passkey. If she hadn't interrupted when she did, he would have died too."

"Did she see who did it?"

He shook his head. "The bathroom window was left open. We figure he climbed out just ahead of her coming in. She had knocked first. He was scared off."

"So she can't give you a description."

"Unfortunately, no. And motel rooms are hell to gather evidence from because hundreds of people come and go through them."

"Footprints outside the window?"

"Blacktopped alley. So far, we have no clues. But hopefully our techs we'll find something useful."

"What about that?" she asked, pointing to the bagged screwdriver.

"We'll get what we can from it."

Rennie wanted to ask him if he had any suspects in mind but was afraid of what his answer would be.

"As soon as Wick wakes up, I'll need to question him, find out what he knows," he said.

"I understand, but keep in mind that he fought for his life last night. He'll need rest. I don't want my patient to be agitated."

"I wouldn't do anything to jeopardize Wick's recovery," he said irritably.

"I'll trust you not to. Now, I must excuse myself. I have another operation scheduled in half an hour."

"But you look exhausted," Grace exclaimed.

"I just need some breakfast." She smiled at Grace Wesley, whom she had liked instantly, then turned back to the detective. "Obviously you and Mr. Threadgill are more than professional associates."

"Friends. Virtually family."

"Then I'll leave word with the ICU nurses that if you call they're free to give you an update on his condition."

"I would appreciate that consideration. Thank you."

"You're welcome."

Grace Wesley thanked her again for saving Wick's life.

The detective said a clipped "I'll be in touch," then punched the Down button on the elevator.

Rennie went back into Wick's cubicle and asked the nurse if he had shown any signs of coming around. "He's moaned a couple of times, Doctor. That's all."

"Please page me when he does. I'll be in the OR, but as soon as he wakes up I want to know about it."

"Of course, Dr. Newton."

Before leaving, she gazed down at her patient, but curbed the impulse to brush a wayward strand of hair off his forehead.

She showered in the locker room and put on fresh scrubs, then went to the cafeteria on the ground level. She had a breakfast of scrambled eggs, toast, and orange juice, but she ate it only because she needed fuel, not because she wanted it or enjoyed tasting the food.

Back on the surgical floor, she reviewed her next patient's charts and spoke to her briefly. "Your oncologist and I agree that the tumor is contained. Once that section of bowel is removed, you're prognosis is very good."

The woman thanked her groggily as the anesthesiologist administered the heavy sedative into her IV.

Rennie scrubbed methodically. It felt good to be performing a task that was familiar and routine. Her carefully organized life had slipped out of her control. Ever since she heard about Lee's murder, ever since the appearance of the roses in her living room, nothing had been in order.

But, she thought as she scrubbed ruthlessly between her fingers, she could get back that control. All she needed to do was focus on her work. Work was her handle on life. Get a grip on her work and she had a grip on her life.

In the operating room, she was slicing through adipose tissue on the patient's abdomen when the assisting resident surgeon said, "Heard you had some excitement around here this morning."

"Our Dr. Newton is a regular heroine," said the scrub tech.

Rennie, whose mind was on her task, asked absently, "What are you talking about?"

"It was all over the news this morning."

Rennie glanced at the anesthesiologist, who'd spoken from his stool behind the patient. "What was on the news?"

"How you saved the cop's life."

The resident said, "Threadgill's brother died in the line of duty a few years ago. You prevented him from doing the same."

"Except that this Threadgill wasn't on duty at the time," said one of the circulating nurses.

"I don't know anything about him," Rennie said coolly. "Suction, please. I responded to an emergency, that's all."

"According to the news, the girl was beyond help," the anesthesiologist remarked.

The talkative resident picked up the story. "I heard straight from the paramedics who responded to the nine-one-one call that she was found in the cop's bed. Apparently whoever attacked Threadgill killed her first."

"Jealous boyfriend?"

"Or husband."

"Could be. The way they've pieced it together, Threadgill was in the shower."

"Speaking for myself," the resident quipped, "I always have a cigarette first. Then shower. What about you, Betts? Do you smoke after sex?"

"I don't know," replied the circulating nurse. "I've never looked."

Everyone laughed.

The scrub tech bobbed her eyebrows above her mask.

"If this cop looks anything like the picture they printed in the newspaper, I'd say the girl died smiling."

"Could we please get back to business here?" Rennie snapped. "What's her pressure?"

The anesthesiologist replied in a subdued, professional tone. Rennie's brusqueness had quelled the joking. She kept her head down, her concentration focused on the surgery. But when her pager chirped, she asked the circulating nurse to check it for her.

"It's surgical ICU, Dr. Newton."

"Would you call them, please?"

She listened as the nurse placed the call. "Okay, I'll tell her." She hung up.

"Threadgill's waking up."

"Thanks."

Although she sensed the raised eyebrows above the masks, no one dared to comment. From there the talk related only to the procedure they were performing. Finally Rennie withdrew her hands and nodded for the assisting surgeon to clip the last internal suture. She probed the area with her gloved finger to make certain all the sutures held. "Looks good."

"Perfect," he said. "Excellent job, Dr. Newton."

"Thank you. Would you mind closing up for me?"

"Your wish is my command."

"Thanks. Good job, everyone."

She peeled off her bloody gloves and pushed through the door, knowing that as soon as it closed behind her she would be the topic of speculative conversation. Let them wonder, she thought.

She reported the satisfactory results of the operation to the patient's anxious family, then hurried to the locker room, took a second shower, and reached the ICU just as the nurse was urging Wick to cough up his breathing tube.

He suffered the choking sensation all patients did, but eventually the thing was out. "Now, that wasn't so bad, was it, Mr. Threadgill? You did real good."

He moved his lips but the nurse couldn't hear him, so she leaned down close. When she straightened up, she was chuckling. "What did he say?" Rennie asked.

"He said, 'Get fucked.'"

"You don't have to tolerate that from him."

"Don't worry about it, Doctor. I've got a husband and four sons."

Rennie took her place at Wick's bedside. "Wick, do you know where you are?"

He grunted an unintelligible reply. She placed her stethoscope on his chest and listened for several moments. "You're doing fine."

"Thirsty."

"How about some ice chips?" She looked across at the nurse, who nodded and left on the errand. "We'll start you out on ice chips, Wick. I don't want you to drink anything yet and get nauseated."

He grunted again and was struggling to open his right eye, unaware that it was swollen shut. He would be groggy and disoriented for hours yet. "How's the pain, Wick? I can increase the dosage of your pain medication." He mumbled something else she couldn't interpret. "I'll take that as a yes."

The nurse returned with the cup of crushed ice and a plastic spoon. "Give him a few spoonfuls every time he wakes up." She made the necessary notations on his chart. Before leaving she said, "I'll be either here or at my office. Page me if there's any change."

"Certainly. Oh, Dr. Newton, I think he wants to speak to you."

Rennie returned to Wick's bedside. He groped for her hand. Despite the IV port that was taped to the back of his hand, his grip was surprisingly strong. She leaned down close. "What is it, Wick?"

He whispered only one word.

"Lozada."

Detective Wesley frowned at her from the other side of his cluttered desk. "Anything else?"

"Just that. 'Lozada,'" Rennie repeated.

"When was this?"

"Around noon today."

"And you're just now telling me?"

"I had to sort it out first."

"Sort what out?"

Other personnel in the Criminal Investigation Division appeared to be going about their business, but Rennie was aware that she was an object of curiosity. "Is there someplace we can talk more privately?"

Wesley shrugged and indicated for her to follow him. He led her into the same room where the interrogation had been videotaped. They sat in the same seating arrangement. She didn't particularly like the implication that she was once again being placed in a defensive position, but she didn't remark on it. Instead she immediately resumed the conversation.

"Could that mean it was Lozada who attacked Wick last night?"

"Oh, you think so?"

She felt her cheeks turn warm. "Apparently that's not a news flash to you."

"Hardly, Doctor."

"May I ask you a question?" He shrugged with indifference. "What is it about me that rubs you the wrong way?"

He shifted in his chair. "Nothing."

"That's not true. You've disliked me from the get-go. Why?"

"Why don't you just tell me what's on your mind, Dr. Newton? What did you 'sort out' this afternoon?"

"The day of Lee Howell's funeral, I received a bouquet of roses. This was the enclosure card."

She opened her handbag and took out a plastic bag in which she'd placed the small white card. It was the second piece of evidence she had collected that day, although she tried not to think about having to pull the screwdriver from Wick's back.

Wesley took the bag from her, looked at the card and read the single typed line, but his reaction wasn't what she had expected. In fact, he didn't react at all. His expression remained unchanged.

"Evidently this comes as no surprise to you, either."

"I didn't know it had accompanied a bouquet of roses sent to you the day of Howell's funeral."

"But you recognize the card, don't you? How could you? It's been . . ." She stopped, looked at him aghast. "You weren't content just to watch my house—you searched it. You did, didn't you?"

"Not me."

She sat back as though pushed by an invisible hand. "Wick."

Wesley said nothing.

Her head dropped forward. She stared at her hands, which no amount of cream or lotion could keep moisturized because of the antiseptic soap she scrubbed with.

Wick had been inside her house, rummaging through her drawers, going through her things. Before or after they'd met? she wondered. Although it didn't matter. Her privacy had been violated, and, worse, Wick had been the one who'd violated it.

After a brief but strained silence, she raised her head and looked at Wesley. "The card came from Lozada. He personally delivered the roses. He broke into my house and left them for me to find."

"How do you know?"

"He told me."

"Told you?"

"He's called me several times. I've asked him not to. I've insisted that he leave me alone. But he keeps calling."

"And says what?"

"Read the card, Detective. He developed a crush on me during his trial. He stared at me constantly, every moment he was in the courtroom. To the point where it became noticeable and embarrassing. Apparently he's now deluded himself into thinking that I reciprocate his romantic interest."

"Because of the verdict?"

"I suppose. Who knows why? He's crazy."

He harrumphed. "Lozada is a lot of things, but crazy isn't one of them." He watched her for a moment. "Why are you telling me all this now?"

"I'm afraid that he killed Dr. Howell. I think he learned that Lee was named chief of surgery over me, so he killed him as a favor for me. He told me he wanted to return the favor I did him."

"By acquitting him?"

"A twelve-person jury acquitted him."

His deep shrug said *If you say so.* "Go on."

"Lozada is the one who told me about your surveillance. He's been watching me too. He saw Wick follow me home yesterday afternoon. I guess Lozada followed him around the block to the stakeout house. Then he called me. He enjoyed telling me that my newfound friend is a cop."

"Wick would argue that."

"What do you mean?"

"Never mind. Why didn't you tell us about Lozada last night when you confronted us?"

"Because I didn't want you to think what you're thinking."

"Which is?"

"That I'm in cahoots with Lozada!" she exclaimed. "That is what you're thinking, isn't it? You think I contracted him to kill Lee. And now . . . now Wick. That's why you objected to my operating on him."

"You were angry at us. At Wick in particular."

"So you think I called this paid assassin, who just so happens to have a crush on me, and instructed him to stab Wick in the back with a screwdriver?"

Wesley stared at her impassively. He was a seasoned policeman with years of experience. Confessions came in all forms. No doubt he thought she was unburdening herself of guilt.

"If that's your allegation, it's too absurd even to deny," she said.

"Then what are you doing here?"

"After Wick spoke Lozada's name, everything became clear. I saw things as you've been seeing them. Lee gets a promotion I wanted. He gets killed. I told Wick I never wanted to see him again. An attempt is made on his life.

When it crystallized in my mind, I came straight here, only stopping at home long enough to retrieve that card."

"Why did you save it?"

"I'm not sure. I destroyed the roses. Maybe I saved the card because I thought I might need . . . proof."

"Meaning that from the beginning you suspected Lozada of killing Howell."

"No. It wasn't until a few days after Lee's funeral, after I received the roses, that Lozada called me for the first time. He asked if I had enjoyed them. I didn't know until then who had sent them."

He gave her a retiring look. "Come now, Dr. Newton."

"I swear I didn't."

"You didn't have an inkling?"

"All right, possibly. Subconsciously. I knew of no one else who could or would have broken into my house."

"Yet when you learned it was Lozada, you still didn't contact me. Why not?"

"Because of the tone of the interrogation you conducted in this room. I was afraid it would confirm your suspicions of my involvement."

"You had information that might have led to Lozada's arrest and you failed to come forward with it."

"Which was a mistake."

"Why didn't you come running to me waving that card and saying 'I think I know who murdered my friend and why'?"

"I could have been terribly wrong. I could have impeded your investigation, sent you down the wrong path."

"No, I don't think that's it, Dr. Newton. I think you hoped that we would solve the mystery of Dr. Howell's murder all by ourselves. Without your help. Isn't that right?" His eyes probed hers. "You didn't want your name attached to a man's violent death." After a meaningful pause, he added, "A second time."

"Ah." She lowered her head again, but only for an instant, then met his incisive gaze defiantly. "You know about Raymond Collier."

"Some. Want to tell me more about it?"

"You've got your resources, Detective, and I'm sure you'll put them to good use."

"You can count on it." He crossed his arms over his chest and tilted his head. "There is something that puzzles me. I'm wondering how you got seated on that jury. Didn't the lawyers question the prospective jurors, ask if there were any arrest records? Weren't you sworn to tell the truth?"

"Raymond Collier's death was a tragic accident. I don't have a police record. And during voir dire nobody asked if I had been involved in an accidental shooting when I was a minor."

"Well that was convenient, wasn't it?"

She stood up. "I can see you neither value nor want my help."

"On the contrary, Dr. Newton. It's been an enlightening conversation."

"Will you arrest Lozada now?"

"When I get my hands on enough evidence to back up an arrest and indictment."

"What do you mean *when*? This morning my hands were soaking in all the evidence you need. Wick's blood. And I've handed you the weapon."

"It'll be thoroughly analyzed by the lab, and as we speak detectives are hot on the trail of its origin, but I can tell you what they'll find. They'll find that it is decades old and that, when new, it could've been bought at any hardware store on the continent and probably beyond. Between then and now, God knows how many hands have come into contact with it. It won't be traced to anybody."

"The girl was shot. What about the gun?"

"Left at the scene and in our possession. But it'll be like the screwdriver. It's cheap and it's old and reliable only at close range. In this case four to six inches. The user knew we couldn't trace it to him. We'll try, but it won't do any good."

"You know it was Lozada," she cried softly. "Wick can identify him."

"Can he? I don't question that Wick suspects him. He would be the number one suspect on anyone's list. He and Wick are bitter enemies."

Judging by Lozada's tone of voice whenever he spoke Wick's name, she had gathered as much. "What happened between them?"

"It's a police matter."

A matter he obviously chose not to divulge to her. "Can't you at least take Lozada into custody for questioning?"

He scoffed at that. "With no probable cause? He'd love that. It would virtually ensure he would never be tried. I'll only arrest him if Wick can positively identify him as his assailant. But I can almost promise you that Wick didn't see him.

"And just as I expected, that motel room is so chock-full of trace evidence it could belong to Lozada or to anyone else who's ever cleared the threshold of that room, me included. Anything we retrieve from there would never hold up in court.

"Even evidence we retrieved off the other victim, the girl, is no good to us. Dozens of people saw her having

physical contact with several men in that bar, including
Wick. We cleaned her fingernails and got only grit. There
was nothing on her that she couldn't have picked up by casual contact."

"She was in the wrong place at the wrong time."

"Definitely, but that's not all. She had a connection to
Lozada," Wesley said. "Her job was cleaning his penthouse
and she bragged to her co-workers that they were intimate."

"Then what more proof do you need?"

"Oh, we've got lots of proof that she came into daily
contact with Lozada's clothing, his bed linens, his carpet,
his everything. That's more a liability than an advantage.
All his defense lawyer would have to argue is that she could
have picked up the evidence at any time, and he would be
right. So much for our proof."

He gave her a wry look. "Why don't you tell me what
kind of proof a jury would need to convict Lozada, Madam
Forewoman?"

"What about blood on his clothing?"

"You know better than I do that all the significant
bleeding was internal because he didn't withdraw the
weapon. If Lozada got any on him, which is doubtful, by
the time we got a search warrant he would have destroyed
the clothing. There was blood from the victim's neck in the
previous case. Was the prosecution able to produce it on
any of Lozada's belongings?"

"No," she replied. "And his defense attorney made certain we jurors knew that." She was thoughtful for several
seconds, then asked, "What about DNA? That would be virtually indisputable. What about semen? Saliva?"

He shook his head. "He would never be so careless. But

even if he were, he and the girl could have been together earlier in the day, not necessarily in that motel room."

He didn't say whether they'd found Wick's DNA on the girl, and Rennie didn't ask. "It seems I've wasted your time."

She stood and pulled open the door, killing all chatter in the room beyond. Every head turned. She hesitated, but Wesley nudged her forward. "Before you go I'd like you to see something."

He directed her back to his desk, where he picked up a photograph. "The girl's name was Sally Horton. She was twenty-three."

She had to ask. "Had Wick known her long? Were they friends?"

"For about twenty minutes. The bartender saw her approach him and introduce herself. Wick left the bar with me. I'll have to ask him what happened after that. But whatever went down and regardless of the length of time she spent with Wick, Lozada disapproved." He passed her the photograph.

Rennie witnessed death on a routine basis. She had seen the havoc that disease or machine or a weapon could wreak on a human body. Often the damage defied belief and looked like something out of a gruesome horror movie made by a producer with a vivid and sick imagination.

She expected a photograph similar to the ones the jury had been shown during the trial. A bloated face, protruding tongue, bulging eyes. But Sally Horton appeared untouched except for two dark spots in her forehead.

Rennie returned the photograph to Wesley's desk. "If I had told you about Lozada earlier, he might have been in jail and she wouldn't have been killed. Is that why you showed me the picture?"

"That, yeah. But also to warn you."

"I already know that Lozada is dangerous."

"So is getting involved with Wick."

Chapter 17

When Lozada first heard about it on TV news, he'd been furious.

How could Rennie have saved Wick Threadgill's life after he had gone to so much trouble and placed himself at such risk to rid her of him? Women! He would never understand them. Nothing you did for them was ever enough.

Whenever any cop was killed, it made news. Other cops rallied. The black armbands were brought out. Pictures of the widowed and the orphaned made the front page. The general public grieved as though they'd lost a friend. The fallen man was hailed a hero.

But to hear them tell it on TV this morning, Wick Threadgill could walk on water. The reports cited various crimes that Threadgill had solved, seemingly all by himself, Batman and Dick Tracy rolled into one. He had been all but drummed off the force, but that was downplayed.

Rennie was touted as the gifted surgeon who had

worked valiantly to bring him back from the brink of death. She brought to the operating room at Tarrant General the trauma-treatment experience she had gained in war-torn countries while participating in international programs like Doctors Without Borders.

Lozada had been so upset by these blatantly biased news stories that he couldn't even enjoy playing with his scorpions. His worst enemy was receiving accolades. Rennie was working against him. He hadn't felt this frustrated since a paramedic had saved his baby brother after he'd shoved a ball down his throat.

It had been Christmas morning of his sixteenth year. His brother was thirteen but had the mind of a two-year-old. One of his gifts from Santa had been a foam baseball and a plastic bat. He was playing with them beneath the decorated tree. Their parents were in the kitchen checking on the Christmas ham.

Lozada had sat watching his brother for several minutes and decided that his world would be so much nicer without him in it. The idiot had thought it was a game when Lozada crammed the foam ball into his mouth. He hadn't uttered a sound. He put up no resistance whatsoever.

The life had almost gone out of his brother's trusting eyes when Lozada heard his parents returning from the kitchen. He started hollering for them to come quickly, that baby brother had put his new baseball in his mouth. Nine-one-one was called and the kid was spared. His parents had wept with relief, held the boy close all day, and said over and over again what a blessing he was.

It had been a rotten Christmas Day. Even the ham had burned.

Ironically, he could have saved himself the trouble of

trying to kill his brother. A mere six months later, his parents had been flying the kid to Houston to consult with yet another witch doctor—didn't these people know when to quit?—when their commuter plane crashed into an East Texas swamp during a thunderstorm. Everyone on board perished. How had he gotten so lucky?

But Lozada wouldn't leave Wick Threadgill to fate.

For one thing, he wouldn't deny himself the satisfaction of killing him. Already he'd had to sacrifice the leisurely planning of it. Only yesterday he had resolved to take his time and devise something special for Threadgill. But last night it had become clear that he must act without delay. He hated like hell having to accelerate his plans. You didn't drink a decanter of Louis XIII like a can of soda. He was being deprived of the savoring. But if it meant Threadgill would be dead sooner rather than later, he could accept that.

Although faced with a few tactical problems last night, he had planned quickly and acted swiftly. The would-be exotic dancer had been easy to entice. She had believed him without question when he told her he had a friend who liked threesomes—was she game? "If he's as cute as you, you bet!"

She had balked at taking her car instead of his, but she had consented quickly enough when he said, "On second thought, let's just forget about it."

He knew where Threadgill was staying. It was the rathole where the FWPD normally stashed paid trial witnesses, visiting law enforcement personnel, new recruits, and such. For verification all he'd had to do was call and ask to be connected to Wick Threadgill's room. He'd hung up while the phone was ringing, but he had confirmed Threadgill's lodging.

He had Sally park in a supermarket parking lot two
blocks away from the motel, and they'd gone the rest of
the way on foot. When she asked why, he told her he
wanted to surprise his friend. She bought it.

Wick's pickup was parked outside Room 121. Lozada
scanned the parking lot to make certain no one else was
about. Most of the rooms were dark. The few where lights
were on had the drapes drawn.

He motioned the girl forward. "You go first. I want you
to be the first thing he sees when he opens the door."

She knocked, but after waiting for several seconds, she
pressed her ear to the door. "I think I hear the shower."

She'd been impressed when he opened the lock with
his credit card. Signaling for her to be very quiet, he ushered her inside and told her to lie down on the bed. She
obliged him and had been suppressing a fit of giggles
when he shot her twice in the forehead. He considered
cutting out her tongue as he had promised to do if she
talked about him, but it would have been messy. Besides,
the shower faucets were turned off.

In hindsight, he should have used the silenced pistol
on Wick, too. One pop in the ear as he came out of the
bathroom, another between the eyes to make sure. But
where was the fun in that? He'd wanted Wick to realize
that he was going to die.

On the other hand, the screwdriver was a good choice.
He'd found it in an old toolbox in the rear storage room
of his TV repair shop. Practical, rusty, antiquated, untraceable.

Another thing he might do differently: He would have
made that jab fatal instead of recreational. Rather than
making it instantaneous and stabbing Wick in the heart as
he'd done Howell, he'd wanted to play with Threadgill.

That turned out to be a bad call. He hadn't had time to finish the job, thanks to the motel maid. Who cleans rooms at 4:30 in the morning?

By the time she had dialed 911, he was back at the supermarket. He'd driven Sally's car to where they'd made the exchange. He had left the keys in it, retrieved his SUV, and parked it in the undesignated space of a garage, then walked to the hotel coffee shop for breakfast. He was having a last cup of coffee when the first reports of the murder appeared on the morning news shows.

All that work and nothing to show for it, he thought now. The bastard hadn't died. And Rennie had helped him survive. Why? Why had she saved him? She had been furious with him. She had told him she never wanted to see him again. She hated him.

Or did she?

He remained in his condo all day, too dispirited to go out. He called his ultra-private voice-mail number and had a message that said a job was his for the asking. The contract was so important to the client that Lozada could name his own price. Ordinarily the prospect would have excited him, but even the promise of a lucrative job with a built-in bonus didn't lift him out of his doldrums.

He was superior to Wick Threadgill in every way. He had class. He doubted Threadgill could even spell it. He was a millionaire. Threadgill scraped by on a cop's salary. He wore designer clothes. Threadgill dressed like a saddle tramp. He wanted to place Rennie on a pedestal. Threadgill wanted to use her to get to him.

It simply didn't tabulate. How could she possibly prefer Threadgill to him?

He was still sulking when the early edition of the evening news came on. Nothing had happened that day to supplant the lead story of Sally Horton's murder and the near-fatal attack on Wick. After recapping the morning's events, the talking head said, "A press conference was held today at Tarrant General, where Dr. Rennie Newton answered the questions of reporters."

That segued into videotape of the press conference. Rennie was standing behind a podium and was flanked by two somber men in dark suits who were probably hospital administrators. She squinted against the glare of video lights as she acknowledged one of the eager reporters.

"Dr. Newton, what's Mr. Threadgill's current condition?"

"He's stable," she replied. "Which is encouraging. He was critical this morning. He had a penetration wound in his back that did a lot of damage to surrounding tissue."

In the right hands, a Phillips screwdriver would do that to a person. Lozada's lips curled into a smirk of gratification.

"Was the wound potentially fatal?"

"In my opinion, yes. Lifesaving measures were taken immediately. Our trauma team did an excellent job."

"Was this attack related to the unsolved murder of Mr. Threadgill's brother three years ago?"

"I don't know anything about that."

"Is Wick Threadgill still on leave from the police department?"

"That's a question for the police."

"Is he—"

She held up her hands for quiet. "I responded to an emergency call this morning. For a time, I didn't even know the patient's name. I don't know anything about Mr. Threadgill's career or his family history. I did my job. Beyond that, I can't tell you anything more."

The video ended there. The talking head returned

with a brief summation and then moved on to the next story.

Lozada switched off the TV set but sat there and thought about Rennie's statement, "I did my job."

Of course! She hadn't saved Threadgill because she liked him. She had only been doing her job. He'd had nothing against most of the people he'd killed. He hadn't even known them, but that hadn't stopped him from doing what he was paid to do. Rennie had simply been going about her work with the same professional detachment he had when he went about his.

And wasn't she fantastic, the way she'd handled the media? Coolly professional, unfazed and unimpressed by the media exposure. She was extraordinary.

Oh, she was tired. He could tell that. He'd seen her looking better. But even disheveled and fatigued she was still beautiful and desirable. He wanted her. He would have her soon. Surely after this she would appreciate the depth of his devotion to her.

Suddenly he was ravenously hungry and felt like going out.

He poured himself a tequila and took it with him into the black marble shower. After showering and shaving his head and body, he let the water stream for another ten minutes. Following that thorough rinsing he disassembled the drain, cleaned every component of it with disposable wipes, then flushed them down the toilet.

He replaced the drain. He wiped the shower stall dry with a towel and placed it in a cloth bag. On his way out he would drop the bag into a chute that emptied into a bin in the building's basement. A laundry service collected the bags twice daily. He never left a used towel in his bathroom.

He finished his drink while dressing in a pair of hand-tailored linen slacks and a silk T-shirt. He liked the feel of the silk against his skin, liked the way it caressed his nipples, as soft and sensual as a woman's tongue. He hoped Rennie would like his tattoo.

He topped off the outfit with a contrasting sport coat. He was overdressing for the Mexican restaurant, but he felt like celebrating. He called down to the parking valet and asked that his Mercedes be brought from the garage.

Before leaving his condo he placed one more call.

The valet had the Mercedes waiting for him and was holding the driver's door open. "Have a good evening, Mr. Lozada."

"Thank you."

Knowing that he looked great and that the young man probably envied him, Lozada tipped him generously.

Chapter 18

The instant she stepped off the elevator she saw the roses.

It would have been impossible for her to miss them. The bouquet had been placed on the ledge of the nurses' station. Nurses and aides had obviously been awaiting her arrival to see her reaction. All were wearing expectant smiles.

"They're for you, Dr. Newton."

"They were delivered about half an hour ago."

"You could barely see the delivery boy behind them. Aren't they gorgeous?"

"Who's your secret admirer?"

"He's not a cop." This from the policeman that Wesley had posted outside Wick's ICU. "No cop could afford them, that's for sure."

Rennie didn't give the bouquet another glance. "There must be some mistake. They're not for me."

"B-but there's a card," one of the nurses stammered. "It's got your name on it."

"Get rid of the roses and the card. The vase. All of it."

"You want us to throw them away?"

"Or distribute them among the patients. Take them to the lobby atrium, the chapel, put them on the dinner menu. I don't care. Just get them out of my sight. I need Mr. Threadgill's chart, please."

The group, no longer smiling, dispersed. The policeman slunk back to his post. One of the nurses carried away the heavy arrangement. Another passed Rennie the requested chart and bravely followed her into Wick's cubicle.

"He's been waking up for longer periods of time," the nurse told her. "He hates the spirometer." Patients were forced to blow into the machine periodically to keep their lungs clear.

His vitals were good. She checked the dressing covering his incision. He moaned in his sleep when she peeled the bandage off to take a look. After replacing the bandage, she asked the nurse if he'd had anything to drink.

"Just the ice chips."

"If he asks for something again, let him have sips of Sprite."

"Widschumburohn."

Rennie moved to the left side of the bed, the one he lay facing. "Come again?"

"Burohn. In the schpirte." Barely moving his head, he tried to locate her with his single eye. To make it easier on him, she sat on the edge of the chair beside the bed.

"Do bourbon and Sprite mix?"

"Don' care."

She smiled. "I think you're well medicated already."

"Not enough."

The nurse bustled out to get the Sprite. Wick readjusted his head so that his face wasn't half buried in the pillow. "Did you do this to me, Rennie?"

"Guilty."

"Then you're off"—he winced, sucked in his breath—"off my Christmas card list."

"If you can joke you must be feeling better."

"Like hammered shit."

"Well, that's what you look like."

"Ha-ha." His eye closed and it remained closed.

Rennie stood up and applied her stethoscope to several spots on his chest.

"Are you getting a beat?" he asked, which surprised her because she thought he had drifted off again.

"Loud and strong, Mr. Threadgill." She sat back down in the chair. "Your lungs sound clear, too, so keep blowing into the spirometer when the nurses ask you to."

"Sissy stuff."

"But pneumonia isn't."

"Rennie?"

"Yes?"

"Was I shot?"

"Stabbed."

He opened his eye again.

"With a screwdriver," she told him.

"Damage?"

"Considerable but reparable."

"Thanks."

"You're welcome."

"My balls hurt."

"I'll see that you get an ice pack for them."

It surprised her that a single eye could pack such malice into a dirty look.

"They're swollen," she explained. "Blood collects in the testicles after an injury like yours."

"But they're okay?"

"They're okay. This is a temporary condition."

"You swear?"

"Give them a few days. They'll return to normal."

"Good, good." He closed his eye. "Funny conversation."

"Not-so-funny pain, though. So I've been told."

"Rennie?" He reopened his eye. "Did they get him?"

She shook her head.

"Fuck."

Rennie remained where she was, seated beside the bed. Again she thought he had gone back to sleep when he mumbled, "My face. Hurts like hell. Wha'd he do to it?"

"Apparently he attacked you from behind."

"Right."

"You fell forward and landed hard on your cheek. Your chin was busted open, but it didn't require stitches. You're bruised and swollen, but no bones were broken."

"So I'll be as handsome as ever?"

"And as conceited, I'm sure."

He smiled but she could tell that any facial expression caused him discomfort.

The nurse returned with the soft drink in a foam cup and looked at Rennie strangely when she took it from her. Few surgeons ministered to patients this way. She pressed the bent straw against Wick's lips. He took several careful sips, then angled his head back slightly to signal that he was done.

"Is that it for now?" she asked.

"Don' wanna throw up."

Then he remained quiet and she was certain this time that he had gone back to sleep. Even after the nurse left the room, Rennie stayed. The next thing she knew, a soft voice was asking, "How's he doing?"

She looked up to find Grace Wesley standing just outside the door. Rennie hadn't heard her approach, hadn't noticed anything, hadn't been aware of the passage of time. How long had she been staring into Wick's battered face?

Quickly she came to her feet. "He's, uh, he's better, actually. Talking coherently when he wakes up. He had some sips of Sprite." She set the cup of soda on the rolling bed tray. It seemed incriminating somehow to be caught holding it. "He's sleeping now."

"Is it okay if I come in?"

"Of course."

"I don't want to disturb."

"I doubt you will. He's out of it."

Grace Wesley was attractive and slim. She wore her hair in a small chignon on the back of her head, a minimalist style that was flattering only to someone with her high cheekbones and delicate features. Her almond-shaped eyes bespoke intelligence and integrity. She had a quiet and gentle way about her. Earlier, Rennie had noticed that Grace's slightest touch had a calming effect on her brawny husband.

She moved to the foot of Wick's bed and for several moments watched him sleep. "It's hard for me to believe that's Wick," she said, smiling. "I've never seen him inert. He never even sits still for more than a few seconds at a time. The man's in constant motion."

"I've noticed that too." Grace turned and looked at her quizzically. "Of course I don't know him well," Rennie was quick to qualify. "Not well at all. But I gather you do."

"Wick was a senior in high school when Oren, my husband . . ."

Rennie nodded.

"When Oren and Wick's brother Joe entered the police academy. We became good friends with Joe. He invited us to a high school basketball game 'to watch my kid brother play,' he said." She laughed softly. "Wick fouled out."

"He's an aggressive competitor?"

"And a hothead. Volatile, easily set off. But when he loses his temper he's usually just as quick to apologize."

They were quiet for a time, then Rennie said, "I didn't know about his brother until today when a reporter asked me about him."

"Joe died three years ago. None of us is over it. Especially Wick. He thought Joe could do no wrong and loved him very much."

The nurse came in to replace an IV bag. They suspended their conversation until they were once again alone. "I understand that Joe was . . ."

"Murdered," Grace said bluntly.

In one blinding instant of clarity, it connected. Rennie said, "Lozada."

"That's right. Lozada."

"How'd he get off?"

"He was never indicted."

"Why not?"

Grace hesitated, then took a step closer to Rennie and spoke more softly. "Dr. Newton, I asked my husband what was going on between the two of you this morning. I sensed the strong undercurrents."

"Two weeks ago I served on a jury that acquitted Lozada."

"Oren explained that."

"Your husband resents me for the outcome of that trial. Especially now. Lozada took one friend from him, and almost took another." She looked down at Wick. "If the jury had arrived at a different verdict, Wick wouldn't have been attacked and that young woman who was killed last night would be alive."

"May I ask you something?" Grace asked quietly. When Rennie turned back to her, she said, "If you could do it all over again, would you still vote to acquit Lozada?"

"Based on what I knew then, or on what I know now?"

"On what you knew then."

Rennie gave the question the same degree of consideration she had given that final and fateful vote. "Based strictly on what I knew then and the charge the judge gave us, I would be compelled to vote for acquittal again."

"Then your conscience should be clear, Dr. Newton. You can't be held responsible for Lozada's attack on Wick."

Ruefully she said, "Tell your husband that."

"I already did."

Rennie was taken aback. Grace smiled her gentle smile and reached out to press Rennie's hand. "I'll go now. But when Wick wakes up please tell him that I was here."

"I'll be going soon too, but I'll leave word with the nurses to be sure and tell him."

"Do you know when he'll be moved to a regular room?"

"In a day or two, if he continues to do well. I'm watching him closely for any sign of infection."

"What can I tell my girls?"

"You have daughters?"

"Two. Very lively ones."

"How nice for you."

"They begged to come with me tonight, but Oren didn't want them to leave the house."

Rennie didn't need to ask why. Wesley feared for their safety, feared Lozada might not be satisfied with an attempt on Wick's life. He had posted policemen at various places throughout the hospital, and now she noticed two more on the other side of the glass wall of Wick's ICU. No doubt they were Grace Wesley's bodyguards.

"My girls adore their Uncle Wick," she was saying. "If there were a poster of him, it would be on the wall of their room along with their other heartthrobs."

"Tell them their Uncle Wick is going to be all right."

"We have you to thank for that. The girls are dying to meet you."

"Me?"

"I told them all about you. Afterward, I overheard them talking together. They've now decided to become surgeons. They want to save people as you saved Wick."

Rennie was so touched she didn't know what to say. Grace must have sensed that. She let her off with a quick good-bye. The two policemen flanked her as they walked to the elevator.

There was no trace of the roses when Rennie returned to the nurses' station. Inside the circular enclosure sat several desks, computer terminals, monitoring machines, file cabinets, and general clutter. She didn't know where to begin looking for what she needed, and apparently she looked at a loss.

"Can I help you find something, Dr. Newton?"

"Uh, yes."

Several drawers were searched before a tin of medicated lip balm was located. Rennie took it with her into Wick's ICU. He was still sleeping, breathing evenly. She sat down in the chair at his bedside, but it was at least a full minute before she uncapped the small tin and released a pleasant aroma that hinted of vanilla.

She had noticed earlier that Wick's lips were dry and cracked. This wasn't an unusual side effect of surgery and loss of fluids. In fact it was quite common. But Wick's lips had looked *exceptionally* dry. She had thought an application of lip balm might help. What was wrong with that?

Who was she arguing with?

She rubbed the surface of the salve with the pad of her index finger, making several tight circles in it, until the friction and her own body heat warmed and softened it. She dabbed the salve on his lower lip, then the upper one, barely making contact, touching him so gingerly it hardly counted as touching.

When both lips had been dotted with the fragrant salve, she withdrew her hand. Hesitated. Then she touched his lower lip again, except this time she didn't break contact. Slowly, she spread the balm from one corner of his mouth to the other, then back again. She did the same with the upper lip, following the masculine contour, staying within the shape of it with the painstaking care of a child who would be scolded if she colored outside the lines.

And just as she was about to retract her hand again, he woke up. The eye contact was electric.

Neither said anything. They remained perfectly still, with her index finger resting on the seam of his lips. Rennie held her breath, realizing that his deep and even breathing had also ceased. She strongly felt that if either one of them moved, something would happen. Something momentous. Exactly what, she didn't know. In any case, she didn't dare move. She wasn't certain she could. His blue gaze had an immobilizing effect on her.

They remained frozen in that tableau for . . . how long? Later she couldn't remember. It lasted until Wick's left eye closed against his pillow. She actually heard his eyelashes brush against the pillowcase. She didn't resume breathing until after he had.

Then she pulled back her hand, clumsily recapped the tin of lip balm, and left it on the bed tray. She didn't look at him again before leaving the ICU. "Call me if there's any change," she instructed brusquely as she returned his chart to the nurses' station.

At the elevator, the policeman on guard held open the door and addressed her shyly. "Dr. Newton, I just wanted to say . . . well, Wick's a great guy. A few years back, one of my kids got hurt. Wick was first in line to donate blood. Anyhow, I wanted to tell you thanks for pulling him through this morning."

Rennie attributed the tear to exhaustion. She hadn't realized how tired she was until the elevator began its descent. She leaned against the rear wall of it and closed her eyes. That was when she felt the tear roll down her cheek. She wiped it away before reaching the ground floor.

As she moved through the hospital exit, another policeman surprised her by following her out. "Is something wrong?"

"Wesley's orders, ma'am. Doctor," he said, correcting himself.

"Why?"

"I didn't ask, and he didn't say. I figure it's something to do with Threadgill."

The officer walked her to her car, checked the backseat, looked beneath it. "Drive safely, Dr. Newton."

"Thank you, I will." He continued watching her until she had gone through the gate.

She had driven several blocks before she noticed the cassette. It was protruding from the audio player in the dashboard. She stared at it, mystified. She never played cassettes, always CDs.

At the next stoplight, she pulled it out to check the label. There was none. She could see the tiny spools of audiotape through clear plastic. Dismissing the sense of foreboding that came over her, she inserted the cassette and punched the arrow indicator for Play.

Strains of piano music filled the car, along with the husky tones of a female torch singer.

"I've got a crush . . ."

Rennie struck the controls with her fist, banging it against them repeatedly until the music stopped. She was trembling, primarily with anger, but also with fear. Having policemen posted around the hospital hadn't deterred Lozada from placing this tape in her car. How the hell had he managed it? Her car had been locked.

She groped inside her leather satchel in search of her cell phone, but all she succeeded in doing was dump the contents of her satchel onto the floor. She reasoned that by the time she stopped and found her phone she could be home. She would call Wesley from there.

She sped through two red lights after glancing right and left to check for oncoming traffic. She wheeled into her driveway at an imprudent speed. The garage door took an eternity to open. It had barely cleared the roof of her car when she drove under it. She used the transistor to reverse it, and it began to close behind her before she even cut her car's engine.

Leaving her spilled possessions on the floor, she clambered out and hit her back door at a dead run. She burst into her kitchen, then drew up short.

Flickering light shone through the connecting door to the living room. No light source in her living room produced that kind of light. So what was going on? Until she knew, the sensible thing to do would be to back out the door, reopen the garage, and run down the center of the street, waving her arms and yelling for help.

But she wasn't going to run screaming from her own house. To hell with that!

She left the back door standing open. She took a butcher knife from a drawer. Then she crossed the kitchen and entered the living room. Candles, hundreds, it seemed, but probably closer to dozens, flickered in clear-glass containers of every shape and size. They had been placed on every available surface, filling the air with a heady floral fragrance and making the room appear ablaze.

On her coffee table was another bouquet of red roses. And from the CD player, music in stereo. Another version. Another artist. But the same classic Gershwin tune. Lozada's theme song.

She was breathing hard through her mouth, and she

could hear the pounding of her heart above the music. She took a cautious step backward, rethinking the advisability of handling this herself. Maybe she should escape through the kitchen door after all.

She calculated the time it would take to get help. Back through the kitchen. Out the door. Punch the garage door switch on the wall. Duck beneath the door. Down the driveway and into the street. Or through the hedge to Mr. Williams's house. Calling for help. Involving other people. Involving the police.

No.

She walked to the sound system and turned off the music. "Come out and face me, why don't you?"

The shouted words echoed back to her. She listened closely, but it was difficult to distinguish any sound except those of her own harsh breathing and hammering heartbeat.

She moved toward the hallway, but paused at the end of it. It stretched before her, dark and ominous, seemingly much longer than it actually was. And because he had made her afraid in her own sanctuary she became even angrier. Anger propelled her forward.

She moved quickly down the hall and reached for the light switch in her home office. The room was empty, with nowhere to hide. She pulled open the closet door. Nothing in there but her stored luggage and travel gear. Again, there was nowhere for a grown man to hide.

From there she went into her bedroom, where more candles flickered. They cast wavering shadows on the walls and ceiling, against the window blinds that, because of him, she now kept closed at all hours of the day and night. She looked under the bed. She went to the closet and opened the door with a flourish. She thrashed through the hanging clothes.

The bathroom was also empty, but her shower curtain, which she always kept open, was drawn. Too angry now to be afraid, she shoved it aside. Another arrangement of roses rested on the wire shelf spanning her tub.

She swung at the vase and sent it crashing into the porcelain tub. The racket was as loud as an explosion.

"You bastard! Why won't you leave me alone?"

She marched back into the bedroom and went around blowing out the candles until she feared the smoke would set off the alarm. She retraced her steps through the living room but left the candles burning for now. In the kitchen she closed the back door and locked it, returned the knife to the drawer.

She found a half full bottle of Chardonnay in the fridge, poured most of it into a glass, then took a long drink. Closing her eyes, she pressed the cold glass against her forehead.

She debated whether to call Wesley. What would be the point? She couldn't prove that Lozada had broken into her home any more than Wesley could prove that he had murdered Sally Horton and attempted to kill Wick.

On the other hand, if she didn't report this and Wesley somehow found out about it . . . Right. Much as she dreaded doing it, he should be notified.

She raised her head, opened her eyes, and saw her reflection in the window above the sink. Standing behind her was Lozada.

She'd only thought she was too angry to be afraid.

Chapter 19

□□□□□□□□□□

He took her by the shoulders and turned her around to face him. His eyes were so dark the pupils were indistinguishable from the irises.

"You seem upset. I wanted to please you, Rennie, not upset you." His voice was soft. Like a lover's.

Her mind was racing down twin tracks of terror and fury. She wanted to lash out at him for disrupting her systematized life. Equally as much she wanted to cower in fear. But either reaction signaled weakness, which she didn't dare let him see. He was a predator who would sense his prey's weakness and take full advantage of it.

He took the wineglass from her and pressed the cup of it against her lips. "Drink."

She tried to turn her head aside, but he gripped her jaw with his other hand and held it in place while he tipped the glass. She felt the wine cold against her lips. The glass clinked against her teeth. Wine filled her mouth.

She swallowed, but not all of it. Some dribbled over her chin. As he wiped it away with his thumb, he smiled at her.

Rennie had seen that kind of smile all over the world. It was an abuser's smile for the abused. It was the smile of a cruel husband for the wife he had beaten beyond recognition. The enemy warrior's smile for the girl he had raped. The father's smile for the virgin daughter he'd had castrated.

It was a possessive and condescending smile. It announced that the abused one's free will had been taken away, and that, through some perverse reasoning, she should be happy about it, even grateful for her abuser's tolerance.

That was Lozada's smile for her.

He tipped the wineglass toward her lips again, but she couldn't endure that smile any longer and swatted the glass away. The wine sloshed over his hand. His eyes narrowed dangerously. He raised his hand, and she thought he was about to strike her.

But instead he lifted his hand to his mouth and licked off the wine with obscenely suggestive strokes of his tongue.

His evil smile turned into a soft laugh. "No wonder you didn't want it, Rennie. It's cheap. A terrible vintage. One of my first projects will be to introduce you to really fine wines."

He reached around her to set the glass of wine on the counter. His body pressed against hers and held. His nearness smothered her. She couldn't breathe and she didn't want to. She didn't want his cologne to be recorded in her olfactory memory bank.

She willed herself not to push him away. A flashback to the photo of Sally Horton enabled her to remain still and endure the pressure of his body. Lozada probably wanted her to struggle. He would welcome an excuse to assert himself as the dominator. Abusers thrived on reasons to justify their cruelty.

"You're trembling, Rennie. Are you afraid of me?" He leaned even closer. His breath ghosted across her neck. He was erect and rubbed himself against her suggestively. "Why would you be afraid of me when I want only to make you happy? Hmm?"

Finally he moved back and, with an air of amusement, took a long look at her, from the top of her head to her shoes and back up. "Maybe before we tackle wine education we should start with something more basic. Like your wardrobe." Placing his fingers on her collarbones, he stroked them lightly. "It's a sin to hide this figure."

His eyes lowered to her breasts and lingered there, and somehow that was worse than if he had actually touched them. "You should wear clothes that hug your body, Rennie. And the color black to offset your pale hair. I'll buy you something black and very sexy, something that shows off your breasts. Yes, definitely. Men will want to fondle you, but I'll be the only one who will."

Then his eyes returned to her face and his tone became teasing. "Of course you're not looking your best today. You've been working very hard." His fingertip traced the dark crescents beneath her eyes. "You're exhausted. Poor dear."

She swallowed the gorge that had filled her throat when he described his fantasy. "I am not your dear."

"Ah, the lady speaks. I was beginning to wonder if you'd lost the capacity."

"I want you to leave."

"But I just got here."

That was a lie, of course. It had taken him at least an hour to place all the lighted candles in her living room. Where had he been hiding when she searched the house?

As though reading her mind, he said, "I never give away trade secrets, Rennie. You should know that about me." He pinched her chin playfully. "We do, however, have a lot to talk about."

"You're right. We do."

Pleased, he smiled. "You go first."

"Lee Howell."

"Who?"

"You killed him, didn't you? You did it as a favor to me. And the attack on Wick Threadgill. That was you too, wasn't it?"

He moved like quicksilver. He raised her blouse with one hand and ran his hand over her breasts and around the inside of the waistband of her skirt. She shoved against his chest with all her strength. "Get your hands off me." She slapped at his searching hands.

"Stop that!" He grabbed her hands and pulled them hard against his chest. "Rennie, Rennie, stop fighting me." His voice was gentle; his grip wasn't. "Shh, shh. Relax."

She glared up at him.

In a deceptively soft and reasonable voice, he apologized. "I'm sorry I had to do that. A few years ago the police used an undercover policewoman to try and trap me. I had to make sure you weren't wearing a wire. Forgive me for getting a little rough. How's this? Better now?"

He let go of her hands and squeezed her shoulders, his strong fingers flexing and relaxing rhythmically, massaging her like an attentive husband who'd just learned that his wife had had a long and tiring day.

"I'm not working for the police."

"I would be terribly disappointed in you if you were."
His hands squeezed a little harder. His expression turned
malevolent. "Why is it you've been spending time with
Wick Threadgill?"

She made a face of dislike. "I didn't know he was a cop.
He deceived me to use me."

"So why did you work so hard to save his life?"

Wesley's words of warning came back to her. Sally Horton had been an innocent pawn in the blood rivalry between Wick and Lozada. She had died for the role she had
unwittingly played. "That's what they pay me for," she said
flippantly. "I don't always get to choose my patient. In this
case, fate chose me. I drew the short straw. I couldn't let
him bleed out there in the emergency room."

His eyes searched hers. He curved his hand around her
throat. His thumb found her carotid and stroked it. "I
would be very unhappy if you were to cheat on me with
Wick Threadgill."

"There's nothing between us."

"Has he ever kissed you?"

"No."

"Touched you like this?" He caressed her breast.

Her throat was too tight to speak. She shook her head.

"That cop has never been this hard for you, Rennie,"
he whispered, pressing himself against her. "He never
could be this hard for you."

"Hands in the air, Lozada!"

Oren Wesley barged in, followed by two other officers,
service pistols drawn and aimed. The three fanned out
into a semicircle around them.

"Hands up, I said! Now, move away from her!"

Rennie was dumbfounded. But as Lozada complied
with the order his face became a placid mask. Within sec-

onds he'd been transformed into an identical replica of himself, the kind of perfect effigy that would appear in a wax museum. He revealed no anger, surprise, or concern. "Detective Wesley, I didn't know you stayed up this late."

"Assume the position."

Shrugging negligently, Lozada leaned forward upon the kitchen table. His hands were splayed near a basket of fruit where the bananas were getting too ripe. It was a bizarre thought to register when a would-be rapist and reputed killer was being patted down in her kitchen, but Rennie found it a welcome distraction.

The policeman who had the honors retrieved a small handgun from Lozada's pants pocket. "It's registered," Lozada said.

"Handcuff him," Wesley instructed. "He'll have a knife in an ankle holster." While one of the policemen was dragging Lozada's hands to the small of his back for cuffing, the other knelt and raised his trousers leg. He slid a small, shiny knife from the sheath. Lozada's expression never changed.

Wesley looked across at her. "You all right?"

Still too astonished to speak, she nodded.

One of the policemen was reading Lozada his Miranda rights, but he was looking at Wesley over the cop's head. "What am I being arrested for?"

"Murder."

"Interesting. And who was the alleged victim?"

"Sally Horton."

"The chambermaid in my building?"

"Save the innocent act for the jury," Wesley said, giving Rennie a glance. "You also stabbed Wick Threadgill in attempted murder."

"This is a farce."

"Well, we'll see what turns up in our investigation, won't we? In the meantime, you'll be a guest of the county."

"I'll be out by morning."

"As I said, we'll see." Wesley motioned with his head for the other pair of policemen to escort him out.

Lozada smiled back at Rennie. "Good-bye, love. See you very soon. I'm sorry about this interruption. Detective Wesley loves to grandstand. It's compensation for other deficiencies." As he drew even with Wesley, he said, "I think your dick was buried with Joe Threadgill."

One of the policemen shoved him hard in the back. They disappeared through the door into the living room. Rennie sagged against the counter.

"Thank you."

"Don't mention it."

"You said you wouldn't arrest him until you had solid evidence. Does that mean—"

"All this means is that I wore my sergeant down. He agreed to me bringing Lozada in while we're running our traps. If we get real lucky—and luck seems to be in short supply when we're trying to nail Lozada—something incriminating will turn up."

"I take it nothing has so far."

He gave a noncommittal shrug. "We can't hold him indefinitely without arraigning him, but we'll drag it out for as long as possible. Unless we can collect some hard evidence to support Wick's allegation, it would amount to a pissing contest in court. If the DA would even take it to court."

"He would have to, wouldn't he? If Wick identified Lozada as his attacker?"

"The DA's office might be reluctant to take only Wick's

word for it to the grand jury. They would factor in the history between Wick and Lozada, which sorely reduces Wick's credibility. Besides, they're not too fond of him over there."

"The DA's office? How come?"

A cop poked his head though the door and spoke to Wesley. "He's on his way to lockup."

"I'm right behind you."

The policeman withdrew. Rennie followed Wesley into her living room, where the candles still burned. Their scent was cloying. She went to one of her front windows and opened it so the room could air out. Several patrol cars were pulling away from the curb in front of her house, strobes flashing.

Pajama-clad neighbors had congregated on the sidewalk and were talking among themselves. Mr. Williams was in the middle of them, holding center stage and gesturing theatrically.

"How did you know Lozada was here, Detective? Are you still watching my house?"

"No. We got a call. Your neighbor. A Mr. Williams. Said something weird was going on."

God, this was a nightmare.

Wesley stood in the center of the room, taking a slow look around. The roses didn't escape his notice. When he finally came back around to Rennie, he said, "I talked to a hospital board member today. He said you had accepted the position vacated by Dr. Howell."

Her chin went up a notch. "I gave them my decision this afternoon. After my meeting with you. I didn't see that accepting made any difference. You were going to continue believing that I hired Lozada to kill Lee whether I took it or not."

He gestured toward the roses. "Congratulations."

"This wasn't a celebration, if that's what you're thinking. All this was here when I arrived home from the hospital. He broke in again."

"You didn't call to report it."

"I didn't have a chance."

He looked down at her rumpled clothing. "He was terrorizing me," she exclaimed. "He has this, this mad notion that I'm going to become his lady love." She told him everything that Lozada had said to her, even the most embarrassing parts. "He manhandled me. He thought I might be wearing a wire."

"A wire?"

"When I mentioned Lee Howell's murder, he searched me. He was afraid I was working for you to try to trap him."

"Well, we both know how wrong that is."

Disliking his snide tone, she said, "Detective, I did not invite him here. Why would you automatically assume that I had?"

"Did you break something?"

"In the bathroom. He'd left another of those bouquets in my bathtub. I was so angry I knocked it over."

"Mr. Williams was in his backyard waiting for his dog to do his business. He heard the crash and tried to call you, see if you were okay." Wesley spied the cordless telephone on the end table.

Rennie picked it up, then held it out toward Wesley. There was no dial tone. It had been disconnected for so long that the obnoxious beeping alert had played itself out.

"I guess he didn't want to be disturbed," she said quietly.

"I guess not."

She returned the telephone to its usual place on the table, then drew her hand back quickly. "Should I have touched that?"

"He doesn't have fingerprints. Anyhow, it doesn't matter. We already know that Lozada was here, and this isn't a crime scene."

"Since when did breaking and entering stop being a crime? He came in and made himself at home."

"Yeah. Mr. Williams told the nine-one-one dispatcher that he looked right at home. After reporting the disturbance, he said, 'Wait, never mind, I can see her and a man through the kitchen window. It appears that nothing's wrong, that she knows him very well.' Something like that. However, this dispatcher was on the ball. She recognized your name and address, knew I—"

"Had been spying on me."

"So she called me. Said she'd just had a curious nine-one-one from your neighbor. You and a man were getting it on in the kitchen."

"Hardly how I would describe it. I was afraid if I resisted I would wind up like Sally Horton."

"You might have."

"Then why do you always put me on the defensive?"

He only looked at her before turning away. "I need to be on my way."

As he headed for the door she rushed after him, grabbed his arm, and brought him around. "I deserve an answer, Detective."

"Fine. Here's my answer," he said tightly. "You haven't given me any reason to trust you, Doctor, but you've given me a lot of reasons not to."

"What would convince you I'm telling the truth? Would

you have been convinced if Lozada had killed me tonight?"

"Not really," he returned with a blasé shrug. "Before Sally Horton became his victim, she was his lover."

Chapter 20

∎∎∎∎∎∎∎∎∎∎∎

He wants only to make her happy."

"Are you kidding?"

"Stop looking at me like that, Wick," Oren complained. "*I* didn't say it. *She* said *he* said it."

Wick had stayed in ICU for two days. For the past five, he'd been in a private room that afforded a view of the downtown skyline. He was able to lie on his back now. It still hurt like hell, especially when he was forced to get up and walk around, which was at least twice a day.

Each of those hikes, as he called them, was an ordeal equivalent to climbing Everest. It took him five minutes just to get out of bed. At first he was able only to shuffle around his room, but earlier today he had managed to make it to the end of the hall and back, which the nursing staff claimed was a major breakthrough. Big woo. They commended his progress. He cursed and asked them where they stored their Nazi uniforms. When he returned to bed, he was sweating and feeling as helpless as a new-born.

He looked forward to the pain medication that was regularly dispensed. It didn't eliminate the pain but made it tolerable. He could live with it if he didn't think about it too much and focused on something else. Like Lozada.

This morning he'd been taken off the IV. He'd been glad to get rid of it, but then the nurses had begun bullying him to take in lots of fluids. They brought him fruit juice in little plastic cups with foil lids. He hadn't succeeded in opening one yet without spilling half of it.

"Are you eating?" Oren asked.

"Some. A little. I'm not hungry. Besides, you wouldn't believe the crap they try to pass off as food."

His cheek was still the color of an eggplant going bad, but the swelling had gone down enough for him to see out of both eyes. For instance, he could see that Oren's eyebrow was in its critical-arch position. "What?" he asked grouchily.

"How're your privates?"

"Fine thanks, how're yours?" For several uncomfortable days he had straddled an ice pack, but, as Rennie had promised, his balls had returned to their normal size.

"You know what I mean," Oren said.

"They're okay. Wanna check 'em out?"

"I'll take your word for it." Oren shifted his weight from one foot to the other. "I haven't had a chance to tell you. I'm sorry about your chin."

"Least of my problems."

"Yeah, but I shouldn't have hit you."

"I struck first."

"Stupid of both of us. I apologize."

"Noted and accepted. Now get back to what you were saying about Lozada and his fixation on Rennie."

"I've told you already," Oren complained.

"Tell me again."

"Jesus, you're cranky. They haven't taken the catheter out yet, have they?"

"This afternoon. If I can pee they'll leave it out."

"What if you can't?"

"I can. I will. If I have to squeeze it out, I'll pee. No way are they putting that thing back in while I'm conscious. I'd jump out the window first."

"You're such a crybaby."

"Are you going to tell me or what?"

"I've told you. I've repeated it word for word several times. The neighbor said they looked cozy with each other. Dr. Newton says that Lozada was terrorizing her, that she was afraid to fight him off for fear that he would do to her what he'd done to Sally Horton."

Wick sank back into his pillow and closed his eyes. The reminder of what had happened to that girl was painful. He would never forget seeing her lying dead. While he'd been enjoying a shower, she had been killed in cold blood.

Leaving his eyes closed, he said, "She makes sense, Oren. Lozada's a threat to her. Especially if he thinks it comes down to a choice between him and me, and she's favoring me."

"I don't suppose she's talked to you about it."

"No. If you hadn't told me what went down the other night, I wouldn't even know about it."

He couldn't figure Rennie's attitude, and that was the primary reason he was so grumpy. Yeah, he hurt. Yeah, the food was lousy. Yeah, he was ready to be peeing on his own. Yeah, he didn't like walking around bare-assed and feeble.

But what really had him bothered was Rennie's aloofness. She came in every morning and every evening, usually with her head down, her eyes on his chart rather than on him. "How are you, Mr. Threadgill?" Always the same ho-hum inflection.

She gave his incision a cursory inspection, asked how he was feeling and nodded absently to whatever answer he gave her, like she wasn't really listening and didn't really give a damn. She told him that she was pleased with his progress, then smiled mechanically and left. He realized that he wasn't her one and only patient. He didn't really expect preferential treatment.

Well, maybe he did. A little.

He'd been heavily medicated when he was in the ICU, but he remembered her sitting near his bedside and giving him sips of Sprite. He remembered her applying the lip balm. He remembered the way they had looked at each other and how long that look had lasted and how significant it had seemed.

Or had any of that actually happened?

Maybe he'd been so drugged out he'd been hallucinating. Had it been a pleasant dream he'd mistaken for reality? Possibly. Because that was, after all, the night Oren had caught her and Lozada in a "cozy" clench in her kitchen.

Damned if he knew what was going on with her.

"When she's on her rounds she's all business," he told Oren. "We haven't even talked about the weather."

"It's hot and dry."

"Looks it."

"She took that chief of surgery position."

"I heard," Wick said. "Good for her. She's earned it."

Oren continued to look at him meaningfully. "That doesn't signify anything, Oren."

"I didn't say it did."

"You didn't have to."

A nurse came in with another container of juice. "I'll drink it later," he told her. "I promise." She didn't look convinced, but she set it on the bed tray and left. He offered the juice to Oren.

"No thanks."

"Cranberry apple."

"I'm fine."

"You sure? Forgive me for saying so, but you don't look too healthy yourself." Oren had arrived looking wilted not only from the summertime heat, but ragged out in spirit as well. "What's up?"

Oren shrugged, sighed, glanced out the window at the hazy view before coming back to Wick. "The DA called about an hour ago. The big cheese himself. Not an assistant."

Wick had guessed that Oren's glumness had something to do with their case against Lozada. If he'd had good news to impart, he would have imparted it before now.

Discomfort made getting bad news worse. He adjusted himself to a more comfortable position that favored his sore right side. "Let's hear it."

"He says that what we've got on Lozada is weak. Not enough to take to the grand jury. In any case, he refused to."

Wick had guessed as much. "He came to see me yesterday. A pillar of goodwill and good cheer right down to his Italian loafers. Brought those." He gestured at a tacky bouquet of red, white, and artificially blue carnations.

"He went all out."

"I gave him a full account of what happened the night I was stabbed. Told him that as sure as I was still breathing, it was Lozada."

"How'd he react?"

"Let's see, he tugged at his turkey wattle, scratched his temple, rubbed his gut, frowned, expelled his breath through his pursed lips, and winced several times. He looked like a guy who had gas and was trying to figure out a polite way to fart. He told me that I was making some serious allegations. 'Well, no shit,' says I. 'Murder and attempted murder are pretty fucking serious.' He had trouble looking me in the eye as he left. He didn't come right out and say it—"

"He's not a politician for nothing."

"But I gathered from all his seeming distress that he had problems with my story."

"He did."

"Such as?"

"I won't bore you with the details," Oren said. "God knows he bored me with them. For about thirty minutes he stammered and stuttered, and did that bellows bit with his cheeks, but basically . . ."

"No soap."

Oren fiddled with the tricolored satin ribbon tied around the ugly carnations. He glanced at Wick askance. "You gotta look at it from his standpoint, Wick."

"The hell I do! Until he has to have six units of blood, until his nuts swell to the size of bowling balls and he's got a tube shoved up his dick, don't talk to me about his standpoint."

"I know you're gonna be pissed when I say this—"

"So don't."

"When it comes right down to it, he's right."

"If I could slug you right now, I would."

"I knew you'd get pissed." Oren sighed. "Look, Wick, the DA plays it safe, yes, but—"

"He's a pussy!"

"Maybe, but he's justified this time. When you boil it down, we've got nothing hard on Lozada."

"Lozada," Wick sneered. "He's got everybody running scared, doesn't he? You think he's not laughing his ass off at us?"

Oren gave him several seconds to cool off before continuing. "Everything in our hopper is circumstantial. Lozada knows you. He knew Sally Horton. That's a link, but it doesn't provide motivation. If, by some weird fluke, the grand jury did indict him, we could never make a case out of that. I was given three days to come up with something. Same as always, he didn't leave a trace. I've got nothing."

"Except my word on it."

Oren looked pained. "The DA factored in your background with Lozada. He hasn't forgotten what happened. That reduces your credibility."

Arguing a point so blatantly valid would be futile.

Oren sat down on the green vinyl armchair and stared at the floor. "I've got no choice but to release him. It wasn't easy, but I got search warrants. We've tossed his place. Nothing. Clean as a freaking whistle. Even his scorpions look sanitary. His car, same thing. Not a trace of blood, fibers, anything. We've got the weapons, but they could belong to anybody. No eyewitnesses except you, and you've been discredited. Besides, by your own account, you didn't actually see him."

"I was too busy leaking blood into my gut."

"His lawyer is already making a hell of a racket about police harassment. He says—"

"I don't want to hear what he says. I don't want to hear a goddamn word about that son of a bitch's civil rights being violated, okay?"

A long silence ensued. After a time, Oren glanced toward the corner near the ceiling. "TV work all right?"

Wick had muted the sound when Oren came in. The picture was little more than colored snow, but images could be detected if you looked hard enough. "Sucks. No cable."

They stared at the silent program for several moments before Oren asked if it was a good show.

"Those two are mother and daughter," Wick explained. "The daughter slept with the mother's husband."

"Her father?"

"No, about her fourth stepfather. Her real father is the father. The parish priest. But nobody knows that except her mother and the priest. He hears his daughter's confession about boinking her mother's husband and freaks out. He blames the mother for being a bad influence, calls her a slut. But he's guilt-ridden because he hasn't been there for his daughter. As a father—I mean as a dad. He's been her priest since he christened her. It's sorta complicated. He went to her house, for christsake." Wick's last statement didn't relate to the soap opera, but Oren knew that.

"I can't rule out the possibility that she invited him there, Wick."

He didn't even honor that with a comeback. He let his hard stare say it all.

"I said it's only a possibility." Averting his head, Oren muttered something else that Wick didn't catch.

"What was that?"

"Nothing."

"What?"

"Nothing."

"*What?*"

"He was feeling her tit. Okay?"

He wished he hadn't asked, but he had. He'd pressured Oren into telling him, and Oren had, and now he was gauging Wick's reaction. He kept his expression as passive as possible. "She was afraid to fight him off."

"That's what Grace said too, but neither of you was there."

"Grace?"

"Oh, yeah." Oren gestured expansively. "My wife has become Dr. Newton's number one fan."

"I knew they had met. All Grace said to me was that she was glad I was in such capable hands."

"I get slightly more than that at home. I get an earful about how I'm judging the doctor too harshly and unfairly. Grace thinks I'm holding a grudge because she served on that jury."

For the first time since Oren walked into his room, Wick came close to smiling. He liked to think of Grace giving his partner an earful. If there was anyone on earth Oren would listen to, it was his wife, whom he not only loved but also respected for her insight. "Grace is a smart lady."

"Yeah, well, she didn't see the romantic setting that I did. She hasn't seen this, either."

From the breast pocket of his sport jacket, Oren withdrew several sheets of paper that had been folded together lengthwise. He laid them on the bed tray next to the untouched juice. Wick made no move to pick up the sheets.

"In all the excitement of recent days you might have forgotten that Dr. Newton fatally shot a man when she was sixteen."

"It didn't escape your memory, though, did it?"

"Don't you think it needs to be checked out before we submit her name for sainthood? I contacted Dalton PD, along with the county sheriff's office. It's all in there."

Wick resented the incriminating sheets on the bed tray and was reluctant to read them. "Why don't you summarize it for me."

"Ugly. Very ugly," Oren said. "Daddy walked in seconds after the two shots were fired. Raymond Collier was dead. Died instantly. T. Dan asserted that his big bad business partner had tried to seduce his sweet baby girl. She shot him to protect her virtue. Clear-cut self-defense."

"It could've gone down that way."

"It could've, but unlikely. Especially since she'd been going down on Collier."

"Oh, good segue, Detective."

Oren ignored the remark. "A good question for her would be why she chose to protect her virtue on that particular day."

"Did anyone ask her?"

"I don't know. I doubt it. Because here's where it gets really interesting. No one was formally questioned. There was no hearing, no inquest, no nothing. T. Dan had deep pockets. Apparently he threw enough money around to bury the thing quicker than it took for Collier's body to get cold. His death was ruled an accident . . . at the scene. Case closed. Everybody went home happy, including Collier's widow. She left Dalton for her new, completely furnished condo in Breckenridge, Colorado. She made the trip in her shiny new Jag."

Wick thought it through, then said, "You talk about re-duced credibility. I don't believe any of it."

"Why not?"

"The police department and sheriff's office admitted to sweeping a fatal shooting under the rug?"

"No. Their reports were brief, but official. There was no evidence to support anything other than an accident. But I tracked down the former cop who was first on the scene."

"Former?"

"He left law enforcement to install satellite dishes. But he remembered driving out to the Newtons' house that day in response to the summons. He said it was the weird-est thing."

"What?"

"Their behavior. Whether it was accidental or inten-tional, if you'd just shot somebody stone dead, wouldn't you be upset? A little rattled? Shed a few tears? Show some remorse? At the very least do a little nervous hand-wringing?

"He said Rennie Newton sat there cool as a cucumber. Those big green eyes of hers stayed dry. And she's sixteen, remember? Kids that age are usually excitable. He said she never faltered as she talked him through what had hap-pened.

"T. Dan and Mrs. Newton sat on either side of her. T. Dan lambasted Collier for attempting to rape his daughter. Just went to show, he said, how you never really knew some-one as well as you thought you did. The mother cried softly into a hanky. She had heard nothing, seen nothing, knew nothing, and would the officers care for something to drink. The ex-cop said it was downright spooky, like being in an episode of *The Twilight Zone*."

Wick tried to imagine a sixteen-year-old Rennie giving a calm account of killing a man, even accidentally. He couldn't. He couldn't imagine the incorrigible teen Crystal had described either, or the nymphet who had enticed a married man. Nothing he had heard about her past life coincided with her present one.

Oren said, "I'd better be shoving off. Let you catch a nap. Can I get you anything before I go?"

Wick shook his head.

"I don't mind going down to the magazine shop and—"

"No thanks."

"Okay then. I'll come back with Grace tonight. Sometime after supper. Think you're up to a visit from the girls?"

"Sure, that'd be great."

"They've been bugging us to bring them to see you. I promise we won't stay long."

Wick forced a smile. "I'll look forward to it."

Oren nodded and headed for the door, but he paused with his hand on the handle. "No bullshit now, Wick. Fair enough?"

"Fair enough."

"Man to man, not partner to partner."

Wick frowned with impatience. "What is it?"

"You've got it bad for her, don't you?"

Wick turned his head toward the window and the familiar view. "I don't know."

Oren swore softly.

"Just go, why don't you?" Wick said. Suddenly he was very weary. "You've said what you came to say."

"Almost. I have a couple more things to say."

"Lucky me."

"Rennie Newton saved your life. No two ways about it. And I'll always be grateful to her for that."

Wick turned back to him. "What's the 'but'?"

"That ex-cop in Dalton? He said he couldn't believe that anybody could take a life, even the life of a bitter enemy, and be so emotionally detached from the act. She was so cold, he said, it still gives him chills to think about it."

Chapter 21

Wick glared at the man with the white lab coat and white smile who breezed into his hospital room like he owned the place. "Who're you?"

"I'm Dr. Sugarman. How are you feeling this evening, Mr. Threadgill?"

"Where's Dr. Newton?"

"I'm making her rounds tonight."

"How come?"

"I understand the catheter came out today. How was that?"

"Oh, it was great. I hope I get to do it again tomorrow."

The doctor flashed another white smile. "Everything okay now?"

"I could out-pee you. Where's my regular doctor?"

"I'm a regular doctor."

And a comedian too, Wick thought sourly.

Dr. Sugarman nodded his approval over whatever he read on Wick's chart, then closed the cover. "I'm glad I'm finally getting to meet the hospital's celebrity patient. Saw you on TV. You had it rough there for a while, but you're making excellent progress."

"Glad to hear it. When can I get out of here?"

"Anxious to be leaving us?"

What kind of sappy question was that? Wick could have throttled him. He didn't like him or his big white smile. And where was Rennie? Why wasn't she making her rounds? She deserved a night off like everyone else, but why hadn't she mentioned to him that she wouldn't be here tonight? Did she not want him to know?

Lozada is released from jail and Rennie takes the night off. It was an unpleasant thought and he hated himself for thinking it.

His dark expression must have conveyed to Dr. Sugarman that he should practice his bedside manner on a more agreeable and appreciative patient. His Colgate smile faltered. "Dr. Newton will make the final decision on your release, but it shouldn't be more than a couple more days. Barring any unforeseen complications." The doctor shook hands with him and left.

"What a turkey," Wick muttered.

The Wesleys arrived. As promised, Oren limited the visit to fifteen minutes, but there was no limit to the girls' energy and exuberance.

They brought him chocolate-chip cookies that they had baked themselves and weren't satisfied until he ate two. Grace had arrived with a shopping bag. "Pajamas. I don't know if they'll let you wear them yet, but you'll have them just in case. I got slippers, too."

He grabbed her hand and kissed the back of it. "Marry me?"

Her daughters squealed with laughter and had to be

admonished to settle down. They chattered nonstop, and they were wonderful, but they wore him out. He was ashamed for being relieved when they gave him hugs and said their good-byes.

Oren didn't talk business until after his family had moved into the hallway, out of earshot. He told Wick that Lozada was again free. "Sarge wouldn't authorize surveillance on him. And after tonight he's pulling the guards from the hospital."

"You're putting me on alert."

Oren nodded solemnly. "Watch your back. After tonight you won't be protected by the FWPD."

That was fine and dandy with Wick. He didn't want police protection, because in exchange for it he would have to give up his freedom. After hearing the DA's decision today, he had concluded that the authorities were no contest for Lozada. Jurisprudence was carried out within moral boundaries, and Lozada operated under no such restraints.

If Wick wanted Lozada he would have to go after him alone. To level the playing field, he must go after him ruthlessly, with a mind-set like Lozada's. He couldn't do that if he were constantly monitored and guarded.

He asked about his pickup truck.

Oren's brow lowered suspiciously. "What about it?"

"I'd like to know where it is."

"Why?"

"Because it's my truck," Wick replied testily.

Reluctantly, Oren told him that it was at his house. "I took the liberty of checking you out of the motel. Once the CSU guys were finished with your room, I packed up everything and took it outta there."

Wick wanted to ask specifically about his pistol, but

didn't. No sense in giving Oren more to worry about. "Thanks. I wasn't looking forward to going back into that room."

"I figured. All your stuff's locked up in your truck. It's parked in my driveway."

"Keys?"

"I've got them and your wallet in a safe place inside the house."

Safe from whom? Wick wondered. Safe from him? Again he didn't ask. "Thanks, partner." Oren didn't return Wick's guileless smile, probably guessing that it was disingenuous.

After that, Wick impatiently endured the long, boring evening hours. Eventually the traffic in the corridor outside his room subsided. Dinner trays were collected and placed on trolleys that were shuttled back to the kitchen. Doctors completed their rounds and left for home. Visitors departed. Personnel went through a shift change. The hospital settled down for the night.

At eleven o'clock a nurse came in to give him a pain pill. "You want your blinds drawn?"

"Please. Sun comes in through there in the morning."

As she moved to the window, he remarked offhandedly, "Too bad about Dr. Newton."

The nurse laughed. "Too bad? I wish I could take vacation at the drop of a hat."

"Vacation? Oh, I thought Dr. Sugarman said she was under the weather."

"No, she's taking some vacation days, that's all."

He twirled his finger near his temple. "This medication makes me goofy."

"It can do that."

"When will Dr. Newton be coming back?"

"She didn't clear her schedule with me," the nurse said around a wide grin. "But don't worry. Dr. Sugarman is a sweetheart."

While she fiddled with the blinds, Wick pretended to swallow the pill. He set the empty drinking cup on his bed tray and she rolled it away.

Readjusting his head on the pillow, he yawned. "Nighty-night."

"Good night, Mr. Threadgill. Rest well."

Darkness had fallen by the time Lozada let himself into his condo. He was pleased to see that his instructions had been carried out. His home was as quiet and serene as a church.

Upon hearing from his lawyer that it had been searched, he had known what to expect. He'd had residences searched before, as early as high school when narcs came into his house one night with a search warrant, hoping to find drugs. They had succeeded only in looking like fools and terrorizing his parents and idiot brother. Since then, he'd had other houses searched with the same storm-trooper enthusiasm.

So he had made arrangements from his jail cell through his lawyer for a cleaning service to put his condo back together, then to sanitize it against police contamination. He had also arranged to have it swept for electronic surveillance devices.

"It's clean," his lawyer had reported as they celebrated his release over drinks at the City Club. "In every sense of the word."

The attorney never inquired as to Lozada's guilt or innocence. Lozada paid him an exorbitant annual retainer, which enabled him to represent Lozada exclusively and play a lot of golf. He could also afford to live the lifestyle of a rich playboy. Lozada's culpability was last on his list of priorities.

"But it's clean only for the time being," he warned. "Be careful who goes in and out of your place from now on."

Lozada didn't need to be cautioned about that. Already he had notified the building's concierge that he would no longer be availing himself of the housekeeping services it provided. He had hired his own housekeeper, who came highly recommended by one of his former— and very satisfied—clients. He was assured that the young man brought excellent skills to the position and could be trusted implicitly.

Nor would he entertain women at home—except for Rennie, of course. He had used that stupid girl, that Sally Horton, because she was convenient, a careless indulgence, as it turned out. He would go out for sex until he had Rennie here with him.

He had been making such good progress with her until Wesley had come charging in, gun drawn like the main character in a silly detective show. What a laugh. Hadn't he realized how ridiculous he looked?

Rennie hadn't been amused. She had seemed mortified to have a group of clumsy cops invading her home, spoiling the surprise he had staged for her. No, she hadn't looked at all happy about the unannounced arrival of Wesley and company.

After spending a half hour of quality time with his scorpions, he took a long shower to wash away all remnants of jail. He shaved carefully, since he hadn't trusted his skin to the dull razor the county provided, then went through the ritual of cleaning out the drain and disposing of the towels.

He enjoyed a couple of tequilas and ate the dinner he ordered from his favorite restaurant. Delivery service wasn't extended to any other patrons, but it was included in Lozada's VIP treatment.

Over a nightcap, he dialed Rennie's number. Eventually her voice mail answered. "This is Dr. Newton. Please leave your name and number. If this is an emergency—"

He hung up. He wanted to see her urgently, but she might not think his desire qualified as an emergency. As he sipped his drink, he tried twice more to reach her, at the hospital and at home, with no success.

Ah well, he thought, tomorrow was soon enough. He would invite her to dinner. It would be their first official date. He smiled at the thought of walking into a fine restaurant with her. He would take her to Dallas. Someplace very upscale, elite. He would buy a sexy black dress for her tomorrow and surprise her with it. He would help her dress, from the skin out, so that everything would be perfect and to his liking. She would be gorgeous, breathtaking. He would wear his new suit. They would turn heads. Everyone would see what Lozada had done for himself.

After spending three nights on a cot with an odorous mattress, he looked forward to sleeping in his own wide bed. Naked, he slid between the silky sheets and luxuriated in their cool caress against his hairless skin. He fell asleep rubbing himself, thinking of the stirring sound Rennie had made when she felt the strength of his erection.

He slept like a baby until he was awakened by the insistent ringing of his doorbell.

Sneaking out of the hospital was much easier than Wick would have thought.

The hardest part was getting into the new pajamas Grace had brought him. By the time he got the damn things on, he was damp with perspiration and so weak he was trembling. He resisted the temptation to lie down and rest for a few minutes, afraid that if he did he wouldn't get up again.

The nurses were too busy performing clerical duties at the central desk to notice when he crept from his room. During his walk down the hall earlier, he had noted the location of the fire exit. Fortunately, it wasn't too far from his room. He made it into the stairwell undetected. Gripping the metal railing every step of the way, he walked down four flights. His knees were rubbery by the time he reached the ground floor.

No one accosted him. The cops posted as guards would have easily recognized him, but he slipped past them unseen. One was flirting with the nurses at the emergency-room admitting desk and the other was napping in his chair.

So much for security.

The nearest commercial area was two blocks from the hospital. He started walking but hadn't gone far when he realized that the two blocks might just as well have been the distance of a marathon. It was as difficult for him to cover that distance as it would have been for him to go twenty-six miles. He was wobbly and faint, and his back throbbed in protest of each step, but he pushed on.

When he entered the 7-Eleven, the turbaned man working the counter regarded him with unconcealed fright.

"I know I look ridiculous," Wick said quickly. "Can you believe it? The wife's pregnant. Got a craving for a Butterfinger fifteen minutes after I fell asleep. So I'm driving here in my PJs to get her a damned Butterfinger—I mean, hell, we have Snickers in the pantry, but, no, it *had* to be a Butterfinger. Anyhow, I ran out of gas up there on the freeway about fifty yards from the exit ramp. Had to walk down, and it's hotter than hell outside even at this time of night." Sweat had stuck the pajama jacket to his chest. He pulled it away from his skin and fanned himself. "Can I please use your Yellow Pages? I need to call a taxi."

Possibly the only words of the whole monologue that the foreign gentleman understood were "Yellow Pages." He slid a well-worn copy across the counter along with a soiled and sticky telephone.

After placing his call, Wick sat down to wait on a folding fishing stool and passed the time by perusing the wide selection of body-builder magazines. Only one other customer came in. He bought a pack of cigarettes and left without giving Wick a second glance.

When the taxi pulled into the parking lot, Wick said, "Much obliged," and waved good-bye. He didn't know who was more relieved to see the taxi, him or the nervous cashier. He left without a Butterfinger.

Luckily, the Wesleys' house was dark. What Oren didn't know was that he kept a spare key in a magnetized box on the underside of his pickup's fender. He retrieved it, although getting up and down was an effort that caused him to gasp in pain. Several times he was forced to pause for fear of passing out.

He unlocked his truck and rummaged through the pockets of his packed clothing in search of money. Finally he scrounged up enough to cover his cab fare. The series of delays hadn't set too well with the driver, who peeled away with an angry spate of obscenities and an even angrier squeal of tires.

Wick waited in the shadow of the house to see if the noise had awakened Oren. He gave it a full five minutes, but no one came out to investigate. Wick got into his truck and turned the ignition key. The engine growled to life. He got the hell out of there.

He drove to the empty parking lot of an elementary school, where he exchanged the pajamas for street clothes and the slippers for a pair of athletic shoes. He was constantly on the lookout for Oren's car, or a police patrol unit, but apparently he had made good his escape.

From the elementary school he drove straight to Rennie's house and parked at the curb. The front porch light was on, but the house was dark. "Too bad." She was about to be awakened. He eased himself from the cab of his truck with all the agility of an octogenarian invalid.

At her door, he leaned heavily on the bell, and, when that got no response, he banged the brass knocker. He waited thirty seconds before pressing his ear to the door and listening through the wood. Nothing but silence. "Dammit!"

But if he were in Rennie's situation, would he be answering the front door in the middle of the night?

He moved toward the garage and studied the horizontally sectioned door. Having followed Rennie home last Sunday, he knew she had an automatic opener. He tested the handle anyway. Without the programmed transmitter, the door was secure.

He slipped around the corner of the house—hoping that an insomniac neighbor didn't mistake him for a thief—and moved along the side of the garage toward the rear of the house. His exploration was rewarded. There was a door into the garage from the backyard. Miracle of miracles, it had a window.

Cupping his hands around his eyes, he peered inside. It was dark, but he knew that had her car been inside he would've been able to see it. The garage was empty. She wasn't at home.

Trembling with fatigue, he retraced his steps to his truck. The task of climbing inside seemed insurmountable, but he managed it—barely. His skin was clammy, and he feared he might toss his cookies. Literally. Stephanie and Laura's homemade chocolate chips. The headrest was tempting. He hurt too bad to sleep, but if he could just close his eyes and rest for a few minutes . . .

No, he had to move and keep moving until he found Rennie.

Second on his list of places to look: Trinity Tower.

Lozada's face was a mask of cold fury when he opened the door to his condo.

"I'm sorry to disturb you, Mr. Lozada, but I have an urgent message for you." The concierge extended to him a sealed envelope with the building's discreet logo embossed in gold in the upper left corner.

Lozada had been having a delicious dream about Rennie. The first peal of his doorbell had jolted him awake. A handgun was weighting down the pocket of his robe. Shooting the messenger became a literal temptation.

He snatched the envelope from the man. "What kind of message? Who's it from?"

"He didn't give me his name, sir. I asked, but he said you would know him."

Lozada ripped open the envelope, removed a stiff note card, and read the so-called message. There was no question who had written the succinct poem.

"He was here?"

"Only a few minutes ago, Mr. Lozada. He left after writing that and asking that I hand-deliver it to you immediately. The man didn't look at all well. When he first came in, I thought he was intoxicated. He was certainly confused."

"In what way?"

"Initially he said he had a message for your guest."

"Guest?"

"That's what I said, Mr. Lozada. I told him that to my knowledge you had come in alone this evening and that no visitors had been announced except for the food delivery. I checked the log book to be sure."

Threadgill had played this moron like a fiddle.

"I offered to ring you, but he said no, then asked to borrow the stationery and a pen."

"All right, you've delivered the message." Lozada was about to close the door when the concierge raised his hand.

"One more thing, Mr. Lozada." He coughed lightly behind his fist. "You'll receive an official notice in writing, but I suppose this is as good a time as any to tell you."

"Tell me what?"

"I've been appointed to advise you that the building's homeowners' association convened earlier today and voted unanimously that you . . . that they . . ."

"What?"

"They want you out of the building, sir. In light of recent allegations, they're demanding that you vacate within thirty days."

Lozada wasn't about to demean himself by arguing with this nobody. "You can tell the other homeowners to go fuck themselves. I own this penthouse and will live here for as long as I fucking well please."

He slammed the door in the man's face. Striding angrily to the built-in slate bar, he poured himself a straight shot of tequila. He didn't know which had made him madder and insulted him more, being asked to move out of the prestigious address or Wick Threadgill's juvenile dare:

The roses were red;
My blood, too.
Come get me, asshole.
I'm waiting for you.

Chapter 22

When Rennie arrived at her ranch, the first thing she did was saddle Beade and go for a long, galloping ride. Following that, she spent two hours in the barn grooming the horses. They didn't need grooming, but it was therapeutic for her.

Earlier in the day, Oren Wesley had made a courtesy call informing her of Lozada's imminent release from jail. "You're releasing him?"

"I have no choice." He explained the district attorney's decision. "I warned you that the charge might not stick. Wick claims it was Lozada, but without hard evidence—"

"What about his breaking into my house?"

"There was no sign of forced entry, Dr. Newton."

"But he broke in," she insisted.

"If you wish, you could come down and file a complaint."

"What good would it do?"

What had become clear to her was that she couldn't

rely on the judicial system to take care of Lozada for her. The problem was hers and she must solve it. But how?

Then there was the matter of Wick. She was still angry with Wick the cop, who deserved her scorn. But Wick the man was her patient who deserved the best medical care she could provide. How was she to reconcile the two?

Out of respect for Dr. Howell, the board had set a date two weeks hence for her formal assumption of the chief of surgery position. She wanted to move into that job with a clear slate, with her life in perfect order, free of problems. She needed time away to think things through and plot a course of action.

Her last-minute decision to take a few days off had required some deft maneuvering by her able office staff, but they juggled the schedule so that her patients were only moderately inconvenienced. Dr. Sugarman returned the favor she had done him a few months ago by agreeing to oversee the care of her post-op patients who were still in the hospital, Wick among them.

She had packed in a hurry and made good time driving. The horseback ride had provided a temporary reprieve from her troubling thoughts. Toby Robbins arrived shortly after she returned to the house. "You didn't have to come right away, Toby," she told him as soon as she answered the door. Earlier she had called him to report a loose board on the corral gate.

"I feel bad about overlooking it."

"It's no big deal. It'll keep."

"I'd just as soon get it fixed now. Unless this is a bad time for you."

"Now is fine."

He looked beyond her at the pieces of luggage still

standing on her living room floor. "Staying for a while this time?"

"A few days. Let me show you that loose board." They went down the front steps together. On the way to the corral he retrieved a metal toolbox from the bed of his pickup truck. "How's Corrine?"

"Fine. She's giving the devotional at the church ladies' luncheon next Thursday. She's got butterflies."

"I'm sure she'll do fine."

He nodded, glanced at Rennie, then said, "We read about you in the paper this week."

"Don't believe everything you read, Toby."

"It was all good this time."

This time. She didn't know if the qualifier had been intentional. The old rancher remembered newspaper stories about her that hadn't been so flattering, the ones about the fatal shooting of Raymond Collier.

Before inheriting his ranch from his parents, Toby had lived in Dalton and occasionally had done odd jobs for T. Dan. When he took over the ranch, it had a modest herd of beef cattle, but, with careful management, he had increased it and prospered when other ranchers had succumbed to drought or economic recessions of one origin or another.

Through the years, he had stayed in touch with Rennie. He knew she was interested in having a weekend getaway, a place where she could keep horses, so he had notified her when the ranch neighboring his went on the market. She saw it only once before signing a contract for the asking price.

Toby no longer needed the additional income that came from doing odd jobs for her. She supposed he worked for her because he was a good neighbor, a nice man, or simply because he liked her.

Or maybe he was kind to her because he had known T. Dan so well.

"Here. See?" She showed him the gate, wiggling the loose slat, then stepping aside so he could get to it. He inspected it, then hunkered down and took a hammer from his toolbox. He used the forked end to pry the rusty nails out of the loose holes.

"That guy, the one whose life you saved . . ."

"Wick Threadgill."

"Wasn't he the fella I met out here?"

"That's right."

"What do you think of him?"

"I don't."

She had answered too quickly and defensively. Toby squinted up at her from beneath the brim of his hat.

"Uh, listen, Toby, if you'll excuse me, I think I'll go back inside and start putting things away. Come say goodbye before you leave."

"Will do."

She was busy in the kitchen an hour later when he approached the back door and knocked. "Come on in."

He stepped inside and removed his hat. "Some of the other boards had loose nails, too. I replaced them all. Solid as a rock now."

"Thank you. How about something cold to drink?"

"No, thanks. I best get going so Corrine won't have to hold supper for me. Next week sometime I could come over and give that gate a coat of fresh paint."

"That would be nice. Want me to buy the paint?"

"I'll bring it with me. Same white okay?"

"Perfect."

"Are you going to be okay here, Rennie?"

"Why wouldn't I be?"

"No reason."

He had his reasons, all right. She could tell by the way he nervously threaded the brim of his hat through his fingers and stared at the toes of his scuffed work boots.

"What's on your mind, Toby?"

Raising his head, he gave her a direct look. "You've been mixed up lately with some pretty raunchy characters. If you don't mind my saying so."

"I don't mind. I agree. I think raunchy would be a mild adjective for Lozada."

"Wasn't talking about just him. That Threadgill was kicked off the police force, you know."

"He took a leave of absence."

Toby's shrug said *Same thing.* "Well, anyhow, me and Corinne have been worried about you."

"Needlessly, Toby, I assure you. I haven't been mixing with these people voluntarily. My path crossed with Lozada's by happenstance. My association with Mr. Threadgill is purely professional. His profession as well as mine. That's all."

His expression was skeptical.

"I've been protecting myself for a long time, Toby," she added softly. "Since I was sixteen."

He nodded, looking embarrassed for having resurrected bad memories. "It's just sort of a habit, you know, for me and Corinne to look out for you."

"And I can't tell you how much your concern means to me. Has always meant to me."

"Well," he said, replacing his hat, "I'm off. If you need anything give us a holler."

"I will. Thanks again for repairing the gate."

"Take care, Rennie."

She sipped a glass of wine as she cooked herself a meal of pasta and marinara. As she ate, she watched the sun sink into the western horizon. Afterward she carried her bags upstairs to unpack. Here in the country she wasn't persnickety. She tossed undies into drawers without folding them. She hung clothes in the closet willy-nilly, in no particular order. Out here she yielded to a rebellious streak—against her structured self.

These tasks completed, she went from room to room looking for something to do. Now that she had the desired free time, she didn't know how to fill it. TV had nothing interesting to offer. She wasn't inspired to watch a movie from her library of DVDs. She tried to read a new biography, but found the subject dull and the writing pretentious. She wandered into the kitchen, looking more for something to occupy her than for something to eat. Nothing looked appetizing, but because she was there she opened a box of cookies and nibbled on one.

A benefit of being in the country, far removed from city lights, was the panoply of stars. She ventured outside to gaze at the nighttime sky. She located the familiar constellations, then spotted a satellite and tracked its arc until she could no longer see it.

She crossed her yard and entered the corral through the gate Toby had repaired. Although she knew his intentions had been good, and that his concern was sincere, his caution had left her feeling restless and even a little jittery as she went into the dark barn.

Usually the familiar smells of hay and horseflesh comforted her. T. Dan had put her astride a pony about the time she had learned to walk. Ever since, horses had played an important role in her life. She had never experienced any fear of them and loved being in their environment.

Tonight, however, the cavernous barn seemed ominous. The shadows were abnormally dark and impenetrable. As she moved from stall to stall, the horses nickered and stamped skittishly. They had been groomed and fed. They were dry. There was no approaching storm. She spoke to them in a low and soothing voice, but it sounded counterfeit to her own ears and must have conveyed to them her own disquiet. Like her, they were unsettled for no apparent reason.

Rather than being comforted by the animals, they increased her uneasiness because they seemed to share it. Upon returning to the house, she did something she had never done before. She locked all the doors and windows, then double-checked to make certain she hadn't overlooked any. Upstairs, she showered, but she realized she was rushing through it.

She, who had waded through snake- and croc-infested African rivers, was now afraid to shower in her own tub? Annoyed with herself for buying into the spookiness, she turned out the light with a decisive click and got into bed.

She slept lightly, as though expecting the noises that eventually awakened her.

"What the . . . ?"

Wick gripped the steering wheel of his pickup. He acknowledged that his mind was sluggish from exhaustion. There were probably a few grains of pain medication still swimming around in his bloodstream, gumming up his thought processes. He was a little slow on the uptake, but it sure seemed to him that the steering wheel had frozen up in his hands.

For several seconds he was stumped. Then he looked at the gas gauge.

"Son of a bitch!"

He was out of gas. In the middle of frigging nowhere. In the freaking wee hours of the morning. He was out of gas.

It had never occurred to him to check the gauge before leaving Fort Worth. Once he'd left Trinity Tower reasonably certain that Rennie wasn't shacked up in the penthouse with Lozada, once he'd left the concierge with the envelope and a ten-dollar bill guaranteeing its speedy delivery, he'd wanted only to get clear of the city before Oren saw that his driveway was minus one pickup truck or a nurse discovered that the hospital bed was shy one patient.

During the drive he'd had a hell of a time keeping his eyes open. Usually he was an aggressive driver who cursed slowpokes. He thought radar traps were a violation of the Constitution. But tonight he had stayed in the outside lane, yielding the faster lanes to long-haul truckers and motorists who hadn't experienced a life-threatening assault barely a week ago.

It was a broad assumption that Rennie had gone to her ranch. She could be on her way to anywhere in the world, but if she was taking only a few days of vacation, the ranch would be his first guess, so that was where he was headed.

He didn't know exactly what he was going to say to her when he got there, but he would figure it out as he went along. Nor could he predict what her reaction would be to his unannounced arrival. She had saved his hide on the operating table, but she might still be inclined to flay it off him for his lying and spying.

Whatever, he would deal with it. The important thing was that he was almost there.

Or so he'd thought until he ran out of gas.

He twisted the wheel as hard as his diminished strength would let him and steered the truck onto the narrow shoulder. He let it roll to a complete stop. Without the air conditioner it was already getting uncomfortably warm in the cab. He rolled down the window for ventilation, but that only let in more hot air.

The interstate was at least eight miles behind him. He estimated he still had a good ten miles to go before he reached the cutoff to Rennie's place. If he could run, he could cover that much distance in an hour, say an hour and ten minutes max. But he couldn't run. He could barely walk. Hobbling, it would take him hours to go that far, if he didn't collapse first, which he surely would.

He supposed he could use his cell phone to call a service station on the interstate. But service stations on the interstate usually didn't provide roadside assistance, much less deliver gasoline. Getting a wrecker here would take forever. Besides, he had no money or credit cards because Oren had his wallet in a safe place inside his house. The road wasn't going to be well traveled until daybreak, and that was still a few hours away. Basically, he was stuck.

As soon as the sun came up, he could start walking to Rennie's ranch and hope that a Good Samaritan would come along and give him a lift. It was too dark to see his reflection in the rearview mirror, but if he looked anywhere near as bad as he felt, he looked like someone in dire need of mercy.

He could use the hours until dawn to rest. With that blessed thought in mind, he leaned back against the headrest and closed his eyes. But it didn't take long for him to

realize that until he got horizontal, his back was going to
continue throbbing so badly he wouldn't even be able to
doze. He cursed himself for choosing bucket seats over a
bench seat.

Wearily he unlatched his door. Pushing it open required all his strength. He took several deep breaths before stepping out, unsure that his legs would support him.
They did, but they were shaky. Leaning heavily against the
side of the truck, he made his way to the rear of it and lowered the tailgate, which seemed to weigh a million pounds.

Besides being a heavy bastard, it was as hard as a slab of
concrete. Try getting comfortable on that, he thought.
"Shit." If he didn't lie down he was going to fall down.

He looked at his surroundings. Not a light to be seen
in any direction. Across the road and beyond a barbed-
wire fence was a cluster of trees. Ground was softer than
metal, right? Definitely. And ground beneath trees might
be softer than open ground because it would retain more
moisture, right? Hell if he knew, but it sounded good.

Before leaving his truck he retrieved his duffel bag, another heavy bastard, and dragged it along behind him as
he trudged across the road. He lay down on the ground
and scooted beneath the bottom strand of barbed wire. He
could never have bent double and stepped through it.

The darkness had been deceptive. The grove was farther away than it had appeared. The silence was total except for his own labored breathing, but if breaking a sweat
were noise-producing, he would've been making a terrible
racket. He was drenched. And he was afraid that the blackness advancing from his peripheral vision had nothing to
do with it being nighttime.

When he finally reached the trees, he dropped the duffel bag against the trunk of one and sank to his knees be-

side it. Then he went down on all fours and hung his head between his shoulders. Sweat dripped off his nose, off his earlobes. He didn't care, he didn't care if he melted, he didn't care about anything except getting prone. He lay down in the dry grass. It pricked him through his shirt, but he could live with that as long as he could close his eyes.

He turned his cheek into the stiff canvas duffel and imagined that it was a woman's breast. Cool and soft and fragrant with good-smelling talc. Goldleaf and Hydrangea maybe.

He was sleeping dreamlessly. Only something really startling could have pulled him out of a sleep that deep. Something *really* startling, like "Move and you're a dead man."

He moved anyway, of course. First he opened his eyes, then he rolled onto his back to orient himself and locate the source of the warning.

Rennie was standing about twenty yards from him holding a rifle to her shoulder, looking into the scope. He sat bolt upright.

"I told you not to move."

Then she fired.

Chapter 23

□□□□□□□□□□□□□

The bobcat fell dead from the tree.

It missed falling on Wick only by a couple of feet. Its hard landing sent up puffs of dust. There was a bloody hole in the center of its chest. Inside Wick's, his heart was thundering.

He swallowed with difficulty. "Nice shot."

Rennie came and knelt beside the carcass. "He was so pretty." Except for the lethal incisors, the animal did indeed look like an overgrown house cat with a beautiful pelt. Rennie stroked the soft tuft of white fur at the base of its ear. "I hated to shoot him, but he looked about to pounce. For months he's been killing lambs and pets. This morning he got into my stable."

"I didn't know he'd prey on something as large as a horse."

"He wouldn't. He was probably looking for something small, like mice, or a rabbit. But he spooked the horses and got as scared as they were, wound up scratching one.

I heard the ruckus and reached the barn in time to see him scamper out. For the past hour I've been tracking him."

"And he tracked me."

For the first time, she looked across at him. "You were easy prey."

"The walking wounded."

"The nearly dead. What the hell are you doing here, Wick?"

"Sleeping. Or was." He nodded toward the rifle propped on her knee. "Do you ever miss?"

"Never. Are you going to answer me?"

"What am I doing here? It's a long story. But the punch line is that my truck ran out of gas. I hope you're not afoot."

She stood up and gave a shrill whistle. He was impressed. He'd never known a woman who could whistle worth a damn. But that wasn't the extent of her talents. A few seconds later, a mare trotted toward the grove.

"Wow, just like in the movies," he said. The horse stopped a cautious distance away from the dead bobcat and stamped nervously. "I'm not sure I can get on her without a saddle."

"You're not getting on her at all. I am." Rennie turned and started walking away toward the horse.

"You're going to abandon me here? With this animal carcass?"

"I didn't invite you."

Poetry in motion. That's what it was to see her sink her fingers into the mare's thick mane and pull herself up far enough to throw her right leg over. She accomplished this in one fluid motion, without dropping the twenty-two. She nudged the horse with her heels and the mare danced a dainty circle, head and tail held high.

"You're coming back for me, right?" He thought he saw Rennie smile, but the sun wasn't fully up yet, so he might have imagined it. With a movement of her knees that was almost undetectable, she nudged the mare into a gallop.

So sure was he that she would come back for him that he was asleep before horse and rider disappeared over the horizon.

He didn't know how long he slept. It could have been fifteen minutes or fifteen hours. When he opened his eyes, Rennie was beside him again. She was wrapping the bobcat in a thick, quilted furniture pad. When she noticed him watching her, she said, "I'm not going to leave him for them to pick apart."

He looked up through the branches of the tree. Buzzards were circling overhead. "They might be waiting for me to croak."

"They might be."

She picked up the bundle and carried it to a pickup he'd never seen her drive. He figured it must be restricted to ranch usage because it showed signs of wear and tear. By the time she had placed the bobcat in the bed and closed the tailgate, he had managed to stand up, using the tree trunk for support. He leaned down to pick up his duffel.

"I'll get that," she said, and started back for it. "You get in the truck."

As they passed one another he thought of saluting her, but at the last second he thought better of it.

Of course, her getup offset her military bearing. She had on a red tank top, the kind she slept in, a pair of butt-snug blue jeans, and cowboy boots. Her hair was loose and tangled. He guessed that the disturbance in her stable had caused her to jump from bed and pull on the jeans and boots before racing outside. Whatever, it was a fashion statement that won his approval.

Sliding beneath the barbed-wire fence was only slightly easier to do in daylight than in darkness. By the time he reached the pickup and had managed to climb into the cab, he had broken out in a cold sweat and was trembling.

Rennie returned with his duffel and unceremoniously threw it into the bed of the truck with the dead bobcat. She climbed in and cranked the ignition. She noticed him looking through the rear window into the bed of the pickup.

"Something wrong?"

"No. I'm just glad you didn't toss me back there too."

"I thought about it."

"What about my truck?"

"I've got a gas can."

She didn't outline her plan of how and when they were going to get the gas from her gas can into his truck, but he didn't ask. She pulled out onto the road and drove for at least a mile before saying, "I know Dr. Sugarman didn't release you from the hospital."

"Where did he buy all those teeth?"

"Did you just walk out?"

"Hmm."

"What about the guards?"

"I wouldn't want to be in their shoes when Oren discovers I'm gone."

"He doesn't know?"

"He might by now."

"He'll be upset?"

"Volcanic."

"Because he knows you need another couple days in the hospital."

"Because he knows I'm going after Lozada on my own." She looked at him sharply. "Then why'd you come here?"

"Find you, find him. He'll come after you, Rennie, and, like me, this is the first place he'll look."

"He doesn't know about this place."

"He will. Eventually. He'll find you. He won't stop until he does. He's got too much of himself, of his ego, invested in you. He'll come."

They said no more. When they reached the house, she parked the pickup close to the front steps. She came around and assisted Wick out of the truck and onto the porch, then opened the door and motioned him inside.

They stepped directly into a spacious living room that was furnished and decorated in Texas chic. Lots of leather and suede, all very tasteful and expensive. Thick rugs on the hardwood floors. Fringed throw pillows. The pieces were large and comfy, inviting one to sit and relax for hours in front of the fireplace, reading the magazines that were scattered—scattered?—on accent tables.

A Mexican saddle of black tooled leather with lots of silver detailing stood in one corner, displayed and spot-lighted as a sculpture might be. A boldly striped horse blanket served as a wall hanging. Wick loved it. "This is nice."

"Thank you."

"It doesn't look like you."

She met his gaze. "It looks exactly like me. Are you hungry?"

"I thought about starting on the bobcat."

"This way."

She led him into the kitchen, which held even more surprises. In the center was a work island with open shelving underneath. On the surface was a small copper sink where red and green apples had been left to drain after being rinsed. Cooking pots hung from an iron rack overhead. An opened box of cookies had been left on the counter.

"Soup or oatmeal?"

Painfully, he lowered himself into a chair at the round wood table. "Those're my choices?"

"Unless you were serious about the bobcat. Then you're on your own."

"What kind of soup?"

It was cream of potato and might have been the best food he'd ever eaten in his life. Rennie had started with canned condensed, but she added half and half, butter, and seasonings, then topped off the crockery bowl with grated cheddar and put it in the microwave long enough for the cheese to melt. Her motions were economic and skilled. Like a surgeon's.

"That was haute cuisine after hospital food," he said as he polished off a second piece of toast. "What's for lunch?"

"You'll sleep through lunch."

"I can't rest yet, Rennie. I didn't bust out of the hospital, and then bust my ass to get here, just to go to sleep as soon as I arrived."

"Sorry. That's what you need and that's what you're going to do. I've never had a patient look as bad as you and survive. I should call nine-one-one and have an ambulance take you to the county hospital immediately."

"I would immediately leave."

"That's why I haven't already called." She finished rins-

ing out his dishes and dried her hands. "Let's get you upstairs and undressed."

"I slept, Rennie. Under the tree."

"How long?"

"Long enough."

"Not near long enough."

"I'm not going to sleep."

"Yes you are."

"You'd have to drug me."

"I did."

"Huh?"

"When you went to the bathroom, I ground a strong
painkiller and a sleeping pill into your soup. Any minute
now you'll catch quite a buzz."

"Goddammit! I'll fight it off."

She smiled. "You can't. It's going to knock you on your
can. You'll be more comfortable if you let me get you into
bed before it does."

"We've got to talk, Rennie."

"We will. After you've had some sleep."

She put her hand beneath his elbow and hauled him
out of the chair. Or tried. His legs were already wobbly and
there was a distinct tingling in his toes that he knew was in-
duced by narcotics, not hyperventilation.

"Put your arm across my shoulders." He did as she instructed. She slipped her arm around his waist and lent
support as she guided him back through the living room
toward the open staircase along the far wall.

"I'm catching a buzz, all right," he said about midway
up. "My ears are ringing. How long before this wears off?"

"Depends on the patient."

"That's not an answer."

On the second floor a wide gallery overlooked the liv-

ing room. Several doors opened onto the gallery. She led
him through one of them into a bedroom. The bed was
unmade. "Is this your room?" he asked.

"It's the only bedroom that's furnished."

"I get to sleep in your bed?"

She propped him against an armoire. "Lift your arms."
He did and she pulled his T-shirt over his head. Then she
knelt and helped him out of his shoes. "Now take off your
pants and lie down."

"Why, Dr. Newton, I would've thought you'd be more
subtle. That you'd . . . What's that?" She'd taken something from the bottom drawer of the armoire.

"That is a syringe." Coming to her feet, she held it up
and tapped the clear plastic tube. "And you're about to get
a butt-load of antibiotic."

"I don't need it."

"We aren't going to argue about this, Wick."

No, she didn't appear to be in any mood to argue. He
couldn't have argued with her anyway. His tongue had become about as nimble as a walrus. His legs had turned to
columns of jelly. It was a struggle to keep his eyes open.

He unbuttoned his fly, dropped his jeans, and stepped
out of them. She probably had expected him to be wearing underwear. Well, too damn bad, Dr. Newton. He strut-
ted—as much as he could strut in his drugged state—to
the bed and lay down.

"On your stomach, please."

"You're no fun at all," he grumbled thickly.

Rennie swabbed a spot on his hip with alcohol, then
jabbed the needle into his muscle.

"*Son of a*—"

"This might hurt."

"—*bitch*! Thanks for the damn warning." He clenched

his teeth and waited out the injection, which seemed to take forever.

Laying the empty syringe on the nightstand, she said, "Stay where you are. I'm going to clean your incision."

He thought of something clever to say, but forgot it before he could form the words. The pillow was feeling awfully good.

He was vaguely aware of her bathing his incision with cold liquid, then applying a fresh bandage. It dimly registered when she covered him with a sheet and light blanket. The room seemed to grow gradually darker. He opened his eyes only long enough to see her at the windows where she was closing the shutters. For a millisecond before she shut the louvers, he saw her in silhouette against the bright outdoor light. It detailed her shape. She wasn't wearing a bra.

He groaned, Sweetjesus.

Or maybe he didn't.

When he woke up he was lying on his back, favoring his right side. The room was empty, but light was leaking from beneath the closed bathroom door. He checked the windows. The shutters were still drawn.

God, what had she given him? How long had he been asleep? All day? Two days? Three?

Just then the light went out beneath the bathroom door. It was eased open soundlessly. Rennie stepped through, bringing the smell of soap and shampoo with her. She looked toward the bed and saw that he was awake and watching her.

"I'm sorry. I shouldn't have used the hair dryer. I was afraid it might wake you up, but you were sleeping so soundly I took the chance."

"What time is it?"

"Going on six."

Her bare feet made whispering sounds on the hard-wood floor as she moved to the edge of the bed. "How are you feeling?"

When she bent down to take a closer look at him, her hair fell forward to curtain both sides of her face. She swept it over one shoulder to keep it out of her way. "Can I bring you anything?"

Hair, eyes, skin, lips. She was a beautiful woman. He had thought so the first time he'd laid eyes on her in Oren's eight-by-tens. That's when the desire took root and the lying began. He had lied to Oren and to himself, first about his opinion of her, then about his objectivity. It had died when she turned to him at the wedding reception. He had known in that instant that his professionalism was done for. It sank right along with him into the depths of her green eyes.

During his career he had dealt with all types of women, from hookers to homemakers. Cheats and liars and thieves and saints. Women who dressed in power suits and made it their mission in life to symbolically de-ball every man with whom they came into contact, and women who undressed for the amusement and entertainment of men.

Oren had been right when he said that he'd never had an unremarkable encounter with a woman. All had been memorable for one reason or another, from his adoring kindergarten teacher, to the policewoman who had pronounced him the biggest asshole she'd ever had the displeasure of knowing, to Crystal the waitress. He never failed to make an impression.

Good or bad, he had an innate awareness of females that was reciprocated. It was just one of those things, a component of himself that he'd been born with and more or less took for granted, like his palm print or his crooked front tooth.

He had slept with some of those women—he had slept with a lot of them. But he had never desired one as much as he desired Rennie Newton. Nor had one ever been so forbidden. She had meant trouble to him from the start, and she would mean trouble to him from here on.

None of that mattered, though, when strands of her hair brushed against his bare chest. Common sense and conscience didn't stand a chance.

"Ah, hell," he growled. Curving his hand around the back of her neck, he drew her head down to his.

It was a full-blown kiss from the start. No sooner had his lips touched hers than he pressed his tongue between them. He probed her mouth lustily. Her breath was warm and rapid against his face, and that urged him on. He tilted her head, found more heat, more sweetness, wet delight.

His hand moved up from her neck and spread wide over the back of her head. His other hand settled on her rib cage. Against his thumb he could feel the soft weight of her breast. Then the center of it, growing firm at his touch, responding, becoming harder beneath his stroking.

"No!"

Backing away, she shook her head furiously. She stared at him for several ponderous seconds, then turned and fled—the only way to describe the speed with which she left the room.

Chapter 24

He showered. He shaved with one of Rennie's pink razors. In the mirror above the bathroom sink, he didn't look quite as frightening as he had before the long sleep. The dark rings under his eyes had lightened and the sockets weren't as deep.

But he was no Prince Charming. His hospital pallor emphasized the discoloration on his cheekbone. And when was the last time he'd had a haircut? "Screw it," he said to his reflection as he left the bathroom.

Rennie was in the kitchen. She glanced over her shoulder when he walked in. "You found your duffel bag?"

"Yeah, thanks." She had placed it at the foot of the bed so he would have a change of clothes.

"How do you feel?"

"Better. Thanks. For everything. Except the shot. My butt's sore."

"I'm sure you're thirsty. Help yourself to anything in

the fridge." She was dredging boneless chicken breasts in seasoned breading and placing them in a Pyrex dish.

He took a carton of orange juice from the refrigerator, shook it, and twisted off the cap. "Okay to drink from the carton?"

"Not in this house."

"I used your toothbrush."

"I have extras."

"Why am I not surprised?"

"Glasses are in the cabinet just behind you."

The juice tasted good. He drained the glass and re-filled it. "What did you do with the bobcat?"

"Called the game warden. He came out and picked him up. He congratulated me."

"You provided a valuable community service."

She gazed into near space for a moment. "It didn't feel like that. It felt like killing." She washed her hands, moved to the oven and turned it on, then went to the vegetable sink and picked up a chopping knife. She used it to ges-ture toward a cell phone lying on the counter. "It's rung several times."

"Jeez, I don't even remember where I last had it."

"It was in your truck."

"Where's my truck?"

"In the garage out back."

He looked through the window and spotted the build-ing. It was a smaller version of the barn. The double doors were closed. "How'd you manage to get it here?"

"I rode Beade over, carrying the gas can. Then I tied him to the tailgate and drove back slowly."

"It would have been easier if you'd waited on me to go with you."

"I didn't think you wanted anyone to know you were here."

He studied her for a moment. "That's not quite accurate, is it, Rennie?"

She stopped slicing tomatoes and looked across at him.

"*You* didn't want anyone to know I was here."

She returned to her task. "Do you like tomatoes in your salad?"

"Rennie."

"Some people don't."

"Rennie."

She dropped the knife and confronted him. "What?"

"It was only a kiss," he said softly.

"Let's not make a big deal of it, all right?"

"I'm not, you are. You're the one who went tearing out of the bedroom like it had caught fire."

"So you would stop mauling me."

"Mauling you?" he repeated in a raised voice. "*Mauling* you?"

"The night we met—no, the night you arranged for us to meet—I told you then, straight out and in language a child could understand that I wasn't interested in . . . all that."

Masculine pride kicked in. Wick rounded the work island so it would no longer be between them. "Well that's a switch for you, isn't it? One kiss and I'm mauling you, but back in Dalton you were quite the party girl. What did you call it then?"

She recoiled as though he'd struck her, but that initial reaction lasted only a second before her facial expression turned hard. "You must have had a locker-room chat with your pal Detective Wesley."

"Only after I heard all about you from folks in Dalton.

You're remembered there, Sweetcheeks. Because you used to do a lot more than kiss the locals, didn't you?"

"You're so well informed—why ask me?"

"You did *considerably* more than kiss."

She backed down and looked away. "I'm not like that now."

"Why not? Seems to me like you were having one hell of a good time. Tongues in Dalton are still wagging about your topless cruise through town in your red Mustang convertible. But I get your nipple ripe and you freak out."

She tried to go around him, but he executed a quick sidestep and blocked her path. "You had all those horny cowboys at the rodeo panting after you. And their daddies, and their uncles, and probably even their grandpas."

"Stop it!"

"And you knew it, too, didn't you? You liked keeping 'em steaming in their jeans."

"You don't know—"

"Oh, yeah, I do. Guys know. We have ugly names for girls like you, Rennie. Doesn't stop us from wanting what you advertise, though. How many hearts were broken when you set your sights on Raymond Collier?"

"Don't—"

"Then when that affair went south, you shot and killed him. Is that what turned you off mauling?"

"*Yes!*"

Her shout was followed by a sudden, reverberating silence. She turned away from him and leaned forward against the counter. She put her hand to her mouth and kept it there for several moments. Then, very unsurgeon-like, she seemed at a loss what to do with her hands. She crossed her arms over her midsection and hugged her elbows; she wiped her palms on her thighs; she finally picked up the baking dish of chicken and placed it in the oven. After setting the timer, she returned to chopping tomatoes.

Wick continued to watch her with the single-mindedness of the buzzards that had circled the carcass of the bobcat. He refused to drop this subject. He felt entitled to peel away just one of her multiple layers. He wanted at least a glimpse of who she was and what had made her so compulsively neat, what had made her so disinclined to touch another human being except in the sterile security of an operating room. He wanted to see, if only for an instant, the real Rennie Newton.

"What happened in your father's study that day?"

The knife came down hard and angrily on the chopping block. "Didn't Wesley share the details with you?"

"Yes. And I read the police report."

"Well then."

"It didn't tell me shit. I want to hear what happened from you."

She finished with the tomatoes and rinsed off the knife. As she dried it on a tea towel, she looked at him sardonically. "Prurient curiosity, Wick?"

"Don't do that," he said, keeping a tight rein on his anger. "You know that's not why I'm asking."

She braced her arms on the countertop and leaned toward him. "Then why *are* you asking? Explain to me why it's so bloody important for you to know about that."

He leaned forward to narrow the space between them. "You know why, Rennie," he whispered. There was no way his meaning could have escaped her. But just in case it did, he covered the back of her hand with his palm and encircled her wrist with his fingers.

She lowered her head. It appeared to him that she was

staring at their hands, but all he could see was the crown
of her head, the natural part in her hair. Half a minute
passed before she withdrew her hand from beneath his.

"Nothing good can come of this, Wick."

"*This* being the weird triangle we have going? You, me,
and Lozada?"

"There's no such triangle."

"You know better, Rennie."

"The two of you had a score to settle before you ever
heard of me."

"That's true, but you've added another dimension."

"I'm not involved in your feud," she said adamantly.

"Then why did you leave town?"

"I needed some time off."

"You heard Lozada was released from jail."

"Yes, but—"

"And you beat it here within hours of his release. Looks
to me like you're hiding from him."

His cell phone rang. He picked it up and read the
caller ID, then swore under his breath. "I might as well get
this over with." He carried the phone with him through
the living room and out onto the front porch. He answered as he sat down in the swing. "Hey."

"Where the hell are you?"

"No hello?"

"Wick—"

"Okay, okay." He sighed heavily. "I just couldn't take
that hospital anymore, Oren. You know I don't handle in-
activity well. Another day in that place and I'd've wigged
out. So I left. Retrieved my truck from your house and
drove most of the night. Reached Galveston this morning
around, hmm, five or so, I guess. Been asleep most of the

day and got a whole lot more rest listening to the surf than I would have in the hospital where real rest is impossible."

After a significant pause, Oren said, "Your place in Galveston is locked up tighter than a drum."

Oh, shit. "How do you know?"

"Because I asked the police there to check it."

"What for?"

"I'm waiting for an explanation, Wick."

"Okay, on my way home I took a little detour. What's the big deal?"

"You're with her, aren't you?"

"I'm a big boy, Oren. I don't have to account to you for my—"

"Because she's coincidentally flown the coop too. From the hospital. From her house. Her obliging neighbor told me that he saw a man who looked seriously ill and malnourished knocking on her door in the middle of the night."

"Does that guy keep vigil at his window or what?"

"He's become a valuable informant."

"My, my, Oren. Talking to Galveston police. Talking to nosy neighbors. You've been busy today."

"And so has Lozada."

"Oh yeah? Doing what?"

"Terrorizing my family."

His name was Weenie Sawyer. Only someone of Weenie's diminutive size would have tolerated such a derisive name. Weenie did so only because he had no choice. He was defenseless.

He had acquired the name in second grade when he'd wet himself in the classroom. During a geography lesson on Hawaii a seeming river of urine had charted a course down his leg. To the amusement of his classmates, what wasn't absorbed by his sock had formed a puddle beneath his desk. He'd wanted to die on the spot, but he had had the rotten luck of living through it. That afternoon he had been dubbed Weenie by a pack of bullies led by the scourge of the school yard, Ricky Roy Lozada.

The nickname had stuck to this day. And so had Lozada's bullying. Weenie audibly groaned when he opened his door and saw Lozada standing on the threshold.

"May I come in?"

The formality was a mockery. Lozada asked only in order to remind Weenie that he didn't need an invitation. He pushed past Weenie and entered the cramped, poorly ventilated apartment where Weenie sometimes confined himself for days without going out. For self-protection, Weenie existed in a universe of his own making.

"This isn't a good time, Lozada. I'm having dinner." On a TV tray next to the La-Z-Boy a bowl of Cap'n Crunch was growing soggy.

"I wouldn't interrupt, Weenie. Except that this is very important."

"You always say that."

"Because my business is always important."

Lozada's torture of his unfortunate classmate hadn't ended that afternoon in second grade, but had continued through their high school graduation. Weenie's size, his perpetual squint, and his meek personality were open invitations to torment and ridicule him. He was almost too easy a target. Consequently Lozada had treated him as a forgettable pet, one he could scold and neglect, or grace and praise, at whim.

Every class has a computer whiz, and in their class it

had been Weenie. While computers and microchip technology bored Lozada, he was nevertheless aware of the ad-
vancements being made. As the viability of computer
usage increased, so had Weenie's value to him.

Nowadays Weenie's livelihood was designing Web sites.
He liked the work. It was a rewarding creative outlet. He
could do it alone, at home, on his own schedule. He billed
his clients four times the number of hours it required him
to complete a job, but they were so pleased with the result
that none ever questioned the amount of the invoice. It
was a lucrative business.

But that income was paltry compared to what Lozada
paid him.

Weenie's computer setup occupied one whole room of
his apartment and rivaled NASA's in sophistication. He
put most of his money back into his business, buying state-
of-the-art equipment, upgrades, and gadgets. He could dis-
sect a computer with the precision of a pathologist, then
reassemble it with new and improved specifications. He'd
never met one he didn't like. He knew how they worked.
Furthermore, he understood how they worked.

With a minimum of mouse clicks, he could enter any
secret chat room, generate a deadly virus, or crack any security code. If Weenie had possessed any imagination or
larcenous impulses, he could potentially control the world
from this old, ugly, smelly, cluttered apartment in a rundown neighborhood in the shadow of downtown Dallas.

Lozada thought it a woeful waste of talent. Weenie's
level of know-how should belong to someone who would
exploit it, someone with panache and style and *cojones*.

Had Lozada been in another field, he could have used
Weenie's genius to steal huge quantities of money with little chance of getting caught. But where would be the chal-

lenge? He much preferred the personal involvement his occupation required. He relied on Weenie strictly to provide him with information on his clients and his targets.

He told Weenie that was what he was after tonight. "Information."

Weenie pushed up his slipping eyeglasses. "You always say that, too, Lozada. And then the person I get you information on winds up dead."

Lozada fixed a cold stare on him. "What's wrong with you tonight?"

"Nothing." He picked at a crusty scab on his elbow. "What makes you think something's wrong?"

"You don't seem very glad to see me. Didn't I pay you enough last time?"

"Yeah, but . . ." He sniffed back a nostril full of mucus. "I've got no quarrel with the money."

"Then what's the matter?"

"I don't want to get into trouble. With the law, I mean. You've been in the news a lot lately, or haven't you noticed?"

"Have you noticed that it's all been good news?"

"Yeah, but this time, I don't know, the police seem to be closing in tighter. That Threadgill's got it in for you."

"He's the least of my worries."

Weenie looked plenty worried. "He comes across as a man with a mission. What if they, you know, link us? You and me."

"How could they do that?"

"I don't know."

Lozada remembered that whining tone from elementary school. It had annoyed him then, and it annoyed him even more now. He was in a hurry, and this conversation was wasting precious time.

"What I mean is," Weenie continued, "I don't want to become an accessory. I was watching *Law and Order* the other night. And they charged this guy with being an accessory before the fact. He went down for almost as long as the guy who did the actual killing. I want no part of that."

"You're afraid?"

"Damn right I'm afraid. How long do you think a guy like me would last in prison?"

Lozada looked him up and down. He smiled. "I see your point. So you'll have to be doubly careful not to get caught, won't you?"

Weenie went through his routine of nervous twitches again with the eyeglasses, the scab, the snot in his nose. He avoided making eye contact. Lozada didn't like it.

"Sit down, Weenie. I'm in a hurry. Let's get started."

Weenie seemed to consider refusing, but then he reluctantly sat down in the rolling desk chair in front of the bank of computer terminals, all of which were oscillating with a variety of screen savers.

"Rennie Newton," Lozada told him. "Doctor Rennie Newton."

Again Weenie groaned. "I was afraid you were going to say that. I saw her being interviewed on the news about that cop. What do you want to know?"

"Everything."

Weenie went to work. His nose stayed within inches of the screen as he squinted into the glare. His fingers struck the keys with impressive speed. But Lozada wasn't fooled. He could tell Weenie was dillydallying. It went on for at least five minutes. Occasionally he mumbled with frustration.

Finally he sat back and said, "Bunch of dead ends. Truth is, Lozada, there's not much on her."

Lozada slipped his hand into his pants pocket and removed a glass vial with a perforated metal cap. He unscrewed it slowly, then upended the vial over Weenie.

The scorpion landed on Weenie's chest. He shrieked and reflexively tried to roll back on the chair's casters, but Lozada was standing behind it, trapping Weenie between him and the computer table. He clamped his hand to Weenie's forehead, pulled his head back, and held him still while the scorpion crawled over his chest.

"He's been mine only a short while. I've been waiting for the perfect time to show him off. Isn't he a beauty?"

Weenie emitted a high-pitched squeal.

"All the way from India, meet *Mesobuthus tamulus*, one of the rare species of scorpions whose venom is toxic enough to cause death in humans, although it may take days for a sting victim to die."

Weenie's glasses had been knocked askew. His eyes rolled wildly as they tried to focus on the vicious-looking scorpion crawling up his chest. "Lozada, for the love of God," he gasped.

Lozada calmly released him and chuckled. "You aren't going to pee on yourself again, are you?"

He calmly scooped the scorpion onto a sheet of paper, then formed a cone and funneled it back into the vial. "There now, enough fun, Weenie," he said as he replaced the perforated cap. "You've got work to do."

Chapter 25

∎∎∎∎∎∎∎∎∎∎∎∎

You don't like it?"

Wick looked up from his plate. "Uh, yeah. It's great. Just . . . I think that potato-soup breakfast filled me up." He tried to smile but knew he failed.

They'd taken their dinner trays out onto the patio behind the house and had watched the sunset while they ate, in silence for the most part. In fact, they hadn't exchanged more than a few inconsequential sentences since Wick's telephone conversation with Oren.

She stood up with her tray and reached for his. "Finished, then?"

"I can carry in the tray."

"You shouldn't. Not with your back."

"It doesn't hurt anymore."

"Will you just give me the tray?"

He relinquished it and she took it into the house. He heard her moving around in the kitchen, water running, the fridge door being opened and closed. Background noise for his preoccupation.

When Rennie returned, she brought with her a bottle of white wine and set it on the small table between their two teak chairs. He said, "That'll hit the spot."

"You don't get any." She poured wine for herself into the single glass she had brought out.

"Why not?"

"The medication."

"You slipped me another mickey in my chicken breast? Or was it in the wild rice?"

"Neither. Because I don't know what you take."

"What do you mean?"

"For the panic attacks."

He thought about playing dumb. He thought about flat-out denying it. But what would be the point? She knew. "I don't take anything. Not anymore." He turned away and stared across the landscape. "How'd you know?"

"I recognized the symptoms." His gaze moved back to her and she softly confessed, "Borderline compulsive obsessive. Back, years ago. I never counted each heartbeat, or every footstep, nothing that extreme. But everything had to be just so, and to a great extent still does. It's all about being in control."

The topic under discussion made him terribly uncomfortable. "I had a . . . a few . . . what you'd call episodes, I guess. Rapid heartbeat, shortness of breath. That's all. A lot of shit happened to me all at once. Major life changes." He gave an elaborate shrug. "The shrink seemed to think there was nothing to it."

"There's no reason to be ashamed, Wick."

"I'm not ashamed." His brusqueness implied just the opposite.

She gave him a long look, then said, "Well, anyway, the drugs I gave you today would be compatible with anything you happened to be taking. Just so you know."

"Thanks, but as I said, I'm off that stuff."

"Maybe you should go back on it."

"Why's that, *Doctor*?"

"Because if you weighed five pounds less, I don't think the earth's gravity could keep you in that chair."

He made a conscious effort to stop fidgeting.

"Why don't you just tell me what Wesley told you?" she said.

Again, he turned his head aside and gazed out across the rear of her property. It was a pretty spread, the kind of place he'd love to have if he could ever afford it, which he never could. He wasn't, nor had he ever been, materialistic. Greed wasn't one of his flaws. But a place like this, this would be nice to have.

The pasture beyond the near fence was dotted with mature trees, mostly pecan. A stream cutting diagonally across the pasture was lined with tall cottonwoods and willows that swayed in the south breeze. The breeze had cooled the evening off, making it comfortable to be outdoors.

After being cooped up in the hospital for a week, he had welcomed her suggestion that they take their dinner onto the patio. But he hadn't enjoyed the al fresco meal as much as he should have. Oren's news had spoiled his appetite.

"Grace Wesley left her school office today around four-thirty," he began. "The last couple of weeks, she's been getting things ready for the upcoming term, same as the rest of the faculty. Except that Grace is extremely conscientious. She's usually the last one to leave the building, as she was today. When she got into her car, Lozada was sitting in the backseat."

Rennie sucked in a quick breath and held it.

"Yeah," he said. "Scared her half to death."

"Is she . . ."

"She's okay. He never lifted a finger to her. He just talked."

"Saying what?"

"He wanted to know where I was, where you were."

"Does she know?"

"No, and that's what she told him. But he must not have believed her." He looked over at Rennie. She folded her arms across her middle as though bracing for what was coming. "He told her it would be in her best interest to tell him what he wanted to know, and when she said she couldn't, he remarked on how pretty her daughters were."

Rennie bowed her head and supported it in her hand, her middle finger and thumb pressing hard against her temples. "Please, please don't tell me that—"

"No, the girls are all right too. It was a warning. A veiled threat. But a real one because he knew a lot about them. Their names, favorite activities, friends, places they like to go.

"Grace started crying. She's a strong lady but, like all of us, she has a breaking point, and her family is it. Oren says she didn't fold, didn't beg or plead. But somehow she must have persuaded him that she didn't know anything. He got out of her car and into his. He even waved her good-bye before driving off.

"Grace immediately called Oren on her cell. Within minutes the girls were collected and put under police guard. Grace, too. Oren was . . . well, you can imagine."

They were quiet for a time. Crickets were tuning up for the night.

"He wants Grace and the girls to go stay with her mother in Tennessee," he continued. "Even while he was talking to me he was packing their bags. Over their protests. I could hear the girls fussing in the background and Grace saying that if he thought she was going to leave him alone, he could just think again. Nor, she said, was she going to be frightened away from her home by a homicidal freak like Lozada."

"What do you think?"

"Oh, he's a freak, all right."

"You know what I mean. Should she leave?"

He shrugged. "I can see both sides."

"So can I. Having met Grace, seen them together, it doesn't surprise me that she would refuse to leave her husband in a time of crisis."

"Not only that, Rennie. If Lozada wants to hurt Oren's family, he will. A trip out of state would be only a minor inconvenience." They exchanged a long look.

Then suddenly Wick left his chair and began to pace the width of the flagstone patio. "Lozada. He really is the lowest turd in the shit pile. He's threatening women and children now? I mean, what kind of lowlife . . . You know what I think? I think he's got no balls, that's what I think. He attacks in the dark like those goddamn scorpions he keeps."

"Scorpions?"

"He gets his victims in the back. In the *back*. Think about it. He choked the banker to death from the back. He stabbed me in the back. The only one he's met face-to-face in daylight is a woman, and he threatened her children. He's never faced a man. I wish to God I could get a crack at him face-to-face."

"That could prove dangerous."

He shot her a bitter look. "You and Oren are reading from the same script. I was already out of your porch swing and on my way to the garage to get my truck and return to Fort Worth, but Oren told me if I so much as crossed the city line, he'd have me arrested."

"For what?"

"He didn't specify, but he meant it. He said the only thing he needed to make a bad situation worse was a hotheaded avenger. He said the only good thing about Lozada's terrorizing Grace was his choosing to do it when I was out of town."

"He did it *because* you were out of town."

He stopped pacing and turned to her. "Did you eavesdrop on our conversation? Because that's exactly what Oren said. He thinks Lozada threatened Grace in the hope of smoking me out."

"I'm sure he's right."

He raked his fingers through his hair. "I'm sure he is too," he mumbled. "Lozada would expect me to ride in like the cavalry"

"Making you a target that would be hard for him to miss."

"Especially if I was the aggressor. Lozada would love nothing better than for me to come after him. If I did, he could drop me and then claim self-defense."

Rennie agreed with a nod, which agitated him further. He resumed pacing. "Oren hoped I'd gone back to Galveston. He wasn't too happy to learn I was still this close to Fort Worth."

"With me."

"I've told him there's no way that you and Lozada are, or ever were, in cahoots."

"Does he believe you?" His hesitation in answering gave him away. She said, "Never mind. I know he thinks I'm shady."

Wick didn't belabor the point. He returned to his chair, picked up the bottle of wine, and took a drink from it. She didn't stop him. He then leaned toward her. "Lozada upped the ante today when he messed with Grace. Attacking me is one thing. Going after her, Oren's kids, that's another. I'm gonna get this son of a bitch, Rennie. For good.

"And it can't be done through legal channels. I've learned that lesson several times over. Now Oren realizes it too. We can't rely on the system. It's let us down. We've got to get him some other way. We've got to forget the law and start thinking like Lozada."

"I agree." He registered his surprise, and she continued, "You thought I left town to escape him. That I ran in fear when I learned that he'd been released from jail. You thought I had come here to hide. Well, you're wrong. I left because I needed time to plan how I was going to free myself from him. I refuse to live in fear, especially in fear of a man.

"Lozada has invaded my home. Twice. He killed my friend Lee Howell. He killed Sally Horton and tried to kill you, and, so far, he's gotten away with it. He got away with killing that banker, and I helped him do that."

"You were a juror. You voted according to your conscience."

"Thanks for the endorsement, but I regret that decision now. Lozada seems to be immune to the law, but he's not invincible, Wick. He's not bulletproof."

"And you're a damn good shot." His grin collapsed when he saw the drastic change in her expression. "I was referring to the bobcat, Rennie, not to what happened in Dalton."

She formed a half smile and nodded acknowledgment. "I have no intention of shooting anybody, even Lozada. I don't want to wind up in prison myself."

"I'd rather not either, although I'm committed to eliminating him no matter what it costs me."

"Because of your brother?" When he nodded, she added, "Was that one of the life-changing things that happened to you all at once?"

"That was the major one."

He leaned back and laid his head against the chair cushion. The sky had turned an inky purple. Already he could see stars. Thousands more than were visible in the city. Even more than he could see on the Galveston beach where commercial lights reduced stars to dim reminders of what they should look like.

"Joe and Lozada had actually known each other in school. Or rather they knew *of* each other. They attended rival high schools but graduated the same year. Joe was a star athlete and student leader. Lozada was a hoodlum, hell raiser, drug dealer. They saw each other occasionally at places where teens hang out.

"They only clashed once, when Joe broke up a fight between Lozada and another guy. They exchanged words, but it amounted to no more than that. Joe became a cop. Lozada became a hired killer. Both excelled at what they did. They were destined to collide. It was only a matter of time."

He reached for the wine bottle and took another

drink, hoping it would relieve the throbbing pain in his back, which had returned with a vengeance.

"Fast-forward a few years. Joe and Oren were working a high-profile homicide case. Typical Texas tale. Socialite wife of wealthy oilman whacked on terrace of mansion.

"The husband was conveniently out of town and had a long list of indisputable alibis. Since nothing had been disturbed, nothing stolen, it stunk of a murder-for-hire. Joe and Oren leaned heavily on the husband, who had a very demanding, very expensive twenty-two-year-old mistress in New York.

"Figuratively speaking, the murder had Lozada's fingerprints all over it, but they couldn't link him to the husband. Joe hammered the guy, and each time he questioned him, he cracked a little more. Joe was relentless, kept at him. He was this close to splitting the thing wide open."

He was quiet for a time before continuing. "The last time I saw Joe, we met for a cup of coffee. He told me he could taste the man's fear. 'I'm close, Wick. Close.' He predicted that the guy was gonna crash and burn soon, and when he did, Joe would have his ass as well as Lozada's. The oilman was a schmuck, he said. Pussy-whipped by this brat in New York. His dick had done him in. Joe said you could almost feel sorry for him.

"'But that Lozada dude is bad news, little bro. I'm talking real bad news.' Joe's words exactly. He said Lozada killed for pleasure more than for money. He liked killing. Joe said he was gonna do the world a favor and put that heartless, hairless son of a bitch away for life.

"I remember us clinking our coffee cups in a toast to his success. Which, apparently, Lozada also thought was coming down soon. He must've sensed the oilman was close to ratting him out.

"That same evening, Oren left the office a few minutes behind Joe. When he got to the parking lot, he noticed that Joe's car was still there. The driver's door was standing open. Joe was just sitting there, staring through the windshield. Oren remembers walking toward the car and saying, 'Hey, what's up? I thought you'd be gone by now.'"

He paused to inhale a deep breath and let it out slowly. The darkness was now complete. The moon was a sliver hanging just above the horizon.

"Joe was already dead when Oren found him. I was hosting a party at our house that night. Oren and Grace came to tell me." He leaned forward, planted his elbows on his knees, and lightly tapped his lips with his clasped hands.

"You know what I wonder about most, Rennie?" Turning his head, he looked at her and realized that she hadn't moved since he began talking. "You know what really puzzles me?"

"What?"

"I wonder why Lozada didn't kill the oilman instead. That would have shut him up. Why didn't he do him instead of Joe?"

"Joe posed the greater threat. Killing the oilman would have been a temporary fix to a long-range problem. Lozada knew Joe wouldn't give up until he had him."

"His twisted form of flattery, I guess."

"Why was he never charged and brought to trial for Joe's murder?" she asked.

But Wick's cell phone rang, sparing him from having to answer.

                *   *   *

He opened the phone and put it to his ear. "Yeah?"

He listened for a few seconds, glanced at Rennie, then left his chair and moved to the edge of the patio, keeping his back to her. "No, we haven't talked about it yet," she heard him say as he stepped off the flagstones and moved even farther away from her.

Taking the hint that he wanted privacy, she went inside and finished cleaning the kitchen. She wondered what unpleasant developments Detective Wesley would tell them of this time.

Through the window above the kitchen sink, she could see Wick pacing along the fence line. She shared his restlessness. She felt she should be taking action, doing something, but she just didn't know what to do.

In the living room, she switched on an end-table lamp and took up her favorite spot in the corner of the sofa. She flipped through a magazine, but neither the pictures nor the text registered. She was preoccupied with thoughts of Wick.

He was in perpetual motion, just as Grace Wesley had said. Yet he had a habit of making his point by holding a stare for an interminable length of time. Once his blue eyes locked with yours, it was difficult to escape their intensity.

He was clever and glib and funny and had self-confidence to spare. But he wasn't superficial. He felt things deeply. He had loved his brother, and the loss was still a raw, open wound. Every hour Lozada went unpunished was like salt to that wound. He seemed to hate Lozada as much as he had loved Joe, and that was a perilous level of emotion to keep contained. Lozada should be very afraid of Wick Threadgill.

She identified with the rage that drove him to get even.

Her vengeance had taken an altogether different form, but she understood Wick's compulsion to seek it. She also pitied him for it, because finding retribution is a lonely, all-consuming business.

She hadn't wanted to like Wick Threadgill, but she did. She hadn't wanted to forgive him for tricking her, but she had. She hadn't wanted to be attracted to him, but she was. She had known that if she ever kissed him once, she would want to again. She had, and she did. And if that kiss was any indication of how fervently he made love, she wanted to experience it.

"Rennie?"

She sat up straight and cleared her throat. "In here."

His boot heels made clomping sounds against the hardwood floor. He took the opposite end of the couch but perched on the very edge, as though he might spring off it at any moment. "What are you doing?"

She indicated the open magazine in her lap.

"Horse magazine?"

"Hmm."

"Anything new and interesting in the world of horses?"

"What did he say, Wick?"

He expelled a breath and ran his hand around the back of his neck. "I need a massage."

"It wouldn't be good for your wound."

"Just my shoulders. I've got a crick in my neck from sleeping under that tree last night. How 'bout some massage therapy for your favorite patient?"

"More bad news?"

"Not really. Where'd you get the saddle?"

"It was a prize."

"For barrel racing?"

"You know about my barrel racing?" Reading his guilty

expression, she said, "Of course you know. Yes, I won the saddle for barrel racing."

"Good-looking saddle. But don't those silver studs make for an uncomfortable ride?"

"Wick, if Oren's news wasn't that bad, why are you stalling?"

"Okay," he said curtly. "I'll tell you what we talked about. But I want you to know up front that it wasn't my idea."

"I'm not going to like it, am I?"

"I seriously doubt that you are."

She looked at him expectantly, but still he hesitated. "For heaven's sake, how bad can it be?"

"Oren thinks we should pretend to be lovers." He bobbed his head for additional punctuation.

She stared at him for several moments, then began to laugh. "That's it? That's the brilliant plan to snare Lozada?"

He took offense at her laughter. "What's the matter with it?"

"Nothing. As every dime novelist and C-movie producer will attest." She laughed harder, but he didn't join in. "Come on, Wick. Don't you think that idea is a trifle clichéd? We try and make Lozada jealous. He devises some horrible punishment, and when he attempts it, we nab him. Is that the gist of this grand scheme?"

"Basically," he said stiffly.

She shook her head in disbelief. "Lord help us."

"I'm glad you can laugh, Rennie, because I can't. Lozada's disappeared. His Mercedes is in the parking garage, so he's using an unknown means of transportation. He hasn't been spotted in his favorite restaurants, hasn't been seen at his place in Trinity Tower since last night. The concierge told Oren that the homeowners' association has asked him to vacate."

"Then maybe he just moved out."

"And maybe that bobcat you dropped this morning will resurrect tonight." He got up and began to roam the living room aimlessly. "Lozada wouldn't have complied with an eviction request from his neighbors. That place is one of his status symbols, like his hand-tailored suits and that hundred-thousand-dollar set of wheels.

"Being asked to leave would be the worst kind of affront and would make him mad as hell. And who's he going to blame for being undesirable to Fort Worth's elite? You guessed it. Me. Us. He's pissed at us for vanishing, especially if he knows we're together. He's pissed at us for making news and getting him kicked him out of his building. Now nobody knows where he is. And all of that makes me real nervous."

When she was certain his outburst was over, she apologized. "I didn't mean to make light of the situation, Wick. I know how serious it is. I only have to think about Grace to be reminded. But let's be reasonable. Lozada wouldn't fall for a corny charade like that."

He came to stand directly in front of her, forcing her to tilt her head back to look at him. "Okay then, let's hear your idea. I assume you have a workable alternate plan. You said you came here to think of a way to get him out of your life. Has the fresh country air stimulated the gray matter?"

She lowered her head. "You don't need to be insulting."

"Considering your recent laughter, I can't believe you have the gall to look me in the eye—in the fly, rather—and say that."

He headed for the kitchen. Rennie went after him. By the time she got there he was downing a bottle of water.

"You're limping. Does your back hurt?"

"And then some."

"You said it didn't."

"I lied."

"Not for the first time."

They stared at each other in hostile silence. She was the first to break it. "All right, what are we supposed to do? Hold hands on the corner of Fourth and Main? Gaze at each other over candlelight dinners? Slow-dance till dawn? What?"

"Don't forget mauling," he said. "I could maul you some more."

Heat rushed to her face, but she remained where she was. To stalk away angrily would only give the incident the importance she had told him it didn't have.

Swearing softly, he set the bottle of water on the counter and rubbed his tired eyes. "I'm sorry. You're always making me say things that make me feel like shit after I say them."

"It's all right. I should never have used that term for what . . ."

He lowered his hand from his eyes and looked at her. "For what . . . What?"

"You weren't mauling me."

He fixed her with one of those immobilizing gazes until she willed herself to look away. "You'd better tell me more about Oren's plan."

"Uh, yeah." He shook his head as though to remind himself what they'd been talking about. "He said we might get Lozada on a stalking charge. If we can put him away for that, even for a while, we'd have more time to build a case against him for the murder of Sally Horton and the attack on me. But—"

"I was afraid there would be one."

"No one else has heard these calls you claim he made." She was about to object when he held up his hands, palms out. "Bear with me. I'm thinking like our DA's office. I can hear some fresh-out-of-law-school ADA asking for the evidence of these calls, and we have none. True?"

"True. But I have that note that came with the roses."

"It didn't contain a threat."

"He broke into my house."

"Oren and two other cops saw you and Lozada in a clinch."

"I was afraid if I resisted I'd wind up like Sally Horton."

"There was no sign of forced entry at your house, Rennie."

"There was no sign of forced entry when you broke in either."

He was taken aback. "You know about that?"

"I guessed, and Wesley confirmed it with a stony silence."

"Oren didn't tell me you knew." He hung his head and rubbed the back of his neck again. "It's a wonder you didn't let me bleed out."

"I didn't know about the illegal search until after I'd saved your life."

His head came up quickly. She smiled wryly to let him know she was kidding. He returned the smile. "Lucky for me."

"Getting back to the stalking angle," she said, "how effectual is it if I can't prove Lozada's been harassing me?"

"We'd have a better chance of getting a charge to stick

if something happened in another locale. The allegation would have stronger legs if he followed you somewhere."

"Like here."

He shook his head. "He could say you had invited him. It would be his word against yours."

"Then where?"

"My place in Galveston. He sure as hell wouldn't be on any guest list of mine. How soon can you be packed?"

Chapter 26

Oren answered on the first ring. Wick told him they had decided to go along with his plan.

"Dr. Newton is okay with it?"

"No," Wick said. "No more than I am. It's hackneyed and Lozada would have to be a moron to fall for it."

"But no one has a better idea."

"I do. Arm me to the teeth and let me hunt down the bastard and blow him away."

"That plan could sorely affect your quality of life in the future."

"Which is the only reason I'm agreeing to this one. Rennie is of the same mind. It's not an ideal strategy, but it's the only one we've got going. On the plus side, it smacks Lozada right where it'll hurt most—in his ego."

"That's why it just might work."

"What did you and Grace decide?"

"The girls went. Grace stayed."

Wick smiled into the telephone. "Good for Grace."

"Yeah, well . . . Listen up. By the time you get to your place in Galveston, there'll be men watching it around the clock. Don't look for them. You won't see them. I hope not, anyway."

"Will you be coming down?"

"Would you invite your best buddy to a lovefest with your new squeeze?"

"I don't know. How kinky are we gonna get?"

"Wick."

"Sorry. I got it." If Lozada spotted Oren, he would know it was a setup.

"I'll be in touch by phone 'round the clock," Oren continued. "Keep your eyes open and check in often. If you hear a seagull fart, I want to know about it."

"Are you sure? 'Cause if they fart as much as they shit—"

"Will you stop messing around? This isn't funny."

"I know. All joking aside." And he meant it.

"Lozada's gone underground, Wick. You know what usually happens when he disappears for a few days."

"A body turns up."

"I don't like it."

"Neither do I. However, I don't think he could find us this soon."

"But it's possible. I've got people all over town talking up your affair with the surgeon who saved your life. Word has probably reached him that you and Dr. Newton are a hot item."

"Oh, he'll turn up. I'm sure of that." He hadn't told Oren or Rennie about the red flag he'd waved in Lozada's face in the form of a nursery rhyme. Lozada wouldn't be able to resist the dare.

He signed off with Oren, then went outside to take a

look around. He walked the perimeter of the house, around the barn and garage, checked inside both. Nothing seemed to be amiss. When he came back in, he and Rennie checked all the windows and doors to be certain they were locked. She wasn't overwrought, but she had the good sense to be cautious.

"Who would have thought my stint as a juror would result in this?"

"You didn't know the defendant was going to develop a crush on you."

"That word implies an innocent, almost childlike infatuation. This is far beyond that. This is . . ."

When she seemed at a loss for the right word, Wick summed it up. "Lozada."

"Even his name sounds menacing." In a subconscious gesture, she rubbed her arms as though she were chilled. "Did he honestly expect me to be flattered by his creepy attention?"

"Absolutely."

"How could he be that arrogant? He was on trial for murder. Capital murder that carried a death sentence. In that situation who could be thinking of romance?"

"No one who's rational. Only someone with Lozada's delusions of grandeur. He thinks of himself as the winning quarterback."

"In the Super Bowl for professional assassins."

"Something like that. He's one of the best at what he does. As far as we know he hasn't gone international, but why should he? He can make more money with less risk working out of Fort Worth, USA. Besides, most of the guys who do that kind of killing work deep undercover, which isn't Lozada's style. Why should he hassle with popping public officials and having entire governments and Interpol on his tail? He's a big fish in a relatively small pond."

"So what woman wouldn't welcome his attention. That's his thinking?"

"Exactly," he said. "Add to that his quest for the best. He grew up middle class. His only sibling was severely retarded and physically handicapped. His parents depleted their resources providing for him.

"So to Lozada, acquisitions are a big thing. He sees himself as a well-paid businessman who can recognize and afford the finest of everything. To complete the package, he wants a classy woman by his side."

"What about scorpions?"

"He collects them. Yeah, gives you the heebie-jeebies, doesn't it? They're sort of like his mascot. They're nocturnal, they kill their prey at night. He wouldn't collect anything like coins or stamps or even art because that would be too ordinary. He prides himself on being exceptional."

She tilted her head and regarded him thoughtfully. "You've analyzed him thoroughly, haven't you?"

"I haven't been idling my time away since leaving the department. Contrary to what Oren believes, I've been busy. I've collected everything on Lozada I could get my hands on."

"Such as?"

"Public-school records. He was psychologically profiled when he was in junior high school, roughly when his criminal career began. That's where I got most of the background stuff. His sociopathic behavior, the superiority complex, have been consistent throughout his life. I've studied him inside out. Psychologically speaking, I probably know him better than I know myself."

He paused, then said grimly, "One thing I didn't know

was that he was sleeping with Sally Horton. If I had, I would have warned her to stay away from him, and from me, and I'd have been watching my back that night. If he thinks you and I are lovers..." He didn't need to say more. "Sally Horton wasn't even important to him. You're very important, Rennie."

"And I've betrayed him with another man."

"That's how he'll see it. Don't underestimate the danger you're in. Oren has got cops and informers spreading juicy gossip about us. Lozada won't be able to tolerate our being together. You've cheated on him, and I've stolen one of his play-pretties."

"But I'm not his anything, except an obsession."

"If he *thinks* you're his, you're his."

"Over my dead body."

"I'd like to avoid that." He tipped up her chin so that they were looking directly at one another. "Say the word and I'll call Oren back, tell him we'll get Lozada by some other means, some way that doesn't put you in danger. I came here last night to warn you, to urge you to get far away until Lozada is out of the picture one way or the other."

"That could take a long time."

"I don't think so," he said, thinking again of the note he'd sent to Lozada last night.

"I'm already in danger, Wick. With or without you, I spurned him. Besides, I can't just up and leave my responsibilities. No, let me put it another way. I *won't*."

"All right then, how soon can you be ready?"

"You aren't thinking of leaving tonight?"

"As soon as you get packed."

"Packing isn't the issue. You're less than twenty-four

hours out of the hospital and you left days before you should have."

"I'm fine."

"You're not fine. Your back is stiff and sore. You can't walk across a room without grimacing. Imagine driving across the state. You have no stamina, and I'm still afraid of infection and pneumonia, both of which could be fatal. You might've popped some stitches."

"You said the incision looked fine."

"There are many more sutures inside than out. Promise me that at the first sign of tenderness in your abdomen, you'll tell me."

"I'll tell you. If I start feeling really rotten between here and Galveston, I'll stop at the nearest hospital."

"We're not leaving tonight," she said stubbornly. "I've deferred to you and Wesley on the police matters. But your health is my domain. We're going nowhere until you've had more rest. End of argument."

They shared the bed since he refused to leave her downstairs alone to sleep on the couch. He said, "It's a police matter to which you should defer. End of argument."

Being a true-blue gentleman, he kept his pants on and lay outside the covers. He dozed, but falling into a deep sleep just wasn't going to happen tonight, partially because he had slept so long during the day, partially because he was alert to every sound, partially because he was trying to think with the guile of Lozada, and partially because he was acutely aware of Rennie sleeping beside him.

The features of her face and the contours of her body had relaxed in sleep. One hand rested outside the covers, near him. It lay palm up, the slender fingers curved inward. It looked susceptible and defenseless, not like the strong, skilled hand of a surgeon. She was the most self-reliant and capable woman he'd ever met. He admired her accomplishments. But he also felt protective of her.

And he wanted to make love to her.

God, did he. He wanted to because . . . well, because he was a man and that was what men wanted to do with women. But it wasn't just that. His humor, charm, even anger, had failed to pierce her hard shell of self-containment. Dented it perhaps, but hadn't broken through. Would he be able to reach her if he penetrated her body? It was a provocative thought that left him agitated on several levels.

She shrank from his touch, but he didn't think it was because she disliked him. The reaction was a self-imposed conditioned reflex, part of that control she was so hung up on, a legacy of the Raymond Collier incident. Passion had landed her in a terrible fix. That didn't necessarily mean that she was any less passionate. She just no longer submitted to it.

In spite of her reserve, he could imagine her flushed with arousal. Today when he kissed her, for a few incredible seconds, it hadn't been all one-sided. She hadn't permitted herself to kiss him back, but she had wanted to. And that wasn't the pompous disclaimer of a braggart who'd kissed a lot of women.

He hadn't imagined that catch in her breath or that almost-but-not-quite surrendering of her tongue. Her skin had felt feverish even through her clothes. He hadn't had to coax a response from her, either. Two strokes of his thumb and her nipple was hard, ready to be drawn into his mouth.

He stifled a groan by pretending to clear his throat. Beside him, Rennie slept on, undisturbed and unaware of his misery. He rolled onto his side to face her. If she woke up and challenged him, he could truthfully claim that his back had begun to ache. He couldn't really see her anyway. It was too dark in the room.

But he could feel her soft breath, and he didn't need to see her in order to feed his fantasies. During those long nights of surveillance he'd had plenty of time to memorize the features of her face.

He summoned up the memory of her removing the dress she'd worn the night of the wedding. Were those inadequate patches of lavender lace the lingerie of a dispassionate woman? Hell no.

One by one, moving slowly, he undid the buttons of his fly. If she woke up now, she would raise the standard for freaking out, because his back wasn't all that was stiff. He was grateful that his sexual apparatus hadn't suffered permanent damage and had resumed full, operational capacity, but it seemed to be trying to prove itself better fit than before the injury.

That pressure having been relieved, he closed his eyes and willed himself if not to sleep, at least to clear his mind and rest. He would not remember how good that kiss had tasted, or how perfectly her breast had molded to his hand. He would not think of her, warm and soft, under the light covers, or of that sweet place where she would be even warmer and softer. Taking him in. Enveloping him.

A horse nickered, waking him with the impact of a clanging alarm clock. He lay perfectly still, eyes open, holding a lungful of air he didn't dare exhale for fear of missing another sound. He didn't have to wait long before hearing another equine snuffle.

The noises hadn't awakened Rennie. She continued to sleep soundly. Despite the soreness in his back, he came off the bed with the alacrity of a cat and picked up his pistol where he'd left it within easy reach on the nightstand. He tiptoed to the window, pressed himself against the adjacent wall, and leaned forward only far enough to look out.

He watched for several moments but detected no movement in the yard or in the clearing between the rear of the house and the barn, but instinct told him something was going on inside that building. Maybe a mouse had spooked one of the horses. Maybe the bobcat had a mate who'd come looking for him. Or maybe Lozada was paying them a call.

He crept across the bedroom and, after checking first to see that Rennie was still asleep, slipped from the room and moved soundlessly across the gallery. At the top of the stairs he paused to listen. He waited for a full sixty seconds but heard nothing except his own pulse beating against his eardrums.

He took the stairs as rapidly as possible but was mindful of creaking treads that would give away his presence. The living room appeared just as they'd left it several hours ago. Nothing had been disturbed. The front door was locked and bolted.

His pistol was cradled between raised hands as he approached the door leading into the kitchen. He hesitated, then sprang into the room and swept it with his outstretched hands. It was empty, as was the walk-in pantry.

He unlocked the back door and slipped through, walking in a ninety-degree crouch but still feeling exposed. He took cover behind the patio chair in which he'd sat earlier. It wasn't very substantial cover, but darkness also provided concealment. He blessed the skinny moon.

He waited and listened. Soon the unmistakable sounds

of movement came from within the barn. He slipped from behind the chair and covered the distance at a run. When he reached the barn, he flattened himself against the exterior wall, hoping to meld into its shadow. He also needed it for support. He was dizzy, out of breath, sweating profusely, and his back felt like he'd been impaled on a railroad spike.

That's what a few days in the hospital would do for you, he thought. Make you a weakling. Against any foe stronger than a pissant, he might be in trouble. But he had a pistol, and it was fully loaded, and, at the very least, he was going to give the bastard a fight.

He inched along the wall until he reached the wide door, where he stopped to listen. And what he heard bothered him, because he heard absolutely nothing. But the silence was heavy, not empty; he sensed another presence. He knew someone was in there. He knew it in his gut.

Whoever it was had stopped whatever he'd been doing. Something, maybe his own keen instinct, had alerted him to Wick's presence. He was now listening for Wick with the same intensity that Wick was listening for him.

The standoff stretched into its second minute. Nothing moved. There wasn't a sound. Even the horses had become completely still and silent inside their stalls. The atmosphere was thick with expectation. Wick felt the weight of it against his skin.

Acrid sweat ran into his eyes. It trickled down his rib cage and between his shoulder blades. It stung his incision. His hands, still gripping his pistol, were slippery with it. He reasoned he could either stand there and slowly dissolve or he could end it here, now.

"Lozada! Have you got balls enough to face me like a

man? Or are we gonna continue this silly game of hide-and-seek?"

Following a short silence, a voice came to him from the other side of the wall. "Threadgill?"

It wasn't Lozada. Lozada had refined his voice into a low-pitched purr. This one had the nasal intonation of a Texas native. "Identify yourself."

The man stepped from behind the wall into the opening. Wick's hands tensed around the pistol and kept it aimed at head level. Toby Robbins raised his hands. "Whoa, cowboy."

His easygoing manner didn't faze Wick. Cops had died when fooled by that. "What the hell are you doing sneaking around in the dark?"

"I could ask you the same thing, couldn't I? But since you're the one with the firearm, I'll be pleased to answer first. If you'll direct that thing somewhere else."

"Not until I hear why you're in Rennie's barn."

"I was checking on things."

"You gotta do better than that."

"Heard one of her horses got a nasty scratch from a bobcat."

"Who told you?"

"Game warden. I came to check it out, see if I ought to call the vet."

"At this time of night?"

Toby Robbins glanced toward the eastern horizon where by now the sky was blushing pink. "It's practically lunchtime."

Wick glanced toward the gate. It was closed and locked, no vehicle parked beyond it. "How'd you get here?"

"Walked."

He looked down at the man's feet. He was wearing athletic shoes rather than cowboy boots.

Robbins tapped the left side of his chest. "The cardiologist recommends at least three miles a day. That's about a round trip between our place and Rennie's. I like to get the miles in before it gets too hot."

Reluctantly Wick lowered the pistol and stuffed it into the waistband of his jeans. Or would have if they'd been buttoned. Hurriedly he did up his fly with one hand. "You know, Robbins, I ought to go ahead and shoot you just for being stupid. Why didn't you call first? Or turn on a light, for godsake?"

"The light switch is in the tack closet. It was locked. Rennie keeps an extra key above the door. I was looking for it when I heard you. Didn't know it was you. Thought it might be another bobcat."

Wick eyed the older man distrustfully. He didn't think he was lying, he just wasn't telling the whole truth. "Rennie told me she put antiseptic on the scratch and thought it would heal up in a day or two. If she had thought the horse needed a vet, she would have called one."

"Doesn't hurt to get a second opinion."

Robbins turned and reentered the barn. Despite his bare feet, Wick followed. As long as he stayed in the center aisle he would be okay. As stables went, Rennie's was as clean as an operating room.

Robbins went straight to the tack closet and ran his hand along the top of the doorjamb. He came away with a key. He unlocked the closet door, reached inside, and, an instant later, the overhead lights came on.

Paying no attention to Wick, he entered a stall, speaking softly to the mare as he moved in behind her. He located the scratch on the horse's rear leg, then hunkered down to examine it more closely.

When he'd finished, he left the stall, moving around Wick as though he were an inanimate object. He returned to the closet, switched off the lights, locked the closet door, and replaced the key where he'd found it.

Wick fell into step behind him. When they got outside, he said, "That scratched mare wasn't your only reason for coming over here this morning, was it?"

The older man stopped and turned. He gave Wick a look that could've scoured off paint, then he moved to the corral fence and leaned against it. For the longest time he kept his back to Wick and focused on the sunrise. Eventually he fished a small pouch of tobacco and rolling papers from the pocket of his plaid shirt that had white pearl snaps in lieu of buttons.

He spoke to Wick over his wide shoulder. "Smoke?"

"Sure."

Chapter 27

Robbins shook tobacco from the cloth pouch onto the strip of paper and carefully passed it to Wick, who tapped the tobacco into a straight line down the center of the paper, moistened the edge of it with his tongue, then tightly rolled it into a cigarette.

Robbins watched him with interest. Wick figured that by knowing how to roll his own he had elevated the cattleman's opinion of him. In the older man's eyes he had adequately performed a rite of passage.

Wick silently thanked the high school friend who'd taught him the skill by rolling joints—until Joe found out. After the beating he'd taken from Joe, he had decided that smoking anything was bad for his health.

Robbins rolled his own smoke. He struck a match and lit Wick's first, then his own. Their eyes met above the glare of the match. "This another of your cardiologist's recommendations?"

Robbins inhaled deeply. "Don't tell my wife."

It was damn strong tobacco. It stung Wick's lips, tongue, and throat, but he smoked it anyway, pretending to be a pro at it. "You weren't surprised to see me here."

"The game warden told me Rennie had company. I figured it was you."

"Why?"

Robbins shrugged and concentrated on his smoking.

"You came here this morning to check on Rennie, didn't you? See if she was okay."

"Something like that."

"Why would you think I'd harm her?"

The older man looked off into the distance for a moment before his unnerving gaze resettled on Wick. "You might not mean to."

Wick still resented the man's implication. "Rennie's a grown woman. She doesn't need a guardian. She can take care of herself."

"She's fragile."

Wick laughed, which caused him to choke on the strong smoke. To hell with this. He ground out the cigarette against a fence post. "Fragile isn't a word I would free-associate with Rennie Newton."

"Goes to show how ignorant you are then, doesn't it?"

"Look, Robbins, you don't know me from shit. You don't know anything about me. So don't go making snap judgments about me, okay? Not that I give a flying—"

"I knew her daddy."

The curt interruption silenced Wick. Robbins was giving him a look that said *Shut up and listen*. He backed down.

Robbins said, "Before I inherited this place from my folks, I lived in Dalton and did some work for T. Dan. He was a mean cuss."

"That seems to be the general consensus."

"He could be a charmer. He had a smile that didn't stop. Came on to you like he was your best friend. A glad-hander and backslapper. But make no mistake, he was always looking out for number one."

"We've all known people like that."

Robbins shook his head. "Not like T. Dan. He was in a class by himself." He took a last greedy drag on his cigarette, then dropped it on the ground and crushed it out with the toe of his shoe. The cross-trainers looked incongruous with his cowboy attire, with him. John Wayne in Nikes.

He turned to face the corral and propped his forearms on the top rail of the fence. Wick, hoping to have some light shed on Rennie's secrets, moved to stand beside him and assumed a similar pose. Robbins didn't acknowledge him except to continue talking.

"Rennie was a happy little kid, which is a wonder. T. Dan being her daddy and all."

"What about her mother?"

"Mrs. Newton was a nice lady. She did a lot of charity work, was active in the church. Hosted a big party every Christmas and did the house up real pretty. A Santa Claus handing out candy to the kids. Stuff like that. She kept T. Dan's house running smooth, but she knew her place. She didn't interfere with his life."

Wick got the picture. "But you said Rennie was happy."

Robbins gave one of his rare smiles. "Me and Corinne always felt a little sorry for her. She tried so hard to please everybody. Skinny as a rail. Towheaded. Eyes bigger than the rest of her face."

They still are, Wick thought.

"Smart as a whip. Polite and knew her manners. Mrs.

Newton had seen to that. And she could ride like a pro before she got to grade school." Robbins paused for several
moments before saying, "The hell of it was, she thought
her daddy hung the moon. She wanted so bad for him to
pay attention to her. Everything she did, she did to win T.
Dan's notice and approval."

He clasped his hands together and in the faint morning light studied the callused, rough skin on the knuckles
of this thumbs. Wick saw that one of his thumbnails was
completely dark from a recent bruise. He would likely lose
the nail.

"Everybody in Dalton knew T. Dan messed around. It
wasn't even a secret from Mrs. Newton. I figure she made
her peace with his womanizing early in the marriage. She
bore it with dignity, you might say. Ignored the gossip as
best she could. Put up a good front.

"But Rennie was just a kid. She didn't understand the
way it was supposed to be between a loving man and wife.
She didn't know any different, because her parents' marriage had always been the way it was. They were pleasant to
one another. Rennie wasn't old enough to realize that the
intimacy was missing."

He glanced over at Wick, and Wick knew it was to make
sure he was still paying attention. He was getting to the
crux of the story.

"Rennie was about twelve, I think. A rough time for a
girl, if my wife is any authority on the subject, and she
seems to be. Anyhow, Rennie surprised T. Dan in his office
one afternoon. Only she was the one who got the surprise."

"There was a woman with him."

"Under him, on the sofa in his office. Rennie's piano
teacher." He paused and stared straight into the new sun.

"That was the end of the happy childhood. Rennie wasn't a kid anymore."

Crystal, the waitress in Dalton, had told Wick that Rennie went hog wild about the time her female parts took form. But her emerging sexuality hadn't been the cause of her personality change at puberty. It had been the discovery of her father's adultery.

The rebellion made sense. Probably Mrs. Newton had been having mother-daughter talks with Rennie about sex and morality. Rennie had caught her father violating the principles her mother was trying to instill. The experience would have been disillusioning, especially since she worshiped her dad.

It was also a catalytic event. Her promiscuity as a teen had been a fitting punishment for her philandering father and for her mother who turned a blind eye it. The innocent girl had discovered her father in flagrante delicto with her piano teacher, and, as a consequence, became the town slut.

As though following Wick's train of thought, Robbins said, "These days they call it 'acting out.' So Corinne tells me. I think she heard the term on TV. Whatever they call it, Rennie changed overnight. Became a holy terror. Grades went to the cellar. For the next several years she was out of control. Nothing in the way of punishment seemed to take. She defied teachers, anyone with the least bit of authority. T. Dan and Mrs. Newton revoked privileges, but it didn't do any good."

"Her father gave her a red Mustang convertible," Wick said. "I call that sending a child mixed signals."

"She probably blackmailed him into getting her that automobile. Rennie knew she had the upper hand and she exercised it. T. Dan lost his parental authority when she

saw him humping her piano teacher. She was on a fast
track to hell."

"Until she was sixteen."

Robbins turned his head and looked at him. "You
know about Collier?"

"Some. I know Rennie fatally shot him. She was never
charged with a crime. It was never even investigated as a
crime. The whole thing was swept under the rug."

"T. Dan." Robbins said it as if the name alone summa-
rized the explanation.

"I can't say my heart bleeds for Raymond Collier," Wick
said. "What kind of scumbag has an affair with a sixteen-
year-old girl who obviously needed good parenting, strict
discipline, and counseling?"

"Don't be too quick to judge him. If Rennie set her cap
for a man, she was hard to resist."

Wick's eyes sharpened on Robbins, who shook his head
wryly. "No, not me. I was a Dutch uncle to her. I wanted to
scold her, knock some sense into her, not bed her. But it
was another story with Raymond Collier."

"What was he like?"

"I didn't know him well, but most folks seemed to like
him okay. Had a good head for business. That's why T. Dan
was partnering with him on a big commercial real estate
deal. But he had a weakness."

"Women."

"Not women. Only one. Rennie," the older man said
grimly. "He was obsessed with her. Like that James Mason
movie."

"*Lolita.*"

"Right. I guess she knew how Collier felt about her.
Sensed it, you know, the way women can. She—"

"Why didn't I get the memo for this meeting?"

Wick and Robbins turned in unison. Rennie was crossing the yard toward them. Her hair was still damp from her
shower, indicating that she had rushed to dress and join
them. "I saw you from the bedroom window. You've had
your heads together for a long time." Her eyes dropped to
the pistol tucked into his waistband.

"I nearly shot him." Wick tried to smile convincingly,
but his mind was still on everything Robbins had told him.

Robbins gave her one of his typically laconic explana-
tions for why he was there. "Heard you got that cat with
one shot straight through the heart. Folks around here
who've lost livestock will be thanking you."

"Do you think I should have called the vet to look at
Spats?"

"No," Robbins replied. "You were right. The wound
isn't deep, and it's clean. Should be closed up in no time."

Her eyes cut to Wick, then back to Robbins. "I'm going
to be away for a couple of days. Would you mind looking
after things until I get back?"

The old man hesitated long enough for it to be noticeable. Finally he said, "Happy to. Can I reach you at the
Fort Worth number if something comes up?"

"Galveston," Wick said. "I have a place down there. I'll
leave you the number." Rennie didn't seem too pleased
with him for sharing that.

"I'm going to check on Spats," she said. "I think she
should probably stay in her stall one more day, but I'll let
the others out into the corral."

"I'll be over this evening to put them up," Robbins told
her.

She headed toward the open door of the barn, then
glanced back as though expecting Robbins to follow her.

"Be right there," he told her. "I need to get that phone number."

"You can always reach me on my cell."

"Doesn't hurt to have two numbers. Just to be on the safe side."

She seemed reluctant to leave them alone again, but she turned and went into the barn. Wick looked at Robbins, but he wasn't sure he wanted to hear any more about Rennie's fatal seduction of Raymond Collier. "You've got something to add?"

"Yeah, I do," Robbins said. "There's something maybe you should know. It may not matter to you, but I hope it will."

When he hesitated, Wick gave an inquisitive shrug.

Robbins glanced over his shoulder toward the barn, then said in a low voice, "After that business with Collier, Rennie didn't pick up where she left off. She didn't go back to being the way she was before."

Wick didn't comment and waited him out.

"You're right, Threadgill, I don't know you from shit, but I know you're trouble. I read the newspapers. I watch TV. I don't much like you hanging around Rennie."

"Too bad. You don't get a vote."

"Especially with this character Lozada being involved."

"It's because of him that I'm hanging around."

"That the only reason?" His eyes bored into Wick's. "Me and Corinne have been looking after Rennie for a long time. We don't plan to stop now." He inclined his head, moving in closer. "You've got a big gun and a big mouth, but you're dumber than this fence post here if you don't get what I'm telling you."

"I'd get it if you'd say it straight out."

"All right. Rennie's worked hard to get where she's at

in her career. I've seen her take chances on horseback that seasoned cowboys and stunt riders wouldn't take. She flies off to the other side of the world, goes to places where there's fighting and God knows what kind of pestilence, and she never shows an ounce of fear.

"But," he said, taking a step closer, "I've never seen her in the company of a man. She's certainly never let one spend the night." He took in Wick's bare chest and made a point of looking down at the fly he had hurriedly buttoned. "I hope you're decent enough, man enough, to handle that responsibility."

When Rennie came in from the corral, Wick was watching coffee drip from the filter basket into the carafe. Barechested and barefoot, he was wearing only blue jeans. His handgun was lying on the counter next to the Mr. Coffee. None of this was compatible with her safe, familiar kitchen, and all of it was disconcerting.

"Is there something wrong with the coffeemaker?"

He shook his head with chagrin. "I'm just so anxious for it I've been counting the drips."

"Sounds good to me, too." She took two mugs from the cabinet.

"Spats okay?" he asked.

"Just as Toby said."

"He hates my guts."

She passed him a mug. "Don't be silly."

"I'm not. And my feelings aren't hurt. I'm just stating a fact. Did he go home?"

"He just left."

The last of the coffee gurgled into the carafe. Wick filled her mug, warning "It's cops' coffee. Strong."

"Doctors have the same kind." She sipped and gave him a thumbs-up.

"Robbins makes a very serious business out of looking after you. He warned me to keep my grubby paws off you."

"He said no such thing. I know he didn't."

"Not in so many words."

She took another few sips of her coffee, then set her mug on the counter. "Turn around and let me check your incision."

He turned, set the heels of his hands on the edge of the counter, and leaned forward. "Can't fool me. You just want to look at my ass."

"I've seen it."

"And?"

"I've seen better."

"Now *that* hurts my feelings."

The human body held few mysteries for Rennie. She had studied it, learned it, seen it in every condition, size, color, and shape. But yesterday when she saw all of Wick's body stretched out on her bed, it had made an impression. And not from a medical standpoint. His torso was long and lean, his limbs well proportioned. No body she had ever seen had the appeal of his, and she had struggled for professional detachment when she touched it.

She removed the old bandage and gently probed his incision. "Tender?"

"Only when you poke it. It's starting to itch."

"A sign of healing. A medical miracle considering your shortage of bed rest."

"When will you remove the stitches?"

"A few more days. Stay put and finish your coffee. I might just as well clean it during one of your rare periods of immobility."

"No more shots," he called to her as she left the room.

She retrieved the supplies from upstairs and was actually surprised to find him still in place when she returned. She told him so.

"Doctor's orders."

"Yes, but I can't believe you followed them. You're not exactly an ideal patient, Mr. Threadgill."

"Why are Toby and Corinne Robbins so protective of you?"

"They've known me since I was a little girl."

"So have a lot of other people in Dalton. I don't see anyone else hovering around you and warding off satyrs like me."

"I doubt Toby Robbins knows what a satyr is."

"But you do, don't you, Rennie?"

"You're not a satyr."

"Was Raymond Collier?"

He was baiting her, trying to get her to talk about it. She wasn't ready to talk about it. She doubted she would ever be ready to talk about it with Wick. Where would she even begin? With the day she had discovered her father's adultery? Could she make Wick understand how shattering it had been to realize the hypocrisy she'd been living with and stupidly accepting?

Or would she begin with Raymond? How he used to follow her. How his longing gaze had never strayed from her if they were in the same gathering of people, including his wife. How she had loathed his calf eyes and moist hands before she realized that she could use his obsession to punish her father. No, she couldn't talk about that with Wick.

"There," she said as she placed a new bandage over the

incision. "All done, and actually you were fairly cooperative this time."

Before she could move away, he took one of her hands
in each of his and pulled them around him, to the front of
his body, so that she was hugging him from behind.

"What are you doing, Wick?"

"Who was your ideal patient?"

She dismissed the question with a light laugh, something not easily accomplished with her breasts flattened
against his back, her hands splayed over the crisp hair on
his chest, and her center growing warm from the contact
with his rump.

He had covered her hands with his, holding them captive against him. His skin—not his epidermis, but his
skin—felt warm and vital against her palms. Beneath her
left hand she could feel the strong beating of his heart. For
someone accustomed to listening to hearts beat every day,
the rhythm of his had a strange effect on her. It was making her own beat faster against the strong muscles of his
back.

"Shouldn't we be preparing to leave, Wick? I thought
you were in a hurry to get away."

"Your ideal patient. I want to hear about him or her, or
we'll stand here until I do, and you know that I'm just stubborn enough to mean it." For emphasis he pressed down
on her arms at his sides, forcing a tighter hug.

In surrender, she rested her forehead in the shallow
depression between his shoulder blades. But it was far too
comfortable, far too nice, so it lasted for only a few brief
seconds before she raised her head.

"It was a she. A thirty-four-year-old woman. She was a
victim of the World Trade Center attack. I was in Philadel-

phia on September the eleventh, attending a conference. I drove straight to New York and arrived late that evening.

"She was one of the few who'd been pulled from the rubble still alive, but her injuries were severe and numerous. I worked on her internal injuries. A specialist amputated her leg. For twenty-four hours we didn't even know her name. She had no identification on her and wasn't lucid enough to tell us who she was. But subconsciously she knew she was being helped. Every time I took her hand, trying to let her know that she was safe, that someone was taking care of her, she would squeeze my hand.

"Finally, she regained consciousness enough to give us her name, which we matched with a family, one of thousands desperately seeking information. She was from Ohio and had been on a business trip. Her husband and three children had an emotional reunion with her in the hospital. In the midst of it, she looked at me. Her eyes spoke with such eloquence she didn't have to say anything."

At some point during the telling, she had rested her cheek against Wick's back. He was stroking the backs of her hands where they still rested on his chest. "You saved her life, Rennie."

"No," she said thickly. "I couldn't. She died two days later. She knew she was going to die. We had told her it was doubtful she could survive such massive damage. She was thanking me for extending her life long enough for her to see her family. She wanted to tell them good-bye. It took an act of will and tremendous courage for her to live even that long. Her love for them was stronger than her pain. So when you asked who my ideal patient was, she immediately came to mind."

Several moments elapsed before he said, "I think

you're incredible, Dr. Newton. No wonder the Robbinses think so highly of you."

She recognized the statement as a transition. He wanted to know about her relationship with Toby and Corinne, and this was his roundabout way of asking. What would be the harm in telling him that much? He probably knew anyway. It was possible that Toby had told him during their extended conversation at the corral fence and Wick wanted to hear her version of it.

This time when her forehead came to rest between his shoulder blades, she kept it there. "After Raymond Collier, my parents enrolled me in a boarding school in Dallas. The first Christmas I was there, they went to Europe. Mother didn't want to go, or so she claimed. But there was no arguing with T. Dan. As part of my punishment for the trouble I'd caused, I was left at school to spend the holiday alone.

"Somehow, Toby and Corinne found out. They showed up on Christmas morning. They brought their children, goodies, presents, and tried to make me happy. They've been seeing to my happiness ever since. If he comes across as overly protective, I think it's because he still sees me as a lonely abandoned girl on Christmas."

"What happened in your father's study that day, Rennie?"

She raised her head and withdrew her hands from beneath his. "If we're going to Galveston, we should be going."

He came around and took her by the shoulders. "What happened, Rennie?"

"Wesley will blame me for any delay" was her only answer.

"Did he rape you? Try?"

Angered by his tenacity, she flung off his hands. "God, you never give up!"

"Did he?"

"Isn't that what my father told the police?"

"Yes. And from what little I know of T. Dan Newton, lying would be the least of his sins. He'd lie to the police and smile while doing it. Now, what caused you to shoot Raymond Collier?"

"What does it matter?"

"It matters because I want to know, dammit! It matters because you're so damned and determined to keep the secret your daddy's money got buried. And it matters because I'm working on a two-day hard-on that I can't do anything about. Not without you accusing me of mauling you and getting death threats from your neighbor Toby."

He had backed her into a corner, literally—she was wedged into the right angle formed by intersecting cabinetry—and he had backed her into a corner emotionally. She came out fighting.

"Raymond never forced me to do anything. Not that afternoon. Not ever. If you want to invent a myth about attempted rape because that somehow sanitizes it in your mind and makes you feel better about me, then fine. But that's not the way it was.

"Raymond and T. Dan became partners on a land deal when I was fourteen. He started coming around a lot, spending time with us. I knew the impact I had on him. I teased him unmercifully. Under the guise of an affectionate older man, he seized every opportunity to touch me. I encouraged it and laughed about it later. He had this . . . this naked yearning that I thought was hilarious." She paused to take a breath. "Still think I'm 'incredible,' Wick? Just wait. There's more."

"Stop it, Rennie."

"Oh no, you wanted to know. You wanted relief for your hard-on. Well this ought to cure it. For two years I tormented that poor man. Then, about a week before that wretched day, I had a quarrel with my father. I don't even remember what I'd done, but he took away the keys to my car and grounded me for a month.

"So I got back at him by sleeping with his business partner. That's right, Wick. I called Raymond from a motel and told him that if he wanted me he could have me, but that he had to come right then. I was waiting for him."

She brushed tears of shame off her hot cheeks, but it was too late to stop now. The words continued to bubble out of her. "Raymond came to the motel and I went to bed with him. Just like I went to bed with all of them. Everything you've heard about Rennie Newton is true. You probably haven't heard a fraction of what there is to tell. Sometime when I haven't got a killer breathing down my neck, we'll get together and split a bottle of wine, and I'll detail for you all my sexual escapades. It'll be like telling ghost stories, only better.

"But this is the one story that seems to have you itching for the lowdown. And rightly so, because it was the worst thing I ever did. Daddy punished me, but I showed him, didn't I? I showed him but good."

Chapter 28

Reportedly, Wesley had been relieved to hear that she and Wick had passed the night safely and that there'd been no trace of Lozada. But since they'd left the ranch he had called Wick at half-hour intervals even though Wick had assured him he would be notified immediately if they spotted Lozada at any point on the long drive to Galveston.

Wick had insisted on taking his pickup, and he had insisted on driving. It would be a difficult and exhausting trip for him as a passenger. Driving would add more stress and strain, but she hadn't quarreled with him about it.

They avoided talking at all.

The tension between them since their last conversation was pulled so taut that one cross word could cause it to snap like an overextended rubber band. And Wick had resumed wearing one around his wrist.

She was staring out the passenger window looking disinterestedly at the scenery speeding by when his cell phone rang for the umpteenth time. "Jesus, Oren, give it a rest," he said.

"Extend to the detective my warmest regards," she said drolly.

"Yeah?"

Rennie sensed the change in Wick instantly. She turned away from the window and saw that his free hand had tightened around the steering wheel and his lips were set in a thin, straight line.

His voice, however, was incongruently pleasant. "Well, well, well, Ricky Roy. Haven't seen you in a while. Of course the last time we shared space I didn't exactly see you, did I?"

Just knowing that Lozada was on the other end of the call caused Rennie to shudder. The fear she'd felt that evening in her kitchen was still a fresh memory. Had he been brutal or raving, he wouldn't have frightened her nearly as much, but his complacency had been terrifying.

Wick steered the pickup off the highway. "I hate to be the one to break it to you, Ricky Roy, but backstabbing someone is really a chicken-shit thing to do." When the truck came to a full stop, he pushed the gear stick into Park. "But I'm as good as new now. Pity I can't say the same for Sally Horton. Sally Horton, asshole. You remember. The girl you killed the night you tried to kill me."

Rennie could hear Lozada's silky laughter coming through the phone. She unfastened her seat belt, moved closer to Wick, and motioned for him to hold the phone away from his ear so she could listen in.

"You must still be on mind-altering painkillers,

Threadgill," he said. "I don't know what you're talking about."

"Then let me clarify it. You're a cowardly woman killer."

Lozada was too clever to fall for such obvious baiting. "I read that you had barely survived an assault of some kind, and that you would have died if you hadn't received excellent emergency care."

"Rennie Newton is an excellent surgeon."

"A good fuck, too."

Rennie reacted as though she'd been struck. She looked at Wick but could only see herself reflected in the lenses of his sunglasses.

"Is she there with you now?" Lozada asked.

"If she weren't you wouldn't be calling me, would you?"

"Strange, isn't it? You and I sharing a woman. Although," he continued smoothly, "it's not surprising that Rennie is attracted to both of us. Danger turns her on. Like when her friend Dr. Howell died. She described to me the violent way he died, and during the telling she got wet."

Rennie made a lunging grab for the telephone, but Wick caught her wrist and pushed her hand away. He shook his head furiously.

"That was only the second time we were together," Lozada said. "She was a wild one that night. Even I could barely keep up with her."

"That doesn't surprise me," Wick said as though bored. "I always figured your murder weapons were substitutes for physical shortcomings."

Lozada tsked. "That was a cheap shot. Unworthy of even you."

"You're right. I should have come right out and called you an impotent slug-dick."

Lozada laughed. "It really bothers you that I had her first, doesn't it? I bet you wonder how you compare. I once made her come just by licking her nipples. Can you do that?"

Rennie covered her ears, but she could still hear Wick say, "You know, Ricky Roy, I'm beginning to think you're trying to come on to me with all this dirty talk. What's the point of this call anyway?"

She didn't hear what Lozada said, but Wick's response to it was, "Wrong. If you were finished with her, you wouldn't be making this call. You're jealous and can't stand it that she's with me now. Eat your heart out, asshole."

He clicked off, practically threw the phone up onto the dashboard, and cursed viciously.

"He's lying," she said gruffly.

He shifted the pickup into Drive and checked for oncoming traffic, then pulled back onto the highway.

"He's lying, Wick."

He still didn't acknowledge her.

"He's manipulating you, and you're letting him!"

He turned to her then and she could feel his eyes probing hers from behind the sunglasses. But all he said was "Buckle your seat belt."

Although he disliked Wick Threadgill hanging up on him, Lozada was chuckling as he clicked off his cell phone. The call had accomplished what he'd wanted. The only thing more gratifying would be to hear the conversation going on between them now. He would love to know if the seeds of doubt he'd planted had taken root in Threadgill's mind.

Rennie had probably been listening in. She would be denying everything and Threadgill would be finding her denials hard to believe. Especially since he knew all, if not more, of what Lozada's own investigation had uncovered about the young Rennie Newton.

In another life he might have been a cop, he thought philosophically. He definitely had the instincts of an undercover detective. He had turned these intuitive skills one hundred eighty degrees to serve his own needs, but he would have made as good an investigator as Oren Wesley or Joe Threadgill or little brother Wick. And, unlike them, he wasn't constrained by conscience or legality.

For instance, had the waitress at the Wagon Wheel Café in Dalton not been so cooperative, he might have followed her home and tortured answers out of her before killing her.

As it turned out, however, Crystal had been a gushing fountain of information. At first she had thought it curious that he was the second man in so many weeks to inquire about Rennie Newton.

"Funny that you're askin' 'bout her."

Lozada had picked at his plate of greasy enchiladas and said nonchalantly, "How so?"

"There was another fellow in here not long ago. I think it was a Sunday. He'd known her in college, he said. He was a real cutie pie." She winked. "Rennie missed out on him, same as she did on you, Mr. Tall, Dark, and Handsome."

"Thank you. What did the other guy look like?"

She had described Wick Threadgill from his mop of blond hair to his scuffed cowboy boots. When he told

Crystal that this dreamboat was a cop, she had been miffed. "Now *that* pisses me off," she exclaimed. "I fell for every word of his BS!"

He told her that Wick was an investigator for a sleazy medical malpractice lawyer. "His sole job is to dig up dirt on defending doctors." Crystal fell for the story just as she'd fallen for whatever line Threadgill had given her. "Don't blame yourself, Crystal. He can be very convincing."

"Dadgum right. Must've been those big blue eyes of his." Her gaze turned wary. "You some kind of investigator too?"

He gave her his best smile. "I'm a freelance writer. I'm doing an article on Dr. Newton. About her volunteer work in underprivileged countries."

"Well, if you ask me, all her volunteering won't make up for her past shenanigans," she said with a righteous sniff. Then for the next half hour she had regaled him with stories about the licentious Rennie Newton. "Don't guess we should've been surprised when she shot poor ol' Raymond."

Oh, yes, his trip to Dalton yesterday had been very worthwhile and informative. He had even come away with a complementary piece of chocolate meringue pie, packed up for carry-out.

Weenie Sawyer had come through for him. The threat with the scorpion had rendered all kinds of information, such as new and useful facts regarding Wick Threadgill, including the place of his last credit-card charge, which happened to be located in the town where, according to other computer data, Rennie Newton had been born and reared.

He had also learned how much property tax she paid

on her ranch in a neighboring county, that she was quite a horsewoman, and that she had competed in rodeo barrel racing in her hometown. That is, when she wasn't fucking for sport.

Now, feeling flush with the success of his phone call to the former cop, he turned up the volume on the CD player in his SUV and inhaled deeply, wondering when he would catch the first whiff of coastal air.

Wick unlocked the door and it swung open on rusty hinges. He motioned her inside. "Don't expect too much."

"It'll be fine."

"I don't earn a six-figure surgeon's salary."

"I said it's *fine.*"

"Kitchen's there. Bedroom and bath through there. Make yourself at home."

"I'd like to shower."

"I don't guarantee hot water. Clean towels—if there are any—will be in the cabinet above the commode."

Without another word she went through the door into the bedroom, closing it behind her. "Never mind, Your Highness, I'll bring in the bags by myself," he muttered.

He returned to the pickup, consciously telling himself to act naturally and not to look around for the police personnel posted to watch them. He hauled the two bags from the bed of the pickup, wincing at the pinching pain in his back.

Twice Rennie had offered to drive. The first time he had declined the offer and politely thanked her for the courtesy. The second time he had snapped at her. That was after Lozada's call, when their strained silence had

turned into hostile coexistence. The last three hours of
the trip had seemed like thirty. The tension had found
his weak spot and settled in. Every time he felt so much
as a twinge, he cursed Lozada.

With no regard for his guest's privacy, he pushed
open the bedroom door and went in. He could hear the
water pipes knocking in the bathroom. A naked and
soapy Rennie would be the best thing ever to grace that
sorry shower, but he'd be doing himself a favor not to
think about Rennie either naked or soapy or at all.

He tossed the bags onto the bed, then went to the bureau and opened the bottom drawer. Beneath a jumbled
pile of his oldest and most comfortable shorts he located
the mike and transmitter that had been planted there for
him. Wesley had told him where they would be hidden.
They would keep him in constant communication with
the surveillance team.

He inserted the earpiece and spoke into the minus-
cule microphone. "We're here."

"Ten-four. We see you."

"Who's this?"

"Peterson. I'm heading the operation."

"Threadgill."

"Pleased to meet you."

"Where are you?"

"Best you don't know," Peterson said. "Don't want to
tempt you into looking for me and giving us away."

"Hey, Wick, how was your trip?"

"Long. Who's this?"

"Plum."

"Hey, Plum. I didn't know Oren had sent down any of
his guys."

"It's a coordinated effort between Fort Worth and

Galveston PDs. Lozada was a suspect in a murder case here. Organized crime bigwig who was trying to get legalized gambling in here. Some said a church group hired Lozada."

"I'd vote for a competing organized crime bigwig."

"Me too," Plum said. "No church group could afford Lozada. Anyhow, it's an unsolved murder on their books down here, so they were willing to help us out."

"Glad to have you, Plum. Thank God it's you and not Thigpen."

"Kiss my ass, Threadgill."

"Oh, Jesus," Wick groaned. "Tell me no."

"And, while you're at it, kiss the doctor's sweet ass for me."

"I'd volunteer for that," said an anonymous voice.

"Animals," growled a distinctly female voice, obviously a policewoman.

Thigpen said, "Hey, Threadgill, leave the mike on. We want to hear everything."

"Okay, that's it," Peterson cut in sharply. "Shut up, all of you, unless you've got something to report."

"Bye-bye, boys and girls. Have fun," Wick taunted.

"Up yours," he heard Thigpen whisper.

He kept the earpiece in so he could hear their warnings, but he turned off the mike. Rennie emerged from the bathroom, wrapped in a towel. When she saw him, she pulled up short. "I forgot that my bag is still—" He motioned toward the bed. "Oh. Thank you."

He could have taken it to her. He didn't. He could have excused himself and left the room. He didn't. Instead, he let her cross the room and get her bag and carry it into the bathroom with her, which she did with amazing dignity for a woman who was wet from head to toe and covered only by one of his skimpy towels.

The rear view was just as good as the front, and he enjoyed the hell out of it, although he wondered uneasily if he was turning into a slimmer, cleaner version of Pigpen.

Wick was in the kitchen when Rennie rejoined him. "Did something die in here?"

He glanced at her over his shoulder. "An opened package of bologna. Found it in the bottom drawer of the fridge. Real slimy. Do you want to eat out or in, honey?"

"Whatever."

"No, you decide, sweetheart."

"All right, since you asked, I'd rather eat in so I don't have to dress up."

"Do you like steak?"

"Filet mignons."

"Naturally," he said as he added filets to what she had determined was a grocery list. "Only the best for you."

"Is this how you're going to be, Wick?"

He looked over at her and asked innocently. "How am I being?"

"Sarcastic. Snide. Because if so, I'm leaving. You, Wesley, and Lozada can go to the devil. I don't know why I consented to this. Lozada probably won't even show."

Wick turned away from her and stared through the salt-encrusted window. "You're wrong, Rennie. He'll show. I don't know how or when, but he'll show. You can count on it."

The dark conviction with which he spoke made her wish for a return of his sarcasm.

At least the solemn reminder of why they were there leveled the chip on his shoulder that had been there since the call from Lozada. He insisted that she go with him to the supermarket. As he ushered her to his pickup, he said, "Lovers on a getaway do chores and run errands together."

She was glad he had insisted she go along. The house was a dreary place, and she hadn't relished the thought of being there alone, anticipating an appearance by Lozada and knowing that she was under constant observation by undercover officers.

Even sitting in the passenger seat of Wick's truck she felt conspicuous. When they stopped for a traffic light she said, "I haven't noticed anyone watching us."

"They're there."

"Can they hear us?"

"Not if I don't engage the mike."

He had explained the tiny, clear earpiece he was wearing. "Are they saying anything now?"

"The blue van two cars back just passed us off to the gray Taurus over there signaling to turn left."

She forced herself not to look and instead leaned forward to change the station on the radio.

"Very good, Rennie."

"I'm trying." As she sat back she smiled at him. He surprised her by reaching across the seats and stroking her cheek with the backs of his fingers.

"What's that for?"

"For show. Just in case the cops aren't the only ones who have us in their sights."

That was an unnerving possibility, so she didn't protest when Wick threw an arm across her shoulders and stayed close as they walked from the parking lot into the store where he played the role of attentive and affectionate lover. He smiled at her a lot, and nudged her

shoulder playfully, and asked her opinion about everything he placed in the basket, and showed off for her by
juggling a trio of oranges.

They shared a cone of frozen yogurt, and when they
were in line to check out, he held a *Sports Illustrated* in
one hand and read an article while his other hand massaged her neck with the absentmindedness of someone
accustomed to doing it. Had she been observing them,
she would have been convinced that they were two people in love and comfortable with the relationship.

The sun was going down by the time they returned to
the house. "I'll start the charcoal. While it's smoldering,
let's go down to the water."

"I didn't think to bring a suit."

"Then I guess you'll have to skinny-dip."

She shot him a retiring look and headed for the bedroom. "I brought some shorts. They'll do."

When she came out a few minutes later, Wick had exchanged his jeans for a pair of baggy shorts with a stringy
hem. The low-slung shorts made his chest look even
wider, his waist more tapered. She made a point of not
looking at his tanned, muscled calves.

He, on the other hand, took one look at her and said
a soft but emphatic, "Damn."

Her face turned warm. She had changed into a black
knit top with thin straps and a pair of faded denim shorts.
The outfit—or perhaps Wick's reaction to it—made her
feel more self-conscious than she had wearing only the
towel.

"Let's go." He turned and headed for the door.

"What about those?" She pointed to the communication apparatus he'd left lying on the coffee table alongside his pistol.

"Shit. Almost forgot."

He had to put his shirt back on so he could clip the mike inside the collar and hide the thin cable to the ear-piece. He stuck his handgun into the waistband of the shorts. It was covered by his long shirttail.

Holding hands, they walked to the shore and waded into the strong tide of the Gulf. It was twilight. Only a few stragglers were on the beach. "Afraid of sharks?" he asked.

"In water this shallow?"

"That's where most attacks occur."

"Don't we have a better chance of getting struck by lightning?"

"Or getting popped by Lozada."

She tugged on his hand, pulling him to a stop. When he was facing her, she said, "He was lying, Wick. Those things he said were not true."

"Shh." Apparently someone was speaking to him through the earpiece. He pulled her into a close em-brace and nuzzled her neck. "There's a man moving at seven o clock, but don't turn around. Keep up the act. But if something happens, if all hell breaks loose, you hit the surf, Rennie. Got that?"

She nodded.

He angled back, but kept his hands loosely on her waist. The current surged against their legs. Their bodies swayed together. For balance, he assumed a wider stance, placing her feet between his. He kissed her cheek just beneath her ear. His hands moved down to her hips. Another wave caught them just behind the knees. Re-flexively she reached for him so she wouldn't lose her bal-ance. She could feel the tension in his biceps. He was playing his role well, but he was primed for action.

Then he said, "Not our man."

It had been a false alarm, but they remained as they were, with her hands resting on his upper arms and his on her bottom. Beneath her feet, the sand shifted with the current. She felt like she was losing ground and that the only solid thing in the universe at the moment was Wick's blue stare.

"He was lying, Wick."

"I know. I—"

"*Do* you?"

"For a few minutes there—"

"You believed him."

"Not really. Okay, for maybe half a second he had me going. He probably guessed that you were listening and said those things to embarrass you. But even if you weren't listening, he knew they would rile me. And they did. He got to me, and I acted like a jackass. I realized it about ninety seconds later, but was—"

"Too bull-headed to admit it."

"Am I allowed to complete a sentence here?"

"I'm sorry. What did you want to say?"

"I wanted to say that the way he talked about you is reason enough for me to want to kill him. And that . . ."

"What?"

"That I'm going to kiss you now and make it look like I mean it."

He dipped his head and settled his mouth on hers. His tongue slipped easily past her lips and moved against hers in what felt like a mating ritual, ancient and elemental. A wave took her unawares from behind and pushed her against him. Middles bumped together. And stayed.

"Oh man," he groaned. His fingers flexed tighter on her hips, held her firmly against him.

A burst of heat spread through her center. It all felt too good. So she pulled back. "Wick, I can't . . ." The words stuck in her throat. "I can't keep my balance."

He set her away from him. "That's enough for now anyway."

But as they walked back toward the house, his face was hard and set, his stride was long and angry, and she didn't believe for an instant that it had been enough.

Chapter 29

□□□□□□□□□□□

They were so ridiculously transparent.

Did those undercover yahoos think he wouldn't spot them? They might just as well be wearing neon vests. The stocky bitch and her hairy companion sweeping their metal detector across the sand. Please. And the fat guy fishing from the pier. His hat was too new and his technique too clumsy. The three guys and a girl having a tailgate cookout were working way too hard at having a good time. The others were just as obvious.

Lozada had spotted them all from the passenger seat of the realtor's van. She was fiftyish, friendly, and eager to please. He had seen the billboard advertising her as Galveston Island's most successful real estate broker. He had called her from his car.

Thanks to Weenie Sawyer's research, he knew the location of Wick's house. He mentioned the vicinity to the realtor as an area where he was interested in buying a lot on which to build a beach house for his wife and four children. He had requested a late evening appointment. They had met at her office and she had driven him here in one of the company's vans. The logo painted on the side was a familiar sight; it was plastered all over the island. Police wouldn't give the van a second glance.

Now, while she prattled on about the excellent investment opportunities of beachfront property, Lozada picked out the cops on the beach.

He dismissed them as insignificant amateurs and focused on Rennie and Wick. Walking in the surf. Holding hands. How sweet. How romantic. All staged to draw him out and slap him with some trumped-up charge.

But what really rankled was that this newfound romance of theirs wasn't just a futile police operation, as he had originally thought. It was real and, as such, it was an affront. His blood pressure soared when he saw Wick groping her. Even from this distance he could tell their kiss wasn't playacting. Which only affirmed that Rennie was a whore.

She had been a whore from her youth. She had spread her legs for every lout in that miserable little town where she'd grown up, and now she was spreading them for Wick Threadgill, days after Lozada had professed his affection. He sorely regretted that now. Why hadn't he realized sooner that she was a whore, undeserving of him and his attention?

He had been tricked by her. During his trial she had noticed his attraction and had played games with him. She had used her cool, aloof demeanor to taunt him and make herself desirable.

Well he didn't want her anymore. She had proved herself unworthy.

Oh, he still wanted to fuck her. And when he did, he

would make it hurt. By the time he got through with her she would understand that nobody toyed with Lozada and got away with it. Maybe he would force Threadgill to watch. Oh, yes. Threadgill would pay dearly for taking what Lozada had claimed as his.

"Mr. Smith?"

"Yes?"

"I asked if you had prearranged financing."

He'd almost forgotten that the realtor was there. He turned to her and thought seriously about snapping her neck. Quickly and painlessly she would be dead and he would have let off some steam. But he had never let spontaneity overrule sound judgment. He was better disciplined than that.

Answering as the mild-mannered Mr. Smith, he said, "Financing would be no problem."

"Excellent." She launched into the next phase of her sales pitch.

He would have to wrap up this appointment soon. From the safety of the van he had seen everything he needed to see. Twilight had turned into full-blown darkness, his favorite time. He looked forward to the busy night ahead.

"How was your steak?"

"Perfect."

"Glad you liked it." Wick propped his forearms on the edge of the table and rolled the glass of wine between his palms. "The Merlot was a good choice."

"Yes, it was."

"Can't say much for the glass." His collection of mismatched glassware hadn't included wine balloons, so they'd drunk from juice glasses.

"I didn't mind."

He swirled the ruby liquid in the glass. "Know what I think?"

"What?"

"If this were a blind date, it would be a bust."

She smiled ruefully. "It's hard to make casual conversation when you're on display. I feel like a goldfish."

They had sat out on the deck while the steaks were grilling and the potatoes were baking on the coals. They had sipped wine, said little, listened to the swish of the surf.

The glider had squeaked each time Rennie's bare foot gave it a gentle push. Those shorts made her legs look about nine miles long. There were small dots of salt on her thighs where splashes of seawater had dried. Wick's attention had often strayed there.

A young dog had wandered up to the deck, no doubt attracted by the aroma of the cooking meat. She got down on his level, scratched him behind the ears, and laughed the laugh of a child when he tried to lick her face. She played with him until his master whistled sharply. He charged off obediently, but then stopped and looked back at her wistfully, as though he hated to leave her, before disappearing into the darkness to rejoin his owner.

About every five minutes the undercovers would check in with Peterson, one by one. He could hear them in his earpiece. If Lozada was anywhere on Galveston Island, he was remaining invisible. He wasn't registered at any hotel, motel, or bed-and-breakfast. Wick wasn't surprised.

Peterson gave him signals to send them. "If y'all are okay in there, scratch your nose." Put your right hand in your pocket. Stretch. Stuff like that. But it reached the point where he could tune out the voices in his ear. If an emergency arose, he would react appropriately, but for the time being he minded the bacon-wrapped filets and spent the rest of the time looking at Rennie.

When the steaks were done, they brought the meal indoors. Once while they were eating, her bare foot had made contact with his calf beneath the table. She hadn't excused herself for the accidental touch, which was progress of a sort. But she hadn't acknowledged it either. She pretended it hadn't happened.

She had discovered a yellowed candle in a drawer and had placed it on a saucer in the center of the table to create a romantic atmosphere and help obscure the ugliness of his kitchen. But the only thing the candlelight really enhanced and made look good was Rennie.

When her hair was loose, like now, she had a habit of combing her fingers through it. She wasn't even conscious of doing it, but he was conscious of it because he liked watching it sift through her fingers and fall back onto her shoulders. *Liquid moonlight*, he thought, and wondered when he'd become a poet.

The candlelight deepened the triangular shadow at the base of her throat and the cleft between her breasts. Throughout the evening he had tried to ignore the shape they gave the fitted black knit top, but some things were beyond human endurance, and for him, that was one.

The meal had been satisfying and tasty. His stomach was full, but another hunger gnawed at him. He should have known better than to kiss her again. It had been unnecessary. It had been overkill. Their little sunset stroll in the surf would have been just as romantic a scene without the kiss. The only thing it had accomplished was to make him want her with an ache that was damn near killing him.

She drained the wine from her juice glass and looked across at him. "You're staring."

"I'm trying to get my fill."

"Your fill?"

"Of you," he said. "Of looking at you. Because once this is over, however it comes down, you're going to return to your life, and I'm not going to be in it. Am I, Rennie?"

Slowly, she shook her head no.

"That's why I'm staring."

She pushed back her chair and picked up her place setting, but as she passed him on her way to the sink he reached out and caught her arm.

"Relax, Rennie. You may get lucky. Lozada could kill me."

She yanked her arm free, carried the dishes to the sink, and set them down hard. "That was a horrible thing to say."

"You'd care?"

"Of course I'd care!"

"Oh, right, right. You're in the lifesaving business, aren't you? Which I find odd . . . since you court death."

She laughed shortly. "I court death?"

"All the time. You're reckless. You take unnecessary risks."

"What in the hell are you talking about?"

"No alarm system in either of your houses. Downright foolish for a woman who lives alone. Riding bareback and jumping fences. Dangerous no matter how skilled an equestrian you are. Going to places in the world where every day is a field day to the Grim Reaper. You flirt with him, Rennie."

"You've had too much wine."

He stood and joined her near the sink. "You don't live life, Rennie, you defy it."

"You're either drunk or crazy."

"No, I'm *right.* Self-sufficient Rennie, that's you. No friends or confidantes. No socializing. No nothing except those goddamn invisible walls you erect every time someone gets too close.

"You even keep your patients at arm's length. Isn't that why you chose surgery over another field of medicine? Because your patients are unconscious? You can treat them, heal them, without any emotional involvement on your part."

Peterson asked into the earpiece, "Hey, Threadgill, everything all right in there?"

"He's famous for losing it," Thigpen said.

"I'd like to know what he's saying to her," the policewoman said. "I don't like his stance."

Wick ignored them. "You shower affection on your horses. You turn to mush over a puppy dog. You mourn a wild animal you were forced to put down. But if you make skin contact with another human being, you either ignore it or run from it."

"That's not true."

"Oh, it's not?"

"No."

"Prove it."

He bent over the table and blew out the candle, pitching the kitchen into darkness. He yanked out the earpiece, then, curving an arm around her waist, pulled her against him.

"Wick, no."

"Prove me wrong." His lips hovered above hers, giving her an opportunity to protest again. When she didn't, he kissed her. Tempering his anger, he gently rubbed her lips apart then went seeking her tongue with his. When they touched, he deepened the kiss. He fit himself into the vee of her thighs.

She pulled her mouth free and turned her face away. "Wick . . ."

He trailed kisses down the column of her throat, lightly nipping her skin with his teeth.

She placed her hands on his shoulders and dug her fingers in. "Please."

"I could say the same thing, Rennie."

He lowered his head and kissed the swell of her breast above her neckline.

"No." She pushed him hard.

Wick's arms fell to his sides. He backed away from her. Their harsh breathing soughed through the darkness. He heard Peterson cursing him through the earpiece where it dangled on his chest.

He tried to keep his anger in check, but arousal had fueled it and there was no putting it down yet. With a distinct edge, he said, "I just don't get it."

"What don't you get?"

"Why you keep saying no."

"I have the option of saying no."

A growl of frustration rose out of his throat. "It's so goddamn good, Rennie. What's not to like?"

"I do like it."

Thinking he hadn't heard her correctly, he reached for the wall switch and turned on the lights. "What?"

She blinked against the sudden glare, then met his bewildered gaze. She said huskily, "I never said I didn't like it."

He stared at her with such profound incomprehension

that it didn't even register with him that a cell phone was ringing until she asked, "Is that yours?"

He groped for the phone clipped to his waistband and then shook his head. "Must be yours."

She went to get her phone. Wick reinserted the earpiece and caught the tail end of a blistering condemnation. He switched on the microphone. "Calm down, Peterson. We're fine."

"What's going on, Threadgill?"

"Nothing. A little electrical problem when we tried to turn on the lights. A fuse or something."

"Everything's all right?"

"Yeah, I'm about to wash the dishes and Rennie's talking on her—"

He broke off when he turned and read the expression on her face. "Hold on, guys. Someone just called her on her cell."

She was holding on to the small phone with both hands. She listened for possibly fifteen seconds more, then slowly lowered it and disconnected.

"Lozada?" Wick asked. She nodded. "Son of a—what did he say?"

"He's here."

"He told you that?"

She raised her hand to her throat in a subconsciously self-protective gesture. "He didn't have to. He let me know that he had seen us."

"Are you guys getting this?" Wick asked into the mike. After receiving acknowledgments through the earpiece, he motioned for Rennie to proceed.

"He said that I should wear black more often. That it was a good color for me. He asked if you could cook a decent steak."

"He's that close?"

"Apparently."

"What else?"

She looked at him meaningfully, with appeal. Slowly he raised his hand and switched off the mike. There would be hell to pay later, but he was more concerned about Rennie than he was about having the Galveston PD miffed at him.

"They're raising bloody hell in my ear, but they can't hear you. Go ahead. Tell me what he said."

"He said . . . vulgar things. About you and me. Us. Together."

"Like the things he said earlier today?"

"Worse. He said that before I . . . before I . . ." She crossed her arms over her middle and hugged her elbows. "Paraphrasing, he said that before I become too enamored of you, I should ask how you fucked up the investigation of your brother's murder."

"She was too embarrassed to give it to me word for word. I imagine it was awfully crude."

Oren was so tired his eyeballs hurt. He massaged them as he listened to Wick's account of Lozada's most recent contact with them.

"He brought up the investigation of Joe's murder and how I botched it because, like earlier today when he lied about Rennie and him being lovers, he's trying to cause a rift between us."

"Is it working?"

"Not in that sense, but we're both a little frayed around the edges. She's in the shower now. Her second since we got here. She's clean, I'll give her that."

"I'm more interested in Lozada's whereabouts than in

Dr. Newton's hygiene. None of those undercovers spotted him?"

"Neither hide nor hair."

"How could he get close enough to watch you cooking steaks without them seeing him? Binoculars, I guess."

"Or he could be buried in sand up to his eyeballs ten feet from the front door. With Lozada you can't rule out anything. He's not going to be caught by following procedure. Peterson seems competent enough, but—"

"You're not cooperating."

"He said I'm not cooperating?"

"You're taking offense?"

"I don't like being tattled on like I'm a kid."

"Then stop acting like one. He said you rarely leave the mike on and only have the earpiece in about half the time."

"I have it in *at least* half the time."

"You joke? Those people down there have put their lives on the line for you," Oren said angrily. "Keep in mind that if Lozada's that close to you, he's probably marked them."

Oren heard him sigh heavily. "I know, I thought about that. And I'm not joking. Really. I appreciate what they're doing, and that's no bullshit."

"It wouldn't hurt to tell them that."

"I'll make it a priority."

"It may be that Lozada has spotted them and they're the only reason he hasn't attempted something."

"I thought of that too," Wick said.

"One thing puzzles me."

"Just one?"

"Why the phone calls? This isn't Lozada's MO. It seems

out of character for him, almost careless. He's never warned a victim before."

Wick thought about it for a moment. "This time he isn't doing it for the money. It's not a job, it's personal."

Grace stuck her head through the door and looked at him inquisitively. He motioned her in. She sat near him on the sofa and laid her head on his shoulder. He lifted her hand to his lips and kissed it. He died a little every time he thought of what Lozada could have done to her had he chosen to.

Into the phone he said, "Well, at least we know he's in Galveston. An APB has already been issued."

"I hope they've been warned to approach with caution. What will he be arrested for?"

"Since he made that call today and it was obscene, both you and Dr. Newton can testify to his stalking her. If we can find him, we can bring him in on that."

"It's a flimsy charge, Oren."

"But it's all we've got."

"Okay, I'm gonna go smooth Peterson's feathers now," Wick said. "Over and out."

After hanging up, Oren filled Grace in on the latest development.

"How's Dr. Newton handling it?"

"He says she's okay. Clean."

"He likes her."

"He likes her looks."

"More than that. I think he might have really fallen this time."

"In love?" he scoffed. "What else is new? Wick's been in love with every woman he's ever taken to bed. His love affairs begin with an erection and end with a climax."

"And that makes him unique?" she said, laughing. "That speaks for most men."

"Not me."

"You're not most men."

He kissed her hand again. "I miss the girls."

"Me too. I talked to them this afternoon. They're having a great time. Mom's keeping them entertained, but they miss their friends and are already asking how many more days until they can come home."

"No time soon, Grace. If there's a chance in hell that Lozada—"

"I know," she said, patting his chest. "And I agree completely. I explained it to them."

"Did they understand?"

"Maybe not completely, but when they're parents they will. Now come to bed."

"I can't sleep now. I gotta go back to the office."

She stood up and tugged on his hand. "Since when is sleep all we do in bed?"

"Sorry, hon. I'm too tired to be any good in that department."

She leaned down and kissed him, saying sexily, "Leave everything to me."

"The policewoman's in the kitchen."

"She and I had a heart-to-heart. We won't be disturbed unless it's an emergency."

He was tempted, but he checked his wristwatch and frowned. "I promised to be back in half an hour."

Grace smiled and reached for him. "Hmm, I do love a challenge."

It was forty-five minutes before he returned to his desk at headquarters, and, although he hadn't even napped, he

felt considerably refreshed after thirty minutes in bed with
Grace. God, he loved that woman.

He knew before asking that there had been no further
word from Galveston. Had there been, he would have
been called or paged. But he asked anyway. "Nothing," another detective reported. "But there's a guy been waiting
here to see you."

"What guy?"

"Over there."

The unkempt, bespeckled individual sitting in the
chair in the corner with his shoulders hunched was gnawing on his index finger cuticle as though it were going to
be his last meal.

"What's he want?" Oren asked.

"Wouldn't say."

"Why me?"

"Wouldn't say that either. Insisted on talking to you
and only you."

Oren looked at the man again, but he was certain he'd
never seen him before. Surely he would have remembered. "What's his name?"

"Get this. Weenie Sawyer."

Chapter 30

Rennie came up on one elbow. For the past half hour Wick had been standing at the bedroom window, looking out. Motionless, he stood with one arm propped just above his head on the window jamb, the other hanging loosely at his side. In that hand he held his pistol. His weight was shifted to his left foot, favoring his right side. His shorts rode low on his hips. The bandage over his incision showed up very white in the dark room.

"Is something wrong?" she whispered.

He looked at her over his shoulder. "No. Sorry I disturbed you."

"Did you hear—"

"No, nothing." He walked back to the bed and set his pistol on the table. "Other than the periodic check-ins by the undercovers, it's been quiet."

"No word about Lozada?"

"No word. I wish the son of a bitch would show himself and get it over with. This waiting is driving me nuts." He lay down beside her and stacked his hands behind his head.

"What time is it?" she asked.

"Still an hour before sunrise. Were you able to sleep?"

"I dozed."

"That was about it for me, too."

For the sake of the microphone that hung loosely on his chest, he was lying, just as she was. They had lain side by side all night, silent and tense, each fully aware that the other was awake but, for their individual reasons, not daring to acknowledge it.

"You should get some sleep, Rennie."

"I learned to live on very little my first year of internship. It scares me now to think of how many patients I treated while virtually asleep on my feet."

"Did you always know you wanted to be a doctor?"

"No. Actually it wasn't until my second year in college that I decided to go pre-med."

"Why then?"

"It sounds banal."

"You wanted to help your fellow man?"

"I told you it sounded banal."

"Only if you're a beauty pageant contestant."

She laughed softly.

"I don't think it's a trite explanation at all," he continued. "That's the reason I wanted to be a cop."

"I would have thought you wanted to follow in your big brother's footsteps."

"That too."

"It was a good career choice, Wick."

"You think?"

"I can't see you sitting behind a desk for eight hours a day. Eight minutes a day. I should have known you were lying when you tried to pass yourself off as a computer software salesman."

"Sorry about that."

"You had a job to do."

"I still do."

Which brought them around to the subject of Lozada again. She rolled onto her side to face him. "What do you think he'll do?"

"Honestly?"

"Please."

"I don't have the slightest idea."

"What about Detective Wesley?"

"Oren doesn't know either. I've been studying Lozada for years, but the only thing I know with any certainty is that when he strikes, we won't see it coming. It'll be like the sting from one of his scorpions. We won't see it coming."

"Chilling thought."

"Damn right it is. That's what makes him so good." They were quiet for a time, then he turned his head and looked across at her. "Did he sexually abuse you, Rennie?"

"He tore my shirt open to see if I was wearing a wire. He thought—"

"Not Lozada." With a deliberate motion, he switched off the mike. "T. Dan."

"What? No! Never."

"Anyone?"

"No. What made you think that?"

"Sometimes when girls turn promiscuous in their teens it's because they've been abused as children."

She smiled sadly. "Stop trying to find justification for my misdeeds, Wick. There is none."

"I'm not trying to justify them, Rennie. Any more than

I'd try to justify why I attempted to nail every girl I possibly could. And did."

"The rules are different for boys."

"They shouldn't be."

"No, but they are."

"Not in my rule book. Believe me, I'm in no position to cast the first stone, or even to visit the rock pile." He slid his hand from beneath his head and reached for one of hers. "What I'm having trouble understanding is why you're punishing yourself for things you did twenty years ago."

"What's the statute of limitations on self-chastisement?"

"Pardon?"

"How long since Joe's murder?"

He released her hand and bounded off the bed. "Not the same."

"No, it's not. But it's relevant."

He propped his hands on his hips. "Lozada sparked your curiosity. Is that it? He warned that before you . . . how was it you paraphrased? Before you become too enamored of me, you—"

"Before I take it up the ass. That's what he said."

He dropped the belligerent pose, sighed, and raked his fingers through his hair. He sat down on the edge of the mattress with his back to her and propped his forearms on his knees. Head lowered, he massaged his forehead. "I'm sorry, Rennie. You shouldn't have had to listen to that." He added quietly, "And I shouldn't have made you repeat it."

"Doesn't matter. My reason for asking about Joe has nothing to do with Lozada."

"I know."

"What happened when he was killed?"

He took a deep breath, releasing it on a long, slow exhalation. "At first I was too stunned to think. I couldn't take it in, you know? Joe was dead. My brother was gone. Forever. He'd been there all my life. And suddenly he was a body in the morgue with a tag on his toe. It seemed"— he spread his hands as though trying to grasp the right word—"unreal."

He stood up and began pacing the length of the bed. "It didn't really sink in until the funeral two days later. In the meantime, Oren was working around the clock, despite his own grief, trying to build a case against Lozada. He had the CSU turn over every pebble in that parking lot, look under every blade of grass in the adjacent lawn, in a search to find anything that could remotely be tied to Lozada. Before Oren could obtain a search warrant or have just cause even to bring him in for questioning, he needed something, a shred of evidence that would place Lozada at the scene.

"Then just before the funeral, Oren told me they'd finally found something. A silk thread. A single thread, maroon in color, no more than two inches long, had been found at the scene. The lab had already analyzed it and determined that it came from very expensive goods, the kind sold in this area only in the most exclusive stores. The kind Lozada wore. If they could find a garment made of that fabric in his wardrobe, they'd have him.

"The turnout for the funeral was incredible. Cops show up to honor fallen cops, you know. There wasn't enough room in the church to accommodate the crowd. The church choir sang, and angels couldn't have done it better. The eulogies were unbelievably moving. The minister's message was comforting.

"But I didn't hear a word of it. None of it. Not the

songs, the eulogies, the message about eternal life. All I could think about was that incriminating silk thread."

He had made his way back to the window and resumed his original pose, staring out toward the ocean. "I lasted through the grave-site service, the final prayer, the twenty-one-gun salute. Grace and Oren hosted the wake. More than a hundred people crowded into their house, so it wasn't hard for me to slip out unnoticed. This was before Trinity Tower. Lozada lived in a house near the TCU campus. I busted in, even though he was there at the time.

"You can probably guess what happened. I tore his place to pieces. Ripped through his closet like a madman. Upended drawers. Ransacked the whole house. And you know what he was doing all that time? Laughing. Laughing his ass off because he knew I was destroying any chance we had of bringing him to trial for Joe's murder.

"When I didn't turn up the piece of clothing I had hoped to find, I went after him. That scar above his eye? Courtesy of me. He wears it proudly because it signifies his biggest victory. To me it represents my lowest point. I honestly believe I would have killed him if Oren hadn't shown up and physically pulled me off him. I owe Oren my thanks—and my life—for that. And the only reason Lozada didn't kill me and claim self-defense is because he knew the torture it was going to be for me to live with this."

He came around slowly and his eyes connected with hers through the darkness. "You have me to thank for all the trouble Lozada's caused you. If I hadn't lost my temper along with my sanity, he would be on death row and you wouldn't be in this mess."

He chuckled softly and spread his arms to encompass the small room. "And I wouldn't be in this one. I wouldn't be living in a hovel, licking my wounds and wearing a rubber band around my wrist to ward off panic attacks like a—"

"Human being," she said, interrupting. "You said it yourself, Wick. A lot of shit happened to you all at once. Everything you felt, everything you feel now, is human."

"Well, sometimes I'm a little too human for my own good." He gave her a weak smile and she returned it. Then he grimaced and swore softly. Reaching for the microphone, he switched it on. "Yes, I hear you. Jesus, do you think I'm deaf? What's up?" He listened for a moment then said, "Nothing here either. I'm coming out to get some air. Don't shoot me."

He moved past her to retrieve his pistol and cell phone, then headed for the door. "I'll be right outside. If you hear or see anything, holler."

Sleep was out of the question, so she dressed and was in the kitchen making coffee when he came back in. He was moving quickly. His expression was purposeful.

"What's the matter?"

"We're leaving, Rennie. Now. Get dressed." Then he saw that she was already dressed. "Get your things together. Hurry."

"Where are we going? What's happened?"

He kept moving, through the kitchen, through the living room and into the bedroom where he began stuffing discarded clothing back into his duffel. "Wick! Tell me. What's going on? Has Lozada done something?"

"Yeah. But not in Galveston."

He told her nothing more because he didn't know anything more.

Oren had called him on his cell phone while he was outside breathing in sea air in an attempt to clear his head and his conscience. Telling Rennie about his fuckup had left him with a mixed bag of feelings.

On the one hand, it had been cathartic to talk about it. She was a damn good listener. On the other, talking about it had reminded him that he was the idiot who had secured Lozada's freedom. He would carry the guilt of that until Lozada was behind bars. Or, better, dead.

Knowing that Lozada was out there mocking his futility made him feel incompetent. Oren's call had left him feeling powerless.

"We don't believe Lozada's still in Galveston," Oren had said.

"Why not?"

"We have good reason to believe he's no longer there."

"What's with the prepared speech and double talk? This isn't a press conference. What's up?"

"Do you have access to Dr. Newton's cell phone?"

"Why?"

"For the next few hours, it might be best if she didn't receive any phone calls."

"Why?"

"Let me sort this out and I'll get back to you."

"Sort what out?"

"I can't tell you until I sort it out."

"What do you mean you can't tell me? Where are you?"

"Ever heard of a Weenie Sawyer?"

"Who the devil—"

"Ever heard of him?"

"No! Who is he?"

"Never mind that now. It can keep. You stay put. Keep the doctor occupied. Have a picnic on the beach or something. Peterson's going to keep his people in place just in case we're wrong. I've got to go now, but I'll be in touch."

"Oren—"

He had hung up and when Wick tried to dial him back, his line was busy. He called the Homicide Division and was told that Oren couldn't be reached but he would be given a message.

He had deliberated for maybe ten full seconds before he returned to the house and alerted Rennie that they were leaving immediately. *Picnic on the beach, my ass,* he thought. If the FWPD was closing in on Lozada, he wanted to be in on the action, although he couldn't blame Oren for wanting to keep him away until it was a done deal.

Maybe it wasn't so smart to drag Rennie along, but what if Oren *were* wrong and Lozada was still in Galveston? It was possible that Lozada had duped them into thinking he'd left Galveston for just that purpose, to lure Wick back to Fort Worth and clear his way to Rennie. Wick didn't have enough confidence in Peterson and his crew to protect her. He certainly wouldn't entrust her to Thigpen. Which left him no alternative but to take her back with him.

Why had Oren suggested that he confiscate her cell phone? Knowing his partner must have a good reason for such a strange request, Wick had placed it in his duffel bag while she was in the bathroom. She didn't miss it until they were on the far side of Houston and heading north up I-45.

"I think you had it with you in the kitchen," he lied.

"I'm always so conscientious about keeping it with me. How could I have left it?"

"It's too late now to go back for it."

About every ten miles, she questioned him about the phone call that had prompted them to leave so abruptly. "Wesley didn't tell you anything else?"

"Nothing else."

"Only that he doesn't think Lozada is still in Galveston."

"That's what he said."

"We know he was there last night."

"I guess he could have made a quick round trip. He could have left sometime after calling you."

"And Wesley said nothing else?"

"Rennie, what he said to me hasn't changed since the last ninety-nine times you've asked."

"So where are we going?"

"To your ranch. I'll drop you there. Make sure Toby Robbins is available to keep an eye on you. Then I'll go into Fort Worth and find out what the hell is going on."

"You can take me to the ranch, but only so I can get my Jeep. I'll drive myself to Fort Worth."

"No way. You stay where—"

"I have work to do."

"Bullshit. You're on vacation, remember?"

"I'm going back."

"We'll argue about it when we get there."

The argument never took place.

When they arrived at her ranch a little before noon, they were shocked to see several vehicles, including a sheriff's squad car, parked inside her gate. Wick recognized Toby Robbins's pickup among them.

"What in the world is going on?"

"Stay in the truck, Rennie."

Of course she didn't. Before he could stop her, she was out of the pickup and running toward the gaping barn door.

"Rennie!" He bolted out his own door. But when his feet hit the ground, a pain knifed through his back. It took his breath for a second, but he struck out after Rennie in a hobbling run. She had too much of a head start for him to catch her. He watched her disappear into the barn.

Then he heard her screams.

Chapter 31

She didn't remember it ever raining this hard in August. Today's aberrant weather would probably set state records. The clouds had rolled in from the northwest at about two o'clock, providing unexpected and welcome relief from the sun and heat. But it wasn't a passing thundershower. It had begun as a hard, steady rain and hadn't let up.

Rennie sat on a hay bale with her back propped against the door of Beade's empty stall. Beyond the barn door, the rainfall looked like a gray curtain. Gullies had been gouged into the hard, dry earth. Channels of rainwater filled puddles that had formed in natural depressions. Rain had washed away the tire tracks left by the cattle truck that Toby had arranged to haul off the carcasses.

Carcasses. Her beautiful horses. All that magnificent power, beauty, and grace reduced to carcasses.

She wept without restraint, sobbing audibly, shoulders shaking. Her heart was broken. Not only for her loss, which was enormous, but for the sheer cruelty of the act. She wept over the wanton waste of those five beautiful, living creatures.

She wept to the point of exhaustion. When her weeping subsided, she remained as she was, listless, eyes closed, tears drying on her cheeks, listening to the hypnotic patter of raindrops striking the roof.

Sounds of his approach were eclipsed by the rainfall, but she sensed his presence. She opened her eyes and saw him standing in the open doorway of the barn, seemingly impervious to the torrent beating down on him.

He had offered to assist with the removal of the carcasses but had been reluctant to leave her alone. Toby had suggested calling Corinne to sit with her, but she had declined. She'd wanted to be alone for a while. He had seemed to understand that and had honored her wishes.

Nevertheless, he had asked a sheriff's deputy to remain parked at her gate until his return and had told her to stay inside the house, rifle nearby, with the door bolted. And for a while she had complied. But the barn had seemed the only appropriate place in which to mourn. Taking a throw from the sofa, she had used it as protection from the rain as she ran to the barn. Either the deputy hadn't seen her or had elected to leave her undisturbed.

Taking advantage of the solitude, she had grieved for each of the animals individually, then as a group. They had been her family. She had loved them as children. And now they were gone. Destroyed maliciously.

She didn't know how long she'd been here in the barn alone, but Wick would consider any amount of time too long. He would be angry at her for leaving herself unprotected.

He stepped inside and started down the center aisle.

His boots squished rainwater. It had plastered the old T-shirt to his skin, making a mold of his torso. His blue jeans were soaked through, too, and clung to his legs. His hair was dripping rainwater and lay flat against his skull.

He stopped a few feet away from her. Contrary to what she had expected, his expression wasn't angry, but anguished. His eyes weren't hard with annoyance, but soft with compassion. He stretched out his hand, clasped hers, and pulled her to her feet. Before her next heartbeat, she was in his arms and his mouth was possessively taking hers.

This time she gave herself over to it. She went with what had been her inclination the first time he'd kissed her. Mouth, hands, body—all responded. She pushed her fingers up through his wet hair and clutched his head, kissing him back hotly and hungrily, with desire finally unleashed.

She worked the clinging T-shirt up his chest and ran her hands over his wet skin, enmeshing her fingers in the curled hair, brushing his nipples. Then she dipped her head and kissed his chest, her lips skipping over it lightly, greedily. Hissing swear words of surprise and arousal, his large hand closed around her jaw, lifted her mouth back up to his, and made love to it.

When at last they broke apart, she clawed at his T-shirt until, together, they had it off. "Get close to me, Wick. Please. Be close to me."

He peeled her top over her head and brought her up against his bare chest. His skin was wet, cool; hers felt very hot against it, an erotic contrast.

He buried his face in her neck. His arms enveloped her. She felt the imprint of all ten of his fingers on her back as he held her hard and flush against him. She worked her hands between their bodies. It was difficult to unfasten the metal buttons of his jeans because the wet fabric was stubborn, but she stayed with the task until they were all undone and she was touching him.

His breathing was harsh and loud in her ear as he walked her backward until she was pinned between him and the door of the stall. They kissed ravenously while he dealt with the zipper of her slacks. He pushed them down, along with her underpants. When her legs were free, he lifted her up.

With one thrust he was inside her. "My God, Rennie," he gasped and was about to withdraw.

"No!" She slid her hands over his butt and drew him deeper into her, rocking her hips against him. He rasped her name again and began to move. He stroked them toward a climax that seized them quickly and simultaneously.

Supporting her on his thighs, he gradually lay her on the throw she had brought from the house and stretched out above her. He brushed loose strands of hair off her face and lowered his head to kiss her. "Wick—"

"Hush."

His lips moved over her face delicately, caressing each feature in turn. She tried to follow them, to capture them with her own for a kiss. But they were elusive, moving from ear to eyelid to temple to cheek to mouth. His breath was warm and sweet on her skin as he traced a slow path to her breasts.

He touched her nipple with his lips, sipped at it tenderly, then tugged it into his mouth. The other was reshaped by his hand, the nipple fanned with feather-light strokes until it was stiff and flushed and even then he continued to fondle her.

She moved restlessly beneath him, but when she reached for him, he stretched her arms high above her head and traced kisses on the underside of her arm from her wrist to her armpit. By the time he returned to kissing her breasts, she was aching to have him inside her again.

But he withheld. Sliding his hand between her thighs, he found her center. He drew small circles on it with his fingertip. The lightest of touches, yet it created an exquisite pressure inside her.

Darkness closed in around her. Her limbs began to tingle. There was a quickening in her middle. "Wick . . ."

He timed it perfectly and was nestled deep inside her when she climaxed. Wave after wave of sensation pulsed through her, each more pleasurable than the one before it, until she heard, as from a great distance, her own choppy cries of ultimate release.

Eventually, when she opened her eyes, Wick was smiling down at her. He kissed her softly on the lips, whispering, "Welcome back."

Feeling him still full and firm inside her, she squeezed him from within. He winced with pleasure. "Again." And then, almost inaudibly, "Jesus. Again."

He bridged her head with his arms. His deep blue eyes held hers as he began thrusting into her smoothly and powerfully. She ran her hands over his back, loving the feel of his skin. It emanated vitality. Her fingertips felt the currents of energy that made him unable to remain still, that made him Wick.

She was careful not to caress his incision because she didn't want to detract from his pleasure, even with an unpleasant reminder. Her hands skimmed over it to the small of his back, which dipped gracefully before swelling into his hips. She pressed his buttocks with her palms, and when he came, she held him tightly within the cradle of her thighs. Drawing his head down beside hers, she held it fast until his body relaxed.

The rain had decreased to a sprinkle. They dodged puddles on their way back to the house. "The sheriff's car is no longer there," she observed.

"When I saw you in the barn, you were crying but you were all right. I sent him away."

"Why?"

"I wanted to be alone with you."

"So you thought it might happen?"

He placed his arm across her shoulders and hugged her close. "A guy can hope."

The phone was ringing when they entered the house. It was Toby Robbins asking after Rennie. Wick assured him that she all right. "Still upset but holding up."

"Can I speak to her?"

Wick passed her the telephone. "Hello, Toby. I'm sorry you had to be the one to find them. It must have been horrible."

Earlier she had been too traumatized to talk about it. Wick could hear only one side of the conversation now, but he knew Toby was giving her his account of finding the horses dead in their stalls when he arrived to let them into the corral.

Rennie listened for several minutes in silence, then said, "I can't thank you enough for making all the arrangements. No, the authorities haven't made an arrest. Yes," she said quietly, "Lozada is definitely a suspect." Then Wick heard her say "Sandwiches?"

He pointed to the Tupperware container on the table and whispered, "Corinne sent them back with me."

"We were just about to sit down to them," Rennie said into the telephone. "Please thank Corinne for me."

After she hung up, Wick said, "I forgot about the sandwiches during my mad search through the house looking for you."

"I'm sorry I alarmed you."

"Alarmed me? Scared me shitless is more like it." He motioned her into a kitchen chair. "Hungry?"

"No."

"Eat anyway."

He coaxed her into half a ham sandwich and a glass of milk. After their meal he went around the house checking doors. "A locked door won't stop him," Rennie said.

"I'm only checking out of habit. Lozada won't come back here."

"How can you be sure?"

"Criminals often return to the scene, whether to gloat or to see if they overlooked something, whatever. But as you know, Lozada isn't a common criminal. He's too smart to return to the scene. He did what he wanted to do here."

"Punish me for being away with you."

"I told you that when he struck we wouldn't see it coming."

"But my horses," she said, her voice cracking. "He knew what would hurt me most, didn't he?"

Wick nodded. "He's done the deed. If I thought he would come back, I wouldn't have left you here with only a sheriff's deputy posted at the gate."

"Then why were you so frightened when you couldn't find me in the house?"

Grimly he said, "I've been known to be wrong."

They went upstairs. He switched on the nightstand

lamp. The pale light cast deep shadows on her face, emphasizing her weariness. "How 'bout a hot shower?"

"You read my mind."

The shower was a time for leisurely exploration. He was delighted and surprised by her lack of modesty and the access she gave him. Nor was she shy about caressing him.

He asked her if she liked hairy chests, and she showed him how much she liked his.

She apologized for one breast being slightly larger than the other, which gave him an opportunity to weigh and measure them with his hands and mouth.

She ran her tongue across his crooked front tooth and told him she really got off on that.

They kissed often, sometimes playfully with the water splashing on their faces, sometimes deeply and with feeling. They caressed each other with slick, soapy hands. And once, after she'd had her way with him, he knelt in front of her, nuzzled her thighs until they parted and then made provocative use of his tongue.

The foreplay was stimulating and left their bodies buzzing, but they didn't take it too far. It resulted only with their holding each other very close.

Afterward, they got into bed and were lying spooned together when she said, "At least they didn't suffer. Lozada didn't torture them."

"Try not to think about it." He pushed aside a handful of her hair and kissed the back of her neck.

Lozada had killed the horses using the same efficiency, and probably the same detachment, with which he'd killed Sally Horton—a couple of bullets through the brain. Wick didn't have to wonder why Lozada hadn't dispatched him that neatly. He'd wanted him to suffer. He had probably planned to stab him more than once with that screwdriver, let him die slowly and painfully.

Lying next to Rennie like this, he was very glad to be alive, and he knew that he was alive only because Lozada had unwisely decided that for Wick Threadgill only a protracted execution would do.

"Rennie?"

"Hmm?"

"You . . ." He searched for a tactful way of putting it. "You were so . . ."

"It almost stopped you."

She lay facing away from him, her hands beneath her cheek. He stroked her arm. "I'm not registering a complaint." He laid a soft kiss on her shoulder. "It was like a . . . a fantasy. A gift. Like you'd never—"

"I haven't been with anyone since the tragedy with Raymond Collier."

That's what he had surmised, but hearing her say it lent this moment, this day, even more significance. Had she told him before he'd made love to her, he would have been astonished. He probably wouldn't have believed her.

"That's a hell of a long time to pay penance, Rennie."

"Not penance. It was a conscious decision. I felt that after what happened, I didn't deserve to have a normal and fulfilling sex life."

"That's nuts. Collier got what he had coming. You were a child."

She laughed dryly. "With my track record? Hardly. No way could I be called a child."

"Maybe a child in desperate need of guidance."

She gave a small shrug of concession.

"Collier was the grown-up. He had no business messing with you. If he did have this sexual obsession for you, he should have stayed away from you, got his own counseling, something. He made a conscious decision too, Rennie, and the consequences of it were his own fault. Whatever caused you to pull that trigger—"

"I didn't."

Wick's heart jumped. "What?"

"I didn't shoot him. I never even touched the pistol. Not until afterward, that is. When the police were already on their way. I held the pistol then, but it didn't make any difference because they never tested it for fingerprints. They never looked for gunpowder residue on anyone's hands. Nothing."

"Who would have had gunpowder residue, Rennie?" When she didn't say anything, he spoke the name that was blaring inside his head. "T. Dan."

She hesitated, then gave a quick nod.

"Son of a bitch!" Wick sat up so he could look down at her, but she kept her head on the pillow, staring straight ahead, giving him nothing except her profile. "He shot Collier and let you take the blame?"

"I was a minor. T. Dan said there would be less mess if I admitted to shooting Raymond in self-defense."

"*Did* he try to rape you?"

"I had been avoiding him since that one time I met him at the motel. I was disgusted with him, and more so with myself. I wouldn't agree to see him, wouldn't even talk to him on the telephone. He showed up at the house that afternoon. I wasn't happy to see him. I don't know why I took him into T. Dan's study. Maybe subconsciously I wanted him to catch us together. I don't know. Anyhow, when my father walked in on us, Raymond was trying to kiss me. He was crying, pleading with me not to refuse him."

"T. Dan fired and asked questions later, is that it? He walked in, read the scene wrong, and thought he was protecting you from being raped?" She didn't answer. "Rennie?"

"No, Wick, protecting me wasn't his reason for firing. Raymond was a savvy businessman. My father was in partnership with him because he was smart. He was relying on Raymond to make them a lot of money on a real estate deal. So when he came in and saw Raymond clinging to me, he was furious. He told him he was making a fool of himself by crying like a baby over 'a piece of tail.'"

Wick's jaw bunched with anger. "He said that? About his sixteen-year-old daughter?"

"He said much worse than that," she said quietly. "Then he went to his desk and took the revolver from the drawer. When the smoke cleared, literally, Raymond lay dead on the floor."

"He murdered him," Wick said in disbelief. "In cold blood. And got away with it."

"T. Dan forced the gun into my hand and told me what to tell the police when they arrived. I went along because . . . because at first I was too stunned to do otherwise. Later, I realized that it was, ultimately, my fault."

"No one ever contested T. Dan's story? Your mother?"

"She never knew the truth. Or if she did, she never let on that she did. She never questioned anything T. Dan told her. No matter what happened, she kept up appearances and pretended that all was well and harmonious in our household."

"Un-fucking-believable. All this time you've assumed the blame and guilt for T. Dan's crime."

"His crime, Wick, but my blame. If not for me, Raymond wouldn't have died. I think about that every day of my life."

Wick expelled a heavy breath and lay back down. She had carried this burden just as he had borne the guilt for letting Lozada escape prosecution. Both of them had suffered severe consequences for behaving irresponsibly. Maybe they should learn to forgive themselves. Maybe they could help each other to forgive themselves.

He placed his arm around her but, unlike before, she held her body stiff and didn't adjust to the contours of his.

"Are you flattered that you're my first lover in twenty years?"

Softly he said, "I'd be lying if I said I wasn't."

"Well, you shouldn't be. There were so many others."

"It doesn't matter, Rennie."

Turning only her head, she looked at him over her shoulder. Her expression was nakedly vulnerable. He was reminded of what Toby Robbins had said about her eyes being larger than the rest of her face when she was a child.

"Doesn't it, Wick?"

He shook his head. "What matters to me," he whispered, "is that you're with me now. That you trust me enough to be here with me like this."

She turned and took his face between her hands. "I was afraid of you. No, not of you. Of the way you made me feel."

"I know."

"I fought it."

"Like a tigress."

"I'm glad you didn't give up on me." She touched his hair, his cheek, his chin, his chest.

They continued nuzzling until they fell asleep.

When he woke up hours later, he was very hard. Rennie must have sensed it because her eyes opened seconds after his. They gazed at each other across the width of the pillow.

He reached for her hand and drew it down to his lap. She closed her fingers around him and rolled her thumb across the glans, discovering a bead of moisture. One nudge of his knee and she separated her thighs. Moving closer, he propped her thigh on his hip, opening her. She was wet, but knowing that she was probably tender, he held back and didn't enter her.

Instead he covered her hand that was holding his penis and, guiding her, positioned it so she could caress herself with the tip. Connecting in that most intimate way, her eyes conveyed to him an immensity of feeling. And it was incredible. The sensations were new and novel, and holding back was a delicious agony in itself.

He was almost past the point of endurance when she slipped only the tip of his penis within the lips of her sex and came around it warmly and wetly while her hand milked him. He wouldn't have thought it was possible to have a more satisfying climax than the ones they had already shared. He'd been wrong.

He hugged her close and breathed in the scent of her hair, her skin, their lovemaking. He wished for the honor of killing T. Dan Newton for sentencing this beautiful, talented woman to twenty years of self-sacrifice and loneliness for a crime she hadn't even committed. He wanted to give her enough happiness to make up for all that lost time. He wanted to be with her every day for the rest of their lives.

But first they had to survive Lozada.

Chapter 32

▪▪▪▪▪▪▪▪▪▪▪

That's him. Do you recognize him?"

Wick looked into the interrogation room. "Never seen him before."

"I hadn't either," Oren said. "Not until he came in here the other night ready to hand over the goods on Ricky Roy Lozada."

"*I've* got the goods on Ricky Roy Lozada. My great-aunt Betsy's got the goods on Ricky Roy Lozada. Where Lozada is concerned, 'the goods,' have been got for a long time. Trouble is, they're worthless."

"Calm down," Oren said. "I know you're upset about Dr. Newton's horses."

"Damn right I am."

"Nobody could've predicted he would do that."

"Why wasn't someone watching her house?"

"It's not in our city, not even our county."

"Don't give me any bullshit about jurisdiction, Oren. You staked out Galveston cops at my house there."

Oren dragged his hand down his tired face. "Okay, maybe it was an oversight. How is Dr. Newton bearing up?"

"She insisted on going back to work today. Said that's what keeps her grounded. We drove in early from her ranch. I dropped her at the hospital just before coming here."

"Hmm."

Wick gave him a sharp look. "What?"

"Nothing."

"So okay, let's see what this bozo has to say."

As he reached for the doorknob Oren caught him by the arm. "Hold up. Don't go charging in there with steam coming out your ears."

"I'm cool."

"You're anything but cool, Wick."

Everyone in the FWPD Criminal Investigation Division knew that Wick Threadgill was among them that morning. Everybody, at least all the homicide detectives, knew that Oren Wesley's scheme to attract Lozada to Galveston had been a dismal failure. While Threadgill and the lady surgeon were playing footsie on the beach, Lozada had doubled back and killed her stable of fine horses. That's why Wesley had egg on his face, and you could fry one on Threadgill's ass.

Wick was aware of the attention he had attracted. If he'd had a bull's-eye painted on the back of his shirt he couldn't have felt more conspicuous. It hadn't been easy for him to enter the CID or even to walk into police headquarters. He had felt right at home and ill at ease at the same time.

Since his departure, the turnover of personnel hadn't been that considerable, so he knew many. Some spoke to him and even shook his hand as though genuinely glad to

see him. Others looked at him askance and kept their hel-
los low-key. Wick understood. A police department was as
political as any other bureaucracy. Everyone watched his
own back. A friendly greeting to an officer on indefinite
leave might be misinterpreted by those who recommended advancement. Anyone concerned about his next
promotion wouldn't jeopardize his chances by mingling
with a persona non grata like Wick Threadgill.

As though validating his paranoia and self-consciousness,
it seemed that everyone on the entire third floor, upon
hearing his and Oren's raised voices, had stopped what
they were doing and were watching with frank interest to
see how this scene between the former partners was going
to play out.

Wick threw off Oren's hand. "I said I'm cool."

"I just don't want—"

"Are we gonna do this or not?"

Oren glanced over his shoulder at their attentive audience, then opened the door to the interrogation room
and waved Wick in. Weenie Sawyer was seated at the far
end of the small table. He was jiggling both legs, his bony
knees bobbing up and down as rapidly as synchronized
sewing-machine needles. His teeth were doing a number
on a fingernail.

When he saw Wick he paled, which was remarkable
considering that his complexion was already the pasty
color of a toad's belly. "What's he doing here?"

"You know Mr. Threadgill?" Oren asked pleasantly.

The man's eyes darted from Wick to Oren then back to
Wick. "I recognize him from the pictures in the newspaper."

"Good. Then there's no need to make formal introductions." Oren sat down adjacent to Weenie.

Wick pulled out a chair at the opposite end of the table, turned it around, and straddled it backward. He glared at the little man. "So you're the sniveling little shit who's been doing Lozada's research."

The diminutive man seemed to shrivel even smaller. He looked over at Oren. "Why's he here?"

"He's here because I invited him."

"What for?"

"So he could hear what you have to tell us."

Weenie swallowed hard. He squirmed in his seat. "I . . . I've been thinking about it. It's not too smart for me to be here and talking to you without a lawyer."

"Come to think of it, you're right," Oren said. "Maybe you'd better go hire you one. When you do, give us a call." He made to stand.

"Wait, wait!" Weenie divided another nervous glance between them. "If I get a lawyer is the deal still on?"

Wick practically came out of his chair. "Deal?" He looked at Oren. "You made a deal with this dickhead?"

"Remember, Wick, you're only here because you promised not to interfere."

"Well *you* promised that this asshole was our ticket to getting Lozada."

"I think he is. But not without—"

"A deal," Wick said, fuming. "What did you offer him?"

"Immunity from prosecution."

He swore under his breath. "That's bullshit. That's what that is."

"Then what's your idea?"

Wick gave Weenie a scornful once-over. "He's a little too big to throw back. Why don't we bread him in cornmeal and deep-fry him?"

Sweat popped out on Weenie's face. He looked wildly

at Oren. "He's crazy! Everybody says so. Lozada says so. Lozada says he went 'round the bend when his brother died."

In a blur of motion, Wick practically vaulted the length of the table. He lifted Weenie out of his chair by his scrawny neck and pushed him backward, hard up against the wall, and held him there. The little man squealed like a trapped mouse.

"My brother didn't *die*."

"Wick, have you lost your mind? Let him go!"

"He was *murdered*, you puny little cocksucker."

"Wick, I'm warning you."

"Murdered by your pal Lozada."

Weenie's face had turned beet red. His feet danced uselessly a few inches above the floor. He rolled terrified eyes toward Oren. The detective had hold of Wick's arm, trying to break his grip on Weenie's neck.

"Wick, you're going to kill him. Let him go," he said, straining the words through clenched teeth. He literally tried to peel Wick's fingers from around Weenie's neck. When that didn't work, when Weenie's eyes began to bug out of his head, Oren rammed his elbow into Wick's ribs.

His breath whooshed out. Immediately he released Weenie, who sank to the floor. Cursing expansively and holding his injured right side, Wick bent double.

Oren was breathing hard. "I'm sorry I had to hurt you, but goddammit, you just never learn, do you?"

Weenie remained crouched on the floor, whimpering, but their attention was on each other, not on him.

Wick straightened up, gasping with the effort. "You do that again and I'll—"

"Shut up and listen, Wick. For once. *Listen*." Oren took

several breaths to control his own temper. "You're still having issues with anger management."

Wick laughed. "Issues? Anger management? Where'd you hear that? On *Oprah*?"

Oren shouted over him. "Has your rage blinded you to the fact that you're making the same mistake you made before? You want Lozada to escape prosecution again, you go right on doing what you're doing."

Thigpen opened the door and cautiously poked his head inside. "Everything okay in here?"

"None of your goddamn business!" Wick roared.

Oren told him everything was fine.

"What's the matter with him?" The detective was looking at Weenie, who was still on the floor, mewling and wiping his nose on his sleeve.

"He's okay."

Thigpen gave a dubious shrug, then withdrew and pulled the door closed after him.

Wick continued as though there'd been no interruption. "I've got a temper. I admit it. What you refuse to admit is that when it comes to Lozada, you've got no balls, Oren."

"Speaking of balls, yours should be good and blue by now."

Sparks shot from Wick's eyes. His hands formed fists at his sides. "What are you getting at?"

"Nothing."

"No. Oh, no. We're way past insinuations. Why don't you come right out and say what's on your mind?"

"Okay. You're sleeping with a suspect. Aren't you?"

"If you're referring to Rennie Newton, yes. I am. And loving every second of it. But she's not a suspect."

"I haven't eliminated her as a suspect in the murder of Dr. Howell. Have you forgotten about that?"

"It was Lozada."

"Who could have been hired by her."

"He wasn't."

"Did she ever tell you about that card that she kept in her nightstand?"

"The enclosure card? I found it, remember?"

"Right, right. It came with the roses that Lozada sent her."

Wick spread his arms wide and shrugged. "What's your point?"

"I'm curious is all. When she discovered that Lozada was the sender of those roses, why didn't she tear up the card? Destroy it along with the flowers. Throw it away."

"She was saving it as evidence."

"Or as a keepsake. See, after I dismissed it as evidence, she took it back. Far as I know she still has it."

Wick thought about that for maybe a split second, then shook his head emphatically. "She despises Lozada. He gives her the creeps."

"Yeah, so she's said. Tell me, Wick, did you start believing her before or after she screwed your brains out?"

Wick advanced a step. "I warned you once, Oren. Now I'm telling you for the last time, if you ever want to call yourself my friend again, if you ever called my brother your friend, you won't make remarks like that about Rennie. Ever."

Oren didn't back down. "Funny you should mention Joe. Because if he were here, he'd be telling you the same thing. He'd be the first to tell you that you're over the line. You can't be both cop and lover boy to a suspect."

"She's not a suspect," Wick repeated loudly. "She's a victim."

"You sure? You seem to have forgotten that she shot a man."

"She didn't."

"What?" Oren exclaimed.

"She didn't shoot Raymond Collier. Her father killed him. She took the blame."

"Why?"

"Because T. Dan told her to."

Oren barked a laugh. "You believe that?" He laughed again. "She gives you this sob story that nobody can corroborate and you believe her?"

"That's right."

"Uh-huh. And when she told you this, was she blowing in your ear? Or just plain blowing you?"

Wick launched himself at Oren and both flew backward onto the floor. Weenie shrieked. Wick landed a few punches, but he wasn't anywhere near up to full strength and Oren had always been the heavier and stronger of the two. He fought back with a vengeance and without deference to Wick's injury.

When he had Wick somewhat subdued, he struggled to his knees and pulled his service revolver from his shoulder holster. He pointed it down at Wick. Tears of pain smarted in his eyes, but he could see the bore of Oren's handgun clearly enough.

Upon hearing the commotion, several other plainclothesmen rushed into the room. "Back out!" Oren ordered. "Everything's under control."

"What happened?"

"Just a little misunderstanding. It stays in this department, understood?" When no one said anything, he shouted, "*Understood?*"

There were murmurs of consent.

Oren motioned with his pistol. "Get up, Wick."

"I'm not believing this. You pulled a goddamn gun on me?"

"Come on. Up. It might be a good idea if you went in the tank for a while. Cool off." Oren glanced toward the door. "Thigpen, you got a pair of cuffs handy?"

"Not fucking hardly," Wick growled. He surged to his feet and head-butted Oren's belly. He heard the scuffle of feet behind him and knew the other officers were scrambling to assist Oren. Wick had the momentum, however, and succeeded in backing Oren into the wall. He placed a forearm across his throat while with the other hand he tried to wrest the pistol away from Oren.

"Take back what you said about Rennie."

Oren struggled just as hard as he.

The other cops were trying to pull Wick off, but he had adrenaline working for him. "Take it back!" His shout reverberated off the walls of the small room.

But it wasn't as loud as the gunshot. That deafened him.

Chapter 33

∎∎∎∎∎∎∎∎∎∎∎∎∎

Weenie had wet himself. It was the definitive humiliation. The second-grade nightmare had been revisited to validate his cruel nickname. There was only one variation— today no one had noticed the dark stain on the front of his trousers. They'd been too busy trying to control the pandemonium.

Following the gunshot all hell had broken loose, and that was how Weenie had managed to escape. There were advantages to being small in stature and easily forgettable. In the aftermath of the shooting he'd been the last thing on anyone's mind.

When he saw an opportunity to slip out of the interrogation room, he had seized it. He'd used the fire-escape stairs rather than taking the elevator. It wasn't until he had exited the building that he realized he'd peed himself.

What had he been thinking when he decided to go to Fort Worth? Dallas had the more colorful reputation, but Fort Worth was wilder and woollier by far. The people over there thought they were still living in the wild, wild West. He'd barely survived thirteen years of its public school system and he should have known better than to cross into that testosterone-charged territory again.

All the way home—and the thirty-mile distance between the two cities had never seemed so far—he'd expected a squadron of police cars to come screaming after him.

But the FWPD had much bigger problems to deal with than one missing would-be confessor who had come to his senses. A bleeding cop was a major event, especially since it had been another cop who'd made him bleed. Probably no one in that room would even remember that Weenie Sawyer had been there to witness the shooting.

Even so, he was taking no chances. He figured he was long overdue a relocation. He would start looking for another place. All he needed was space for his lounger, TV, and bed, and enough electricity to support his computer setup. When he moved he wouldn't leave a forwarding address.

In the meantime, a vacation to a tropical Mexican clime sounded good. Acapulco. Cancún. Someplace where he needed more sunscreen than *pesos.* He'd go out to DFW Airport and hop terminals until he found an available flight to a destination where he could enjoy peace and obscurity until things settled down.

With unsteady hands he unlocked his front door. He tossed his keys onto his TV tray and entered his bedroom in a rush. He groped beneath his bed for his suitcase. It was covered by a thick layer of dust, but he set it on his bed, unlatched the top and raised it, then turned toward his narrow closet.

He screamed in fright.

"Hello, Weenie." Lozada was leaning against the opposite wall, arms and ankles crossed, looking perfectly relaxed. And deadly. Noticing the stain on the front of Weenie's trousers, he grinned. "Did I startle you?"

"H-hi Lozada. How's it going? I was just—"

"About to pack." He gestured toward the suitcase. "Going somewhere? But then you've already been somewhere, haven't you, Weenie?"

"Been somewhere? No." He was trying very hard to keep his teeth from chattering.

"I've been calling you for a day and a half."

"Oh, I was, uh . . . my phone's out of order."

Indolently Lozada unfolded his arms and legs and crossed to the rickety table beside Weenie's bed. He lifted the receiver of the telephone. The dial tone buzzed loudly.

Weenie swallowed. "Son of a gun. They must've got it working again."

Lozada replaced the receiver and came to stand close to him. "I was getting worried about you, Weenie. You rarely leave this dump of yours. So where have you been?"

Weenie had to crane his neck to look up into Lozada's face. He didn't like what he saw. "I-I'm sorry I wasn't around. Did you need me for something?"

Lozada ran his index finger along Weenie's hairline. "You're sweating, Weenie."

"Uh, listen, whatever you wanted me to do, I'll do it for free. No charge. You know, because I wasn't here when you—"

"You've peed your pants, Weenie. What made you nervous enough to lose bladder control?"

Lozada removed a switchblade from his pocket. With a flick of his wrist and a deadly click, he opened it inches from Weenie's face. The small man whimpered in terror.

"You'd better tell me what's got you so shaken." Lozada began to clean beneath his fingernails with the knife. "I'd hate to hear it from somebody else. If you withheld information from me, I'd be very disappointed in you."

Weenie considered his options, which were, basically, life or death. His life wasn't much, but it beat the alternative. "Th-that Threadgill?"

"What about him?"

"He shot what's-his-name. The black guy. Wesley."

Lozada's eyes narrowed to slits of mistrust.

Weenie's head bobbed on his skinny neck. "He did. He shot him. I saw it. I was there."

"Where?"

"At the police station in Fort Worth. The big one downtown. They hauled me in for questioning," he lied. "But don't worry. I didn't tell them anything. Honest, Lozada. They tried several tactics to get me to talk, but—"

"Skip that. What about Threadgill shooting Wesley? I don't believe you."

"I swear," Weenie said, his voice going shrill. "First he went for me. Nearly choked me to death and would have if Wesley hadn't pulled him off. Then they got into an argument over that doctor."

He recounted their quarrel almost word for word. "Wesley said some things about her that didn't sit well with Threadgill. He attacked Wesley. Wesley pulled his pistol and threatened to have Threadgill locked up until he cooled off. Threadgill was having none of it and went for Wesley again. They were in a struggle for the pistol when it went off.

"Cops came running in, all trying to figure out what had happened. There's blood all over Wesley. Threadgill's going berserk, yelling, 'No, no, Jesus, no!' Stuff like that.

He was trying to get to Wesley, but other cops were holding him back." Weenie paused to push up his slipping eyeglasses.

"I don't think Threadgill meant to shoot him. It was an accident. But the other cops heard a heated argument before the gunshot, so they figured, you know, it was intentional. And Threadgill was a wildman. It took several men to handcuff him and haul him outta there."

"Wesley's dead?"

"I don't know. I sneaked out before the ambulance got there, but somebody had a handkerchief stuffed into the wound and it looked bad. He was gut shot, I heard somebody say."

Lozada backed up a bit and Weenie relaxed considerably when he retracted the blade of the knife. But Lozada's stare was still activating his sweat glands.

"A shooting at police headquarters is big news, Weenie. How come I haven't heard any bulletins?"

"They talked about that. Even during all the hullabaloo, everybody kept saying, 'This is contained, understand? Contained. It's a department matter.' They want a tight lid kept on it. Makes sense. A cop shooting a cop. They don't want the public to know about it. They'll probably tell the people at the hospital that Wesley's gun accidentally fired while he was cleaning it. Or something."

Weenie nervously cracked his knuckles. He wondered about the departure time of the last plane to Mexico. Did you need a passport to enter Mexico or would a driver's license do?

"She kept my card?"

"Huh?"

Irritably Lozada snapped his fingers in front of Weenie's face as though to wake him up, then repeated the question.

"Oh yeah, a card you sent with some roses? Wesley thinks the lady has a thing for you. That's what pissed off Threadgill. Wesley said she was playing him like a fiddle. Not in those words, but—"

"Do you masturbate?"

"Beg pardon?"

Before Weenie could blink, his male parts were suspended over the razor-sharp blade of Lozada's knife. "Do you—"

"What are you talking about?" Weenie screeched.

"You might not miss it for sex, but you'll be pissing like a woman if you don't tell me what you were doing in an interrogation room being questioned by Wesley and Threadgill."

Weenie was up on tiptoes, trying to maintain his balance. If he faltered, he'd be a eunuch and any chance he had of fulfilling his fantasies with an amiable señorita would be dashed. "I was afraid of getting into trouble."

"So you ratted me out."

"No, I swear. God as my witness."

"There is no God." Lozada raised the knife blade another centimeter and Weenie squealed. "There is only Lozada and the laws of physics, one of which is the law of gravity. If I cut off your balls, Weenie, they'll drop like marbles."

"I went there to see what kind of deal I could make," he sobbed. "You know, in case they ever linked me to you. But then, Wesley got all worked up over some phone call you had made to Dr. Newton's cell phone. They thought you were in Galveston."

"I was."

"Then he got word that her horses had been shot. Miles from Galveston. Confused the hell outta them all. Anyhow, Wesley slapped me in a holding cell and sorta forgot about me, I guess. Until this morning. He let me shower. Gave me breakfast. Put me in this room and told me to wait.

"When he came back, Threadgill was with him. I told them I had changed my mind, that I wanted a lawyer. You know the rest. I swear I didn't tell them anything." He was crying now, blubbering like a baby, but he couldn't help it.

Lozada withdrew the knife. "The only reason I'm not killing you is because I don't know how to destroy your computers and be certain I'm also destroying all the data they contain."

Weenie wiped his nose with the back of his hand. "Huh?"

"Get to it, Weenie," Lozada said softly.

Weenie swallowed convulsively. "You want me to destroy my computers?" Lozada might just as well have asked a mother to smother her child. Weenie had been prepared to take a vacation from his computers for a while, but to destroy them was beyond his imagining. He couldn't do it.

Lozada's hand barely moved, but Weenie felt a slight tug at his crotch and a sudden draft. When he looked down he saw that his pants had been split open from inseam to waistband. The knife was poised just below his crotch. The blade gleamed wickedly.

"Get to work, Weenie, or your foreskin is next."

Weenie had been circumcised, but, at the moment, that seemed a rather insignificant detail.

As soon as Rennie alighted from the elevator on the ground floor of the hospital, she heard her name.

Grace Wesley was entering the atrium lobby through the revolving doors. Rennie tried to catch the elevator and hold it for her, but the doors had closed and it had already begun its ascent.

Grace rushed up to her. "Please don't tell me he's dead."

"No, he's still with us." Grace's knees buckled and she might have collapsed had Rennie not been there to lend support. "He's still listed as critical, but they think he's going to make it."

Grace covered her mouth to stifle a sob of relief. "Thank God, thank God. You're sure?"

"I talked to the them just now as they were wheeling him out of surgery."

Grace blotted her eyes with a tissue. "I was so afraid that by the time I got here . . ." She was unable to speak aloud the horrible thought.

Rennie reached for her hand and squeezed it tightly. "I heard you'd gone to Tennessee to see your daughters."

"A Nashville policewoman met my flight and told me what had happened. I never even left the airport. Took the next flight back. Oren's supervisor met me at DFW and drove me straight here." She paused. "You said 'they.' "

"What?"

"You said 'they' think Oren's going to make it."

"I was referring to the surgical team."

"I thought you—"

"I wasn't even allowed to observe, much less perform the surgery. Under the circumstances that would have been very awkward. But he had an excellent team working on him."

"I would have requested you."

"Thanks for that." Moved to tears, Rennie turned away and punched the elevator button again.

"Is it true, Rennie? Wick did this?"

Sadly she lowered her head, nodding.

Grace said, "That's what I was told, but I thought there must be some mistake. I can't believe it."

"Neither can I. It's . . . incomprehensible. What could have driven him to do this? The two of them have been through so much together, been such good friends. Wick thinks the world of your husband." Head still down, she rubbed her eyes. "Detective Wesley is in ICU and Wick's in jail."

"He's in love with you."

Rennie's head came up quickly.

"He is." Grace held Rennie's astonished stare until an elevator arrived and the doors slid open. "I've got to go."

"Yes. By all means."

Grace quickly boarded the elevator. Rennie waited until the doors had closed before she turned to go. Yesterday's unseasonable rain was a memory. It was blistering hot on the doctors' parking lot. She would never again traverse it without thinking of Lee Howell. His murder had been cataclysmic, but this tragic chain of events had really begun when she'd announced the jury's verdict. "We find the defendant not guilty."

Her house was dark when she arrived. As always, she drove her Jeep into her garage and entered through the kitchen door. She went straight to the refrigerator and got a bottle of water. She stood at the kitchen sink until she had drunk all of it.

She passed through her living room, went down the dark hallway and into her bedroom. She switched on the nightstand lamp and undressed. When she was down to her underwear, she went into the bathroom and turned on the tub faucets. She chose a scented gel and took a long shower.

Wrapped in her favorite, most comfortable robe, she went back into the kitchen and poured herself a glass of wine. She carried it with her into the living room and sat down in her favorite spot in the corner of the sofa.

She sipped her wine and thought back to the night she'd fallen asleep here and later had been called to an emergency at the hospital. The patient had had a critical stab wound to the back.

Wick. She had caused him so much pain. Wesley too. He and his whole family. And now . . . God, now.

Her head fell back against the sofa cushions. She closed her eyes, but tears slid through her eyelids and rolled down her cheeks. They had all suffered because of her and that damned verdict.

She sat there for a long while, with her head back and her eyes closed. That was how he found her.

Or rather, that was how she was when she sat up, turned, and said, "Hello, Lozada." He was standing behind the sofa, inches away, looking down at her. "I've been expecting you."

He smiled, pleased. "Have you, Rennie?"

Hearing him say her name, seeing that reptilian smile, almost made her throw up the wine. Placing the glass on the coffee table, she stood up and came around the end of the sofa to face him. "I knew you'd come when you heard about what happened to Oren Wesley."

"Your boyfriend can't control his temper. An unfortunate character trait. It was only a matter of time before he self-destructed. Wesley?" He shrugged. "His problem is choosing the wrong friends."

"How'd you find out? It hasn't been on the news. Security was so tight at the hospital that only a handful of staff knew Wesley's identity and the nature of his injury. You must have an informant in the FWPD. Who told you?"

"A little birdy," he whispered. "He's a cowardly little birdy. I didn't believe him at first, but I've checked out the sad tale, and, alas, it's true."

He reached out to finger a strand of hair that lay against her chest. She forced herself not to recoil, but he must have sensed her revulsion because he smiled that smile again. "You look lovely tonight."

"I don't look lovely at all. I'm tired. Weary, actually. Of everything."

"Your trip must've been exhausting."

"How'd you do it?"

"Do what, my dear?"

"How'd you get from Galveston to my ranch before daybreak?"

"I told you before, Rennie, I don't reveal trade secrets. If I did, I'd soon be out of business."

"It was quite a feat."

He laughed. "I don't have wings, if that's what you're thinking."

When her palm connected with his cheek, it made a sound as emphatic as an exploding firecracker.

"That's for killing my horses."

No longer laughing or smiling, he gripped her wrist so hard she cried out in pain. He whipped her around and thrust her hand up between her shoulder blades. His breath was hot against her ear. "I ought to kill you right now for doing that."

"You're going to kill me anyway, aren't you?"

"How could I possibly let you live, Rennie? You have

only yourself to blame. You should have allowed me to cherish you the way I wanted. Instead you chose to be manhandled by that crude cowboy ex-cop." He drew her tighter against him and pushed her hand up higher. "After an insult like that, you leave me no choice but to kill you both. I'm only sorry he's in jail so he won't get to watch you die. But one can't have everything."

The pain was considerable, but she didn't struggle. She didn't even whimper. "They should've locked you up years ago, Lozada. Not for being a killer, but for being insanely delusional. Don't you get it? I wouldn't have had you near me even if Wick Threadgill didn't exist. You're a creep."

He clicked open the switchblade and placed it across her throat. "Before I finish with you, you'll be begging me to spare your life."

"I'll never beg you for a damn thing. I might have pleaded with you to spare my horses, but you didn't give me a chance. When you killed them, you played your trump card as far as I'm concerned. I'm over you, Lozada. I'm over being afraid of you."

"Oh, I doubt that." Lowering the knife, he patted the flat side of the blade against her nipple.

Reflexively she sucked in a quick breath.

"See?" he chuckled. "You're very afraid, Rennie."

It was true. She was terrified, but still she refused to show it. "I won't fight you, Lozada. For twenty years, every day of my life has been a bonus. I won't beg you to let me live. If that's what you're waiting for, you're only wasting your time."

"Such courage. And for that, I hate to kill you, Rennie, I really do. You're a remarkable woman. I hope you understand how badly I feel about the way our affair must end."

"We never had an affair, Lozada. As for understanding, I understand that the only way you can get a woman's attention is to terrorize her."

He drew her tighter against him and ground his crotch against her bottom. "Feel that? That's what gets women's attention. Plenty of women."

She remained silent.

"Say pretty please, Rennie." He slid his tongue down the length of her neck. "Say pretty please and I may let you suck it before I kill you."

"Oh, Lo-za-da."

At Wick's singsong voice, Rennie felt him start.

"Yeah, that's right. That's the barrel of my three-fifty-seven in your ear. Blink and you're history."

"Please blink, Lozada. Pretty please," Oren Wesley taunted from the connecting kitchen door. His handgun was aimed directly at Lozada's head.

"Drop the blade!" Wick ordered.

Lozada chuckled and raised the razor edge back to Rennie's throat. "Go ahead and pull the trigger, Threadgill. If you want to see her blood gush, shoot me."

"That's just like you, you chicken-livered son of a bitch. Using a woman to save your ass. Attacking her from behind, too. Another of your—what you'd call it?—unfortunate character traits.

"But if that's the way you want it, Ricky Roy, fine by me," he said easily. "When I fire, Oren will, too. See, we've been practicing all day. Ever since we staged that little scene for your pal Weenie. Messy as hell, all that fake blood and all, but obviously convincing.

"Now, here's what'll happen. Our bullets will enter your skull. His may be a thousandth of a second behind mine. But pretty damn near simultaneous, wouldn't you say, Oren?"

"That's what I'd say."

"They might even intersect at some point, Ricky Roy, but in any case, your brains will spatter like shit from a tall goose."

"She'll be dead by then," Lozada said.

"Let her go, Lozada."

"Not a chance."

"What do you think, Oren?" Wick said. "Are you tired of this crap?"

"I'm tired of this crap."

"Me too." And with his left hand, Wick fired a small pistol into Lozada's right elbow, point blank. Bone shattered. Nerves and blood vessels were severed. The switchblade fell from useless fingers. Rennie dropped to the floor, as she had been instructed to do. Lozada spun around, left hand raised, thumb extended, jabbing toward Wick's eye socket. Wick fired the .357 directly into his chest.

Lozada's eyes widened with astonishment. Then Wick said, "This is for Joe," and fired a second time.

Lozada fell backward onto the floor.

Rennie crawled over to him and immediately checked his neck for a pulse.

"His heart's still beating." She ripped open his shirt.

"Leave him."

She looked up at Wick. "I can't."

Then she turned back to Lozada and set about trying to save his life.

Chapter 34

It was eight o'clock the following morning before Rennie left the hospital. Wick was outside waiting for her in his pickup truck with the engine running. He leaned over and opened the passenger door for her.

They had timed her departure to coincide with Oren's press conference so the media would be occupied and she could make a clean getaway. As they pulled away from the hospital, they saw news vans lining the street and a cluster of reporters and cameramen surrounding the lobby entrance.

"What's he telling them?" she asked.

"That the FWPD pulled off a flawless sting operation, with the cooperation of Tarrant General Hospital personnel. One of the city's most notorious criminals, one Ricky Roy Lozada, died from gunshot wounds he received while resisting arrest."

Before turning him over to paramedics, Rennie had heroically worked to keep his heart beating. She had ridden in the ambulance with him to the emergency room, but upon their arrival he was pronounced dead. Wick had personally escorted his body to the morgue.

Rennie had then insisted on examining Wick, even ordering a CAT scan to check for internal bleeding. He'd told Oren not to hold back, to make their fight look authentic. Oren had taken him at his word. He felt like a punching bag, but Rennie's examination had turned up nothing worrisome.

"Oren's going to try and keep your name out of the story," Wick told her.

"I will appreciate that."

"But it might be unavoidable, Rennie."

"If it's unavoidable, then I'll deal with it."

Their destination had been predetermined. She wouldn't be returning to the house in which Lozada had died. Once they were headed west on the interstate, Wick reached for her hand. "I died a thousand deaths while he was holding that knife on you."

"I was afraid that something had happened to detain you, that you and Oren wouldn't be in place. When I got home I was tempted to look in the kitchen pantry and under the bed to make sure you were there."

"Hell couldn't have kept me away."

"It was a daring plan, Wick."

"I just thank God it worked."

He had resolved that he and Rennie had no hope of a future until the problem of Lozada was resolved. In other words, until he was taken out of the picture. And that had been the key phrase: out of the picture. His mind had snagged on those four words. It occurred to him that if Lozada thought he was out of the picture, and Oren was out of the picture, he would make a move on Rennie.

"The toughest part of the plan for me was the necessity of placing you in danger."

"But I was already in danger."

"That's the conclusion I finally drew. And you were going to remain in danger unless and until I forced Lozada's hand." Yesterday morning, he had got up well before dawn, called Oren, and outlined the plan. Oren had liked the idea, made a few suggestions of his own, and put things into motion.

"How did you convince Oren that I wasn't the femme fatale he believed me to be?" Rennie asked.

"I didn't have to. Lozada did that when he killed your horses. Actually I think Oren had made up his mind long before that and was just being mule-headed. Believe me, Rennie. If he hadn't been totally convinced of your innocence and his misjudgment, he would never have pulled this sting. And by the way, he sends his apology for all the ugly things he had to say about you in order to convince Weenie Sawyer.

"Who, by the way, was a lucky break for us. If not for him, we might have had to wait for days, me in jail, Oren in the hospital pretending to be gravely wounded, before Lozada got the news and acted on it.

"We had Sawyer tailed to his place in Dallas, and when the stakeout team saw Lozada there, they called in a heads-up. After Lozada left, they moved in and arrested Weenie. He was lying on his bed crying because Lozada had forced him to hammer his computers to bits. He started confessing his complicity even before they got the cuffs on."

"Will there be any repercussions for you?"

"For shooting Lozada? No. Oren had me reinstated before we went in to question Weenie."

She turned to him with surprise. "So you're officially a cop again?"

"I'm thinking about it."

"What's there to think about?"

"All the shit that goes with it."

"There's shit with every job, Wick."

"Not a very encouraging maxim," he said wryly.

"It boils down to one question." He looked across at her. "Do you love the work more than you hate the shit?"

He didn't have to think about it for long. "I love the work."

"There's your answer."

He nodded thoughtfully. "Now that I'm finally able to bury Joe, really bury him, it'll be different, I think."

"I'm sure it will be. It's your calling." She laughed softly, "And speaking of callings, Grace may have missed hers. She should have been an actress. She put on quite a performance at the hospital."

"I heard you both did."

"I don't know if Lozada saw it or not."

"I don't know either, but every scene had to be staged and played out as though it were real. If Lozada had been watching the hospital and Grace hadn't rushed to Oren's bedside, he would have smelled a rat."

Noticing her yawn, he said, "You've been up all night. Why don't you try and sleep the rest of the way?"

"What about you?"

"I napped between all those unnecessary tests my doctor put me through."

Smiling, she closed her eyes. She woke up when he stopped the truck at the gate and got out to open it. After driving through, he parked at the front steps.

Rennie looked toward the barn. "That was always my first stop."

He stroked her cheek. "Try not to think about it."

"I'll always think about it."

He got out and came around to open her door, but he blocked her from getting out. "What?" she asked.

"When I was in your bedroom, waiting to make my move on Lozada . . ."

"Yes?"

"I heard you say something to him that I thought was strange. You said that every day of your life for the past twenty years had been a bonus." He removed her sunglasses so he could see into her eyes. "And I just wondered what you meant by that, Rennie." She lowered her head, but he placed his finger beneath her chin and raised it, forcing her to look at him. "You didn't finish the story, did you?"

He could see she wrestled with lying about it, but his will won out. She took a deep breath. "When T. Dan fired?"

"Yes?"

"He wasn't aiming at Raymond."

He stared at her for a moment, and then when misapprehension cleared and he understood what she was saying, he expelled his breath slowly. "Jesus."

"My father was much angrier at me than he was at Raymond. Raymond had lost interest in their business deal, had lost his edge. When T. Dan saw us together and realized that I was the reason for Raymond's preoccupation, he regarded me only as an obstacle that had to be eliminated."

She paused for a moment and stared vacantly into near space. "He was my father and I had adored him. He'd broken my heart with his infidelity. He had betrayed my mother, our family. He was a selfish, self-serving scoundrel."

She laughed bitterly and shook her head. "But, Wick, you know what's really funny? Or tragic. I still loved him. In spite of everything. If I hadn't, I wouldn't have tried so hard to anger and upset him by doing the very things he did. I wouldn't have seduced his business partner. I loved him," she repeated sadly.

"But his land deal meant more to him than I did. He whipped himself into a froth and was angry enough to kill me. He would have if Raymond hadn't jumped in front of me just as T. Dan fired. So, you see, I meant it literally when I told you if not for me Raymond wouldn't have died. He died saving me from my own father.

"Afterward, I was in shock. I went along with everything T. Dan told me to do, said everything he told me to say. Soon after the incident he sent me away. Maybe the sight of me pricked his conscience, or maybe I was an unhappy reminder of the land deal that got away. I don't know. But until the day he died, we never spoke of that afternoon again."

Wick pulled her toward him and when she resisted he said, "Uh-huh. No way. You're not going to retreat, withdraw, and pull on your hair shirt." He tucked her face into his neck and stroked her head. "It happened twenty years ago. It's long past, you've atoned for it a thousand times over, and T. Dan is frying in hell. He can't hurt you anymore, Rennie. I won't let him."

He held her close for several moments before setting her away. "I'm glad you told me. It explains a lot. The need to be in control. The thumbing your nose at danger because you could have died at sixteen. I just hope that you'll cut back on some of that daredevil bullshit. I can't be running around all the time covering your ass. Speaking metaphorically, of course."

She laughed. Or sobbed. It was difficult to tell because there were tears in her eyes but she was smiling. He helped her out of the truck and together they climbed the steps. As he pushed open the front door, he said, "How 'bout breakfast?"

"Sounds good."

He reached around her to close the door and trapped her between it and him. "Breakfast. Every morning for the rest of our lives."

She smiled at him sadly. "Wick—"

"Now wait. Before you start raising objections, hear me out." He cupped her cheek with his hand. "I'll be your best friend for the rest of your life. I'll try my damnedest to heal that part of you that still hurts. I'll be an ardent and faithful lover. I'd father your children, gladly. And I would protect you with my life."

"You already have."

"You saved me, too, Rennie. And not just on the operating table. I was in a wretched state when Oren came to Galveston. Being lured into a case involving a mysterious lady surgeon was the best thing that ever happened to me."

She smiled, but her eyes were still clouded with doubt. "I don't see how we could ever work."

"Come to think of it, you may be right," he sighed. His hand moved to the top button of her blouse and undid it. "I throw temper tantrums and you're cool under pressure. I'm a slob, you insert the tabs on your cereal boxes. I'm poor, you're rich."

By the time he had enumerated those fundamental differences, all the buttons were undone and so were her slacks. Leaning into her, he kissed the side of her mouth. "We make no sense at all."

She tilted her head to give his lips access to her throat. "Except what Grace said."

He pulled her earlobe gently through his teeth. "What did Grace say?"

She tugged the shirttail from his waistband and ran her hands up over his chest. "That you're in love with me."

"Smart Grace."

"So you are?"

"I are." Her soft laugh became a low moan when he unclasped her bra and took her breasts in his hands.

"Then there's my work."

"There is that." His tongue stroked her nipple.

"It's very demanding."

He caressed her tummy with the backs of his fingers, down past her navel. "I guess you're right." He turned his hand and slid it into her underpants. "We've got nothing going for us." She was wet and receptive, and as he slipped his fingers into her, he captured her mouth in a searing kiss.

A few minutes later, Rennie lay sprawled on top of him on the sofa. The clothes that hadn't been removed in time were damp, wrinkled, and twisted around them. Strands of her hair were wrapped around his neck. He was balancing with one foot on the floor. They were flushed and breathless, and excitement still pulsed where their bodies remained joined.

He panted a few breaths. "You were saying?"

He felt her smile against his chest as she asked drowsily, "Pancakes or eggs?"

HELLO, DARKNESS

prologue

Up until six minutes to sign-off, it had been a routine shift.

"It's a steamy night in the hill country. Thank you for spending your time with me here on 101.3. I've enjoyed your company tonight, as I do each weeknight. This is your host for classic love songs, Paris Gibson.

"I'm going to leave you tonight with a trio of my favorites. I hope you're listening to them with someone you love. Hold each other close."

She depressed the button on the control board to turn off her microphone. The series of songs would play uninterrupted right up to 1:59:30. During the last thirty seconds of her program, she would thank her listening audience again, say good night, and sign off.

While "Yesterday" played, she closed her eyes and rolled her head around on her tense shoulders. Compared to an eight- or nine-hour workday, a four-hour radio show would seem like a snap. It wasn't. By sign-off, she was physically tired.

She worked the board alone, introducing the songs she had selected and logged in before the show. Audience requests necessitated adjustments to the log and careful attention to the countdown clock. She also manned the incoming telephone lines herself.

The mechanics of the job were second nature, but not her delivery. She never allowed it to get routine or sloppy. Paris Gibson the person had worked diligently, with voice coaches and alone, to perfect the Paris Gibson "sound" for which she was well known.

She worked harder than even she realized to maintain that perfected inflection and pitch, because after 240 minutes on air, her neck and shoulder muscles burned with fatigue. That muscle burn was evidence of how well she had performed.

Midway through the Beatles classic, one of the telephone lines blinked red, indicating an incoming call. She was tempted not to answer, but, officially, there were almost six minutes left to her program, and she promised listeners that she would take calls until two A.M. It was too late to put this caller on the air, but she should at least acknowledge the call.

She depressed the blinking button. "This is Paris."

"Hello, Paris. This is Valentino."

She knew him by name. He called periodically, and his unusual name was easily remembered. His speaking voice was distinctive, too, barely above a whisper, which was probably either for effect or disguise.

She spoke into the microphone suspended above the board, which served as her telephone handset when not being used to broadcast. That kept her hands free to go about her business even while talking to a caller.

"How are you tonight, Valentino?"

"Not good."

"I'm sorry to hear that."

"Yes. You will be."

The Beatles gave way to Anne Murray's "Broken Hearted Me."

Paris glanced up at the log monitor and automatically registered that the second of the last three songs had begun. She wasn't sure she'd heard Valentino correctly. "I beg your pardon?"

"You will be sorry," he said.

The dramatic overtone was typical of Valentino. Whenever he called, he was either very high or very low, rarely on an emotional level somewhere in between. She never knew what to expect from him, and for that reason he was an interesting caller. But tonight he sounded sinister, and that was a first.

"I don't understand what you mean."

"I've done everything you advised me to do, Paris."

"I advised you? When?"

"Every time I've called. You always say—not just to me, but to everybody who calls—that we should respect the people we love."

"That's right. I think—"

"Well, respect gets you nowhere, and I don't care what you think anymore."

She wasn't a psychologist or a licensed counselor, only a radio personality. Beyond that, she had no credentials. Nevertheless, she took her role as late-night friend seriously.

When a listener had no one else to talk to, she was an anonymous sounding board. Her audience knew her only by voice, but they trusted her. She served as their confidante, adviser, and confessor.

They shared their joys, aired their grievances, and sometimes bared their souls. The calls she considered broadcast-worthy evoked sympathy from other listeners, prompted congratulations, and sometimes created heated controversy.

Frequently a caller simply needed to vent. She acted as a buffer. She was a convenient outlet for someone mad at the world. Seldom was she the target of the caller's anger, but obviously this was one of those times, and it was unsettling.

If Valentino was on the brink of an emotional breakdown, she couldn't heal what had led him to it, but she might be able to talk him a safe distance away from the edge and then urge him to seek professional help.

"Let's talk about this, Valentino. What's on your mind?"

"I respect girls. When I'm in a relationship, I place the girl on a pedestal and treat her like a princess. But that's never enough. Girls are never faithful. Every single one of them screws around on me. Then when she leaves me, I call you, and you say that it wasn't my fault."

"Valentino, I—"

"You tell me that I did nothing wrong, that I'm not to blame for her leaving. And you know what? You're absolutely right. I'm not to blame, Paris. *You* are. This time it's *your* fault."

Paris glanced over her shoulder, toward the soundproof door of the studio. It was closed, of course. The hallway beyond the wall of windows had never looked so dark, although the building was always dark during her after-hours program.

She wished Stan would happen by. Even Marvin would be a welcome sight. She wished for someone, anyone, to hear this call and help her get a read on it.

She considered disconnecting. No one knew where she lived or even what she looked like. It was stipulated in her contract with the radio station: She didn't make personal appearances. Nor was her likeness to appear in any promotional venues, including but not limited to all and any print advertising, television commercials, and billboards. Paris Gibson was a name and voice only, not a face.

But, in good conscience, she couldn't hang up on this man. If he had taken to heart something she'd said on air and things hadn't turned out well, his anger was understandable.

On the other hand, if a more rational person disagreed with something she had said, he simply would have blown it off. Valentino had vested in her more influence over his life than she deserved or desired.

"Explain how it's my fault, Valentino."

"You told her to break up with me."

"I never—"

"I heard you! She called you the night before last. I was listening to your program. She didn't give her name, but I recognized her voice. She told you our story. Then she said that I had become jealous and possessive.

"You told her that if she felt our relationship was constricting, she should do something about it. In other words, you advised her to dump me." He paused before adding, "And I'm going to make you sorry you gave her that advice."

Paris's mind was skittering. In all her years on the air, she'd never encountered anything like this. "Valentino, let's remain calm and discuss this, all right?"

"I'm calm, Paris. Very calm. And there's nothing to discuss. I've got her where no one will find her. She can't escape me."

With that statement, sinister turned downright scary. Surely he didn't mean literally what he'd just said.

But before she could speak her thought aloud, he added, "She's going to die in three days, Paris. I'm going to kill her, and her death will be on your conscience."

The last song in the series was playing. The clock on the computer monitor was ticking toward sign-off. She cut a quick glance at the Vox Pro to make certain that an electronic gremlin hadn't caused it to malfunction. But, no, the sophisticated machine was working as it should. The call was being recorded.

She wet her lips and took a nervous breath. "Valentino, this isn't funny."

"It isn't supposed to be."

"I know you don't actually intend—"

"I intend to do *exactly* what I said. I've earned at least seventy-two hours with her, don't you think? As nice as I've been to her? Isn't three days of her time and attention the least I deserve?"

"Valentino, please, listen—"

"I'm over listening to you. You're full of shit. You give rotten advice. I treat a girl with respect, then she goes out and spreads her legs for other men. And you tell her to dump me, like I'm the one who ruined the relationship, like I'm the one who cheated. Fair's fair. I'm going to fuck her till she bleeds, then I'm going to kill her. Seventy-two hours from now, Paris. Have a nice night."

chapter one

Dean Malloy eased himself off the bed. Groping in darkness, he located his underwear on the floor and took it with him into the bathroom. As quietly as he could, he closed the door before switching on the light.

Liz woke up anyway.

"Dean?"

He braced his arms on the edge of the basin and looked at his reflection in the mirror. "Be right out." His image gazed back at him, whether with despair or disgust, he couldn't quite tell. Reproach, at the very least.

He continued staring at himself for another few seconds before turning on the faucet and splashing cold water over his face. He used the toilet, pulled on his boxers, and opened the door.

Liz had turned on the nightstand lamp and was propped up on one elbow. Her pale hair was tangled. There was a smudge of mascara beneath her eye. But somehow she made deshabille look fetching. "Are you going to shower?"

He shook his head. "Not now."

"I'll wash your back."

"Thanks, but—"

"Your front?"

He shot her a smile. "I'll take a rain check."

His trousers were draped over the armchair. When he reached

for them, Liz flopped back against the heaped pillows. "You're leaving."

"Much as I'd like to stay, Liz."

"You haven't spent a full night in weeks."

"I don't like it any better than you do, but for the time being that's the way it's got to be."

"Good grief, Dean. He's sixteen."

"Right. Sixteen. If he were a baby, I'd know where he was at all times. I'd know what he was doing and who he was with. But Gavin is sixteen and licensed to drive. For a parent, that's a twenty-four-hour living nightmare."

"He probably won't even be there when you get home."

"He'd better be there," he muttered as he tucked in his shirt-tail. "He broke curfew last night, so I grounded him this morning. Restricted him to the house."

"For how long?"

"Until he cleans up his act."

"What if he doesn't?"

"Stay in the house?"

"Clean up his act."

That was a much weightier question. It required a more complicated answer, which he didn't have time for tonight. He pushed his feet into his shoes, then sat down on the edge of the bed and reached for her hand. "It's unfair that Gavin's behavior is dictating your future."

"*Our* future."

"Our future," he corrected softly. "It's unfair as hell. Because of him our plans have been put on indefinite hold, and that stinks."

She kissed the back of his hand as she looked up at him through her lashes. "I can't even persuade you to spend the night with me, and here I was hoping that by Christmas we'd be married."

"It could happen. The situation could improve sooner than we think."

She didn't share his optimism, and her frown said as much. "I've been patient, Dean. Haven't I?"

"You have."

"In the two years we've been together, I think I've been more than accommodating. I relocated here without a quibble. And even though it would have made more sense for us to live together, I agreed to lease this place."

She had a selective and incorrect memory. Their living together had never been an option. He wouldn't even have considered it as long as Gavin was living with him. Nor had there been any reason to quibble over her relocation to Austin. He had never suggested that she should. In fact, he would have preferred for her to remain in Houston.

Independently, Liz had made the decision to relocate when he did. When she sprang the surprise on him, he'd had to fake his happiness and conceal a vague irritation. She had imposed herself on him when the last thing he needed was an additional imposition.

But rather than opening a giant can of worms for discussion now, he conceded that she had been exceptionally patient with him and his present circumstances.

"I'm well aware of how much my situation has changed since we started dating. You didn't sign on to become involved with a single parent of a teenager. You've been more patient than I had any right to expect."

"Thank you," she said, mollified. "But my body doesn't know patience, Dean. Each month that passes means one less egg in the basket."

He smiled at the gentle reminder of her biological clock. "I acknowledge the sacrifices you've made for me. And continue to make."

"I'm willing to make more." She stroked his cheek. "Because, Dean Malloy, the hell of it is, you're worth those sacrifices."

He knew she meant it, but her sincerity did nothing to elevate his mood, and instead only increased his despondency. "Be patient a little longer, Liz. Please? Gavin is being impossible, but there are reasons for his bad behavior. Give it a little more time. Hopefully, we'll soon find a comfort zone the three of us can live within."

She made a face. "'Comfort zone'? Keep using phrases like that and, next thing you know, you'll have your own daytime TV talk show."

He grinned, glad they could conclude the serious conversation on a lighter note. "Still headed to Chicago tomorrow?"

"For three days. Closed-door meetings with folk from Copenhagen. All male. Robust, blond Viking types. Jealous?"

"Pea green."

"Will you miss me?"

"What do you think?"

"How about I leave you with something to remember me by?"

She pushed the sheet away. Naked and all but purring, lying on the rumpled bedding on which they'd already made love, Elizabeth Douglas looked more like a pampered courtesan than a vice-president of marketing for an international luxury-hotel chain.

Her figure was voluptuous, and she actually liked it. Unlike most of her contemporaries, she didn't obsess over every calorie. She considered it a workout when she had to carry her own luggage, and she never denied herself dessert. On her the curves looked good. Actually, they looked damn great.

"Tempting," he sighed. "Very. But a kiss will have to do."

She kissed him deeply, sucking his tongue into her mouth in a manner that probably would have made the Viking types snarl with envy. He was the one to end the kiss. "I've really got to go, Liz," he whispered against her lips before pulling back. "Have a safe trip."

She pulled up the sheet to cover her nudity and pasted on a smile to cover her disappointment. "I'll call you when I get there."

"You'd better."

He left, trying to make it look as if he wasn't fleeing. The air outside settled over him like a damp blanket. It even seemed to have the texture of wet wool when he inhaled it. His shirt was sticking to his back by the time he'd made the short walk to his car. He started the motor and set the air conditioner on high. The radio came on automatically. Elvis's "Are You Lonesome Tonight?"

At this hour there was virtually no traffic on the streets. Dean slowed for a yellow light and came to a full stop as the song ended.

"It's a steamy night in the hill country. Thank you for spending your time with me here on 101.3."

The smoky female voice reverberated through the interior of the car. The sound waves pressed against his chest and belly. Her voice was perfectly modulated by eight speakers that had been strategically placed by German engineers. The superior sound environment made her seem closer than if she'd been sitting in the passenger seat beside him.

"I'm going to leave you tonight with a trio of my favorites. I hope you're listening to them with someone you love. Hold each other close."

Dean gripped the steering wheel and rested his forehead on the back of his hands while the Fab Four yearned for yesterday.

As soon as Judge Baird Kemp retrieved his car from the Four Seasons Hotel parking valet and got in, he wrestled loose his necktie and shrugged off his jacket. "God, I'm glad that's over."

"You're the one who insisted we attend." Marian Kemp slipped off her Bruno Magli sling-backs and pulled off the diamond clip earrings, wincing as blood circulation was painfully restored to her numb earlobes. "But did you have to include us in the after party?"

"Well, it looked good for us to be among the last to leave. Very influential people were in that group."

Being a typical awards dinner, the event had run insufferably long. Following it, a cocktail party had been held in a hospitality suite, and the judge never passed up an opportunity to campaign for his reelection, even informally. For the remainder of their drive home, the Kemps discussed others who had been in attendance, or, as the judge derisively referred to them, "the good, the bad, and the ugly."

When they arrived home, he headed for his den, where

Marian saw to it that the bar was kept well stocked with his favorite brands. "I'm going to have a nightcap. Should I pour two?"

"No thank you, dear. I'm going up."

"Cool the bedroom down. This heat is unbearable."

Marian climbed the curved staircase that had recently been featured in a home-design magazine. For the photo, she'd worn a designer ball gown and her canary-diamond necklace. The portrait had turned out quite well, if she did say so herself. The judge had been pleased with the accompanying article, which had praised her for making their home into the showplace it was.

The upstairs hallway was dark, but she was relieved to see light beneath the door of Janey's room. Even though it was summer vacation, the judge had imposed a curfew on their seventeen-year-old. Last night, she had flouted the curfew and hadn't come in until almost dawn. It was obvious that she'd been drinking, and, unless Marian was mistaken, the stench that clung to her clothing was that of marijuana. Worse, she'd driven herself home in that condition.

"I've bailed you out for the last time," the judge had bellowed. "If you get another DWI, you're on your own, young lady. I won't pull a single string. I'll let it go straight on your record."

Janey had replied with a bored, "So fucking what?"

The scene had grown so loud and vituperative that Marian feared the neighbors might overhear despite the acre of manicured greenbelt between their property and the next. The quarrel had ended with Janey stomping into her room and slamming the door, then locking it behind her. She hadn't spoken to either of them all day.

But apparently the judge's most recent threat had made an impression. Janey was at home, and by her standards, it was early. Marian paused outside Janey's door and raised her fist, about to knock. But through the door she could hear the voice of that woman deejay Janey listened to when she was in one of her mellow moods. She was a welcome change from the obnoxious deejays on the acid rock and rap stations.

Janey tended to throw a tantrum whenever she felt her privacy was being violated. Her mother was disinclined to disturb this tenuous peace, so, without knocking, she lowered her hand and continued down the hallway to the master suite.

Toni Armstrong awoke with a start.

She lay unmoving, listening for a noise that might have awakened her. Had one of the children called out for her? Was Brad snoring?

No, the house was silent except for the low whir of the air-conditioning vents in the ceiling. A sound hadn't awakened her. Not even the soughing of her husband's breath. Because the pillow beside hers was undisturbed.

Toni got up and pulled on a lightweight robe. She glanced at the clock: 1:42. And Brad still hadn't come home.

Before going downstairs, she checked the children's rooms. Although the girls got tucked into their separate beds each night, they invariably wound up sleeping together in one. Only sixteen months apart, they were often mistaken for twins. They looked virtually identical now, their sturdy little bodies curled up together, tousled heads sharing the pillow. Toni pulled a sheet up over them, then took a moment to admire their innocent beauty before tiptoeing from the room.

Toy spaceships and action figures littered the floor of her son's bedroom. She carefully avoided stepping on them as she made her way to the bed. He slept on his stomach, legs splayed, one arm hanging down the side of the bed.

She took the opportunity to stroke his cheek. He'd reached the age where her demonstrations of affection made him grimace and squirm away. As the firstborn, he thought he had to act the little man.

But thinking of him becoming a man filled her with a desperation that was close to panic.

As she descended the staircase, several of the treads creaked, but Toni liked a house with the quirks and imperfections that gave it character. They had been lucky to acquire this house. It was in a good neighborhood with an elementary school nearby. The price had been reduced by owners anxious to sell. Parts of it had needed attention, but she had volunteered to make most of the repairs herself in order to fit the purchase into their budget.

Working on the house had kept her busy while Brad was getting settled into his new practice. She'd taken the time and effort to do necessary repairs before finishing with the cosmetic work. Her patience and diligence had paid off. The house wasn't only prettier in appearance, but sound from the inside out. Its flaws hadn't been glossed over with a fresh coat of paint without first being fixed.

Unfortunately, not everything was as easily fixable as houses.

As she had feared, all the rooms downstairs were dark and empty. In the kitchen, she turned on the radio to ward off the ominous pressure of the silence. She poured herself a glass of milk she didn't want and forced herself to sip it calmly.

Maybe she was doing her husband a disservice. He might very well be attending a seminar on taxes and financial planning. He had announced over dinner that he would be out for most of the evening.

"Remember, hon," he'd said when she expressed her surprise, "I told you about it earlier this week."

"No you didn't."

"I'm sorry. I thought I did. I intended to. Pass the potato salad, please. It's great, by the way. What's that spice?"

"Dill. This is the first I've heard of a seminar tonight, Brad."

"The partners recommended it. What they learned at the last one saved them a bundle in taxes."

"Then maybe I should go, too. I could stand to learn more about all that."

"Good idea. We'll watch for the next one. You're required to enroll in advance."

He'd told her the time and location of the seminar, told her not to wait up for him because there was an informal discussion session following the formal presentation and he didn't know how long it would last. He had kissed her and the kids before he left. He walked to his car with a gait that was awfully jaunty for someone going to a seminar on taxes and financial planning.

Toni finished her glass of milk.

She called her husband's cell phone for the third time, and as with the previous two calls, got his voice mail. She didn't leave a message. She thought about calling the auditorium where the seminar had taken place, but that would be a waste of time. No one would be there at this hour.

After seeing Brad off tonight, she had cleaned up the dinner dishes and given the children their baths. Once they were in bed, she had tried to go into Brad's den, but discovered that the door to it was locked. To her shame, she'd torn through the house like a woman crazed, looking for a hairpin, a nail file, something with which she could pick the lock.

She had resorted to a screwdriver, probably damaging the lock irreparably, but not caring. To her chagrin, there had been nothing in the room to validate her frenzy or her suspicion. A newspaper ad for the seminar was lying on his desk. He'd made a notation about the seminar on his personal calendar. Obviously he had been planning to attend.

But he was also very good at creating plausible smoke screens.

She had sat down at the desk and stared into his blank computer screen. She even fingered the power button on the tower, tempted to turn it on and engage in some exploration that only thieves, spies, and suspicious wives would engage in.

She hadn't touched this computer since he had bought one exclusively for her. When she saw the labeled boxes he'd carried in and placed on the kitchen table, she had exclaimed, "You bought another computer?"

"It's time you had your own. Merry Christmas!"

"This is June."

"So I'm early. Or late." He shrugged in his disarming way. "Now that you have your own, when you want to exchange email with your folks, or do some Internet shopping, or whatever, you won't have to work around me."

"I use your computer during the day when you're at the clinic."

"That's my point. Now you can go online anytime."

And so can you.

Apparently he had read her thought because he'd said, "It's not what you're thinking, Toni." Here he had propped his hands on his hips, looking defensive. "I was browsing in the computer store this morning. I see this bright pink number that's small, compact, and can do just about everything, and I think, 'Feminine and efficient. Just like my darling wife.' So I bought it for you on impulse. I thought you'd be pleased. Obviously I was wrong."

"I am pleased," she said, instantly contrite. "It was a very thoughtful gesture, Brad. Thank you." She looked askance at the boxes. "Did you say *pink?*"

Then they'd laughed. He'd enfolded her in a bear hug. He'd smelled like sunshine, soap, and wholesomeness. His body had felt comfortable, familiar, and good against hers. Her fears had been assuaged.

But only temporarily. Recently they had resurfaced.

She hadn't booted up his computer tonight. She'd been too afraid of what she might find. If a password had been required for access, her suspicions would have been confirmed, and she hadn't wanted that. God, no, she hadn't.

So she had done her best to restore the busted doorknob, then had gone to bed and eventually to sleep, in the hope that Brad would awaken her soon, brimming with knowledge about financial stratagems for families in their income bracket. It had been a desperate hope.

"I've certainly enjoyed your company tonight," the sexy voice on the radio was saying. "This is your host for classic love songs, Paris Gibson."

No seminar lasted until two o'clock in the morning. No therapy-group meeting lasted until the wee hours either. That had been Brad's excuse last week when he had stayed out most of the night.

His explanation had been that one of the men in his group was having a difficult time coping. "After the meeting, he asked me to go get a beer with him, said he needed an understanding shoulder to cry on. This dude has a *real* problem, Toni. Whew! You wouldn't believe some of the stuff he told me. I'm talking *sick*. Anyhow, I knew you would understand. You know what it's like."

She knew all too well. The lying. The denials. The time unaccounted for. Locked doors. She knew what it was like, all right. It was like this.

chapter two

This was creeping her out. Like, *really* creeping her out.

He'd been gone for a while now, and she didn't know when he would be coming back. She didn't like this scene and wanted to leave.

But her hands were tied. Literally. And so were her feet. The worst of it, though, was the metallic-tasting tape he had secured over her mouth.

Four—maybe five—times in the past several weeks, she had come here with him. On those occasions they had left drained of energy and feeling mighty good. The expression "screwed their brains out" sprang to mind.

But he had never suggested bondage or anything kinky. Well . . . nothing *too* kinky. This was a first and, frankly, she could do without it.

One of the things that had first attracted her to him was that he seemed sophisticated. He had been a definite standout in the migratory crowd comprised mostly of high school and college students looking for drink, dope, and casual sex. Sure, now and then you had your pathetic old geezer lurking in the bushes wagging his weenie at anybody unfortunate enough to glance his way. But this guy was nothing like that. He was way cool.

Apparently he had thought she was a standout, too. She and her friend Melissa had become aware of him watching them with single-minded interest.

"He might be a cop," Melissa speculated. "You know, working undercover."

Melissa had been on a real downer that night because she had to leave for Europe the following day with her parents, and she couldn't imagine anything more miserable. She was trying like hell to get glassy-eyed stoned, but nothing had taken effect yet. Her outlook on everything had been sour.

"A cop driving that car? I don't think so. Besides, his shoes are too good to be a cop's."

It wasn't merely that he had looked at her. Guys always looked at her. It was the *manner* in which he had looked at her that had been such a major turn-on. He'd been leaning against the hood of his car, ankles crossed, arms casually folded over his midriff, perfectly still and, despite his intensity, seemingly relaxed.

He didn't gawk at her chest or legs—consistently the objects of gawking—but looked straight into her eyes. Like he knew her instantly. Not just recognized her, or knew her by name, but knew *her,* knew everything there was to know about her that was important.

"Do you think he's cute?"

"I guess," Melissa replied, self-pity making her indifferent.

"Well, I think he is." She drained her rum and Coke, sucking it through the straw in the provocative way she had perfected by practicing for hours in front of her mirror. Its suggestiveness drove guys crazy and she knew it, and that's why she did it.

"I'm going for it." She reached behind her to set the empty plastic cup on the picnic table where she and Melissa had been sitting, then came off it with the sinuous grace of a snake sliding off a rock. She shook back her hair and gave the hem of her tank top a tug while drawing a deep, chest-expanding breath. Like an Olympic athlete, she went through a preparatory routine before each big event.

So it had been she who had made the first move. Leaving Melissa, she had sauntered toward him. When she reached the car, she moved in beside him and leaned back against the hood as he was doing. "You have a bad habit."

Turning only his head, he smiled down at her. "Only one?"

"That I know of."

His grin widened. "Then you need to get to know me better."

With no more invitation than that—because, after all, that was the reason they were there—he took her arm and ushered her around to the passenger side of his car. In spite of the heat, his hand was cool and dry. He politely opened the door and helped her into the leather-upholstered seat. As they drove away, she shot Melissa a triumphant grin, but Melissa was rummaging through her pouch of "mood enhancers" and didn't see.

He drove carefully, with both hands on the wheel, eyes on the road. He wasn't gaping at her and he wasn't groping and that was certainly a switch. Ordinarily, the minute she got into a guy's car, he'd start grabbing at her, like he couldn't believe his good fortune, like she might vaporize if he didn't touch her, or change her mind if he didn't hurry up and get on with it.

But this guy seemed a bit detached, and she thought that was kinda cool. He was mature and confident. He didn't need to gape and grope to assure himself that he was about to get laid.

She asked his name.

Stopping for a traffic light, he turned to look at her. "Is it important?"

She raised her shoulders in an exaggerated shrug, the rehearsed one, the one that pushed her breasts up and squeezed them together better than any Wonderbra could have. "I guess not."

He left his eyes on her breasts for several seconds, then the light changed and he went back to driving. "What's my bad habit?"

"You stare."

He laughed. "If you consider that a bad habit, then you really need to get to know me better."

She had placed her hand on his thigh and in her sultriest voice said, "I look forward to it."

His place was a major letdown. It was an efficiency apartment in a guest hotel. A tacky red banner strung across the front of the two-story building advertised special monthly rates. It was in a seedy neighborhood that didn't live up to his car or clothes.

Noticing her disappointment, he'd said, "It's a dump, but it's all I could find when I first moved here. I'm looking for something else." Then he added quietly, "I'll understand if you want me to take you back."

"No." She wasn't about to let him think she was a stupid, prissy high school girl with no spirit of adventure. "Shabby chic is in."

The apartment's main room served as both living area and bedroom. The galley kitchen was barely shoulder width. The bathroom was even smaller than that.

In the main room was a bed and nightstand, a four-drawer bureau, an easy chair with a floor lamp beside it, and a folding table long enough to accommodate an elaborate computer setup. The furnishings were garage-sale quality, but everything was neat.

She went over to the table. The computer was already booted up. With only a few clicks of the mouse, she found what she anticipated finding. She smiled at him over her shoulder and said, "So you weren't out there tonight by accident."

"I was out there tonight looking for you."

"Specifically?"

He nodded.

She liked that. A lot.

The Formica bar separating the kitchen from the living area was used as shelving for photographic equipment. He had a 35-millimeter camera, several lenses, and various attachments including a portable tripod. It all looked intricate and expensive, out of place in the crummy apartment. She picked up the camera and looked at him through the viewfinder. "Are you a professional?"

"It's only a hobby. Would you like something to drink?"

"Sure."

He went into the kitchen and returned with two glasses of red wine. Cool. Wine showed that he had refined tastes and class. It didn't jibe with the apartment either, but she figured that his explanation for it was a lie. This probably wasn't his main residence, only his playground. Away from the wife.

Sipping her wine, she glanced around. "So where are your pictures?"

"I don't display them."

"How come?"

"They're for my private collection."

"'Private collection'?" Grinning at him slyly, she twirled a strand of hair around her finger. "I like the sound of that. Show me."

"I don't think I should."

"Why not?"

"They're . . . artistic."

He was looking at her in that straightforward way again, as though measuring her reaction. His stare caused her toes to tingle, her pulse to race, and that hadn't happened in a long time in the company of a guy. It was usually she who created tingles and racing hearts. It was rare and wonderful to be the one unsure of exactly what was about to take place. Exciting as shit.

Boldly she declared, "I want to see your private collection."

He hesitated for several seconds, then knelt down beside the bed and pulled a box from beneath it. He removed the top and took out a standard photo album bound in faux black leather. As he came to his feet, he hugged it close to his chest. "How old are you?"

The question was an affront because she prided herself on looking much older than she was. She hadn't been carded in years—but a glimpse of the butterfly tattoo on her right breast usually made a bouncer too stupid to ask for an ID. "What the hell difference does it make how old I am? I want to see the pictures. And anyway, I'm twenty-two."

Clearly he didn't believe her. He even tried unsuccessfully to hide his smile. Nevertheless, he set the album on the table and stepped away from it. Trying to appear nonchalant, she walked over to it and flipped open the cover.

The first photo was graphic and startling. From the angle at which the close-up had been taken, she assumed—correctly, she discovered later—that it was a self-portrait.

"Are you offended?" he asked.

"Of course not. Do you think I've never seen one erect?" Her response wasn't nearly as blasé as she made it sound. She wondered if he could hear her pounding heartbeat.

She turned the page to the next shot and then to the next, until she had gone through the entire album. She studied each photograph, pretending to be as analytical as an art critic. Some were in color, some in black and white, but all except the first one were of naked young women provocatively posed. Anyone else might have considered them obscene, but she was too sophisticated to get uptight over exposed genitalia.

But by no stretch were they "artistic" studies of nudes. They were nasty pictures.

"Do you like them?" He was standing so close behind her now she could feel his breath in her hair.

"They're okay."

Reaching around her, he flipped back through several of the pages until he came to a particular shot. "This one's my favorite."

She didn't see anything that made this girl so special. Her nipples looked like mosquito bites against a flat, bony chest. You could count every rib and her hair had split ends. She had zits on her shoulders. A veil obscured her face, probably for good reason.

She closed the album, then turned to him and gave him her most seductive smile. Slowly she pulled her tank top over her head and dropped it to the floor. "You mean it's been your favorite up till now."

He caught his breath, then released it on a staggering exhalation. Moving slowly, he took her hand and placed it beneath her breast so that she was cupping it in her palm as though offering it to him.

He gave her the sweetest, most tender smile she'd ever seen. "You're perfect. I knew you would be."

Her ego soared. "We're wasting time." She unzipped her shorts and was about to remove them when he stopped her. "No, leave them there, low on your hips. Just like that." Quickly he reached for his camera. Apparently it was loaded with film and ready to fire, because he put his eye to the viewfinder.

"This is going to be great." He moved her closer to the floor lamp near the easy chair and adjusted the dingy shade, then backed away and looked through the camera again. "Lower the shorts just a little more. There. Right there."

He clicked off several shots in rapid succession. "Oh, lady, you're killing me." He lowered the camera and looked at her with pure delight. "You're a natural. You must've done this before."

"I've never posed professionally."

"Amazing," he said. "Now go sit on the edge of the bed."

He knelt on the floor in front of her and positioned her the way he wanted her. Legs. Hands. Head. Before he picked up the camera again, he kissed her inner thigh, sucking her skin against his teeth and leaving a mark.

For another hour, the picture taking continued along with the foreplay. By the time they actually did it, she was past ready. Afterward he refilled their wineglasses and lay beside her, stroking her gently all over and telling her how beautiful she was.

She had thought, *Now, here's a guy who knows how to treat a woman.*

When they finished their wine, he asked if he could take more pictures. "I want to capture your afterglow."

"So you'll have the before and after?"

He laughed and kissed her quickly and with affection. "Something like that."

He dressed her—yes, he had personally dressed her as she used to dress her dolls. He returned her to the park on the lake where they'd met and saw that she got safely into her car. As he closed the door, he kissed her lips softly. "I love you."

Whoa! That had taken her aback. A hundred guys had told her they loved her, but usually as they were fumbling to get a rubber on. More often than not these professions of love took place within the steamy interior of their cars or pickups.

But love had never been proclaimed softly, tenderly, and meaningfully. He'd even kissed the back of her hand before he let her go. She'd thought that was awfully sweet and gentlemanly.

They'd been together several times since that first night, and it was always good kicks. But soon, and predictably, he'd started whining. Where were you last night? Who were you with? I waited for hours, but you never showed up. When can I see you again?

His possessiveness took the fun out of being with him.

Besides, the newness and novelty had begun to wear off. His photography didn't seem exotic anymore, just weird and often creepy. It was time to bring this to a halt.

Maybe he sensed that she'd decided to break it off tonight, because it had started off badly. They'd quarreled immediately after he picked her up. From there things had grown progressively worse.

He'd gone bizarre and scary on her with this bondage shit. Leaving her tied up for what was going on hours now. What if this dump caught on fire? What if there was a tornado or something?

She didn't like it. She wanted out of here. The sooner the better.

Before he left, he had at least turned on the radio and tuned it to Paris Gibson's program. That provided her with some company. She didn't feel quite as abandoned as she would have felt in a total silence that accompanied the total darkness.

So she lay there listening to Paris Gibson's voice and wondering when the hell he was coming back and what other fun and games he had in mind.

chapter *three*

The red light on the control board went out. Valentino had hung up.

It was several seconds before Paris realized that the only sound she heard was that of her own heartbeat. The music had stopped. On the log monitor she saw a series of zeros where descending numbers should be counting down the time remaining on a song. How long had she been broadcasting dead air?

With twenty-three seconds left in her program, she depressed her microphone button. She tried to speak. Couldn't. Tried again.

"I hope you've enjoyed this evening of classic love songs. Please join me again tomorrow night. I'll be looking forward to it. Until then, this is Paris Gibson on FM 101.3. Good night."

By depressing two control buttons, she was off the air. Then she was off her tall swivel stool like a shot, yanking open the heavy studio door, racing down the dark hallway, and barreling into the engineering room.

Except for a box of take-out fried chicken on Stan's desk, the room was empty. She continued running down the hall, turning right at the first intersection of corridors and literally slamming into Marvin, who was dragging a dirty rag along an interior windowsill.

She gasped, "Have you seen Stan?"

"No." One thing you could say about Marvin—he was a man of few words. If he spoke at all, it was in monosyllables.

"Has he already left?"

This time, he didn't even give her a verbal reply, only a shrug.

Leaving the janitor, she ran to the men's rest room and pushed open the door. Stan was at the urinal. "Stan, come here."

Stunned by the interruption, he whipped his head around. "What— I'm sorta busy here, Paris."

"Hurry up. This is important."

She rushed back to the studio and wheeled her stool over to the Vox Pro. It recorded each incoming call for optional playback. There was also a mandatory recording made of everything that went out over the air. But that was another machine and another matter. Right now, she was interested only in the telephone call.

"What's going on?" Stan strolled in, looking at his wristwatch. "I've got plans."

"Listen to this."

"Remember, my shift ends when you sign off."

"Shut up, Stan, and listen."

He leaned against the edge of the control board. "Okay, but I really need to be leaving soon."

"Shh." Valentino had just identified himself. "This is a repeat caller."

Stan appeared more interested in the crease of his linen trousers. But when Valentino told her she would be very sorry, her coworker's eyebrows shot up. "What's that mean?"

"Listen."

He was quiet through the remainder of the recording. When it ended, Paris looked at him expectantly. He raised his narrow shoulders in a quick shrug. "He's a kook."

"That's it? That's your assessment? He's a kook?"

He snuffled. "What? You don't think he's *serious*?"

"I don't know." Turning, she punched the hot-line button on the board. That was the telephone line provided for the deejays' personal use.

"Who're you calling?" Stan asked. "The cops?"

"I think I should."

"Why? Nutcases call you all the time. Wasn't there one just last week who wanted you to be a pallbearer at his mother's funeral?"

"This is different. I talk to a lot of people every night. This one . . . I don't know," she added uneasily.

When her 911 call was answered, she identified herself and gave the operator a brief description of what had happened. "It's probably nothing. But I thought someone should hear this conversation."

"I listen to your program on my nights off, Ms. Gibson," the operator said. "You don't sound like the type to panic. There'll be a squad car there shortly."

Paris thanked her and hung up. "They're on their way."

Stan winced. "Do I have to hang around?"

"No, go on. I'll be fine. Marvin's still here."

"Actually he's not. He split. I saw him leaving on my way here from the men's room, where I was rudely interrupted midstream. A surprise like that, a guy could get hurt, you know."

She was in no mood for Stan tonight. "I doubt you'll suffer any damage." She waved him out. "Go on. Just lock the door behind you. I can let the police in."

Her nervousness must have conveyed itself and made him feel like a deserter. "No, I'll wait with you," he said glumly. "Go brew yourself some tea or something. You look rattled."

She *was* rattled. Tea sounded like a good idea. She headed for the employee kitchen, but never made it. An obnoxious buzzer sounded throughout the building, announcing that someone was at the main entrance.

Reversing her direction, she rushed toward the front of the building and was relieved to see two uniformed policemen on the other side of the glass door. Never mind that they appeared to be fresh out of the academy. One of them looked too young to shave. But they were all business and introduced themselves with stiff-lipped laconism.

"Thank you for coming so quickly."

"We'd been out this way and were headed back when we got

the call," one explained. He and his partner were looking at her strangely, as most people did when they first met her. The sunglasses made them instantly curious.

Without acknowledging either her glasses or their curiosity, she led Officers Griggs and Carson through the labyrinth of dark corridors. "There's a recording of the call in the studio."

The unremarkable exterior of the building hadn't prepared them for the electronic sophistication of the studio. They gazed about them with curiosity and awe. She brought them back on track by introducing Stan. Their acknowledgments were clipped. No one shook hands. Paris used the mouse on the Vox Pro computer to play Valentino's recorded call.

No one spoke while they listened. Officer Griggs stared at the ceiling, Carson at the floor. When it ended, Griggs raised his head and cleared his throat, seemingly embarrassed by Valentino's crude language. "Do you get calls like this often, Ms. Gibson?"

"Weird and kooky sometimes. Heavy breathers and dirty propositions, but nothing like what you've just heard. Never anything threatening. Valentino has called before. He tells me about a wonderful new girlfriend, or a recent breakup that left him heartbroken. He's never said anything like this. Never anything even close to this."

"You think it's the same guy?"

They all turned to Stan, who had ventured the idea.

He continued, "Somebody else could have borrowed the name Valentino because they've heard him on your show and know that he's a regular caller."

"I guess it's possible," Paris said slowly. "I'm almost positive that Valentino's voice is disguised. It never sounds quite natural."

"That's not a common name either," Griggs said. "Do you think it's legit?"

"I have no way of knowing that. Sometimes a caller is reluctant to give even a first name, preferring to remain totally anonymous."

"Do you have a way of tracing calls?"

"Ordinary caller ID. One of our engineers added software to

the Vox Pro that would give us a readout of the number, if it was available. Each call is also date and time stamped."

She brought up the information on the computer screen. There was no name, but a local telephone number, which Carson jotted down.

"This is a good start," he said.

"Maybe," Griggs said. "Considering what he called to say, why would he use a traceable number?"

Paris read between the lines. "You think it was a hoax?"

Neither of the policemen answered her directly. Carson said, "I'll call the number, see if anyone answers."

He used his cell phone, and after listening through numerous rings concluded that no one was going to pick up. "No voice mail either. Better call it in." He punched in digits, then while he was giving Valentino's number to whomever was on the other end, Griggs told her and Stan that the number would be traced.

"But my guess is that it was a guy using a name he'd heard on your program and just trying to get a reaction out of you."

"Like the sickos who make obscene phone calls," Stan said.

Griggs bobbed his cropped head. "Exactly like that. I bet we find a lonely drunk or a group of bored kids trying to have some fun by talking dirty, something like that."

"I hope you're right." Paris hugged herself and rubbed her arms for warmth. "I can't believe someone would do this as a joke, but I certainly prefer a joke to the alternative."

Carson disconnected. "They're on it. Shouldn't take long."

"You'll let me know what they find out?"

"Sure thing, Ms. Gibson."

Stan offered to follow her home, but it was a halfhearted offer and he seemed relieved when she declined. He bade them good night and left.

"How can we contact you when we know something?" Griggs asked as they wended their way through the building, toward the entrance.

She gave him her home telephone number, emphasizing that it was unlisted. "Of course, Ms. Gibson."

It surprised the two policemen that she was the one to lock up the building for the night. "Are you here alone every night?" Carson asked as they walked her to her car.

"Except for Stan."

"What does he do and how long has he worked here?"

He doesn't do much of anything, she thought wryly. But she told them that he was an engineer. "He's on standby if anything should go wrong with the equipment. He's been here for a couple of years."

"Nobody else works the night shift?"

"Well, there's Marvin. He's been doing our janitorial service for several months."

"Last name?"

"I don't know. Why?"

"Never can tell about people," Griggs said. "Do you get along with these guys all right?"

She laughed. "Nobody gets along with Marvin, but he's not the type to make a scary phone call. He only speaks when spoken to, and then he more or less grunts."

"What about Stan?"

She felt disloyal talking about him behind his back. If she spoke candidly, it wouldn't be a flattering description, so she told them only what was relevant. "We get along fine. I'm sure neither of them had anything to do with that call."

Griggs smiled at her and closed his small notebook with a decisive snap. "Doesn't hurt to follow up."

Her home telephone was ringing when she let herself in. She rushed to answer. "Hello?"

"Ms. Gibson, it's Officer Griggs."

"Yes?"

"Did you get in okay?"

"Yes. I just disengaged my alarm. Have you learned anything?"

"That number belongs to a pay phone near the UT campus. A squad car was dispatched to check it out but nobody was around. The phone's outside a pharmacy that closed at ten. Place and parking lot were deserted."

In effect, they were back to where they had started. She had hoped they would trace the number to a sad and lonely individual like Griggs had described, a lost soul who had threatened her and an imaginary captive in a dire attempt to get attention.

Her initial misgivings returned. "So what now?"

"Well, there's not really anything to be done unless he calls again. I don't think he will, though. It was probably someone just trying to rile you. Tomorrow night, we'll have squad cars patrolling the area around that phone booth, watching for anyone lurking in the vicinity."

That wasn't satisfactory, but it was all she was going to get. She thanked him. He and his partner had done what was expected of them, but she wasn't ready to concede that Valentino's call was a prank and nothing to worry about. Even the origin of the call was worrisome. Wouldn't someone seeking attention leave obvious clues so that he could be traced and identified, chastened by the police, maybe even written up in the newspaper?

Valentino had used a public telephone so the call couldn't be traced. He didn't want to be identified.

That disturbing thought was uppermost in her mind as she made her way through the living area of her house, down the hallway, and into her bedroom. As always when she returned home from work, the rooms were dark and silent.

The houses neighboring hers were also dark and hushed at this hour, but there was a difference. In those houses, the prayers of children had been heard before they were tucked in. Husbands and wives had kissed good night. Some had made love before settling beneath their blanket. They shared a bed, body heat, dreams. They shared their lives. Darkness was relieved by nightlights, small beacons of comfort that shone in rooms littered with toys and shoes, with the accoutrements of busy family life.

The nightlights in Paris's house only emphasized the sterile neatness of the rooms. Her movements were the only source of sound. She slept alone. That wouldn't have been her first choice, but that's the way it was, and she had come to accept it.

Tonight, however, the solitude was unnerving. And the cause was Valentino's call.

She'd had years of experience listening to voices, picking up nuances in speech, detecting underlying messages, separating truth from lies, and hearing more than what was said out loud. She was able to draw several conclusions about a person based strictly on his or her inflections. Calls had left her feeling happy, sad, reflective, annoyed, and, on occasion, downright angry.

None had left her feeling afraid. Until tonight.

chapter *four*

*H*er limbs were beginning to cramp from being held in one position for so long, and an itch on the sole of her foot was driving her nuts. Her face hurt and she could feel it swelling. She ached all over.

That son of a bitch, she thought, unable to curse him out loud because of the tape over her mouth.

Why had she ever thought he was so special? It wasn't like he took her to fabulous places and spent money on her. They'd never been anywhere together except this place, and it was a rathole.

She didn't know anything about him, not where he worked, not even his name. She'd never learned his name even by accident. It wasn't printed on anything in the apartment, no subscription magazines or mail, nothing. He remained nameless, and that should have been her first clue that he wasn't classy and intriguing, but just flat-out, freaking weird.

The second time they were together, he had defined the nature of their relationship. Laid down the ground rules, so to speak. He had opened the conversation while spreading baby oil over her, hoping to achieve a special effect in a series of photographs.

"Your friend . . . the one you were with the night we met."

"You mean Melissa?" she'd asked, feeling a stab of jealousy. Was he wanting to invite Melissa to join them in a ménage à trois? "What about her?"

"Have you told her about us?"

"I haven't had a chance. Her folks made her go to France with them for vacation. I haven't seen or talked to her since the night I met you."

"Have you told anyone about me and what we do here?"

"Oh, sure. I announced it over breakfast to my parents." His poleaxed expression made her giggle. "No, silly! I haven't told anyone."

"That's good. Because this is so special, I like thinking that you and I are each other's best-kept secret."

"We are each other's secret. I don't even know your name."

"But you know me."

He stared deeply into her eyes, and she was reminded of her first impression of him, that he could see straight into her innermost being. He apparently had felt the instantaneous connection that she had. After all, he'd told her that first night that he loved her.

The secrecy was probably necessary because of a wife who knew nothing about his "hobby." She envisioned his missus as a missionary-position-only prude who would never understand, much less consent to, his need for variety and excitement. Pictures of Mrs. No-name masturbating? Get real. Never in a million. Probably not even a bare-boob shot.

That night his lovemaking had been especially ardent. He was focused, you might say, not just his camera. She lost count of the number of times they did it, but it was always different, so it never got boring. He couldn't get enough of her and told her so. It was a heady experience, being practically worshiped by a man so classy he could probably have any woman. She had thought she would never want it to end.

But that had been then.

Each time she saw him, his jealousy increased, until it began to irritate her and rob her of the pleasure of being with him. No matter how good the sex was, it wasn't worth the hassle he gave her about other men.

She had thought about standing him up tonight, but then changed her mind. He was going to take it hard whenever she told him she didn't want to see him anymore. She dreaded a scene, but better to put him out of his misery sooner rather than later.

He had been waiting for her at the appointed place. And, unlike the night they'd met, he didn't look at all cool and relaxed. He was agitated and edgy. The moment she joined him in his car, he started in on her. "You've been with somebody else, haven't you?"

She supposed she should be flattered that he was jealous, but she had a headache and was in no mood for the third degree. "Do you have a joint?" Having learned that she was fond of smoke, he always had some for her.

"In the glove compartment."

There were three in a Ziploc bag. She lit one and inhaled deeply. "Best thing for a headache." Sighing, she laid her head on the headrest and closed her eyes.

"Who was he?"

"Who was who?"

"Don't jerk me around."

His tone brought her head up.

"You've already been with someone tonight, haven't you?" His fingers were clenching the steering wheel. "Don't bother lying about it. I know you've just had sex with someone else. I can smell him on you."

At first she was surprised and a bit unnerved that he knew. Had he been spying on her? But the uneasiness soon gave way to anger. Why was it any of his business who and when she screwed?

"Look, maybe getting together tonight isn't a good idea," she'd said. "I'm PMSing and I don't need any shit from anybody. Okay?"

His anger dissolved instantly. "I'm sorry I raised my voice. It's just . . . I thought . . ."

"What?"

"That we had something special here."

That's when she should have told him that she didn't want to see him again. Right then he'd given her an opportunity, but, damn it, she hadn't taken it. Instead she'd said, "I don't like you ragging me about where I go, what I do, and who I do it with. I get enough of that at home." She leaned back and pulled deeply on the joint. "Either chill or take me back to my car."

He chilled. He was subdued, even a little sullen, when they reached the apartment. "Want some wine?"

"Don't I always?"

She was already high from the weed. Might as well go all out and get really wasted. One mercy fuck, then she'd tell him they needed to cool it for a while—read *forever*—then she'd get the hell out of here and never come back.

His computer monitor was the only source of light in this room where the shades were always drawn. One of the more graphic photos of her was on his screen saver.

Seeing it, she said, "Tsk, tsk. That's definitely one of the 'afterglows,' isn't it? I'm such a naughty girl. Naughty but nice, right?" She winked at him as she accepted the glass of wine he brought from the kitchen.

She drank it like water, burped loudly and wetly, then extended the empty glass toward him in an impertinent request for a refill.

"You're acting like a slut." He calmly took the glass from her and set it on the nightstand. Then he slapped her. He slapped her so hard that tears came to her eyes even before the rocket of pain from her cheekbone reached her brain.

She cried out, but was too shocked to articulate a word.

He pushed her back onto the bed. She landed hard. The room seemed to tilt. She was more wasted than she'd thought. She struggled to get up. "Hey! I don't—"

"Oh, yes, you do."

He splayed his hand over her chest, holding her down while he wrestled with his belt and fly. Then he began tearing at her clothing. She swatted his hands, kicked at him, and called him every name in the book, but he wouldn't be stopped.

He pushed himself into her with such force that she screamed. He covered her mouth with his hand. "Shut up," he hissed, so close to her face she felt a shower of spit.

She bit into the flesh beneath his thumb. He yelped and withdrew his hand. "You bastard," she yelled. "Get off me."

To her astonishment, he began to laugh softly. "You fell for it. You thought I was serious."

She stopped struggling. "Huh?"

"I was just fulfilling your rape fantasy."

"You're crazy."

"Am I?" He thrust hard into her. "Can you honestly say you don't like it?"

"Damn right. I hate it. I hate you, you son of a bitch."

That caused him to smile, because in spite of what she said, she was responding. When it was over, each was exhausted and glistening with sweat.

He recovered first and went for his camera. "Stay just as you are," he said as he clicked off the first shot.

The flash seemed exceptionally bright. She was good and truly stoned.

"Don't move," he told her. "I have an idea."

Move? She was too lethargic to move. Her entire body throbbed, starting with her cheekbone—how was she going to explain a bad bruise?—and all the way down to her splayed thighs. Christ, she still had her sandals on. How funny was that? But she was too tired to trouble herself with taking them off. Besides, he had told her not to move.

Maybe she dozed for a minute or two. Next thing she knew he was back, bending over her, pulling her wrists together.

"What's that?" She roused herself and saw that he was using a necktie to bind her wrists together.

"A prop for a photograph. You've been a bad girl. You need to be punished." He climbed off the bed and picked up his camera and adjusted the focus.

That's when it began to get creepy and she felt the first twinges of apprehension. She had struggled to sit up. "Have I mentioned that I'm not into bondage?"

"This isn't bondage, this is punishment," he said absently as he moved to the lamp. He adjusted the shade, setting it first at one angle, then another, causing shadows to shift across her body.

Okay. Enough of this. She'd had it. After tonight, no more of him. Posing for him had been fun. It had been something different and, admittedly, it had been a kick to later look at the pictures of herself.

But he was getting too possessive and too . . . too out there.

"Look," she recalled saying sternly, "I really want you to untie my hands now."

Finally satisfied with the lighting, he began setting up the tripod.

Taking another tack, she softened her tone. "I'll do anything you want. You know I will. All you have to do is ask. Anything."

He still didn't seem to be listening. While he was distracted, she had inched toward the edge of the bed, calculating the distance to the door. But when she looked at it, something struck her as odd, and a cold dart of fear went through her when she realized that there was no doorknob on this side. Only a brass disk where the doorknob should have been.

That's when he had stopped tinkering with the camera. No doubt sensing her alarm, he had smiled down at her. "Where do you think you're going?"

"I want you to untie me."

"You moved and spoiled the lighting," he chided gently.

"Lighting, my ass, I'm *leaving*."

Her cheerleading days had paid off. She came off the bed with surprising strength and agility. But she didn't get far. He caught her by the hair and yanked her back, then shoved her down onto the bed.

"You can't keep me here," she'd cried.

"You just had to ruin it, didn't you?"

"Ruin what?"

"Us."

"There isn't any 'us,' you sick wacko."

"You had to cheat on me. Just like the others. Didn't you think I'd find out? I listen to Paris Gibson, too, you know. She put your call on the air. Thousands of people heard you telling her that you felt smothered by my possessiveness. You were going to take her advice and dump me, weren't you?"

"Oh, Jesus."

He'd stood over her, both fists clenched at his sides as though he were forcibly suppressing his rage. "You can't treat people like toilet paper and get away with it, you know."

And because he had become so freaking scary, she had wisely shut up.

He had taken a few more photos, then decided that her feet also needed to be tied. She had fought him as if her life depended on it, but he'd eventually slapped her so hard her ears rang. That was the last thing she heard.

When she came to, she was spread-eagled, her hands and feet tied to the bed frame beneath the box springs, her mouth taped shut. The apartment was empty. He was gone. She was alone, and no one knew where she was.

Over the passing hours, she had devised a dozen means of escape, but dismissed the ideas almost as soon as she conceived them. None was workable. She was helpless to do anything but wait for him to come back for more of his sick sex games.

Jesus, she thought, *what have I gotten myself into?*

"I hope you've enjoyed this evening of classic love songs. Please join me again tomorrow night. I'll be looking forward to it. Until then, this is Paris Gibson on FM 101.3. Good night."

Great. Now she didn't even have Paris to keep her company.

chapter five

Gavin Malloy was awfully drunk. The pleasant buzz from the cheap tequila wasn't quite so pleasant any longer. It was too hot to be drinking tequila shots. He should have stuck to beer. But he had needed something strong and nasty to drown his depression.

The hell of it was, he was still depressed.

The evening had been spoiled for him early on. His drinking had accomplished nothing except to make him light-headed, sweaty, and nauseous. Blearily he looked toward a clump of scraggly cedar trees and wondered if he could cover the distance over the rocky ground before he puked. Probably not.

Besides, he'd seen a couple disappear behind the trees a while ago. If they were still doing what they'd gone there to do, they wouldn't appreciate him hurling on them. Talk about coitus interruptus.

He chuckled at the thought.

"What're you laughing at?" his new friend asked, nudging him in the gut, which caused the tequila to slosh. The guy's name was Craig something. If he'd ever heard his last name, he'd forgotten it. Craig drove a Dodge Ram pickup, the biggest one made. Jet black. Fully loaded. It was one badass truck.

Gavin, Craig, and several others had been hanging out in the bed of the pickup for hours, waiting for something to happen. A group of girls had come by earlier, drunk some of their tequila, showed them just enough skin to get them excited, then wandered away with promises to return. So far they hadn't.

"What's funny?" Craig asked again.

"Nothing. Just thinking."

"'Bout what?"

What had he been thinking? He couldn't remember. Must not've been very important. "My old man," he said around a belch. Yeah, his old man had been in the back of his mind all night, bothering him like an itch he couldn't reach.

"What about him?"

"He's gonna shit 'cause I went out tonight. He grounded me."

"That sucks."

"You got grounded?" another guy jeered. "What are you, twelve?"

Gavin didn't know his name, only that he was an asshole with bad skin and worse breath who thought he was a lot cooler than he was.

Gavin had moved to Austin from Houston a week after the spring semester ended. Finding a new crowd during summer break hadn't been easy, but he had joined this group, who accepted him once they learned he was a guy who liked to party as much as they did.

"Awww, Gavin's scared of his daddy," the jerk taunted.

"I'm not scared of him. I just dread having my ass chewed again."

"Save yourself the hassle." This from the optimist who'd showed them earlier his inventory of condoms. "Wait till he goes to bed before you sneak out."

"I tried that already. He's a freaking bat. He's got like built-in radar or something."

This conversation was making the lousy evening lousier. Nothing could cheer him up tonight, not more tequila, not even the return of the girls, and chances were excellent that they weren't going to come back as promised. Why would they waste their time on losers like this bunch, like him?

He stood up, swaying dangerously. "I'd better split. If I'm lucky, he won't be home yet. He's with his girlfriend."

He waded through the others, then jumped off the tailgate. But he miscalculated the distance to the ground as well as the weakness in his knees and wound up facedown in the dirt.

His new buddies howled. Weak with laughter himself, he struggled to get upright. His T-shirt was so wet with sweat that when he tried to dust himself off, he left streaks of mud across the front of it.

"Tomorrow night," he told his friends as he staggered away. Where had he left his car?

"Don't forget tomorrow is your turn to bring the booze," Craig called.

"I'm broke."

"Steal it from your old man."

"I can't. He checks the bottles."

"Jesus, is he a cop in his spare time?"

"I'll see what I can do," Gavin mumbled as he turned in the general direction of where he'd parked.

"What if Miss Hotpants comes looking for you?" It was the asshole, calling to him in a singsong voice. His grin was ugly and goading. "What should we tell her? That you had to go home to your daddy?"

"Get fucked."

The obnoxious kid hooted. "Well, it's for sure you won't. Not tonight anyway."

One of the others muttered, "Shut up, dickhead."

"Yeah, give it a rest," the condom guy said.

"What? Wha'd I do?"

Craig spoke softly. "She dumped him."

"She did? When?"

Gavin moved out of earshot, which was just as well. He didn't want to hear any more.

He located his car. It wasn't that difficult to spot among all the others because it was a piece of shit. No badass pickup or sports car for him. Oh, no, nothing like that for Gavin Malloy. And you could forget a motorcycle. That wasn't going to happen as long as his old man was in charge, and probably not as long as he was drawing breath.

His car was a snore. It was a sensible, good-mileage means of transportation that would spoil the racy image of a Mormon soccer mom. And he was expected to be grateful for it.

He'd gotten a lecture when he expressed his low opinion of it. "A car isn't a toy, Gavin. Or a status symbol. This is a reliable first car. When you've proved that you're responsible enough to take care of it and use it safely, I'll consider an upgrade. Until then . . ." Blah-blah-blah.

The thing was an embarrassment. When the fall semester started at his new school, he would probably be laughed off campus for driving this heap. The dorkiest of the dorks wouldn't want to be seen with him.

In his present condition, he had no business driving anything and was just sober enough to realize it. He concentrated hard on keeping the center stripe in focus. But that only seemed to increase his dizziness.

He was still several blocks from home when he was forced to pull over, get out, and vomit. He spewed a torrent of tequila on some poor sucker's flower bed that formed a neat circle of color around the mailbox. Someone would have a disgusting surprise when they came out to get the mail tomorrow. To say nothing of the mailman.

Coordination shot, he climbed back into his car and drove the remainder of the way to the new house his dad had bought for them. It wasn't bad. In fact, Gavin kinda liked it. Especially the pool. But he didn't want his dad to know he liked it.

He was relieved to see that his old man's car wasn't in the driveway. But Gavin wouldn't put it past him to have laid a trap, so he slipped into the house through the back door and paused to listen. His dad would love to catch him sneaking in so he could ground him for longer, take away his cell phone, his computer, his car, and make his life even more miserable than it was.

That was his parents' main mission in life—to make *him* miserable.

Satisfied that the house was empty, he went to his room. His old man must still be with Liz. Screwing like rabbits, no doubt.

They never did it here in his dad's bed. Did they think he was stupid, that he didn't know they were having sex when they spent the evening at her place?

It was easy to imagine Liz in bed. She had a hot body. But his old man? Rutting? No way. Gavin couldn't imagine anything more gross.

In his bedroom he turned on his computer even before he switched on the desk lamp. He couldn't fathom life without a computer. How had people survived before them? If his dad really wanted to punish him, that's the privilege he would revoke.

He checked for email. There was one from his mom, which he deleted without reading. Anything she had to say was salve for her conscience and he didn't want to hear it.

You'll come to realize that this is best for all of us.

You and your future are our main concerns, Gavin.

Once you have adjusted to the change . . .

Sure, Mom. Whatever you say, Mom. Bullshit, Mom.

He sat down at the desk and began composing an email letter. But not to his mother. His anger with her was mild compared to the animosity he felt for the recipient of this letter. Not that he planned on sending it. And because he didn't, he poured out all the anger that had been roiling inside him for days.

"What makes you think you're so hot anyway?" he wrote. "I've seen better. I've *had* better."

"Gavin?"

When the overhead light flashed on, he nearly jumped out of his skin. He quickly exited his email before his old man could read what was on his screen. He pivoted in his chair, hoping he didn't look guilty. "What?"

"I'm home."

"So?"

"You okay?"

"Why wouldn't I be? I'm not a kid."

"Did you eat some dinner?"

"Oh yeah," he said, smacking his lips. "Microwaved leftover pizza."

"You were invited to join Liz and me. You chose not to."

"Bet that broke your heart."

In the even, unruffled voice Gavin hated, his dad said, "If I hadn't wanted you to come along, I wouldn't have invited you." He came into the room. Gavin thought, *Oh, great.* "What've you been doing all evening?"

"Nothing. Surfing the net."

"What's that on your shirt?"

Perfect. He'd forgotten about the filth on his T-shirt. Dirt. Probably vomit, too. Ignoring the question, he turned back to face the computer. "I'm busy."

His dad took him by the shoulder and turned him around. "You went out. Your car isn't in the same place it was when I left and the hood is warm."

Gavin laughed. "You're checking the temperature of my car's engine? You need to get a life."

"And you need to get with the program." His father said this in a raised voice, which was rare. "You stink of vomit and you're drunk. Driving drunk, you could've killed somebody."

"Well, I didn't. So relax and leave me alone."

Dean stuck out his hand, palm up. "Give me your car keys."

Gavin glared at him. "If you think taking my keys will keep me cooped up in here, you're wrong."

Dean said nothing, just kept his hand extended. Gavin fished the keys from the pocket of his jeans and dropped them into his father's palm. "I hate the damn car anyway, so no big loss."

His dad pocketed the keys but didn't leave. He sat down on the edge of the unmade bed. "Now what?" Gavin groaned. "One of your famous lectures on how I'm pissing my life away?"

"Do you think I enjoy punishing you, Gavin?"

"Yeah, I think you do. I think you get off on being the big, bad father, having me to boss around. You enjoy telling me everything I'm doing wrong."

"That's ridiculous. Why do you say that?"

"Because you've never done anything wrong in your whole goddamn life. Mr. Perfect, that's you. It must be boring as shit to be so right all the time."

He was surprised to see his dad smile. "I'm far from right all the time and nowhere near perfect. Ask your mother. She'll tell you. But I know I'm right about one thing."

His dad paused and looked at him hard, probably hoping he would ask what that one thing was. He could wait till hell froze over. Finally he said, "It's right that you're living with me now. I'm glad you are. I want you here with me."

"Right. I'm sure you're just thrilled over the new living arrangements. You love having me around, cramping your style, getting in the way."

"In the way? Of what?"

"Of everything." The exclamation caused his voice to crack. He hoped his dad didn't mistake it for emotion, which it sure as hell wasn't. "I'm in the way of your life. Your new job. Liz."

"You're not in the way, Gavin. You're my family, my son. Liz and I wanted you with us tonight."

He scoffed. "For a cozy dinner? Just the three of us. Your new family. Then what? What was I supposed to do when you took her home? Wait in the car while you went inside for a quick blow job?"

He knew instantly that he'd gone too far. His dad wasn't one to fly off the handle when he got angry. He didn't lose his temper, rant and rave, stomp around, yell, or throw things. Instead, Mr. Self-control went very still. His lips narrowed and something funny happened to his eyes that made them seem to harden and sharpen and go right through you like steel picks.

But apparently there was a limit to his old man's restraint, and he'd just reached it.

Before he had even processed all this, his father was on his feet, and he was on the receiving end of a backhanded smack that caught him hard across the mouth and split his lip.

"You don't want to be treated like a kid? Fine. I'll treat you like an adult. That's what I would have done to any grown man who said something like that to me."

Gavin struggled to hold back tears. "I hate you."

"Well, too bad. You're stuck with me." He went out, soundly pulling the door shut behind him.

Gavin launched himself out of the chair. He stood in the

center of his messy room, bristling with anger and frustration. But realizing he had nowhere to run, and no means of running if he had somewhere to go, he threw himself onto his bed.

He made swipes at the snot, tears, and blood that had mingled on his face. He felt like blubbering. He wanted to draw himself into the fetal position and cry like a baby. Because his life sucked. All of it. He hated everything and everybody. His dad. His mom. The city of Austin. Women. His stupid friends. His ugly car.

Most of all he hated himself.

chapter six

Without making it too obvious, Sergeant Robert Curtis was trying to see past the dark lenses of her sunglasses. Catching himself staring, he hastily held a chair for her. "Forgive my lack of manners, Ms. Gibson. I'll admit to being a little starstruck. Have a seat. Can I get you some coffee?"

"I'm fine, thanks. And I'm hardly a star."

"I beg to differ."

Curtis was a detective for the Austin Police Department's Central Investigative Bureau. He was fiftyish, compactly built, and neatly turned out, down to a polished pair of cowboy boots, the heels of which added a couple of inches to his stature. Although he was still no taller than she, he gave off an air of authority and confidence. A sport jacket was hanging on a coat tree, but his necktie was tightly knotted beneath a starched collar. His cuffs were monogrammed with his initials.

On the walls of the small enclosure were a detailed map of the state, another of Travis County, and a framed diploma. The built-in desk was nearly completely covered with paperwork and computer components, but somehow avoided looking messy.

Curtis sat down at his desk and smiled at her. "It's not every morning of the week I get visited by a radio personality. What can I do for you?"

"I'm not sure you can do anything."

Now that she was here, ensconced with a detective in his

compact cubicle where he doubtless worked long hours, serving the public by snaring felons, she was second-guessing her decision to come.

Things that happened at two o'clock in the morning took on a different complexion in daylight. Suddenly, coming here seemed like a melodramatic and somewhat self-centered reaction to what probably amounted to a crank phone call.

"I called in a 911 last night," she began. "Actually early this morning. Two patrolmen, Griggs and Carson, responded. I have a case number for your reference." She gave him the number that Griggs had left with her.

"What kind of 911, Ms. Gibson?"

She gave him an account of what had happened. He listened attentively. His expression remained open and concerned. He didn't fidget as though she were wasting his time on something trivial. If he was faking his interest, he did it very well.

When she finished, she removed a cassette tape from her handbag and passed it to him. "I went to the station early this morning and made a copy of the call."

Insomnia had claimed her until dawn, when she finally surrendered to it. She got up, showered and dressed, and was back at the radio station by the time Charlie and Chad, the morning drive-time deejays, were reading the seven o'clock news headlines.

"I'll be happy to listen to your tape, Ms. Gibson," Curtis said. "But this department investigates homicide, rape, assault, robbery. Threatening phone calls . . ." He spread his hands wide. "Why'd you come to me?"

"I read your name in yesterday's newspaper," she admitted with chagrin. "Something about your testifying at a trial. I thought I'd get more personal attention if I asked to speak with a particular detective rather than just showing up without an appointment."

Now he looked chagrined. "You're probably right."

"And if my caller does what he threatens to do, it will fall to this department to investigate, won't it?"

Sobering instantly, Curtis left his chair and stepped outside the cubicle. He called across the room at large, asking if anybody had a cassette recorder handy. Within moments another plain-clothes detective appeared with one. "Here you go."

He regarded Paris with patent curiosity as he handed the machine to Curtis, whose brusque, "Thanks, Joe," was as good as a dismissal. The other man withdrew.

Sergeant Curtis had been a random selection, but she was glad she'd come to him. He obviously had some clout and wasn't reluctant to use it.

He returned to his seat and inserted the tape into the recorder, saying in an undertone, "I see word has gotten around as to who you are."

Maybe, Paris thought. Or maybe the detective was simply wondering why she hadn't removed her sunglasses. This wasn't a particularly bright environment. In fact, it was a room without windows.

Curtis and the other detective probably assumed that she wore the sunglasses like a celebrity would, to conceal her identity in public or to add to her mystique as a media personality, that she wore them to shut others out. It would never occur to them that she wore the glasses to shut herself in.

"Let's see what Mr. . . . what was it? Valentino? . . . has to say for himself." Curtis pressed the Play button. *This is Paris. Hello, Paris. This is Valentino.*

When the tape ended, Curtis tugged thoughtfully on his lower lip, then asked, "Mind if I play it again?"

Without waiting for her consent, he rewound the tape and restarted it. As he listened, he frowned with concentration and rolled his University of Texas class ring around his stubby finger.

At the end of the tape, she asked, "What do you think, Sergeant? Am I reading too much into a crank call?"

He asked a question of his own. "Did you try to call the number?"

"I was so stunned, I didn't think of calling back immediately, but I suppose I should have."

He dismissed her concern with a wave. "He probably wouldn't have answered anyway."

"He didn't when Carson called later. No voice mail either. Just an unanswered ring."

"The number on the caller ID, you say it was traced to a pay phone?"

"I'm sure the details are in the report, but Griggs told me that a patrol car in that area had been dispatched to check out the phone booth. But by that time—at least half an hour, maybe more—whoever placed the call was gone."

"Somebody could have seen him at the phone booth. Did the patrolmen ask around?"

"There was nobody to ask. According to Griggs, the area was deserted when the patrol car arrived." Curtis's questions were validating her concern, but that only increased her anxiety. "Do you think Valentino was telling the truth? Has he kidnapped a girl he plans to murder?"

Curtis made balloons of his ruddy cheeks before expelling a long breath. "I don't know, Ms. Gibson. But if he has, and if he sticks to his three-day deadline, we don't have time to sit around and talk about it. I don't want another kidnap-rape-murder case on my desk if I can possibly avoid it." He stood up and reached for his jacket.

"What can we do?"

"We start by trying to determine if he's for real or just a nut trying to win the attention of his favorite celebrity." By now he was ushering her through the maze of similar cubicles toward the set of double doors through which she'd entered the CIB.

"How do we make that determination?"

"We go to the authority on the subject."

Just as Dean was leaving the house, Liz called from the Houston airport. "You're already in Houston?"

"My flight from Austin was at six-thirty."

"Brutal."

"Tell me." After a short pause, she asked, "What happened with Gavin when you got home last night?"

"Your basic open warfare, both sides scoring hits and suffering casualties."

He balanced the cordless phone between chin and shoulder and poured himself a glass of orange juice. He'd lain awake for hours last night, and when he finally did fall asleep, he'd gone comatose. His alarm had been going off for half an hour before it awakened him. No time to brew coffee this morning.

"Well, at least he was home when you got there," Liz said. "He hadn't disobeyed."

Not wanting to recount his argument with Gavin, Dean harrumphed a nonverbal agreement. "What time is your first meeting in Chicago?"

"As soon as I arrive at the hotel. I hope O'Hare isn't too hairy and I can get through it quickly. What have you got on tap today?"

He outlined his day. She said she needed to run, that she'd just wanted to say hi before her flight to Chicago. He told her he was glad that she'd caught him and wished her a safe flight. She said, "I love you." And he replied with, "Love you, too."

After disconnecting, Dean bowed his head, closed his eyes, and tapped his forehead—hard—with the telephone as though he were paying some kind of unorthodox self-flagellating penance.

Rather than getting his day off to the good start that Liz had obviously intended, her call put him out of sorts. Add the blasted heat and Austin's rush-hour traffic, and he was in a testy mood when he reached his office fifteen minutes late.

"Good morning, Ms. Lester. Any messages?"

Dean shared the secretary with several other people. She was competent. And friendly. His first day on the job, she had informed him that she was the divorced mother of two daughters and that it was okay for him to call her by her first name.

Unless his eyes were deceiving him, and he didn't think they were, since his arrival her necklines had gotten progressively lower and her hemlines higher. This gradual reduction of textiles could be in correlation with the rising summertime temperature, but he doubted it. Just to be safe, he had stuck to calling her Ms. Lester.

"Messages are on your desk. A fresh pot of coffee is brewing. Soon as it's ready, I'll bring you some."

Fetching him coffee wasn't in her job description, but this morning he was glad she'd volunteered. "Great, thanks."

He went into his office and closed the door, discouraging further conversation. He slung his jacket onto the wall rack, loosened his tie, and unbuttoned his collar button. He sat down at his desk and riffled through his messages, happy to see there were no urgent ones. He needed a few minutes to decompress.

He swiveled his desk chair around and adjusted the window blind so he could see out. The sunlight was glaring, but that wasn't why he dug his fingers into his eye sockets, then wearily dragged his hands down his face.

What was he going to do about Gavin? How many times could he ground him? How many more privileges could he revoke? How many more scenes like the one last night could they withstand? Arguments such as that inflicted damage that was often irreparable. Could any relationship survive constant onslaughts like that?

He sorely regretted smacking him. Not that Gavin hadn't deserved it for the insulting crack he'd made. Still, he shouldn't have struck him. He was the grown-up and he should have behaved as such. To lose his temper like that was juvenile. And dangerous. Loss of control could wreak havoc, and he knew that better than anyone.

Besides, he was determined to be a positive role model for Gavin. He didn't want to preach to him, but to set a good example. Last night, he had sent the wrong message on how to manage anger, and he was sorry for it.

He ran his fingers through his hair and wondered what was taking the coffee so freaking long.

Should he send Gavin back to his mother? "Not an option," he muttered out loud. No way. For a long list of reasons that included welshing on the agreement he and Pat had reached about their son, but the main one being that Dean Malloy deplored failure. At anything. He threw in the towel only when absolutely forced to.

Gavin had told him—more like *accused* him—of always being right. He'd said that it must be boring as shit to be so right all the time. *Hardly, Gavin,* he thought cynically. He didn't feel right about anything. Obviously he wasn't doing right by his son.

Or by Liz. Not by a long shot was he doing right by Liz. How long could he put off doing something about that?

"Dr. Malloy?"

Thinking that Ms. Lester was bringing the long-awaited, high-octane coffee, he kept his back to the door. "Just set it on the desk, please."

"There's someone here to see you." Dean swiveled his chair around. "Sergeant Curtis from CIB asked for a minute of your time," the secretary told him. "Is it all right if he comes in?"

"Certainly." He'd met the detective only once, but he'd seemed like a stand-up kind of guy. Dean knew that he was a hard-working and well-respected member of the Austin PD. He stood up as Curtis walked in. "Good morning, Sergeant Curtis."

"Just plain Curtis. That's what everybody calls me. Do you prefer Doctor or Lieutenant?"

"How about Dean?" They met in the center of the office and shook hands.

"Is this a bad time?" Curtis asked. "I apologize for barging in on you unannounced, but this might turn out to be important."

"No problem. Coffee is on the way."

"Make that coffee for three. I'm not alone." Curtis stepped back into the open doorway and motioned someone forward.

Despite her sunglasses, Paris feared that her expression was no less revealing than Dean's.

He appeared to be as dumbfounded as she'd been a few moments ago when she read his name on the office door she was about to enter, unaware, unprepared, unbolstered, and unable to stop the inevitable.

He gaped at her for several seconds before managing to articulate a startled, "Paris?"

Curtis divided a surprised look between them.

"Should I bring more cups, Dr. Malloy?"

That from the secretary.

Dean's gaze remained fixed on Paris as he replied, "Please, Ms. Lester."

The secretary withdrew, leaving Paris, Dean, and the detective standing frozen in an awkward tableau like actors who had forgotten their lines. Finally Curtis placed his hand beneath her elbow and nudged her forward. Unwillingly she went farther into the office, into Dean's space.

And like any space Dean had ever occupied, he dominated it. Not just physically, with his above-average height and broad shoulders, but with the strength of his personality. Immediately one sensed that this was a man of principle, unshakable conviction, and unwavering determination. He could be your staunchest ally or your most feared adversary.

Paris had experienced him as both.

Her throat had constricted, as though every blood vessel leading from her heart had converged there. The oxygen in the room seemed insufficient. She was breathing with difficulty while striving to appear perfectly composed.

Dean wasn't doing so well either. When it became obvious that shock had robbed him of manners, Curtis motioned Paris into the nearest chair. That snapped Dean out of his daze. "Uh, yeah, please, sit. Both of you."

As they were taking their seats, Curtis said, "I'm not a detective for nothing. I gather you two know each other."

She relied on her voice to earn her living, but it had deserted her. She left it to Dean to do the talking.

"From Houston," he said. "Years ago. I was with the PD and Paris . . ."

He looked at her expectantly, leaving her no option but to take up the explanation. "I was a reporter for one of the television stations."

Curtis raised his pale eyebrows in surprise. "Television? I assumed you'd always been on radio."

She glanced at Dean, then shook her head. "I moved from TV to radio."

Curtis murmured an acknowledgment that said he understood the transition when clearly he didn't understand at all.

"Excuse me." Ms. Lester came in carrying a tray. As she set it on Dean's desk, she asked, "Cream and sugar, anyone?"

They all declined. She filled three mugs from a stainless-steel carafe, then asked Dean if there would be anything else. He shook his head and thanked her.

Curtis watched her leave. When he turned back around he remarked, "I'm impressed. They don't spring for personal assistants in CIB."

"What?" Dean looked at him with confusion, then at the empty doorway. "Oh, Ms. Lester. She's not my personal assistant. She just . . . She's just very efficient. Treats everybody over here like that."

"Over here" referred to the annex next door to the main building of police headquarters. It was accessible through a connecting parking garage, which was the route Paris and Curtis had taken. The detective didn't seem to buy Dean's explanation for the secretary's attention any more than Paris did, but he didn't comment on it further.

Paris wrapped both hands around the steaming mug of coffee, grateful for the warmth it provided. Dean took a gulp of his that probably blistered his tongue.

Curtis said, "I had no idea that I would be reuniting two long-lost friends."

"Paris didn't know about my transfer here," Dean said, watching her closely. "Or if she did—"

"I didn't. I assumed you were still in Houston."

"No."

"Hmm."

Curtis filled the ensuing gap in conversation. "Up until Dr. Malloy joined us, we used civilians and paid them a consulting fee. But for a long time, we'd been needing and wanting a psychologist on staff, a member of the department, someone with experience and training as a cop as well as a psychologist. Early this year, the funding was finally approved and we were lucky enough to lure Dr. Malloy here."

"How nice." She included both of them in her perfunctory smile.

After another short silence, Dean cleared his throat again and addressed the detective. "You mentioned a matter that could be important."

Curtis sought a more comfortable position in his chair. "Are you familiar with Ms. Gibson's radio program?"

"I listen to it every night."

Her head came up quickly and she looked at Dean with surprise. Their eyes connected for several seconds before he turned back to Curtis.

"Then you know she takes call-in requests and such," the detective said. Dean nodded. "Last night, she received a call that disturbed her. With cause." Curtis went on to explain the nature of Valentino's call, then concluded by saying, "I thought you might take a listen and give us your professional opinion."

"I'll be glad to. Let's hear it."

Curtis had brought the cassette player with him. He set it on the desk, rewound the tape, and after several false starts for which he apologized, her voice filled the taut silence: *This is Paris*.

By now she knew the dialogue word for word. As it played, she stared into her coffee mug, but in her peripheral vision she observed Dean. Individual parts of him. All of him. Surreptitiously she looked at his hands resting on the edge of his desk, fingers laced. He was slowly rubbing his thumbs together, and that, just that, caused a quiver deep in her belly.

Only once did she allow herself to look at his face. He'd been gazing into near space, but he must have felt her eyes on him because he focused on her sharply. His eyes still had the capability of making her feel like a butterfly pinned to a corkboard.

At one time, years ago, it had been thrilling to be looked at with that kind of intensity. Now it only made her remember things that should have been long forgotten. It resurrected sensations and emotions she had tried to bury and, until a few minutes ago, thought she had. She returned her gaze to her coffee mug.

When the tape ended, Dean asked if he could have a duplicate made.

"Of course," Curtis replied.

Dean ejected the tape and left the office only long enough to dispatch Ms. Lester on the errand. When he returned, Curtis said, "So you don't think this guy is just blowing smoke?"

"I want to listen to the recording several more times, but my first impression is that it's worrisome at the very least. Ever get a call like this before, Paris?"

She shook her head. "Listeners have reported UFOs, terrorist infiltration, asbestos in their attics. One night a woman called to tell me she had a snake in her bathtub and asked if I knew how to tell if it was poisonous. I get at least one proposal of marriage a week. I've had one offer of donor sperm. Hundreds of obscene propositions. But nothing like this. This . . . this *feels* different."

"Although he's called you before."

"A man identifying himself as Valentino calls periodically. I believe this is the same man, but I can't swear to it."

"Do you think he's someone you know?"

She hesitated before answering. "Honestly? I couldn't sleep last night for thinking about that. But I don't recognize the voice, and I believe I would."

"You would have an ear for voices," Dean said thoughtfully. "But it sounds to me as though he's trying to disguise his."

"To me, too."

"So it *could* be someone you know."

"I suppose. But I can't think of anyone who would play such a horrible prank."

"Have you recently made someone angry?"

"Not that I know of."

"Exchanged words?"

"I don't recall an incident like that."

"Have you said anything that would come across as an affront? To a coworker. Bank teller. Waiter. Grocery sacker. The guy who dries your windows at the car wash."

"No," she snapped. "I don't make a habit of provoking people."

Ignoring her annoyance, he pressed on. "Have you quarreled with a boyfriend? Ended a relationship? Broken someone's heart?"

She glared at him for several ponderous moments, then shook her head.

Serving as a tactful referee in a conflict he didn't understand, Curtis coughed behind his fist. "Couple of rookies, Griggs and

Carson, handled this last night," he told Dean. "They were going to check out the radio station personnel first thing this morning. I'll follow up with them right now, see if they've learned anything. Excuse me."

Before she could protest—and how could she?—Curtis pulled his cell phone from the holster clipped to his belt and left the office.

Instead of warming her hands, the ceramic coffee mug had grown cold within them. She leaned forward and placed it on the edge of Dean's desk, giving the mug and the surface of the desk more focus than either warranted.

Unable to avoid it any longer, she looked at him. "I didn't plan this, Dean. When I came here this morning, I had no idea . . . I didn't know you were in Austin now."

"I could have told you at Jack's funeral. You wouldn't talk to me."

"No, I wouldn't."

"Why not?"

"It would have been inappropriate."

Leaning toward her, he said, softly but angrily, "After seven years?"

Jack had been the first to say that nobody could get to Dean the way she could. She seemed to be the only person on the planet with a knack for gouging a chink in his rigid self-control.

Still sounding angry, he said, "I thought the sunglasses were only for the funeral. Have you still got—"

"I'm not going to talk about this, Dean. I'd leave if I could. If I'd known who Sergeant Curtis was bringing me to see—"

"You'd have turned tail and run. That's your MO, isn't it?"

Before she could form a reply, Curtis returned. "They're checking out the janitor, Marvin Patterson. Nothing solid so far. There appears to be some confusion that they're trying to sort through. Should have some info soon. Stan Crenshaw . . ." Here he paused and looked at Paris. "He's related to the station's owner?"

"He's Wilkins Crenshaw's nephew."

"A nepotistic hiring?"

"To be sure," she said candidly. "Stan does as little as possible and isn't very good at what little he does. His laziness is irritating and often inconvenient for those of us who work with him, but on a personal level we get along. Besides, it couldn't have been either him or Marvin, even if one of them would do such a thing. They were in the building when the call came in."

"Telephones being the high-tech gadgets they are these days, I've got the department's electronics wizard working on that angle. Officers are also talking to the people who work in the nearby pharmacy, seeing if they can pick up something there. Either an employee or a customer who's got a fixation on you. But . . ." He paused to tug on his ear. "We don't actually have the commission of a crime here. Just the threat of one."

"It's a serious threat."

"Right," the detective conceded thoughtfully. "Valentino said he heard the woman talking about him on your show. Do you remember a call like the one he describes?"

"Not off the top of my head. It must have been fairly recent, though, and it was a call that I played on the air. That narrows it down considerably. But I never would have told a caller to 'dump' someone."

"He could've been lying about that," Dean said. She and Curtis looked at him for clarification. "The call from the girl-friend could be an invention to justify—even to himself—what he plans to do to her."

It was a grim surmise. During their reflective silence, Ms. Lester returned with the original tape and the requested duplication. Dean played it again. "Something really bothers me," he said when it ended. "He refers to 'girls,' not women."

"Diminishing a female's status," Curtis remarked.

"In his estimation, it does. That gives us a clue into this guy's mind-set. His basic dislike and mistrust of women comes through loud and clear. If I had to profile him based on no more than this conversation, I'd categorize him as an anger-retaliator rapist."

Apparently Curtis was acquainted with the clinical term. "He's angry with women in general over real or perceived injus-tices."

"Yes. Possibly a result of sexual abuse, even incest. A dangerous motivation," Dean said. "Sex is his method of punishment. That usually translates to violent rape. If he wants to make his victim bleed, as he told Paris, then he'll have no qualms about killing her." His lips formed a grim line, which expressed the apprehension that all were feeling. "Another thing, the only other Valentino I ever heard of was Rudolph."

"The silent-film star," Paris said.

"Right. And his best-known film was *The Sheik*."

"In which he kidnaps and seduces, rather forcibly, a young woman." She knew the movie. She and Jack had seen it at a classic-film festival. "Do you think that's why he's using that name?"

"It could be a coincidence, but I'm not prepared to dismiss it as such." He thought about it only a second longer. "In fact, Curtis, I'm not prepared to dismiss any of this. My recommendation is that you take him at his word."

The detective agreed with a somber nod. "Unfortunately, I agree."

"I'd like to work with you on the case."

"I welcome your input. We'll take Valentino's threat seriously until it proves to be a hoax."

"Or proves to be real," Paris added softly.

chapter *seven*

Judge Kemp granted the defense attorney's request for a thirty-minute recess to consult with his client, hopefully to urge him to accept a plea bargain that would end the trial and free up the judge's afternoon.

He used the half hour to retire to chambers and clip hairs from his nostrils with a tiny pair of silver scissors. He used a mirror with a magnifying power of five times actual size. Nevertheless, it was a delicate procedure. The sudden ringing of his cell phone almost cost him a punctured septum.

A bit irritably, he answered his wife's call.

"Janey's not in her room," she stated without preamble. "She hasn't been there all night."

"You told me she was in when we got home."

"I thought she was because I could hear the radio through her door. It was still on this morning. I thought that was odd, because you know what a late riser she is, but I figured she was sleeping through it.

"I knocked on her door around ten. I wanted to take her to that new tearoom for lunch. That would be something we could do together. And it's a lovely little place, really. Bea and I were there last week and they have an exceptional gazpacho."

"Marian, I'm in recess."

Reigned in, she continued, "She didn't answer my knock. At quarter to eleven, I decided to go in and wake her. Her room was empty and the bed hadn't been slept in. Her car isn't in the garage and none of the help has seen her."

"Maybe she got up early, made her bed, and left the house."

"And maybe the sky will fall this afternoon."

She was right. It was an absurd assumption. Janey had never made a bed in her life. Her refusal to do so was one of the reasons she'd been sent home from summer camp the one and only time they had ignored her protests and insisted she go.

"When did you last see her?"

"Yesterday afternoon," Marian replied. "She'd been lying out by the pool for hours. I persuaded her to come indoors. She's going to ruin her skin. She refuses to wear sunscreen. I've tried to tell her, but of course she won't listen. She says sunscreen is the stupidest thing she's ever heard of because it defeats the purpose.

"And, Baird, I really think you should say something to her about sunbathing topless. I realize it's her own backyard, but there are always workmen around here doing one project or another, and I refuse to allow them a free peep show. It's bad enough she wears a thong, which, if you ask me, looks not only distasteful and unladylike, but terribly uncomfortable."

This time she stopped herself from going off on a tangent. "Anyway, yesterday I coaxed her to come inside during the hottest part of the day. I reminded her that we were going to the awards dinner and that she was restricted to the house. She flounced upstairs without speaking to me, slammed her door, and locked it. Apparently, she left last night sometime after we did, and she hasn't been home since."

He hadn't noticed that Janey's car was missing because he'd left his out front overnight, not parked in the garage. The next time he grounded Janey he would remember to confiscate her car keys. Not that that would stop her from sneaking out of the house and meeting up with those wild friends of hers, whose influence was doubtless the cause of her misbehavior.

"Did you call her cell phone?"

"I get her voice mail. I've left repeated messages."

"Have you checked with her friends?"

"Several of them, but none claims to have seen her last night. Of course, they could be lying to cover for her."

"What about that tart, that Melissa she's been spending so much time with?"

"She's in Europe with her parents."

His secretary knocked softly, then poked her head in and told him that everyone was back in the courtroom.

"Listen, Marian, I'm sure she's just punishing us for punishing her. She wants to give you a scare, and she's succeeding. She'll turn up. It's not as if this is the first time she's stayed out all night."

The last time Janey had failed to come home, she'd come close to being booked into the Travis County jail for public lewdness. She and a group of friends had availed themselves of a hotel's outdoor hot tub. Guests had complained of noise. When hotel security officers checked on the nature of the disturbance, they discovered a bubbling cauldron of young people in varying degrees of drunkenness and nakedness, engaging in all manner of sexual activity.

His daughter was among the drunkest. She was definitely the most naked, according to the Austin policeman who had person-ally fished her out of the water and separated her from the young man with whom she was coupled.

He had wrapped her in a blanket before transporting her home rather than to jail. He'd done it as a favor to the judge, not out of kindness toward the girl who had hurled invectives at him when he delivered her to her parents' doorstep.

The officer had been thanked with a hundred-dollar bill, which had tacitly bought his promise to exclude Janey's name from the incident report.

"Thank God the media didn't get wind of that story," Marian said now, reading the judge's mind. "Can you imagine the damage your reputation would have suffered?" She sniffed delicately and asked, "What are you going to do, Baird?" Thereby effectually dumping the problem into his lap.

"I'm in court all day. I haven't got time to deal with Janey."

"Well, you can't expect me to drive all over Austin looking for

her. I'd feel like a dogcatcher. Besides, you're the one with the contacts."

As well as the hundred-dollar bills, he thought sourly. Over
the last few years, he'd liberally doled out C-notes to ensure that
his daughter's shenanigans remained a private matter.

"I'll see what I can do," he grumbled. "But when she does
reappear—as I'm certain she will—don't forget to page me. I'll
have my pager on vibrate if I'm in court. Punch in three threes.
Then I'll know she's at home and won't waste anyone's time looking for her."

"Thank you, dear. I knew I could depend on you to handle
this."

Curtis invited Dean to join him for lunch and he accepted, but not
naively. He figured the detective was after background information on Paris. He could hardly blame Curtis for being curious,
especially after the charged atmosphere they'd created in his office
this morning.

He wouldn't give him anything, nothing that Curtis couldn't
learn for himself by reading a published bio, but it would be interesting to watch the detective in action.

They were on their way down the steps in front of the building when Curtis was hailed from behind. The young uniformed
cop who had called after him had just emerged from the glass
doors. He offered a breathless apology.

"I hate to hold you up, Sergeant Curtis."

"We're only going to lunch. Do you know Dr. Malloy?"

"Only by reputation. I'm a little late welcoming you to the
Austin PD. Eddie Griggs." He extended his hand. "A pleasure,
sir."

"Thank you," Dean said as they shook hands. "You two take
your time, I'll wait over here in the shade."

"I don't think Sergeant Curtis will mind you hearing this, seeing as how you're working with him on that Paris Gibson call.
That's what this is about. Well, sorta. Indirectly."

"Let's all get in the shade," Curtis suggested.

They moved closer to the building to take advantage of

the sliver of shadow it cast on the blazing sidewalk. Traffic whizzed past on nearby Interstate 35, but the rookie made himself heard.

"You issued a heads-up memo?" he said to Curtis. "About missing persons reports?"

"That's right."

"Well, sir . . . Judge Baird Kemp?"

"What about him?"

"He's got a daughter. High school age. Wild as a March hare. Every now and then she gets a little too wild and crosses the line. She's real well known by cops on patrol after midnight."

He glanced around, checking to see if anyone entering or exiting the building was within hearing distance. "The judge is real generous to any officer who takes her home, keeps her out of jail and her name out of print."

"I get the picture," the detective said.

"So today," Griggs continued, "the judge called in a special request to some of his friends on the force. Seems that Janey— that's her name—didn't come home last night. Everyone's been asked to be on the lookout, and if she's spotted, the judge would be very appreciative to the officer who brought her home."

Dean hadn't yet met the judge, but he knew him by name. One of his first duties in Austin had been to try to talk a prisoner into helping the police apprehend his partner in crime, who, by comparison, was the more evil of the two and was still at large.

The prisoner had refused to cooperate. "I'm not giving them shit, man."

"Them," as opposed to "you," because Dean had placed himself on the prisoner's side, becoming his friend, sympathizer, and confidant. The good cop.

"My trial was rigged! Fuckin' rigged," the prisoner ranted. "You hear what I'm saying, man? That judge swayed the jury. Smug motherfucker."

His regard for his trial judge didn't differ from that of most convicted criminals. They rarely had a kind word for the robed individual who, with a final bang of the gavel, sealed their bleak futures.

Eventually Dean got information from the prisoner that resulted in his partner's arrest, but the man had maintained his low opinion of Judge Kemp, and, based on what Griggs had just told them, Dean thought it might have been justified.

Curtis said, "In this county alone, there could be a hundred teenagers who didn't come home last night, and whose current whereabouts are unknown to their parents. And that would be a conservative estimate."

Dean was thinking of his own teenager, who had alarmed his mother on more than one occasion by not returning home until well into the next day. "I agree. It's too soon to jump to conclusions about one unaccounted-for girl, especially if she makes a habit of staying out."

"Judge Kemp would shit a brick if his 'special request' became an all-points bulletin," Curtis remarked, his distaste showing. "All the same, thanks for telling us about this, Griggs. Good follow-up and good hustle. How come you came in so early today?"

"Putting in overtime, sir. Besides, I hoped I could, you know, help Paris Gibson. She was pretty shook up last night."

"I'm sure she will appreciate your diligence."

Curtis's statement was made tongue in cheek. Apparently, he'd noticed the same thing Dean had—the kid was smitten with Paris.

"Let's give Miss Janey Kemp a few more hours to sober up and find her way home before we link her to Ms. Gibson's caller," Curtis said.

"Yes, sir." The young policeman's manner was so militarily correct, Dean almost expected him to salute. "Have a good lunch, sir. Dr. Malloy."

Curtis continued down the sidewalk, but Dean hung back, sensing that Griggs still had something on his mind. If it concerned Paris, he wanted to know what it was. "Excuse me, Griggs? If something's nagging at you, we'd like to hear it."

It was clear the rookie didn't want to step on the toes of a detective with rank or an officer with an alphabet soup of degrees behind his name and a Dr. in front of it. All the same, he seemed relieved that Dean had invited him to speak his mind.

"It's just that this girl goes looking for trouble, sir." He lowered his voice to a confidential pitch. "One of our undercover narcs at the high school? He says she's great looking and knows it. A . . . a real babe. Says she's made moves on him that almost made him forget he was a badge." Griggs's ears had turned red. Even his scalp was blushing through his buzz haircut.

Hoping to relax the younger man, Dean quipped, "I hate when that happens. One of the reasons I never worked undercover."

Griggs grinned as though happy to learn that Dean was just a guy after all. "Yeah, well, what I'm saying is, she might've placed herself in a situation where something bad could happen."

"Flirted with danger and got more than she bargained for?" Curtis asked.

"Something like that, sir. From what I know of her, she does what she wants to, when she wants to, and doesn't account to anybody. Not even to her folks. Perfect candidate to be slipped some Rohypnol. If she crossed paths with this Valentino, and he's done what he claims, nobody would know it for a while. And that could be bad."

Curtis asked if anyone had looked for Janey Kemp in places where she was known to hang out.

"Yes, sir. That's what the judge wanted done. Covertly, of course. Couple of intelligence officers are on it as well as the regular patrolmen. But it's summer, so the Sex Club meets outdoors more nights than not, and the meeting place changes every few nights to keep narcs and parents—"

"Sex Club?" Dean looked over at Curtis for an explanation, but the detective shrugged. Both looked back at Griggs.

Nervous again, the young officer shifted his weight from one polished shoe to the other. "You don't know about the Sex Club?"

•   •   •

Paris arrived home exhausted. This was normally the time of day she was getting up. Customarily she ate breakfast when everyone else was having lunch. Today she was off her schedule. If she didn't sleep a few hours this afternoon, she would be a zombie by sign-off time tonight.

But after her unexpected reunion with Dean, sleep was unlikely.

She made herself a peanut butter sandwich she didn't really want and sat at the kitchen table, a napkin in her lap, pretending it was an actual meal. As she ate, she sorted her mail.

When she came to the pale blue, letter-sized envelope with the familiar logo in the upper-left-hand corner, she stopped her methodic chewing. She washed down the bite of sandwich with a whole glass of milk, as though fortifying herself for the contents of the envelope.

The three-paragraph letter was from the director of Meadowview Hospital. Politely but firmly, in language that could not be misunderstood, he requested that she retrieve the personal belongings of former patient the late Mr. Jack Donner.

"Since you haven't responded to my numerous attempts to reach you by telephone," the letter read, "I can only assume that you never received those messages. Therefore, let this letter serve to notify you that Mr. Donner's belongings will be removed from the facility if you do not collect them."

Her deadline to comply was tomorrow. Tomorrow. And he meant it. The date was underlined.

While Jack was a patient at Meadowview, Paris had been on a first-name basis with everyone on staff, from the director to the custodian. This read like a letter to a stranger. He'd reached the limit of his patience with her, no doubt because she had ignored his telephone messages.

She hadn't been back to the private nursing facility since the day Jack died inside room 203. In the six months since then, she hadn't had the wherewithal to return, not even to pick up his personal belongings. With very few exceptions, she'd gone to the hospital every day for seven years, but after leaving it that final day, she'd been unable to make herself return.

Her reluctance to do so wasn't entirely selfish. She didn't want to dishonor Jack by remembering him lying in that hospital bed, his limbs withering even though they were exercised every day by Meadowview's capable staff of physical therapists. He'd been no more self-sufficient than a baby, unable to speak anything except gibberish, unable to feed himself, unable to do anything except take up space and rely on dedicated health care professionals to tend to even his most personal needs.

That was the condition in which he'd lived—existed—the last seven years of his life. He deserved better than to be remembered like that.

She folded her arms on the table and laid her head on them. Closing her eyes, she envisioned Jack Donner as he'd been when she met him. Strong, handsome, vital, self-confident Jack . . .

"So you're the new one who's causing such a sensation."

He had spoken from behind her. When she faced him, her first impression was of the cockiness of his grin. Her assigned cubicle in the news room was barely large enough to turn around in. It was crammed with boxes that she was in the process of unpacking. Jack had pretended not to notice that he was contributing to the crowded conditions.

Coolly she repeated, " 'New *one*.' "

"You're being talked about in the front offices. Don't force me to repeat what I've heard and risk a sexual harassment charge."

"I've just joined the news team, if that's what you mean."

"The 'award-winning' news team," he corrected, his grin stretching wider. "Don't you pay attention to our station's promos?"

"Are you in the promotions department?"

"No, I head the official host committee. In fact, I *am* the official host committee. It's my job to welcome all newcomers."

"Thank you. I consider myself welcomed. Now, if you'll—"

"Actually I'm in sales. Jack Donner." He stuck out his hand. They shook.

"Paris Gibson."

"Good name. Stage or yours for real?"

"Mine for real."

"You want to go to lunch?"

His audacity didn't give offense. Instead it made her laugh. "No. I'm busy." She raised her arms to indicate the boxes surrounding her. "It'll take me all afternoon to get this stuff organized. Besides, we just met."

"Oh, right." As he mulled over that dilemma, he gnawed on his lower lip in a manner he probably knew was cute and endearing. Then he brightened. "Dinner?"

She didn't go to dinner with him that night. Or the next three times he asked. In the ensuing weeks she worked her tail off, covering as many stories as the assignments editor would give her. She vied for as much airtime as she could get, knowing that exposure was the only way to build audience recognition of her name, voice, and face.

She was aiming for the evening anchor spot. It might take her a year or two to get there. She had a lot to learn and much to prove, but she saw no reason to set her sights on anything lower than the top. So she was way too busy getting herself established in the Houston television market to accept dates.

And Jack Donner was way too confident that she would ultimately submit to his charm. He was all-American-boy handsome. His personality was engaging, his humor infectious. Every woman in the building, from the college interns to the grandmother who ran the accounting department, had a crush on him. Surprisingly, men liked him, too. He'd held the top sales record for several consecutive years, and it was no secret that he was being groomed for management.

"Upper management," he confided in her. "I want to be GM and then, who knows? One day I might own my own station."

He certainly had the ambition and charisma to achieve whatever he set out to do, and getting a date with her was his primary short-term goal. Finally he wore her down and she accepted.

On their first date, he took her to a Chinese restaurant. The food was dreadful and the service even worse, but he kept her laughing throughout the meal by creating histories for each of the dour wait staff. The more rice wine he drank, the funnier the stories became.

When he opened his fortune cookie, he whistled. "Wow, listen to this." He pretended to read. "Congratulations. After months of trying to seduce a certain lady, tonight you get lucky."

Paris broke open her cookie and pulled out the fortune. "Mine says, 'Disregard previous fortune.'"

"You won't sleep with me?"

She laughed at his crestfallen expression. "No, Jack, I won't sleep with you."

"You're sure?"

"I'm sure."

But after four months of dating, she did. After six months, everyone at the TV station acknowledged them as a couple. By Christmas Jack had asked her to marry him, and by New Year's Day she had accepted.

In February it snowed. Houston, where snow was as infrequent as the Hale-Bopp comet, ground to a halt, which meant that the news teams worked overtime to cover all the weather-related stories, from school closings, to shelter for the homeless, to the myriad hazards of icy roadways. Paris worked for sixteen hours straight, going in and out of the weather, riding in a drafty news van, drinking lukewarm coffee, meeting deadlines.

When she finally got home, Jack was in her kitchen stirring a pot of homemade soup. "If I never loved you before," she said, lifting the lid on the pot and taking a deep whiff, "I do now."

"I'd cook for you every night if you'd move in with me."

"No."

"Why not?"

"We've been over this at least a thousand times, Jack," she said wearily as she pulled off soggy boots.

He knelt down to massage her frozen toes. "Let's go over it again. I keep forgetting your lame excuses. As you know, my dick is longer than my attention span. And aren't you glad?"

She withdrew her foot from between his warm hands. The massage felt entirely too good to be getting while they were having this oft-repeated argument.

"Until we're married, I'm maintaining my independence." Seeing that he was about to press his argument, she added, "And if you keep bugging me about it, I'll postpone the wedding for another six months."

"You're a hard woman, Paris Gibson soon-to-be Donner."

They ate their soup and finished the bottle of wine Jack had opened before her arrival. He didn't even suggest that he spend the night, and she was grateful for his sensitivity to her exhaustion.

As she bade him good night at her door, she noticed that the inch and a half of snow that had immobilized the city was already beginning to melt. All that ass-busting news coverage was made history by a few degrees on the thermometer.

"Thank God tomorrow is Saturday," she said with a sigh as she leaned against the doorjamb. "I'm going to sleep all day."

"Just wake up in time for tomorrow night."

"What's tomorrow night?"

"You're meeting my best man."

Recently he'd told her that his best friend from college was moving back to Houston after getting an advanced degree in something, from an out-of-state university somewhere that right now she couldn't remember. She knew only that Jack was very excited to have his friend returning to the area and couldn't wait to introduce them.

"How's he liking the Houston PD?" she asked around a wide yawn.

"Still too early to tell, he says, but he thinks he's going to like it. We're gonna try to scare up a game of basketball at the gym while you're snoozing the day away. We'll pick you up around seven tomorrow evening."

"I'll be ready." She was about to close the door when she called after him, "I'm sorry, Jack, what's his name again?"

"Dean. Dean Malloy."

Paris sat up, gasping.

She was in her own kitchen, but it took her a moment to orient herself. Revery had given way to dreaming. She'd been in a deep sleep. The angle of the sunlight coming through the window had changed. Her arms were tingling from the lack of circulation that lying on them had caused. Shaking them only heightened the prickling sensation. With a numb hand, she reached for the ringing telephone—the cause of her waking up so abruptly.

Out of habit, she said, "This is Paris."

chapter *eight*

"When was the last time you saw a dentist, Amy?"

"I don't remember. A few years maybe."

Dr. Brad Armstrong gave his patient a stern frown. "That's much too long between checkups."

"I'm scared of dentists."

"Then you haven't been to the right one." He winked at her. "Until now."

She giggled.

"You're lucky I've found only one cavity. It's small, but it needs to be filled."

"Will it hurt?"

"Hurt? I'll have you know that in this office, pain is a four-letter word." He patted her shoulder. "My job is to fix your tooth. Your job is to lie back and relax while I'm doing it."

"The Valium sure helps. I'm already getting sleepy."

"It doesn't take long."

His staff had cleared it with Amy's mother before giving her a low-dosage tranquilizer to relieve her anxiety and make the procedure less stressful for both patient and doctor. Her mother was coming back in a while to drive her home. In the meantime, he was free to look his fill as she drifted into la-la land.

According to her chart she was fifteen, but she was well formed. She had good legs. Her short skirt revealed smooth, tan thighs and muscled calves.

He loved summer. Summer meant skin. Already he dreaded the onset of fall and winter when women gave up sandals for boots, and bare legs for opaque tights. Skirts got longer, and shoulders bared in the summer by halters and narrow straps were covered with sweaters. The only good thing about sweaters was that sometimes they clung, and the suggestion of what was underneath could be wonderfully enticing.

His patient took a deep breath that shifted the paper bib to one side of her chest. He was tempted to lift it and look at her breasts. If she protested, he could always say he was returning the bib to its proper place, nothing more.

But he restrained himself. His nurse might come in, and, unlike his patient, she wasn't loopy on Valium.

He surveyed the girl's legs again. Relaxation had caused them to roll outward, leaving several inches of space between her knees. The stretchy fabric of her skirt fit like a second skin. It molded to the dip between her thighs and delineated the vee. Was she wearing panties? he wondered. The possibility that she wasn't inflamed him.

He also wondered if she was a virgin. Beyond the age of fourteen, few were. Statistically, the odds were good that she had been with a man. She would know what to expect from a man who was aroused. She wouldn't be that shocked if—

"Dr. Armstrong?" His assistant appeared, interrupting the daydream. "Is she ready for the deadening?"

He never let his patients even hear the word "shot."

He came off the low stool on which he'd been sitting, pretending to study the patient's X rays. "Yes. Go ahead. Let's give it ten minutes."

"I'll have everything ready."

He disposed of his latex gloves and went into his private office, closing the door behind him. His skin was feverish. His heartbeat was accelerated. If not for his lab coat, his assistant would have seen his erection. If not for her timely interruption, he might have made a dreadful mistake. And he couldn't afford to make another.

That last time, though—now, that had *not* been his fault.

That girl had been in his chair three times within two months, and with each visit she had become a little friendlier. Friendlier, hell, she'd flirted with him outright. She had known exactly what she was doing. The way she smiled up at him provocatively whenever she was reclined in his chair—hadn't that practically been an invitation to fondle her?

Then when he did, she had raised such a hue and cry it had brought his partners, all the hygienists, and most of the patients running down the hallway and into the treatment room where she stood screaming accusations at him.

If she had been the twenty-five-year-old she appeared to be, instead of the minor she was, those accusations would have been dismissed. As it was, they'd been believed, and he'd been invited to leave the practice. The following morning when he arrived at the office, his partners had met him at the door with a severance agreement that included a check amounting to three months' earnings. Under the circumstances, they considered that fair. Good-bye and good luck.

Sanctimonious pricks.

But the repercussions hadn't stopped there. The girl's parents, incensed that a normal, heterosexual male had responded to the inviting signals transmitted by their sexpot of a daughter, had filed charges of indecency with a child. As if she was a child. As if she hadn't asked for it. As if she hadn't liked having his hand slide between her thighs.

He was dragged into court like a criminal and, on the advice of his inept attorney, forced to apologize to the conniving little bitch. He'd pled guilty to the humiliating allegations in order to receive a "light sentence" of mandatory counseling and probation.

The judge's ruling was much lighter than Toni's, however. "This is the last time, Brad," she'd warned.

Since he had dodged incarceration, wouldn't you assume a celebration was in order? Oh, no. His wife had other plans, which included beating the subject of his "addiction" to death.

"I can't go through another ordeal like this," she told him. Then for hours she'd harped on his "destructive pattern of behavior."

Okay, there had been a few other incidents, like the one at the clinic where he'd first practiced. He had shown a dental hygienist some photographs. It was a joke, for godsake! How was he to know she was a Bible beater who probably thought babies should be born with fig leafs attached to their belly buttons. She had spread such vicious gossip about him, he'd left of his own accord. But Toni still held him responsible.

Finally she had concluded by saying, "Let me make this even clearer, Brad. I *won't* suffer through another ordeal like this. I won't allow our children to suffer through it. I love you," she declared tearfully. "I don't want to divorce you. I don't want to break up our home and family. But I will leave you if you don't get help and control your addiction."

Addiction. So what if he had a strong sex drive? Was that an *addiction?* She'd made him sound like a pervert.

He wasn't a complete fool, though. He knew he had to adapt to the world in which he lived. If society was going to be puritanical, then he must adjust to the accepted rules. He must walk the straight and narrow as defined by church and state, and they were in league on this issue. One misstep beyond their silly boundaries of so-called decency, and you were not only a sinner but an outlaw.

Even the mildest flirtation with another patient could cost him his career. It had taken him eight months to land this job in Austin, long after the severance check had been spent and the savings accounts depleted.

This clinic wasn't as prosperous as the previous one. His current partners weren't as specialized and renowned as his former associates. But the job paid the mortgage. And his family liked Austin, where no one knew the reason for their move here.

For weeks after that courtroom nightmare, Toni had flinched each time he touched her. She had continued sharing a bed with him, although he figured that pretense had been for the kids' benefit.

Eventually she had allowed him to hold her and kiss her, and then, after his group therapy leader had given him a gold star for the progress he'd made toward "healing," she had resumed having sex. She had seemed reasonably content . . . until a few nights ago when he'd been careless enough to stay out all night.

He'd devised a plausible story, and she might have continued believing it if he hadn't been so late getting home last night. The story about the tax seminar didn't fly. He had gone to the seminar and signed in, so there would be a record of his attendance. But he had never intended to stay and had left after the first boring hour.

He'd caught hell for it this morning. Toni shooed the kids from the breakfast table and sent them upstairs to do chores. Then, without any warning, she demanded, "Where were you last night, Brad?"

No lead-in, just that angry, surprise attack that immediately pissed him off. "You know where I was."

"I was up until after two o'clock this morning and you weren't home yet. No tax seminar lasts that long."

"It didn't. It was over around eleven. I met a few guys there. We went out for a beer. Realized we were hungry. Ordered food."

"What guys?"

"I don't know. Guys. We exchanged first names. Joe, I think it was, is an executive at Motorola. Grant or Greg, something like that, owns three paint and body shops. The other one—"

"You're lying," she exclaimed.

"Well, thanks for giving me the benefit of the doubt."

"You haven't earned it, Brad. I tried to go into your office last night. The door was locked."

He stood up, pushing his chair away from the table so angrily it scraped loudly against the floor. "Big deal. The door was locked. I didn't lock it. One of the kids must have. But why were you going in there in the first place? To see what you could find to hold against me? To snoop? To spy?"

"Yes."

"At least you admit it." He expelled a long breath, as though taking time out to get a grip. "Toni, what's wrong with you lately? Every time I leave the house, you put me through a royal grilling."

"Because you're leaving the house more often and you stay

away for long periods of time that you can't, or won't, account for."

"Account for? What, I'm not an adult? I'm not allowed to come and go of my own free will? I have to check in with you if I decide to stop for a beer? When I need to take a piss, shall I call you first and ask permission?"

"It won't work, Brad," she'd said with maddening composure. "I'm not going to let you turn the tables and make me feel bad for asking why you were out until early this morning. Go to work. You're going to be late." That had been her exit line. She had stalked from the kitchen, her spine as straight as if she had a girder up her ass.

He'd let her go. He knew her. Once she reached that stage of righteous indignation, he could grovel for hours and nothing he said or did would appease her. She would stay frosty for days. Eventually she would thaw, but in the meantime . . .

Jesus! Was it any wonder that he wasn't eager to go home tonight? Who wanted to cozy up to a Popsicle? If he erred tonight, Toni was to blame, not him.

Thankfully he had discovered a new outlet for his "addiction." Sex in all its variations was his for the taking. Thinking about what was now available to him, he smiled.

Reaching beneath his lab coat, he stroked himself. He liked to stay semierect, so throughout the day he took sneak peeks at the photographs he kept locked in his credenza drawer, or, if he felt safe from intrusion, he visited favorite websites. Only a minute or two would do the trick. Some people drank coffee for a quick pick-me-up. He'd discovered something a hell of a lot more stimulating than caffeine.

It would be a long afternoon, but the anticipation alone was delicious.

Hurry, nightfall.

chapter nine

When Paris entered the room where they were waiting for her, Dean and the other two men stood up. They had convened in a small meeting room within the CIB that was ordinarily used to interview witnesses or question suspects. It was cramped quarters but confidentiality was assured.

Curtis pulled a chair from beneath the table for Paris. She nodded her thanks to him and sat down. She was still wearing sunglasses. Dean could barely detect her eyes behind the dark gray lenses. He hated to speculate as to why she never removed them.

"I hope it wasn't too inconvenient for you to come back downtown," Curtis said to her.

"I got here as quickly as I could."

In unison they all looked at the wall clock. It was coming up on two P.M. None needed to be reminded that twelve hours of Valentino's deadline had already expired.

The detective motioned to the third man in the room. "This is John Rondeau. John, Paris Gibson."

She leaned forward and extended her hand across the table. "Mr. Rondeau."

As they shook hands, he said, "A pleasure, Ms. Gibson. I'm a huge fan."

"I'm glad to hear that."

"I listen to you all the time. It's a real honor to meet you."

Dean drew a bead on the officer, whom he had met only minutes before Paris's arrival. Rondeau was young, trim, and good looking. A weight lifter, from the looks of his biceps. His face was lit up like a Christmas tree as he gazed at Paris. Plainly, like the rookie Griggs, Rondeau was instantly infatuated with her.

Dean suspected that Sergeant Curtis was, too. They'd gone to lunch at Stubb's. The Austin landmark, famous for its barbecue, beer, and live music, was only a few blocks from police headquarters. They'd walked.

During the lunch period there was no band playing in the amphitheater beneath the live oaks out back, but hungry state capitol personnel and downtown office workers lined up by the dozens to order cuts of smoked meat slathered with fiery sauce.

Opting to not wait for a table, he and Curtis had ordered chopped beef sandwiches and had taken them out onto the wood porch, where they stood in the shade to eat.

Dean had expected Curtis to ask him about Paris, but he'd thought the detective's approach would be subtle. Instead Curtis had dug into his sandwich, then asked him bluntly, "What's with you and Paris Gibson? Old flames?"

Maybe it was Curtis's candor that made him such a crackerjack investigator. He caught suspects off guard. Striving for nonchalance, Dean took a bite of his sandwich before answering. "More like water under the bridge."

"Lots of water, I'm guessing."

Dean continued chewing.

"You don't want to talk about it?" the detective probed.

Dean wiped his mouth with a paper napkin. "I don't want to talk about it."

Curtis nodded as though to say, Fair enough. "You married?"

"No. You?"

"Divorced. Going on four years."

"Kids?"

"One of each. They live with their mother."

"Has your wife remarried?"

Curtis took a drink of iced tea. "I don't want to talk about it."

They'd left it at that and moved the conversation back to the case, which actually wasn't a case yet, but which they feared would become one. But now Dean knew that Curtis was single, and the detective never let pass an opportunity to treat Paris to some show of chivalry.

Paris elicited that kind of attention from men. In all the time he'd known her, he'd never seen her play the coquette. She didn't simper. She didn't flirt or deliberately draw attention to herself or dress provocatively. It wasn't anything she *did*. It was something she *was*.

One glance at her and you wished you had a long time to study her. Her figure wasn't voluptuous like Liz's. In fact, hers was rather angular and boyish, and she was taller than average. Her hair, light brown streaked with several shades of blond, always looked slightly mussed, which was certainly sexy, he supposed. But that alone wasn't enough to rouse male interest.

Maybe it was her mouth. Women got painful collagen injections to achieve that pout. Paris had come by it genetically. Or was it her eyes? God knows they were pretty damn spectacular. Blue and fathomless, they invited you to dive in and splash around, see if you could ever plumb their depths. Not that you could tell anything about her eyes now, hidden as they were behind the sunglasses.

Young John Rondeau didn't seem to mind, though. He was practically transfixed.

"Have you learned something else since this morning?" she asked.

"Yes, but we don't know how significant it is." She had posed the question to Curtis, but by answering, Dean forced her to look at him, which she had studiously avoided doing since she entered the room. "We're here to discuss its validity."

Curtis chimed in, "Rondeau works in our computer crimes unit."

"I don't understand," Paris said. "How do computer crimes relate to what you requested of me?"

"We'll get to that," the detective replied. "I know it appears to have no relevance, and maybe it doesn't."

"On the other hand," Dean said, "it could all tie in together.

That's what we're trying to determine. Are those the cassettes?" He gestured at the canvas tote she had carried in along with her handbag.

"Yes. The Vox Pro holds one thousand minutes of recorded material."

"So when a call comes in, it's automatically recorded?" Curtis asked. "That's how you screen calls, keep people from shouting obscenities to your audience?"

She smiled. "Some have tried. That's why each call is recorded. I then have the option of saving it and playing it on the air, or deleting it."

"How do you transfer the recordings onto cassette?" Dean asked.

"It isn't easy. As a favor to me, one of the engineers figured out a way. Periodically, he dumps—his term, not mine—the recordings off the Vox Pro computer onto cassettes for me."

"Why?"

She shrugged self-consciously. "Nostalgia, maybe. The more interesting conversations could also be useful if I ever put together a demo tape."

"Well, whatever your reasons for saving them, I'm glad you have them now," Curtis told her.

"I hope you understand that you lose quality in the duplication process," she said. "These tapes won't be as clear as the original."

"Doesn't matter," Dean said. "Quality might become an issue later if a voice print becomes necessary. But right now all we want to know is if the call Valentino referenced was real or a fabrication.

"That's why we asked to hear the calls you received during the past week. If there *was* such a call, and if hearing it on your program lighted Valentino's fuse, then we need to trace that call to the woman who placed it."

"If it's not too late," she murmured.

Judging by the expressions around the table, everyone in the room echoed her grim thought.

"Can you remember a call similar to the one Valentino described?" Curtis asked her.

"Possibly. I've been thinking about it since our conversation this morning. I got a call three nights ago. As I was driving here, I listened to it on the cassette player in my car. I marked the cassette and cued the call."

Dean found the marked cassette among the others in the bag, inserted it into the machine, and pressed Play.

This is Paris.

Hi, Paris.

What's on your mind tonight, caller?

Well, see, I met this guy a few weeks ago. And we really hit it off. I mean, it's been hot, hot, hot between us. (A giggle.) Sorta exotic.

That's probably all the detail we need on a family show.

(Another giggle from the caller.) But I like being with other guys, too. So now he's getting jealous all the time. Possessive, you know?

Do you want to take the relationship to another level?

You mean like do I love him? Hell, no. The whole thing has been about fun. That's it.

Perhaps not to him.

Then that's his problem. I just don't know what to do about him.

If you feel that the relationship is constricting, you probably shouldn't be in it. My advice is to make the break as quick and painless as possible. It would be cruel to string him along when your heart is no longer in it.

Okay, thanks.

"That's all," Paris said. "She hung up."

Dean switched off the recorder. For several moments there was a heavy silence, then everyone began talking at once. Curtis pointed to Paris, giving her the floor.

"I was just going to say that this call may have absolutely no connection to Valentino. It was a rather silly conversation. I only put her on the air because she was so animated. I gathered from her voice that she was young. My audience are mostly baby boomers. I've wanted to expand it to include the younger crowd, so when a call from someone obviously younger comes in, I generally use it."

"Did you get the phone number?"

"I checked the Vox Pro. The caller ID said 'unavailable.'"

"Did other listeners respond to your conversation with her?"

"You'll hear a few on the tape. Several offered interesting advice on how she should handle the breakup. Others I thanked for calling but didn't put them on the air and deleted their calls from the Vox Pro."

"I don't remember talking to anyone else this week about a breakup, even off the air. But I talk to dozens of people every night. My memory isn't one hundred percent."

"Do you mind if we keep these tapes for a while?" Curtis asked.

"They're yours. I had duplicates made."

"I think I'll have someone listen to all—how many hours is it?"

"Several, I'm afraid. I went back three weeks. That's fifteen nights on the air, but of course I delete more calls than I save."

"I'll have someone listen, see if there's a similar call that's slipped your mind."

"Did Valentino call in response?" Dean asked.

"That night, you mean? No. He always identifies himself by name. Last night was the first time I'd heard from him in a while. I'm definite on that."

Curtis stood up. "Thank you, Paris. We appreciate your help. I hope coming back downtown wasn't too much of an imposition."

"I'm as concerned as you are."

Apparently, he intended to escort her out, but she remained seated. Curtis hesitated. "Is there something else?"

Dean knew why Paris was reluctant to leave. Her news-gathering instinct had kicked in. She wanted the full story and didn't want to stop until she had it. "I'm guessing she'd like to know what's going on," he said.

"I would, yes," she said with a nod.

Curtis hedged. "It's really a police matter."

"For you it is. But it's a personal matter to me, Sergeant. Especially if Valentino turns out to be someone I know. I feel responsible."

"You're not," Dean said, speaking more sharply than he intended. Everyone looked toward him. "If he's for real, he's a psychopath. He would be doing something like this whether or not he talks to you on the radio."

Curtis agreed. "He's right, Paris. If this guy is wound as tight as he sounds, he would've snapped sooner or later."

Rondeau said, "You're just providing him with a forum, Ms. Gibson."

"And because of that, you're our only link to him." Dean looked over at Curtis where he still stood beside her chair. "That's why I think she has a right to know the leads we're following."

Curtis frowned, but he resumed his seat. Then he looked directly at Paris and, with his characteristic bluntness, stated, "We might have a missing girl."

"'Might'?"

Dean watched her while she listened to Curtis's summary of what Griggs had told them about Judge Baird Kemp's daughter. He already knew the facts, so he was able to tune them out and concentrate on Paris, who was hanging on every word.

Obviously she had cultivated a sizable radio audience, but he wondered if she missed her TV news reporting. Like greasepaint for a stage actor, didn't it get into a person's blood?

She'd been a natural, earning the viewers' confidence with her solid and impartial reporting. She'd been smart enough to know that if she was too cutesy or glamorous they would regard her as an airhead who had probably slept her way into her job. Taken to the other extreme, she would've been thought of as a ball-breaking bitch with penis envy.

Paris had struck the perfect balance. She had been as aggressive a reporter as any of her male counterparts, but without any sacrifice to her femininity. She could've taken her career as far as she chose to take it.

If only.

Her soft exclamation brought him back into the present. "This girl hasn't been seen or heard from for almost twenty-four hours, and her parents are just now becoming worried?"

Dean said, "Hard to believe, isn't it? They haven't formally notified the police, so Janey's disappearance isn't official. But there've been no other missing persons reported. It's a long shot, but it's a coincidence that Curtis and I thought we should investigate."

She quickly connected the dots. "And if it turned out that this caller was the judge's daughter—"

"That's why we asked for the tapes," Dean said. "Did she give you her name?"

"Unfortunately, no. You heard the recording. And the name doesn't ring a bell. If I'd recently heard the name Janey, or Kemp, which is more unusual, I think I would remember. Besides, isn't this a stretch? It's an awfully broad coincidence on which to base an investigation."

"We thought so, too. Until we heard about this Internet club. The Sex Club."

"The *what?*"

Rondeau came to life. "That's where I come in." He glanced at Curtis as if asking permission to continue.

Curtis shrugged. "Go ahead. It's not as if she couldn't find out for herself."

Rondeau launched into his description. "The website has been online for a couple of years. Janey Kemp was one of the . . . founders, I guess you'd say. It started out as a message board where local teens could communicate, more or less anonymously. Using only their user names and email addresses.

"Over time the messages got more explicit, the subject matter racier, until the purpose of it has evolved into what it is now, which is, basically, an Internet personals column. They flirt via cyberspace."

"Flirt?" Dean scoffed. "The messages they exchange are more like foreplay."

The younger cop said, "I didn't want to offend Ms. Gibson."

"She's a grown-up and this isn't Sunday school." Dean looked at her directly. "The Sex Club's sole purpose is to solicit sex. Kids post messages advertising what they've done and what they're willing to do with the right partner. If they want more privacy with someone, they enter chat rooms and talk dirty to each other.

Here's a sample." He opened a folder and removed the sheet he'd printed off the computer in Curtis's office.

She scanned it, registering her dismay. When she looked up, she said, "But these are kids."

"High school mostly," Rondeau told her. "They congregate at a designated spot each night. It's a huge swap meet."

Curtis said, "Part of the fun, it seems, is trying to match individuals with their user names, see if you can figure out who's who."

"And if a couple who've been chatting over the Internet find each other, they have sex," Dean said.

"Or not," Rondeau said, correcting him. "Sometimes they don't like what they see. The other person doesn't live up to expectations. Or someone better comes along in the meantime. No one's obligated to follow through."

"The computer crime guys discovered the website," Curtis said, "and since most of the users are minors, they brought it to the attention of the child abuse unit, which investigates sex offenses against children and child pornography, which falls under the auspices of the CIB." He folded his arms across his stocky torso. "It's a bleed-over investigation, meaning we can put a lot of people on it."

"That's the good news," Rondeau said. "The bad news is that stopping it is virtually impossible."

Paris was shaking her head with incredulity. "Let me make sure I understand. Girls like Janey Kemp go to a designated place and meet up with strangers whom they've teased, via the Internet, into believing they'll have sex."

"Right," Rondeau said.

"Are they insane? Don't they realize the risk they're taking? If they meet their chat room partner, who turns out to be less than a Brad Pitt, and say, 'No thanks,' they're placing themselves at the mercy of a man whom they've inflamed and who is . . . disappointed, to say the least."

"They're hardly at anyone's mercy, Ms. Gibson," the young cop said quietly. "We're not talking nuns here. These are party girls. They frequently charge the men for their favors."

"They ask for money?"

"Not ask. Demand," Rondeau told them. "And they get it. Plenty of it."

This information stunned them into silence. Eventually Curtis said, "What troubles us, Paris, beyond the obvious, is that anybody who applies for membership in this so-called club gets it. Getting a password and access to this website requires only a few clicks of a mouse. That means any sexual predator, any deviate, would know where to go to look for his next victim."

"What's more," Dean said, "his victim would probably go with him willingly. He'd have to put forth very little effort."

"This is alarming whether or not it has a connection to Valentino," she said.

"And we're fighting a losing battle," Rondeau said. "We bust up the kiddie porn rings. But for each one that's busted, dozens more spring up and thrive. We work with the feds, with Operation Blue Ridge Thunder, a nationwide information network that deals specifically with Internet crimes against children. That's more than we can handle. Teenagers consensually exchanging dirty email is a low priority."

Curtis said, "It's like writing tickets for jaywalking, while across town, gang members are shooting each other."

"What about Janey's parents?" Paris asked. "Have they been made aware of this?"

"They've had trouble with her," Curtis replied. "She has a history of misbehavior, but even they probably don't know about all her activities. We didn't want to alert them to a possible connection between her unknown whereabouts and Valentino's call until we had more to go on. We were hoping your audiotape would shed some light."

"It doesn't shed much, does it?" she said. "I'm sorry."

After a discreet knock, the door was opened and another detective poked his head in. "Sorry to interrupt, Curtis. I have a message for you."

He excused himself and left the room.

Paris consulted her wristwatch. "Unless I can be of further help, I should be going."

Rondeau nearly broke his neck getting out of his chair and

helping her with hers. "What time do you have to be at the radio station, Ms. Gibson?"

"Around seven-thirty. And please call me Paris."

"Do you have to do a lot of preparation ahead of time?"

"I select the music myself and prepare my log—that's the order in which songs are played. Another department, called 'Traffic,' has already logged the commercials.

"However, a lot of my programming occurs spontaneously. I never know what song someone from the audience is going to request. But I can insert that song into the log instantly, because we have a computerized library of music."

"Are you ever nervous when you go on the air?"

She laughed and shook her head, making the shaggy hairdo even shaggier and more attractive. "I've been doing it too long to get butterflies."

"Do you operate the equipment all by yourself?"

"If you're referring to the control board, yes. And I man my own telephone lines. I turned down having a producer. I like being a one-woman show."

"When you started, did you have to learn a lot of technical stuff?"

"Some, but, honestly, you probably know much more about the workings of a computer than I know about the physics of radio waves."

The implied compliment brought a silly grin to his face. "Does working alone ever get boring?"

"Not really, no. I like the music. And the callers keep me on my toes. Each broadcast is different."

"Don't you get lonely working alone every night?"

"Actually, I prefer it."

Before Rondeau asked her to father his children, Dean interceded. "I'll walk you out, Paris."

As he ushered her toward the door, she said, "I'd like to stay updated. Please ask Sergeant Curtis to call me when he knows something." Sergeant Curtis. Not him. The snub couldn't be more blatant, and it irritated the hell out of him. He was as much a cop as Sergeant Robert Curtis. *And* he outranked him.

He reached around her to grab the doorknob. But the door opened without his help and Curtis was on the other side of it. His complexion was several shades ruddier than usual. What was left of his pale hair seemed to be standing on end.

"Well, it's hit the fan," he announced. "Somehow a courthouse reporter learned that cops were looking for Janey Kemp. He confronted the judge about it as he was returning from lunch recess. His Honor is *not* happy."

"His daughter's life could be at risk and he's worried about media exposure?" Paris exclaimed.

Dean said, "My thought exactly. I don't give a shit if he's happy or not."

"Fine. You'll have an opportunity to tell him that to his face. We've been ordered by the chief to meet with Kemp and try to smooth his feathers. Right now."

chapter ten

Paris wheeled into the Kemps' circular driveway directly behind Sergeant Curtis's unmarked Taurus. She got out of her car at the same time he got out of his. Before he had a chance to speak, she said, "I'm coming with you."

"This is a police matter, Ms. Gibson."

If he was back to using her last name, he was irked. She held her ground. "I started this ball rolling when I came to see you this morning. If I never hear from Valentino again and the call last night turns out to be a hoax, then I owe you, the Austin police, and especially this family a profound apology. And if it isn't a hoax, then I am directly involved and so are they, which entitles me to speak with them."

The detective looked across at Dean as though seeking guidance on how to handle her when she took a stubborn stance. Dean said, "It's your call, Curtis. But she's good at talking to people. That's what she does."

Coming from a trained negotiator, that was quite a compliment. Curtis considered it for only a moment, then said grudgingly, "All right, but I don't know why you'd want to involve yourself in this any more than you already are."

"I didn't choose to be. Valentino involved me."

She and Dean followed him toward the door. For Dean's ears only she said, "Thanks for backing me up."

"Don't thank me yet." He nodded toward the wide front

door, which was being opened as they made their way up the veranda steps. "Looks like he's been lying in wait."

Judge Baird Kemp was tall, distinguished looking, and handsome, except for his scowl, which he directed toward Curtis, whom he obviously knew by name. "I'm trying to keep a lid on this, Curtis, and what does the Austin PD do? Trot extra cops out to my house. What the hell is going on with you people? And who are they?"

To Curtis's credit, he kept his cool, although his face and neck flushed to a deeper hue. "Judge Kemp, Dr. Dean Malloy. He's the department's psychologist."

"Psychologist?" the judge sneered.

Dean didn't even bother extending the judge his hand, knowing it would be rebuffed.

"And this is Paris Gibson," Curtis said, motioning toward her.

If her name meant anything to the judge, he didn't show it. After giving her a cursory look, he glared at Curtis. "Are you the one who started the false rumor that my daughter is missing?"

"No, Judge, I didn't. You did. When you called one of the cops you've got on the take and told him to start looking for her."

A vein ticked in Kemp's forehead. "I told the chief that I demanded to know who was responsible for leaking that story, which has been grossly exaggerated. He sends me you, a shrink, and a—" He glanced at Paris. "Whatever. Why the hell are you here?"

"Baird, for godsake." A woman emerged from the house and upbraided him with a stern look. "Can we please do this inside where fewer people will have the opportunity of overhearing?" She gave their guests a collective once-over, which was just shy of hostile, then said stiffly, "Won't you come in?"

Again Paris and Dean followed Curtis. They were shown into an elaborately appointed living room that might have been a salon in Versailles. The decorator had padded her budget with an overload of brocades, gilt, beading, and tassels.

The judge marched over to a dainty liquor cart, poured himself a drink from a crystal decanter, and tossed it back as if it was a shot. Mrs. Kemp perched on the delicate arm of a divan as though she didn't intend to stay very long.

Curtis remained standing, looking as out of place as a fireplug in this room of froufrou. "Mrs. Kemp, have you heard from Janey?"

She glanced at her husband before answering. "No. But when she gets home, she'll be in serious trouble."

Paris couldn't help but think the girl could be in much more serious trouble now.

"She's a teenager, for christsake." The judge was still standing, too, glaring down at them as though about to sentence them to twenty years of hard labor. "Teenagers pull stunts like this all the time. Except when *my* daughter does it, it makes headlines."

"Don't you realize that negative publicity only makes a situation worse?"

For whom? Paris was dismayed that Mrs. Kemp's primary concern was publicity. Shouldn't she be more worried about the girl's absence rather than what would be said about it?

Curtis was still trying to be the diplomat. "Judge, I don't know who within the Austin PD spoke to that reporter. We'll probably never know. The culprit isn't going to come forward and admit it, and the reporter is going to protect his source. I suggest we move past that and—"

"Easy for you to say."

"Not at all easy." Dean spoke for the first time, and his tone was so imperative that all eyes turned to him. "I wish the three of us had come here, hat in hand, to beg your forgiveness for an error in judgment, a slip of the tongue, a false alarm. Unfortunately, we're here because your daughter could be in grave danger."

Mrs. Kemp moved off the arm of the divan and onto the seat cushion.

The judge rocked back on his heels. "What do you mean? How do you know?"

"Maybe I should tell you why I'm here," Paris said quietly.

The judge's eyes narrowed. "What was your name again? Are you that truancy officer who kept hassling us last year?"

"No." She reintroduced herself. "I have a radio program. It's on each weeknight from ten to two."

"Radio?"

"Oh!" Mrs. Kemp exclaimed. "Paris Gibson. Of course. Janey listens to you."

Paris exchanged glances with Dean and Curtis before turning back to the judge, who apparently was unfamiliar with her and her show. "Listeners call in and sometimes I put them on the air."

"Talk radio? A bunch of left-wing radicals spouting off about this, that, or the other."

He had to be the most unpleasant individual Paris had ever met. "No," she said evenly, "my show isn't talk radio." She was in the process of describing her format when he interrupted her.

"I get the picture. What about it?"

"Sometimes a listener calls to air a personal problem."

"With a total stranger?"

"I'm not a stranger to my listeners."

The judge raised a graying eyebrow. Apparently he wasn't used to people contradicting or correcting him. But Paris wasn't intimidated by someone she had already formed such a low opinion of.

Being flagrantly rude, he dismissed her and turned back to Curtis. "I still don't understand what a radio deejay has got to do with any of this."

"I think this will help explain." The detective set the portable tape recorder on a coffee table. "May I?"

"What is this?"

"Sit down, Baird," his wife snapped. Paris saw traces of apprehension in the other woman's eyes. Finally the severity of the situation was beginning to sink in. "What's on the recorder?" she asked Curtis.

"We want you to listen, see if you recognize your daughter's voice."

The judge looked down at Paris. "She called you? What for?"

She, along with the others, ignored him as the recording began.

Well, see, I met this guy a few weeks ago.

Paris noticed that Dean was watching Mrs. Kemp closely. Her reaction was immediate, but was it from recognizing the voice, or from the young woman's description of a short-lived but hot, hot, hot fling?

When it ended, Dean leaned toward Mrs. Kemp. "Is that Janey's voice?"

"It sounds like her. But she rarely talks to us with that much animation, so it's hard to tell."

"Judge?" Curtis asked.

"I can't tell for dead certain either. But what the hell difference does it make if it is her? We know she's got boyfriends. She flits from one to the other so fast we can't keep up. She's a popular girl. What's that got to do with anything?"

"We hope nothing," Curtis replied. "But it might tie in to another call that Paris received from a listener." While talking, he exchanged one cassette for another. Before he played the second tape, he said to Mrs. Kemp, "I apologize in advance, ma'am. Some of the language is rather crude."

They listened in silence. By the time Valentino wished Paris a nice night, the judge had his back to the room and was gazing out the front window. Mrs. Kemp was mashing a pale fist against her lips.

The judge came around slowly and looked at Paris. "When did you receive this call?"

"Just before sign-off last night. I called 911 immediately."

Curtis picked up from there and brought them up-to-date. "Janey's the only missing person who's been reported. If that's her talking to Paris earlier in the week, it could correlate."

"If I heard evidence that flimsy in my courtroom, I'd dismiss it."

"Maybe you would, Judge, but I won't," Curtis declared. "After the reporter confronted you, I understand you called off the unofficial search for your daughter. Well, sir, you should know that as we speak, patrolmen are intensifying their search and intelligence officers are tapping every resource."

The judge looked ready to implode. "Upon whose authority?"

"Mine," Dean said. "I made the recommendation and Sergeant Curtis acted on it."

Mrs. Kemp turned to him. "I'm sorry, we weren't formally introduced. I don't know who . . ." He introduced himself again and explained how he had become involved.

"Very possibly this will turn out to be a hoax, Mrs. Kemp. But until we know it is, we should take this caller seriously."

She stood up suddenly. "Would anyone like coffee?" Then before anyone could answer, she rushed from the room.

The judge muttered a string of curses. "Was that necessary?" he asked Dean.

Dean was barely restraining himself. Paris recognized the tension in his posture and the hardening of his jaw as he stood up and confronted the judge. "I hope to God you can file a formal complaint against me. I hope Janey comes waltzing in here and makes me look like a colossal fool. You'll then have the pleasure of calling me one, possibly even getting me fired.

"But in the meantime, your rudeness is unforgivable and your obstinance is stupid. We've been given a seventy-two-hour deadline, and so far you've wasted twenty minutes of it by being a jerk. I suggest we all set aside our egos and focus on finding your daughter."

The judge and Dean stared each other down. Neither submitted to the other in a silent contest of wills. Finally Curtis cleared his throat. "Uh, when was the last time you saw Janey, Judge?"

He actually seemed relieved to have an excuse to break eye contact with Dean. "Yesterday," he replied briskly. "At least Marian saw her then. In the afternoon. We got home late last night. Thought she was in her room. Didn't discover until this morning that her bed hadn't been slept in." He sat down and crossed one long leg over the other, but his insouciance appeared affected. "I'm sure she's with friends."

"I have a son about Janey's age," Dean told him. "He can be a challenge. There are times when you'd think we hated each other. Discounting the normal ups and downs of living with a teenager, would you say you're basically on good terms with Janey?"

The judge looked ready to tell Dean that his relationship with his daughter was none of his business. But he relented and said stiffly, "She's been difficult at times."

"Breaking curfew? Experimenting with alcohol? Going out with kids you'd rather she not associate with? I speak from experience, you understand."

By placing them on common ground, he was gradually breaking down the judge's barriers and Curtis seemed content to let him continue.

"All of the above," the judge admitted before turning to Paris. "Sergeant Curtis said this degenerate has called you before."

"A man using that name has, yes."

"Do you know anything about him?"

"No."

"You have no idea who he is?"

"Unfortunately, no."

"Do you intentionally provoke this kind of lewdness from your listeners?"

The implicating question took her aback. Before she could form a reply, Dean said, "Paris can't be held responsible for the actions of her listening audience."

"Thank you, Dean, but I can speak for myself." She met the judge's censorious stare head-on. "I don't care what you think of me or of my program, Judge Kemp. I don't need or desire your approval. I'm here only because I heard Valentino's message first-hand, and I share Dean—Dr. Malloy's—concern. I respect his opinion both as a psychologist and a criminologist. Sergeant Curtis's investigative skills are unsurpassed. You'd be wise to give serious consideration to what they're telling you.

"As for my opinion, it's based on years of experience. I listen to people in every possible human condition. They talk to me through laughter and tears. They share their joy, sorrow, grief, heartache, exhilaration. Sometimes they lie. I usually can tell when they're lying, when they're faking an emotion in an attempt to impress me. They do that sometimes, thinking it will increase their chances of being put on the air."

She pointed toward the recorder. "He didn't even hint at

being put on the air. That wasn't the reason he called. He called with a message for me, and I didn't get the sense that he was lying or faking it. I don't think it was a crank call. I think he has done, and is going to do, what he said:

"Insult me if it makes you feel better, but, regardless of anything you say, I'm going to do everything within my power to help the police get your daughter returned safely to you."

The taut silence that followed Paris's speech was relieved by the reappearance of Marian Kemp. It seemed she had timed it for just that purpose. "I decided on iced tea instead."

She was followed into the room by a uniformed maid carrying a silver tray. On it were tall glasses of iced tea garnished with lemon and fresh mint. Each glass rested on an embroidered linen coaster. A silver bowl of sugar cubes was accompanied by dainty sterling tongs.

Once they were served and the maid had withdrawn, Curtis awkwardly set his glass of tea on the coffee table. "There's another element to this that you should be made aware of," he told the Kemps. "Does your daughter have a computer?"

Marian replied, "She's on it all the time."

Judge and Marian Kemp listened in stony silence as Curtis told them about the Sex Club. When he finished, the judge demanded to know why his wife had been subjected to hearing about such filth.

"Because we need access to Janey's computer."

The judge erupted with vehement protests. He and Curtis launched into a heated argument over investigative procedure, privacy, and probable cause.

Finally Dean entered the fray. "Doesn't this girl's safety supersede points of law?" His shout silenced them, so he pressed his advantage. "We need a copy of everything on Janey's hard disk."

"I will not permit it," the judge said. "If such a thing as this Sex Club exists, my daughter has nothing to do with it."

"Soliciting to have sex with strangers," Marian Kemp sniffed. "Revolting."

"And speaking as a parent, terrifying," Dean said to her. "But I would rather be informed than ignorant, wouldn't you?"

Apparently not, he thought when neither the judge nor his wife answered. "We don't want to invade Janey's privacy, or yours. But her computer could yield clues to her whereabouts."

"Such as?" the judge asked.

"Friends and acquaintances you don't know. People who send her email."

"If you did discover anything incriminating, it would never be admissible in a court of law because it will have been illegally obtained."

"Then what have you got to worry about?"

The judge had laid that trap for himself and he realized it.

Dean continued, "If Janey has an email address book, which I'm sure she does, we could send out a blanket message to everyone on it, asking if they've seen her, and if they have, urge them to contact you."

"In effect announcing to the world that her mother and I can't keep track of our daughter."

Dean had no love for these people, but he didn't have the heart to state what was glaringly obvious: They wouldn't be here if the Kemps had kept better track of their daughter.

"Her friends will recognize her email address and open the letter," he said. "We'll sign the message from you, not the police, and promise that anyone coming forward with information can remain anonymous."

"Mrs. Kemp," Paris said gently, "an email would reach a lot of people much more efficiently than policemen canvasing Janey's hangouts. Besides, young people get nervous when cops approach even if they're doing absolutely nothing wrong. Janey's friends would be reluctant to talk to a policeman about her. They'd be much more likely to reply to an email."

It was a persuasive point lent even more potency by her mellow voice. Mrs. Kemp looked over at her husband, then back to Paris. "I'll show you to her room." The invitation seemed to include only Paris, who stood when Mrs. Kemp did and followed her out.

Without a word, the judge turned on his heel and stalked toward an adjacent room. From what Dean could see through the doorway before the judge slammed the door behind him, it appeared to be a library or study.

Curtis lightly slapped his thighs as he came to his feet. "That went well, don't you think?"

Dean grinned at the ironic remark, but he sure as hell didn't feel like smiling. "I guess His Honor is divesting himself of the whole ugly matter."

"I'll bet you my left nut he's in there on the phone giving the chief hell about the department's new shrink."

"I don't care. I meant everything I said, and I'd say it again."

"Yeah, well, occasionally I have to testify in his court. I have to play both ends against the middle. But I figure the next time I'm in the witness box, my testimony will be discredited." He ran his hand over his thinning hair. "I'm going outside to make a few calls, see if there's been any news that would make all of us sleep better tonight."

Dean followed him as far as the grand staircase. "I'll wait here for Paris."

"I thought you might."

He didn't have a suitable comeback for the detective's parting shot, so he let it pass. Sliding his hands into the pockets of his trousers, he took in the formal foyer. The floor was marble tile. Overhead was a lavish crystal chandelier that was reflected in the polished wood surfaces of twin consoles facing each other across the wide hall.

Above one of the tables hung an oil portrait of Marian Kemp. And on the opposite wall above the matching table was a painting by the same artist of a girl about seven years old. She was wearing a summer dress of white gauzy fabric. Her feet were bare. The artist had captured sunlight shining through pale blond curls. She looked angelic and achingly innocent.

Dean's cell phone vibrated inside his jacket pocket. He checked the LED and recognized Liz's cell number. He didn't answer, telling himself that now wasn't a good time. She had called twice before. Those hadn't been good times either.

Hearing footsteps in the deep carpeting of the staircase, he looked up to see Paris and Marian Kemp descending. Paris subtly nodded at him. In her hand she was carrying a Zip disk, which she handed over as soon as she reached him. He slid it into his pocket. "Thank you, Mrs. Kemp."

Even though she had cooperated, she hadn't warmed to them. "I'll see you out."

She opened the front door, and when she saw the young woman standing in the driveway with Curtis, she exclaimed, "Melissa! I thought you were in Europe."

Upon hearing her name, the girl turned toward them. She was tall and lanky and was probably attractive underneath the makeup that had been applied with all the finesse of a brave preparing for the warpath.

"Hey, Mrs. K. I just got back."

"She's a friend of Janey's?" Dean asked Marian Kemp.

"Her best friend. Melissa Hatcher."

Behind Paris's car was a snazzy, late-model BMW convertible, but you would never guess by her clothing that this girl came from affluence. She was wearing a pair of denim cutoffs that left ragged strings trailing down her thighs. The waistband had also been cut off, leaving nothing but fringe to hold the shorts on her hipbones. Twin sapphires winked from her pierced navel. The neck and armholes of her T-shirt were oversized, making it no secret that she was wearing nothing beneath it.

Her striped knee socks looked unseasonably heavy, and the black boots laced to her ankles would have been more appropriate on a lumberjack or a mercenary who meant business. Incongruously, the large handbag hanging from her shoulder was a Gucci.

"Have you spoken to Janey since your return?" Marian Kemp asked.

"No," she replied, as though put out by the question. "This guy here's been asking me all these questions. What's going on?"

"Janey didn't come home last night."

"So? She probably just crashed at somebody's place. You know." She shrugged, which slid her T-shirt off one shoulder. She sent a look Dean's way that was unmistakably flirtatious.

"Could you give us some names?"

She turned back to Curtis and eyed him up and down. "Names?"

"Of people Janey might've gone home with?"

"Are you heat?" The detective opened his sport jacket and showed her the ID clipped to his belt. "Oh shit. What's she done?"

"Nothing that we know of."

"She could be in danger, Melissa." Paris moved down the steps to join them.

The girl regarded her curiously. "Danger? What kind of danger? You a cop, too?"

"No, I work for a radio station. I'm Paris Gibson."

Melissa Hatcher's lips were painted a red so dark it was almost black. They fell open in astonishment. "Get out! You're fucking kidding, right?"

"No."

"Oh my God." Her delight was probably the most honest reaction the girl had shown in months. "How cool is this? I listen to your show. When I'm not listening to CDs. But sometimes, you know, you're just not in the mood for CDs. So that's when I turn on your program. Sometimes the music you play sucks, but you are totally bitchin', girl."

"Thank you."

"And I like your hair. Are those highlights?"

"Melissa, do you know if Janey has ever called me while I was on the air?"

"Oh, yeah. Coupla times. It's been a while, though. We called you on Janey's cell and talked to you but we didn't give our names and you didn't put us on the radio. Which was cool, 'cause we were wasted and you could probably tell."

Paris smiled at her. "Maybe next time."

"Has Janey called Paris recently?" Dean asked. Dark eyes lined in darker kohl slid over to him. Paris introduced him to the girl as Dr. Malloy. He stuck out his hand.

She seemed nonplused by the polite gesture, but she shook his hand. "What kind of doctor are you?"

"Shrink."

"Shrink? Jesus, what'd Janey do? OD or something?"

"We don't know. She hasn't been heard from in over twenty-four hours. Her parents are worried about her and so are we."

"We? You a cop, too?"

"Yes. I work for the police department."

"Hmm." Melissa shot them each a suspicious look, and Dean sensed her cautious withdrawal. They were losing her. Despite her being a Paris Gibson fan, her first loyalty would be to her friend. She'd be stingy with information about Janey.

"Like I said, I don't know anything about where Janey is or who she's called 'cause I just got back from France. I've been up for like thirty hours straight, so I'm gonna go home now and crash. When Janey shows up, tell her I'm back, will ya, Mrs. K.?"

Her Gucci bag slung a wide arc as she turned and sauntered toward her car. But just short of reaching it, she suddenly came back around, slapping her forehead with a hand weighed down by sparkling bangles and numerous rings.

"Holy shit, I just got it!" She pointed at Dean. "No wonder you're such a hottie. You're Gavin's dad."

chapter eleven

"Wake up, sleepyhead."

Janey opened her eyes. He was bending over her, his face close to hers, his breath ghosting over her face. He kissed her forehead. She moaned pitiably.

"Did you miss me?"

When she nodded, he laughed. He didn't believe her, and he would be wise not to. Because the first chance she got, she was going to kill the son of a bitch.

She tried to keep the malice she felt from showing in her eyes, having concluded that her best option was to appear submissive. The psycho wanted to play games, wanted her to beg, wanted to dominate her.

So, fine. She would be his contrite little plaything—until he turned his back on her, and then she was going to bash in his skull.

"What's this?" He noticed the stained bedsheet and tsked.

She'd peed herself. What did he expect? He had abandoned her here for God knows how long. She had held her bladder for as long as she could, but ultimately she'd had no choice except to wet the bed.

"You'll just have to change the sheets," he told her.

Okay, I'll remake the bed. Untie me and give me a fresh sheet and I'll strangle you with it.

He brushed aside a strand of her matted hair. "You smell like piss and sweat, Janey. Have you been exerting yourself? Doing what, I wonder?" His gaze roved until it settled on the wall behind the bed. "Hmm. Scars in the paint. You've been rocking the bed so the headboard would knock against the wall, haven't you?"

Damn! She had hoped to annoy a neighbor who would eventually get so angry over the monotonous knocking that he'd come over and demand a stop to it. Then, when he was ignored, he would complain to the manager until the manager checked out the source of the noise.

She would be found and her father would be notified, and he would make certain this asshole never saw the light of day again. They'd lock him in a cell *beneath* the prison and give visitation rights to all the bull queers in the place.

Her daydream of rescue and vengeance died when he pulled the bed several feet away from the wall. "We can't have that, Janey." He bent down and kissed her forehead again. "Sorry to spoil your clever little plan, sweetheart."

She looked at him with a desperation that wasn't entirely feigned. She moaned imploringly.

"Do you need the toilet?"

She nodded.

"All right. But I need your promise that you won't try to get away. You would only get hurt, and I don't want to hurt you."

I promise, she said behind the awful tape.

He unbound her feet first. She had thought the instant they were free she would start kicking and fighting him, but, to her alarm, she discovered that her limbs were rubbery. Her legs were reluctant to move at all, and when they did, they did so sluggishly.

He untied her hands, then lifted her into his arms and carried her into the bathroom. He set her on her feet near the toilet, raised the lid, then gently lowered her onto the seat.

She reached for the tape across her mouth.

"You can remove it," he told her softly. "But if you scream, you'll regret it."

She believed him. It was painful to peel off the tape, but when she had done so, she sucked large drafts of air through her mouth. "I'd like a drink of water, please," she said, her voice a croak.

"Finish here first."

He made no move to leave. To her mortification tears came to her eyes. "Go out and close the door."

He frowned down at her impatiently. "Oh, please. This sudden modesty is absurd. Hurry up before I change my mind and make you wet yourself again."

When she was finished, she asked again for a drink of water.

"Certainly, Janey. As soon as you change your bed. You've left it so nasty. Dreadfully nasty."

She was dying of thirst, so she submissively exchanged the damp sheets for fresh ones. By the time she had completed the task to his satisfaction, she was exhausted and had broken out in a cold sweat.

He made her sit in the armchair, where he could watch her while he stepped into the kitchen and uncapped a plastic bottle of water. She'd hoped for a glass. She could have broken it and shoved a shard of glass into his throat. If she could've found the strength. She was abnormally weak even for someone who'd been lying in bed for hours. Had he drugged her last night? Was he doing so again now? Had he put something in her water?

Actually she didn't care. She was so thirsty, she drank the water greedily.

"Are you hungry?"

"Yes."

He made a pimiento cheese sandwich, then hand-fed it to her, pinching off small pieces one at a time and placing them in her mouth. She thought about biting his fingers, but that would still leave one of his hands free. She hadn't forgotten the slap that had made her vision blur and her ears ring. She didn't want to invite another.

Causing him even momentary pain would give her enormous satisfaction. She would love to sink her teeth into his flesh, draw blood. But in her present condition, it would be impossible to follow that up with a full-fledged attempt to overpower him. The satisfaction she would derive from it would be all too brief and would cost her dearly. Until she could achieve more than just getting him angry and retaliatory, she had best conserve her strength and try to devise a foolproof plan of escape.

When she'd finished the sandwich, he said, "I like you this way, Janey." He stroked her head and used his fingers to comb the tangles out of her hair. "Your submission is very arousing." He touched her nipples lightly. "It makes you so desirable."

He turned away from her only long enough to get his camera. The despised camera. It was the camera that had so intrigued her and made her think he was special. A special pervert, maybe. She hated the sight of that camera now and would like nothing better than to grind it into his face until both his facial bones and the camera had broken apart.

But she was too frightened to resist as he posed her for a series of obscene pictures.

"Get on the bed."

She considered begging, pleading, promising him money, swearing she'd never tell anyone about this, if only he would let her go. But maybe she would have more bargaining power if she did him one more time.

So she lay down on the bed and did exactly what he told her to do. When he was finished, she didn't even have the energy to raise her head. He had drugged her. She was sure of it now.

She watched in dread as he opened the nightstand drawer and removed a roll of duct tape. "No," she whimpered. "Please."

"I hate having to do this, Janey, but you're a whore. Your love isn't pure. You're dishonest. You can't be trusted even to remain quiet."

"I will. I swear."

That was all he allowed her to say before clamping a strip of tape over her mouth. This time he also used the tape to secure her wrists and ankles to the bed frame, winding it so tightly there was absolutely no give.

He showered before he dressed. Standing beside the bed, he calmly threaded his belt through the loops of his trousers. "Are you crying, Janey? Why? You used to be the ultimate party girl."

He stuffed the soiled bed linens into a laundry bag and

picked up his keys. He was almost to the door when he snapped his fingers and turned back. "I almost forgot. I have a surprise for you."

He took an audiocassette from the pocket of his jacket and placed it in the player that was built into his sound system. "I recorded this last night. I think you'll find it interesting." He pressed the Play button, then blew her a kiss and left. He locked the door from the outside.

There were thirty seconds of silence on the tape, then a ringing telephone. It rang several times before Janey heard a familiar voice say, "This is Paris."

"Hello, Paris. This is Valentino."

His name is Valentino?

That was her first thought, because she instantly recognized his voice. It wasn't his normal speaking voice, but the other one, the one he sometimes used when they were in bed. She had thought it was amusing, the way he could lower the pitch of his natural voice, make it whispery, make it sound as though it went with doing something naughty—as it usually had.

Now, hearing that voice in stereo only gave her chills.

Listening as he told Paris Gibson their story from his perspective, Janey breathed rapidly through her nose, watching the machine in fascination, listening to the recording with an anxiety that soon escalated into terror. When he told Paris Gibson his plans for her, she began screaming into the hollow chamber of her taped mouth.

But of course no one could hear her.

Toni Armstrong arrived at her husband's dental office just before closing. One of the other dentists in the practice paused on his way out to speak with her. He apologized for not yet having had her and Brad over for dinner. They exchanged promises to get a date on the calendar soon.

Seemingly Brad had no trouble keeping up appearances. She would do the same for as long as she could.

When she walked into the office, the receptionist was surprised to see her. "I got a baby-sitter and thought I'd treat Brad to an unscheduled dinner out," she explained.

"Oh, golly, Mrs. Armstrong, Dr. Armstrong left a couple of hours ago."

At least to the other woman, her dismay would look like disappointment. "Oh, well, so much for my surprise evening. Did he tell you where he was going?"

"No, but I'm sure he has his cell phone."

"I'll give him a call. Will I be keeping you if I use his office?"

"Not at all. Take your time. I've got some filing to do before I leave."

Since Brad was the newest partner, his was the smallest office, but Toni had done her best to make it attractive. Degrees and diplomas in matching frames formed an attractive arrangement on the wall. Family photographs were tucked among the dental health books on the shelves behind his desk. His desktop was neat.

She hoped the setting was as benign as it appeared.

Sitting down in his desk chair, she commenced her search. All his drawers were locked, but she had anticipated that and had come prepared. A bent bobby pin opened them with minimum effort.

Truthfully, she *had* secured a baby-sitter for tonight. She had taken care with her hair and makeup and had dressed up in the hope of surprising Brad with an evening out—to make amends for this morning.

Throughout the day, their quarrel had haunted her. Brad had left the house angry. She had been hurt as well as angry. Housecleaning, menu planning, and the myriad other chores that filled her days had kept her busy. But nothing could take her mind off their argument and the possibility, however slight, that she might have been wrong.

What if Brad hadn't been lying about where he'd been last night?

Maybe she had gone looking for trouble where none existed. If he had been telling her the truth, how frustrating it must have been for him to try to make himself believed, knowing that she would think the worst.

Chances were slim that he had attended a seminar and gone

for a beer afterward, but in order to hold her family together, she was desperate enough to act on that chance.

So this afternoon, she had hoped to intercept him at the office with a pleasant surprise, an olive branch of a dinner reservation at an Italian restaurant he'd been wanting to try. By spending an evening alone with him, away from the house and kids, with a bottle of wine and lovemaking later on, she had hoped to win his forgiveness for misjudging him and be able to put the ugly episode behind them.

But he wasn't where he was supposed to be. He had left work early without an explanation and without informing anyone of his destination. It was a familiar pattern, a recognizable signal, that made her heartsick and justified her picking the locks on her husband's desk drawers.

A few moments later, her suspicion was validated. Inside the lower drawer of his credenza was a treasure trove of pornography.

The printed material ranged from relatively mild to extremely graphic. Some of the crudest pictures, both in subject matter and composition, surely had been taken by amateur photographers.

Brad was an addict. Like all addicts, he was susceptible to bingeing. And it was during a binge that an addict was capable of doing something he or she wouldn't ordinarily do, like sexually harassing a coworker or fondling a patient who was a minor.

And God only knew what else.

chapter twelve

There was a wet swimsuit on the utility room floor when Dean passed through it on his way into the house. He found Gavin semi-reclined on the sofa in the den. He was desultorily punching the TV remote, changing stations every ten seconds. He was wearing only a towel around his waist and his hair was wet.

"Hi, Gavin."

"Hi."

"Have you been in the pool?"

Without taking his eyes off the television screen, he replied, "No. I just like to sit around in a towel."

"When you take the wet towel to the utility room, you can also pick up the swimsuit you left on the floor."

Gavin punched through another few stations.

Dean said, "Shower, then we'll go eat."

"I'm not hungry."

"Shower, then we'll go eat," he repeated.

"And if I don't, are you going to hit me again?"

The look Dean shot him apparently conveyed his shrinking patience. Gavin threw down the remote and stalked from the room. Just before moving through the door, he whipped off the towel, baring his ass to Dean, literally as well as figuratively. In spite of himself, Dean gave Gavin two points for the symbolic gesture.

Without asking Gavin's preference, he drove to a chain restaurant that was one of their staples. Gavin sulked, responding in monosyllables to Dean's attempts at conversation.

When their order arrived, Dean asked him if his burger was cooked the way he liked it.

"It's fine."

"I apologize for not having more dinners at home."

"Doesn't matter. Your cooking sucks."

Dean smiled. "I can't argue that. You probably miss your mom's homemade pasta sauce and pot roast."

"Yeah, I guess."

"But all you ever seem to want is burgers or pizza anyway."

Immediately on the defensive, Gavin said, "Something wrong with that?"

"No. I had the same diet when I was your age."

Gavin snorted as though to say he didn't realize they had burgers and pizza that far back in ancient history.

Dean tried again. "I saw an old friend today. Do you remember Paris Gibson?"

Gavin looked at him scornfully. "Do you think I'm retarded?"

"It was a long time ago and you were just a boy. I wasn't sure you would remember her."

"'Course I do. Her and Jack. They were gonna get married, but he got killed."

"He didn't get killed. He survived the accident. He didn't die until a few months ago."

"Huh. She's on the radio here now."

Dean was surprised. "So you knew that?"

"Everybody knows that. She's popular."

"Yeah, I understand she has quite a following. She told me today she's trying to cultivate a younger audience. Do you ever listen to her program?"

"I have. Not every night. Sometimes." Gavin dipped a french fry into a glob of ketchup. "Did you call her up, or what?"

"Uh, no. She had a crank call last night from a listener."

"Seriously?"

"Hmm," Dean said around a bite of his grilled chicken. "She

reported it to the police. I was consulted. She and the detective wanted my take on it."

"Detective? Was it that bad?"

"Pretty bad."

He signaled the waitress and asked her to bring Gavin another Coke. For someone who wasn't hungry, he had wolfed down his cheeseburger in record time. "And bring us an order of queso and chips, too, please." Gavin would never ask for more, but Dean knew he was probably still hungry.

"I also saw a friend of yours today," he remarked casually.

"I don't have any friends here. All my friends are in Houston. Where I used to live. In my own house. Until my mother married that jerk."

Here we go, Dean thought. "She had been single for a long time, Gavin."

"Yeah, 'cause you divorced her."

"Funny. Last night you said she divorced me. Actually, you're right on both accounts. We agreed to divorce because we knew it would be best."

"Whatever," Gavin said with a bored sigh and turned his head to gaze out the window.

"Don't you think your mother has a right to be happy?"

"Who could be happy with him?"

Dean wasn't overly impressed with Pat's choice either. Her husband was rather bland, so lackluster that one had to work at having a conversation with him. But he seemed besotted with Pat and she with him.

"So what if he doesn't have a dynamic personality, can't you just be glad that your mother has found someone she cares about, who also cares for her?"

"I'm glad, I'm glad. I'm ecstatic, okay? Can we drop it now?"

Dean could have reminded him that he'd been the one to bring up the topic, but he let it pass. The waitress came with their additional order.

"Anything else?"

She had addressed Gavin, not him, and for the first time, Dean tried to see his son through a young woman's eyes. Parental bliss notwithstanding, Gavin was a good-looking kid. His brown hair had the wavy texture of his mother's and he must secretly like it because—thank God—he hadn't had it sculpted into a bizarre style or had it dyed a color that glowed in the dark.

His eyes were whiskey colored and slightly brooding. You couldn't tell it now when he was slouching, but he was already over six feet tall, and had the strong, lean build and supple grace of a natural athlete.

Dean smiled at the waitress. "We're fine now, thanks." As she moved away, he said, "She's cute."

Gavin glanced at her indifferently. "She's okay."

"Cuter than the young woman I met today." Regarding Gavin closely, he said, "Melissa Hatcher."

Unmistakably, the name registered. Dean was sure of it. But Gavin played dumb. "Who?"

"She said she knew you."

"She doesn't."

"Then why would she say she did?"

"How should I know? She got the name wrong, or mixed me up with someone else." He was fiddling with the drinking straw in his glass of Coke, avoiding eye contact.

"I introduced myself to her and after we had talked for a while, she said, 'You're Gavin's dad.' She knew you."

"Maybe she'd been warned off me 'cause you're a cop."

"You mean, who wants to be friends with a cop's kid?"

He looked at Dean resentfully. "Something like that."

"Janey Kemp?"

This time Gavin couldn't as easily hide his reaction. His expression became guarded instantly. "Who?"

"Janey Kemp. From what I've heard about her, she wouldn't want to be friends with a cop's kid. Do you know her?"

"I've heard of her."

"What have you heard?"

Gavin scooped up a bite of queso and through a mouthful said, "You know. Stuff."

"Like what? That she's wild? Easy?"

"It's been said."

"Have you ever met her?"

"I may've bumped into her a couple of times."

"Where?"

"Jeez, what is this? The Spanish Inquisition?"

"No, I'm saving the thumbscrews for later. Right now I'm just curious to know where you've bumped into Janey Kemp and her friend Melissa. It must have been enough times that my name meant something to her. Even before that, she recognized me because you and I favor each other."

Gavin squirmed in his seat, shrugged his shoulders. "They hang out with all those rich, snooty kids. I've seen them around, is all. At the movies. The mall. You know."

"The lake?"

"Which one? Town or Travis?"

"You tell me."

"I've seen 'em a few times, okay? I don't remember where."

Dean laughed. "Gavin, don't bullshit me. If I were your age, and I had met Melissa Hatcher, and she was dressed anything like she was today, I would remember it in minute detail." He pushed his plate aside and leaned forward. "Tell me what you know about the Sex Club."

Gavin kept his expression blank, but again his eyes gave him away. "The what?"

"Last night, when you disobeyed and went out, did you go to Lake Travis?"

"Maybe I did. So what?"

"I know that kids congregate in specified spots around the lake. Did you see Janey Kemp among the crowd last night? And before you give me some bullshit answer, you should know that she's been missing for over twenty-four hours."

"Missing?"

"She didn't come home after going out last night. No one's heard from her. Late this afternoon, just before I left headquarters, patrol officers discovered her car. It was parked near a lakeside picnic area in a clump of cedar trees. No sign of Janey. Apparently she met someone last night and left with that person. Did you see her? Was she with someone?"

Gavin lowered his eyes to his ravaged plate and stared at it for several moments. "I didn't see her."

"Gavin," he said, lowering his voice, "I know the ironclad rule against ratting on your friends. The same rule applied when I was growing up. But this isn't a matter of loyalty or betrayal. It's much more serious.

"Please don't try to protect Janey or anyone else by holding back information. Drinking, drugs, whatever else was going on last night, I'm not interested in right now. If Janey left with the wrong guy, her life could be in jeopardy. With that in mind, are you absolutely certain you didn't see her?"

"Yes! God!" He glanced around, realizing he'd drawn attention to himself from people at nearby tables. He slumped in the booth and mumbled to his lap, "Why're you picking on me?"

"I'm not picking on you."

"You're being a cop."

Dean took a deep breath. "Okay, maybe. I'm coming to you as a source of information. Tell me what you know about the Sex Club."

"I don't know what you're talking about. I gotta pee." He slid to the end of the booth and was about to leave, but Dean ordered him to stay where he was.

"You've been potty trained since you were three. You can hold it for a few more minutes. What do you know about the Sex Club?"

Gavin rocked back and forth, staring angrily through the window, his expression hostile. Dean thought he would refuse to answer him, but eventually he said, "Okay, I've overheard guys talking about this website where they swap email with chicks. That's all."

"Not quite all, Gavin."

"Well, that's all I know about it. I didn't go to school with these kids, remember? I got ripped up by the roots and transplanted here, so they're not—"

"You've been hanging out with a group of kids almost since the day we moved here. Your 'Oh woe is me, I had to leave my friends' refrain is getting a little tired. You need to think of something else to bitch about.

"In the meantime, this girl may be fighting for her life, and I'm not exaggerating. So stop sulking and feeling sorry for yourself and give me a straight answer. What do you know about this Internet club and Janey Kemp's participation in it?"

Gavin held out for several more moments, then, as though resigned, laid his head against the back of the booth. "Janey meets up with guys she's met over the Internet, and they have sex. She'll do anything. Her and that Melissa."

"So you do know them."

"I know who they are. Lots more girls are in the club. I don't know all their names. They come from schools all over the city. There's this message board and the members talk about what they do."

"Have you joined this club, Gavin?"

He sat up. "No! You have to know how to get in, and I haven't asked 'cause I'd feel like a dork for not knowing already."

"It's not that much of a secret. The department's computer crime unit is on to it."

The boy laughed. "Yeah? What are they gonna do about it? They can't stop it, and everybody knows that."

"Soliciting sex is a crime."

"You would know," he muttered resentfully. "You're the cop."

He parked in a grove of live oak trees where others had left their cars. He had a Styrofoam chest of beer and wine coolers in the trunk. He selected a beer and carried it with him as he strolled toward the lakeshore and the wood-plank fishing pier that extended thirty yards out over the water.

This was tonight's meeting place.

He had come to check things out.

He had dressed to blend into the crowd. The baggy shorts and T-shirt were Gap issue, exactly like the younger people wore. Nevertheless, he kept the bill of his baseball cap pulled down low so it would shadow his face.

Some of the people here tonight were familiar. He'd seen them before at similar gatherings, or in the clubs on Sixth Street and around the university campus. Others were new to him. There were always fresh new faces.

Name your pleasure—drink, drugs, sex—it was available. And tonight you could even indulge in gambling. On the beach, a girl wearing only bikini trunks and a straw cowboy hat was on her knees fellating a guy. Bets were being placed on how long the guy could hold out before climaxing.

He joined the ring of cheering onlookers that had formed around the couple and wagered five bucks. One had to admire the guy's self-control because the girl had know-how. He lost his bet.

Unhurried, he strolled along the pier. He didn't invite attention, but ordinarily he didn't have to, and tonight proved to be no different. He was soon approached by two girls who were acting so lovey-dovey that right away he knew they were on Ecstasy.

They hugged him, stroked him, kissed him on the mouth, told him he was gorgeous, the moon was awesome, the night air was divine, and life was beautiful.

They asked him to hold their clothes while they went skinny-dipping. He watched from the pier as they cavorted like water nymphs, occasionally pausing to wave and throw kisses up to him.

When they came out of the water and dressed—well, partially—he took them to his car and gave them each a beer.

One of the girls fixed her glassy eyes on him. "Do you like to party?"

"I'm here, aren't I?" Clever answer. Noncommittal. Affirmation was only implied.

She fondled him through his shorts and giggled. "I believe you do."

"We *love* to party," the other drawled.

They did, too. Over the course of the next hour, in the back-seat of his car, they showed him just how much the party girls they were. When he finally told them he must go, they were reluctant to say good-bye. They kissed and caressed him and begged him to stay for more fun and games.

He finally disentangled himself and made his departure. As he was steering his car through the makeshift parking lot toward the main road, he noticed a couple of guys looking at him with blatant envy. They must have seen him getting out of his backseat with the two babes, extricating himself from their clinging limbs and drug-induced affections.

Did these losers wish they were as lucky in love as he was? You bet your ass they did.

But he also marked a guy he recognized as an undercover narcotics officer. The cop was thirty, but didn't look a day over eighteen. He was transacting with a known drug dealer through the open window of a car.

What's the difference in the narc buying drugs and what I'm doing? John Rondeau asked himself.

Not a damn thing. To effectively fight a crime, you had to understand the nature and mechanics of it. Ever since his unit had discovered the Sex Club, he had appointed himself to do some research. After hours and on-site, of course.

His ambition was to get promoted to CIB, which was the pulse of the department. That's where all the exciting police work was done, and that's where he wanted to be.

Toward that promotion, he could really distinguish himself with this Kemp case. It had elements that received notice, namely, a celebrity, sex, and minors. Put them together and you had yourself a humdinger of an investigation.

To the computer crime unit, the Sex Club was old hat. They'd known about it for months and, realizing the futility of trying to shut it down, had more or less forgotten about it.

But the messages left on the discussion boards continued to blow Rondeau's mind. He'd made it his duty to check out the situation, see if the members really did what they boasted or simply exchanged their wildest fantasies via email. He had discovered that most of the claims were not exaggerations.

And it was a good thing he had done the research. If he hadn't had hands-on knowledge, he wouldn't have been able to answer intelligently and thoroughly all the questions put to him by Curtis, Malloy, and Paris Gibson this morning. So it really was for the benefit of the PD that he'd been putting in this unpaid overtime, wasn't it?

However, more investigative work was required. It was all about his getting a promotion to CIB. It was his job, his sworn duty. He was working undercover, that's all.

Not surprisingly, Brad Armstrong wasn't at home when Toni returned from his dental office. She explained to the startled baby-sitter that she didn't feel well and that she and Dr. Armstrong had canceled their plans for an evening out. She paid her for five hours.

Three times she had called Brad's cell phone. Three times she'd left voice-mail messages to which he hadn't responded. She fixed the children hot dogs for dinner. After they'd eaten, she played a game of Chutes and Ladders with the girls while her son watched a *Star Trek* rerun.

They were trooping upstairs to take their baths when Brad came in with chocolate bars and bear hugs. For Toni there was a bouquet of yellow roses, which he sheepishly presented to her. "Can we be friends again? Please?"

Unable to look at the insincere apology in his eyes, she lowered her head. He took that as acquiescence and kissed her quickly on the cheek. "Have you eaten?"

"I was waiting for you."

"Perfect. I'll put the kids to bed. You get something on the table. I'm famished."

What she had on the table when he returned to the kitchen wasn't what he expected. The unappetizing display stopped him dead in his tracks. "Where'd you get all that?" he demanded angrily. "Never mind. I know where you got it."

"That's right. I found it this afternoon when I went to your office. Where you were conspicuously absent, Brad. You didn't tell anyone where you were going, and you haven't answered your cell phone for hours. So don't put *me* on the defensive. I refuse to apologize for violating your privacy when this is what your privacy is protecting."

As soon as he was confronted with the evidence of his sickness, the fight went out of him. It was a physical diminishing, a deflation both of spirit and body. He pulled out a chair and sat down at the table, his shoulders slumping, his hands falling list-lessly into his lap.

Toni took a plastic trash bag from the pantry and scooped the collection of sordid photographs and magazines into it. Then she closed it with a twist tie and carried it to the garage.

"I'll take it to a Dumpster in the morning," she told him when she came back in. "I would hate for the bag to come open acci-dentally and our neighbors, or even the garbage collectors, to see what's inside."

"Toni, I'm . . . There's really no defense I can offer, is there?"

"Not this time."

"Are you going to leave me?" He reached for her hand and clasped it damply. "Please don't. I love you. I love the kids. Please don't destroy our family."

"I'm not destroying anything, Brad," she said, pulling her hand free. "You are."

"I can't help myself."

"Which is all the more reason for me to leave and take the children. What if one of them had found those pictures?"

"I'm careful about that."

"You're careful to conceal it the way a drug addict hides his stash or the alcoholic keeps a hidden bottle in case of an emer-gency."

"Oh, come on," he cried.

His contrition was gradually dissipating. Hostile defensive-ness was setting in. Next would come an air of superiority. They'd played this scene many times before. His transition from penitent to martyr was virtually scripted and Toni knew to anticipate each phase of it.

He said, "Comparing a harmless hobby to drug addiction is ridiculous and you know it."

"Harmless? Some of those pictures are of underage girls. They're exploited by corrupt and depraved people for your enter-tainment. And how can you call it harmless when it affects your career, our family life, our marriage?"

"Marriage?" he sneered. "I don't have a wife anymore, I've got a jailer."

"If you continue, you may well wind up in jail, Brad. Is that what you want?"

He rolled his eyes. "I'm not going to jail."

"You could, unless you admit to yourself and to others that you're a sex addict and get the help you need to combat it."

"Sex addict." He snuffled a laugh. "Do you hear how absurd that sounds, Toni?"

"Dr. Morgan doesn't think it sounds absurd."

"Jesus. You called him?"

"No, he called me. You haven't been to the therapy group in three weeks."

"Because it's a waste of time. All those guys talk about is whacking off. Now, I ask you, is that a productive way to spend an evening?"

"It's court mandated that you attend the meetings."

"I guess you're going to tattle to my probation officer. Tell him I've been a bad boy. I haven't been going to therapy with the other pervs."

"I don't have to tell him. Dr. Morgan already did."

"Dr. Morgan is the worst sicko in the group!" he exclaimed. "He's a recovering 'addict' himself. Did you know that?"

She continued unflappably. "Dr. Morgan is required to report more than two consecutive absences to your probation officer. You have an appointment with him tomorrow morning at ten o'clock. It's compulsory."

"I guess it doesn't matter if I cancel patient appointments and get my partners pissed at me."

"That's a consequence you'll have to pay."

"Along with sleeping on the sofa, I suppose."

"I would prefer that you did."

His eyes narrowed into a glare. "I bet you would. Since you obviously don't like anything we do in bed."

"That's not fair."

"Fair? I'll tell you what's not fair. It's having a wife who'd rather snoop than fuck. When was the last time we did? Do you even remember? No, I doubt you do. How can you think of sex when you're so busy spying?"

He came to his feet and advanced on her. He curved his hand around the back of her neck and gave it a squeeze that was too hard to be mistaken for affection.

"Maybe if you put out more often, I wouldn't have to resort to looking at my dirty pictures."

He yanked her forward. She turned her head to avoid his kiss and tried to push him aside. But he backed her against the counter and pinned her there. Shocked, she cried out, "Stop it, Brad. This isn't funny."

Her anger only seemed to excite him. His face suffused with color as he ground his lower body against hers. "Feel that, Toni? Feel good?"

"Leave me alone!"

She pushed him hard enough to send him reeling backward and crashing into the table. Covering her mouth with her hand, she tried to stifle her sobs. She was equally outraged and frightened. She'd never seen him this way. Her husband had become a stranger.

He regained his footing and collected himself, then snatched up his jacket and keys. The house shook with the impact of the slamming door. Toni staggered to the nearest chair and sank onto it. For several minutes she wept softly, not wanting the children to hear.

Her life was falling apart and she was incapable of doing anything about it. Even now she loved Brad. He refused to get help to rid himself of this illness. Why was he intent on destroying the love they'd once had? Why would he willfully choose his "harmless hobby" over her, over his children? Weren't they worth more to him than his—

In a heartbeat, she was out the door to the garage. The trash bag in which she had placed the pornography was gone.

Brad had taken his first love with him.

chapter *thirteen*

Paris had an office at the radio station, which she worked in when she wasn't on the air. Although "office" was an aggrandizing word for the small room. It couldn't claim a single redeeming feature, not even a window. Decades ago the plaster walls had been painted an ugly manila color. The acoustic ceiling tiles sagged and bore generations of water stains. Her desk was made of ugly gray Formica, chunks of which had been gouged out, probably by a previous occupant who was hopelessly depressed over his surroundings.

Nothing in the office belonged to her. There were no framed diplomas on the walls, or posters of vacation destinations fondly remembered, no candid snapshots of grinning friends, or posed family portraits. The room was barren of anything personal, and that was intentional. Pictures and such invited questions.

Who's that?

That's Jack.

Who's Jack? Your husband?

No, we were engaged, but we didn't get married.

Why? Where's Jack now? Is he the reason you wear sunglasses all the time? Is he the reason you work alone? Live alone? Are alone?

Even the friendly prying of coworkers could bring on severe heartache, so she tried to prevent it by keeping her relationships with them strictly professional and her office space devoid of any hints about her life.

The office wasn't without clutter, however. The unsightly surface of her desk was covered by mail. Bags of it were dumped onto it daily—fan letters, ratings charts, inner-office memos, and the endless reams of material sent to her by record companies promoting their newest releases. Since there was no space for even a file cabinet in the room, she sorted and tossed as efficiently as possible, but it was an unending task.

She had attacked the pile of correspondence after making her music selections for that night's show and entering them into the program log. She'd been at it for an hour when Stan materialized in the open doorway. His expression was petulant. "Thanks a lot, Paris."

"For what?"

He came in and closed the door. "Guess who came to see me today?"

"I hate guessing games."

"Two of Austin's finest."

She laid aside her letter opener and looked up at him. "Policemen?"

"And I have you to thank for it."

"They came to your house?" She had thought that either Carson or the eager Griggs would have called Stan only to ask follow-up questions.

He moved aside a stack of envelopes and sat down on a corner of the desk. "They interrogated me and jotted down my answers in little black notebooks. Very gestapoesque."

"Stop dramatizing, Stan."

Because of her return trip to the police station, followed by the upsetting visit with the Kemps, she'd had no time to sleep. Before she could rest, she had to do a four-hour radio program and do it as though nothing was wrong. It was a daunting prospect.

Dealing with Stan's wounded pride wasn't the best use of her limited stamina or the time remaining before the evening deejay turned the broadcast studio over to her.

"This morning, I reported Valentino's call to a detective," she explained. "As it turns out, a young woman from this area is unaccounted for. The police are investigating to see if there's a connection between her disappearance and Valentino's call. They're conducting routine background checks on everyone who's involved, even remotely. So don't take offense. They didn't single you out. Marvin is also on their list of people to talk to."

"Oh, great. I rank right up there with a *janitor*. I feel much better now."

For once she felt his sarcasm was warranted. "I'm sorry. Truly. The police are being thorough because they're as convinced as I am that this was no crank call. I hope we're all overreacting and it turns out to be nothing. But if our hunches are right, a girl's life is at stake. Nevertheless, I regret that you were dragged into this by happenstance."

He was mollified, but only slightly. Stan's first consideration was always Stan. "The police also talked to our general manager. Of course, he immediately called Uncle Wilkins, who in turn called the chief of police and, from what I understand, gave him an earful."

"Then I'm sure you've been cleared of all suspicion."

"I was actually under suspicion?" he exclaimed.

"Figure of speech. Forget it. Go out and buy a new gadget. There's bound to be one on the market you don't have yet. Treat yourself. You'll feel better."

"It's not that easy, Paris. My uncle was even more incensed than I was. He's been talking to the GM off and on all afternoon, wanting to know 'what the hell is going on.' I paraphrase, of course. You can count on being summoned into the inner sanctum yourself."

"I already have been."

The station's general manager had called her on her cell phone as she was leaving the Kemp estate. He had asked for a meeting, but he'd put it in the form of a mandate, not a request. She'd received a dressing-down for not telling him about Valentino's call before notifying the police. His primary concern was the station's reputation.

"I played him the recording of the call," she told Stan. "It disturbed him, as it's disturbed everyone who's heard it. He spoke with Sergeant Curtis, the detective who's heading the investigation."

The GM had talked to Curtis via speakerphone, making Paris privy to their conversation. He had agreed that Paris and everyone at 101.3 should cooperate with the police to the fullest extent, but stipulated that if Janey Kemp's disappearance became a big news story, he wanted the radio station's involvement to be minimized.

Curtis's response had been, "Frankly, sir, I'm more worried about this girl's life than I am your radio station's call letters showing up in the press."

Before she left the GM's office, he had peevishly reminded her that her precious anonymity might soon be blown. She had already thought of that, and hoped it didn't come to pass. For years she had safeguarded her privacy with the fanaticism of a miser protecting his stockpile of gold. She never again wanted to be the pivotal figure in a sensational news story.

But she agreed with Curtis—rescuing Valentino's victim superseded everything else. By comparison, the impact it would have on her life was trivial.

To further pacify Stan, she said, "Rest assured that I received a proper scolding for jumping the chain of command. You weren't the only one who had his hands slapped today. Now, can I please get back to work?"

"It was a wristwatch with a built-in GPS."

"What was?"

"The gadget I bought myself today."

She laughed as he blew her an air kiss and headed for the door. Over his shoulder he said, "Oh, by the way, Marvin called in sick."

"Sick?"

"Switchboard left a message on my voice mail," he called back. "That's all it said."

To her knowledge Marvin had never called in sick before, making her curious about the nature of his sudden illness. She left the mail sorting for another time and headed toward the small employee kitchen at the back of the building.

At this time of night, the building was hushed and dimly lighted. Other station personnel were long gone, their offices dark. Paris was accustomed to the silence, the darkness, and the pervasive odors of dust scorched by electronic equipment, burned coffee, and carpet that had absorbed decades of tobacco smoke before smoking was outlawed in the workplace.

FM 101.3 was owned and operated by the Wilkins media conglomerate, which included five newspapers, three network-affiliated television stations, a cable company, and seven radio stations. The corporate offices occupied the top three floors of an Atlanta skyscraper that was upscale and sleek, with glass pods for elevators and a two-story waterfall in the sterile granite lobby.

This facility, rescued from a bankrupt previous owner, was as far from upscale and sleek as a woolly mammoth. There was no waterfall in the lobby, only a water cooler that gurgled and occasionally leaked.

The unattractive, single-story brick structure was situated on a hill on the outskirts of Austin, several miles from the state capitol dome. The building hailed from the early fifties and looked it. It had passed through the hands of twenty-two penny-pinching owners.

Rundown and tacky, it was virtually overlooked by the corporate suits—except when they reviewed the ratings charts. Appearance wise, FM 101.3 was an unsightly wart on the glossy corporate image. But it was healthfully in the black, a reliable producer of revenue.

Despite the building's shortcomings, Paris liked it. It had soul. It bore up well despite its scars.

After the dark hallways, the flickering fluorescent light in the kitchen seemed excessively bright. It took several seconds for her eyes to adjust to the glare even behind her tinted lenses. She took a teabag from her personal stock in the cabinet and put it in a cup of water she heated in the vintage microwave. The water had barely begun to color when she heard voices.

Looking into the hallway, she was stunned to see Dean trailing several steps behind Stan, who was saying to him, "She didn't tell me she was expecting a visitor."

"She isn't expecting me."

Spotting her, Stan said, "He was tapping on the front door. I didn't let him in until he showed me his cop's badge."

Trying to hide her consternation from her coworker, she said, "Dr. Malloy works with the Austin PD. He was consulted for a psychological assessment of Valentino's tape."

"So he said." Stan looked Dean up and down. "Two for the price of one. A cop and a shrink."

"Something like that," he replied, smiling tightly.

Stan looked from one to the other, but when neither spoke, he must have realized that his company was no longer wanted. He said to Paris, "If you need me, I'll be in the engineering room."

Dean watched as Stan retreated down the hallway. When he was out of earshot, he turned back to Paris. "That's Crenshaw? The owner's nephew? Is he gay?"

"I have no idea. What are you doing here, Dean?"

He stepped into the kitchen, immediately reducing its already limited floor space. "Someone should be here with you during your shift."

"Stan's with me."

"You would trust him with your life?"

She smiled wanly. "You have a point."

"Until we know more about this character calling himself Valentino, you should have police protection."

"Curtis offered to send out Griggs and Carson. I said no."

"I've met Griggs. He seems to be on his toes and a real Boy Scout, but neither he nor . . ."

"Carson."

" . . . has hostage-negotiation training. I should be here if Valentino calls again. If I sense that he's close to losing it, I could talk to him, hopefully persuade him to identify his captive and tell us where he's keeping her."

That being his field of expertise, it was a plausible excuse for his being there. Nevertheless, she questioned his motive. "He may not call. You will have wasted your whole evening."

"It wouldn't be wasted, Paris. I'm also here because I wanted to see you."

"You've seen me."

"Alone."

She set the mug of tea on the stained counter, turning her back to him. "Dean, please don't do this."

He moved up close behind her, and she held her breath, fearing he would touch her. She was unsure as to what her reaction would be if he did, so she didn't want to be tested.

"Nothing has changed, Paris."

She gave a rueful laugh. "Everything has changed."

"When you walked into my office this morning, it came back. All of it. I got slam-dunked just like I did the first time I saw you. Remember? It was the night after the snow."

Houston's snowfall had been reduced to a cold rain that gusted inside when she opened her front door to admit Jack and Dean.

She waved them inside hastily so she could close the door. Jack's introduction got lost in the flurry of their shedding damp overcoats and trying to close stubborn umbrellas that were dripping on her entry floor.

Once she had hung their coats on the coat tree and propped their umbrellas in the corner, she turned and smiled up at her fiancé's best friend. "Let's start over. Hello, Dean. I'm Paris. It's a pleasure to meet you."

"The same goes for me."

His handshake was firm, his smile warm and friendly. He was a couple inches taller than Jack, she noticed. His brown hair was showing signs of premature gray at his temples. He wasn't classically handsome like Jack, but ruggedly so. Jack had told her that Dean had to beat women off with a stick. She could see why. The asymmetric features of his face were arresting. They were counterbalanced by his eyes, which were pale gray and outlined by dark, spiky lashes. An absorbing combination.

He said, "I thought Jack was lying."

"Jack lie? Never!"

"When I asked him what you looked like, he said you would take my breath away. I thought he was exaggerating."

"He does tend to do that."

"He didn't this time."

From across the room, Jack grinned at them. "While you two are discussing my character flaws, I'm going to fix a round of drinks."

They enjoyed a convivial dinner at Jack's favorite steak house. After the meal they migrated to the adjacent bar, where they sat in front of the fireplace and sipped after-dinner coffees. The men regaled her with stories about their college days. Of course, Jack dominated the conversation, but Dean seemed willing to yield him center stage. Jack was a talented, witty storyteller.

Dean was an excellent listener. He asked her about her work, and while she was describing a normal workday, he never broke eye contact. He gave her the attention he would give an oracle divulging the future of mankind. He hung on every word and asked pertinent questions. That was Dean's special gift—making the other person feel as if they had become the center of his universe.

Jack's enjoyment of the evening included imbibing too much brandy. He was sleeping in the backseat when Dean pulled his car to a stop in front of her town house.

"I think we've lost him," he remarked.

She looked back at her fiancé, who was snoring softly through his open mouth. "I think you're right. Will you see him home safely and into bed?"

"As long as I don't have to kiss him good night."

She laughed. "I had heard so much about you from Jack, I already considered you my friend, too. Promise me that you'll join us for another evening soon."

"That's a promise."

"Good." She reached for the door handle.

"Wait. I'll see you in."

Despite her protests, he got out and came around with an umbrella as she alighted from the passenger seat. He walked with her to the front door. He even took her key from her, unlocked the door with his free hand, and waited until she had disengaged the alarm system.

"Thank you for seeing me in."

"You're welcome. What's the date?" he added.

"The date?"

"Of the wedding. I need to put it on my calendar. The best man's gotta be there, you know."

"I haven't set the date yet. Sometime in September or October."

"That long? Jack gave me the impression it would be sooner."

"It would be if he had his way, but I want to use fall colors."

"Yeah, that'd be nice. Church wedding?"

"Presbyterian."

"And the reception?"

"Probably a country club."

"A lot of planning."

"Yes, a lot."

"Hmm."

He seemed not to notice that rainwater dripped off the metal tips of the umbrella frame and splashed onto his shoes. She didn't notice that rain was being blown inside and onto her floor. Even that first night, the look they shared was perhaps several moments too long.

Dean had been the one to eventually break the stare, saying huskily, "Good night, Paris."

"Good night."

Often when future spouses are introduced to long-standing best friends, they despise one another on sight, making it awkward for the one in the middle who loves them both. She had liked Dean from the start.

She hadn't known any better than to consider that a good omen.

Now Dean reached for her hand and turned her around to face him. He looked at her with the same disturbing penetration as he had the night they'd met, and it had the same magnetic effect. She felt her will dissolving and knew that if she didn't fight it immediately, she would be lost.

"Dean, I beg you. Leave this alone."

She tried to step around him, but he blocked her path. "Our circumstances may have changed, Paris, but not what counts."

"What counts is what always has counted. Jack."

"He went through hell," he said. "I know that."

"You couldn't possibly know the hell his life was after that night."

He lowered his face to bring it closer to hers. "That's right, I don't. Because you made it clear I was not to come and see him. Ever."

"Because he wouldn't have wanted you—especially you—to see him that way," she said, her voice cracking. "But take my word for it, his was a living death for seven years before his heart made it official and stopped beating."

"I regret what happened to him as much as you do," he whispered urgently. "Don't you know that? Do you think I could blithely forget? Jesus, Paris, do you think I'm that callous? I've had to live with what happened, just as you have."

He expelled a long breath and pushed his fingers through his hair. He gazed at a spot above her head for a moment before his eyes moved back to her. "But at the risk of making you angry, I have to say this. What happened to Jack was his fault. Not yours, not mine. His."

"The accident wouldn't have happened if—"

"But it *did*. And we can't go back and undo it."

"Guilt management 101, Dr. Malloy?"

"Okay. Yeah. Simply put, I'm not going to let regret eat me alive. I've let it go."

"How nice for you."

"So your method of guilt management is better? Emotionally healthier? You think it preferable to dig a hole and hide in it?" He gave the untidy kitchen a scornful glance. "Look at this place. It's a dark, dirty, dreary rathole."

"I like it."

"Because it's no better than you think you deserve."

When he moved a step closer, her reaction was to hug her elbows tighter as a means of self-defense against his nearness. It was also a defense against the truth of what he was saying. She knew he was right, which only made her more determined not to listen.

"Paris, God knows you're good at what you do here. Your listening audience loves you. But you could've written your own ticket in TV news."

"What do you know about it?"

"I know I'm right. Furthermore, *you* know I'm right."

Unable to look into his persuasive eyes, she lowered her head and stared at the sliver of linoleum flooring between his shoes and hers. She curbed the impulse to grab his lapels and plead with him either to drop the subject or to convince her that she had paid her penance. "I did what I had to do," she said softly.

"Because you felt it was your duty?"

"It was."

"'Was,'" he repeated with a soft emphasis. "What duty do you owe Jack now that he's dead?" He took her by the shoulders. It was the first time in seven years that they had touched. A tide of heat surged through her and she struggled against the compulsion to lean into him and press her body to his.

Instead she said, "Dean, please, don't. I had to make some hard choices, but I made them. As you said, it's done. In any case, I won't argue with you about this."

"I don't want to argue either."

"Or talk about it," she added.

"Then we won't."

"I don't even want to think about it."

"I'll never stop thinking about it."

The timbre of his voice lowered. His fingers closed more tightly around her shoulders. Barely but noticeably he came closer, close enough for their clothing to touch and for her to feel his breath on her hair.

The subject had shifted from Jack's death to a topic that was even more unsettling and better avoided. She dared to raise her head and meet his gaze.

"Why do you hide in the dark, Paris?"

"I don't."

"Don't you? I could barely find my way down that hallway."

"You get used to it."

"'Hello, darkness, my old friend.'"

"You're quoting Simon and Garfunkel?"

"Is that your theme song these days?"

"Maybe you should have been the deejay." She smiled, hoping to lighten the tone of the conversation, but he wouldn't be deterred.

His eyes moved over her face. "You're beautiful, but no one in your listening audience knows what you look like."

"It isn't necessary. Radio is an aural medium."

"But normally radio personalities promote themselves. You have no identity beyond your voice."

"Which is all the identity I need. I don't want to focus attention on myself."

"Really? Then maybe you should dispense with the sunglasses."

"She can't. Her eyes are sensitive to light."

Neither realized that Stan was there until he spoke. As they turned toward him, Dean dropped his hands from her shoulders.

Stan eyed him mistrustfully, but his message was for Paris. "It's five to ten. Harry's going into the news update and final commercial break. You're up."

chapter fourteen

"Hey, Gav!"

Gavin glanced over his shoulder, saw who had hailed him, then waited for Melissa Hatcher to catch up with him. When she got close enough to read his expression, her smile dissolved.

Foregoing any greeting, he said, "Way to go, Melissa. Were you trying to ruin my life, or were you just too stupid to not keep your mouth shut?"

"You're pissed?"

"You bet your ass I'm pissed."

"What for? What'd I do?"

"You told my dad we knew each other."

"So, what's the big deal?"

"The big deal is that we're having a burger at Chili's tonight and he starts in on the Sex Club."

She propped her hand on her hip. "Oh, like I'd tell your dad about the Sex Club. Duh!"

"Well, he heard about it from somebody."

"Probably that other cop. The short, bald one." She puffed on a lighted joint, then offered it to him. "Here. You look in need of some major chilling out."

He pushed the marijuana aside. "What do you know about Janey?"

"She's in deep shit. With her folks. The cops. Everybody." Spotting a group of acquaintances beyond Gavin's shoulder, she waved, calling out, "Hey, y'all, I'm back from France, and have I got stories!"

Gavin sidestepped, blocking her view of the others and forcing her to look at him. "Is Janey really missing?"

"I guess. I mean, that's what your dad told me. By the way, he's hot. Does he have a girlfriend?"

The dope alone couldn't be blamed for her being a mental zero. She hadn't started out with enough gray matter to brag about. "Melissa, what do you know about Janey?"

"Nothing."

"You're her best friend," he argued.

"I've been out of the frigging country," she said crossly. "I haven't seen Her Highness in weeks. All right?" She took another hit of weed. "Look, I've got people waiting for me. Chill, why don't you."

She left him to join a group who had attached a garden hose to a keg of beer and were taking turns guzzling from it. A lot was lost on the ground, but no one seemed to notice or care. There was always more where that came from.

Gavin joined his friends, who were once again congregated in and around Craig's pickup. He surrendered the unopened bottle of Maker's Mark he'd stolen from his dad's liquor cabinet. As busy as his old man was tracking down Janey Kemp, it might be several days before he noticed he was short a bottle of bourbon.

Craig went to work on the red wax seal with his pocketknife. "Did you catch hell last night?"

"And then some." Gavin put his back against the rear fender while his eyes scoured the crowd in search of a familiar face and form.

"You were so wasted."

"Hurled on the way home."

"Oh, man."

"I shit you not." He recounted the incident at the mailbox. "I'm talking projectile vomiting."

Their laughter was interrupted when another of the boys brought up Janey's name. "Y'all hear about her disappearance?"

"It was on the local news," another said. "My mom asked if I knew her."

"Bet you didn't tell her how well you know her."

"Yeah, bet you didn't tell your mom that you know Janey in the biblical sense."

"What do you know about anything biblical?"

"My cousin's a preacher."

"So what happened to you?"

"He tried to save me. It didn't take. Pass the bottle."

The others continued to swap insults along with swigs of the whiskey. Craig climbed out of the truck and came to stand beside Gavin. "What's with you tonight?"

"Nothing."

"Just bummed, huh?" Craig gave him an opportunity to explain his mood, but then gave up with a shrug and joined Gavin's perusal of the crowd. Suddenly, in an excited whisper, he said, "Hey, see that guy over there?"

Gavin looked in the direction Craig indicated and saw a man climbing from the backseat of a car, rearranging his clothes and pulling on a baseball cap. Two girls got out behind him. They were lookers. Barbie-doll types, blond and chesty, although their bony sternums suggested implants.

"Their tits are fake," Gavin remarked.

"Who cares?"

Obviously not Craig, who continued to ogle. "Wonder if the girls know he's a badge?"

Gavin reacted with a start. "A cop? No way."

"I've heard it rumored."

As they watched, the trio engaged in a group hug. Then the man shooed away each girl, but not before giving her an affectionate smack on the butt and a promise to see her again soon.

The girls ambled away, unfortunately in the opposite direction from Craig and Gavin. The man got back into his car, this time in the driver's seat, and as he maneuvered it around Craig's Ram, he and Gavin made eye contact.

"Smug SOB," Craig muttered.

"You're *sure* he's a cop?"

"Ninety-nine point nine percent."

"Then what's he doing here?"

"Same thing we are, and tonight he scored big."

"Yeah, times two."

"Lucky prick." They watched until the taillights disappeared, then Craig said, "I saw you talking to Melissa."

"That's what she's good at. Talking." He told Craig about his dad's chance meeting with her at the Kemp house. "He knows about the Sex Club."

"Don't worry about it," Craig said with a disdainful sniff. "What are they gonna do, seize all the computers?"

"Exactly what I asked my old man. They're pissing in the wind."

Gavin was talking tougher than he felt. Worry gnawed at him like a hunger pain. That's why he had defied his dad once again by leaving the house tonight. He was going to be in trouble anyway, so what the hell? It was a matter of degree.

Weeks ago, planning for an emergency like this, he'd had a spare car key made. As soon as his dad had dropped him off at home and left for the radio station, he was outta there, too. But he didn't feel as cavalier as his defiance implied. He was sick with apprehension over what the next few days might yield.

"Where do you think she is?"

Craig's question broke into his thoughts as though he'd been reading them. "Who, Janey? How the hell should I know?"

"Well, I thought you might."

"Why?"

Craig looked at him with annoyance. "Seeing as how you were with her last night."

As the last few bars of "I'll Never Love This Way Again" faded into silence, Paris spoke into her microphone. "That was Dionne Warwick. I hope you have someone in your life who can look inside your fantasies and make each one come true."

The studio felt claustrophobic tonight and Dean was the reason why. He'd sat for the last three hours and sixteen minutes on a tall, swivel stool identical to hers, far enough away to give her freedom of movement and access to all the controls, but close enough for her to be constantly aware of him. He sat motionlessly and for the most part silently, but his eyes followed her every move.

She felt them especially now when she mentioned fulfilling fantasies. "It's a toasty eighty-two degrees at one-sixteen, but I'll be playing cool classics until two o'clock here on 101.3. Let me know what's on your mind tonight. Call me.

"I've had a request from Marge and Jim, who are celebrating their thirtieth wedding anniversary. This was their wedding song. It's from the Carpenters. Happy anniversary, Marge and Jim."

As "Close to You" began to play, she punched the button to turn off her mike, then glanced across at Dean as she depressed one of the blinking telephone lines. "This is Paris."

"Hi, Paris. My name's Roger."

Throughout the program, each time she had answered one of the phone lines, she and Dean had feared, and yet hoped, that Valentino would be the caller. He'd brought a portable cassette recorder with him. It was loaded and ready to record.

His shoulders relaxed along with hers as she said, "Hello, Roger."

"Can you please play a song for me?"

"What's the occasion?"

"Nothing. I just like the song."

"That's occasion enough. What song would you like to hear?"

Facilely she inserted the requested number into the log, substituting it for one already on deck. Then digging her fists into her lower back, she stood up and stretched.

"Tired?" Dean asked.

"I got virtually no sleep last night and never caught a nap today. You must be tired, too. You're not accustomed to these hours."

"More accustomed than you think. I rarely sleep through a whole night anymore. I doze while listening for Gavin to come in."

"Is he with you for the summer?"

"No, more or less permanently."

She registered her surprise. "Nothing's happened to Pat?"

"No, no, she's good," he said in quick response to her concern. "Doing great, in fact. She finally remarried. He's a nice guy in everyone's opinion except Gavin's."

Paris had met Dean's ex-wife at one of Gavin's Little League games, and she and Jack had once been invited to her house for Gavin's birthday dinner. She remembered her as a petite and pretty woman, but rather serious and structured.

Without her having to ask, Jack had confided to her that Dean had married straight out of college. The union had lasted less than a year. "Really only long enough for them to get Gavin home from the hospital. They were unsuited and knew it and agreed it would be best, even for the kid, if they cut their losses and made a clean break when they did."

Although Gavin had lived with Pat, Dean saw him several times a week and had been actively involved in all phases of his life. He joined Pat at teacher conferences, coached T-ball and soccer teams, participated in and contributed to every aspect of Gavin's development. Following a divorce, a child's upbringing was most often abdicated to the custodial parent. Paris had admired Dean for taking his responsibilities as a father so seriously.

"He and his stepfather weren't getting along?" she asked.

"Gavin's fault. He had moved beyond misbehaving to being downright impossible. Pat and I agreed that he should live with me for a while." He described their tenuous coexistence. "The hell of it is, Paris, I was looking forward to having him with me. I want this arrangement to work."

"I'm sure it will, given time. Gavin is a sweet kid."

He laughed. "Lately, I would beg to differ. But I hope that sweet kid you remember is still in there somewhere behind all that hostility and surliness."

At half past the hour she read a few headlines of news off the information monitor. Following that came several minutes of commercials, during which she took calls. One caller asked her for a date. She graciously declined.

"Maybe you should have accepted," Dean teased. "He sounded desperate."

"Desperately drunk," she said, returning his smile as she deleted the call from the Vox Pro.

The next call came from a giddy couple who'd just become engaged. "He asked me to open a bottle of wine and then handed me a glass with the ring in it." Even her squeal couldn't disguise a charming British accent. "My friends in London won't believe it! We faithfully watched *Dallas* when we were girls and dreamed of someday meeting a handsome Texan."

Laughing because of the young woman's obvious delight, Paris asked what song they wanted her to play.

"'She's Got a Way.' He says Billy Joel could've written it about me."

"And I'm sure he's right. Is it okay if I share our conversation with the listening audience?"

"Fantastic!"

She jotted down their names and answered a few more calls. After the sequence of commercials, she replayed the conversation with the engaged couple and followed it with their requested song, then "Precious & Few," which segued into "The Rose."

Operating the board was second nature to her, so she was able to do all this while continuing her conversation with Dean about Gavin. "What did he say when you told him about meeting Melissa Hatcher?"

"He pretended not to know her."

Paris looked at him inquisitively and he read her thought.

"Yeah, that bothers me, too. Why didn't he want to admit that he knew her? He didn't admit to knowing Janey Kemp either, until I pressed him on it."

"How well does he know her?"

"Not very. At least that's what he told me, but these days I don't always get the truth."

"Not like the time he bent the wheel on his bicycle."

"You remember that?"

"Jack and I had come over to your house for a cookout. Gavin was staying with you that weekend. He'd been riding bikes with neighborhood kids, but came home pushing his. The spokes of his front wheel were bent almost in half. You asked if he'd been popping wheelies and when he confessed, you sent him to his room for the rest of the evening."

"Which might have been punishment enough because he loved being around you and Jack. But I also made him do chores to earn enough money to replace the wheel."

"Tough but good parenting, Dean."

"You think?"

"I do. You made your point about the value of property, but it wasn't the damage to the bike that upset you."

He smiled ruefully. "I'd told him a thousand times not to pop wheelies or jump curbs because it was dangerous. I didn't want him to become an organ donor."

"Right. He could just as easily have busted his head or broken his neck. You were upset over what could have happened, and that's why you were angry."

"I guess I should have explained that to him."

"He knew," she said softly.

He looked across at her and the connection was more than just visual. It lasted through the remainder of the Bette Midler song. As it wound down, Paris turned back to the control board and engaged her mike.

"Don't forget to join Charlie and Chad tomorrow morning. They'll keep you company as you drive to work. In the meantime, this is Paris Gibson with a romantic lineup of classic love songs. The phone lines will be open right up till two o'clock. Call me."

When the next series of songs began, she glanced up at the log monitor. "Only nine minutes left in the program."

"Isn't this about the time he called last night? Right before sign-off?" When she nodded, he said, "Will you be able to talk to him uninterrupted if he does call?"

She pointed to the countdown clock on the screen. "That's the amount of time remaining for everything that's logged to play. Two more selections follow this one."

He calibrated. "So after the last song ends, you'll have barely enough time to say good night and sign off."

"Right."

He glanced at the phone lines on the control board. Three were blinking. "If it's not Valentino, don't engage the caller in a lengthy conversation. Keep the lines open. And if it is him, remember to ask to speak to Janey."

She took a deep breath, checked to see that Dean's finger was on the Record button of the portable machine, then answered one of the phone lines. Rachel wanted to request a song for her husband, Pete, "It Might Be You."

"Ah, Stephen Bishop."

"It was the first song we danced to at our wedding reception."

"It's such a good choice, it deserves a prime spot." Paris promised to play it the following night in the first half hour of her program.

"Awesome. Thanks."

Paris glanced again at Dean before depressing another of the blinking buttons. "This is Paris."

"Hello, Paris."

Her blood ran cold at the sound of his voice. Frantically she cut her eyes to Dean, who started the portable recorder. The Vox Pro screen registered a phone number, which he scribbled down. He stared into the screen as though willing it to give up not just the telephone number but also the image and identity of the caller.

"Hello, Valentino."

"How was your day? Busy?"

"I managed."

"Come now, Paris. Share. What did you do today to keep yourself occupied? Did you think of me at all? Or did you write me off as a crank? Did you talk to the police?"

"Why would I? Unless you let me speak to the girl, I have no reason to believe that she exists and that what you told me last night is true."

"Stop playing silly games, Paris. Of course she exists. Why would I make such a claim if it weren't true?"

"To get my attention."

He laughed. "Well, did it? Will you pay attention this time?"

"This time?"

"You ignored me when I warned you before, and look what happened."

She looked at Dean and shook her head with misapprehension. "What are you talking about, Valentino?"

"Wouldn't you like to know?" he taunted. "Ask me nicely and I may give you a few hints. But you have to ask me *very* nicely. Now, that's an exciting thought." He inhaled deeply, loudly, so she could hear it. "Your voice alone is enough to arouse me. I think about us together, you know. Someday soon, Paris."

She shuddered with repugnance but continued in a bland tone. "I don't believe you have a girl with you. You're all talk and this is a hoax."

Dean nodded approval.

"More games, Paris? I advise against them. You've already squandered twenty-four of your seventy-two hours. The next forty-eight are going to be much more fun for me than for you. As for my captive, she's a little tired, and all her whining and pleading is beginning to grate on my nerves. But she's still a hot fuck, and I'm due."

The line went dead.

"It's not the same number he called from last night," Dean said as he reached for his cell. "Did you notice anything different tonight, Paris? Any change in his inflection or tone from last night?"

Dean was a policeman, she wasn't. Revolted by the call, she was finding it harder to launch into the mode of crime solver. "No," she replied hoarsely. "He sounded the same."

"To me, too, but I thought you might've picked up— Hey, Curtis, he just called," he said into his cell phone. "Different number. Ready?"

As he reeled it off to the detective, Stan pushed open the soundproof door. "Uh, Paris, we've got dead air."

She hadn't realized the music had stopped. Quickly she signaled for quiet and engaged her mike. "Be safe, be happy, love someone. This is Paris Gibson wishing you a good night." She punched a few buttons, then announced, "We're off."

"The creep called again?" Stan asked.

Dean had turned his back to them while he continued his telephone conversation with Curtis.

To Stan she said, "Leave a note for the morning engineers. Ask them to dump the last call on the Vox Pro onto a cassette and make several copies. They'll be better than the one Dean's portable made."

He looked affronted. "I know how to transfer it to cassette, Paris. I could do it right now."

She hesitated, uncertain of his skill. But he looked so crestfallen, she added, "Thanks, Stan, that would be a help."

Dean ended his call, then turned around and grabbed his jacket off the back of the stool and picked up the portable recorder, all in one fluid motion. "The number belongs to another pay phone. Units are already rolling."

"I'm going, too," Paris said.

"Damn straight you are. No way would I leave you alone now."

He pulled open the door. As they rushed out, she called back to Stan. "Could you drop those cassettes off at my house?"

Dean pushed her through the door before Stan had time to answer.

chapter fifteen

Melissa Hatcher was jealous of Janey Kemp for all the reasons that customarily inspire jealousy. Janey was wealthier, prettier, smarter, more popular, and more desired. However, there was one attribute Melissa had that Janey did not: shrewdness.

Had Melissa made Janey her rival, she automatically would have fallen into a distant second place in a two-woman contest. Instead, she had been cunning enough to make Janey her best friend.

But on her first night back from France, when she should have been the center of attention, all anyone wanted to talk about was Janey and her mysterious disappearance. Melissa was miffed. She had tales of the nude beaches on the Côte d'Azur, of the wine she'd drunk and the drugs she'd done. How she'd come to obtain a nipple ring in St. Tropez was a story that would hold an audience captive for half an hour.

But no one was interested in her recent adventures abroad. Janey was the name on everyone's lips, the topic of every conversation.

Melissa didn't believe any of the wild speculations being circulated about her friend's whereabouts. They ranged from her eloping with the Dallas Cowboys rookie quarterback whom she'd met in a club on Sixth Street, to having been kidnapped for ransom that her old man refused to pay, to being snatched by a pervert and made his sex slave.

My ass, Melissa thought resentfully.

If Janey was honeymooning with one of the Dallas Cowboys, she would've made sure that everybody knew about it. Melissa wouldn't put it past the judge to refuse to pay a ransom to kidnappers, but he would do so in front of lights and cameras and use it to campaign for his reelection. And if anybody was being made a sex slave, it was probably the guy who was shacked up with Janey.

Janey was getting stoned. She was getting balled. End of story. When she felt good and ready, she would reappear and gloat over the stir she'd created. She would milk it for all it was worth. That was Janey. She thrived on shocking and agitating people.

How like her so-called best friend, Melissa thought, to steal the limelight on her first night back from Europe. The evening had turned into a real drag, and she was in a sour mood. Having heard enough about Janey to last a lifetime, Melissa decided to go home and submit to jet lag.

But when she spotted the older guy, she changed her mind.

She had seen him before. Her memory wasn't 100 percent reliable, but she was almost positive that Janey had been with him at least once. As galling as it was to admit, he probably would choose Janey over her if Janey was here. Which she wasn't.

So Melissa sauntered over to where he stood leaning against the driver's door of his car, observing. "You going or coming?"

He looked her up and down, then formed a slow grin. "Right now, neither."

She slapped his arm playfully. "I think you took my meaning wrong."

"You didn't intend the double entendre?"

She wasn't sure what that was, so she shrugged and gave him her most beguiling smile. "Maybe."

He was nice looking. Around thirty-five, she'd guess. A little old and geeky, but so what? At least he would be impressed by her travels.

"I just got back from France."

"How was it?"

"Frenchy."

He smiled in appreciation of her wit.

"It was a total blast. I didn't know what the hell they were saying, but I liked listening to them talk. I saw this guy drinking wine with breakfast. Parents give it to their kids, can you believe that? And people sunbathe nude on public beaches."

"Did you?"

She grinned slyly. "What do you think?"

He reached out and brushed her arm. "Mosquito."

"They're vicious tonight. Maybe we should get in your car."

He ushered her to the passenger door and opened it for her, then went around and got in on the driver's side. He started the motor and turned on the air conditioner.

"Hmm, this is much better," she said, wiggling against the cool leather upholstery. "Nice car," she said, taking in the interior. Glancing into the backseat, she asked, "What's that?"

"A plastic trash bag."

"Duh! I know that. What's in it?"

"Want to see?" He reached between the seats and picked up the bag, then set it in her lap.

"It's not dirty laundry, is it?" she asked, and he laughed.

Melissa undid the twist tie and peered inside, then took out a magazine. The title and cover couldn't have been more explicit, but she feigned nonchalance. "In France, you can buy fetish mags like this on every street corner. Nobody thinks anything about it. Can I look?"

"Be my guest."

By the time she'd gone through the magazine, his fingers were strumming the inside of her thigh. He lowered his head to nuzzle her breast. "What's this?"

"My souvenir from France." She raised her top and proudly showed him her nipple ring. "I met this guy on the beach who knew this dentist who does body piercing on the side."

He began to laugh.

"What's funny?"

He flicked the silver ring with the tip of his finger. "Inside joke."

• • •

There were seven calls from Liz on Dean's home telephone voice mail. He listened to all seven.

"I can't imagine why you haven't called me," the last message began. "I've gone beyond angry, Dean. I'm scared. Has something happened to you or Gavin? If you get this message, please call. If I don't hear from you within an hour, I'm going to start calling the Austin hospitals."

The message had been left at 3:20 A.M. There was a similar one on his cell phone voice mail. The last thing he wanted was to talk to Liz. No, the last thing he wanted was to have her start calling the hospitals.

He dialed her cell phone, which she answered on the first ring. "I'm okay," he said immediately. "No one's in the hospital, and you have every right to be mad as hell. Let fly."

"Dean, what is going on?"

He slumped into a chair at his kitchen table and plowed his fingers through his hair. "Work. We've got a crisis situation."

"I haven't heard any news about—"

"Not a national crisis. Not a plane crash, standoff, mass murder, nothing like that. But it's a tricky case. I got involved early this morning . . . yesterday morning, rather. I was consulted as soon as I got to my office, and I've been on it all day. I just got home and I'm beat. None of which is an excuse for not returning your calls."

"What kind of case?"

"Missing girl. Egotistical suspect. He's called and told us what he plans to do to her unless we can locate her before his deadline." He didn't have the energy to tell her more than that. Besides, the details would have included Paris. Liz didn't know about Paris, and this wasn't the time to try to explain a situation of that complexity.

"I'm sorry you had such a hellish day."

"Jesus, Liz, I'm the one who's sorry."

He had much to be sorry for. Sorry for pretending to return her love, and pretending so well that she believed he did. Sorry for not telling her to remain in Houston as she should have done. Sorry for wishing that her trip to Chicago would last longer than a few days.

Lamely he asked, "How did the meetings with the Swedes go?"

"Danes. They accepted my proposal."

"Good. Not surprising, though."

"How's Gavin?"

"He's all right."

"No more arguments?"

"We've avoided bloodshed."

"You sound exhausted. So I'm going to hang up and let you get some rest."

"Again, about today—"

"It doesn't matter, Dean."

"The hell it doesn't. I caused you a lot of unnecessary worry. It matters."

He was angry with her for not being angrier with him. It would have eased his conscience if she'd been royally pissed off. He didn't want her to be understanding. He didn't want to be let off the hook gently. He wanted her to be mad as hell.

But a full-fledged fight would have required energy he didn't have, so he let it drop with a feeble, "Well, anyway, I apologize."

"Accepted. Now go to bed. We'll talk tomorrow."

"I promise. Good night."

"Good night."

He took a long drink straight from the bottle of water in the fridge, then moved through the dark house, toward the bedrooms. There was no light beneath Gavin's door, not even the glow of his computer monitor. He paused to look in.

Gavin was asleep. Wearing only his underwear, he was lying on his back, long limbs flung wide, covers kicked away. He was almost as long as the bed. He was breathing through his mouth, as he'd done since he was a baby. He looked very young and innocent. At sixteen, he was on the borderline between boy and man. But asleep, he seemed much more like a child than a grown-up.

Dean realized, as he stood looking down at his son, that the painful twinge he felt deep inside his chest was love. He hadn't loved Gavin's mother, nor she him, really. But both had loved Gavin. From the day they knew he'd been conceived, they had channeled the love they should have had for each other into the person they had created.

Obviously they had failed to communicate the depth of that love to Gavin. He still didn't believe that correction was for his protection and that discipline wasn't a pleasant pastime for them, but a demonstration of how important he was to them.

Damn it, Dean had wanted to be a good parent. He'd wanted to get it right. He hadn't wanted his son to doubt for one moment of his life that he was loved. But somewhere along the way he must have tripped up, done something wrong, omitted doing something he should have. Now his son held him in contempt and made no secret of it.

Feeling the weight of his failure, Dean backed away from Gavin's bed and quietly closed the door behind him.

The master bedroom was a large room with a high cove ceiling, wide windows, and a fireplace. It deserved better decorating than what he'd done, which amounted to nothing more than basic furnishings and a bedspread. When he'd moved in, he'd told Liz he was saving the decorating for her to do after they married. But he'd been lying to her as well as to himself. He'd never even invited her to spend the night in this bed.

He plugged his cell phone battery charger into a wall socket in the bathroom so it would be handy in case of a call, then stripped and got into the shower and let the hot water pound into him while he mentally reviewed everything that had taken place after Valentino's call.

The race to the pay telephone had been a wasted effort for all concerned—for the cops in the three squad cars who had converged on it, for Sergeant Robert Curtis, who had arrived as neatly dressed as he was during daylight hours, and for Paris and him.

They had arrived shortly after it was confirmed that Valentino was no longer anywhere in the vicinity of the pay phone from which his call had originated. The Wal-Mart store had been closed for hours. The parking lot was a vast desert of concrete. There were no witnesses except for a stray cat who had helped himself to the remnants of a hot dog someone had tossed toward a trash bin, but missed.

"And the cat's not talking," Curtis said wryly as he summed up the situation for them.

He and Paris had joined the detective in his car to conduct a postmortem on the aborted effort to catch Valentino. Paris climbed in the back. He sat in the passenger seat. "I made a cassette recording as the call came in," he told Curtis.

"Let's hear it."

He played the tape once, then rewound it and they listened to it a second time. When it ended, Curtis remarked, "He doesn't seem to know we're after him."

"Which could work in our favor," Dean said.

"Only until tomorrow when it shows up in the newspaper." Curtis turned to Paris. "What does he mean when he says you didn't heed him the last time?"

"Just as I told him, I have no idea."

"You don't recall a previous warning?"

"If I had ever received a call like this, I would have reported it to the police."

"Which is what she did last night." Dean didn't like the way the detective was looking at Paris. "What are you getting at?"

"Nothing. Just thinking."

"Then do us the courtesy of thinking out loud."

Curtis turned to him and seemed ready to take issue with his tone of voice, then must have remembered that Dean outranked him. "I was just thinking about Paris."

"Specifically?"

"How she's gone out of her way to remain anonymous. Which, frankly, I don't get," he said, turning back to her. "Other people in your field are extroverts. Publicity hounds. Their pictures are on billboards. They make personal appearances, stuff like that."

"I'm not like the wild and crazy drive-time jocks. My program isn't hyper like theirs. The music is different, and so am I. I'm the disembodied voice in the dark. I'm the sounding board when no one else will listen. If my listeners knew what I looked like, it would compromise the confidentiality I share with them. It's often easier for people to talk to a stranger than to a trusted friend."

"It's certainly easier for Valentino," he remarked. "If he *is* a stranger to you."

"He may be now, but he doesn't want to remain a stranger," Dean said. Paris and Curtis were sharp enough to know he was referring to Valentino's suggestion that he and Paris would soon be lovers.

Curtis, however, was still following his original train of thought. "You know," he said, "some of those phone sex people are very ordinary looking. Fat, ugly, a far cry from what their voices suggest about them."

Dean knew this wasn't a random observation. "Okay, you've tossed out the bait. I'll bite."

"Instead of lounging on a bed of satin sheets in skimpy lingerie, like they want their callers to fantasize, they're actually in sweats and sneakers, working out of their untidy kitchens. It's all about imagination." He turned to address Paris. "Folks hear your voice and conjure up a mental image of you. I did it myself."

"And?"

"I wasn't even close. I envisioned you dark haired and dark eyed. A fortune-teller type."

"I'm sorry to disappoint."

"I didn't say you disappointed me. You're just not as exotic looking as your voice indicates." He shifted more comfortably in his seat so he wouldn't have to crane his neck to talk to her. "All this is to say that some people may have formed an unwholesome image of you. Valentino appears to be one of those people."

"Paris can't be responsible for a listener's imagination," Dean said. "Especially if he suffers from mental, emotional, or sexual problems."

"Yeah, you said that before." More or less dismissing Dean's comment as irrelevant, the detective continued to address Paris. "Is there a personal reason you want to remain anonymous?"

"Absolutely. To protect my privacy. When you're a television personality, you're always in the public eye, even when you're not on the air. I didn't like that aspect of my work. My life was an open book. Everything I said or did was subject to criticism, or speculation, or judgment from people who didn't know anything about me.

"Radio enables me to stay in the business but out of the spot-light. It allows me to go anywhere without being recognized and scrutinized and to keep my private life just that."

Curtis's harrumph implied that he knew he wasn't hearing the whole story but was willing to let it go for now. "How long did you say you keep the recordings of your phone calls?"

"Indefinitely."

He grimaced. "That's a lot of phone calls."

"But remember, I only save the ones that I feel are worth saving."

"Even at that, we're talking what? Hundreds?" She nodded. He said, "We'd use up a chunk of our remaining forty-eight hours listening to all those calls, trying to find the one Valentino referred to tonight. But if we go in by the back door—"

"By looking at cold cases," Dean said, seeing suddenly where Curtis was headed.

"Right. I called a friend over there." The cold-case unit worked out of a separate building a few miles from headquarters. "He promised to check, see if any of their cases have a similarity to Janey Kemp's."

"And if so, we can check to see if Paris received a call from Valentino around that time."

"Don't get too excited," she cautioned them. "I might not have saved that call. Besides, how could I have dismissed a warning of murder?"

"I doubt he was so blatant the first time," Dean told her. "It's symptomatic of serial rapists to get progressively bolder. They start out cautiously and get more daring with each offense until they're practically courting capture."

Curtis agreed. "That's been my experience."

"Some actually want to get caught," Dean said. "They're begging to be stopped."

"Somehow I don't think Valentino fits into that category," she said. "He sounds very self-assured. Arrogant."

Dean looked across at Curtis and could tell that the veteran detective agreed with her. Unfortunately, so did Dean.

"On the other hand," he said, "he could be manipulating us.

Maybe you don't remember any such call because there wasn't one. Valentino could be trying to distract us with a red herring."

"Could be," Curtis said. "I get the distinct feeling he's laughing up his sleeve." He asked Paris, "What do you know about Marvin Patterson?"

"Until yesterday, only his first name."

"Why?" Dean asked the dectective.

"He's split," Curtis said. "Officers called his place to see if he was at home, told him they were on their way to talk to him. By the time they arrived, Marvin Patterson was gone. Vacated in a hurry. Dirty breakfast dishes in the sink and his coffeepot still warm. That's how fast he cleared out."

Paris asked, "What's he got to hide?"

"We're investigating that now," Curtis replied. "The Social Security number he put on his job application at the radio station was traced to a ninety-year-old black woman who died in a rest home several months ago."

"Marvin Patterson was an alias?" Dean asked.

"I'll let you know when we know."

Paris said, "Marvin, or whatever his name is, may have something to hide, but I don't believe he could possibly be Valentino. He uses that creepy whisper, but he's articulate. If Marvin speaks at all, it's a mumble."

Dean asked her what Marvin looked like. "How old is he?"

"Thirtyish. I've never really paid much attention to his looks, but I would describe him as nice looking."

Curtis said, "Let's wait and see what turns up."

"Has anything useful been found on Janey's computer?" Dean asked.

"Smut. Lots of it. Written by other kids."

"Or predators."

Curtis conceded Dean's point. "Wherever it originated it's raw stuff, especially coming from high school kids. Rondeau printed out her email address book and is in the process of tracing the users."

After that, they'd parted company. Paris's protests against having police protection were overruled. Curtis had already dispatched Griggs and Carson to her house.

"They're both starstruck. If they were guarding the president, they couldn't be taking it more seriously. They'll be parked at your curb all night."

Dean drove her home. "What about my car?" she asked when he refused to return her to the radio station so she could pick it up.

"Ask one of your admirers to retrieve it in the morning."

She directed him to her house. It was located in a wooded, hilly area on the outskirts of downtown. The limestone house was tucked into a grove of sprawling live oaks and garnished with well-maintained landscaping. A curved walkway lined with white caladiums led up to a deep porch. Twin brass light fixtures glowed a welcome from either side of a glossy-black front door.

Incongruous with the coziness of the property was the patrol car parked at the curb. The two young policemen practically leaped from it when Dean and Paris pulled up behind them.

Dean waved back the ever-ready Griggs. "I'll see her in."

He'd insisted on going inside with her, and even though her alarm control panel hadn't registered a disturbance since she set it, he went through every room of the house, looking inside closets, behind shower doors, and even beneath the bed.

"Valentino doesn't strike me as the type who would hide under a bed," she said.

"A rapist often hides in his victim's house, waiting for her to return home. That's part of the thrill."

"Are you trying to frighten me?"

"Definitely. I want you good and scared, Paris. This guy wants to punish women, remember? He's angry with Janey—at least we're still presuming it's Janey—for cheating on him. He's angry with you for taking her side."

"I didn't even know there were sides to be taken."

"Well, that's his skewed perception of it and perception is—"

"Truth. I know."

"The suggestion that you and he would soon be together as lovers actually meant that you would be his next victim. He doesn't differentiate between the two."

She pulled her lower lip through her teeth. "When he's finished with Janey, he'll come after me."

"Not if I can help it." He went to her then and placed his hands on her shoulders. "But until we have him in custody, be afraid of him."

She smiled wanly. "I'm not actually afraid. But I'm not stupid either. I'll be careful."

When she'd tried to move away, he hadn't let her go. "This is the first time in our friendship that we've been in a bedroom together."

"Friendship?"

"Weren't we friends?"

She hesitated for several beats before saying quietly, "Yes. We were friends."

"Good friends."

That's when he had reached up and removed her sunglasses, tossed them into a nearby chair, then anxiously searched her eyes. They were as beautiful as he remembered. Deeply blue, intelligent, expressive. They gazed back at him steadily and with seeming clarity.

He exhaled a deep sigh of relief. "I was afraid that you'd lost sight in one eye, or suffered a serious injury, and that was the reason for the sunglasses."

"No permanent damage was done," she said huskily. "I wasn't even left with noticeable scars. But my eyes are still very sensitive to bright light."

Without breaking their eye contact, he leaned forward to reach behind her for the wall switch. He flicked it down and the room went dark. He remained inclined forward, so they were touching from chest to knees, and when she didn't move away, he slid his hands around her neck and up into her hair. He tilted her face up as he lowered his.

"Dean, don't."

But the words were no more than an uneven sigh against his lips as he settled them upon hers. They parted simultaneously, and when their tongues touched, her groan echoed the hunger behind his own. He backed her against the wall, wanting to feel her and taste her. Wanting.

He curved his arm around her waist and drew her lower body

up against his, increasing the pressure where already the pressure was intense. She broke off the kiss and moaned his name.

He brushed his lips across her eyes, her cheekbones, whispering, "We've waited long enough for this, Paris. Haven't we?"

Then he returned to her mouth and kissed her even more passionately than before. He worked his hand between their bodies and covered her breast. Her nipple was erect even before his thumb found it. He felt her hands tensing on the muscles of his back, felt the upward and forward angling of her hips.

He remembered muttering something unintelligible, even to himself, as he lowered his head, his mouth blindly seeking her breast.

"Ms. Gibson? Dr. Malloy?"

Dean jerked as though he'd been shot. Paris froze, then squeezed out from between him and the wall.

He saw red. "That goddamned rookie. I'm gonna kill him."

And at that moment he had meant it. He might have stormed down the hallway and throttled Griggs with his bare hands—as he'd wanted to do—if Paris hadn't grabbed his arm and held him back. She stepped around him and, straightening her hair and clothing as she went, made her way through the house and into the living room.

Griggs was standing on the threshold of the front door. "You left the front door standing open," he said to Dean, who was only half a step behind Paris. "Everything all right?"

"Everything is fine," Paris told him. "Dr. Malloy was kind enough to check my house."

Griggs was staring at her strangely. Either he had noticed that her color was high and her lips were swollen, or he was surprised by her breathlessness, or he was shocked to see her without her sunglasses, or a combination of all of that.

At that moment Dean was incapable of diplomacy and stated bluntly, "You can leave now." He had never liked cops who pulled rank, but this was one time he did and didn't feel bad about it.

Paris was more gracious. "Dr. Malloy will be leaving momentarily. We both appreciate your diligence."

"Uh, some guy . . . Stan? Dropped these off for you." He extended several cassettes.

"Oh, right. Thank you."

"Just leave them there on the table."

Griggs did as Dean ordered. He took another apprehensive glance in his direction, then scuttled out, pulling the door closed behind him.

Dean reached for Paris again, but she avoided his touch. "That shouldn't have happened."

"The interruption? Or the kiss?"

She shot him a baleful look. "It was more than just a kiss, Dean."

"You said it, not me."

She wrapped her arms around her middle. "Don't read anything into it. It won't be repeated."

He looked at her for several moments, taking in her tense expression, her taut posture, and said quietly, "Don't do this, Paris."

"What? Come to my senses?"

"Don't withdraw. Close up. Shut me out. Punish me. Punish yourself."

"You need to go. They're waiting for you to leave."

"I don't care. I've waited for seven years."

"For what?" she asked angrily. "What were you waiting for, Dean? For Jack to die?"

The words hurt, as she'd known they would. She'd said them deliberately to hurt and provoke him, but he'd be damned before he allowed himself to become either. Tamping down his own anger and keeping his voice calm, he said, "I've waited for a chance to get even this close to you."

"And then what did you expect to happen? Did you expect me to fall into your arms? To forget everything that happened and—"

When she broke off, he raised his brow inquisitively. "And what, Paris? And love me? Is that what you were going to say? Is that what you're so goddamn afraid of? That we might actually have loved each other then and still do?"

She had refused to answer him. Instead she'd marched to her front door and pulled it open.

With watchdogs at the curb, he'd had no choice but to leave.

By now the water in his shower had grown cold, but his body was still feverish with a burning desire to know—if he had been able to wring it out of her—what her answer to his question would have been.

chapter *sixteen*

*J*aney had abandoned her plans for retribution and was focusing strictly on survival.

Her attempts to escape from this room seemed as remote as her memories of childhood birthday parties. She'd seen photographs taken at those parties, but felt no connection with the little girl wearing the silver paper tiara and blowing out candles on a bakery-made cake. Likewise, her memories of trying to escape from her captor, of plotting his punishment, seemed to be vague recollections of someone else. Such courageous strategizing was unimaginable to her now.

She was so weak that even had her arms and legs not been restrained, she couldn't have moved. He hadn't given her food or water the last two times he'd been there. She could live with the hunger but her throat was raw from thirst. She had implored him with her eyes, but her silent pleas were ignored.

He was cheerful and talkative, blasé even. He tilted his head to one side and regarded her with renewed interest. "I wonder if you're missed, Janey. You've treated so many people badly, you know. Especially men. Your special talent, certainly your hobby, has been to get men to desire you and then to humiliate them with a public rejection.

"I'd been watching you for a long time before you approached me that first night. You didn't know that? I had. I figured out your email name: pussinboots. Right? Very clever.

Especially since you enjoy wearing western boots. Your favorites are the red ones, aren't they? You even wore them here one night. Wait! Hold on."

He rummaged around the room until he found the photo album he was seeking. "Yes, here you are in your boots. Only your boots, in fact," he added with a sly grin.

When he turned the photograph toward her, she averted her head and closed her eyes. Which made him angry. "Seriously, do you think anybody is really sorry that you're missing?"

He'd left shortly after that. She had been relieved to see him go but terrified that he would never return. In spite of the tape across her mouth, she sobbed noisily. Or maybe her weeping only sounded loud to her own ears. When she choked, she panicked, wondering if a person could drown in tears.

Get a grip, Janey!

She could do this. She could survive him. She could hold out until rescue came, and it would come soon. Her parents would be turning Austin upside down looking for her. Her daddy was rich. He would hire private investigators, bring in the FBI, the army, whatever it took to find her.

She'd hated some of the diehard cops on the Austin PD force, the ones who gave her a hard time about driving drunk, and disorderly conduct, and the illegal substances often in her possession. If she hadn't been Judge Kemp's daughter, the cops who went by the book would have busted her too many times to count.

But she had also balled a few of Austin's finest, the younger, good-looking officers who had a more liberal outlook than the veterans, like the narcotics officer who worked undercover at her high school. He'd been a challenge to seduce, and when he'd finally surrendered, a letdown.

Nevertheless, she wasn't entirely without friends in the police department. They would be searching, too.

And her tormentor had called Paris Gibson. Why he had, Janey couldn't imagine and didn't care. He was obviously proud of that call, because he had recorded it just so he could play it for her. Had he wanted her to know that he was on a first-name basis with a well-known radio personality? The egotistical idiot. Didn't he know that Paris was on a first-name basis with anybody who called her?

Whatever. The important thing was that he had involved her. She could pull a lot of strings. No one was going to ignore Paris Gibson.

But Janey's burst of optimism quickly fizzled. Time was running out. Her captor had told Paris that he was going to kill her within seventy-two hours. But when had he made that call? How much of that time had already expired? She'd lost all track of the days and rarely even knew if it was daylight or dark. What if she was in hour seventy-one of the seventy-two?

Even if he didn't murder her, she could die of neglect. What if he simply never came back? How long could she survive without food and water? Or what if—and this was her greatest fear— what if he was right and nobody gave a damn that she was gone?

He hadn't enjoyed the comfort of his own bed last night, but Dr. Brad Armstrong was feeling sprightly when he arrived at the dental clinic a half hour before his first appointment.

He'd had a busy night and had snatched no more than a couple hours of sleep. But sleep wasn't the only way one could get energized. A girl with a silver ring through her nipple—now, that could get a man supercharged.

He was chuckling to himself as he entered the building and greeted the receptionist.

"Good morning, Doctor. I assume Mrs. Armstrong located you last evening. She was so disappointed that her surprise date was spoiled."

"We had a quiet dinner together after the kids went to bed, so it worked out okay. Any messages for me?"

"A Mr. Hathaway has called twice, but he didn't leave a message either time. He only asked that you return his call. Shall I get him on the line for you?"

Mr. Hathaway was his probation officer. On his best day, Hathaway was a humorless tight ass who loved peering at people over the top of his granny glasses. His idea of intimidation, Brad supposed. "No thanks, I'll try him later. No other messages?"

"That's it."

Toni must really be upset this time. Ordinarily she would have tried to reach him by now if only to assure herself that he hadn't had a head-on with an eighteen-wheeler, suffered a heart attack, or been mugged and murdered. It was always she who took the initial steps toward making up. Isn't that what a loving, supportive wife was supposed to do when her husband stormed from the house after a quarrel?

So he really couldn't be blamed for anything he'd done last night, could he? He'd broken vows, but his backsliding was more Toni's fault than his. She hadn't even tried to be compassionate and understanding. Instead she had scolded him.

He had a collection of erotic magazines and pictures. Big deal. Some might call the material pornographic, but so what? And maybe his collection was more extensive than the next guy's. Was that grounds for making it into a federal case?

After last night, her next accusation would be that he had played too rough. He could hear her now. *Where is that aggression coming from, Brad? I don't know you anymore.* Toni had many fine qualities, but she lacked a spirit of adventure. Anything novel or experimental frightened her. He'd seen the fear in her eyes last night.

She should take lessons from that girl he'd met at the lake. Melissa, her name was. That's what she'd told him anyway. He certainly hadn't given her his name, but he didn't remember her asking. To an adventurous girl like her, names were unimportant.

He'd seen this one around a lot, with many different partners, so, not surprisingly, she hadn't been shocked by his graphic pictures. In fact, she had demonstrated a sincere appreciation for them. They had really steamed her up. She'd been all over him. That girl was something else, her and her nipple ring. Toni would probably have him committed if he suggested a body piercing. But, damn, what a turn-on.

He settled into his desk chair and booted up his computer. Other people in the office had been curious as to why he'd placed his monitor with the back of it facing out into the room rather than up against a wall so all the cables wouldn't show. He'd contrived an explanation, but the real reason was that it was nobody's business but his what was on his monitor.

He visited his favorite websites, but was disappointed that the material hadn't been updated since yesterday morning. Even so, he scanned them all, looking specifically for women with nipple rings. He didn't find any.

He would do some research later, surf the Internet until he located some new, exotic websites. Maybe a Sex Club member had discovered some interesting ones that he didn't yet know about. Leave it to kids to be at the forefront of discovery.

He entered his password and went into the site. He went straight to the message board and was about to type in an inquiry when someone knocked on his office door, then immediately pushed it open.

"Dr. Armstrong?"

"What?" he said brusquely.

"Sorry," an assistant said. "I didn't mean to disturb you. Your first patient has been prepped."

He forced himself to smile. "Thank you. I'll be there as soon as I finish this email to my mom."

She ducked out. He glanced at the clock. He'd been in the office for over a half hour, but it had seemed like five minutes. "Time flies . . . ," he chuckled to himself. Some men read the stock-market report over their morning coffee, some the sports page. He had another interest. Was that a crime?

He returned to his home page and, just to be on the safe side, engaged the service that deleted all his Internet connections so they couldn't be traced.

He'd treated three patients before he was able to take a break. A newspaper had been left at the coffee bar. He carried it, a doughnut, and a cup of coffee into his office with him. He sipped the coffee, took a bite from the doughnut, and flipped up the front page of the newspaper . . . nearly choking when he saw her picture.

It was a serious portrait, probably last year's school photo. Laughably ironic, she looked demure. She seemed to be staring straight at him in a way that made him want to look away. He couldn't.

Accompanying the picture was a story about her: county judge's daughter—Jesus; high school senior; previous malfeasances; a three-day suspension from school last semester; her mysterious disappearance.

The reporter went into detail about her membership in an Internet club, the purpose of which was to solicit sex partners. It was all there in black and white. The writer described how it worked, the chat rooms, the sexually explicit messages left on the website, the secret gatherings—which were no secret to the members—and the licentious acts that ensued at these meeting places. Anyone with whom Janey had had contact was being pursued and questioned by the police. A reference was made that hinted at a possible connection to Paris Gibson's radio program.

Brad placed his elbows on his desk and clasped his head between his hands.

Sergeant Robert Curtis, who has organized a team of investigators, wouldn't comment on Ms. Kemp's alleged connection to the Sex Club, although Officer John Rondeau of the Computer Crimes Division said that such a connection had not been ruled out.

"We're still exploring that," Rondeau said.

The officers declined to comment when asked about the possibility of foul play.

The write-up also said that Austin PD personnel had refused to comment when asked why a homicide detective was overseeing a missing persons case. The more loquacious Rondeau did tell the reporter, "At this point in time, we've had absolutely no indication of foul play and are assuming that Ms. Kemp is a runaway." Good answer, but it didn't address the question.

There was one quote from Judge Kemp. "Like all teenagers, Janey can be inconsiderate and irresponsible when it comes to notifying us of her plans. Mrs. Kemp and I are confident that she'll soon return. It's much too soon for alarming speculation."

Brad actually jumped when his phone rang. With a shaking hand, he reached for the intercom button. "Yes?"

"Your wife is on line two, Dr. Armstrong. And your next patient has arrived."

"Thanks. Give me five minutes."

He wiped the sweat off his upper lip and took several deep breaths before lifting the telephone receiver. It was time to play meek.

"Hi, hon. Look, before you say anything, I just want you to know how sorry I am about last night. I love you. I hate myself for saying the things I did. That trash bag of stuff? History. I threw it away. All of it. As for the . . . the other . . . I don't know what came over me. I'm—"

"You missed your appointment."

"Huh?"

"Your ten o'clock appointment with Mr. Hathaway. He called here because he's been unable to reach you at your office."

"Christ. I forgot about it." The truth was, he had. He'd come into his office, killed a half hour on the Internet, seen three patients, read the front-page story.

"How could something that important slip your mind, Brad?"

"I had patients," he replied testily. "They're pretty damn important, too. Remember our mortgage? Car payment? Grocery bill? I have a job."

"Which won't matter if you get sent to prison."

He glanced down at the picture of Janey Kemp. "I'm not going to prison, not for missing one appointment with my probation officer."

"He's being lenient. He rescheduled you for one-thirty this afternoon."

She was back on her high horse, talking to him like he was no older than their son. He was a grown-up, by God. "Apparently I'm not getting through to you, Toni. I've got work."

"And an addiction," she snapped.

Jesus, she was cutting him no slack whatsoever. "I told you I got rid of the magazines. I tossed the bunch of them in a Dumpster. Okay? Happy now?"

Rather than sounding happy, her laugh sounded terribly sad. "Okay, Brad, whatever. But you're not fooling anybody. Not Hathaway, and certainly not me. If you don't keep this appoint-

ment, he'll have to report it, and you'll have to face the consequences."

She hung up on him.

"And the horse you rode in on, sweetheart!" he shouted to the
telephone receiver as he slammed it down. He sent his chair
rolling back on its casters as he shot to his feet. Placing one hand
on his hip and rubbing the back of his neck with the other, he
began to pace.

Any other time, he would be really pissed off at Toni for taking such a high-handed tone with him. And he was pissed off.
Matter of fact, he was mad as hell. But Toni would keep. Today
he needed to focus on a much more serious problem.

When you lined it all up, things didn't look so good for him.
He was a convicted sex offender. The charge had been a complete
falsehood and the trial a farce. Nevertheless, it was there on his
personal record.

Last night he'd had sex with a young woman. God help him if
she was under seventeen. Never mind that she was as experienced
as a ten-dollar whore—ten dollar, hell. For round two he'd given
her a fifty-dollar "gratuity." Despite her experience, if she was a
minor, he'd committed a crime. And his wife, who had the ear of
his group therapist and his probation officer, was probably
already yapping to them about his recent violent tendencies.

But what really had him concerned, what was causing his
bowels to spasm, was that he couldn't remember if he'd ever seen
Melissa in the company of Janey Kemp.

chapter *seventeen*

Sergeant Curtis called Paris while she was spreading a piece of toast with peanut butter. "I mentioned cold cases last night?"

"There's one that's similar?"

"Maddie Robinson. Her body was discovered three weeks after her roommate reported her missing. A cattleman found it in a shallow grave in one of his pastures. Middle of nowhere. Cause of death, strangulation with a ligature of some kind. Decomposition was advanced. Scavengers and the elements had done significant damage."

Paris set aside her breakfast.

Curtis continued, "But the coroner was able to determine that the body had been washed with an astringent agent." There was a significant pause before he added, "Inside and out."

"So even if it had been found sooner—"

"The perp had made damn sure any DNA evidence would be compromised to the point of making it negligible. Also no sign of either shoe prints or tire tracks. Probably weather eroded. No clues on clothing because there was none."

Paris felt heartsick for the victim who had suffered such a horrible and ignominious death. She asked Curtis what he knew about her.

"Nineteen. Attractive but not a stunning beauty. She was a student. Her roommate admitted that they weren't exactly nuns. Partied a lot. They went out nearly every night. Here's where it gets really interesting. According to her, Maddie had been seeing someone she referred to as 'special.'"

"In what way?"

"She didn't know. Maddie was vague about what set this guy apart. The girls had been friends since junior high school. Usually confided everything. But Maddie wouldn't tell her anything about this mystery guy except that he was cool and wonderful and special."

"The roommate never saw him?"

"Didn't come to their apartment. Maddie would meet him. The roommate didn't know where. He never even called their apartment phone, only Maddie's cell. The roommate's theory was that he was married, and that was the reason for the secrecy. For all their exploits, she and Maddie had drawn the line at sleeping with married men. Not for moral reasons, but because there was no future in it, she said.

"One day Maddie was in love, the next she announced that she was breaking off the relationship. She told her roommate that he was getting too possessive, which irritated her since he never took her on a real date. The only place they ever went was to his apartment—which she described as dreary—where they'd have sex. She hinted that it had become bizarre, even for her, and she enjoyed novelty. The roommate pressed her for details, but she refused to talk about it. All she'd say was that the affair was over.

"To cheer her up, the roommate prescribed getting laid by someone else. Maddie took her advice. They went out, drank a lot, and Maddie brought a guy home with her. He was later cleared as a suspect.

"Maddie Robinson was last seen on the shore of Lake Travis, where a large group of young people were celebrating the start of summer break. She and the roommate got separated. The roommate went home alone, assuming that Maddie had found a partner for the night. This was nothing unusual. But when Maddie hadn't come home twenty-four hours later, she notified the police.

"I wasn't assigned the case, so it didn't spring immediately to my mind. The trail got cold for the CIB detectives who were investigating, and the case got turned over to the other unit." Summary complete, he took a deep breath.

"So this happened roughly around the time spring semester ended?"

"Late last May. The body was found June twentieth. Do you have recorded calls from that far back?"

"In my files. Shall I bring you duplicates?"

"ASAP. Please."

"Stan?"

He jumped when Paris walked into her office and caught him seated behind her desk. He recovered quickly and greeted her with a glum, "Hey."

She tossed her handbag onto the pile of printed material on her desk. "You're in my seat."

Before coming into her office, she had gone to the storage room and retrieved several CDs containing recorded call-ins that she'd had transferred off the Vox Pro. She'd left them with an engineer and asked him to duplicate their contents onto audiocassettes.

"Cassettes? That's working backward, isn't it?" he'd grumbled.

Without wanting to explain that the CIB was still working with audiocassettes, she simply said, "Thanks," and left before he had an opportunity to refuse her odd request.

"What are you doing in my office?" she asked Stan now as she replaced him in her chair. As he'd done the night before, he cleared a corner of her desk and perched there, uninvited.

"Because I don't rate an office, and this was the most private place to wait."

"For what?"

"My uncle Wilkins. He's in a conference with the GM."

"About what?"

"Me."

"Why, what'd you do?"

He took exception. "How come everybody automatically assumes that I screwed up?"

"Did you?"

"No!"

"Then why is your uncle Wilkins having a conference about you with our GM?"

"Because of that goddamn phone call."

"Valentino's phone call?"

"It churned up some stuff. My uncle flew out here in the company jet early this morning, called and woke me up, ordered me to meet him here, and he meant immediately. So I break my neck to get here, and he's already behind closed doors. I haven't even seen him yet."

"What 'stuff'?"

Rather than answer her question, he asked one of his own. "Do I do a good job around here, Paris?"

She shook her head with amusement and dismay. "Stan, you don't do any job around here."

"I'm here every single weeknight until two o'clock in the freaking morning."

"You're here in body. You occupy space. But you don't do any work."

"Because nothing ever goes wrong with any of the machines."

"If it did, would you know how to correct it?"

"Maybe. I'm good with gadgets," he said petulantly.

" 'Gadgets' isn't exactly the word I would use to describe millions of dollars' worth of electronics. Do you even understand radio technology, Stan?"

"Do *you*?"

"I don't have the title of engineer."

He was a spoiled brat, prone to whining. On any given night she felt like throttling him for his incompetence and casual approach to his job. Ineptitude was forgivable, but indifference wasn't. Not in her book, anyway.

Every time she spoke into her microphone, she was aware that hundreds of thousands of people were listening to her. She was touching them with her voice, in their cars and where they lived. She became a partner in whatever they were doing at the time.

To her the listening audience wasn't just a six-digit number on which to base an advertising rate. Each number represented an individual who was giving her his time and to whom she owed the best programming she could provide.

Stan had never considered the human factor of their audience. Or if he had, it hadn't been translated into work. He'd never shown any initiative. He put in his time, counting the minutes until sign-off, and then rushed out to do whatever it was that he did.

But in spite of all that, she couldn't help but feel sorry for him. He wasn't here by choice. His future had been dictated the second he was born into the Crenshaw family. His uncle was a childless bachelor. Stan was an only child. When his father died, he became the heir apparent to the media empire, like it or not.

No one in the corporation seemed willing to accept or admit that he was uninterested and ill-equipped to assume control when his uncle Wilkins stepped down, which probably wouldn't be until he was pronounced dead.

"I'm learning the business from the bottom up," he told Paris sulkily. "I need to know a little about every aspect of it so I'll be ready when it's time for me to take over. At least that's what Uncle Wilkins thinks."

"What stuff did Valentino's call churn up?"

His mouth twisted into a scornful frown. "It's nothing."

"It was enough to get your uncle Wilkins in a spin."

He heaved a huge sigh. "Before I was assigned—read 'banished'—to this swell radio station, I was working at our TV station in Jacksonville, Florida. Compared to this dump, it was paradise. I had a fling with one of the female employees."

"Then you're not gay?"

He reacted as if he'd been jabbed in the spine with a hot poker. "Gay? Who says I'm gay?"

"There's been speculation."

"Gay? Jesus! I hate these stupid rednecks around here. If you don't drive a dual-axle pickup, drink Bud from a bottle, and dress like the Sundance Kid, you're queer."

"What about the woman in Florida?"

He picked up a paper clip and began reshaping it. "We got

carried away in the office. Next thing I know, she's crying sexual harassment."

"Which was untrue?"

"Yes, Paris, it was untrue," he said, enunciating each word. "The charge was as bogus as her thirty-six-C cups. I didn't coerce her into having sex with me. In fact, she was on top."

"More information than I needed, Stan."

"Anyhow, she filed suit. Uncle Wilkins settled out of court, but it cost him a bundle. He got pissed at *me*, not her. Can you believe that? Said, 'How stupid do you have to be to take your dick out at work?' I asked him if he'd ever heard of Bill Clinton. A remark he didn't appreciate, especially since all our newspapers had endorsed him for president.

"Anyway, that's why I'm here, serving time." He tossed the now-misshapen paper clip into the wastebasket. It made a soft ping when it struck the metal bottom. "And that's why he hopped the company jet and flew here this morning."

Paris could guess the rest. "After you told him about being questioned by the police, Wilkins thought he should come to Austin and make certain this unfortunate episode in Florida didn't rear its ugly head."

"He called it damage control."

"Spoken like a true corporate godfather."

She now had the picture. Stan had been foisted onto 101.3 as punishment for mixing business with pleasure. Uncle Wilkins had omitted telling management about the incident with the company employee, but felt he should explain it now before the Austin PD uncovered it and suspicion was cast on his nephew.

"Was that the only incident, Stan?"

His eyes narrowed as he looked down at her from his lofty angle. "What do you mean?"

"The question was simple enough. Yes or no?"

The starch went out of him then. "That was the only time, and, believe me, I learned my lesson. I'll never touch another employee."

"As an owner, that could make you vulnerable to litigation."

"I wish somebody had warned me about that before I went to Jacksonville."

Paris passed up telling him he shouldn't have had to be warned. That was a policy he should have adopted without being told. She also refrained from calling him a creep for doing it under any circumstances.

He looked across at her with a wounded expression. "Everybody thinks I'm gay?"

How like Stan to prioritize the least important point. "You dress too well."

The electrician who'd duplicated the recordings stepped in to tell her that the cassettes were ready and that he'd left them for her at the lobby desk.

"More cassettes?" Stan said.

"This may not be the first time Valentino heralded a murder by calling me."

"What happened last night after you and Malloy raced out of here? I gather you didn't catch Valentino."

"No, unfortunately." She told him about the pay phone at the Wal-Mart store. "Patrol cars were there within minutes, but no one was around."

"I heard about the missing girl on the news this morning. Front page of the paper, too."

She nodded, recalling the quote from Judge Kemp. Janey's parents were holding fast to their belief that her absence was by choice, which, to Paris's mind, was a monumental mistake. On the other hand, she hoped they were right.

She stood up and gathered her handbag, preparing to leave. "I'll see you tonight, Stan."

"Who's Dean Malloy?"

The question came from out of the blue and caught her off guard. "I told you. Staff psychologist for the APD."

"Who moonlights as a bodyguard?" He gave her a sardonic look. "When I dropped off those cassettes at your house last night, the cop told me that Malloy was inside with you."

"I'm missing your point."

"Deliberately, I think. Who is Malloy to *you*, Paris?"

If she didn't tell him, he might go digging on his own and learn more than she preferred him to know. "He and I knew each other in Houston years ago."

"Mmm-hmm. I'm guessing you knew each other pretty well."

"Not pretty well, Stan, *very* well. He was Jack's best friend."

Closing the conversation with that, she stepped around him and moved toward the door. But at the threshold, she paused and turned back. "What do you know about Marvin?"

"Only that he's a jerk."

"Is he into computers, the Internet?"

He snuffled. "Like I would know. I haven't exchanged more than a few grunts with him. Why the sudden interest?"

She hesitated, not knowing if Marvin's apparent flight was information that Curtis would want to be shared. "No reason. See you tonight."

Paris and Sergeant Curtis sequestered themselves in a small interrogation room and sat across from each other at a scarred table. On it were the portable recorder he had used the day before and the cassette tapes she had brought from the radio station.

They began their search for Valentino's calls by listening to tapes recorded up to a week before Maddie Robinson's disappearance. Yesterday she and Dean had agreed that Valentino was altering his voice. The affectation made it distinctive and instantly recognizable, thereby allowing her to fast-forward past voices obviously not his.

Curtis left briefly to get them fresh coffees. When he returned, Paris told him excitedly, "I think I've found it. We don't have a date-and-time stamp like we would on the Vox Pro, but it's on a cassette of recordings made about that time. He was especially morose that night, but I aired this call anyway. His statements provoked follow-up calls that kept my phone lines busy for hours."

Curtis resumed his seat. "You made him a celebrity for the evening."

"Unwittingly, I assure you. Ready?" She started the tape.

Women are unfaithful, Paris. Why is that? You're a woman.

When you've got a man practically eating out of your hand, why would you want another? Isn't quality better than quantity?

I'm sorry you're unhappy tonight, Valentino.

I'm not unhappy, I'm angry.

Not every woman is unfaithful.

That's been my experience.

You just haven't found the right woman yet. Would you like to hear a special song tonight?

Like what?

Barbra Streisand sings a wonderful rendition of "Cry Me a River." It's a cliché, but what goes around comes around.

Play the song, Paris. But even if she gets dumped the way she dumped me, it won't be the retribution she should receive.

Paris stopped the cassette and looked across at Curtis, who was thoughtfully twirling his ring around his finger again. He said, "I guess the retribution he felt she deserved was to choke her to death and bury her body in a goddamn cow pasture. Excuse my French."

Paris lowered her head into her hands and massaged her temples. "I never would have gathered from what he said that he was plotting to kill her."

"Hey, don't beat yourself up over this. You're not a mind reader."

"I didn't detect a real threat in what he said."

"No one would have. And anyway, we're still guessing. Valentino may have no connection whatsoever to Maddie Robinson."

She lowered her hands and looked at him. "But you think they're connected, don't you?"

Before he could answer, John Rondeau pushed open the door. He smiled brightly at Paris. "Good morning."

"Hi, John."

He seemed pleased that she remembered his name. "Making progress?"

"We think so."

"So am I." He looked at Curtis. "Can I see you outside for a minute?"

Curtis got up. "Back in a sec."

"I'll see if I can find any other calls from Valentino."

The detective left with the younger man and was gone much longer than a sec. By the time he returned, she had scored again. "This call is on the same cassette, which means they couldn't have come in more than a few days apart.

"He's a totally different Valentino. Very upbeat. He claims that the unfaithful lover is 'out of his life' and he stresses the word 'forever.' You'll hear on the tape the difference in his mood." Sensing that Curtis was only half-listening and seemed distracted, she paused to ask, "Is something wrong?"

"Maybe. I hate to think this might be bad, but . . ." He ran his hand around the back of his thick neck as though it had suddenly begun to ache. "I suppose you know that Malloy has a son."

"Gavin."

"You know him?"

"I knew him as a little boy. I haven't seen him since he was ten." Curtis's anxiety was evident. She felt a stab of fear for Dean. "Why, Sergeant? What about Gavin? What's happened?"

chapter eighteen

"Gavin?"

"Yeah?"

Dean pushed open his son's bedroom door and went in. "Boot up your computer."

"Huh?"

"You heard me."

Gavin was lying on his bed watching ESPN. He should have something more constructive to do than watch a replay of a soccer game between two European teams. Why wasn't he up and dressed, doing something rather than lazing in bed?

Because I haven't made him, Dean thought.

He had a lazy son because he'd been a lazy parent. Trying to make Gavin get off his butt hadn't been worth the quarrels that invariably followed. Lately, to avoid a hassle, he'd let a lot of things go. He shouldn't have. He wasn't trying to win a popularity contest with Gavin. He wasn't his buddy, his pastor, or his therapist. He was his father. It was past time for him to start exercising stricter parental authority.

He snatched the remote control from Gavin's hand and switched off the television set. "Boot up your computer," he repeated.

Gavin sat up. "What for?"

"I think you know."

"No I don't."

The disrespectful tone and insolent expression stoked Dean's temper. He felt it smoldering like a nugget of coal inside his chest. But he wouldn't yield to it. He would not.

He said tightly, "We can go straight to the police station, where they're waiting to interrogate you about Janey Kemp's disappearance, or you can boot up your goddamn computer so at least I'll know what we're up against when I get you down there. Either way, your days of jerking me around are over."

He had stayed home this morning to organize and type his notes on a suspect he had interviewed several days ago. The detective overseeing that case was growing impatient with the delay.

He knew that if he went to his office, he couldn't have concentrated on anything except Paris and the case in which she was involved. He couldn't have kept himself out of the CIB, where he knew she and Curtis would be listening to her tapes.

So he'd called Ms. Lester, told her he would be working at home, and forced himself to tackle the overdue report. He had just finished it when Robert Curtis called and gave him what could be life-altering news.

"The police want to question me?" Gavin asked. "How come?"

Dean had been clinging to a thread of hope that John Rondeau had made a grave error, but Gavin's worried expression was a dead giveaway that the information was correct.

"You lied to me, Gavin. You're an active member of the Sex Club. You've exchanged numerous email letters with Janey Kemp, and, based on what you two wrote back and forth, you know her a hell of a lot better than you led me to believe. Do you dispute any of this?"

Gavin was now seated on the edge of his mattress, his head hanging between hunched shoulders. "No."

"When was the last time you saw her?"

"The night she disappeared."

"What time?"

"Early. Eight or so. It was still light."

"Where?"

"At the lake. She's always there."

"Had you arranged to meet her there that night?"

"No. She'd been giving me the leper treatment for the last few weeks."

"Why?"

"She's like that. Gets you to like her and then, you know, you're history. I heard she's been seeing this other guy."

"What's his name?"

"Don't know. Nobody does. Rumor is he's older."

"How old?"

"I don't know," Gavin whined, becoming impatient with all the questions. "Thirty-something, maybe."

"So what happened the other night?"

"I went up to her and we started talking."

"You were mad at her." Gavin looked up at him, silently asking how he knew that. "In your last email to her, you called her a bitch. And worse."

Gavin swallowed hard and dropped his head again. "I didn't mean anything by it."

"Well, that's not how the police are going to see it. Especially since she's been missing since that night."

"I don't know what happened to her. Swear to God I don't. Don't you believe me?"

Dean desperately wanted to, but he resisted the urge to go easy on him. Now wasn't the time to turn soft. Gavin needed him to be tough, not Mr. Nice Guy. "We'll get to the part about believing you later. Boot up your computer. I need to see how bad it is."

Reluctantly Gavin moved to his desk. Dean noticed that he typed in a user name and a password to get in, which would've been unnecessary if he had nothing to hide.

The home page of the Sex Club had been designed by amateurs. It was the cyberspace-age version of rest room wall graffiti. Dean motioned Gavin aside. He sat down in the desk chair and reached for the mouse.

"Dad," Gavin groaned.

But Dean ignored him and went straight to the message board. Curtis had given him the names Gavin and Janey had used: blade and pussinboots, respectively. For ten minutes, he scrolled

186 • SANDRA BROWN

through the messages, stopping to read the ones written by his son and the judge's daughter. It was difficult reading.

The last message Gavin had emailed her was crude, insulting, and, now, incriminating. Sick at heart, Dean closed the website and turned off the computer. For several moments he stared into the blank monitor screen, trying to link the writer of what he'd just read with the little boy he had taught to use a baseball glove, the kid with the gap-toothed smile and sprinkling of freckles across his nose, the youngster whose biggest problem used to be foot odor.

Dean couldn't afford the time to indulge in his personal despair now. He must save it for later. More imperative was clearing his son of all suspicion.

"This is one time you had better come clean with me, Gavin. I want to help you, and I will. But if you lie to me, I'll be hamstrung and unable to help you. So no matter how bad it is, is there anything else I should know?"

"Like what?"

"Anything about Janey and you. Did you actually ever have sex with her?" He nodded toward the computer. "Or was this only talk?"

Gavin looked away. "We did it once."

"When?"

"Month ago, six weeks," he said, raising his shoulders. "Not long after I met her. But we'd already been exchanging emails. I was the new kid in town. I think that's the only reason she was interested in me."

"Where did this take place?"

"A whole bunch of us met at some park. I can't remember the name of it. She and I broke away from the group, got in my car." Resentfully, he added, "Didn't you ever do it in the backseat of a car?"

He was trying to pick a fight. The transference of guilt was a classic distraction tactic that Dean recognized and refused to buy in to. "Did you use a rubber?"

"Of course."

"You're sure?"

"I'm sure. Jeez."

"And you were with her only that one time?"

Gavin rolled his shoulders, pushed back a hank of hair that had fallen over his forehead, looked everywhere except at Dean.

"Gavin?"

He sighed theatrically. "Okay, one other time. She went down on me."

"Same questions."

"Where did it happen? Behind some club on Sixth Street."

"In public?"

"Yeah, sorta, I guess. I mean, we were out in the open, but nobody else was around."

He had a flash image of himself calling Pat and telling her that her baby boy was in jail for public lewdness. *Where were you, Dean?* she would have asked. Where *had* he been while his son was composing smutty letters and getting blow jobs in alleyways?

The self-accusations had to be shelved until later, too. "Those two times? That's it?"

"Yeah, she cooled it, dumped me."

"But you weren't ready to be dumped."

Gavin looked at him as if he was crazy. "Hell, no. She's hot."

"To say the least," Dean said in an undertone. "If there's anything else, you'd better tell me. I don't want any more ugly surprises, something the cops have discovered that you haven't told me."

Gavin wrestled with indecision for at least half a minute before he said, "She, uh . . ." He opened a desk drawer, removed a paperback copy of *The Lord of the Rings,* and took out a photograph that had been secreted between the pages. "She gave me this the other night."

Dean reached for the photograph. He didn't know which astonished him more, the girl's graphic pose or her shameless smile. He slipped the picture into his shirt pocket. "Get showered and dressed."

"Dad—"

"Hurry. I've been instructed to have you there by noon. A lawyer is meeting us there."

Finally, the gravity of his predicament seemed to have penetrated layers of adolescent insolence. "I don't need a lawyer."

"I'm afraid you do, Gavin."

"I didn't do anything to Janey. Don't you believe me, Dad?"

His sullenness had dissolved. He looked young and scared, and Dean experienced that same twinge in his heart that he had felt the night before when he watched him sleep.

He wanted to embrace him and assure him that everything would be all right. But he couldn't promise that because he didn't know it to be true. He wanted to tell him that he believed him implicitly, but, unfortunately, he didn't. Gavin had betrayed his trust too many times.

He wanted to tell him he loved him, but he didn't say that either. He was afraid that Gavin would rebuke him for it being too little too late.

Paris had been pacing the hallway for more than an hour, waiting. Nevertheless, she reacted with a start when Dean emerged through the double doors of the CIB, where he, Gavin, and an attorney had met with Curtis and Rondeau in an interrogation room.

He looked surprised to see her. "I didn't know you were here."

"I couldn't leave until I knew that Gavin was all right."

"So you know?"

"I was with Curtis listening to the tapes when . . ." She stopped, unsure of what she should say.

"When my son became a suspect?"

"As far as we know, no crime has been committed and Janey is with a friend."

"Sure. That's why Curtis is putting Gavin through the wringer."

She pushed him toward a bench and made him sit down. It was an ugly, sad-looking piece, a cheap metal frame supporting a blue vinyl cushion with the stuffing poking up through numerous cracks. Probably it had been mindlessly picked at by the restless hands of witnesses, suspects, and victims who had occupied this same bench while despairing over their fate or that of someone they loved. They wouldn't have been in this place unless their lives had been upended, perhaps permanently.

"How is Gavin handling it?" she asked softly.

"He's subdued. Not giving off any attitude, thank God. I think it's finally sunk in that he's in deep shit."

"Only because he exchanged sexually explicit emails with Janey. So did a lot of others."

"Yeah, but Gavin has demonstrated a real creative flare," he said with a bitter laugh. "Did they show you any of the stuff he'd written?"

"No. But even if I'd read it, it wouldn't have changed my opinion of him. He was a terrific little boy, and he'll be a fine young man."

"Two days ago I thought breaking curfew was a major offense. Now . . . this. Jesus." Sighing, he propped his elbows on his knees and covered his face with his hands.

Paris placed her hand on his shoulder. It was instinctive. He needed to be touched, and she needed to touch him. "Have you called Pat?"

"No. Why upset her if it turns out to be nothing except some dirty emails?"

"Which I'm sure is exactly what it'll turn out to be."

"I hope. Twice he talked us through his actions that night. The accounts didn't vary."

"Then he's probably telling the truth."

"Or his lie has been well rehearsed."

Staring straight ahead, toward the open staircase across the hall, he tapped his clasped fingers against his lips. "I talk to liars every day, Paris. Most people lie to one degree or another. Some don't even realize they're lying. They've said or believed something for so long that it becomes their truth. It's my job to filter out their bullshit until I get to the real truth."

When he paused, Paris remained silent, giving him an opportunity to organize his thoughts. The warmth of his skin radiated up through his shirt and into her palm where it still rested on his shoulder.

"Gavin admits to driving home drunk," he said. "He admits to stopping along the way to barf in someone's yard and to disobeying me by leaving the house in the first place.

"He owns up to liking Janey, or at least liking what they did together. He says he talked to her that night and tried to persuade her to go somewhere with him. She shot him down cold.

"He got mad, said things, some of which I can't believe came out of my son's mouth. He confesses to being furious when he left her, but he insists that he did. He says he joined a group of guys and remained with them, drinking tequila, until he left for home. He didn't see Janey again."

Turning his head, he locked gazes with her. "I believe him, Paris."

"Good."

"Am I being naive? Is that wishful thinking?"

"No. I think you believe him because he's telling the truth." She gave his shoulder a light squeeze of reassurance. "Is there anything I can do?"

"Have dinner with us tonight. Gavin and me."

Not expecting that, she quickly removed her hand from his shoulder and looked away. "I work at night, remember?"

"There's plenty of time to have dinner before you go to the station. We'll start early."

She shook her head. "I have something to do this afternoon that can't be postponed. Besides, I don't think it's a good idea."

"Because of what happened last night?"

"No."

"Yes."

Vexed by his perception, she said, "Okay, yes."

"Because you know that if we're together it's going to happen again."

"No it won't."

"It will, Paris. You know it will. Furthermore, you want it to just as much as I do."

"I—"

"Dean?"

Upon hearing his name, they sprang apart. A woman had just

alighted from one of the elevators and was coming toward them. There was only one word to describe her: stunning.

Her tailored suit emphasized her curvy figure rather than detracted from it. Excellent legs were shown off by a fashionably short skirt and high heels. Lip gloss and mascara were her only makeup, and no more than that was needed. She wore no jewelry other than discreet diamond studs in her ears, a slender gold chain at her throat, and a wristwatch. Her pale, shoulder-length hair was parted down the middle, the style loose, classic, and uncomplicated. A California girl in a power suit.

Dean shot to his feet. "Liz."

She graced him with a dazzling smile. "Everything went so well in Chicago, I wrapped things up a day early. Made all my flight connections and thought I would surprise you with a late lunch. Ms. Lester told me I could find you here, and apparently I did pull off a surprise."

She hugged him, kissed him on the mouth, then turned and gave Paris an open and friendly smile. "Hello."

Dean made a terse introduction. "Liz Douglas, Paris Gibson."

Paris didn't remember coming to her feet, but she found herself standing face-to-face with Liz Douglas, whose handshake was firm, like a woman accustomed to conducting business primarily with men. "How do you do?" Paris said weakly.

"A pleasure to meet you. Are you a policewoman? Do you work with Dean?" She was trying to see past Paris's tinted lenses and probably had assumed she was an undercover officer.

"No, I work in radio."

"Really? Are you on the air?"

"Late night."

"I'm sorry, I don't—"

"No need to apologize," Paris told her. "My program comes on when most people are already in bed."

After a brief but awkward lapse in conversation, Dean said, "Paris and I knew each other in Houston. Years ago."

"Ah," Liz Douglas said, as though that was an explanation that clarified everything.

"You'll have to excuse me. I'm late for an appointment." Paris turned to Dean. "Everything will be fine. I know it will. Please tell Gavin hello for me. Ms. Douglas, nice to meet you." She walked quickly away, toward the elevators.

Dean called her name, but she pretended not to hear and kept walking. As she disappeared around the corner, she heard Liz Douglas say, "I get the distinct impression I interrupted something. Is she in some sort of trouble?"

"Actually, I am," he replied. "Gavin and I."

"My God, what's happened?"

By then an elevator had arrived. Paris stepped into it and was grateful to find herself the sole passenger. She leaned against the back wall as the doors slid closed. She didn't hear any more of Dean's conversation with Liz. But she didn't need to. The familiarity with which they'd kissed said a lot.

He would no longer need her hand on his shoulder. He had Liz to console him now.

Gavin knew that if he lived to be a hundred, this would go down as the worst day of his life.

For this visit to the police station, he had dressed in his nicest clothes, and his dad hadn't even had to tell him to. They were probably ruined now because for the past hour and a half he'd been leaking sweat from every pore. The BO would never come out.

On TV and in movies, suspects under interrogation made themselves look guilty with their body language. So he tried not to fidget in the uncomfortable chair, but sat up straight. He didn't let his eyes dart about the room, but looked directly at Sergeant Curtis. When asked a question, he didn't elaborate, but spoke truthfully and concisely, although the subject matter was embarrassing.

He took his dad's advice—now was not the time to withhold information. Not that he was trying to cover up anything. They already knew about the emails, the Sex Club, all that. He didn't know Janey Kemp's whereabouts or what had happened to her. He was as clueless about her fate as they were.

Yes, he'd had sex with her. But so had every guy he'd met since coming to Austin, with the exception of his dad and the men in this room.

All but one. And more than Curtis's persistent questions, it was that one who was making him sweat. He'd been introduced as John Rondeau.

The instant Rondeau walked into the room Gavin recognized him. After all, he'd seen him just last night with two busty babes, climbing from the backseat of a car. And it sure as hell hadn't been a prayer group.

There was no mistaking that the young cop had recognized him, too. When he saw Gavin, his eyes had widened slightly but returned to normal in a nanosecond. Then he had clapped a warning stare on Gavin that made his scrotum shrink and snuffed any comment he might have made about having seen this guy before.

The others, including his dad, probably took Rondeau's stare as stern disapproval of the emails he had swapped with Janey. But Gavin knew better. Gavin knew Rondeau was threatening him with severe consequences if he betrayed his extracurricular activities to his superiors.

Gavin felt even more afraid when Curtis asked his dad to leave the room. Lately, his old man had been a real hard-ass, constantly riding him about one thing or another. It had gotten to where Gavin dreaded the sight of him, knowing he was about to receive a lecture on something. But he was glad to have his dad on his side today. And no matter how bad the situation became, Gavin knew he wouldn't abandon him.

He remembered once when they'd gone to the Gulf Coast for a long weekend. His dad had cautioned him about swimming out too far. "The waves are stronger and higher than they look from the beach. There's also a strong undertow. Be careful."

But he'd wanted to impress his dad with what a good swimmer and body surfer he was. Next thing he knew, he couldn't touch bottom and the waves just wouldn't let up. He panicked and floundered. He went under, knowing he was doomed to a death by drowning.

Then a strong arm closed around his chest and hauled him to the surface. "It's okay, son, I've got you."

He sputtered and struggled, still trying to find a footing.

"Relax against me, Gavin. I won't let you go. I promise."

His dad towed him all the way back to shore. He didn't bawl him out when they got there either. He didn't say, "Stupid kid, didn't I tell you? When are you going to listen and learn?"

He'd just looked real worried while he thumped him on the back until he'd coughed up all the seawater he'd swallowed. Then he had wrapped him in a beach towel and hugged him tight against his side for a long time. Not saying anything. Just staring out across the water, holding him close.

When the weekend was over and his mom had asked if everything had gone okay, his dad had winked at him while telling her that everything had been fine. "We had a great time." He never did tell her that Gavin would've been a goner if he hadn't saved him.

Gavin trusted him to be there to grab him if he sank today, too. His dad was like that. A good person to have around during a crisis.

That's why it had stressed him when the detective asked his dad to wait outside while they talked to Gavin alone. "I'll leave, but only if the lawyer stays," his dad had stipulated.

Curtis had agreed. Before he left, his dad had looked at him and said, "I'll be right outside, son," and Gavin was confident that he would be.

After he left, Curtis had looked at him so hard, he'd begun to squirm in his seat despite his determination not to. He was beginning to wonder if the detective had gone mute by the time he said, "I know it's hard to talk about certain things in front of your dad. Girls and sex. Stuff like that."

"Yes, sir."

"Now that your father isn't here, I'd like to ask you some questions of a more personal nature."

More personal than they'd already been? You gotta be kidding me. That's what he'd thought, but he'd said, "Okay."

But the questions were basically the same ones his dad had asked him before they left the house. He responded to Curtis just as candidly. He told him about the times he and Janey had had sex.

"You didn't engage in any sexual activity with her that last night you saw her?"

"No, sir."

"Did you see her having sex with anyone else?"

What, did they think he'd watch? Did they really think he was that sick? "I wouldn't have gone up to her and started talking if she'd been with another guy."

"Did you touch her?"

"No, sir. I tried to take her hand once, but she pulled it back. She told me I was needy, and that my neediness had gotten to be a real pain."

"That's when you called her a bitch and so forth?"

"Yes, sir."

"What was she wearing?"

Wearing? He couldn't remember. When he called up an image of her, he saw only her face, the sultry eyes, the smile that was both inviting and cruel. "I don't remember."

Curtis looked over at Rondeau. "Can you think of anything else?"

"Where'd you get the picture of her?"

Gavin dreaded looking directly at him, but he did. "She gave it to me."

"When?"

"That night. She said, 'Get over it, Gavin.' Then she gave me the picture. A 'souvenir,' she called it. When I got to missing her, I could use it, you know, to get off."

"Did she tell you who took the picture?"

"Some guy she's been seeing."

"Did she say his name?"

"No."

"Did you ask?"

"No."

Curtis waited to see if Rondeau had anything else he wanted to ask, but when he sat back, satisfied, Curtis stood up. "That's it for now, Gavin. Unless you can think of anything else."

"No, sir."

"If you do, notify me or tell your father immediately."

"I will, sir. I hope she's found soon."

"So do we. Thank you for your cooperation."

As promised, his dad was waiting outside the CIB, but Gavin was surprised to see that Liz was with him. Immediately she rushed toward him. She asked if he was all right and smothered him in a hug.

"I've gotta go to the bathroom," he mumbled and moved away before anyone could stop him.

No one was at the urinals. He slipped into one of the stalls and checked for feet beneath the partitions. When he was sure he was alone, he bent over the toilet and vomited. He hadn't had much to eat today, just some cereal for breakfast, so mostly he spewed bile and then had the dry heaves until the blood vessels in his neck seemed on the verge of bursting. The spasms were so violent, they made his torso sore.

Fear had caused him to vomit once before. When he was fourteen, he had sneaked his mother's car out. She was on a date with the man she'd ultimately married. Since she had abandoned him to go to dinner with that loser, Gavin had felt it served her right if he drove her car illegally.

He'd gone only as far as the nearest McDonald's, where he'd scarfed down a Big Mac. On his way home, only a block from his house, a neighbor's new golden retriever darted right into the path of his car. The puppy had been the talk of the neighborhood. He was cute and friendly, and when Gavin had gone down to meet him a few days earlier, he had licked his face enthusiastically.

He had braked in time to prevent a tragedy, but he had come close enough to killing the puppy that as soon as he got home, he'd thrown up his ill-gotten meal. His mom never knew that he'd taken the car out, and the puppy had grown into a dog that still thrived. Beyond a guilty conscience, he hadn't had to face any consequences.

He hadn't been as fortunate this time.

He flushed the toilet twice before leaving the stall. At the sink he splashed double handfuls of cold water over his face, rinsed his mouth out several times, then bathed his face some more before turning off the faucet and straightening up.

Before he could even register that Rondeau was there, the cop had one hand on the back of his head and the other in an iron grip around his wrist and was pushing his hand up between his shoulder blades.

chapter nineteen

Rondeau shoved Gavin's face against the mirror. It struck with such impact, Gavin was surprised the glass didn't crack. He wasn't sure about his cheekbone. The pain brought unmanly tears to his eyes. His arm felt like it was being wrenched from his shoulder socket. Gasping, he said, "Let go of me, asshole."

Rondeau hissed directly into his ear, "You and I have a secret, don't we?"

"I know your secret, Officer Rondeau." His lips were smushed against the mirror, but he could make himself understood. "While you're off duty from the police department, you fuck high school girls."

Rondeau rammed his hand up higher between Gavin's shoulder blades, and in spite of Gavin's determination not to show any fear, he cried out. "Now let me tell you your secret, Gavin," he whispered.

"I don't have a secret."

"Sure you do. You'd had your fill of that little bitch's games. You figured it was time she was taught a lesson. So you arranged to meet her. She got abusive and you got mad."

"You're crazy."

"You were so enraged, so humiliated, you lost it, Gavin. In the state of mind you were in, I can't hazard to think what you did to her."

"I didn't do anything."

"Of course you did, Gavin," he said smoothly. "You had the perfect motive. She dumps you, then makes you a laughingstock. She ridiculed you on the message board, for everybody to read. A 'dickless dud.' Isn't that how she referred to you? You couldn't have that. You had to shut her up. Forever."

Rondeau's salesmanship made the scenario sound plausible. Gavin panicked at the thought of how many other policemen, including Sergeant Curtis, Rondeau could convince.

"Okay, she was making fun of me, and I was mad at her," he said. "But the other is crap. I was with friends that night. They'll vouch for me."

"A bunch of rednecks and jocks stoned on tequila and grass?" Rondeau scoffed. "You think anything they testify to will hold up in court?"

"Court?"

"I hope you've got another alibi lined up, Gavin. Something stronger than the testimony of those losers you hang out with."

"I don't need an alibi because I didn't do anything to Janey except talk to her."

"You didn't hit her on the head with a tire iron and roll her body into the lake?"

"Jesus! No!"

"You're not shitting bricks every waking moment, wondering when her body will be discovered? I'll bet I can find somebody who will testify to seeing you and Janey in a struggle."

"They'd be lying. I didn't do anything."

Rondeau stepped even closer, mashing Gavin's thighs against the sink. "Whether you did or not, I really don't care, Gavin. They can let you go, or they can send you away for the rest of your life, it makes no difference to me. But if you rat me out, I'll make sure you look guilty as shit. I'll lead them to believe—"

"What the hell is going on?"

Gavin felt the rush of air immediately after hearing his dad's booming exclamation from the doorway. He yanked Rondeau away from him and slammed him against the tile wall, then used his hand like a staple against Rondeau's neck to hold him there.

"What the hell do you think you're doing?" His voice reverberated off every hard surface of the room. "Gavin, are you all right?"

His cheek was throbbing and his shoulder hurt like hell, but he wasn't going to complain in front of Rondeau. "I'm okay."

His dad looked him over, as though to reassure himself that he wasn't seriously hurt, then turned back to Rondeau. "You'd better make this good."

"I'm sorry, Dr. Malloy. I've been reading that stuff your son wrote. It just . . . It's disgusting, some of it. I've got a mom, a sister. Women shouldn't be talked about like that. When I came in here to take a leak, I saw him and just blew my cool, I guess."

Gavin wouldn't have wanted to be in Rondeau's shoes. His dad was practically breathing fire into his face and his hand hadn't relaxed its pressure on his throat. Rondeau's face was turning red, but he stood stock-still, as though afraid that if he moved, he could set off an eruption of wrath that he would be powerless to combat.

Finally, Dean lowered his hand, but his eyes were just as effective at keeping Rondeau nailed to the wall. His voice was quiet and controlled, but menacing. "If you ever touch my kid again, I'll wring your fucking neck. Do you understand me?"

"Sir, I—"

"*Do you understand me?*"

Rondeau swallowed, nodded, then said, "Yes, sir."

Despite his meekness, it was several moments before Dean released him from his stare and stepped back. He extended his arm toward Gavin. "Let's go, son."

Gavin glanced at Rondeau as he walked past him. The young cop might have convinced his dad that he'd experienced an uncontrollable surge of righteous indignation for which he was truly sorry.

But Gavin wasn't fooled. Rather than creating more trouble for himself, he would keep Rondeau's dirty little secret. What did he care if the cop led a double life that included screwing under-age girls? The girls hadn't seemed to mind.

Once they'd left the rest room, Gavin took a glimpse at his dad. His jaw was clenched and he looked ready to make good on his threat to wring Rondeau's neck. He was glad that he wasn't on the receiving end of that simmering anger.

He figured that his cheekbone would soon be sporting a bruise, and possibly it was already beginning to discolor because the moment Liz saw them, she knew something had happened.

"What's wrong?"

"Nothing, Liz," Dean told her. "Everything's fine, but I have to skip lunch. Sergeant Curtis has paged me."

Apparently, while he was in the john heaving up his guts, his dad had filled her in on what was going on.

"There's somebody he wants me to talk to. I'm sorry you cut your trip short only to rush back to this mess."

"If it's your mess, it's my mess," she said.

"Thanks. I'll call you at home tonight."

"I'll be glad to wait until you're free."

Dean shook his head. "I have no idea how long I'll be. This could take the rest of the afternoon."

"Oh, I see, well . . ." She looked so disappointed Gavin felt sorry for her. "You're too valuable around here for your own good. Would you like me to drive Gavin home?"

Inwardly Gavin groaned, *Please no.* Liz was okay. She was certainly great to look at. But she tried too hard to make him like her. Often her efforts were so transparent that he resented them. He wasn't a little kid who could be won over with bright chatter and excessive interest in him.

"I appreciate the offer, Liz, but I'm going to send Gavin home in my car."

Gavin whipped his head toward his dad, thinking he must not have heard him correctly. But no, he was passing him his car keys. Two nights ago, he had made Gavin surrender the keys to his rattle-trap. Now he was entrusting him with his expensive import.

This demonstration of his trust meant more than when he had threatened Rondeau with death. Protecting your kid was required, but trusting him was a choice, and his dad had chosen to trust him when he had given him no reason to. If fact, he'd given him every reason not to.

It was something he needed to think about and analyze. But later, when he was alone.

"I'll call you when I'm ready to leave, Gavin. You can come back and get me. Does that sound like a plan?"

His throat was awfully tight, but he managed to squeak out, "Sure, Dad. I'll be waiting."

Even though her present situation was chaotic, Paris didn't use it as another excuse to postpone the necessary trip out to Meadowview.

And perhaps after kissing Dean last night, guilt also had motivated her to call the director of the perpetual care facility and tell him that she would be there at three o'clock.

When she arrived promptly, he was in the atrium entrance to greet her. As they shook hands, he looked abashed and apologized for the tone of the letter she had received the day before.

"In hindsight I wish my wording hadn't been quite so—"

"No apology necessary," she told him. "Your letter prompted me to do something I've needed to do for months."

"I hope you don't think I'm insensitive to your grief," he said as he led her down the hushed corridor.

"Not at all."

Jack's personal effects had been placed in a storage room. After unlocking the door, the director pointed to three sealed boxes stacked on a metal shelving unit. They weren't large and didn't contain much. Paris could easily have carried them all to her car, but he insisted on helping her.

"I'm sorry for any inconvenience my delay has caused you and the staff," she said as they placed the boxes in the trunk of her car.

"I understand why you'd want to stay away. The hospital couldn't hold good memories for you."

"No, but I never had to worry about the treatment Jack received here. Thank you."

"Your generous donation was thanks enough."

After settling Jack's outstanding medical bills, she had donated the remainder of his estate to the facility, including the sizable life insurance policy he had obtained when they became engaged. She was the beneficiary, but she could never have kept the money.

She and the director had parted company in Meadowview's parking lot, under a broiling sun, knowing it was doubtful they would ever see each other again.

Now the three boxes sat on Paris's kitchen table. There would never be a good time to open them, and she would rather have it over and done with than continue to dread it. Using a paring knife, she slit the packing tape on all three boxes.

In the first were pajamas. Four pair, neatly folded. She'd bought them for him when he was first admitted to Meadowview. They were soft now from being laundered countless times, but they still had the cloying, antiseptic smell she associated with the hallways of the hospital. She closed the box.

The second contained mostly papers, those notarized, triplicate documents from insurance companies, county courthouses, hospitals, medical and law offices, which reduced Jack Donner to a Social Security number, a statistic, a client, an entry for an accountant to tabulate.

As executor of his will, she'd had to deal with all the legalities inherent in a person's demise. All the wherefores and hereins were past tense now, the documents obsolete. She had no need or desire to read them again.

Only the third box remained. It was the smallest of the three. Even before opening it, she knew the contents would be the most upsetting because the articles inside were Jack's personal possessions. His wristwatch. Wallet. A few favorite books, which she had read aloud to him during her daily visits to Meadowview. A framed photograph of his parents, who were already deceased when Paris met him. She had thought it a blessing that they hadn't lived to see their only child so reduced.

Shortly after moving him to Meadowview, she had emptied his house. His clothes she had given to a charity. Then, steeling herself, she had sold his furniture, his car, snow skis, bass-fishing boat, tennis racquets, guitar, eventually the house itself, to pay the astronomical medical bills that the insurance didn't cover.

So this was all that Jack Donner had owned when he died. He'd been left with nothing, not even his dignity.

His wallet was soft from wear. His credit cards, long expired, were still in their slots. Behind a plastic shield, her own face smiled up at her. Noticing a sliver of paper behind the photo, she pinched it out. It was a newspaper clipping that Jack had folded several times so it would fit behind her picture.

She unfolded it and saw another picture of herself. Only this one wasn't a flattering studio portrait. This one had been snapped by a photojournalist. He had captured her looking tired, bedraggled, and disillusioned as she stood gazing into the distance, her microphone held forgotten at her side. The headline read, "Career-making Coverage."

Tears blurring her eyes, she rubbed the edges of the clipping between her fingers. Jack had been proud of the job she'd done, proud enough to save the newspaper article about it. At any point in time afterward, had he realized the cruel irony of his pride in her work on that particular story?

Funny, that a total stranger to them, someone they never even met, would have such a catalytic impact on their lives. His name was Albert Dorrie. He changed Jack's and her destiny the day he decided to hold his family hostage.

It had been an uneventful Tuesday until the story broke just before lunchtime. When those in the newsroom heard that a woman and her three children were being held at gunpoint in their home, they were galvanized into action.

A cameraman was assigned to go to the scene. As he hastily gathered his equipment, the assignments editor ran a quick inventory of his available reporters. "Who's free?" he barked.

"I am." Paris remembered raising her hand like a schoolgirl who knew the correct answer.

"You've got to record the voice-over for that colon cancer prevention story."

"Recorded and already with the editor."

The veteran newsman rolled his cigarette, which was never lighted inside the building, from one side of his nicotine-stained lips to the other while contemplating her with a scowl. "Okay, Gibson, you get on it. I'll send Marshall to take over for you when he finishes at the courthouse. In the meantime, try not to fuck up too bad. Go!"

She piled into the news van with the video cameraman. She was hyper, anxious, excited to be covering her first late-breaking story. The video photographer facilely navigated Houston freeway traffic while humming Springsteen.

"How can you be so calm?"

"Because tomorrow there'll be some other nutcase, doing something equally psychotic. The stories are the same. Only the names change."

To some extent, he was right, but she figured his mellow mood was largely due to the joint he was smoking.

Barricades had been placed at the end of a street in a middle-class neighborhood. Paris leaped from the van and ran to join the other reporters who were clustered around the SWAT officer currently acting as spokesperson for the Houston PD.

"The children range in age from four to seven," Paris heard him say as she wedged herself into the mass. "Mr. and Mrs. Dorrie have been divorced for several months. She recently won a child custody dispute. That's all we know at this time."

"Was Mr. Dorrie upset over the custody ruling?" one reporter shouted.

"One would assume, but that's only speculation."

"Have you talked to Mr. Dorrie?"

"He hasn't responded to our attempts."

Paris's cameraman had caught up with her. Reaching through the crowd, he passed her a microphone that was connected to his camera.

"Then how do you know he's in there, holding his family at gunpoint?" another reporter asked.

"Mrs. Dorrie called in a 911 and was able to convey that message before she was disconnected, we believe by Mr. Dorrie."

"Did she say what kind of firearm he has?"

"No."

Paris asked, "Do you know what Mr. Dorrie hopes to gain by this?"

The SWAT officer said, "At this time, all I know for certain is that we have a very serious situation on our hands. Thank you."

With that, he concluded the briefing. Paris turned to the cameraman. "Did you get my question on tape?"

"Yep. And his answer."

"Such as it was."

"The newsroom called. They're gonna come to you live in three minutes. Can you think of something to say?"

"You focus the camera, I'll think of something to say."

She staked out an advantageous spot from which to do her live cut-ins. The Dorrie house could be seen in the background at the far end of a narrow, tree-lined street, which on any other afternoon would probably have been serene.

Now it was thronged with emergency vehicles, police units, news vans, and people who had come to gawk. Paris asked one of the Dorries' neighbors if she would talk to her on camera about the family, and the woman happily consented.

"I always thought he was a nice man," the woman said. "Never woulda thought he'd snap like this. You just never know about people. Most are crazy, I guess."

An hour into the standoff, Paris spotted Dean Malloy arriving in an unmarked car. He seemed impervious to onlookers and walked with confident determination as uniformed officers escorted him past the gaggle of reporters and toward the SWAT van that was parked midway between the barricade and the house. Paris watched him enter the van, then called her assignments editor and reported this update.

"Will you shut the hell up!" he shouted to the voices in the background. "Can't hear myself think." Then to Paris, "Who is he again?"

She repeated Dean's name. "He's a doctor of psychology and criminology, on staff with HPD."

"And you know him?"

"Personally. He's trained to negotiate with hostage takers. He wouldn't be here if they didn't think they needed him."

She went live with this breakthrough, scooping all the other stations.

By hour three of the standoff, everyone was growing a little bored and perversely wishing that something would happen.

Paris got a lucky break when she noticed a small woman standing at the edge of the crowd of spectators. She was being supported by a man at her side while she wept copiously but silently.

Leaving her microphone and cameraman behind, Paris approached the couple and introduced herself. Initially the man was antagonistic and told her bluntly to get lost, but the woman finally identified herself as Mrs. Dorrie's sister. At first she was reluctant to talk, but Paris eventually learned the stormy history of the Dorrie marriage.

"This background information could be very useful to the police," she told the woman gently. "Would you be willing to talk to one of them?"

The woman was wary and frightened. Her husband remained hostile.

"The individual I have in mind is not an ordinary policeman," she told them. "He's not a SWAT officer. His sole purpose in being here is to see that your sister and her children come out of this situation unharmed. You can trust him. I give you my word."

Minutes later, Paris was trying to coax a uniformed policeman to carry a note to the SWAT van and hand-deliver it to Dean. "He knows me. We're friends."

"I don't care if you're his sister. Malloy's busy and doesn't want to talk to a reporter."

She signaled her cameraman forward. "Are you rolling tape?"

"I am now," he said, swinging his camera up to his shoulder and looking into the eyepiece.

"Be sure to get a close-up of this officer's face." She cleared her throat and began speaking into the microphone. "Today Officer Antonio Garza of the Houston Police Department impeded efforts to rescue a family being held hostage by an armed gunman. Officer Garza declined to convey an important message to—"

"The hell you doing, lady?"

"I'm putting you on TV as the cop who screwed up a hostage rescue."

"Give me the friggin' note," he said, snatching it from her hand.

It was a long, agonizing quarter of an hour before Dean stepped from the van and walked toward the barricade. He batted aside microphones thrust at him as he scanned the faces in the crowd. When he saw Paris waving at him from outside her station's news van, he made a beeline toward her.

"Hello, Dean."

"Paris."

"I wouldn't ever take advantage of our friendship. I hope you know that."

"I do."

"I wouldn't have drawn you away if I didn't think this was vitally important."

"So your note indicated. What have you got?"

"Let's get inside."

They scrambled into the back of the van, where she had persuaded Mrs. Dorrie's sister and brother-in-law to wait. She made introductions. Space was limited even though the cameraman had remained outside. Paris didn't want to spook them with the camera and lights.

Dean hunkered down in front of the distraught woman and spoke quietly and calmly. "First of all, I want you to know that I'm going to do everything within my power to keep your sister and her family from getting hurt."

"That's what Paris said. She gave us her word that we could trust you."

Dean cast a quick glance at Paris.

"But I'm afraid the policemen will storm the house," the woman said, her voice breaking emotionally. "If they do, Albert will kill her and the children. I know he will."

Dean asked, "Has he threatened their lives before?"

"Many times. My sister always said he would wind up killing her."

He listened patiently to what she had to impart, interrupting only when he needed a point clarified, gently prodding her when she faltered. The van grew warm and stank of marijuana. Dean seemed unaware of the uncomfortable surroundings, of the sweat that beaded his forehead. His eyes never wavered from the sobbing woman's face.

He asked pertinent questions and must have committed her answers to memory because he wrote nothing down. When she had told him everything she knew that could be relevant, he thanked her, reassured her that he was going to bring her sister and the children out safely, then asked her if she would stay close by in case he needed to speak to her again. She and her husband agreed.

As they emerged from the stuffy van, Paris passed Dean a bottle of water. Absently he drank from it as they walked toward the barricade. A deep worry line had formed between his eyebrows.

Finally she ventured to ask if the interview had been helpful.

"Absolutely. But before it can help, I've got to get Dorrie to talk to me."

"You have his cell number now."

"Thanks to you."

"I'm glad I could help."

Garza and other uniformed policemen held back the crowd of reporters calling questions to Dean as he stepped through the barricade. He started to walk away, but paused long enough to turn back and say, "You did good, Paris."

"So did you."

She remained where she was, watching him until he disappeared into the SWAT van, then called her assignments editor and told him what had happened.

"Good work. Helps to have friends in high places. Since you've got a rapport with the head kahuna, stay put, see it through to the end."

"What about Marshall?"

"I've made it your baby, Paris. Don't disappoint me."

An hour later, she learned along with all the other media that Malloy was finally in conversation with Dorrie. He had persuaded the man to let him speak to Mrs. Dorrie, who had tearfully told him that she and the children were still alive, physically unharmed but terribly frightened.

Paris went live with that report at the top of the five o'clock news. She repeated it at six o'clock because there'd been no further developments and, at the conclusion of the newscast, did a general recap of the events that had taken place throughout the long day. She also fielded extemporaneous questions from the anchors.

Jack arrived at seven with burgers and fries for her and her cameraman. "Who's been smoking weed?" he asked.

"She has," the cameraman replied as he popped a french fry into his mouth. "Can't get her off the stuff."

But when he finished his meal and stepped from the van, he hesitated. "Jack, about the . . . uh . . ."

Jack smiled guilelessly. "I don't know what you're talking about."

The cameraman was visibly relieved. "Thanks, man."

When they were alone, Paris shot Jack a look of vexation. "A fine manager you'll make."

"A good manager instills loyalty." His easy grin turned to an expression of concern as he reached out and stroked her cheek. "You look exhausted."

"My blusher wore off hours ago." Recalling Dean's disregard for his personal discomfort, she added, "How I look on camera doesn't seem very important in light of what I'm reporting."

"You've done a fantastic job."

"Thanks."

"No, I mean it. The station is all abuzz."

That morning, when she'd left in the news van, she had approached the story as an opportunity to strut her stuff, win some attention, create the buzz Jack had mentioned.

Over the course of the day, that had changed. The turning point had been Dean's conversation with Mrs. Dorrie's sister. It had opened her eyes to the grim reality of the story, given names to the people involved, made it a human tragedy rather than a vehicle to propel her career forward. It seemed distasteful to benefit from the misfortune of others.

"Have you seen Dean any more?" Jack asked, breaking into her thoughts.

"Only once. He came out midafternoon to ask Mrs. Dorrie's sister about the children's favorite foods, toys, games, pets. He wanted to personalize his conversations with Mr. Dorrie."

Jack frowned thoughtfully. "It'll be personalized for Dean if this goes south."

"All he can do is his best."

"I know that. You know that. Everybody knows that except Dean. Mark my words, Paris. If five people don't walk out of that house, he'll beat himself up over it."

Jack hung around for another hour, then left with her promise to call him if the situation changed. It didn't. Not for hours. She was sitting in the passenger seat of the van, organizing her notes and trying to find a new angle to the story, when Dean tapped on the windshield.

"Has something happened?" she asked.

"No, nothing. Sorry if I alarmed you," he said, coming to stand beside the open window. "I just had to get out of that van for a while, get some fresh air, stretch my legs."

"Jack said to tell you to hang in there."

"He came around?"

"To bring us burgers. Have you had anything to eat?"

"A sandwich. But I could stand a drink of water."

She passed him a bottle. "I've been drinking from it."

"Like I care." He took a long swallow, recapped it, and handed it back to her. "I have a favor to ask. Would you call Gavin? Whenever I'm involved in something like this, he gets scared." He gave her a fleeting smile. "Too many cop shows on TV. Anyhow, tell him you've talked to me and assure him that I'm okay."

Reading the question in her eyes, he added, "I've already spoken to him. So has Pat. But you know how kids are. He'll come nearer to believing it if it comes from someone not his parent."

"I'll be happy to. Anything else?"

"That's it."

"Easy enough."

His necktie had been loosened and his shirt sleeves were rolled back to his elbows. He propped his forearms in the open window, but turned his head in the direction of the house. He stared at it for a long while before he said softly, "He may kill them, Paris."

She didn't say anything, knowing that she wasn't expected to. He was confiding his worst fear to her, and she was glad he felt comfortable enough with her to do that. She only wished she could think of a reassurance that didn't sound banal.

"I don't know how a man could shoot his own children, but that's what he says he's going to do." Lowering his head to his clasped hands, he rubbed his thumb across his furrowed brow. "Last time I talked to him, I could hear one of the little girls crying in the background. 'Please, Daddy. Please don't shoot us.' If he decides to pull that trigger, there's not a goddamn thing I can say or do to stop him."

"If it weren't for you, he probably would have pulled the trigger already. You're doing the best you can." Then, without any forethought, she touched his hair.

He raised his head immediately and looked at her, possibly wondering how she knew that he was doing his best, or needing to hear that he was. Or maybe just to verify that she had touched him.

"Word filters back to us, you know," she said in a voice barely above a whisper. "From other cops. They all think you're incredible."

In a voice equally low, he asked, "What do you think?"

"I think you're pretty incredible, too."

She would have smiled, as one friend to another, but a smile seemed inappropriate for a multitude of reasons. The situation, for one. The tightness that had seized her chest until she could barely breathe, for another. But especially because of the intensity of feeling with which Dean was looking at her.

As on the night they met, the stare stretched into more than just an exchange between friends. Only this time it lasted even longer and the gravitational pull between them was much stronger.

She would have lowered her hand, which was still raised, an exposed culprit that had acted of its own volition. But lowering it would only have made its transgression more noticeable and lent it the meaning she didn't dare acknowledge.

Later she wondered if they'd have kissed if his pager hadn't beeped.

But it did and broke the spell. He checked the LED. "Dorrie's asking to talk to me." Without another word, he sprinted to the van.

It was midnight before he finally negotiated the release of the children. Dorrie was afraid that SWAT officers were going to rush the house. Dean assured him that he wouldn't allow that to happen if he would let the kids leave. Dorrie agreed on the condition that Dean come as far as the porch and carry them away from the house himself. Of course, Paris didn't know the terms of this negotiation until the crisis was over.

She was talking to Mrs. Dorrie's sister when the cameraman came jogging over to them and said, "Yo, Paris, Malloy is walking up to the house."

With her heart in her throat, she watched as Dean stood, his hands raised high into the air, at the edge of the porch. No one could hear what he and Dorrie said to one another through the door, but he remained in that vulnerable position for what seemed to her an eternity.

Eventually the door was opened from inside the house and a little boy slipped through, followed by an older girl carrying a smaller child. All were crying and shading their eyes against the bright lights aimed at the house.

Dean placed his arms around their waists and, carrying them against his body, delivered them to the Child Protection Services caseworkers who were standing by to receive them.

One of Dorrie's bargaining points, Paris learned later, was that the children were not to be handed over to his sister-in-law, who'd always hated him and had tried to turn his wife against him.

When Paris did a stand-up reporting the children's release, her voice was hoarse with fatigue and her appearance ragged, but a spirit of optimism had rejuvenated everyone at the site.

She concluded her stand-up by remarking on that mood shift. "For hours it seemed as though this standoff might have a tragic ending. But police personnel are now hopeful that the release of the children unharmed signifies a breakthrough."

Her last word was punctuated by two loud gunshots. The noise silenced Paris and other reporters doing similar stand-ups. In fact, she had never experienced a silence that sudden and that profound.

It was shattered by the third and final shot.

Paris stared at the clipping one last time, then refolded it exactly as Jack had done and replaced it behind her photograph in his wallet. She returned the wallet to the box, sick with the knowledge that if Jack had ever connected the night of the standoff to what transpired afterward, he might not have saved the clipping, but would have ripped it to shreds.

chapter *twenty*

She was a small woman. The hands twisting the damp tissue could have belonged to a child. Her legs were crossed at the ankles and tucked beneath the chair. She was as jittery as a piano student at a recital, awaiting her turn to play.

Curtis introduced them. "Mrs. Toni Armstrong, this is Dr. Dean Malloy."

"How do you do, Mrs. Armstrong?"

Curtis was being as gallant with her as he had been with Paris. "Can I get you something to drink?"

"No thank you. How long do you think this will take? I've got to pick up my children at four."

"I'll have you out of here well before then."

Prior to this meeting, Dean had been briefed for all of thirty seconds, the time it had taken him to walk to Curtis's cubicle after seeing Gavin and Liz off. He didn't have a clue as to why he'd been summoned to sit in on this interview. He remained standing, propping himself against the wall, for now a silent observer.

Mrs. Armstrong wasn't the shrinking violet her dainty appearance implied. It must have appeared to her that she was being ganged up on, because she put a stop to the pleasantries and cut to the chase.

"Mr. Hathaway said you had asked to see me, Sergeant Curtis, so I'm here. But no one has explained why you wanted to talk to me. Should I call my lawyer? Is my husband in some kind of trouble that I don't know about?"

"If he is, we don't know about it either, Mrs. Armstrong," Curtis replied smoothly. "But he has violated the terms of his probation, correct?"

"That's right."

"And Hathaway says you've recently noticed other troubling behavior."

She lowered her head. "Yes."

Curtis nodded sympathetically. "Hathaway called one of the SOAR officers, who then brought your husband to my attention."

Dean was beginning to see where this was going. SOAR—Sex Offender Apprehension and Registration—was under the auspices of the CIB. The detectives who specialized in sex offenses would know about Curtis's investigation. Too often those crimes and homicide overlapped.

"Could you please fill me in on the background?" Dean asked.

"Eighteen months ago Bradley Armstrong was convicted of molesting a minor and sentenced to five years' probation, mandatory group therapy, and so forth. Lately he's been skipping meetings.

"His probation officer scheduled two appointments with him today. He didn't show. Mrs. Armstrong notified his attorney, who went to his office—he's a dentist—to urge him to comply, get his act together. He'd split, although he had appointments with patients scheduled for this afternoon. Nobody knows where he is. He isn't answering his cell phone."

Toni Armstrong said, "I'm glad Hathaway called you. I'd rather Brad be arrested for violating his probation than . . . than for something else."

"Like what?" Dean asked.

"I'm afraid he's on the brink of committing another offense. He's doing everything he's not supposed to do."

Curtis, sensing that a rapport had been established, offered Dean his desk chair. Once he was seated, he said, "I know it's difficult for you to talk about this, Mrs. Armstrong. We're not trying to make the situation harder on you. In fact, we'd like to help."

She sniffed, nodding. "Brad is collecting pornography again. I found it in his office. I can't crack his computer because he's constantly changing the password to keep me out, but I know what I would find. It came out during his trial that he had bookmarked dozens of websites. And I'm not talking about artistic or elegant erotica. Brad goes for the very hard-core stuff, especially if the girls are in their teens.

"But that's not the worst of it. I haven't even told his probation officer all of it." She smiled at Dean wanly. "I'm not sure why I'm telling you. Except that I want Brad stopped before he gets into real trouble."

"What didn't you tell Mr. Hathaway?"

In fits and starts, she told them about her husband's frequent absences from his office and home, his lies, and his justifications for his actions. "All of which I know are signs that he's losing control over his impulses."

Dean agreed with her. These were classic bad signs. "Has he become defensive when you try to talk to him about it? Overly sensitive and angry? Does he accuse you of being suspicious, of not trusting him?"

"He turns every argument away from himself and tries to throw the blame on me for being unsupportive."

"Has he become violent?"

She related what had taken place in their kitchen last night.

When she finished, Dean asked quietly, "You haven't seen him since he stormed out?"

"No, but we spoke by phone this morning. He apologized, said he didn't know what had come over him."

"Has he ever been rough with you before?"

"Not even playfully rough. I've never seen him like that before."

Another bad sign, Dean thought.

She must have read the concern in his expression. Her eyes bounced between him and Curtis. "I still haven't been told why I'm here."

"Mrs. Armstrong," Curtis said, "does your husband ever listen to late-night radio?"

"Sometimes," she replied hesitantly.

"Has he ever disappeared before?"

"Once. Just after his patient's parents charged him with molesting their daughter. He was missing for three days before he was found and arrested."

"Where was he found?"

"In a motel. One of those residence places. He said he went into hiding because he was afraid no one would believe his side of the story."

"Did you?" Dean asked.

"Believe him?" Sorrowfully she shook her head. "That wasn't the first time a patient or coworker had complained about inappropriate behavior or touching. Different dental practices, different cities, even. But the same complaint.

"Brad's behavior leading up to that incident was similar to what it has been recently. Only this time, it's more pronounced. He's not trying so hard to hide it. He's more defiant, and that's making him reckless. That's why it was so easy to follow him."

"You followed him?"

Simultaneously with Dean's question, Curtis asked when this had taken place.

"One night last week." She rubbed her forehead as though ashamed of the admission. "I can't remember exactly. Brad had called from his office and said he wouldn't be coming home until late. He made up an excuse, but I saw through it. I asked a neighbor to watch my children.

"I got to his office before he left, so I was able to trail him from there. He went to an adult book and video store and stayed for almost two hours. Then he drove out to Lake Travis."

"Where specifically?"

"I don't know. I would never have found the area if I hadn't been following him. It wasn't a developed area. No homes or commercial buildings around. That's why I was surprised to see so many people there. Mostly young people. Teenagers."

"What did he do there?"

"For the longest time, nothing. He just sat in his car, watching. There was a lot of drinking, messing around, pairing off. Eventually Brad got out and approached a girl." She lowered her head. "They talked for a while, then she got into the car with him. That's when I left."

"You didn't confront him?"

"No," she said, smiling ruefully. "I was the one who felt dirty. I just wanted to get away from there, go home and take a long shower. Which is what I did."

In deference to her embarrassment, neither Dean nor Curtis said anything for a moment. Finally Curtis asked, "Could you identify the young woman you saw with him?"

She thought about it for a moment, then shook her head. "I don't think so. All that registered with me was that she was probably still in high school. It was dark, so I never got a good look at her face."

"Blond or dark hair? Tall, petite?"

"Blond, I think. Taller than me but shorter than Brad. He's five-ten."

"Could this be her?" Curtis reached for the picture of Janey Kemp that had run in the newspaper and held it out to her.

She looked at it and then at them individually. "Now I know why you wanted to see me," she said, her eyes filling with fear. "I read about this girl. A judge's daughter who's missing. That's it, isn't it? That's why I'm here."

Rather than answer her, Curtis said, "Did you ever tell your husband what you'd seen, that you had him cold?"

"No. I pretended to be asleep when he came in that night. The next morning, he was cheerful and affectionate. Teasing the kids, making plans with them for the weekend. Being the perfect husband and daddy."

She was contemplative for a moment. Dean sensed that Curtis was about to break into her thoughts with another question, but he subtly motioned for him to hold off.

Eventually Toni Armstrong raised her head and spoke directly to Dean. "Sometimes I think Brad actually believes his lies. It's as if he's living in a fantasy world where there are no consequences for his actions. He can do as he pleases without fear of getting caught or paying a penalty."

That was the most disturbing thing she'd told them. Dean doubted that she realized that, but Curtis did. When Dean glanced over at him, the detective was frowning thoughtfully.

He knew, as Dean did, that the profiles of serial killers and sexual predators typically included an elaborate fantasy life, one that was so compelling and so real to them that they acted it out. They often believed themselves to be above the laws of a society that had grievously wronged them, and answered only to a god who understood, and even sanctioned, their perversity.

Curtis cleared his throat. "I appreciate your time, Mrs. Armstrong. Since the subject matter is so upsetting, I especially appreciate your candor."

But she wasn't going to be whisked away that easily. "I've told you some awful truths about my husband, but he could not be involved in the disappearance of this young woman."

"We have no reason to believe that he is. None. As I said, we're following numerous leads." Curtis paused, then added, "With assistance from you, we could eliminate him as a suspect."

"How could I help?"

"By letting our experts try to crack his computer. Get into his files, see what they find. This girl was heavily into a website where sexually explicit messages are posted. She made a lot of contacts that way. If she and your husband never corresponded, then chances are slim that he knew her."

She thought about it, then said, "I won't agree to that until I've consulted Brad's attorney."

Curtis accepted the condition but didn't look happy about it.

Dean's opinion of Mrs. Armstrong went up another notch. She was no pushover. This toughness probably hadn't been in her nature before the difficulties brought on by her husband's addiction. She'd had to acquire it in order to hold on to her sanity and survive.

Curtis waited as she got out of the chair and walked her out of the cubicle. "Thank you for obliging us, Mrs. Armstrong. I hope your husband is located soon and that he gets the help he needs."

"He could not be the man you're looking for."

"Probably not. Besides, we're not sure that Janey Kemp has met with foul play. But, as you've no doubt learned, all prior offenders come under suspicion any time a sex offense is alleged. Your husband picked a bad time to miss an appointment with his probation officer, that's all."

That wasn't all, and she was smart enough to realize it. But she was also too polite to call Curtis a liar to his face. Instead, she told them good-bye.

"Nice lady," Curtis remarked once she was out of earshot.

"Intelligent, too." Curtis looked at Dean for elaboration. "Her husband is on a downward spiral, and she knows it. She also recognized your bullshit for what it was. In spite of what you told her, you obviously think there could be a connection between Armstrong's disappearance and Janey's."

"Can't rule it out." Curtis eased himself into his desk chair and indicated the other one to Dean. He took a Baby Ruth from a glass canister on his desk and offered one to Dean.

"No thanks."

As he unwrapped the candy bar, Curtis said, "Armstrong's own wife saw him solicit a minor for sex. He went to that remote place on the lake for that specific purpose. And how did he know to go there? Only one way."

"The Sex Club," Dean said.

"Exactly. He probably uses the message board like a menu. Whets his appetite by reading what's posted there, then goes out looking for the girl who posted it. And the girl Toni Armstrong saw him with matches Janey Kemp's general description."

"*Very* general," Dean said. "She described half the high school girls in and around Austin."

"All the same, it's a coincidence that cuts very close. You agree?"

Dean raked back his hair. "Yeah, yeah, I agree."

He had felt empathy for Toni Armstrong. He identified with hoping to God you were right to believe in the innocence of a loved one in whom you had little trust.

"If she doesn't volunteer his computer soon, I'm going to

request a court order," Curtis told him. "Rondeau may be able to track Armstrong through Janey's email address book, but it'll take longer. In the meantime, I've put everyone on alert that I want to talk to Dr. Armstrong as soon as he surfaces. We've already put out an APB on his car."

"Speaking of which, any lab results back from Janey's car?"

Curtis grimaced. "Evidence overkill. They collected trace evidence of every fiber, either natural or manufactured, known to man. Carpet, clothing, paper. Every frigging thing. It'll take weeks to sort it all out."

"Fingerprints other than Janey's?"

"Only several dozen. They're searching for matches. Maybe we'll get lucky and one of them will be Brad Armstrong's. They also collected traces of soil, food, plants, and controlled substances. You name it, we found it, and we can readily identify it. But if we'd collected evidence from a KOA campground, it couldn't be more scattershot.

"The girl practically lived in her car. According to her friends, even her own parents, she entertained in it extensively. She ate, drank, slept, and screwed in it. The only thing we've matched with certainty is a human hair, and it matches one we took from her hairbrush in her bathroom at home. Oh, and a speck of dried fecal matter. Identified as canine, which makes sense because we also collected several dog hairs that match those of the family pet."

"I don't remember seeing or hearing a dog."

"Stays in the laundry room. The judge is allergic." Curtis finished his candy bar, wadded up the wrapper, and tossed it into the trash can. "That's it so far."

"Nothing was found that sheds light on what happened to her," Dean remarked.

"No sign of a struggle, like ripped clothing or scuff marks on the interior surfaces. Only one hair, not like a clump that had been pulled out. No broken fingernails that would indicate resistance. No blood. The gas tank was half full, so she hadn't run out. No malfunction of the motor. Sufficient air in all the tires. It appears she left the car under her own power and locked it behind her."

"Intending to come back," Dean added thoughtfully. "What about other tire tracks in the area?"

"You know how many people have signed on to the Sex Club website at one time or another? Several hundred. I think every last one of them was congregated there that night. Say two or three rode together, you've still got a hundred vehicles. We've made a few imprints and are running down the makes and models, but it's going to take days, if not weeks, which we don't have.

"And matching DNA samples, even once we've isolated them, takes time. A lot of time. It sure as hell can't happen in"—he consulted his wall clock—"less than thirty-six hours."

"What about the photograph she gave Gavin? Any leads from that?"

"Taken with a film camera, not digital. The film wasn't developed at your corner one-hour photo."

"Our guy has his own darkroom?"

"Or uses someone else's. I've got several people working that angle, trying to track down suppliers of photographic paper and chemicals, but again—"

"Time."

"Right. And our amateur shutterbug may not buy his products over the counter. He could get them by mail order or buy them online." His thinning crew cut certainly didn't need smoothing, but he ran his hand over it as though it did. "Something else to toss into the gumbo, remember Marvin the janitor?"

"What about him?"

"Aka Morris Green, Marty Benton, and Mark Wright. Along with Marvin Patterson, those are the aliases we know of."

"What's his story?"

"Real name Lancy Ray Fisher. In and out of JV court numerous times on petty charges. At age eighteen he did time in Huntsville for grand-theft auto. Got the sentence reduced by ratting out a cell mate who had boasted to Lancy Ray about a murder. But once free, assorted felonies followed, for which he served minimum sentences, usually by plea bargaining. Best known for bad checks and credit card theft."

"Where is he?"

"Don't know. We're still looking and so is his parole officer. He dove underground when we called ahead. Griggs and Carson got an ass chewing for that. Anyhow, Marvin's avoidance of us leads me to believe that violating parole isn't his only crime and that cleaning the toilets at the radio station isn't his sole source of income."

"Or that he's got something worse to hide," Dean said.

"We got a warrant and searched his place. No computer."

"He could've taken it with him."

"Could've, but he left behind other goodies."

"Like?"

Curtis ran down a list of electronics that would be hard to come by on an average janitor's salary. "Mostly sound equipment. Fancy stuff. We also carried out boxes of crap we're still sorting through. But here's where it gets really interesting. One of those felonies I mentioned? Sexual assault. His DNA is on record."

"If you could match him to trace evidence found in Janey's car—"

"If I had the time to match it, you mean."

Dean shared the detective's frustration. It was an upside-down case. They had good leads, but no crime and no victim. They were looking for an abductor without knowing for certain that Janey Kemp had been abducted. They were working under the assumption that she was being held against her will, that her life was in peril, but for all they knew—

A fresh thought struck Dean. "What if . . ."

Curtis looked at him, prompting him to continue. "Say it. I'm open to any ideas at this point."

"Is it possible that Janey herself is behind this?"

"For attention?"

"Or fun. Could she have put a male friend up to calling Paris just for kicks, just to see how far it would go and what would happen?"

"It's not that far-fetched an idea. But it's not original either. I went over to the courthouse this morning to talk to the judge and—"

"He's carrying on business as usual?"

"Right down to the black robe," Curtis said with dislike. "He clings to the notion that Janey is doing this to spite him and his wife. Come the election in November, the judge doesn't need any adverse publicity. Clean family image and all that. He thinks Janey is trying to scotch his chances to keep his seat on the bench."

"Damn."

"What?"

"I'm thinking like Judge Kemp now?"

Curtis chuckled. "And you could both be right."

They mulled it over for several seconds before Dean said, "I don't think so, Curtis. Valentino convinced me. Either Janey's anonymous prankster friend knows enough psychology to pass for the real thing, or he is."

"I have to think he is."

"Janey kept an appointment with this guy. They met in a designated place. She secured her car and rode away with him."

"It would appear," Curtis said.

"Which is consistent with Gavin's story."

The detective stared thoughtfully at the toe of his polished boot. "Gavin could've taken her somewhere in his car so they'd have privacy to thrash things out."

"And instead, Gavin thrashed her? Is that what you're thinking?"

Curtis looked up and shrugged as though to say, *Maybe*.

"After talking briefly to Janey, Gavin joined his friends. He gave you a list of names and numbers. Have you checked with them?"

"Working on it."

The detective's noncommittal answer irritated Dean even more. "Do you think he could disguise his voice enough to sound like Valentino? Don't you think I'd be able to identify my own son's voice?"

"Would you want to identify it?"

Dean could withstand criticism. Sometimes his analysis of a suspect, a potential witness, or a cop in trouble wasn't received well and made him unpopular with fellow officers. It was an accepted hazard of his job.

But this was the first time his integrity had come into question. Ever. And it made him madder than hell. "Are you accusing me of obstructing justice? You think I'm withholding evidence? Do you want a strand of Gavin's hair?"

"I may later."

"Any time. Let me know."

"I meant no offense. The thing is, you hold back a lot, Doctor."

"For instance?"

"You and Paris Gibson. There's more there than you let on."

"Because it's none of your goddamn business."

"The hell it's not," Curtis said, his ire rising to match Dean's. "This whole thing started with her." He leaned forward and lowered his voice so that anyone beyond the cubicle couldn't overhear. "You two were a dynamic duo during a standoff situation down in Houston. Made all the papers, TV news."

"People died."

"Yeah, I heard that. Tore you up pretty bad. You took some time off to get your head on straight."

Dean fumed in silence.

"Not long after that, Paris's fiancé, your best friend—something else you failed to mention—becomes incapacitated. She quits TV news and devotes herself to taking care of him, and you—"

"I know the history. Where'd you get your information?"

"I have friends in the HPD. I asked," he replied without apology.

"Why?"

"Because it occurred to me that maybe this Valentino business stems from all that."

"It doesn't."

"You're sure? Valentino's hang-up seems to be unfaithful women. Do you think an attractive and vital woman like Paris remained faithful to Jack Donner for the whole seven years she cared for him?"

"I don't know. I lost contact with her and Jack after they left Houston."

"Entirely?"

"She wanted it that way."

"I don't get it. You were going to be best man at their wedding."

"Your Houston source was very thorough."

"He didn't tell me anything that wasn't in print. Why did Paris ask you to stay away?"

"She didn't ask, she insisted. She was abiding by what she thought Jack would want. We'd been athletes together in college. Buddies, and all the physical rowdiness that implies. He wouldn't have wanted me to see him so debilitated."

Curtis nodded as though it was a valid answer, but maybe not a complete one. "And something else that strikes me as curious," he said. "The sunglasses."

"Her eyes are sensitive to light."

"But she wears them in darkness, too. She had them on last night when you arrived at the Wal-Mart store. It was the middle of the night and there wasn't even a full moon." Curtis fixed an incisive look on him. "It's almost like she's ashamed of something, isn't it?"

chapter twenty-one

Stan would rather have had an appointment with a proctologist than with his uncle Wilkins. Either way, he was going to get his ass reamed, but at least a proctologist would wear gloves and try to be gentle.

Their meeting place, the lobby bar of the Driskill Hotel, was in Stan's favor. Since Wilkins planned to fly back to Atlanta that evening, he hadn't booked a suite. *Thank God,* thought Stan as he entered the downtown landmark. It was unlikely that his uncle would flay and fillet him in a public arena. Wilkins hated scenes.

The hotel lobby was as tranquil as a harem during afternoon-nap time. The stained-glass ceiling provided subdued illumination. One tended to walk as quietly as possible across the marble mosaic floors. Nor did one wish to disturb a single glossy frond as one passed a potted palm. Sofas and chairs invited one to languish on the deep cushions and enjoy the flute solo filtering through invisible speakers.

But at the center of this oasis of cool serenity squatted a poisonous toad.

Wilkins Crenshaw was well under six feet tall, and Stan suspected he wore elevator lifts in his shoes. His gray hair had a yellowish tint and was so sparse that it barely concealed the age spots on his waxy scalp. His nose was overly wide, which matched fleshy lips, the lower one curling downward. He bore a resemblance to an amphibian of the ugliest genus.

Stan figured his uncle's appearance was the main reason he had stayed a bachelor. The only appeal Wilkins might hold for the opposite sex would be his money, which was the second reason he was still single. He was too stingy to share even a small slice of his financial pie with a spouse.

Stan also guessed that his uncle had been a nerdy outcast in the military academy to which he and his father had been sent by his grandfather. From there the brothers had been given no option other than attending the Citadel. Upon graduation each had served a stint in the air force. Then, having earned the appropriate degrees and done their patriotic duty, they had been allowed to join the family business.

At some point during these passages into manhood, the nerdy Wilkins had turned mean. He had learned to fight back, but his weapon of choice was brainpower, not brawn. He didn't use his fists, but he had a remarkable talent for instilling fear. He fought dirty and took no prisoners.

He didn't stand when Stan joined him at the small round cocktail table. He didn't even greet him. When the pretty young waitress approached, he said to her, "Bring him a club soda."

Stan despised club soda, but he didn't change the order. He would do his best to make this meeting as painless as possible. Smiling pleasantly, he began with flattery. "You're looking well, Uncle."

"Is that a silk shirt?"

"Uh, yes."

It was a family trait to dress well. As though to compensate for his physical shortcomings, Wilkins was always immaculately garbed and groomed. His shirts and suits were tailor-made, mercilessly starched and steamed. A wrinkle or loose thread didn't stand a chance.

"Do you go out of your way to dress like a queer? Or do you just come by that faggoty look naturally?"

Stan said nothing, only nodded his thanks to the waitress when she delivered his club soda.

"You must've inherited that flamboyant style of dress from your mother. She liked ruffles and such. The more the better."

Stan didn't dispute him, even though his shirt wasn't in the least flamboyant, not in style or color. And he seriously doubted his mother had ever worn a ruffle in her life. She'd never looked anything except perfectly correct. She'd had excellent taste and in his opinion remained the most beautiful woman he had ever seen.

But arguing any of this would be pointless, so he changed the subject. "Did your meeting with the GM go well?"

"The place is still making money."

Then why, Stan wondered, was he scowling? "The latest ratings were very strong," he remarked. "Up several points over the previous period."

He'd done his homework so he could impress his uncle with this quote. He only hoped Wilkins didn't quiz him by asking the dates of the last ratings period or to explain what a point was.

His uncle gave a noncommittal grunt. "That's why this business with Paris Gibson is so upsetting."

"Yes, sir."

"We can't have our radio station involved."

"It's not exactly *involved,* Uncle. Only peripherally."

"Even to a minor extent, I don't want us connected to something as unsavory as a teenage girl's disappearance."

"Absolutely not, sir."

"That's why I'm going to tear your fucking head off and piss down the hole if you had anything at all to do with making those phone calls."

Uncle Wilkins had learned something besides meanness from his days in the military. He'd learned to express himself in language that could not be misinterpreted. The crudeness of his statement was topped only by its effectiveness.

Stan quailed. "Why would it even cross your mind that I could—"

"Because you're a fuckup. You have been since your mother expelled you. From the moment you drew breath, she knew you were a mewling little turd. I think that's why, when she got sick, she just lay down and died."

"She had pancreatic cancer."

"Which gave her a good excuse to finally rid herself of you.

Your father also knew you weren't worth spit. He didn't want to be burdened with you. That's why he sucked so hard on his pistol, it blew the back of his head off."

Stan's throat closed. He couldn't speak.

Wilkins was relentless. "Your father was weak to begin with and your mother made him weaker. He felt it was his duty to remain married to her even though it was her personal goal to fuck every man she met."

Cruelty was his uncle's lifeblood. Having experienced it for thirty-two years, Stan realized he should be used to it. He wasn't. He glared at Wilkins with unmitigated hatred. "Father had affairs, too. Constantly."

"More than any of us know, I'm sure. He poked every woman he could in order to convince himself that he still could. Your mother didn't permit him in her bed. He seemed to be the only man she had an aversion to."

"Besides you."

Wilkins closed his hand so tightly around his glass of bourbon that Stan wondered why the crystal didn't break. He had scored a direct hit and it felt good. He knew exactly where his uncle's disdain for his mother was coming from. Countless times, Stan had heard her laugh lightly and say, "Wilkins, you're such a disagreeable toad."

Coming from his mother, who adored men, that was a colossal put-down. Moreover, she had never shown any fear of Wilkins, and that would be the ultimate insult. He thrived on making people afraid of him. With her, he had failed utterly. Stan delighted in reminding him of it.

A slurp of bourbon restored him. He said, "Considering your dysfunctional parents, it's little wonder you have problems with sex."

"I don't."

"All evidence being to the contrary."

Stan's face turned hot. "If you're talking about that woman in Florida—"

"Who you tried to hump over her fax machine."

"That's her version," Stan said. "It wasn't like that. She was all over me until she got cold feet, afraid someone was going to walk in."

"That's not the only time I've had to bail you out because you couldn't keep your pants zipped. Just like your father. If you had half the aptitude for business that you do for fornicating, there would be more money in the till for all of us."

That, Stan suspected, was the crux of Uncle Wilkins's animosity. He couldn't touch the sizable trust fund Stan's parents had set up for him, which included not only what he had inherited upon their deaths, but a large share of the corporation's earnings ad infinitum. The terms were irrevocable and irrefutable. Even Wilkins with all his power and influence couldn't invalidate his trust and steal his fortune.

"That time at the country club swimming pool, what were you trying to prove when you exposed yourself to those girls? That you could get it up?"

"We were eleven years old. They were curious. They begged me to see it."

"I guess that's why they went screaming to their parents. I had to shell out a few grand to keep the incident under wraps and to keep you from being permanently banned from the club. You got expelled from prep school for whacking off in the shower."

"Everybody whacked off in the shower."

"But only you got caught, which indicates an absence of self-control."

"Do you intend to parade all my adolescent indiscretions past me? Because if you do, I'm going to order a drink."

"We haven't got time for me to parade all your indiscretions past you. Not during this meeting." He checked his wristwatch. "I'll be leaving shortly. I told the pilot I wanted wheels up at six."

May you crash and burn, Stan thought.

"What I want from you," Wilkins said, "is a denial that you've been making dirty phone calls to that woman deejay."

"Why would I do that?"

"Because you're a sick little fucker. It cost me a fortune for your shrink to tell me what I already knew. Your parents created a mess—you. And left me with the job of cleaning it up. I'm just glad that—so far at least—all your 'indiscretions' have been with women."

"Stop it," Stan hissed.

He wished he had the nerve to leap across the table, take hold of his uncle's short, fat neck, and squeeze until his bulging frog eyes popped from their sockets and his tongue protruded from his fat lips. He would love to see him dead. Grotesquely, painfully dead.

"I didn't make those phone calls," he said. "How could I? I was in the building with Paris when those calls came through from public telephones miles away from the station."

"I've checked it out. It's possible to reroute calls, make it look like they're coming from one phone when they actually originate on another. Usually a disposable cell phone, one that's been stolen perhaps. Makes the calls virtually untraceable."

Stan was flabbergasted. "You checked out how it could be done, even before you asked me if I'd been doing it?"

"I haven't gotten to where I am by being stupid and careless like you. I didn't want one of your so-called indiscretions blowing up in my face. I don't want to be left looking like a schmuck for trusting you to keep your dick where it belongs. As it is, I've got to answer to the board of directors for paying you a salary when it's a challenge for you to replace a lightbulb."

Wilkins fixed him with an unwavering stare and held it until Stan said, "I didn't rig any phone calls."

"The only thing you're good at is tinkering with gadgets."

"I didn't rig any phone calls," he repeated.

Wilkins eyed him shrewdly as he took another drink from his glass. "This Paris. Do you like her?"

Stan kept his expression impassive. "Yes, she's okay."

His uncle's stare turned harder, meaner, and, as usual, Stan yielded to it. He always did, eventually. And he hated himself for it. He *was* a mewling little turd.

He fiddled with the soggy cocktail napkin beneath his untouched club soda. "If you're asking me if I've ever entertained sexual thoughts about her, then yes. On occasion. She's attractive and has that whiskey voice, and we spend hours alone together every night."

"Have you tried with her?"

He shook his head. "She made it plain she's not interested."

"So you did try and she turned you down."

"No, I never tried. She lives like a nun."

"Why?"

"She was engaged to this guy," he said in a tone that conveyed his exasperation over the uselessness of this conversation. "He was in a private hospital up near Georgetown, north of here. Very exclusive. Anyhow, Paris went to see him every day. People around the station told me she did this for years. He died not too long ago. She took it hard and still isn't over it. Besides, she's not the type who could, you know . . ."

"No, I don't know. Not the type who could what?"

"Who could be seduced."

Wilkins stared at him for an interminable length of time, then peeled enough bills from his money clip to cover their tab. He placed them beneath his empty glass as he stood up. Reaching for his briefcase, he looked down his wide, unsightly nose at Stan.

"'Seduce' is a word that means you have to persuade a woman to have sex with you. Not at all confidence inspiring, Stanley."

As his uncle moved away, Stan said under his breath, "Well, at least I'm not so butt ugly I have to pay for it."

Stan learned one thing from the meeting. There was nothing wrong with his uncle's hearing.

The mobile home was no longer mobile. In fact, it had been in place for so many years that one corner of it listed. In front, a cyclone fence enclosed a small yard where nothing grew except Johnsongrass and sticker patches. The only nod toward landscaping were two cracked clay pots from which sprouted faded plastic marigolds.

A neighbor kid had kicked a soccer ball over the fence and into the yard but had never bothered to retrieve it. It had long since deflated. A two-legged charcoal grill that had been bought at a garage sale years before had been propped against the exterior wall of the house. The bottom of it was completely rusted out. The television antenna on the roof was bent almost to a right angle.

It was derelict, but it was home.

Home to three neglected and foul-tempered cats who'd never been housebroken, and a slattern who was addicted to coffee and Winstons, which she continually puffed in spite of the wheeled oxygen tank to which she was connected by a cannula.

She was wheezing heavily when the door to the mobile home creaked open, causing a wedge of sunlight to cut across the picture on her television screen. "Mama?"

"Shut the goddamn door. I can't see my TV with that light shining on it, and my story's on."

"You and your stories." Lancy Ray Fisher, aka Marvin Patterson, came in and shut the door behind him. The room was plunged into foggy darkness. The black-and-white picture on the television set improved, but only slightly.

He went straight to the refrigerator and looked inside. "There's nothing in here to eat."

"This ain't the Luby's Cafeteria and nobody invited you."

He scrounged around until he came up with a slice of bologna. On top of the fridge there was a loaf of white bread. He pushed aside one of the cats so he could get to it, then folded the bologna into a stale slice. It would have to do.

His mother said nothing else until the soap opera went into a commercial break. "What're you up to, Lancy?"

"What makes you think I'm up to something?"

She snorted and lit a cigarette.

"You're going to blow yourself up one of these days, smoking around that oxygen tank. I only hope I'm not here when you do."

"Make me one of them sam'iches." He did and as he passed it to her, she said, "You only come around when you're in trouble. What'd you do this time?"

"Nothing. The landlord is repainting my apartment. I need a place to stay for the next few days."

"I thought you were hot and heavy with some new girlfriend. How come you ain't staying with her?"

"We broke up."

"Figures. She find out you're a con?"

"I'm not a con anymore. I'm an upstanding citizen."

"And I'm the queen of Sheba," she wheezed.

"I've cleaned up my act, Mama. Can't you tell?"

He held his arms out to his sides. She looked him up and down. "What I see is new clothes, but the man underneath 'em ain't changed."

"Yes I have."

"You still making them nasty movies?"

"Videos, Mama. Two. That was years ago, and I only did it as a favor to a friend."

A friend who had paid him in cocaine. For as much as he could snort, all he had to do was get naked and screw. But then Lancy had started screwing one of the "actresses" off the set as well as on, and the jealous director began complaining about the size of his "package." In a medium where size mattered, Lancy just wasn't making the grade. "Nothing personal, you understand."

But of course Lancy had taken it personally. They'd had a parting of the ways, but not before Lancy made the director bleed and beg that his own package be left intact.

That had been a long time ago. He didn't do hard drugs now. He didn't play in dirty videos. He had improved every aspect of himself.

But apparently his mother didn't think so. "You're just like your daddy," she said as she noisily chewed her sandwich. "He was a shifty bastard, and you got the same sneaky look about you. You don't even talk natural. Where'd you learn to talk so fancy all of a sudden?"

"I'm working at the radio station. I listen to people on the radio. I've picked up speech patterns from them. I've been practicing."

"Speech patterns, my ass. Wouldn't trust you as far as I could throw you."

She went back to watching her soap. Lancy moved down the narrow hallway, stepping around piles of cat shit, and squeezed into the tiny room in which he slept when he was between incarcerations or employment, or at times like this when he needed to disappear for a few days. This was his last resort.

He knew his mother searched the room each time he left, so when he pried up the loose vinyl tile beneath the twin bed, he did so with the fear of what he would find. Or, more to the point, not find.

But the cash, mostly hundred-dollar bills, was there in the small metal box where he'd stashed it. Half of it rightfully belonged to a former partner, who'd been convicted of another crime and was now serving a prison sentence. When he got out, he would come looking for Marty Benton and his share of the loot. But Lancy would worry about that when and if the time ever came.

The amount had shrunk considerably from what it was originally. He'd used a sizable portion of it to buy his car and new threads. He'd rented an apartment . . . well, two, actually. He had invested in the computer that was now inside the trunk of his car.

His mother would rag him about throwing away good money on a foolish contraption like a computer when she was still watching her stories in black and white. She didn't understand that in order to succeed at any endeavor, legal or ill, a person had to be computer savvy. Lancy had trained himself to be. To avoid the old bitch's harping, he would take his laptop inside and access the Internet through his cell phone only when she was asleep.

He counted his cash, stuffed several of the bills into his pocket, then returned the rest to their hiding place under the floor. This was his emergency fund, and he hated like hell having to tap into it now. Although this definitely qualified as an emergency.

Shortly after being released from his last incarceration, he'd landed a good job, but had been too stupid to appreciate it. One of the dumbest things he'd ever done was steal from the company. Not that he had thought of it as stealing, but his boss sure as hell had.

If he'd asked to purchase the cast-off equipment for a nominal amount, the boss probably would have told him to take what he wanted, that he was welcome to it. But he hadn't asked. He had reverted to his old ways. Catch as catch can. Get it while the get-tin's good. One evening before leaving work, he had helped himself to the obsolete equipment, thinking no one would miss it.

But somebody had. He, being the only ex-con on the payroll, was the first person the boss suspected. When accused, he confessed and asked for a second chance. No dice. He was fired and had escaped criminal charges only because he returned everything he'd taken.

The experience had taught him several lessons, primarily never to tell the truth on a job application. So when Marvin Patterson applied for the job at the radio station, he checked the No box to the questions about arrests and convictions.

Lousy as it was to mop up after other people, that job had been a boon. When he got it, he felt that fate, or his fairy godmother, or some power beyond himself had compelled him to steal that stuff. If he hadn't been fired from that first job, he wouldn't have had the way cleared for him to work at 101.3.

Not only had the janitorial job been gainful employment that kept his parole officer pacified, it had kept Lancy from having to deplete his stash. And, most important, it had allowed him to be near Paris Gibson every night.

Unfortunately, there was no returning to that job now. Nor could he go back to his apartment, write a check on Marvin Patterson's bank account, or use an ATM to withdraw from it, all of which were surefire ways of letting yourself be found when you didn't want to be.

The minute those cops called telling him to stay put, that they were on their way over to talk to him about harassing Paris Gibson with a dirty phone call, he knew his goose was cooked. Just like that, he'd become an ex-con again and had acted accordingly. He'd grabbed his cell phone, his computer setup, some clothing, and cleared out.

His first stop had been his second residence, a dump of a place that he kept leased under an assumed name. What might seem like an unnecessary luxury had proved itself to come in handy.

But as he approached the parking lot, he spotted a police car at the IHOP across the street. He had driven past without pulling in. He told himself it was probably just a coincidence, that if the cops were lying in wait for him to show up there, they wouldn't be in marked cars. But he was taking no chances.

He had destroyed Marvin Patterson's fake IDs. Hello, Frank Shaw.

He'd swapped the license plates on his car, too, switching them for some he had stolen months ago.

No matter what anybody said about reform and rehabilitation, no cop, or judge, or decent, law-abiding citizen was going to extend to an ex-con the benefit of the doubt. You could swear on the Good Book that you were a changed man. You could beg for an opportunity to prove yourself. You could promise to become a contributing member of the community. It didn't matter. Nobody gave a con a second chance. Not the law, or society, or women.

Especially women. They'd do all manner of sex with you but got squeamish when it came to a criminal record. There they got finicky. There they drew the line. Did that make sense?

Not to Lancy. But whether or not it was reasonable, that was the rule. Since he didn't conform to the rule, he had tried changing himself into a man who did. He dressed better, talked better, treated women like a gentleman would.

So far, the transformation hadn't met with stunning success. He'd had a few promising prospects, but eventually they'd gone the way of his other relationships. It was like there was a stain on him that could be seen only by women.

He just couldn't make them like and respect him. Starting with his own mother.

chapter twenty-two

"We know this is last minute, but we're hoping you'll go to dinner with us."

Paris looked from Dean to Gavin. In seven years, he had grown tall, lean, and handsome. His hair had darkened slightly and the bone structure of his face was more defined, but she would have recognized him even on sight.

"This is a cliché," she said, "and you'll hate me for saying it, but I can't believe you're so grown up." She clasped one of his hands between hers. "It's so good to see you again, Gavin."

With a mix of embarrassment and shyness, he said, "It's good to see you, too, Ms. Gibson."

"When you were nine, Ms. Gibson was appropriate. Coming from you now it makes me sound ancient. I'm Paris from now on, okay?"

"Okay."

"How about dinner?" Dean asked.

"I've already got something started."

He raised his eyebrows expectantly, putting her on the spot and giving her little choice except to say, "There's plenty if you and Gavin don't mind eating in."

"It will be a welcome change." Dean nudged Gavin across her threshold. "What are we having?"

"You weaseled an invitation out of me and now you're choosy?"

"Anything but liver or rutabagas."

"Angel-hair pasta with pork tenderloin and veggies. No rutabagas."

"My mouth is already watering. What can we do to help?"

"Uh." Suddenly she felt at a loss. It had been so long since she had entertained, she'd forgotten how. "We could all have something to drink."

"Sounds good."

"I have a bottle of wine . . ." She gestured toward the back of the house.

Dean said, "Lead the way."

In the kitchen, she assigned him the job of opening the Chardonnay, while she poured a Coke over ice for Gavin. Dean made himself right at home. She and Gavin were more awkward with the situation. "There's a CD player in the living room," she said to him. "But I'm not sure I have any music you'll like."

"I'll like it. I listen to your show sometimes."

Pleased to know that, she told him where to find her CD player. He left the kitchen for the living room. As soon as he was out of earshot, she said to Dean, "Am I to acknowledge the bruise on his face or not?"

"Not."

It had been impossible not to notice the dark bruise and slight swelling beneath Gavin's right eye. Naturally she'd wondered how he had come to have such a painful-looking injury. But Dean seemed angry and upset about it, so she changed the subject by asking how Gavin's meeting with Curtis had gone.

"Curtis said Gavin stuck to his original story, telling him nothing that he hadn't told me. He and Janey argued, then he joined a group of friends. Never saw her again."

"Does Curtis believe him?"

"Noncommittal. He didn't detain Gavin, which I take as a positive sign. Also, Valentino has a mature voice. I don't think Gavin could pull that off, even if he tried. And where would Gavin be holding a girl hostage? He doesn't have access to a place. He would have had to kill her that night and— Jesus, listen to me." He braced his hands on the edge of the counter and stared into the bottle of wine.

"Gavin had nothing to do with Janey's disappearance. I just know that, Dean."

"I don't think he did either. But I also never would have guessed he was doing the other stuff. It's been disconcerting, to say the least, to discover that my son has been leading a secret life."

"To some extent, don't all teenagers?"

"I suppose, but I've made it easy for him. I wanted him to like living with me, so I've soft-pedaled the discipline. It didn't seem like I was going easy on him, but I suppose I haven't been as diligent or consistent as I should have been. Gavin took advantage of that."

Turning his head to address her, he added, "With all my psychological training, shouldn't I have realized that I was being conned?"

Just then Gavin called from the living room, "Is Rod Stewart okay?"

"Great," Paris called back. Then to Dean, she said, "Cut yourself some slack. It's a child's duty to try and bamboozle his parents. As for discipline, techniques from a textbook don't always translate to real life."

"But how can it be this hard to get right?"

She laughed softly. "If it were easy, if one system worked for every child, a lot of so-called experts would be out of work. What would they discuss on afternoon talk shows? Think of the chaos, to say nothing of the economic crisis, that well-behaved and obedient children would create."

After winning a smile from him, she dropped the joking. "I'm not making light of your concern, Dean. In fact, it's admirable. Gavin may have gotten off track, but he'll turn out all right."

He poured wine into the two stemmed glasses she had set out and handed one to her. "We can hope." He clinked their glasses.

She looked at him over the rim of hers as she took a sip. "He comes by it naturally, you know."

"What's that?"

"Gavin isn't the only master manipulator in the Malloy family."

"Oh?"

"Very crafty of you, showing up here with him in tow after I had already declined a dinner invitation."

"It worked, didn't it?"

"As a psychologist, how would you classify a man who uses his child to get a dinner invitation out of a woman?"

"Pathetic."

"How about two-timing?"

Dean's smile faltered. "You're referring to Liz."

"Did you tell her about your dinner plans for tonight?"

"I told her I needed to spend time with Gavin."

"But you didn't mention me."

"No."

"She seemed to have a rightful claim to your evenings."

"She has had, yes."

"Exclusive claim?"

"Yes."

"For how long?"

"Couple of years."

That came as an unpleasant shock. "Wow. When I knew you in Houston, your affairs lasted no more than a couple of weeks."

"Because the woman I wanted was taken."

"We're not talking about that, Dean."

"The hell we're not."

"We're talking about you and Liz. A two-year relationship implies—"

"Not what you're thinking."

"What is *Liz* thinking?"

"Dad?" From the open doorway, Gavin hesitantly interrupted them. He was extending a cell phone to Dean. "It's ringing."

"Thanks." He reached for the phone and read the incoming number on the LED. "Gavin, help Paris."

He left the kitchen before answering the phone, causing Paris to wonder if the call had been from Liz.

"What would you like me to do?" Gavin offered.

"Set the table?"

"Okay, sure. My mom made me do it all the time."

She smiled at him. "I remember whenever Jack and I went to your dad's house for dinner and you were there, that was your chore."

"Speaking of, I, uh, haven't had a chance to tell you. I'm sorry about him, you know, dying."

"Thank you, Gavin."

"I liked him. He was cool."

"Yes he was. Now," she said briskly, "do you think we should use the dining room, or eat here in the kitchen?"

"Kitchen's okay with me."

"Good." She showed him where the napkins, dishes, and cutlery were kept and he began setting the table while she sautéed the vegetables and strips of pork. "Are you looking forward to school this year?"

"Yeah. Well, I mean, I guess. It'll be tough, not knowing anybody."

"I can relate. My dad was career army." She filled a pot with water to boil the pasta. "We moved all over the map. I went to three different elementary schools and two junior highs. Luckily he retired, so I got to attend only one high school. But I remember how hard it was to be the new kid."

"It sucks."

"You'll adjust in no time. I remember when you had to switch Little League teams, midseason. You went from being a Pirate to a—"

"Cougar. You remember that?"

"Very well. Your coach had to quit."

"His job transferred him to Ohio or someplace."

"So all the boys on his team were divided up among the others. You weren't at all happy about it, but it turned out to be the best thing that could've happened. The Cougars needed a good shortstop, and you filled that position. The team went on to be district champs."

"Just city," he said modestly.

"Well, to hear your dad talk, it was the World Series. For

weeks all Jack and I heard from him was 'Gavin did this, Gavin did that. You should've seen Gavin last night.' Drove us nuts. He was so proud of you."

"I made an error in one of the playoff games. The other team got a run because of it."

"I was at that game."

"That's why it sucked so bad. Dad had invited y'all to come watch me. I'm sure he could've killed me, then died of embarrassment."

She turned away from the range and looked at him. "Dean was most proud of you then, Gavin."

"He was proud of me for screwing up?"

"Hmm. In the next inning, you hit a double that batted a runner in."

"I guess that made up for it."

"Well, yes, to the fans and your teammates. But when Jack thumped your dad on the back and told him that you had redeemed yourself, Dean said you had redeemed yourself by getting right back into the game. He was more proud of the way you handled the mistake than he was of your hitting a double."

Turning back to the stove, she put the angel-hair pasta into the boiling water. When she turned back around, Gavin was still frowning skeptically. She nodded. "Truly."

And when she said that, she experienced a moment of realization. *Listen to yourself,* she thought. After making a mistake, Gavin had gotten right back into the game. He hadn't slunk into the dugout and spent the remaining innings on the bench, grinding his cleats into the dirt while beating himself up over his error.

Last night Dean had said he hadn't let his guilt and regret eat him alive. He had let it go.

Maybe there was a lesson to be learned from these Malloy men.

Dean returned to the kitchen, interrupting her disquieting thoughts. "That was Curtis." He glanced at Gavin as if reluctant to talk about the case in front of him, but he continued without asking Gavin to excuse himself. "The case has gone stale on him."

"What's happening?"

"He's got intelligence officers trying to run down Lancy Fisher."

"Who?"

"You know him as Marvin Patterson." He gave them a brief summary of Marvin's colorful criminal career. "He's wanted for questioning. And so is a Bradley Armstrong, a convicted sex offender who has violated his probation and flown the coop. He's got men checking into the telephone angle to see if it can be figured out how Valentino is rerouting calls. And Rondeau . . ."

He paused to glance at Gavin, who ducked his head.

"He's still working the computer side of this thing. They didn't find a computer in Marvin's place, but they found discs and CDs, so more than likely he took a computer with him. All this to say that Curtis is stuck in neutral. Since nothing new has turned up, I suggested to him that we see if we can provoke Valentino."

"Into doing what?"

"Poking his head out."

"How?"

"Through you."

"Me? On the air?"

"That's the idea. If you sing Janey's praises, make her out as a victim, maybe he'll call you to justify himself. He may talk longer and inadvertently give us a clue to his location or identity.

"The point is to keep the emphasis on Janey," he continued. "Personalize her. Repeat her name frequently. Make him think of her as an individual, not just his captive."

She looked at him doubtfully. "Do you think that tactic will work with Valentino?"

"Not entirely, no. But it'll also offend his ego if this is all about her instead of him. He wants to be the star, the one everybody's talking about. So by making her the focus, he may not be able to resist coming out to say, 'Hey, look at me.'"

Paris glanced at the clock.

Dean spoke her thought out loud. "Right. We've got just over twenty-four hours to stop him from doing what he threatened. Tonight could be the last chance we'll get to change his mind. He shouldn't be nudged into doing something extreme, which could have tragic results. But possibly you could persuade him to release her."

"That's not an easy assignment, Dean. There's a fine line between goading and persuading."

He nodded somberly. "I almost regret coming up with the idea because of that."

"What does Curtis think?"

"He jumped on the idea. Gung ho on it. But I reigned him in, told him it wasn't going to happen unless you were one hundred percent comfortable with it."

He came to stand closer to her. "Before you make a decision, there's something else to think about, and it's no small consideration. In fact, it's a major one. Valentino started out angry with you. He's doing this to punish you as well as the woman who wronged him. If you begin pressuring him, on any level and in any manner, he's likely to get angrier and you'll be the target. He's already made one veiled threat."

"Are you trying to talk me out of it?"

"Sounds like that, doesn't it?" he said with a wry smile. "Don't give a thought to disappointing Curtis or me. Taking risks is part of our job, but you didn't sign up for it. This has got to be your call, Paris. You say nix it, it's nixed. Think about it. You can give me your answer after dinner."

"I don't have to think about it. I'll do or say whatever is needed to get that girl home safely. But I'll need your guidance."

He reached for her hand and gave it a firm, quick squeeze. "I'll be right there with you, coaching you on what to say. I'd be there with you anyway."

Aware of Gavin watching them with interest, she turned away from Dean, announcing, "The pasta's ready."

"Hello? Brad, is that you? If so, please talk to me."

He hadn't planned what he would say when his home phone was answered, but he had been compelled to call if only to assure himself that his family was still there. As soon as he heard one of their sweet voices, he figured he'd think of something appropriate.

But upon hearing the tremor in his wife's plea, Brad Armstrong couldn't say anything. Her evident distress undid him. His throat seized up and he couldn't speak. He clenched the phone in his sweaty hand and considered hanging up.

"Brad, say something. Please. I know you're there."

He expelled a breath that was half sob, half sigh. "Toni."

"Where are you?"

Where was he? He was in hell. This shabby room had none of the amenities of the lovely home she had made for him and the kids. There was no sunlight in this room, no good smells. Here the blinds were tightly drawn, blocking out all light except for what came from one feeble bulb in the lamp. The room stank, mostly of his own despair.

But his surroundings weren't the worst of it. The real hell was his state of mind.

"You must come home, Brad. The police are looking for you."

"Oh, God." He had feared it, but having his fear realized made his stomach roil.

"I went to the police station this afternoon."

"You did what?" he asked, his voice breaking. "Toni, why did you do that?"

"Mr. Hathaway had to report you to SOAR." She explained how she had wound up in the office of a detective, but he was so distraught he caught only a portion of what she said.

"You talked about your own husband to the police?"

"In an effort to help you."

"Help me? By sending me to prison? Is that what you want for me and our children?"

"Is that what *you* want for them?" she countered. "You're the one who's destroying our family, Brad. Not me."

"You're getting back at me for last night, aren't you? That's what this is about. You're still angry."

"I wasn't angry."

"Then what do you call it?"

"Frightened."

"Frightened?" he snorted. "Because I wanted to make love?

From now on, should I alert you in advance that I want to have sex?"

"It wasn't about sex, and it certainly wasn't lovemaking, Brad. It was aggression."

He rubbed his forehead, and his fingers came away wet with sweat. "You don't even try to understand me, Toni. You never have."

"This isn't about me and my shortcomings as a wife and human being. It's about you and your addiction."

"All right, all right, you've made your point. I'll go back to group therapy. Okay? Call the police and tell them you made a mistake. Tell them we had an argument and this was your way of getting back at me. I'll talk to Hathaway. If I suck up to him, he'll be lenient."

"It's too late for apologies and promises, Brad."

The finality and conviction with which she spoke alarmed him to an even greater extent.

"You've already been given more chances than you deserve," she continued. "Besides, it's no longer in my hands or Mr. Hathaway's. It's a police matter now, and I have no choice but to cooperate with them."

"By doing what?"

"Giving them access to your computer."

"Oh, Jesus. Oh, Christ. You do have a choice, Toni. Don't you see that you're going to ruin me? Please, honey, please don't do this."

"If I don't give them permission to get into it, they'll get a court order or a search warrant, whatever is required. It's really not up to me."

"You could . . . Listen, I could tell you how to clear it so they couldn't find anything. Please, Toni? It's not hard. A few clicks of the mouse, that's it. It's not like I'm asking you to rob a bank or something. Will you do that for me, honey? Please. I'm begging you."

She said nothing for a time, and he held his breath hopefully. But tonight his wife was springing one ugly surprise after another on him.

"One night last week I followed you out to Lake Travis, Brad."

Blood rushed to his head as his penitence turned to rage. "You were spying on me. I knew it. You admit it."

"I saw you with a high school girl. You and she got into your car. I can only presume that you had sex with her."

"You're goddamn right I did!" he shouted. "Because my wife cringes every time I touch her. Who could blame me for getting laid where and when I can?"

"Have you ever been with that girl who's missing? The judge's daughter. Janey Kemp?"

His breathing sounded abnormally rapid to his own ears, and he wondered if it sounded that way to Toni—or to anyone else who might be listening in. That possibility struck terror in him. Why was she asking him about Janey Kemp?

"Do the cops have the house phone tapped?"

"What? No. Of course not."

"While you were making chummy with the cops, did you set me up to get caught? Are they eavesdropping on this conversation? Is this call being traced?"

"Brad, you're talking crazy."

"Wrong, I'm not talking at all."

He disconnected, then dropped the cell phone as though it had painfully stung his hand. He began to pace the stuffy, claustrophobic room. They knew about him and Janey. They had found out, just as he had feared they would.

That . . . that Curtis. Sergeant Curtis. Is that who Toni said she had talked to this afternoon? Wasn't he in charge of investigating Janey's disappearance?

He'd been afraid of this. As soon as he saw her picture on the front page of this morning's paper, he had known it was only a matter of time before the police would be looking for him. Someone would have seen him with Janey and reported it.

Now he would have to be very careful about where he went. If he was spotted, he could be arrested. That couldn't happen. That *could not* happen. In jail, other prisoners did terrible things to men like him. He'd heard stories. His own lawyer had told him about the horrors that awaited a sex offender in prison.

God, he was in a fix. And he had Janey Kemp to thank for it, the teasing little slut. Everyone was against him. Janey. His wife, the raging nag. Hathaway, too, who wouldn't know what to do with a boner if he ever got one, which was unlikely. The parole officer was jealous of Brad's success with women. Out of spite, he would happily hand him over in handcuffs to be taken straight to prison.

But Brad's rage was short-lived. His fear returned, overwhelming him. Sweating profusely, gnawing his inner cheek, he paced the room aimlessly. This business with Janey could spell real trouble for him.

He should've stayed away from her. He saw that clearly now. He had known her by reputation even before she approached him the first time. He had read the messages posted about her on the Sex Club website, knew she was as sexually adventurous as he. He also knew she was a spoiled, rich brat who treated former lovers like dirt and poked fun at them on the Internet message board.

But he had been flattered that one of the most desired girls in the Sex Club had come on to him. What was he supposed to do, turn her down? What man could? Even knowing that he might be dooming himself, he hadn't been able to resist her allure. It was worth the danger that being with her posed.

Indulging his fantasies came with accepted risks. He knew he was courting disaster each time he picked up a high school girl, or fondled a patient, or jerked off in a video store, but the risk of getting caught contributed to the thrill.

He constantly challenged himself to see how much he could get away with. Paradoxically, his desire fed on gratification. The farther his escapades took him, the deeper he wanted to explore. Novelty was fleeting. There was always another boundary to cross, one more step to take.

But as he agonized in his private hell, he realized that he might have carried *this* fantasy one step too far.

chapter twenty-three

"*Boo!*"

Paris, who had just stepped into the dark hallway from the snack room, reacted by sloshing hot tea over her hand. "Damn it, Stan! That wasn't funny."

"I'm sorry. Jeez. I wasn't really trying to scare you." He rushed into the tiny kitchen and tore several paper towels off the roll. "Need butter? Salve? The emergency room?"

She blotted the tea off her hand. "Thanks, but no."

"I can't see your eyes, but I get the impression you're glaring."

"That was a silly thing to do."

"Why're you so jumpy?"

"Why're you so juvenile?"

"I said I was sorry. I'm just feeling exuberant tonight."

"What's the occasion?"

"Uncle Wilkins is winging his way back to Atlanta. Anytime there are several states between us, it's cause for celebration."

"Congratulations. But, just for the record, I don't like being scared. I never think it's funny." Stan fell into step behind her as she made her way back to the studio. Once they were in the light, she saw the bruise. "Ouch, Stan, what happened to your face?"

Gingerly he touched the spot at the side of his mouth. "Uncle smacked me."

"You're joking, right?"

"No."

"He struck you?" she exclaimed, then listened with dismay as he told her about their meeting in the lobby of the Driskill.

At the end of his account, he shrugged indifferently. "What I said pissed him off. It's not the first time. No big deal."

Paris disagreed, but Stan's relationship with his uncle was none of her business. "All around me, men are getting punched today," she muttered, thinking of Gavin's unexplained bruise. She sat down on her stool and glanced at the log monitor to see that she still had over five minutes of music on deck.

Without being invited to, Stan took the other stool. "Are you spooked by this Valentino business?"

"Wouldn't you be?"

"Uncle Wilkins asked if I was your mystery caller."

She cut a glance toward him as she stirred a packet of sweetener into her tea. "You're not, are you?"

"As if," he replied. "Although I am sexually maladjusted. At least according to Uncle Wilkins."

"Why would he think so?"

"Bad genes. Mother was a slut. Father was a lecher. Uncle hires hookers he thinks no one knows about. I suppose he thinks the apple didn't fall too far from the tree. But aside from being a sexual deviate, he thinks I'm a royal fuckup."

"He told you that?"

"In so many words."

"You're a grown man. Why do you take that crap from him? You certainly don't have to stand for his slapping you."

Stan looked at her as though she was deranged. "How do you suggest I stop it?"

He had a knack for making her want to throttle him one minute and pat him consolingly the next. A lot of juicy gossip had been circulated when Stan's father committed suicide. If there was any basis to it whatsoever, the Crenshaw family was indeed dysfunctional on many levels. It wasn't surprising that Stan had psychological issues that needed sorting out.

As the last of the songs wound down, she signaled him to be quiet and engaged her mike.

"That was Neil Diamond. Before that Juice Newton was

singing about 'The Sweetest Thing.' I hope you were listening, Troy. That song was a request for you from Cindy. I'll be taking other requests until two o'clock. Or, if you have something on your mind, I invite you to share it with me and my listeners. Please call."

From that she went directly into two minutes of commercials.

"Do you think he'll call tonight?" Stan asked after she'd turned off her mike.

"I assume you mean Valentino. I don't know. It wouldn't surprise me."

"No clues as to who he is?"

"The police are investigating several possibilities, but they have little to go on. Sergeant Curtis is hoping he'll call tonight, maybe say something that would give them fresh leads." She looked at the blinking telephone lines on the control board. "I know another call from him could be valuable, but it gives me the creeps to talk to him."

"Now I really feel bad about scaring you. I was teasing."

"I'll survive."

"Holler if you need me." He headed for the door.

"Oh, Stan, Dr. Malloy will be arriving shortly. Would you please keep an eye on the front door and let him in?"

Stan did an about-face and returned to the stool. "What's with you and the studly shrink?"

Paris shushed him and answered one of the phone lines. "This is Paris."

The male caller requested a Garth Brooks song from the sound track of the movie *Hope Floats*. "For Jeannie."

"Jeannie sounds like a lucky girl."

"It's on account of you that we're together."

"Me?"

"Jeannie was offered this job out in Odessa. Neither of us had told the other how we felt. You advised her not to leave before telling me her feelings. She did, and I told her I felt the same, so she stayed at her job here and we're getting married next year."

"I'm glad it worked out so well."

"Yeah, me, too. Thanks, Paris."

She inserted "To Make You Feel My Love" into the program

log and answered another line. The caller requested that she send a happy birthday wish to Alma. "Ninety? My goodness! Does she have a favorite song?"

It was a Cole Porter tune, but within seconds Paris had located it in the computerized music library and programmed it to play behind the Brooks ballad.

After taking care of that business, she looked over at Stan. "Are you still here?"

"Yes, and my question stands. And don't tell me you and Malloy are old friends from Houston."

"That's exactly what we are."

"How'd you meet?"

"Through Jack. Their friendship outlasted college."

"But it didn't outlast you." She whipped her head toward him. "Ah, just a wild guess, but a correct one, I see."

"Get lost, Stan."

"I take it that this is a sensitive subject."

Exasperated, and knowing that he would bug her about this until she was forthcoming, she asked, "What do you want to know?"

"If Malloy was such a good friend of yours and Jack's, I want to know why I never heard of him until last night."

"We drifted apart when I moved Jack here."

"Why did you move Jack here?"

"Because Meadowview was the best health care facility for his particular needs. Jack was unable to maintain a friendship. I was busy overseeing his care and establishing myself in this job. Dean had his own busy life in Houston, including a young son. It happens, Stan. Circumstances affect friendships. Haven't you lost touch with some of your friends in Atlanta?"

Undeterred, he said, "Jack was the reason you gave up a career in TV news and came to work at this dump?"

"Around the time of his accident, I made a career change. Okay? Satisfied? Therein lies the whole story."

"I don't think so," he said, his eyes narrowing on her. "It sounds logical, even plausible, but it's too pat. I think you're leaving out the shadings."

"Shadings?"

"The nuances that make for a really good story."

"I'm busy, Stan."

"Besides, nothing you've told me explains the electricity that was arcing between you and Malloy last night. It nearly singed my eyebrows. Come on, Paris, give," he wheedled. "I won't be shocked. You've glimpsed the ugly underbelly of my family and nothing could be more scandalous. What happened with the three of you?"

"I've told you. If you don't believe me, that's your problem. If you want shadings, invent your own. I really don't care as long as it keeps you occupied. In the meantime, can't you find something productive to do?"

She returned her attention to the board, the phone lines, the log monitor, and the studio information monitor, where a new weather report had been submitted by a local meteorologist.

Stan sighed with resignation and moved toward the door once again. Speaking over her shoulder, Paris called to him, "Don't touch anything breakable."

But as soon as he walked out, her flippancy dissolved. She tossed her tea, which was now tepid and bitter, into the trash can. She wanted to choke Stan for resurrecting disturbing memories.

But she couldn't dwell on them. She had her job to do. Engaging her mike, she said, "Once again, happy birthday to Alma. Her request took us back several generations, but every love song is a classic here on FM 101.3. This is Paris Gibson, your host until two o'clock tomorrow morning. I hope you'll stay with me. I enjoy your company. I also enjoy playing your requested songs. Call me."

She and Dean had agreed that she wouldn't address any remarks to Valentino or mention Janey until he arrived. They'd left her house at the same time, but he was going to drive Gavin home before coming to the station.

Dinner had gone well. By tacit agreement, they didn't talk about the case in which they had all become involved. Instead their conversation touched on movies, music, and sports. They laughed over shared memories.

As they were leaving, Gavin thanked her politely for the dinner. "Dad's a lousy cook."

"I'm no Emeril either."

"You come closer than he does."

She could tell that Dean was pleased by how well she and Gavin had gotten along and how relaxed their dinner together had been. She had felt very mellow herself, and she had drunk only a half glass of Chardonnay—her limit on a worknight. Her enjoyment was lessened only by knowing that she'd kept them away from Liz Douglas for the evening.

During the next series of commercials, she cleared the phone lines. Each time she depressed a blinking button, she did so with dread, which made her angry with Valentino. He had made her afraid to do the work that had been her salvation. This job had kept her grounded during the seven years she had overseen Jack's health care. She'd been able to endure those interminable days spent at the hospital only by knowing that she could escape to the radio station that night.

She received a call from a young woman named Joan, whose personality was so bubbly Paris decided to put her on the air. "You say you're a Seal fan."

"I saw him once in a restaurant in L.A. He looked super cool. Could you play 'Kiss From a Rose'?"

Moving by rote, she slipped the request behind three songs already on the log.

What was keeping Dean? she wondered. He was putting up a good front, but she could tell he was deeply worried about Gavin's connection to Janey Kemp. Any parent who loved his child would be concerned, but Dean would blame himself for Gavin's misconduct and look upon it as a failure on his part.

Just as he had assumed blame when Albert Dorrie's standoff with Houston police resulted in tragedy.

There it was again. Another reminder. No matter how hard she tried to avoid it, her mind kept going back to that. To that night.

Dean showed up at her condo eighteen hours after Mr. Dorrie had made orphans of his three children by killing first his estranged wife and then himself.

He arrived unannounced and apologetic. "I'm sorry, Paris. I probably shouldn't have come over without calling first," he said as soon as she opened the door.

He looked as if he hadn't even sat down during the last eighteen hours, much less slept. His eyes had sunk into the dark circles surrounding them. His chin was shadowed with stubble.

Paris had rested very little herself. Most of the day had been spent in the TV newsroom, where she had edited together an overall perspective of the incident for the evening newscasts.

Tragically the story wasn't that unusual. Similar incidents happened routinely in other cities. It had even happened in Houston before. But it had never happened to *her*. She had never witnessed something like that up close and personal. Being on the scene and living through it was far different from reading about it in the newspaper or listening with half an ear to television news reports while preoccupied and doing something else.

Even her jaded cameraman had been affected. His ho-hum attitude was replaced by dejection when the news van followed the ambulance bearing the two bodies to the county morgue.

But no one who had experienced it took the calamity to heart the way Dean did. His despair was etched deeply into his face as Paris motioned him inside. "Can I get you something? A drink?"

"Thanks." He sat down heavily on the edge of her sofa while she poured each of them a shot of bourbon. She handed him a highball glass and sat down beside him. "Am I keeping you from something?" he asked dully.

"No." She motioned down at her white terry-cloth spa robe. Her face was scrubbed clean; she'd let her hair dry naturally after a long soak in the tub. He usually didn't see her like this, but she wasn't concerned about her appearance. Things that had seemed important twenty-four hours ago had paled into insignificance.

"I don't know why I came," he said. "I didn't want to be out, with people. But I didn't want to be alone either."

"I feel the same."

She had begged off spending the evening with Jack. He'd been desperate to cheer her up and help take her mind off what she'd been through. But she wasn't yet ready to be cheered up. She wanted time to reflect. Furthermore, she was exhausted. Going to a movie or even to dinner seemed as remote as flying to the moon. Even making small talk with Jack would have required energy she didn't have.

Talking didn't seem to be the purpose of Dean's visit. After those few opening statements, he sat staring into near space, taking periodic sips from his highball glass. He didn't fill the silence with pointless conversation. Each knew how rotten the other felt about the way the standoff had ended. She guessed that, like her, he derived comfort just from being near someone who had shared the tragedy.

It took him half an hour to finish his whiskey. He set the empty glass on the coffee table, stared at it for several seconds, then said, "I should go."

But she couldn't let him leave without offering some consolation. "You did everything you could, Dean."

"That's what everybody tells me."

"Because it's true. You did your best."

"It wasn't good enough, though, was it? Two people died."

"But three lived. If not for you, he probably would have killed the children, too."

He nodded, but without conviction. She stood up when he did and followed him to the door, where he turned to face her. "Thanks for the drink."

"You're welcome."

Several seconds ticked by before he said, "I caught your story on the six o'clock news."

"You did?"

"It was good."

"Trite."

"No, really. It was good."

"Thank you."

"You're welcome."

Holding her with a stare, his eyes seemed to implore her in a way that she knew her own must mirror. Emotions that she couldn't deny, but had held in rigid check for months, erupted inside her. By the time Dean reached for her, she was already opening her lips to receive his kiss.

Later, when she relived it and was able to be brutally honest with herself, she realized that she had wanted him to kiss her, and that if he hadn't initiated it, she would have.

She had to touch him or die. The need for him was that essential.

Dean must have felt the same. His mouth mated with hers possessively and hungrily. Pretense and politeness were shattered. The constraints of conscience snapped. Tension that had been building for months was given vent.

She threaded her fingers up through his hair. He unknotted the tie belt of her robe and when he slid his hands inside, she didn't protest but rose up on tiptoes to bring their bodies flush against each other. They fit. And the perfection of it brought a temporary end to the kissing and they just held each other, tightly.

Paris's mind spun with sensual overload. The cold metal of his belt buckle against her belly. The texture of his trousers against her bare thighs. The fine cotton of his shirt against her breasts. His body heat seeping into her skin.

Then his lips sought hers again. As they kissed, his hand moved to her breast. His thumb brushed her distended nipple, then he bent his head to take it into his mouth, sucking it with urgency. Gasping his name, she clutched his head against her.

As he lowered her to the floor, she undid the buttons on his shirt and pushed it off his shoulders, but that's as far as it got before he was kissing her again. Between her thighs she felt him grappling with his belt and zipper.

The tip of his penis nuzzled her pubic hair, probed, and then was inside her.

His fullness stretched and filled her. He settled his weight onto her and she absorbed it gladly, squeezing his hips between her thighs. The pressure was incredibly sweet. The sounds that rose up from her chest were a joyous mix of laughter and weeping.

He kissed away the tears that leaked from the corners of her eyes, then clasped her head between his strong hands and laid his forehead against hers, rolling it gently back and forth as they exchanged the air they breathed and the ultimate intimacy.

"God help me, Paris," he said raspily, "I just had to be inside you."

She slid her hands beneath his clothing and pressed his buttocks with her palms, drawing him even deeper into her. He hissed a swift intake of air and began to move. With each smooth thrust, the intensity of the pleasure increased. And so did the meaningfulness. Cradling her chin in one hand, he tilted her face up for a kiss.

He was still kissing her when she came, so that her soft cries were released into his mouth. Within seconds he followed her. And still, they clung to each other.

Their separation was gradual and reluctant. As the physical ecstasy began to recede, the moral significance of what they had done encroached. She tried to stave it off. She wanted to rail at the unfairness of it. But it was inexorable.

"Oh, Lord," she moaned, and, turning onto her side, faced away from him.

"I know." He placed his arm across her waist and drew her back against his chest. He kissed her neck lightly and brushed strands of hair off her damp cheeks.

But his hand froze in the act when her telephone rang.

Earlier she had set her answering machine to pick up, so she could monitor calls. Now Jack's voice blared from the speaker, making him a third presence in the room.

"Hi, babe. Just calling to check on you, see how you're faring. If you're asleep, never mind calling me back. But if you're up and want to talk, you know I'm willing to listen. I'm worried about you. Dean, too. I've been calling him all evening, but he's not answering any of his phones. You know how he is. He'll be thinking it was his fault that the standoff turned out the way it did. I'm sure he could use a friend tonight, so I'll keep trying to reach him. Anyway, love you. Rest well. 'Bye."

For the longest time, neither of them moved. Then Paris disentangled herself from Dean and crawled as far as the coffee table, where she pressed her head against the wood, hard enough to hurt.

"Paris—"

"Just go, Dean."

"I feel as badly as you do."

She looked at him over her shoulder. It was bare; she had dragged her robe along behind her like a bridal train. Frantically she tugged up the sleeve to cover the exposed slope of her breast. "You couldn't possibly feel as badly as I do. Please leave."

"I feel bad for Jack, yes. But I'm damned if I regret making love to you. It was destined to happen, Paris. I knew it the minute I met you, and so did you."

"No, no I didn't."

"You're lying," he said quietly.

She snuffled a laugh. "A minor offense compared to fucking my fiancé's best man."

"You know that's not what this was. It would be much easier for us if that's all it was."

That was true. Behind the shame, her heart was breaking from the despair of knowing that it would never happen again. Perhaps she could have forgiven herself a simple tumble, a hormonal rush, a temporary fall from grace. But it had been far too meaningful to dismiss and forgive.

"Just leave, Dean," she sobbed. "Please. Go."

She laid her head on the table again and closed her eyes. Scalding tears rolled down her cheeks as she listened to the rustle of his clothing, the jangle of his belt buckle, the rasp of his zipper, and his muffled footfalls on the carpet as he walked to the door. She endured a purgatorial silence until she heard the door open, then close quietly behind him.

"Paris?"

With a start, she looked behind her, toward the studio door. Dean was standing there, as though he had materialized from out of her memory.

She'd been so lost in thought, it took several seconds for her to process that this was the here and now, not an extension of her reverie. She swallowed thickly and motioned him in. "It's okay. My mike's not on."

"Crenshaw said I could come in if I didn't make any noise."

He sat on the stool beside hers, and for one insane moment,

she felt like throwing herself at him, taking up where they had left off in her recollection. His scruff that night had left whisker burns on her skin. Within a few days they had faded. But the sensual imprints made on her mind had never gone away. Last night's kiss had revealed how vivid and accurate they were.

"Nothing yet from Valentino?"

She shook her head to answer him, but also to clear it of the persistent sensual tweaks. "Did you get Gavin home all right?"

"With orders that he's not to leave, and I don't think he'll disobey me tonight. It shook him up to be questioned at the police station today. He was certainly on his best behavior tonight. Of course, he was trying to impress you."

"Well, he succeeded because I was impressed. He's great, Dean."

He nodded thoughtfully. "Yeah."

She watched him for a moment, noticing the worry line that had formed between his eyebrows. "But?"

He brought her into focus. "But he's lying to me."

chapter twenty-four

Sergeant Robert Curtis was working overtime. He was ensconced in his cubicle inside the CIB, where only one other detective was burning the midnight oil, on a robbery case.

The radio on Curtis's desk was tuned to FM 101.3. He was listening to Paris Gibson's voice while reading the information he'd gleaned about her suspended television career and departure from Houston. His friends in the HPD had been thorough, faxing him everything that had ever been printed about Paris, Jack Donner, and Dean Malloy. It was interesting stuff.

The search of Lancy Ray Fisher's, aka Marvin Patterson, apartment had yielded some surprises, too, specifically, a box of cassette tapes, all of Paris Gibson's radio program.

Now, why, the detective asked himself, would a con cum janitor have such a burning interest in Paris that he would collect recordings of past programs when he could listen to her live every night?

Lancy's mother hadn't provided any insight.

An intelligence officer, having weeded through miles of red tape and reams of records, had located her. Currently she lived in a mobile-home park in San Marcos, a town south of Austin.

Curtis himself had made the thirty-minute drive there. He could have dispatched another detective to conduct the interview, but he'd wanted to hear firsthand why Mrs. Fisher's son, Lancy, living under the alias Marvin Patterson, was seemingly obsessed with Paris Gibson.

The interior of Mrs. Fisher's domicile was even worse than the exterior portended, and she was as untidy and inhospitable as her home. When Curtis showed her his ID, she was at first suspicious, then belligerent, and, finally, abusive.

"Why don't you take your sorry ass outta here? I got nothing to say to no goddamn cop."

"Has Lancy been to see you recently?"

"No."

Curtis knew she was lying, but he got the impression that there was no love lost between mother and son and that she would welcome a chance to air her complaints. Rather than challenge the truthfulness of her reply, he remained quiet and tried to pick the cat hair off his trousers while she sucked on a cigarette and he waited until she decided to unload.

"Lancy's been a thorn in my side since he was born," she began. "The less he comes around me, the better I like it. He lives his life and I live mine. Besides, he's gone and got uppity."

"Uppity?"

"His clothes and such. Drives a new car. Thinks he's better'n me."

Which wouldn't be saying much, Curtis thought. "What make and model is his car?"

She snorted. "I can't tell one Jap car from another."

"Did you know he was working at a radio station?"

"Sweeping up is what he told me. He had to take that job after getting fired from his other one on account of stealing. That was a good job and he went and blowed it. He's dumb as well as no'count."

"Did you know he used an assumed name?"

"Wouldn't surprise me what that boy did. Not after he was a cokehead and all." Leaning forward, she wheezed in an undertone, "You know, that's why he did them dirty movies. To get dope."

"Dirty movies?"

"My neighbor lady? Two rows over? She come running over here one night not long ago, says she's seen my boy, Lancy, wagging his thing in some nasty movie she rented at the video place. I called her a fuckin' liar, but she said, 'Come see for your own-self.'"

She sat up straighter, striking the righteous pose of a recent convert with only contempt for the unshriven. "Sure enough, there he was, nekkid as a jaybird, doing such as I ain't never saw did before. I's embarrassed to death."

Curtis feigned sympathy for a mother whose son had gone astray. "Does he still work in the, uh, film industry?"

"Naw. Don't do drugs no more either. Leastways he says he don't. It was a long time ago. He was just a kid. But still." She lit another cigarette. Curtis would leave there feeling and smelling like he had smoked three packs himself.

"What name did he use when he made the movies?"

"Don't remember."

"What were the titles of the movies he was in?"

"Don't remember and don't want to know. Guess you could ask my neighbor. And how come an old lady like her is watching trash like that anyway? She ought to be ashamed of herself."

"Does Lancy have a lot of girlfriends?"

"You don't listen too good, do you? He don't tell me *nuthin'*. How would I know anything about girlfriends?"

"Has he ever mentioned Paris Gibson?"

"Who? That a boy or a girl?" Her puzzled reaction was too genuine to have been faked.

"Doesn't matter." He stood up. "You know, Mrs. Fisher, that aiding and abetting is a felony."

"I ain't aided or abetted nobody. I done told you Lancy ain't been here."

"Then you won't mind if I look around."

"You got a warrant?"

"No."

She blew a gust of smoke up at him. "Oh, what the hell. Go ahead."

It wasn't a large place, so except for having to avoid hissing cats and their droppings, his walk through it didn't take long. Nor did it take him long to determine that someone had slept in the spare bedroom. The narrow bed had been left unmade and there was a pair of socks on the floor beside it. When he knelt down to pick up one of the socks, he noticed the loose floor tile beneath the bed. It came right up with a little nudge of his pocketknife.

Replacing what he found there exactly as he'd found it, he rejoined Mrs. Fisher in what passed for the living room. He asked who the socks belonged to.

"Lancy must've left them last time he was here. Long time ago. He never did pick up after hisself."

Another lie, but he'd be wasting his time to dispute it. She would continue lying. "Do you know if Lancy has a computer?"

"He thinks I don't know about it, but I do."

"What about a cassette recorder?"

"Don't know about that, but all them modern contraptions are a waste of good money, if you ask me."

"I'm going to leave you my card, Mrs. Fisher. If Lancy comes here, will you call me?"

"What's he done?"

"Avoided questioning."

"'Bout what? Can't be anything good."

"I'd just like to talk to him. If you hear from him, you'd be doing him a favor to notify me."

She took his business card and laid it on the cluttered TV tray beside her reclining chair. He didn't quite catch what she muttered around the cigarette dangling from her lips, but it didn't sound like a promise to do as he asked.

He was anxious to get into the fresh air and away from the potential of being blown to smithereens when her oxygen tank exploded, but at the door he paused to ask one further question. "You said that Lancy got fired from a good job for stealing."

"That's what I said."

"Where was he working?"

"The telephone company."

As soon as he got into his car, Curtis contacted the San Marcos PD, explained the situation, and asked them to keep surveillance on Mrs. Fisher's mobile home. He then got another detective in his own unit busy running down Lancy Ray Fisher's employment record at the telephone company.

Traffic on northbound Interstate 35 was reduced to a crawl because of road work, so by the time he reached headquarters, the information he'd sought was already available. Fisher's employment records at Southwestern Bell were in his real name. He'd been an excellent employee until he'd gotten caught stealing equipment.

"High-tech stuff at the time," the detective reported. "More or less obsolete now because the technology changes so quickly."

"But still useable?"

"According to the expert, yeah."

Armed with that information, Curtis bumped Lancy Ray Fisher up to the viable suspect list and turned his attention to the materials he'd been faxed from Houston.

Included were copies of newspaper articles, transcriptions of TV news coverage, and materials printed off the Internet. They told a tragic story and filled in some of the gaps that Malloy had been averse to filling.

For instance, Curtis now understood why Paris Gibson wore sunglasses. She had suffered an injury to her eyes in the same auto accident that had robbed Jack Donner of his life—except for a beating heart and minimal brain function.

Paris had been riding on the passenger side of the front seat, with her seat belt buckled. When the car struck the bridge abutment at a high rate of speed, air bags deployed. But they weren't any help against flying glass from the windshield, which was supposed to have been shatterproof, but wasn't, especially not when the 185-pound driver of the vehicle was catapulted through it.

Jack Donner was not wearing his seat belt. The air bag retarded his ejection from the car, but didn't prevent it. He sustained severe head trauma. The damage was irreparable and extensive. He was rendered physically helpless for the remainder of his life.

His mental capacity was limited to reacting to visual, tactile, and auditory stimulation. The responses were feeble, on the level of a newborn, but enough to prevent him from being classified as brain dead. No one could pull the plug.

Reportedly, his friend Dr. Dean Malloy of the HPD had

been first on the scene. He had been following Mr. Donner in his own car, had witnessed the accident, and had made the 911 call from his cell phone. By all accounts, he was a caring and self-sacrificial friend, who for days following the accident kept vigil outside Ms. Gibson's hospital room and Mr. Donner's ICU.

The last follow-up story on Jack Donner's tragic fate reported that Paris Gibson had recovered from her minor injuries and, having resigned from her position at the TV station, was moving Donner to a private nursing facility.

She was quoted as thanking all her friends, associates, and fans who had sent flowers and cards wishing her and her fiancé well. She would miss her job and all the wonderful people in Houston, but her life had taken an unexpected turn, and now she must follow a new path.

There was no mention of Dean Malloy in the final story, an omission that practically screamed at Curtis. When one disappears from the radar screen of a strong and lasting friendship, there's got to be a good reason.

No deep, dark mystery there. He'd seen the way Malloy looked at Paris Gibson and vice versa. With I-want-to-see-you-naked lust. But it was also the care they took *not* to look at each other that gave away a yearning that went deeper than just the physical. It was the avoidance that incriminated them. If this was visible to him after having known them for only two days, it must have been glaringly obvious to Jack Donner.

Conclusion: In a love affair, three was one too many.

As he listened to Paris's program, his anger mounted.

She made no mention of him, of Valentino.

But she talked endlessly about Janey Kemp. She went on about how badly her parents wanted her to be returned to them unharmed. Told about her friends, who were worried for her safety. Extolled her virtues.

What a farce! Janey had told him how much she despised her parents, and the feeling was mutual. Friends? She made conquests, not friends. As for virtues, she was without them.

But to hear Paris tell it, Janey Kemp was a saint. A beautiful, charming, friendly, kind American ideal.

"If you could only see her now, Paris," he said in a whispered chuckle.

Janey disgusted him so much now that he had stayed with her only briefly today. She didn't look beautiful and enticing anymore. Her hair, once bouncy and silky, had looked like old rope coiled about her head. Her complexion was sallow. The eyes that could be sultry or scornful at will were now dull and lifeless. Barely acknowledging his presence in the room, she had stared vacantly and unblinkingly, even when he snapped his fingers an inch from her nose.

She seemed half dead and looked even worse. A shower would improve things, but he just couldn't be bothered with carrying her into the bathroom to wash her.

He couldn't be bothered with much of anything except dealing with this jam he'd gotten himself into. Time was running out for him to arrive at a workable solution. He had extended to Paris a seventy-two-hour deadline, and if he had any character at all, any sense of pride, he really should stick to that timetable.

Janey had become more of a liability than he had anticipated. There also remained the question of what to do about Paris.

He really hadn't looked beyond bringing Janey here and using her the way she begged to be used. She was a whore who advertised her willingness to try anything. He had called her bluff, that's all. Her boasts hadn't been empty ones either. She'd proved herself to be a gourmand of debasement.

He hadn't seriously planned on this ending with her demise, any more than he had planned to kill Maddie Robinson. That's just the way his relationship with Maddie had evolved. She'd said, "I don't want to see you anymore," and he had made certain that she wouldn't. Ever. When you looked at it that way, she had decided her fate, not him.

As for Paris, he hadn't thought much beyond placing that first call and telling her that he had taken action against the woman who had wronged him. He had wanted to frighten her, rattle her, and hopefully make her aware of her intolerable smugness. Who

was she to dispense advice on love and life, sex and relationships?

What he hadn't anticipated was that his phone call to her
would launch a police investigation and become the media event
that it had. Who would have thought everyone would get so
uptight over Janey, when she was getting exactly what she had
asked for?

No, it had grown into something much larger than he had
bargained for. He felt himself losing control of the situation. To
survive, he must get back that control. But where to start?

One way would be to release Janey.

Yes, he could do that. He could dump her near her parents'
house. She didn't know his name. He could clear out this room so
that if she ever brought the cops to the "scene of the crime," he
would be long gone. He would have to stop going to the meeting
places of the Sex Club or risk being seen by her, but finding action
was never a problem. The Sex Club was only one resource.

It wasn't a perfect plan, but probably the best course of action
left to him. He would call Paris tonight at the appointed time and
tell her that he'd only wanted to toy with her, make her realize
that she shouldn't play with people's emotions and hand out glib
advice. *I never dreamed you would take me seriously, Paris. Can't
you take a joke? No hard feelings, okay?*

Yes, that was definitely a workable plan.

" . . . here on FM 101.3," he heard Paris say, interrupting his
thoughts. "Stay with me until two A.M. I just got a call from
Janey's best friend, Melissa."

Melissa.

"Melissa, would you like to say something to the listening
audience?" Paris asked.

"Yeah, I just, you know, want Janey back safe," she said.
"Janey, if you can hear this and you're okay, come home.
Nobody's gonna be mad. And if someone out there is holding
my friend against her will, then I have to tell you that's totally
uncool. Let her go. Please. We just want Janey back. So . . . I guess
that's it."

"Thank you, Melissa."

Wait, was he supposed to be the *villain* of this piece? He hadn't done anything to Janey Kemp that she hadn't wanted done. And Paris wasn't the snow princess she wanted everyone to believe either. She was no better than anyone else.

He dialed a number he knew by heart, knowing that this call couldn't be traced to his cell. He'd made certain of that.

"This is Paris."

"The topic tonight is Dean Malloy."

"Valentino? Let me speak to Janey."

"Janey is in no mood to talk," he said, "and neither am I."

"Janey's parents wanted me to ask you—"

"Shut up and listen to me. If you and your boyfriend don't move quickly, you'll have *two* deaths on your consciences. Janey's. And Jack Donner's."

"I'd feel better if you stayed at my house until this is over. I've got an extra bedroom. Nothing fancy, but you'd be comfortable. And safe."

Dean had insisted on following her home and seeing her inside. As before, Valentino's call had been routed through a deserted pay phone, which provided no leads. The police were now convinced that he never went near those pay phones.

This call had been most disconcerting because he had sounded even angrier and edgier than before. He had alluded again to Janey's death. And of course the reference to Dean and Jack had been an alarming new element. Either Valentino was excellent at guessing, or he knew with certainty that Jack's death implicated her and Dean to some extent.

"Thanks for the offer, but I'll be safe here." She went through her front door ahead of him. Once inside, he switched on a table lamp. She immediately turned it off. "I feel like a goldfish with the lights on. They can see in."

Dean glanced at the squad car parked at her curb. "Griggs has a replacement, I see."

"His night off. Curtis told me the personnel would be different but that this team of officers was just as vigilant." As Dean closed the door, she asked, "What about Gavin?" Valentino had spoken about Dean with such disdain, they were concerned not only for his and Paris's safety, but for Gavin's as well.

"Taken care of. Curtis dispatched a squad car to my house. I called Gavin and told him to expect it."

"Liz?"

"I didn't think officers were necessary, but I called and gave her a heads-up. Told her to be sure her alarm was set and to call me if anything unusual happened."

"Maybe she's the one who should be staying in your spare bedroom."

Rather than picking up the gauntlet, he said, "That's another conversation, Paris."

She turned and headed for the kitchen. He followed. It was two-thirty in the morning, but they were too troubled to sleep. "I'm going to have some hot chocolate," she said. "Want some?"

"It's eighty degrees outside."

She gave him a take-it-or-leave-it look.

"Juice?" he asked.

While her water was heating in the microwave, she poured him a glass of orange juice and took a package of cookies from the pantry. "What do you think he's lying about?"

"Valentino?"

"Gavin. Earlier tonight, you told me you thought he was lying to you. We got busy with all the calls coming in and never got around to finishing the conversation."

He stared into his glass of juice for a moment, then said, "That's the hell of it. I don't know what he's lying *about,* I just know that he is."

After stirring a packet of instant cocoa mix into her cup of hot water, she motioned for him to bring the cookies and follow her into the living room. She took one corner of the sofa, he the other. The package of cookies was placed on the cushion between them. The lamp stayed dark, but the glow from the porch lights came through the front windows, so they could see well enough. She removed her sunglasses.

"Do you think he's lying about his activities that night?" she asked.

"By omission, maybe. I'm afraid that there was more to his meeting with Janey than he wants to share."

"Like that they had sex?"

"Possibly, and he doesn't want anybody to know."

"Because that would make his story of leaving her to join friends less credible."

"Right." Dean munched a cookie. "But realistically, how could he be Valentino? It doesn't sound like him. He doesn't know about us." He looked over at her. "That part, anyway. He doesn't have the technical skills to reroute telephone calls."

"I asked Stan about how that technology works."

"How would he know?"

"He likes gadgets, expensive toys. Don't give me that look," she said when his eyebrow formed an inquisitive arch. "He's not Valentino. He hasn't got the balls."

"What do you know about his balls?"

"Please," she groaned. "Do you want to hear this or not?"

He gave a noncommittal harrumph as he reached for another cookie.

She continued, "Stan said it wouldn't be hard to do. Anyone with access to some equipment could probably learn how to do it over the Internet."

"What about somebody who had worked for the phone company?"

"It would probably be a snap. Why?"

"Before becoming a janitor, Marvin Patterson was an installer for Southwestern Bell."

Dean had followed her home from the radio station in his own car. During the drive, he'd had a lengthy cell phone conversation with Curtis. He recounted for her now everything that the detective had learned about Lancy Fisher.

"He had a collection of audiotapes? Of my show? What could that mean?"

"We don't know," Dean replied. "That's why Curtis has intelligence guys out tapping all their informers, trying to find the shy Mr. Fisher. We've got plenty of questions for him, number one being why the preoccupation with you."

"Which comes as a shock. He never showed the least bit of interest in me. Kept his head down and rarely spoke."

"Strange behavior for a former actor."

"Actor? Marvin?"

"He appeared—all of him—in a couple of porno videos."

"What!" she exclaimed. "Are you sure we're talking about the same man?"

He told her what Curtis had learned from Lancy Fisher's mother. "None of which explains why he taped your show every night. Or so it seems. He had ninety-two cassettes in all. Not very good quality, Curtis said. Probably recorded directly off the radio. Hours of love songs and Paris Gibson's sexy voice. It could be that Marvin just jerked off while listening to you. But that's a lot of jerking off."

"Spare me that image, please."

"Did he ever—"

"Nothing, Dean. He never mumbled more than a few words to me. Never even looked me in the eye that I can recall."

"Then as far as this case goes, he may be as innocent as the driven snow. He may have disappeared only because he's an ex-con and as such has a natural aversion to police interrogations even if he's got nothing to hide."

He paused and watched her closely for several moments, long enough for her to ask, "What?"

"Curtis has become a regular Sherlock Holmes into our past."

She blew on her hot cocoa, but she'd suddenly lost her appetite for it. "What's the good news?"

"There isn't any. He told me straight out that he knew the facts behind your leaving Houston. The accident. Jack's head injury. Your resignation from TV. And so forth."

"That's all?"

"Well, he stopped with that, but the silence that followed was teeming with curiosity and insinuation."

"Let him insinuate all he wants."

"I did."

She set her cup on the coffee table, then with a heavy sigh laid her head against the sofa cushion. "I'm not surprised by his curiosity. He's a detective, after all. And he didn't even have to dig very deep. Just scratch the surface and there's my life for all to see."

"I'm sorry."

She smiled faintly. "Doesn't matter. Other aspects of this are more important. Namely, Gavin." Leaving her head against the cushion, she turned it to look at Dean. "What happened to his face today?"

"I didn't hit him, if that's what you're getting at."

Affronted by his tone and the statement itself, she shot bolt upright. "That's not at all what I was 'getting at.'" Retrieving her mug of cocoa, she angrily stalked from the room, saying as she went, "Lock the door on your way out."

chapter twenty-five

With jerky, angry motions, Paris rinsed out her cocoa mug, then switched off the light above the kitchen sink. When she turned, Dean was standing in the open doorway, silhouetted against the faint light coming from the living room.

"I'm sorry I snapped at you."

"That's not what made me mad," she said. "It's that you would think that *I* would think that you had hit Gavin."

"But I did, Paris."

The admission stunned her into silence.

"Not today," he continued. "Several days ago. He provoked me, I lost my temper and backhanded him across the mouth."

Her anger evaporated as quickly as it had formed. "Oh. Then I struck a nerve, didn't I?" After a beat, she added softly, "I know what happened that time at Tech."

He looked at her sharply. "Jack told you?"

"He told me enough. But only after I'd commented on your rigid self-control."

He slumped against the doorjamb and closed his eyes. "Well, my self-control failed me the other night with Gavin, and again today with Rondeau."

"Rondeau?"

He told her about the scene he'd interrupted when he went into the men's room. "He had Gavin's face shoved up against the mirror. That's what caused the bruise on his cheek. I wanted to kill the guy."

"I would have wanted to myself. Why would he do such a thing?"

"He said he had a mother and a sister, and the obscene messages that Gavin had left on the website offended him so much that when he saw him, he lost it. A sorry excuse that stank of bullshit."

"Does Curtis know about this?"

"I didn't tell him, and I can't see Rondeau confessing."

"You're going to let the matter drop?"

"No. Hell no. But I'll deal with Rondeau in my own way and without any interference from Curtis." He laughed without humor. "Going back to our detective friend, he's a dogged cuss. He's not going to give up until he knows everything about our 'cozy little trio,' as he put it."

"Meaning you, me, and Jack."

"He's not dense, Paris. He knows there's more to the story than what was reported in the media, and much, much more that we're not telling him."

"It's none of his business."

"He thinks it is. He thinks Valentino may harken back to that."

She tried to turn away, but he reached for her and turned her back around. "We've got to talk about this, Paris. We didn't address it when we should have, seven years ago. If we had, Jack might not have gotten drunk that night. We should have gone to him, sat him down, and told him—"

"That we had betrayed him."

"That we had fallen in love, that neither of us had set out to, but it had happened, and that's just the way it was."

"So sorry, Jack. Rotten luck. See ya 'round."

"It wouldn't have been like that, Paris."

"No, it would have been worse."

"Worse than what, for godsake? Worse than how it ended?"

He took a deep breath and continued in a quieter, more reasonable tone of voice. "Jack was smarter than you gave him credit for. And a lot more perceptive. He could tell we were avoiding each other. Didn't you know he would want to learn the cause of it?"

Of course, he was right. She had sold Jack short by thinking that if she pretended nothing had changed, he would never learn that everything had. His fiancée and his best friend had made love. Their relationships—hers with Jack, his with Dean, hers with Dean—had been irrevocably altered. They couldn't revert to the way things had been. She'd been naive to think they could.

"I thought . . . thought . . ." She lowered her head and massaged her temple. "I don't remember what I thought, Dean. I just couldn't go to him and say, 'Remember the night after the standoff, and I told you that I wanted to be alone? Well, Dean came over to my place and we had sex on the living room rug.'"

Instead she'd taken a more subtle approach and declined each time Jack tried to get the two of them together. Her excuses became increasingly lame. "Eventually Jack demanded to know why I didn't like you anymore."

"I had a similar conversation with him," Dean said. "He asked me if you and I had crossed swords during the standoff. Had the crisis brought out the cop in me and the reporter in you, and never the twain shall meet. I told him he was way off base, that we liked and respected each other a lot. So he put it to the test with that surprise dinner."

Yes, that fateful dinner, she thought. Jack had arranged for them to meet at one of their favorite restaurants. She and Dean had arrived independently, not expecting to see the other there.

Being face-to-face for the first time since that night was as awkward for them as she had feared it would be. Making eye contact was difficult, but she couldn't keep herself from looking at him, and each time she did, she caught him stealing a glance at her. Yet their conversation had been stilted and formal.

"That dinner was an endurance test for me," Dean said. "You had rebuffed all my attempts to talk to you."

"It had to be a clean break, Dean. I didn't trust myself even to talk to you on the phone."

"Jesus, Paris, I was dying on the inside. I needed to know what you were thinking. If you were all right. If you were pregnant."

"Pregnant?"

"We hadn't used anything."

"I was on the pill."

"But I didn't know that." He smiled with chagrin. "Selfishly, I hoped you had conceived."

She couldn't admit to him even now that she'd clung to the same vain hope and was disappointed when she'd gotten her next period. A baby would have forced her to tell Jack the truth. It would have been her and Dean's justification for having to hurt him. But it hadn't happened.

"I went through hell agonizing over the state you were in when I left you that night," he was saying. "And suddenly there you were, sitting three feet across the dinner table from me, and I still couldn't ask or say anything I wanted to.

"And that wasn't all. Deceiving Jack was killing me," he continued. "Every time he told another joke, or threw his arm around me and called me his good buddy, I felt like Judas."

"He was trying his best to make it a fun evening. Ever the social chairman."

Jack had seemed determined to ignore the awkwardness between them. He had drunk too much, talked too loud, laughed too hard. But during dessert, he finally gave up and demanded to know what was going on.

"Look, I've had it with you two, okay?" he'd said. "I want to know, and I want to know now. What happened to make you so uncomfortable around each other? I'm guessing that either (a) you had a tiff during that standoff, or (b) you've been seeing each other behind my back. So tell me what the squabble was about, or fess up."

Thinking he'd made a clever joke, he folded his arms on the table and grinned at them in turn.

But Dean didn't respond to Jack's grin, and she'd felt as if her face would crack if she attempted a smile. Their silence spoke volumes. Even so, it was several moments before realization struck Jack, and when it did, it was a painful thing to watch. His grin collapsed. He looked first at her, almost quizzically. Then he looked at Dean as though willing him to laugh and say something like "Don't be ridiculous."

But when neither of them said anything, he realized that out of his jest had emerged the truth. "Son of a bitch," he said. He surged to his feet and sneered at Dean, "Dinner's on you, friend."

Apparently Dean had been following her thoughts because he said, "I'll never forget the look on his face when he put it together."

"Nor will I."

"In my haste to follow him out and try to stop him from getting behind the wheel of his car, I knocked over my chair. By the time I got it upright, the two of you had disappeared."

"I don't remember running through the restaurant after him," she said. "But I vividly remember catching up with him in the parking lot. He yelled at me, told me to leave him alone."

"But you didn't."

"No, I begged him to let me explain. He only glared at me and said, 'Did you fuck him?'"

Dean dragged his hand down his face, but the gesture did little to rub the regret from his features. "From all the way across the parking lot, I heard him say that. I heard you telling him that he shouldn't drive, that he was too drunk and too angry."

Heedless of her pleas, Jack had gotten into his car. She'd run around to the passenger side and luckily had found it unlocked. "I got in. Jack ordered me out. But I refused and instead buckled my seat belt. He cranked the motor and floored the accelerator."

They were silent for a time, lost in the recollections of that horrible night. Dean was the first to speak.

"He had every right to be furious with us for sleeping together. If our roles had been reversed, I . . . God, I don't know what I would have done. Torn him limb from limb probably. He was hurt and angry, and if he'd wanted to kill himself over it, there's really nothing we could have done to stop him, that night or on any future night. We wronged him, Paris. We'll live with that for the rest of our lives. But he wronged you when he drove off with you in that car."

He placed his hands on either side of her neck and caressed it with his fingertips. "That's what I blame him for. He could have killed you."

"I don't think it was his intention to kill anybody."

"Are you sure?" he asked gently. "What did you say to each other during those two minutes between the restaurant parking lot and that freeway overpass?"

"I told him I was sorry that we had hurt him. I told him that we both loved him, that it had been an isolated incident, a physical release after a traumatic experience, that if he could forgive us, it would never, ever happen again."

"Did he believe you?"

A tear slid unchecked down her cheek and she said huskily, "No."

"Did *you* believe you?"

She closed her eyes, squeezing out fresh tears. Slowly she moved her head from side to side.

Inhaling deeply, Dean drew her to his chest and stroked her hair.

"Maybe I should have said more," she said.

"Lied to him?"

"It might have saved him. He was enraged. Beyond reason. I tried to get him to pull over and let me drive, but he speeded up instead. He lost control of the car. He didn't drive into that abutment on purpose."

"Yes he did, Paris."

"No," she said miserably, not wanting to believe it.

"If a driver loses control, he reflexively stomps on the brake. I was right behind you. His brake lights never came on." He tilted her head back, forcing her to look at him. "Jack loved you, I don't doubt that. He loved you enough to want you as his wife. He loved you enough to fly into a jealous rage when he found out that you'd been with me.

"But," he said with emphasis, "if he had loved you the way he should have, unselfishly and unconditionally, he never could have considered taking you out along with him. As pitiful as his last years were, I never forgave him for trying to kill you."

His saying that made her love him all the more. And she did love him. From the moment they met, she had realized that her loving Dean Malloy was inevitable. But yielding to it had been impossible then, and it was impossible now. Other people had always stood between them. Jack, certainly. Now Liz.

She worked herself free of his embrace and said, "You should go now."

"I'm staying here tonight."

"Dean—"

"I'll sleep on the living room sofa." He held up his hands in surrender. "If you don't trust me to keep my hands off you, you can lock your bedroom door. But I'm not leaving you alone as long as there's a lunatic out there harboring a grudge against you."

"I can't imagine how he knew that Jack's death is on my conscience."

"And mine."

"What happened between you and me is certainly not public knowledge, and I've never discussed it with anyone."

"He probably did some research on you and surmised the cause of Jack's accident, just as Curtis did."

"Jack's accident could have been caused by any number of things," she argued.

"But only one would have busted up our friendship. It's not that much of a mind teaser, Paris. Valentino has got an ax to grind with unfaithful women. If he's concluded that you cheated on Jack with me, then you personify his nemesis. Even if it were a wrong assumption, Valentino has made it his reality and that's what he'll act on." He shook his head stubbornly. "I'm staying."

He napped on the sofa until dawn, when he silently let himself out of the house. He waved to the two officers sitting in the patrol car still parked at the curb, making certain they were aware of his departure.

He had hardly slept. He looked and felt as if he had been up most of the night. But this was an errand that couldn't wait. He didn't want to postpone it even for the time it would take to go home for a shower and a shave.

He rang the bell twice before he heard the dead bolt click on the other side of the door. Liz peered sleepily through the narrow crack allowed by the brass chain lock, then closed the door only long enough to unlatch it.

"It's unforgivable of me to show up at this time of morning," he said as he stepped inside.

"I forgive you." She wrapped her arms around his waist and snuggled against him. "In fact, this is a lovely surprise."

He hugged her. Beneath the silk robe, which was all she had on, her body felt warm, soft, and womanly. But he wasn't in the least aroused.

She eased back far enough to look up into his face, while keeping her lower body pressed intimately against his. "You look a little the worse for wear. Long night?"

"You could say so."

"Something new with Gavin?" she asked, her concern showing.

"No. He's not totally out of the woods yet, and until he is, I'll be apprehensive. But he's not the reason I'm here."

Her ability to read people had taken her far in her career and it didn't fail her now. After studying him for a moment longer, she said, "I was going to offer you some TLC in bed. But I think I should offer to make coffee instead."

"Don't bother. I can't stay long."

As though to shore up her pride, she dropped her arms to her sides, straightened her posture, and shook back her tousled hair. "Long enough to sit down at least?"

"Of course."

She led him to her living room sofa, where she claimed a corner, tucking her bare feet beneath her hips. Dean sat on the edge of the cushion and propped his elbows on his knees. On the drive over, he had rehearsed several ways to broach the subject, but had ultimately decided that there was no graceful way. He respected her too much to lie. He had decided to be forthright.

"For a long time now—months anyway—I've allowed you to believe that we would eventually get married. It's not going to happen, Liz. I'm sorry."

"I see." She took a deep breath and let it out slowly. "Do I at least get to know the reason?"

"At first I thought I had a classic case of cold feet. After being a bachelor for fifteen years, I thought the idea of marrying again was causing me to panic. So I didn't say anything, hoping that the misgivings would go away. I didn't want to quarrel about it or upset you unnecessarily."

"Well, I certainly appreciate your sensitivity to my feelings."

"Do I detect some sarcasm?"

"Definitely."

"I suppose I deserve it," he said. "I've just broken what amounted to an engagement. You don't have to be nice."

"I'm glad you think so, because I'm working my way up to a hissy fit."

"You're entitled to one."

She glared at him angrily, but then the hauteur returned. "On second thought, I'm not going to get into a fight with you. Histrionics would make it easier for you to storm out of here and never look back. Instead I'm going to put you on the spot. Because I believe I deserve a full explanation."

Actually he *had* hoped for a fight, during which they would swap invective and destroy any affection they'd ever felt for each other. A fight would have been swifter, cleaner, less painful for her, and easier for him. But Liz had slammed shut that cowardly escape hatch.

"I'm not sure I can explain." He spread his hands wide, indicating how futile it was to try. "It's not you. You're as smart and beautiful and desirable as the day I met you. More so."

"Please spare me the I'm-not-worthy-of-you speech."

"That's not what this is," he said testily. "I mean all of that sincerely. It's not about you. It's about *us*. It just isn't where I am, Liz."

"You don't have to tell me that. Lately you haven't been that involved whenever we've made love."

"Funny, I didn't hear you complaining."

"You're trying to pick a fight again," she said sternly. "Don't. And don't be stung by the criticism. It's not your performance that's at issue. It's your emotional detachment."

"Which I acknowledge."

"Is it because of Gavin and his coming to live with you? The additional demands on your time?"

"Gavin provided me with a good excuse to pull back," he admitted. "I'm not proud of the fact that I used him."

"Nor should you be. But this isn't about him either, is it?"

"No."

"Someone else, then?"

He turned his head and looked at her directly. "Yes."

"You've been seeing someone else?"

"No. Nothing like that."

"Then what, Dean? What *is* it like?"

"I love someone else."

She was silenced by the simplicity of his statement. She stared at him for several moments, assimilating it. "Oh. You love someone else. Did you ever love me?"

"Yes. On many levels I still do. You've been an important and vital part of my life."

"Just not the grand passion of it."

"When we started seeing each other, I honestly thought . . . I hoped that . . . I tried . . ."

"You tried," she said around a bitter laugh. "Just what every woman wants to hear."

The sarcasm was back, but it was forced. She had picked up a throw pillow and was hugging it to her chest, literally and figuratively giving herself something to hold on to. He felt he should leave now before his brutal honesty wounded her pride more than it was already wounded.

But as he stood up to leave, she said softly, "The woman in the sunglasses. The one you were talking to at the police station. Paris?" Raising her head, she looked up at him. "Come now, Dean, don't look so shocked. If I were blind, I still would have known that you and she had been lovers."

"Years ago. Only once, but . . ."

"But you never quite recovered."

He matched her sad smile. "No. I never did."

"Just out of curiosity, when did you start seeing her again?"

"The day before yesterday."

Her lips parted in wordless surprise.

"That's right. This alienation of feelings, for lack of a better term, started long before she entered the picture. Seeing her just confirmed what I already knew."

"That you weren't going to marry me."

He nodded.

"Well, thank God you didn't." Tossing the throw pillow aside, she came to her feet. "I don't want to be anybody's second choice."

"And you shouldn't be." He reached for her hand and squeezed it. "I apologize for taking up two years of your biological clock."

"Oh, it's probably for the best," she said flippantly. "What would I do with a baby when I went on a business trip? Take it along in my briefcase?"

She was making light of it, but he knew she was deeply disappointed. Maybe even heartbroken. She was too proud to make a spectacle of herself by crying. And perhaps, just perhaps, she cared too much for him to lay a guilt trip on him.

"You've got a lot of grace, class, and style, Liz."

"Oh, yeah. Out the wazoo."

"What'll you do?"

"Today? I think I'll treat myself to a massage."

He smiled. "What about tomorrow?"

"I didn't sell my house in Houston when I relocated here."

"You didn't?"

"You assumed that I had, and I never set you straight. Maybe I felt intuitively that I would need a safety net. Anyway, as soon as I can arrange it, I'll move back."

"You're special, Liz."

"So are you," she replied gruffly.

He leaned forward and kissed her cheek, then headed for the door. When he reached it, he turned back. "Be well." And, saying that, he left.

chapter twenty-six

"Hello?"

"Is this Gavin?"

"Yes."

"It's Sergeant Curtis. Did I wake you up?"

"Sorta."

"Sorry to disturb you. I couldn't reach your dad on his cell. That's why I'm calling the house phone. May I speak with him, please?"

"He's not here. He stayed over at Paris's house last night." Gavin regretted it the instant the words were out. Being the suspicious person he was, Curtis would jump to the wrong conclusion.

"We had dinner at her place," he explained. "After her program, you know, because of Valentino's latest call, Dad thought she shouldn't be alone."

"Cops are guarding her house."

"I guess my dad didn't think that was enough."

"Obviously."

Gavin decided to quit while he was ahead, afraid he might say too much. Anyway, why was it Curtis's business where his dad spent the night?

"Okay then, I'll try and reach him there," the detective said. "I have her unlisted number."

"I could give him a message," Gavin offered.

"Thanks, but I need to speak to him personally."

He didn't like the sound of that. Did Curtis have to speak personally to his dad about something relating to him? "Any news on Janey?"

"I'm afraid not. I'll talk to you later, Gavin."

The detective clicked off before Gavin could even say goodbye. He got up and went to the bathroom, then looked through a window on the front of the house and saw that the police car was still parked at the curb.

Was he the only one who appreciated the irony of their protecting him from Valentino, while at the same time suspecting him of being Valentino?

It was too early to get up, so he went back to bed, but discovered he couldn't sleep. Until Janey was found, he was going to be quarantined at home. He might just as well resign himself to that. It could be worse, though. If not for his dad, they probably would have put him in jail.

Considering that his dad had caught him in several lies and discovered his membership in the Sex Club, he wasn't suffering overly much. Last night, with his dad and Paris, it hadn't been half bad.

He'd almost dreaded seeing her after so many years. What if she'd changed and now acted like an old person? He was afraid she'd have big, stiff hair and too much jewelry, that she'd be gushy and sappy, going on and on about how much he'd grown, make a big to-do over him like his mother's relatives always did at family get-togethers.

But Paris had been cool, just like he remembered her. She was friendly, but didn't overdo it like Liz did. She didn't talk down to him either. Even when he had known her before, she had talked to him like an equal, not like a kid.

Jack had always addressed him as Skipper, or Scout, or Partner, something cute, and had talked to him boisterously, like he was a baby who had to be entertained. Jack had been okay, but of the two, he had liked Paris better.

He had liked Paris better than the girls his dad had dated then, too. He remembered thinking that if Jack wasn't in the picture, how cool it would be if his dad liked Paris as a girlfriend.

His mom had thought that maybe he did.

She'd never talked to him about it, of course, but he had overheard her say once to a friend that she thought Dean had a "thing" for Paris Gibson, and that he only dated other women because she belonged to Jack Donner.

At the time, he'd been too young to understand the implications. Nor had he been particularly interested in the relationships between grown-ups. But after having seen how anxious his dad had been to get to her house last evening, how he'd checked himself out in the rearview mirror before they left the car, he thought his mom might have been right. He'd never seen his dad consult a mirror before meeting Liz.

For as long as he could remember, his parents had been divorced. As a kid, he had gradually begun to comprehend that his family wasn't like the ones in TV commercials where the mommy and daddy ate breakfast together, and walked on the beach holding hands, and rode in the same car, and even slept in the same bed. He noticed that in other houses on his block, the daddy was there all the time.

He asked questions of both parents, and after they had explained the meaning of divorce, he had fervently hoped that his parents would get back together and live in the same house. But the older he got, the better he came to understand and accept that a reconciliation was an extremely dim possibility. Dumb kid that he was, he had continued to hope.

His dad had dated lots of women. Gavin forgot most of their names because none had lasted very long. He'd heard his mom talking to his grandmother about the "flavor of the month" and knew that she was referring to his dad's girlfriends.

His mom hadn't dated nearly as much, so it was surprising that she was the one to remarry. Her remarriage had dashed all hope that his parents would, somehow, miraculously reunite. That's when he'd gotten really mad at her and had determined to make her life with her new husband miserable.

Looking back, it had been a stupid, childish way to behave. He'd been a real jerk. His mom must have loved the guy or she wouldn't have married him. She didn't love his dad anymore.

Gavin had heard her tell his grandmother that, too. "I'll always love Dean for giving me Gavin," she had said, "but we made the right decision early on to split up."

He figured his dad didn't love his mom either, and maybe never had. He tried to picture his parents as a couple, and it just didn't look right. Like two pieces from different puzzles, they didn't fit. It hadn't worked originally and it never would.

Live with it, Gavin, he thought.

His mom was happy now in her second marriage. His dad deserved to be happy, too. But Gavin didn't think Liz was the one who was going to make him happy.

He drifted off, thinking about it, but before he was completely asleep, the doorbell rang.

Jesus! Why was everybody up so frigging early this morning?

He made his way to the front door and unlocked it. To his regret, he didn't check to see who had rung the bell before he opened the door. John Rondeau was standing on the porch.

Gavin's eyes darted past him to the squad car at the curb. He was comforted to see that it was still there. The cops inside were noshing on doughnuts. No doubt a gift from Rondeau.

"Don't worry, Gavin, your protectors are in place."

Rondeau's pleasant tone of voice didn't fool him. Not for a second. His cheekbone had finally stopped throbbing, but it was still sore and would remain discolored for days. Rondeau outweighed him by probably thirty pounds. He knew firsthand that the son of a bitch was capable of violence. But he'd be damned if he'd cower.

"I'm not worried about anything," he retorted. "Especially you. What do you want?"

"I wanted to add something to what I told you yesterday."

"If my dad finds out you're here, he'll whip your ass."

"That's why this is such a good time, because I know he's not at home." He was smiling, so to anyone looking, including the cops licking sugar glaze off their fingers, this would appear to be a chat between friends. "If you decide to tell anybody about my—"

"Crimes."

His smile only widened. "I was going to say extracurricular activities. If anybody hears about that from you, it won't be you I come after."

"I'm not afraid of you."

Ignoring that, Rondeau said, "I'll skip you and go straight for your old man."

"Is that supposed to be a joke? Because it's freaking funny." Gavin snorted derisively. "You're a computer geek."

"I'm working my way out of that unit and into the CIB."

"I don't care if they make you chief, you haven't got the balls to have a face-off with my dad."

"I wasn't talking about attacking him myself. That would be stupid because he would be watching for that. But what about some psycho jailbird he has to interview?

"Malloy goes into jail cells all the time, you know," he continued smoothly. "Talking to junkies and rapists and homicidal maniacs, trying to get information from them, manipulating them into confessing. What if one of them was tipped off that Dr. Malloy was coming on to his woman, making moves on her while he's in jail?"

"You're getting even funnier."

"Like the way he moved in on his best friend Jack Donner with Paris Gibson."

Gavin's next smart-alecky retort died on his lips. "Says who?"

"Curtis, for one. Says anyone with a grain of sense who can add two and two together. Your dad fucked his best friend's fiancée, which caused Jack Donner to try and commit suicide."

"You're making that up."

"If you don't believe me, ask him." Rondeau clicked his tongue against the roof of his mouth. "It's an ugly story, isn't it? But it fuels any rumor I might start among the jail population that Dr. Malloy, despite all his buddy-buddy tactics, is not to be trusted, especially with a lonely and susceptible female.

"You get my drift, Gavin? Cops get set up to die by other cops all the time. We're human, you know. We make enemies among ourselves. It happens," he said, shrugging. "He wouldn't see it coming, but he'd be just as dead and you'd be just as orphaned."

Fear struck Gavin's heart. "You get out of here," he said thickly.

In no apparent hurry, Rondeau pushed himself away from the doorjamb. "Okay, I'll leave you now. But I strongly urge you to think about what I said. You're nothing. You're dog shit on my shoe, not worth my time and effort. But if you rat me out," he said, poking Gavin's bare chest hard with the knuckle of his index finger, "Malloy goes down."

Paris's eyes came open slowly, but when she saw Dean sitting on the edge of her bed, she sat bolt upright. "What's happened?"

"Nothing new. I didn't mean to startle you."

She was relieved to know that there was no bad news, but her heart was still pumping hard from her initial fright and now from having Dean sitting on her bed. Not having quite regained her breath, she asked, "How was the sofa?"

"Short."

"Did you sleep at all?"

"Some. Not much. Mostly I worked, made some notes on Valentino's profile."

As tired as she'd been, it had taken her a long time to fall asleep, knowing that he was in the next room. It had hovered in her subconscious and had prevented her from getting a restful sleep. "I feel like coffee."

He nodded, but he didn't move and neither did she. The silence stretched out as they continued to gaze at each other across the narrow strip of bed separating them.

"Should have locked my bedroom door after all?" she asked in a voice barely above a whisper.

"Definitely. Because, as it turns out, I can't keep my hands off you."

He reached for her and she stretched toward him, but just before their lips met, she said, "Liz—"

"Not a factor."

"But—"

"Trust me, Paris."

She did, giving herself over to his kiss—his untempered, possessive, delicious kiss. Placing her hands on his stubble-covered cheeks, she tilted her head to change the angle of their lips and invited more intimacy. He pushed aside the blanket and sheet covering her and pressed her onto the pillows, following her down, lying close beside her.

He drew back in order to look at her, taking in her unglamorous tank top and boxers. "Fancy sleepwear."

"Designed to inflame."

"It's working," he growled.

She explored his face with her fingertips, smoothing his eyebrows, stroking the straight line of his nose, then tracing the shape of his lips and touching the shallow cleft at the bottom of his chin.

"Your hair is grayer," she remarked.

"You're wearing yours shorter."

"I guess we've both changed."

"Some things have." His eyes moved to her breasts and when he caressed her through the tank top, her nipple tightened. "Not that. That I remember."

He kissed her again, except with more urgency than before. Splaying his hand over her bottom, he lifted her onto the erection that strained against his trousers.

A rush of fluid heat spread through her lower body and into her thighs. It had been years since she had experienced that aching desire to be filled. She sighed with joy over feeling it again, and moaned with longing to have that desire assuaged.

"We've waited long enough," he said, rolling back only far enough to reach for his fly. "Too damn long."

But they would wait longer. Her telephone rang.

Both froze. They locked gazes, and each knew without having to say anything that she must answer the call. Too many things were at stake. Dean flopped onto his back and blistered the ceiling paint with his curses.

Paris pushed her tangled hair from her eyes and reached for the cordless phone on her nightstand. "Hello?" She mouthed to Dean that it was Curtis. "No . . . no, I was awake. Is there news?"

"Of a sort," the detective said brusquely. "None about

Valentino or Janey directly. Brad Armstrong and Marvin Patterson are still at large. But actually I'm calling for Malloy. I understand he's there."

With more composure than she felt, she said, "Just a moment. I'll get him."

She covered the mouthpiece as she extended the telephone toward Dean. He looked at her inquisitively, but she raised her shoulders, saying, "He didn't say."

He took the telephone from her and said a curt good morning to the detective. Paris got up and went into the bathroom, closing the door behind her. She showered quickly and put on a robe before going back into the bedroom. Dean was no longer there and the telephone had been returned to the battery charger.

She followed sounds into the kitchen. Dean was scooping coffee grounds into the paper filter. Hearing her behind him, he glanced at her over his shoulder. "You smell good."

"What did Sergeant Curtis want?"

"Coffee will be ready in a few minutes."

"Dean?"

"Gavin told him I was here. He had called my house because he couldn't reach me on my cell. When I went to see Liz this morning—"

"You went to see Liz this morning?"

"At dawn. I turned off my cell and forgot to turn it back on. As a courtesy to her, I didn't want a phone call to interrupt what I had to tell her."

Paris said nothing but felt the pressure of a dozen questions wanting to be asked. He calmly removed two coffee mugs from her pantry and only then turned to face her. "Which was that I wouldn't be seeing her again."

She swallowed hard. "Was she upset?"

"Mildly. But not shocked. She'd seen it coming."

"Oh."

He must have read her mind, because he said quietly, "Don't blame yourself for the breakup, Paris. It would have happened anyway."

"Are you . . . okay with it?"

"Relieved. I was unfair to her by letting it go on for so long."

The coffeemaker gurgled, signaling that the coffee was almost ready and giving her a graceful way to change the subject. She went to the fridge for a carton of half-and-half. "What did Curtis want?"

"Only to give me a status report."

"On the case?"

"No, on my employment with the APD. I've been placed on indefinite suspension."

chapter twenty-seven

"Hi, Mama, it's Lancy."

"Christ, what time is it?"

"Nearly nine."

"Where're you at?"

Last evening he had returned to the mobile-home park through a back gate and had parked two rows away from the lane on which his mother's home was situated. Risking barking dogs and skittish neighbors who would welcome a chance to shoot first and ask questions later, he'd sneaked between the narrow lots.

His reconnoitering seemed a bit melodramatic, but it was a precaution that proved to be unwarranted. He spotted the unmarked police car immediately. It was parked about thirty yards from his mother's patch of lawn. Anyone inside the no-frills sedan had an unrestricted view of her front door. It was a good thing he had gone to her trailer and dipped into his piggy bank when he had.

He had slinked back to his car and returned to Austin because he didn't know where else to go. He had called a neighbor, who was as trustworthy as anyone among Lancy's few acquaintances. He confirmed what Lancy suspected—the police had tossed his place. "I saw them carrying out boxes of stuff," the neighbor reported.

The tapes of Paris Gibson's shows would be in those boxes. *Shit!*

Now, disregarding his mother's question, he asked, "Have any cops come around?"

"Guy named Curtis. From Austin."

"What did you tell him?"

"Nothin'," she grumbled, "'cause I don't know nothin'."

"Did he search the trailer?"

"He poked around. Found your socks."

"Did he take them with him?"

"What would he want your dirty socks for?"

"Go to the window and look out toward the south end of the street."

"I'm in bed," she whined.

"Please, Mama. Do me this favor. See if there's a dark-colored car parked down the street."

She griped and cursed, but the telephone clattered when she obviously dropped it on her bedside table. She was gone an inordinate amount of time. When she finally returned, she was wheezing like a bagpipe. "It's there."

"Thanks, Mama. I'll talk to you later."

"I don't want none of your trouble rubbing off on me, Lancy Ray. You understand me, boy?"

He replaced the greasy receiver on the hook of the pay telephone. Thrusting his hands in his pockets and hunching his shoulders, he walked down the breezeway of the residence motel. Beneath the bill of his baseball cap, his eyes furtively watched for squad cars that he expected to appear at any moment with a squeal of brakes and shouts for him to freeze.

After learning that he couldn't hide in his mother's place, he had returned to his secret apartment to spend the night. He'd driven past it once. There'd been no police car at the IHOP across the street or anywhere else that he could see.

He got in without being detected, but it was hardly a comfortable refuge. It stank. It was dirty. It made him feel dirty.

He'd been up all night, and it had been a long one.

"You're screwed, blued, and tattooed this time, Lancy Ray," he muttered to himself as he unlocked the door and once again slipped back into the dank, dark lair of a wanted man.

• • •

Curtis's shiny cowboy boots were propped up on his desk, his ankles crossed. He was concentrating on the hand-tooled pointed toe of one of them when a yellow legal tablet landed on the desk an inch away from it. He turned to find Paris Gibson standing behind him. Even though she was wearing her sunglasses, he could tell by her body language that she was in a major snit.

"Good morning," he said.

"You're going to kowtow to that egomaniacal fool?"

He removed his feet from his desk and motioned her into a chair. She declined the offer and remained standing. He said, "That fool is a powerful county judge."

"Who has the police department in his pocket."

"It wasn't my decision to suspend Malloy. I couldn't even if I wanted to. He outranks me. I was just the messenger."

"Then let me rephrase," she said. "Judge Kemp has the *gutless* police department in his pocket."

Withstanding the insult, he addressed the issue. "The judge went straight to the top with his complaint. After he and Mrs. Kemp heard you talking about their daughter on the radio last night, he went into orbit. Or so I was told. He called the chief at home, got him out of bed, demanded that Malloy be fired for publicly maligning his daughter, dragging the family name through the dirt, and mishandling a delicate family situation, which should have been dealt with privately. He also cited conflict of interest since Gavin Malloy had been brought in for questioning."

"How did he know about that?"

"He's got moles within the department. Anyway, he threatened to sue everything and everybody if Malloy wasn't removed not only from the case, but from the APD. The chief wouldn't go that far, but he did agree that a temporary suspension was called for. Just until things cool down."

"Just to pacify the judge."

Curtis conceded with a shrug. "I got the edict from the chief before dawn this morning. He asked—make that *ordered*—me to notify Malloy since I was the one who'd brought him in to work the case. That was my punishment, I guess."

"I said nothing except flattering things about Janey last night," Paris argued. "In fact, I went out of my way not to allude to her bad reputation, the Internet club, any of that. We were trying to humanize her to Valentino, portray her as a helpless victim with friends and family who care about her."

"But the Kemps wanted to avoid all media, remember? Even a mention of Janey's disappearance. So your going on the radio, under the advice of the police department's staff psychologist, and talking about her, looked like defiance of their wishes."

"Dean told me that you were very keen on the idea."

"I admitted that to the chief."

"So why didn't the judge demand that you be fired, too?"

"Because he doesn't want to antagonize the whole department. He knows I've got a lot of friends on the force. Malloy hasn't been here long enough to cultivate that kind of loyalty.

"Besides, the judge wanted to get back at you, too. You and Malloy went to his house more or less as a team. He just didn't have the guts to criticize you publicly because of your popularity. It might be bad PR with voters to speak out against Paris Gibson."

"Leaving Dean the scapegoat," she concluded. "Has the media learned of his suspension?"

"I have no idea. If it gets out, you can bet Kemp will exploit it."

She sat down, but not because she was placated. He could tell that by her resolute expression as she leaned forward and spoke directly, to his face. "You go to your chief and tell him that I insist that he retract Dean's suspension. Immediately. Furthermore, if a story about it makes the news today, I'll be on the radio *tonight* talking about the self-serving political machine that drives this police department.

"I'll tell the public about the graft, officers receiving bribes in exchange for not making arrests when they're warranted, and about the department's blatant favoritism toward the wealthy and powerful.

"In four hours, I could do a lot of damage, more I think than even Judge Kemp could do. For all his chest thumping, I doubt if several hundred thousand people have even heard of him. But I have that many loyal listeners every night. Now, who do you think wields the most influence, Sergeant Curtis?"

"Your program isn't political. You've never used it as a soapbox."

"I would tonight."

"And tomorrow Wilkins Crenshaw would fire you."

"Which would win me even more public support and sympathy. It would become a media wildfire that I would fan for weeks. The Austin PD would have a tough time restoring John Q. Public's confidence."

Curtis couldn't see her eyes well behind the tinted lenses, but he could see them well enough. They weren't even blinking. She meant what she said.

"If the decision were up to me . . ." He raised his hands helplessly. "But the chief may not bend."

"If he refuses, I'll call a press conference. I'll be on television by noon. 'Paris Gibson goes public.' 'The first time seen on TV in seven years.' 'The face behind the voice revealed.' I can hear the promos now."

Curtis could hear them, too. "The story about Malloy may already have gotten out."

"Then your chief will issue a press release saying that it was a huge misunderstanding, overly eager reporting by someone misinformed, et cetera."

"Did Malloy send you to champion his cause?" She didn't even deign to answer and he didn't blame her. Malloy wouldn't stoop to that. Curtis had only taken the cheap shot because he didn't have any real ammunition against her arguments. "All right, I'll see what I can do."

"Take this with you," she said, pushing the legal pad toward him.

"What is it?"

"The work Dean was doing last night. He stayed up most of the night profiling Janey's kidnapper and rapist while the judge was plotting to have him discredited and fired.

"It should make for interesting reading. Your chief will realize what an asset he has in Dr. Malloy and what an egregious mistake it would be to take him off this case. Of course, Dean may tell you all to go to hell, and I wouldn't blame him. But you can try and persuade him to come back."

"You're pretty sure of our compliance."

"I'm sure only of how wise one becomes when it's a matter of covering one's own ass."

"I'll think about it and get back to you." Dean depressed the button on his cell phone, ending the call. "Meanwhile," he added under his breath, "go fuck yourself." Noticing Gavin's stunned reaction to his language, he chuckled. "Your generation didn't coin the phrase, you know."

They were having a late breakfast at a coffee shop when the chief of police himself called to nullify his suspension.

"Earlier this morning, he was ready to fire me," he told Gavin as he dug back into his omelet. "Now I'm an asset to the department. An excellent psychologist as well as a highly trained officer of the law. A cross between Sigmund Freud and Dick Tracy."

"He said that?"

"It was almost that ridiculous."

"If you're back on the case, won't Janey's dad be pissed?"

"I don't know how the department is going to deal with the judge, and I don't care."

"Do you want to keep working there?"

"Do you want me to?"

"*Me?*"

"Do you like it here, Gavin?"

"Does it matter?"

"Yes."

Gavin idly stirred his glass of milk with a plastic straw. "It's okay, I guess. I mean, it hasn't been too bad living here."

Dean knew that was probably as close to a yes vote as he was going to get. "I'd hate to leave this job before giving it a fair shake," he admitted. "I think I can do a lot of good here. Austin's a happening place. I like the city, the energy of it. Great music. Good food. Fine climate. But I also like having you living with me. I want you to continue to. So can we work out a deal?"

Gavin regarded him warily. "What kind of deal?"

"If I try out the job, will you try out the high school? I don't mean just attend it, Gavin. I mean really apply yourself, make friends, participate in school activities. You'll be required to put forth as much effort at school as I'll be putting into my job. Do we have a deal?"

"Can I have my computer back?"

"As long as I have access to it at any time. From now on, I'll monitor how much time you spend on it, and how you use it. That's a nonnegotiable point. Another condition is that you must take part in some school activity or sport. I don't care if you play croquet, so long as you don't spend all your free time locked inside your bedroom or just hanging out."

He gave Dean a fleeting glance across the table, then looked back down into his plate. "I was thinking about maybe going out for basketball."

Dean was pleased to hear it, but he didn't want to overreact and jinx it. "We've got the perfect driveway in back of the house for a basket. Want to see about putting one up so you can get in some shooting practice?"

"Sure. That'd be good."

"Okay, then. We understand each other. And just so you know, I broke it off with Liz."

Gavin's head came up. "You did?"

"Early this morning."

"That was kinda sudden, wasn't it?"

"Actually, I've been thinking about it for some time."

Gavin began playing with the straw again. "Was it not working out because of me? Because I live with you now?"

"It was because I didn't love her as much as I should have."

"You didn't want to make the same mistake twice."

It pained Dean for his son to think of his marriage to Pat as a mistake, although he was precisely right. "I suppose you could put it that way."

Gavin mulled it over for a moment. "Did Paris figure into it?"

"Hugely."

"Yeah, I thought so."

"Are you cool with that?"

"Sure, she's great." He took the plastic straw out of his glass and began bending and twisting it. "Did you sleep with her while she was engaged to Jack?"

"What?"

"You want me to repeat it?"

"That's a very personal question."

"That means yes."

"That means I'm not going to discuss it with you."

Gavin sat up straighter and looked at him with resentment. "But it's okay for you to pry into *my* sex life. I have to tell you what I did and who I did it with."

"I'm a parent and you're a minor."

"It's still not fair."

"Fair or not, you— Damn!" Dean said when his cell rang again.

He checked the caller ID, saw Curtis's number, and considered not answering. But Gavin had slumped into the corner of the booth and was staring sullenly out the window. It would probably be a one-sided conversation with him from here on anyway.

Dean answered on the fourth ring. "Malloy."

"You talk to the chief?" Curtis asked.

"Yes."

"You staying?"

Although he'd made his decision, he didn't see any reason to jump through hoops for them. "I'm considering it."

"Whether you do or not, I need you to come in."

"I'm having breakfast with Gavin."

"Bring him with you."

Dean's heart jumped. "What for? What's happened?"

"The sooner you can get here, the better. I just got some bad news."

• • •

Curtis didn't beat around the bush. "Your friend Valentino jumped his deadline. Janey Kemp's body was discovered half an hour ago in Lake Travis."

Reflexively Dean reached for Paris's hand and gripped it hard. He'd been surprised to see her waiting in Curtis's cubicle when he and Gavin got there. She told him she had been summoned just as he had, with no more explanation than he had received.

Curtis had arrived a few minutes behind them. He'd asked Gavin if he would wait for them with another detective in one of the interrogation rooms. As his son was led away, Dean had a strong sense of foreboding. Justifiably, as it turned out.

"Two fishermen found her nude body partially submerged beneath the root system of a cypress tree. I was called immediately and rushed out there. Although she hasn't been officially identified, it's her.

"The crime scene unit is combing the place. The ME is examining the body, even before he moves it. Hopes to get something. She looks pretty bad," he said with a heavy sigh. "Bruises on her face, neck, torso, and extremities. What appear to be bite marks . . ." He glanced at Paris. "Several places."

"How did she die?" Dean asked.

"We won't know until the autopsy. The ME estimated that she hadn't been in the water more than six or seven hours, though. Probably put there sometime last night."

"If you had to guess . . ."

"I'd guess strangulation, like Maddie Robinson. The bruises on Janey's neck match the ones she had. On the other hand, the two could be unrelated."

"Sexual assault?"

"The ME will also determine that. Again, if I had to guess, I'd say very likely."

They were silent for a time, then Paris asked softly, "Have the Kemps been notified?"

"That's why I was late getting here. I stopped at their house. The judge was still fuming over the chief's reversed decision and thought I had come to make amends. When I told them about the body, Mrs. Kemp collapsed, but she wouldn't allow him to console her.

"Each blamed the other. They shouted accusations. It was an ugly scene. When I left they were still going at it. I'm meeting them at the morgue in an hour to get a positive ID, and I don't look forward to it."

He stared into near space a moment, then said, "They wouldn't win a popularity contest with me, but I have to admit I felt sorry for them. Their only child has been brutalized and murdered. God knows what she endured before she died. I couldn't help but think about my own daughter, how I'd feel if somebody did that to her, then dumped her in a lake for fish to feed on."

Dean saw from the corner of his eye that Paris had pressed her fingers vertically against her lips as though to forcibly contain her emotion. "Why did you want to see Gavin?" he asked Curtis.

"Will he submit to a lie detector test?"

"Bad time for a joke, Sergeant."

"I'm not joking. We're no longer shooting in the dark. I've got a dead girl. I've got to tighten the screws."

"On my son?"

"He was one of the last people to see her alive."

"Except the person who kidnapped and killed her. Have you checked out Gavin's alibi?"

"His friends, you mean? Yes, we ran down several of them."

"And?"

"Unanimously they vouched for Gavin, said he was with them. But they were drunk and high, so their memories were fuzzy. None could nail down the time he joined them or the time he left."

"You're only subjecting Gavin to this because he's the one suspect who's available," Dean said angrily.

"Unfortunately, you're right," the detective admitted with chagrin. "So far there's been no sign of Lancy Ray Fisher even though we've staked out his apartment and his mother's place. One interesting thing turned up on his bank statement, though.

There were several canceled checks made out to a Doreen Gilliam, who teaches high school drama and speech."

He looked at them meaningfully before adding, "Ms. Gilliam moonlights by giving private lessons out of her home. Lancy, aka Marvin, has been taking speech and diction lessons."

"*Speech* lessons?" Paris exclaimed. "He rarely spoke."

Curtis shrugged.

"To aid in disguising his voice, maybe?" Dean asked.

"That was my thought," Curtis said.

"He worked for the telephone company and would have the know-how to reroute calls," Dean mused out loud. "And he's fixated on Paris or else why the tapes?"

"One of the first things I'm going to ask him when he's brought in," Curtis said. "Finding this body raises the bar considerably, so off come the kid gloves. With everybody. I hadn't heard back from Toni Armstrong, so I obtained a search warrant for their house. I made Rondeau personally responsible for cracking Brad Armstrong's computer. In my book, he's got a real good shot at being our man. His own wife testified that she caught him picking up a teenage girl.

"I've pulled in the sheriff's office, the Texas Rangers, and the Texas Highway Patrol. Every law-enforcement officer in the city and surrounding area is on the lookout for Armstrong as well as Lancy Ray Fisher. In any case, we're not putting the squeeze exclusively on Gavin."

"Is that supposed to make me feel better?" Dean asked. "My son being lumped in with a sex offender and a porn star? And since you can't find them, you're requiring Gavin to take a lie detector test."

"Not requiring, requesting."

Paris laid her hand on his arm. "Maybe you should agree to it, Dean. It will clear him."

He wanted to believe it would turn out like that. But Gavin was holding something back. It was only a gut instinct, but it was strong enough to make him afraid of the secret Gavin was keeping.

Curtis was frowning down at the folder on his desk that Dean guessed contained crime scene photos of Janey Kemp's body. "The evidence we have on Gavin is circumstantial. Nothing hard. You'd be within your rights to refuse the test." He looked up at Dean, and Dean recognized the detective's challenge for what it was.

"Fuck that. Gavin takes your damn test."

chapter twenty-eight

"Paris, it's Stan."

"Stan?"

"You sound surprised. You gave me your cell number months ago, remember?"

"But you've never called it."

"Only in case of an emergency, you said. I just heard about Janey Kemp on the news. I called to see if you're all right."

"I can't describe how awful I feel."

"Where are you?"

"At the downtown police station."

"I bet it's hopping. Did the body give up any clues to who did it?"

"I hate to disappoint you, Stan, but the only gruesome detail I know is that she's dead."

"Do you plan on doing your program tonight?"

"Why wouldn't I?"

"The GM notified Uncle Wilkins about the body. They discussed it and thought that, with everything that's happened, you might want to take the night off, replay a tape of an old show."

"I'll call the GM later and talk to him myself. But if anyone asks, tell them that I'll do the program live as always. Valentino is not going to scare me off."

"He's done what he said he was going to do, Paris. Do you think he'll call again?"

"I hope he does. The more he talks to me, the better chance we have of identifying him."

"Too bad you couldn't have caught him before he killed her." After a pause, he added, "Guess I shouldn't have reminded you of that, huh? I'm sure you already feel bad enough for being the one who set him off in the first place."

"I've got to go, Stan."

"Are you mad? You sound mad."

"I just don't want to talk about it anymore right now, okay? I'll see you tonight."

She clicked off. He wished he could have kept her talking longer because it tied up his phone line. If his uncle continued to get a busy signal, he might become discouraged and stop calling.

Ever since he'd learned that Janey Kemp's body had been discovered, Uncle Wilkins had been phoning periodically. He pretended to be concerned about the station's involvement, but Stan knew the reason for the frequent calls—Uncle Wilkins was checking up on him.

He should never have admitted to being attracted to Paris. You'd think that was all his uncle had heard during their meeting. He'd been referring to it ever since.

During their last telephone conversation, Wilkins had said in his most menacing voice, "If you've done anything perverse or inappropriate . . ."

"I've been an altar boy around her. I swear to God."

How could he have behaved otherwise with Paris? She wasn't rude, but she never acted particularly happy to see him. Sometimes, even when she was talking to him, she seemed preoccupied, as though she had something on her mind that was more important or interesting than him.

He was certain that if he'd ever made a move on her, she would have cut him off at the knees. She'd never invited even the slightest flirtation. In fact, she often looked through him, as though he wasn't there. Much like his parents, she treated him with a casual disregard that was as hurtful as an outright rejection. He was always an afterthought.

His chance for a romance with Paris had always been

remote. But it had been totally squelched when Dean Malloy entered the picture. Malloy was an arrogant son of a bitch, confident of himself and his appeal to the opposite sex. He would never need to coerce a secretary into raising her skirt or cajole a date into bed.

Fact of life: Things came easier to men like Malloy.

Another fact: Women like Paris were attracted to men like that.

People like Paris and Malloy had never known a day of rejection. It would never occur to them that love and affection didn't come as easily to others as it did to them. They shone like bright little planets, without an inkling of what it was like to be someone who could only orbit around them. They had no idea the lengths to which someone would go to attain the adoration they took for granted.

No idea.

Gavin's head was bowed so low, his chin was almost touching his chest. "In the lake?"

"Her body is being transported to the morgue, where it will undergo an autopsy to determine the cause of death."

Gavin raised his head. The news of Janey's death had caused him to go pale. He swallowed with difficulty. "Dad, I . . . You gotta believe me. I didn't do it."

"I believe that. But I also believe just as strongly that you're keeping something from me."

Gavin shook his head.

"Whatever it is, wouldn't you rather tell me than have it come out during a lie detector test? What don't you want me to know?"

"Nothing."

"You're lying, Gavin. I know you are."

The boy surged to his feet, fists clenched. "You have no right to accuse someone of lying. You're the biggest liar I know."

"What are you talking about? When have I lied to you?"

"My whole life!" Dean watched in dismay as tears sprang to his son's eyes. Angrily, Gavin swiped at them with his fists. "You. Mom. Always telling me you loved me. But I know better."

"What's makes you say that, Gavin? Why do you think we don't love you?"

"You didn't want me," he shouted. "You got her pregnant by accident, didn't you? And that's the only reason you got married. Why didn't you just get rid of me and save yourselves the trouble?"

He and Pat had never specifically discussed how much they would tell Gavin if he ever asked this question. Perhaps they should have. She wasn't here to consult, so Dean was left to answer his son's tortured questions alone. Despite the embarrassment it might cause Pat, and himself, he decided Gavin deserved the unmitigated truth.

"I'll tell you everything you want to know, but not until you sit down and stop looking at me like you're about to go for my throat."

Gavin battled with indecision for several moments, then plopped back into the chair. His expression remained belligerent.

"You're right. Your mother was pregnant when we got married. You were conceived during a weekend fraternity party in New Orleans."

Gavin laughed bitterly. "Jeez. It's even worse than I thought. Were you college sweethearts at least?"

"We had dated a few times."

"But she wasn't someone you . . . not someone special."

"No," Dean admitted quietly.

"So I was a mistake."

"Gavin—"

"Why didn't you use something? Were you drunk or just stupid?"

"A little of both, I guess. Your mother wasn't on the pill. I should have acted more responsibly."

"Bet you shit when she told you."

"I'll admit that it came as a shock. For your mother as well as me. She was about to graduate and launch her career. I was beginning grad school. Her pregnancy was a hurdle neither of us had counted on at that time in our lives. But—and I want you to believe this, Gavin—abortion was never even considered."

He could tell by his son's expression that he wanted desperately to believe that, but was still finding it difficult to accept. Dean couldn't blame him. Perhaps he and Pat had been wrong to not discuss this with Gavin once he was old enough to understand how women became pregnant. If they had explained it to him, he wouldn't have developed insecurities about his self-worth, and harbored such resentment toward them.

"Nor was adoption discussed. From the start, Pat planned to have you and keep you. Thank God she paid me the courtesy of telling me that I had fathered a child. And when she did, I insisted that you have my name. I wanted to be in your life. Although neither of us wanted to marry the other, I wanted to make you legally mine. She finally agreed to go through with the ceremony.

"We didn't love each other, Gavin. I wish I could tell you otherwise, but it wouldn't be the truth, and that's what you've asked for and I think that's what you deserve to hear. We liked each other. We were companionable and respected each other. But we didn't love each other.

"We did, however, love you. When I held you for the first time, I was nothing short of awed and overjoyed. Your mother felt the same. She and I lived together until you were born.

"During that time, we tried to convince ourselves that love would eventually blossom and that we'd come to realize we wanted to be together for the rest of our lives. But it wasn't going to happen and both of us knew it.

"We cried on the day we finally agreed that staying together would only make for three unhappy people and postpone the inevitable. It was in your best interest that we split sooner, before you could even remember, rather than later. So when you were three months old, she filed for divorce."

He spread his hands wide. "That's it, Gavin. I think it would help if you also talked to your mother about this. Understandably, she didn't want you to know because she didn't want you to think badly of her. I don't want that either. She wasn't a party girl who slept with every guy on campus. That weekend was the last fraternity party we would ever attend because we were both about to graduate. We got wild and crazy and . . . it happened.

"Your mother sacrificed a lot in order to raise you as a single parent. I know you're upset with her for marrying now, but that's just too damn bad. Pat's not only your mother, she's a woman. And if you're entertaining some childish fear that her husband is going to replace you in her life, you're wrong. Believe me, he couldn't. No one could."

"I don't think that," he said, speaking to his lap. "I'm not an idiot. I know she needs love and all that."

"Then maybe you should stop sulking about it and tell her that you understand."

He gave a noncommittal shrug of his shoulders. "I just wish you'd told me, you know, before now. I knew anyway."

"Well, if you knew anyway, and it didn't make a significant difference in your life, then why are you using it as an excuse now?"

His head snapped up. "An excuse?"

"Lasting marriages don't necessarily make for happy homes, Gavin. Lots of kids who live with both parents have a far worse childhood than you've had, and, believe me, I know this.

"You're using your accidental conception as an excuse to behave like a jerk. That's a cowardly cop-out. Your mother and I are human. We were young and reckless and made a mistake. But isn't it time you stopped brooding over *our* mistake and started accepting responsibility for your own?"

Anger infused Gavin's face with color. He breathed heavily through his nose. But tears had once again collected in his eyes.

"I love you, Gavin. With all my heart. I'm grateful for the mistake your mother and I made that night. I'd willingly die for you. But I refuse to let you use the circumstances of your birth to distract me from what is more imperative and, right now, considerably more critical."

He moved his chair closer to the one in which Gavin sat and planted his hand firmly on his shoulder. "I've talked to you frankly, man to man. Now I want you to act like a man and tell me what you've been holding back."

"Nothing."

"Bullshit. There's something you're not telling me."

"No there's not."

"You're lying."

"Get off my back, Dad!"

"Not until you tell me."

His features reflected the turmoil within as he wrestled with his fear and possibly his conscience. Finally he blurted out, "Okay, you want to know? I was in Janey's car with her that night."

Paris checked her wristwatch. She'd been waiting outside the CIB for over an hour. Dean's attorney, whom she recognized from the day before, had arrived. He'd disappeared through the doorway and into the department. Beyond that, she knew nothing of what was going on. She didn't know if they'd begun Gavin's lie detector test or not.

Lack of sleep was beginning to catch up with her. She leaned her head against the wall behind the bench and closed her eyes, but still she couldn't rest. Haunting thoughts crowded her mind. Janey Kemp was dead. A sick, twisted individual had killed her, but Paris felt partially responsible.

As Stan had so tactlessly reminded her, Valentino had been motivated by the advice she'd given Janey. If only she hadn't aired Janey's call-in that night, Valentino wouldn't have heard it.

But tragically, he had. Once he'd issued his threat to punish Janey, what could she, Paris, have done differently? What could she have said to prevent him from taking the final step and killing her?

"Ms. Gibson?"

She opened her eyes. Before her stood a petite woman who was evidently in distress. Her face, though very pretty, was drawn. She was holding her handbag in a death grip. The skin was stretched so tightly across her knuckles, they looked like bare bone. Anguish had reduced her from dainty to frail. Although she was putting up a brave front, she looked about as stalwart as a dandelion puffball.

Paris immediately tried to ease the stranger's apprehension with a smile. "Yes, I'm Paris."

"I thought it was you. May I join you?"

"Of course." Paris made room for her on the bench and the woman sat down. "I'm sorry, I . . . Have we met?"

"My name is Toni Armstrong. Mrs. Bradley Armstrong."

Paris recognized the name, of course, and immediately understood why the woman was discomfited. "Then I know why you're here, Mrs. Armstrong," she said. "This must be awfully difficult for you. I wish we were meeting under pleasanter circumstances."

"Thank you." She was hanging on to her composure by a thread, but she did hold on, and that earned her Paris's respect. "When the police searched our house, they overlooked this." She removed a CD from her handbag. "Since they confiscated Brad's computer, I thought I should hand this over, too. It could have something important on it."

A confusing thought caused Paris to frown. "Mrs. Armstrong, how did you recognize me?"

Even with all the news coverage the story of Janey's disappearance had generated, Paris's picture had been kept out of it. Wilkins Crenshaw had personally intervened and put pressure on the local media to not use her photograph. Paris had no delusions: He wasn't concerned for her. He wanted to protect the reputation of the radio station. In any case, the local media had agreed to extend that professional courtesy. She wasn't sure how long their largess would last.

Toni Armstrong nervously wet her lips and ducked her head. "This CD from Brad's computer was only the excuse I gave myself for coming to see Sergeant Curtis. The real reason is that I didn't tell him everything yesterday."

Paris said nothing, her silence inviting Toni Armstrong to continue.

"Sergeant Curtis asked me if Brad ever listened to late-night radio. I said yes, sometimes. He went on to ask something else and never came back to that subject. Your name wasn't mentioned, so I didn't volunteer that we—Brad and I—had known you from Houston."

Her eyes were imploring, almost as though willing Paris to

remember on her own so she wouldn't be required to recount the circumstances under which they'd become introduced.

"I apologize, Mrs. Armstrong. I don't remember ever meeting you."

"You and I never actually met. You were Dr. Louis Baker's patient."

Suddenly Paris's memory crystallized. How could she not have remembered his name? Of course, Armstrong was an ordinary name. Neither Curtis nor Dean had mentioned that their suspect Brad Armstrong was a dentist.

"Your husband's a dentist? *That* dentist?"

Toni Armstrong nodded.

Paris inhaled a swift breath. "I'm so sorry."

"You don't owe me an apology, Ms. Gibson. What happened wasn't your fault. I didn't blame you. You did what you had to do. Brad felt differently, of course. He said that you . . . that you had flirted with him, led him on." She smiled sadly. "He always says that. But I never thought for a moment that you had encouraged him to do what he did."

Paris had gone to Dr. Louis Baker for some dental work, but when she arrived at the clinic, she was informed that he'd been called away on a family emergency. Her choice was to reschedule or let one of his partners treat her. The appointment had been postponed twice, she was already there, so she opted to see the other dentist.

She remembered Brad Armstrong as a nice-looking man with an engaging manner. Since she was scheduled for several procedures, some of which might be uncomfortable, he'd suggested using nitrous oxide to help her relax.

She'd agreed, knowing that "laughing gas" had no lasting effect as soon as one stopped inhaling it and that it was safe when administered in a clinical environment. Besides, if a numbing shot was required, she would just as soon not know when it was coming.

Soon she was feeling completely relaxed and carefree, as though she was floating. At first she thought she had only imagined that her breasts were being touched. The caress had been featherlight. Surely it was only a false physical sensation brought on by her state of euphoria.

But when it happened a second time, the pressure was distinctly firmer and applied directly to her nipple. There could be no mistake. She opened her eyes and, shaking off her lethargy, removed the small mask from her nose. Brad Armstrong smiled down at her, and the leering quality of his grin convinced her that she had imagined nothing.

"What the hell do you think you're doing?"

"Don't pretend you didn't enjoy it," he'd whispered. "Your nipple is still hard."

Even reclined in the dental chair as she was, she came off it like a shot, knocking over a metal tray of implements and sending it crashing to the floor. An assistant, whom he had sent out on a trumped-up errand, came rushing back into the treatment room. "Ms. Gibson, what's wrong?"

"Have Dr. Baker call me at his earliest convenience," she told her before storming out.

The dentist had called her later that day, expressing his concern. She reported what had happened. When she finished her story, he said with chagrin, "I'm ashamed to say that I thought the other woman was lying."

"He's done it before?"

"I assure you, Ms. Gibson, this will be the last time. You have my utmost apologies. I'll take care of it immediately."

Dr. Armstrong had been dismissed. For several days afterward, Paris had shuddered in repulsion whenever she thought about the incident, but after a time it had faded from her memory. She hadn't thought any more about it until now.

"I assume your husband blamed me for getting him fired."

"Yes. Although he's been forced out of other practices for similar incidents since then, he's always held a grudge against you. While you were still in Houston, he turned off the television set anytime you appeared. He called you ugly names. And when your fiancé got hurt, he said you deserved it."

"He knew about Jack, the accident?"

"And Dr. Malloy. He theorized that it was a love triangle."

Paris exclaimed, a soft "Oh."

"When we moved here and Brad discovered you were on the radio, his resentment flared up again." Mrs. Armstrong lowered her head and twisted the straps of her handbag. "I should have told Sergeant Curtis about this yesterday, but I was so afraid they would think Brad was involved with this missing-girl case."

"She's no longer missing." When Paris told her that Janey Kemp's body had been discovered, Toni Armstrong finally lost her valiant battle against tears.

chapter *twenty-nine*

Anytime John Rondeau crossed paths with Dean Malloy, he went out of his way to be nothing but pleasant. But Malloy treated him with patent animosity. Curtis had noticed. Rondeau had overheard him asking Malloy what the problem was. Malloy had replied with a gruff, "Nothing," and Curtis hadn't pressed him.

As far as Rondeau was concerned, Malloy could glower at him until hell froze over. It was Curtis he wanted to butter up, not Malloy. The psychologist had the higher ranking, but it was Curtis who could recommend Rondeau for CIB.

As for Malloy's kid, he had him right where he wanted him, which was scared out of his skivvies. The results of the lie detector test had been in his favor and had basically cleared him of suspicion. So, one might wonder, why was he still so fidgety?

He was sitting in a chair near Curtis's desk, his shoulders hunched in a self-defensive posture. A bundle of nerves, he couldn't sit still. His eyes darted about fearfully. He looked like he would disintegrate if somebody said "Boo!"

Only Rondeau knew why the boy still looked so scared, and he wasn't telling. Neither was Gavin. Rondeau was confident of the kid's silence. He had frightened him sufficiently that he wasn't about to tattle on him. Brilliant to think of threatening his dad, not him. That had done the trick.

It was crowded inside Curtis's cubicle, where they'd all gathered for a brainstorming session. Curtis was there, of course. Malloy. Gavin. And Paris Gibson.

Rondeau welcomed any opportunity to share space with her, though it was hard for her to notice him with Malloy stamping around repeating ad nauseam that he feared she would be next on Valentino's to-do list.

Rondeau had stumbled on to this meeting when he came to report to Curtis what he'd found on the CD Mrs. Armstrong had hand-delivered to Paris. It wasn't all that earthshaking, but he grabbed any opportunity to impress Curtis and bump up his chances of getting into the CIB.

Paris—innocently, of course—had stolen his thunder before his arrival. What Toni Armstrong had withheld from him while he was searching her house, she had imparted to Paris—her husband had fondled Paris when she'd been his patient.

Had Mrs. Armstrong shared this with him and he'd been the one to bring it to Curtis's attention, it would have been a real feather in his cap. As it was, he'd have to earn that feather by some other means.

"I've got a bad feeling about this guy," Sergeant Curtis was saying of the dentist. "Has he contacted his wife today?" he asked Paris.

"She says no. All her attempts to reach him have been unsuccessful."

"If he called her from his cell, we could place him using satellite," Malloy remarked.

"I'm sure that's why he hasn't done it," said Rondeau, hoping he'd made Malloy sound like a fool. His neck was still sore from Malloy's squeeze yesterday. He and Malloy were never going to be friends, but he didn't consider that any great loss.

"Have you checked out his phone records?" Malloy asked.

"Working on it," Curtis replied. "It'll look really bad for him if he's made repeated calls to the radio station." Turning back to Paris, he asked, "Mrs. Armstrong didn't recognize his voice on the tapes?"

"She's listening to them again, but I'm not sure how reliable her input will be. She's very upset. When I told her about Janey, she underwent an emotional meltdown that I think had been brewing for days."

"Would you recognize Brad Armstrong on sight?"

Paris frowned. "I don't think so. The incident happened a long time ago. I saw him only that one time, and I was high on nitrous oxide."

"Would a photograph be helpful?" Rondeau asked, nudging Malloy aside and wedging himself into the center of the enclosure.

"Possibly," Paris said.

He produced the CD that Toni Armstrong had brought from home and given to Paris. "Apparently Brad Armstrong scanned photos and burned them onto CDs. The ones we found during the search had porno shots taken out of magazines on them.

"But this last one has family photographs on it. I brought it back so it could be returned to Mrs. Armstrong, but it may be useful now. May jiggle your memory, Paris."

"Can't hurt to take a look," said Curtis. He booted up the computer on his desk, then stepped aside so Rondeau could sit down. He was aware of Paris moving in close behind him to get a better look at the monitor screen. He caught a whiff of a clean scent, like shampoo.

He executed the necessary keystrokes and within seconds a snapshot filled the screen. The family of five was posed in front of an attraction at a theme park. Parents and kids were wearing American clothing and American smiles, living the American Dream.

Rondeau turned toward Paris. "Look familiar?"

For several moments, she studied the man in the photograph. "Honestly, no. If I had spotted him in a crowd, I wouldn't have immediately recognized him as the man who fondled me. It was too long ago."

"You're sure you haven't seen him recently?" Malloy asked. "If he resented you as much as Mrs. Armstrong indicated, he might have been stalking you."

"If I have seen him, it didn't register."

Curtis, who was still studying the Armstrong family snapshot, said, "I wonder who took the picture."

"Probably he did," Rondeau said. "A guy who has a scanner and makes a CD photo album—"

"Would be into cameras," Curtis finished for him. He turned to Gavin. "Janey told you her new boyfriend took that picture of her, correct?"

The kid withered beneath the attention of everyone in the room. His left knee was doing a jackhammer number. "Yes, sir. When she gave me the picture, she said he'd taken that one and lots of others. She said he liked taking the pictures almost as much as the sex."

"I don't recall any camera equipment being found during the search of their house," Rondeau said. "But he's got to have a setup or he wouldn't have these family photographs. Some were taken with wide-angle or telephoto lenses."

"Has the lab turned up anything on that photo Janey gave Gavin?" Malloy asked.

Querulously Curtis shook his head. "The only prints on it belonged to Janey and Gavin."

"Sergeant Curtis?" Griggs poked his head in, interrupting.

"In a minute," the detective told him.

"What about the local outlets for photographic supplies?" Malloy asked.

"Still being investigated," Curtis said. "Running down their clients is a time-consuming process."

"You wouldn't think that many people had their own darkrooms," Malloy said.

"Mail-order customers. Faxed-in orders. People ordering on-line. It's a chore."

Griggs interrupted a second time. "Sergeant Curtis, this is important."

But Curtis's mind was moving down a single track. He addressed the detectives who had clustered just outside his cubicle. Some didn't work homicide cases, but he'd asked everyone in the unit for their cooperation and time if they could spare it.

"Somebody determine if there's a darkroom in Brad Armstrong's home. Garage, attic, toolshed, extra bathroom. I don't care how crude." One of the detectives peeled away from the group in a hurry.

"We need Brad Armstrong's telephone records ASAP. Find out what's taking so long." Another detective rushed away to carry out that assignment.

"Print out a picture of him—no family members, just him. Get it to all the TV stations in time for their first evening newscasts. He's wanted for questioning, got it? *Questioning*," he stressed to the detective who reached for the CD that Rondeau helpfully ejected from Curtis's computer.

"Also distribute it to the intelligence officers who're checking out those photo places," Curtis called out across the cubicles. "Have it faxed to all the other agencies that are helping us in the search."

That business dispatched, Rondeau said, "Sir, I apologize for not putting it together sooner."

"Never mind." Curtis, dismissing him in a way that stung, turned to Paris. "His wife will be our best source of information. Are you sure she'll cooperate?"

"Absolutely. Whether or not he's Valentino, she wants him to be found and has promised to cooperate in any way she can."

Curtis bobbed his head at a plainclothes policewoman. "Ask Mrs. Armstrong who takes their family photographs. Make it conversational."

While everyone was distracted, Rondeau looked over at Gavin Malloy and winked. The boy mouthed, *Get fucked.* Rondeau smiled.

"Sergeant?" Griggs was still making a nuisance of himself. "Excuse me?"

Finally Curtis turned to him and growled, "What is it, for christsake?"

"S . . . somebody to see you, sir," he stammered. "And . . . and Ms. Gibson."

"Somebody? Who?"

Griggs pointed across the tops of the cubicle walls. Curtis and Paris followed him through the maze of tiny offices to the double-door entrance where two uniformed patrolmen were holding a handcuffed man between them.

Paris exclaimed, "Marvin!"

• • •

Lancy Ray Fisher was seated at the table in one of the interrogation rooms. Paris sat across from him while Curtis stood at one end and Dean at the other. Even though they'd been focused on Dr. Brad Armstrong, the man she knew as Marvin Patterson remained a viable suspect.

He'd walked into police headquarters and introduced himself to the officers at the lobby desk. Recognizing him instantly, they had put his hands in restraints for his elevator ride up to the third floor. He'd put up no resistance whatsoever. Each time Paris and he made eye contact, he looked away quickly, appearing to be guilty of something.

She was surprised by how nice looking he was without his baggy coveralls and the baseball cap he wore to work. She'd never seen his face in full light. Nor had he seen hers, she reminded herself. Maybe that's why his glances at her weren't only guilty, but also curious.

"Should I get a lawyer?" he asked Curtis.

"I don't know, should you?" the detective replied coolly. "You're the one who called this meeting and insisted on Paris being in on it. You tell me if you need a lawyer."

"I don't. Because I can tell you right off, and it's the God's truth, I had nothing to do with that girl's kidnapping and murder."

"We haven't accused you of having had anything to do with it."

"Then why'd those guys downstairs pounce on me and put me in these?" He thrust his cuffed hands toward Curtis.

Unfazed, Curtis replied, "I'd have thought you'd be used to them, Lancy. You've been in them often enough."

The young man slumped back in his chair, acknowledging the verity of that.

"Marvin," Paris said, getting his attention, "they found tapes of my shows, a large number of tapes, in your apartment. I'd like to know why you had them."

"My real name is Lancy."

"I'm sorry. Lancy. Why did you collect all those tapes?"

Dean said, "To us, it looks like you have an obsessive interest in her."

"I swear, it's not what you're thinking."

"What am I thinking?" Dean asked.

"That it's for some kinky reason. It's not. I . . . I've been studying her." He looked at their baffled faces. "I, uh, I want to be like her. Do what she does, I mean. I want to be on the radio."

If he'd said he wanted to pilot a nuclear submarine through the capitol rotunda, they couldn't have been more astonished.

Paris was the first to recover. "You want a career in radio broadcasting?"

"I guess you think that's crazy, considering my criminal record and all."

"I don't think it's crazy. I'm just surprised. When did you decide on this career path?"

"A couple years back. When I got out of Huntsville and started listening to you every night."

"Why Paris, specifically? Why not another deejay?"

"Because I liked the way she talked to people," he said to Dean. Then he turned back to her. "It seemed like you really cared about the people who called in, like you cared about their problems." Looking abashed, he added, "For a while there, I had it pretty rough. Getting back into life on the outside. You were like my only friend."

Curtis was staring at him with a skeptical scowl. Dean, too, was frowning. But Paris gave him a smile that encouraged him to continue.

"One night this guy called, told you he'd been laid off from his job and couldn't find another. You said it seemed to you that his confidence had suffered, and that's when you should aim the highest, reach the farthest.

"I took the advice you gave him. I stopped trying to get penny-ante jobs and applied at the telephone company. They hired me. I was making good money, enough to pay for voice lessons. Better clothes. A good car. But I got greedy, lifted some equipment I knew I could hock fast. They didn't file charges but they fired me."

He fell silent, as though castigating himself for such a bad judgment call. Paris looked over at Dean. He lifted his shoulders as though to say that Lancy could either be telling the truth or telling a whopper.

"After a few weeks of unemployment," he continued, "I couldn't believe my good fortune when I saw the ad in the paper about a job at the radio station. I didn't care that it was cleaning out the crapper . . . uh, toilets. I wanted to be in that environment any way I could get in. So I could observe you. See how you work. Maybe even pick up some of the technology.

"I rigged a recorder up to my radio at home and had it timed to tape every show. During the daytime, I'd replay the tapes and try to imitate the way you talked. I practiced, trying to get your diction and the rhythm of your speech down. I took more lessons to get rid of my accent."

He shot her a grin. "As you can hear, that's going to take a lot more work. And of course I know I'll never be as good as you no matter how hard I work at it. But I'm determined to give it my best shot. I wanted to . . . I *had* to, what do they call it?"

"Reinvent yourself?" she guessed.

His eyes lit up. "Yeah, that's it. That's why I was using an alias. My real name sounds too much like where I came from."

Curtis tossed a folder onto the table and when Lancy saw that it was his criminal record, he winced. "I know it looks bad, but I swear to God I've put that life behind me."

"It's a long list of wrongdoing, Lancy. Did you find Jesus in Huntsville, or what?"

"No, sir. I just didn't want to be trash for the rest of my life."

Curtis harrumphed, unconvinced.

Lancy glanced around and must have realized that they were still skeptical. He wet his lips and in a tone of desperation said, "I wouldn't do anything to hurt Paris. She's my idol. I haven't made any threatening phone calls. As for that girl who turned up dead, I don't know anything."

Curtis propped a hip on the corner of the table and addressed the younger man in a deceptively friendly way. "You like high school girls, Lancy Ray?"

"Sir?"

"You dropped out of school at sixteen."

"I got my GED while I was in prison."

"But you skipped all the fun of high school. Maybe you're making up for what you missed."

"Like the girls, you mean?"

"Yeah, that's what I mean."

He shook his head emphatically. "I don't pick up underage girls and have sex with them. I'm not perfect, but that's not my thing."

"Do you like women?"

"You mean, over men? Hell, yes."

"You've got a handsome face. Good build. It can get awfully lonely in prison."

Self-consciously Lancy cast a look at Paris, then lowered his head and muttered, "They left me alone. I stabbed one in the . . . in the testicles with a fork. I got a year tacked onto my sentence for it, but they didn't bother me after that."

She was embarrassed for him. She hoped Curtis would let up, but she was afraid that if she interfered he would ask her to leave and she wanted to hear this.

Curtis said, "I met your mother yesterday."

Lancy raised his head and looked directly at the detective. "She's a cow."

"Whoa! Did you hear that, Dr. Malloy? Did that sound like latent hostility toward a female? A resentment—"

"I don't like my mother," Lancy said heatedly, "but that doesn't carry over into my sex life. If that was your mother, would you like her?"

Curtis persisted. "Do you have a girlfriend?"

"No."

"Want one?"

"Sometimes."

"Sometimes," Curtis repeated. "When you get a hankering for a girlfriend, what do you do?"

"What do you mean?"

"Come on, Lancy Ray." Curtis tapped the folder with a blunt index finger. "You were sent up for sexual assault."

"That was a bullshit rap."

"That's what all rapists say."

"This guy, this movie producer—"

"A pornographer."

"Right. We were making triple-X-rated skin flicks in his garage. He got upset when his girl started coming on to me. It was all right for us to . . . you know, while his camera was rolling. But not in private. So he and I got into it and—"

"And you cut him up pretty bad."

"It was self-defense."

"The jury didn't buy it, and neither do I," Curtis said. "When you finished with him, you started in on the girl."

"No, sir!"

He denied it so emphatically and indignantly that Paris had to believe he was telling the truth. "It was him. He worked her over good." He pointed to the folder. "All those things that were done to her, he did."

"They collected your DNA."

"Because she and I had been together earlier that day. He caught us. That's what started the fight."

"His testimony was corroborated under oath by two of the production crew and the girl herself."

"They were all junkies. He fed them dope. I didn't have anything to offer in exchange for them telling the truth."

Dean asked, "Why should we believe your version of this, Lancy?"

"Because I own up to all my other crimes. I did some awful things, but I never beat up a woman."

Paris leaned across the table toward him. "Why did you run away when the officers called to say they wanted to question you? Why didn't you tell them what you're telling us now?"

He sighed heavily and raised his cuffed hands to rub his forehead. "I freaked. I'm an ex-con. That automatically makes me a suspect. Then, I knew if they discovered that I'd been taping your shows, they'd for sure haul me in."

"Why did you leave the tapes behind?"

He smiled shyly. "Because I'm stupid. I panicked and got the hell out of there. Forgot them. Maybe I've lost my criminal instinct. I hope I have."

He had a safe-effacing manner that Paris liked. But Curtis didn't appear to be charmed by it.

"If you had admitted this to us the day before yesterday, we might have come closer to believing you."

Lancy looked at Paris and said earnestly, "I'm telling the truth. I don't know anything about this Valentino character or those phone calls. I don't know anything about Janey Kemp except what I've heard on the news. The only thing I'm guilty of is wanting to learn to do what you do."

"You've been working at the station for months," she said softly, "but you've never even engaged me in conversation. Why didn't you come and talk to me about your ambition? Ask for advice? Guidance?"

"Are you kidding?" he exclaimed. "You're a star. I'm the guy who pushes around the mop bucket. I'd never have worked up my nerve to talk to you. And if I had, you would have laughed at me."

"I would never have done that."

He searched her eyes, behind her lenses. "No, maybe you wouldn't have. I see that now."

"Where've you been all this time?" Curtis asked. "You didn't return to your mom's place or your apartment."

"I keep a . . . I guess you'd call it a—"

"Hideout?" Curtis prompted.

Lancy looked abashed. "Yes, sir. I'll give you the address. You're welcome to search it."

"You can bet we will," Curtis said as he hooked his hand beneath Lancy's arm and hoisted him from the chair. "And while we're at it, you'll be residing with us here."

chapter thirty

It was a great bar for trolling.

It was on the lakeshore, a cedar-shingle place well known to the locals. Fishermen might stumble upon it, but it wasn't a watering hole that would attract tourists or country club golfers. The clientele was comprised mostly of construction workers, cowboys, and biker types. A white-collar professional would feel out of his element, so it was highly unlikely that Brad Armstrong would be spotted here by anyone he knew.

Peanut shells crunched underfoot as he made his way across the dim barroom. It was lighted only by neon signs, nearly all boasting the Lone Star flag and a brand of beer. The shaded fixtures suspended over the billiards tables provided supplemental lighting, but it was obscured by tobacco smoke.

The bubbling Wurlitzer in the corner emanated a revolving rainbow of pastel colors, but there was nothing subtle about the music blaring from it. It was old country, the twangy, wailing, woebegone kind, pre Garth, McGraw, and the like.

Customers drank beer from the bottle, Jack Daniel's, or Jose Cuervo straight. Which was what the girl was shooting when Brad joined her at the bar. He recognized her immediately. That she was here today, now, was a cosmic sign that he was doing nothing wrong.

He glanced down at the two empty shot glasses in front of her and motioned for the bartender to serve up two more. "One for me and one for the lady with the nipple ring."

She turned to him. "How'd you— Oh, hi. Coupla nights ago, right?"

He grinned. "I'm glad you remember."

"You're the guy with all the porno."

His face registered a crestfallen expression. "I was hoping you'd remember me for my . . . other memorable quality."

She licked her upper lip and smiled. "That, too."

"I wouldn't expect to find you in a place like this," he said. "You outclass it."

"I hang out in here sometimes." She cracked a peanut shell between her teeth and daintily ate the nuts. "Before the Sex Club starts gathering." She dropped the shell onto the floor and dusted off her hands. "You don't exactly blend either."

"I think we were destined to see each other again."

"Cool," she said.

Makeup had been slathered on to make her look legally old enough to drink. Either the bartender was fooled or, more likely, didn't care that she was underage. He served the tequila shots that Brad had ordered.

"What shall we drink to?"

She rolled her large, dark eyes toward the ceiling as though the answer might be written in the chemically polluted layer of smoke that hovered there. "How about body piercing?"

Leaning forward, he whispered, "I get hard just thinking about it." He clinked his glass to hers and simultaneously they tossed back the fiery liquor.

This was so damn easy, he thought. Didn't mothers warn their daughters against talking to strangers anymore? Didn't they tell them never, ever to go with a man they didn't know? What was the world coming to? It made him afraid for his daughters.

But thinking about his family killed the mood, so he tucked thoughts of them safely away and ordered another round of tequila shots.

After that one they agreed to leave. He smiled smugly as they passed the pool tables. He was the envy of tough guys with tattoos on their arms and knives attached to their thick leather belts. He'd been successful where apparently they had not. Maybe because his hair was clean.

"It's Melissa, right?" he asked as he held the car door open for her.

Her glossy red lips smiled over his remembering her name. "Where are we going?"

"I've got a room."

"Super."

Ridiculously easy.

Coming out this evening wasn't a wise thing to do, but he couldn't have stayed cooped up another minute or he would have gone crazy. He couldn't return home. Toni had been calling his cell phone at fifteen-minute intervals all day, begging him to come back. The police only wanted to talk to him, she said. *Right,* he thought. *They want to talk to me through iron bars.*

He hadn't answered his phone and he hadn't called her, knowing that the police had probably set up a system of tracking his cell by satellite. The discovery of Janey's body didn't bode well for him. News reports had said that an autopsy was being conducted. Hearing that had nearly sent him over the edge.

He'd fretted, stewed, paced, lambasted his wife for not understanding him, and Janey for being a cock teaser he couldn't resist, even his mother, who'd punished him severely for masturbating when he was little.

Truthfully, he didn't remember such a time, but psychologists had asked him during therapy sessions if he'd been so punished and he'd said yes because that seemed to be the expected and accepted explanation for his sexual preoccupation.

As the news reports went from bad to worse, actually including his name in them, his anxiety increased. He had tried to distract himself by looking at his pornographic magazines, reading the letters and "true" experiences submitted by subscribers. But soon familiarity had made them boring. Besides, his craving wasn't going to be satisfied vicariously.

He was aroused and needed relief. With the pressure he'd been under recently, who could blame him? He resolved that if

334 • SANDRA BROWN

relief wasn't going to come looking for him, he would have to go looking for it.

Now he'd found it.

"This isn't the car you were in the other night," Melissa remarked as she punched through radio stations until she found one playing a thrumming rap song.

The police would've spotted his car, so he had called and ordered one from a rental place that delivered. Not a chain outfit that required all kinds of documentation, but one that, according to their yellow pages ad, would take cash. That signaled to Brad a business that was light on rules and regulations. The only amenity promised was a working air conditioner in all their cars.

While waiting for it to arrive, he'd showered and dressed, splashed on the Aramis, and put a supply of condoms in his pants pocket.

As anticipated, the man who delivered the car looked as if his next stop might be a 7-Eleven store he could rob. Brad flashed him his driver's license and filled out a form with false information. He'd counted out the required deposit and added ten bucks for a tip. The man spoke only limited English and didn't seem to care one way or the other what day Brad promised to return the ten-year-old car to their lot.

"Had we met before?" Melissa asked him now. "Before the other night, I mean. You look familiar."

"I'm a famous movie star."

"That must be it," she said, giggling.

To distract her from that train of thought, he said, "Do you always look this sensational?"

"You think?"

Actually she looked like a whore. The dyed hair was spiked stiffer and higher than it had been the other night. Outside the dimness of the bar, her makeup looked even more garish. Her halter top was made of some flimsy fabric through which he could see her dangling silver nipple ring. Most table napkins were larger than her skirt.

In short, she was asking for it. She should thank him for saving her from being gang-banged by the rednecks in the bar.

He drew her eyes down to his lap. "See what you're doing to me."

She assessed the distention behind his trousers, then said, "Is that the best you can do?" and leaned back against the passenger door. She idly brushed her fingertips across the nipple with the ring piercing it.

The girl knew her stuff. His erection stretched. "I can't watch you and drive."

She gave the nipple ring a teasing yank.

He groaned. "You're killing me, you know that?"

"But you'll die happy."

He reached across the console and slid his hand beneath her skirt, felt the scratch of lace against his fingers, then worked his way past it.

"Hmm. Right there." Melissa closed her eyes. "Don't get stopped for speeding. At least not till after I come."

Gavin was waiting outside the CIB when Dean, Paris, and Sergeant Curtis emerged. His hope was riding on Lancy Ray Fisher. He shot to his feet, asking, "Was he the guy?"

"We don't know yet," his dad told him. "Sergeant Curtis is going to keep him here, ask him some more questions."

Paris glanced at her wristwatch. "If it's no trouble, I'd like to stop at my house before going to the station. I ran out in such a rush this morning."

"I'll drive you and drop Gavin at home on the way," Dean said. "We'll have our cell phones on, Curtis. If anything happens—"

"I'll call right away," he assured them. "I'm going to lean on Lancy Ray."

"With all due respect, I don't believe he's Valentino," Paris said.

The detective nodded. Gavin thought he looked very tired. A blond bristle had begun to sprout from his pink cheeks. "I'm still partial to Dr. Armstrong," he told them, "but I'm not ready to give up on Lancy Fisher just yet. I'll be in touch."

They were turning toward the elevators when Curtis spoke

Gavin's name. His first thought was, *What now?* But he said, "Yes, sir?"

"I'm sorry I had to put you through that today. I know it wasn't any fun."

"It's okay," he said, not really meaning it. It hadn't been okay at all. He'd hated being made to feel guilty when he wasn't. "I hope you find out who did that to Janey. I should've told you from the beginning that she and I were in her car. But I was afraid you'd think, well, what you thought. I guess she met whoever killed her after she got rid of me."

"It appears that way. Are you absolutely certain she never mentioned who she was meeting afterward? A name? Occupation?"

"I'm positive."

"Well, thanks," Curtis said. "I appreciate your cooperation."

His dad nudged him toward the elevators and they left. Gavin sat in the backseat on the way home. Nobody said much, each seemed lost in his own thoughts. When they reached the house, a patrol car with two officers inside it was already parked out front. Inwardly Gavin groaned. He'd had his fill of policemen today. If he never saw one again—except his dad—it would be too soon.

"I don't need baby-sitters, Dad. Or am I still grounded?"

"You're grounded, but the cops are for your protection. They stay until Valentino is caught."

"He's not gonna—"

"I'm not taking any chances, Gavin. Besides, the guards are Curtis's mandate, not mine."

"You could call them off if you wanted to."

"I don't want to. All right?" When his dad was wearing that face, the argument was over. He nodded grudgingly. Then his dad reached over the seat and laid his hand on his shoulder. "I was proud of the way you conducted yourself today."

"At the risk of sounding patronizing, so was I, Gavin," Paris told him.

"Thanks."

"Call my cell immediately if anything happens. Promise me you will."

"I promise, Dad." He climbed out. "'Bye, Paris."

"'Bye. See you soon, okay?"

"Yeah, that'd be great."

He shuffled up the walkway. They didn't pull away until he had let himself in. Unlike his mom and dad, the two of them looked right together. He sorta hoped it would work out between them.

He waved at them from the front door before shutting and bolting it, effectively becoming his own jailer.

"Penny for them."

Paris looked across at Dean. "My thoughts? I was thinking about Toni Armstrong. I feel for her. I like her."

"So do I. Brave lady."

"I think she loves her husband. Deeply. Under the circumstances, that must be very conflicting." Curious, she asked, "From a clinical standpoint, when is a person considered a sex addict?"

"Tricky question."

"I'm sure you can address it, Dr. Malloy."

"All right. If a guy gets twelve hard-ons in a day, I'd congratulate him and probably urge him to try for thirteen. If he *acts* on twelve hard-ons in a day, I'd say that's a little excessive and we could have a problem."

"You're being facetious."

"Somewhat, but there's a basis of truth." His grin relaxed and he became serious. "Sex can become an addiction like anything else can. When the compulsion outweighs common sense and caution. When the activity begins to have a negative effect on one's work, family life, relationships. When it becomes the governing force and the exclusive means of personal gratification."

He glanced at her, and with a nod she prompted him to continue. "It's the same point at which a social drinker becomes an alcoholic. The individual loses control over the craving. Conversely, the craving gains control over the individual."

"Like making him willing to sacrifice a wife and family to get his thrills."

"That doesn't mean that Brad Armstrong doesn't love his wife," he said. "He probably does."

Reflecting on that, she stared through the front windshield. Even behind her sunglasses, she had to squint against the setting sun, which was doing a bang-up job of it. She wondered what Judge and Marian Kemp were doing just now. This spectacular sunset would go unnoticed by them.

"They have a funeral to arrange."

"I'm sorry?" Dean said.

"Thinking out loud. About the Kemps now."

"Yeah," he said with a sigh. "I can't imagine how devastating it would be to lose a child. I've counseled cops who did, but to my own ears, every word I said to them sounded like so much crap. If anything happened to Gavin . . ." He stopped, as though unable to articulate the dreadful thought. Then he said quietly, "I want to be a good parent to him, Paris."

"I know."

"Because of my own dad."

"I know that, too."

"How much did Jack tell you?"

"Enough."

He had told her that Dean's relationship with his father had been volatile. Mr. Malloy had a fierce temper, and Dean usually caught the brunt of it. Sometimes his dad's rages had turned violent.

"Did your father beat you, Dean?" she asked.

"He could give me a hard time, yeah."

"Is that a gross understatement?"

He shrugged with an indifference she knew was phony. "I could take his shit," he said. "When he started in on my mom, that's what I couldn't take."

According to Jack, the defining incident had taken place when Dean's parents visited him for homecoming weekend his sophomore year at Texas Tech. During a party at the fraternity house, Dean's father had picked an argument with him. Dean tried to ignore it, but his father became increasingly vituperative and wouldn't be put off.

His mother, embarrassed for her son, tried to intervene. That's when Dean's father began disparaging her. His words were humiliating and cruel. Heedless of his friends and the other parents looking on, Dean took up the banner for his mother. His dad threw a punch. Before it was over, Dean was straddling Mr. Malloy's chest and, in Jack's words, "pounding the shit out of him."

After that night their relationship became even more antagonistic, and it remained so until his father died.

"I went a little crazy that time at Tech," he said now. "I'd never been like that before, and I haven't lost my temper like that since. If Jack and some of the others guys hadn't pulled me off him, I might have killed him. I wanted to kill him.

"I hated like hell that it happened, because of the embarrassment to my mom. But at least it made the old man think twice before he lit into her again, especially if I was around." He glanced at Paris; she'd never seen him look as vulnerable. "But it scared the hell out of me, Paris. I can't even describe it. A red rage? It consumed me, blotting out everything else.

"My dad launched into fits like that all the time. That night I learned that whatever caused him to be the way he was, it's inside me, too. It came out that once. I live in fear of it happening again."

Reaching across the console, she laid her hand on his arm. "He provoked you in the meanest way. You reacted. But that doesn't mean that you have this latent rage that can ignite in an instant. You're not like him, Dean," she said with emphasis. "You never were and never could be.

"As for Gavin, it's allowed to get angry with him. Kids anger and disappoint and make their folks crazy. That's what they do. It's inherent in being a kid. And it's all right for you to get mad at him when he does.

"In fact, Gavin might doubt that you love him if you didn't get mad at him. He needs to know you care enough to get angry. He's going to test you often, just to reassure himself that you still care." Then she laughed. "Listen to me. You're the psychologist and the parent. I'm neither."

"Everything you're saying is right, though, and I need to hear it."

She smiled at him gently. "As long as you praise him at least as much, if not more, than you punish him, you'll be fine."

He mulled it over for a moment, then winked at her. "Smart as well as beautiful. You're a dangerous woman, Paris."

"Oh yeah, that's me. A regular femme fatale."

"Maybe that's what attracted Lancy Ray Fisher. Your element of mystery appealed to his criminal instinct."

She rolled her eyes. "He wants my job."

"So he says."

"You think he's lying?"

"If he is, he's convincing. He's either sincere or a damn good con artist."

"That was my impression, too."

"What's it like to be someone's idol?"

She gave him a sad smile. "I don't recommend that anyone pattern his life after mine."

Just then his cell phone rang. He answered it with one hand. "Malloy . . . Huh, speak of the devil. No, Paris and I were just talking about him." He mouthed *Curtis* and she nodded.

"What about Lancy's home away from home?" He listened for a moment, then said, "Probably not a bad idea." Curtis had more to tell him, then Dean signed off with, "Okay, stay in touch."

After disconnecting, he updated Paris. "He 'drilled Lancy Ray good,' is the way Curtis put it. But Lancy is sticking to his story."

Officers sent to the apartment where he had been holed up reported that Lancy had been there, but it didn't appear that anyone else had.

"No sign of Janie being held captive there?" Paris asked.

"None. No amateur photo lab. Nothing naughtier than one issue of *Playboy*. So Curtis is hotter than ever for the dentist. He's about to have a heart-to-heart with Toni Armstrong."

"Hmm, what a dilemma for her. On the one hand, she wants her husband apprehended so he can get help, but on the other, she's incriminating him."

"He incriminated himself."

"I know that. I'm thinking as she will. She loves him and wants him to be healed, but if he's beyond healing, how long can she be expected to stand by her man?"

"Good question, Paris."

Too late she realized that what she had said about Toni Armstrong could apply to herself.

Dean pulled his car to a stop at the curb in front of her house. Cutting the engine, he turned to face her, ready to speak, but she cut him off before he could.

"Jack needed me."

"*I* need you."

"Hardly in the same way."

"That's right. You were with him out of obligation. I want you to choose to be with me." He held her stare for several seconds, then pushed open his car door and got out.

As they went up the walkway, she stopped to collect her mail, which had been neglected for the last two days. Once they were inside the house, she tossed the bundle onto the entry table. "Lord knows when I'll get to that. My desk at work is even—"

That was all she had time to say before Dean pulled her into his arms and kissed her. While doing so, he removed her sunglasses and dropped them on the table. Then he embraced her tightly, drawing her up against him. Immediately responsive, her arms slid beneath his to encircle his torso. She dug her fingertips into the muscles of his back.

As his mouth fused with hers, he gathered up the fabric of her skirt until he could stroke her bare thigh. Her insides melted, but she pulled her mouth free of his kiss, gasping, "Dean, I've only got an hour."

"Then that'll be a record for us. So far our sexual encounters have lasted no longer than three minutes." He buried his face in her hair. "This time, I want to see you naked."

Laughing deep in her throat, she moved her head against his. "What if you don't like what you see?"

"Not a chance in hell."

He pushed his hands into her panties and gripped her ass. She made a low sound of pleasure but the voice of reason was louder. "What if Curtis calls?"

"I've learned to live with disappointment. But all the more reason for us to get busy."

Taking her by the hand, he walked purposefully toward the bedroom, dragging her along behind him. A girlish giggle bubbled up from Paris's chest. Her heart began to race. She felt terribly wicked and wonderfully, gloriously alive.

Dean was laughing, too, as he dealt with the stubborn fabric-covered buttons on her top. "Damn these things."

She was more deft. His shirt was soon open and she pressed a kiss against the warm skin just below his left nipple, feeling his heart beating against her lips.

Finally having succeeded with the buttons, he removed her top and unclasped the front fastener of her brassiere. Then his hands were on her, kneading her breasts with his strong fingers.

She watched his face as he looked down at her. His expression was at once passionate and tender as he saw her nipples responding to the glancing touches of his fingertips. His eyes met hers for barely a second before he dipped his head and took one into his mouth.

She unbuckled his belt and lowered his zipper, then worked her hand into the waistband of his underwear. He was velvety smooth, hard, throbbing with life. She rolled her thumb across his glans and he shuddered.

"Paris, stop," he said, stepping out of her reach. "If you . . . You can't do that. I'll come. And I want this to last."

She shrugged off her bra, then reached behind her to unfasten her skirt, pushed it past her hips, and stepped out of it. Feverishly, his eyes moved over her. In one swift motion, he removed his slacks and underwear. She gazed at him with frank appreciation, but when she reached for him again, he staved her off.

Then he dropped to his knees and kissed her through the silk bikini. His hands splayed over her bottom as he held her against his face. The heat and moisture of his breath filtering through the fabric made her weak. He kissed her again. And again. She closed her eyes and used his shoulders to brace herself.

Then the silk seemed to dissolve because the barrier was no longer there. His lips were hot and quick on her a heartbeat before she felt his tongue, separating and seeking and stroking. She gave herself over to the pleasure, and it was immense.

But she retained enough control to beg him to stop when it became critical. He came to his feet and enfolded her in his arms. They held one another tightly, her breasts crushed against his chest, his sex making a deep impression in the softness of her belly.

Finally, they lay down face-to-face on her bed, virgin until now. Her hand coasted over his torso, down past his navel, and into the dense hair surrounding his sex. She drew her finger up the length of his penis. He covered her hand with his and guided it up and down. "Jesus," he groaned.

"I can't quite believe this is happening."

"Me neither." He kissed her nipple, caressed it with his tongue. "I keep thinking that I'll wake up."

"If you do, please leave me in the dream."

He separated her legs and positioned himself between them, then entered her by degrees, giving her body time to accommodate him, pausing to test each new sensation before pressing deeper, until he was sheathed snugly and completely inside her.

Soaked in pleasure, they kept from moving as long as they could endure it, but it only got better when he withdrew, then thrust into her.

chapter thirty-one

Dean shook water from his ear as he raised his cell phone to it. "Malloy."

"Curtis."

"What's up?"

"What's that noise?"

"The shower," Dean replied, turning to wink at Paris, who was rinsing the shampoo from her hair. Head thrown back, soapy water streaming over her breasts and funneling between her legs. God, she was gorgeous.

"You're showering?"

"So I can look as fresh as you. What's up?" he repeated.

"One of the other detectives has been chatting with Lancy Ray. Remember when Paris asked him why all the subterfuge, why he hadn't just come to talk to her?"

"He was shy."

"That . . . and he didn't want to move in on another guy's territory."

"What guy?"

Paris looked at him with puzzlement as she stepped from the shower. He handed her a towel.

"Stan Crenshaw," Curtis said.

That was possibly the only statement that could have diverted his attention from Paris's naked form. "Pardon me?"

"That's right. Lancy Ray was operating under the misconception that Stan and Paris are lovers."

"Where'd he get that?"

"From Crenshaw."

Dean cupped the cell phone's mouthpiece and told Paris to hurry and get dressed. His urgency must have communicated itself to her, because she rushed back into the bedroom. "Tell me," he said to Curtis.

"Crenshaw told the janitor not to bug her. Made up some bullshit about it being company policy that he was the only one allowed access to her, told him she didn't like people staring at her because of her sunglasses, that she liked the darkness for reasons that were nobody's business.

"Lancy Ray wanted to keep his job, so he went along, kept his distance and rarely even spoke to her for fear of Crenshaw getting jealous and having him canned. He said the guy was jealous of anyone who went near her."

"Why didn't Lancy tell us this the first time we talked to him?" Dean asked as he struggled to dress himself with one hand.

"He took it for granted that everyone knew they were a couple."

"My ass. There's something about Crenshaw that isn't right. I knew it the night I met him. He took that proprietary stance with me, too, but I thought he was just a prick."

"Maybe he is just a prick."

"And maybe not. I want him turned inside out, Curtis. I want to know every fucking thing about him, and I don't care who his uncle is or how much money he has."

"I hear you. This time I'm skipping Uncle Wilkins. We're going straight to the Atlanta PD, the district attorney's office, the damn governor of Georgia if necessary. One good thing, he's carrying on business as usual. He's at the radio station. Griggs and Carson are there and just called in."

"We'll be on our way momentarily. Tell those rookies to keep him there if he tries to leave. Have you checked his phone records?"

"Under way."

"Who's doing the digging into his background?"

"Rondeau volunteered."

"Rondeau." Dean made no effort to mask his displeasure.

"He's going to run a thorough computer check."

"He was supposed to have done that already."

"I told him to go deeper this time."

"Would've been nice if he'd dug deeper the first time."

"What's with you and him? I sense tension."

"He's cocky."

"That's it? You don't like his personality?"

"Something like that. Look, we gotta run."

"Maybe Paris shouldn't do her show tonight. Give us a chance to check out Crenshaw."

"Tell her that. She's determined. Besides, I'm not budging from her side. Later."

Before the detective could say more, Dean hung up and hustled Paris out of the house. Once in the car, she asked for details. "From what I could gather, his call was about Stan."

He filled her in on what Lancy Ray Fisher had divulged. She let out an incredulous laugh. "I can't believe it."

"It's not funny."

"No, it's hysterical."

"I don't think so."

"Dean," she said, giving him a fond smile, "in light of recent, ahem, events, I can understand your male posturing. I'm flattered. I wish there were a dragon you could slay for me. But don't waste the machismo on Stan, for heaven's sake. He's not Valentino."

"We don't know that."

"*I* know. He's a prick, just as you said. And it upsets me that he misled Marvin—Lancy. And God knows who else. But he hasn't got the brains or the balls to be Valentino."

"We'll soon see," he said as he whipped his car into the station parking lot.

Griggs and Carson waved from the front seat of the squad car as she unlocked the door. As usual, the building was dark and the offices deserted. Harry, the evening deejay, gave her a thumbs-up through the window of the studio as they went past. Dean had learned the layout of the building and led the way through the dim hallways.

They reached her office, to find Stan seated at her desk, feet propped on the corner of it, desultorily sorting through her mail.

"Stan Crenshaw, just the person I wanted to see," Dean said as he strode in.

Stan lowered his feet from the desk, but they'd barely touched the floor before Dean took him by the front of his shirt and hauled him up from the chair.

"Hey!" Stan objected. "What the hell?"

"We need to have a little talk, Stan."

"Dean." Paris laid her cautionary hand on his arm. He released his grip on Stan's shirt.

"You've been telling lies about Paris."

Taking umbrage, Stan pulled himself up straighter and smoothed his hand over his rumpled shirt. But he might just as well have tried to defy a redwood, and he seemed to realize it. His gaze shifted to Paris. "What's your boyfriend talking about?"

"Lancy said that you told him—"

"Who the hell is Lancy?"

"Marvin Patterson."

"His name is Lancy?"

"You told him that you and Paris were sleeping together."

His head swiveled back to Dean. "No I didn't."

"Didn't you insinuate that you and she were more than coworkers? Didn't you warn him to back off, leave her alone, and not even talk to her?"

"Because I know how she is," Stan declared.

"Is that right?"

"Yeah, that's right. I know she's a private person. She doesn't like to be bothered by other people, especially while she's concentrating on work."

"So you told him to lay off in order to protect her privacy?"

"You could put it that way."

"I don't need you to screen the people I associate with, Stan," Paris said. "I didn't ask you to and I dislike the fact that you did."

"Well, gee, I'm sorry. I was trying to be a friend."

"Only a friend? I don't think so," Dean said. "I think you've been entertaining fantasies about Paris. You've deluded yourself into believing there's a romance between you two somewhere in your future. You're jealous of any other man who expresses an interest in her, even a platonic one."

"How do you know Marvin's interest is platonic?"

"He said it was."

"Oh, and he's to be believed over me? A janitor who's using an alias?" He made a scoffing snort. "You're the one who's delusional, *Doctor*." He headed for the door, but Dean's next words halted him.

"That possessiveness could be a strong motivator."

Stan turned around quickly. "For what?"

"Let's see, creating an ugly situation for which Paris would be partially blamed. Placing her job at risk. Placing her life in jeopardy. Shall I go on?"

"Are you talking about that Valentino business?" Stan asked angrily. "Paris brought that on herself."

"I see. It's her fault that Valentino kidnapped and murdered a seventeen-year-old girl."

"A girl who went asking for trouble."

With deceptive calm, Dean sat down on a corner of her desk. "Then your opinion of women is basically low?"

"I didn't say that."

"No, you didn't come right out and say it, but I sense a large chunk of hostility against the fairer sex lodged deep inside your psyche, Stan. Like a seed caught between two molars. It bugs you like hell, but you can't get it out."

"Wooooo." Stan waggled his fingers an inch from Dean's face. "Don't try that psychological hocus-pocus voodoo on me. There's nothing wrong with me."

Dean's jaw bunched with anger, but his voice remained calm. "So I'm to believe that all your dealings with women have been perfectly normal and problem free?"

"Has any man's dealings with women been perfectly normal and problem free? Have yours, Malloy?" He cut his eyes to Paris. "I think not."

"You're not Dean," Paris said quietly. "He doesn't have your history."

His mocking smugness vanished. In the next heartbeat, he was seething. "Did you tell him about the harassment charge?"

Dean turned to her. "The *what?*"

"At his previous job, a female employee accused Stan of sexual harassment."

Dean gave her a look that said he couldn't believe she hadn't shared this information with him before now. She realized that she'd been wrong not to. Probably she also should have told him about Stan's promiscuous parents and his overbearing uncle's cruelty.

Dean turned back to him. "Obviously you do have issues with women, Stan."

"She was the office whore!" he exclaimed. "She had slept with every other guy who worked there. She gave head to the anchorman under the desk during a newscast. She kept coming on to me and when I responded, she turned into a vestal virgin."

"Why?"

"Because she was more greedy than horny. She saw a way to get her hands on some of my family's money. She cried foul and my uncle paid her to shut up and go away."

Dean assimilated that, then said, "Let's go back to when you 'responded' to her."

"Wait, how come I have to answer your questions?"

"Because I'm a cop."

"Or because you've been in Paris's pants yourself?"

Dean's eyes narrowed dangerously. "Because if you don't answer my questions I'm going to take you downtown and lock you up until you get talkative. That's my official, professional answer. Off the record, my personal answer is that if you say anything like that about Paris again, I'm going to take you outside and smear some of your pretty face on the parking lot."

"Are you threatening me?"

"You bet your skinny ass I am. Now stop dicking around and tell me what I want to know."

Despite what he'd said, Dean wasn't performing a hundred

percent in an official capacity. He wasn't interrogating Stan in the calm, confidence-inspiring manner he usually used with suspects. But Stan probably wouldn't have responded to his usual approach. Taking a harder line with him seemed to be working.

Stan glared at Dean, fired drop-dead looks at Paris, but crossed his arms over his chest as though to protect himself. "I'm going to file charges of police brutality. My uncle will—"

"Your uncle will have more than me to worry about if it turns out you're Valentino."

"I'm not! Don't you listen?"

"When that woman said no to you, did you go ahead and complete the act?"

Stan's eyes darted between them. "No. I mean, yeah. Sort of."

"Well, which is it? Yes, no, or sort of?"

"I didn't force her, if that's what you're getting at."

"But you completed the act?"

"I told you she was the—"

"'Office whore.' So she was asking for it."

"Right."

"For you to rape her."

"You keep putting words in my mouth!" Stan cried.

"And you're going downtown with me. Right now."

Stan backed away from him. "You can't . . ." He looked frantically at Paris. "Do something. If you let this happen, my uncle will have your job."

She didn't even consider questioning Dean. Frankly, she was now afraid of Stan. Perhaps she had misjudged him. She had always thought of him as a worthless, maladjusted screwup, but basically harmless. Maybe he *was* capable of committing the crimes against Janey Kemp.

If he proved not to be Valentino, she would have to face Wilkins Crenshaw's wrath. Undoubtedly it *would* cost her her job. But she would rather lose her job than her life.

Dean took Stan by the arm and turned him toward the door. Stan began to struggle and Dean had his hands full trying to restrain him without handcuffs. When his cell phone rang, he tossed it to Paris so she could answer it for him.

"Hello?"

"Paris?"

She could barely hear over the crude invective Stan was screaming at Dean. "Gavin?"

"I've gotta talk to my dad, Paris. It's an emergency."

Gavin had been whiling away his time watching television, which was the only privilege his dad hadn't revoked. He'd put his favorite movie into the VCR, but the challenges confronting Mel Gibson seemed tame compared to what was happening in his own life.

He was worried about his dad and Paris.

He hadn't felt nearly as dismissive as he'd acted when his dad said that Valentino might come after them. This guy really could intend to harm them and didn't seem afraid to try. He shouldn't be underestimated. Who'd have thought he would murder Janey?

When the house phone rang, he welcomed the distraction. He rushed to answer and did so without even checking the caller ID. "Hello?"

"Why haven't you been answering your cell phone?"

"Who is this?"

"Melissa."

Melissa Hatcher? Oh, great. "I haven't had my cell on. It's been kinda hectic—"

"Gavin, you gotta help me."

Was she crying? "What's the matter?"

"I need to see you, but there's a cop car parked in front of your house, so I drove on past. You gotta meet me."

"I'm not supposed to leave."

"Gavin, this is no bullshit," she fairly shrieked.

"Just come over."

"With cops there? I don't think so."

"Why not? Are you high?"

She blubbered and sniffed, then said, "Can I sneak in through the back?"

He didn't want any part of her crisis, whatever it was. Having to take a lie detector test would clear up a guy's thinking and rearrange his priorities, but quick. He'd made a promise to himself that if he came out of this mess reasonably unscathed, he would cultivate a new circle of friends.

Another major infraction, and he could find himself on his way back to Houston. He didn't want to return to his mother's house. Now that things were square between him and his dad, he looked forward to staying with him, maybe until he graduated from high school.

It was definitely in his best interests to tell Melissa he was busy and hang up. But she sounded really strung out. "Okay," he said reluctantly. "Park on the street behind us and walk between the houses. There isn't a fence. I'll let you in through the patio door. How soon can you be here?"

"Two minutes."

He checked to make certain that both policemen were in the squad car at the front curb, and that one wasn't making his hourly tour around the house, then went into the kitchen and watched for Melissa. When she emerged from the hedge of oleander bushes that separated the two properties, she looked like a trick-or-treater.

Tears had left tracks of black eye makeup down her cheeks. Her clothes looked more like a costume than anything a normal person would wear. It was a mystery to him how anyone could run in the platform sandals she was wearing, but she managed. She skirted the pool and clopped across the limestone terrace. He opened the sliding glass door and she flung herself against him.

He pulled her inside and closed the door. Supporting her against his side, he half-carried her into the den, where he lowered her into a chair. While she babbled incoherently, she continued to clutch at him.

"Melissa, calm down. I can't understand a thing you're saying. Tell me what's going on."

She pointed to the wet bar across the room. "I gotta have something to drink first."

When she tried to get up, Gavin pushed her back down. "Forget it. You can have some water."

He took a bottle from the mini-fridge, and while she drank from it, he remarked, "You're a freak show. What happened?"

"I was . . . was with him."

"Who?"

"The guy . . . the . . . the dentist. That Armstrong."

Gavin felt his jaw drop open. "What? Where?"

"Where? Uh . . ."

She looked around the room as though Brad Armstrong might be standing in a corner of it. Gavin wanted to slap her. How could anybody be so damned dense?

"*Where,* Melissa?"

"Don't holler at me." She rubbed her forehead as though trying to massage the answer out. "A motel. I think the sign out front had a cowboy, or a saddle, something like that on it."

A motel in Austin with a western theme. That narrowed it down to several hundred, he thought caustically. "If you met him there—"

"I didn't. He picked me up in a bar on the lake and drove me there. I was shit-faced. I'd been drowning my sorrow, you know, over Janey, with tequila shots. He showed up, bought me a drink."

"And you went to a motel with him?"

"It wasn't like I didn't know him. I was with him a few nights ago and we hit it off."

"Where was this?"

"That, uh, oh, you know the spot. Where we all go sometimes."

He anxiously motioned for her to continue.

"We did it in his car."

"What kind of car?"

"Today or then? They were different."

"Today."

"Red, I think. Or maybe blue. I wasn't paying much attention either time. He was nice to me. Really got off on my pierced nipple. It's new." She grinned at him and proudly raised her top.

"Nice."

Actually he thought she was grotesque. He'd never liked her

much, had never been attracted to her, but just then, she repulsed him. He also began to question whether she was really hysterical or if this was all an act, a ploy to get inside his house, or more. She was jealous of Janey and could be trying to get some of the attention her murdered friend was receiving.

He pulled her top back into place. "Are you sure it was Brad Armstrong you were with, Melissa?"

"Don't you believe me? Would I go out looking like this on purpose?"

She had a point. "When did you learn that this was the guy the police are looking for?"

"We drove to this motel. Got in bed. He's humping away when I happen to glance across the room at the TV set. It was on, but the sound was muted. And his picture is on the screen. Big as Dallas. Everybody and his dog is out looking for him, and he's balling *me*."

"What did you do?"

"What do you think? I got him off me. I told him I had to leave, remembered I was late for an appointment. He put up an argument. Tried to talk me into staying. The more he talked, the crazier he got. First he called me a tease, then he said I was a cruel bitch, then he totally wigged out. Grabbed me and shook me and said I could go when he was good and finished with me."

She held out her arms to show Gavin the bruises beginning to appear on her biceps. "I'm telling you, Gavin, he went completely nuts. Slapped me, called me a cunt, said I was as much a cunt as Janey Kemp had been. That capped it for me. I started screaming bloody murder, and he let me go. I grabbed my clothes and hoofed it."

"How long ago?"

"Since I ran out? Maybe an hour. I flagged down a guy in a pickup truck and hitched a ride back to my car, then I drove straight here, saw the cop car. All this time I'm trying to reach you on your cell phone. Finally remembered your home number. You know the rest." She gave him an imploring look. "I'm in a bad way here, Gavin. Just one shot of something, please?"

"I said no." He squatted down in front of her. "Did you talk to him about Janey?"

"You think I'm stupid? I didn't want to wind up like her."

"Did you see any pictures of her around?"

"He had the newspapers."

"Any regular photographs?"

"No. But when I first got there, I wasn't looking, and later all I wanted to do was split."

"You said that when you met him earlier this week, he looked familiar. Had you ever seen him with Janey?"

"I'm not sure. Could be I've just seen him lurking in the crowd. He visits the Sex Club website and—"

"He said that?"

"Yeah. And the other night he had this huge stash of porn. He likes to party."

When Gavin reached for the cordless phone and began punching in numbers, she sprang from the chair. "Who're you calling?"

"My dad."

She grabbed the phone from him. "He's a cop. I don't want to get involved with the police. No thank you."

"Then why'd you come to me?"

"I needed a friend. I needed help. I thought I could get it from you. Of course, I didn't know you had dorked out since the last time I saw you. No booze, no—"

"There's a manhunt on for this guy." Angrily Gavin snatched the phone back. "If he's the one who killed Janey, he's gotta be caught."

Her facial features collapsed and she began to whimper and wring her hands. "Don't be mad at me, Gavin. I know they've gotta catch him, but jeez . . ."

He softened. "Melissa, the reason you came to me, out of all your friends, is because you knew I would call my dad. Deep down, you wanted to do the right thing."

She pulled her lower lip through her teeth. "Okay. Maybe. But give me time to flush some stuff. On top of everything else, I don't need to get busted for possession. Where's the bathroom?"

He pointed her toward the powder room in the hallway even as he redialed his dad's cell phone number. It rang four times before it was answered.

He could barely hear the hello above the yelling and what sounded like scuffling in the background.

"Paris?"

"Gavin?"

"I've gotta talk to my dad, Paris. It's an emergency."

chapter thirty-two

"This is Paris Gibson. I hope you're planning to spend the next four hours with me here on 101.3. I'll be playing classic love songs and taking your requests. The phone lines are open. Call me.

"Let's start off our time together with a hit from the Stylistics. It's what falling in love should be about, 'You Make Me Feel Brand New.'"

She shut off her mike. The phone lines were already lighting up. The first caller requested B. J. Thomas's "Hooked on a Feeling." "Since tonight's theme is how we feel when we fall in love."

"Thanks for calling, Angie. It'll be up next."

"'Bye, Paris."

She was going through her normal routine, although tonight wasn't at all normal or routine. It had been almost an hour since Dean had left in a rush to meet Gavin and Melissa Hatcher at the downtown police station.

Immediately after hanging up with Gavin, Dean had dialed Curtis and capsulized Melissa's story. Curtis milked him for information and immediately acted on it.

"It shouldn't be long till we have him in custody," Dean told Paris after concluding his conversation with Curtis. "We can start at the bar where he picked up Melissa. She has an approximate idea of how long it took Armstrong to drive from there to the motel, so that gives us a radius to search within. It's a wide area, but not as wide as before."

Paris had asked him if someone had told Toni Armstrong about this development.

He nodded somberly. "Curtis was with her when he took my call. Their attorney had joined her there." Then he hugged Paris tightly. "He'll soon be in custody, and you'll be safe. It'll be over."

"Except for the memory of what he did to Janey."

"Yeah." He sighed his regret, but his mind was clicking along at a mile a minute, in cop modality. "Curtis says the squad car remains outside until we've got Armstrong. Besides, Griggs practically considers himself your personal bodyguard." He looked over at Stan, who'd been momentarily forgotten. "I guess this lets you off the hook, Crenshaw."

"You're going to regret the way you treated me."

"I already do. I wish I'd kicked your ass while I had a good excuse." He kissed Paris swiftly on the mouth, then rushed out.

Stan followed him from her office, leaving in a huff. She let him go without saying anything. He would pout, but he would survive, and in the meantime she had a program to prepare for. Making amends with Stan could wait until she had more time and he was in a more receptive mood.

Now, at half past the hour, she engaged her mike. "I'll be back after the break with more music. If you have a request, or just something on your mind you'd like to share, call me."

She cut her mike and, sensing a presence, turned on her swivel stool. Stan was standing directly behind her. "I didn't hear you come in."

"I sneaked in."

"Why?"

"I figured as long as you and your boyfriend regard me as a creep, I should behave like one."

It was a typically childish, peevish, Stan-like thing to say. "I'm sorry your feelings were hurt by Dean's allegations, Stan. But admit it. For a while there, you looked like a plausible suspect."

"For rape and murder?"

"I said I was sorry."

"I thought you knew me better than that."

"I thought I knew you better, too," she exclaimed, losing patience with him. "If your behavior had been above reproach, no one would have suspected you. But aside from the sexual harassment charge in Florida, you've been lying about me, telling people we were lovers."

"Only Marvin, or whatever his name is. And not in so many words."

"Whatever you said, you managed to get your message across. Why would you lead anyone to believe that?"

"Why do you think?"

His voice cracked and he suddenly appeared to be on the verge of tears. The emotional display made her embarrassed for him. "I had no idea you felt that way about me, Stan."

"Well, you should have, shouldn't you?"

"I never looked at you as a . . . in a romantic context."

"Maybe those damn sunglasses keep you from seeing what should be obvious."

"Stan—"

"You only saw me as an incompetent whipping boy for my uncle, and a fag."

It was an uncomfortable truth that she couldn't deny, but she did apologize. "I'm sorry."

"For godsake, that makes three times you've said you're sorry. But you don't really mean it. If you wanted to change the way you feel about me, you could. But you don't want to. Especially now that you've got your boyfriend back. He slobbers over you, doesn't he? And you—who have always maintained a hands-off policy—you're suddenly in heat.

"I think you came here straight from bed, didn't you? When have you ever come to work with wet hair? Having fun, Paris? Isn't it nice there's no inconvenient fiancé to eliminate this time?"

"That's a tacky and extremely insensitive thing to say."

Leaning toward her, he smirked. "Did I prick your conscience?"

She had to curl her fingers into fists to keep from slapping him. "You don't know anything about that or about me. This conversation is over, Stan."

She turned back to the control board, checked the countdown clock, looked at the blinking telephone lines. She depressed one of them. "This is Paris."

"Hi, Paris. My name's Georgia."

"Hello, Georgia." She breathed slowly and silently through her mouth in an effort to calm her anger and focus on the business at hand.

"I've been having some doubts about my boyfriend," her caller said.

Paris listened while the young woman whined about her boyfriend's fear of commitment. During the monologue, Paris glanced over her shoulder. The studio was empty. As when Stan had come in, he'd left just as stealthily.

"We've got him!" Curtis shouted from his cubicle in the CIB. "They'll have him here in ten minutes."

Dean met the detective in the narrow passageway between offices. "Did he put up any resistance?"

"The arresting officers got the motel manager to open the door of his room. Armstrong was sitting on the bed, his head in his hands, crying like a baby. Kept saying over and over, 'What have I done?'"

Dean moved toward the exit. "I want to tell Gavin."

"Thank him for me. The lead he gave us narrowed the playing field considerably. And stick around, will ya? I'd like for you to be in on the interrogation."

"I plan to be. I'll be right back."

Gavin and Melissa Hatcher were seated on the same bench outside the CIB where he and Paris had been sitting . . . when was it? Only yesterday? God, so much had happened since then, with the case, with them.

As the double doors swung shut behind him, he gave Gavin and Melissa a thumbs-up. "He's just been arrested. They're bringing him in now. You did well, son." He placed his arm across Gavin's shoulders and gave him a brief hug. "I'm proud of you."

Gavin blushed modestly. "I'm just glad they caught him."

Turning to the girl, Dean said, "Thank you, too, Melissa. Coming forward took a lot of guts."

When Dean had arrived at the police station, Melissa and Gavin were already with Curtis. He and several other detectives were listening to her detailed account of the time she'd spent with Brad Armstrong.

Although she seemed to enjoy being the center of attention, she had looked a fright. Since then, she had washed the streaked makeup off her face and brushed her hair so that it no longer radiated from her head like spikes on a medieval mace. Someone, probably a policewoman, had located a cardigan sweater for her to put on over her sheer halter top, which had proved to be a distraction even to seasoned detectives.

Now she beamed at Dean's compliment, but then wet her lips nervously. "Do I have to see him?"

"We need you to officially identify him as the man who assaulted you."

"It wasn't exactly assault. I was wasted, but I knew what I was doing when I left the bar with him."

"You're a minor. He had sex with you. That's a crime. He also struck you and tried to hold you against your will. We can hold him on those charges while we're waiting for Janey's autopsy report from the medical examiner. I know it won't be easy for you to see him again, but your help is essential. Have your parents arrived?"

"Not yet. They freaked out when I called them, but they weren't as pissed as I would have thought, I guess since I coulda turned up dead, too. Is it okay if Gavin stays with me?"

"If you want him to. Gavin?"

He raised his shoulders in a shrug of consent. "Sure."

"Okay then, Dr. Malloy," Melissa said. "Bring on the pervert. I'll stay as long as you need me."

"This is Paris."

"It's me."

Merely the sound of Dean's voice caused her heart to flutter and brought on a silly smile. "Did you lose the hot-line number I gave you? Why are you calling on this line?"

"I thought I'd see what it was like to be an ordinary listener."

"You might be a listener, but you're certainly not ordinary."

"No? Glad to hear it." There was a smile behind his voice, too, but it soon turned serious. "They've arrested Armstrong. He's due here any minute."

"Thank God." She was relieved, but her heart immediately went out to his wife. "Have you seen Toni?"

"Just a few minutes ago. She's distraught, but I think she's glad we got him before he could hurt anyone else."

"Or himself."

"The possibility of suicide had occurred to me, too. You're getting as good at my job as I am."

"Not even close. Oops, hang on a sec. I've got to do a station ID." She dispatched her business, then came back on the line. "Okay, I've got a few minutes."

"I won't keep you. I promised to call as soon as I knew something."

"And I appreciate it. My program will go a lot smoother now that I know he's been apprehended. I couldn't concentrate, and every time I answered a phone line, I held my breath, afraid it would be him."

"You don't have to worry about that now."

"Is Gavin still with you?"

"He's keeping Melissa company. What he did was great, huh?"

"I thought so."

"Me, too. Shows maturity and a sense of responsibility."

"And trust in you, Dean. That's the most significant breakthrough."

"After a few derailments, I think we're on the right track now."

"I'm sure of it."

"Speaking of misguided youths, Lancy Ray Fisher was released."

"I'm thinking of hiring him."

"I beg your pardon?"

She laughed at his shocked tone. "I've never worked with a

producer, although management has offered me one. It would be a good way for Lancy to learn, get some experience."

"What would Stan think about it?"

"It's not his decision to make."

"Any backlash over what happened earlier?"

She hesitated, then said, "He's brooding, but he'll get over it."

Dean had enough on his mind without her telling him about her most recent altercation with Stan. It had made her uneasy. After everything that had been said, could they mend fences and resettle into a comfortable working relationship? Unlikely.

However, the prospect of dissidence in the workplace didn't upset her as it would have even a week ago. Then, her life had revolved around her job. Anything that affected it had a profound effect on her, because that's all she had. That had changed.

As though following her thoughts, Dean said, "I want to spend the night with you."

The declaration evoked memories of the abbreviated but precious time they'd spent in bed earlier this evening and sent a tingle through her all the way down to her toes. "I'm supposed to disconnect callers who say things like that."

He chuckled. "I want to, but unfortunately I don't know how long I'll be needed here."

"Do what you need to do. You know I understand."

"I know," he said, sighing. "But tomorrow night is a damn long time to wait."

She felt the same. With as much professionalism as she could muster, she said, "Caller, do you have a request?"

"In fact I do."

"I'm listening."

"Love me, Paris."

She closed her eyes and held her breath for a moment, then said softly but emphatically, "I do."

"I love you, too."

John Rondeau took the stairs rather than waiting for the elevator. His email exchanges with a counterpart in the Atlanta PD had yielded new information on Stan Crenshaw, which he was eager to share with Curtis. Rather than forwarding it by email or telephoning, Rondeau wanted to deliver it in person.

But when he reached the CIB, it was humming with activity. For the number of personnel bustling about, it could have been high noon rather than nearing midnight. As a policewoman barreled past him, he hooked his hand in her elbow, bringing her to an abrupt halt. "What's going on?"

"Where've you been?" she said, frowning at him as she extricated her arm. "We got Armstrong. They're about to bring him in."

Rondeau spotted Dean Malloy in conversation with Toni Armstrong and a gray-suited man who had "lawyer" stamped all over him. He found Curtis in his cubicle, hunched over his desk phone and rubbing his palm back and forth across his burred head.

He was saying, "No, Judge, he hasn't confessed, but there's a lot of circumstantial evidence pointing to him. We're hoping the autopsy will produce some DNA, although the body was washed—"

He stopped speaking, apparently having been interrupted. He rubbed his head a little more briskly. "Yes, I'm well aware of how long DNA testing takes, but maybe when Armstrong knows that we're submitting his for a possible match, he'll crack. I certainly will, Judge. By all means. As soon as I know more. My condolences again to Mrs. Kemp. Good night."

He hung up, stared at the receiver for several seconds, then looked up at Rondeau. "What?"

Rondeau raised the file folder he'd brought with him. "Stan Crenshaw. The guy has been a deviant since grade school. Raising girls' skirts. Indecent exposure. Interesting reading."

"I'm sure it is, but he's not Valentino."

"So what do I do with this? Ditch it?"

Standing, Curtis shot his monogrammed cuffs and smoothed down his necktie. "Leave it on my desk."

"Somebody should look at it," Rondeau insisted.

A sudden shift in the atmosphere indicated that something momentous was happening beyond the walls of Curtis's cubicle.

Rondeau followed him out. They wended their way into the center of the CIB.

Rondeau recognized Dr. Brad Armstrong from the family snapshots taken off the CD. Flanking him were two uniformed policemen. Handcuffed, he stood with his head down, his aspect that of a defeated man. He was ushered into an interrogation room. Malloy, the attorney, and Toni Armstrong crowded in. Curtis was the last to enter the room. He closed the door behind him.

Rondeau, feeling rebuffed, tapped the folder against his open palm. If Curtis thought he had Valentino, then he should probably just let it drop and forget Stan Crenshaw.

But what if, after interrogating Armstrong, Curtis determined they had the wrong guy? What if the result of the autopsy cast doubt on or even refuted the circumstantial evidence against him? What if his DNA didn't match any samples they collected from Janey's remains, if they even could since her body had been chemically cleansed?

Reaching a decision, Rondeau left the CIB in a hurry. As he went through the double doors, he spotted Gavin Malloy and a girl seated together on a bench in the vestibule. He had missed seeing them when he came in. From the open staircase, he had turned right to enter the CIB. They were seated to the left of the stairs. At the sound of the doors closing, the girl turned her head toward him.

Oh, shit!

He didn't know her name, but he'd seen her plenty of times. If she recognized him, he'd be up shit creek.

John Rondeau made a dash for the stairs.

"Hey, Gavin, who's that guy?"

"Huh?"

The past few days had caught up with him. His head had been resting against the wall, and he'd been dozing.

Melissa nudged his elbow. "Hurry! Look!"

"Where?"

He raised his head, blinked open his gritty eyes, and looked in the direction of Melissa's pointing finger. Through the metal railing of the staircase, he caught a glimpse of John Rondeau's head just before he cleared the landing below and disappeared.

"His name is John Rondeau."

"Is he a cop?"

"Computer crimes," he muttered. "It was him who ratted out the Sex Club."

"Seriously? Because I've seen him somewhere. In fact, I think I might've balled him."

Terrific, Gavin thought. If she placed Rondeau as someone who hung out and partied with the high school crowd, then blabbed about it, Rondeau might think he was the one who'd fingered him.

"No way. He's got one of those faces that always remind you of somebody else." It wasn't a very good explanation, but it was all he could think of.

Melissa frowned thoughtfully. "Guess I'd have to see his cock to know for sure. But I could swear . . ."

Just then they heard a ping signaling the arrival of an elevator. They turned in time to see a nice-looking, well-dressed couple step around the corner and into their view.

Melissa stood up.

"Your folks?" Gavin asked, surprised by how presentable and respectable they appeared. He'd been expecting the Osbornes, not June and Ward Cleaver.

Awkwardly, Melissa wobbled toward them on her platform sandals, self-consciously tugging down her short skirt. "Hi, Mom. Hi, Dad."

Their arrival couldn't have been better timed. Gavin wanted nothing more to do with Rondeau, and that extended even to talking about him. He hated being the keeper of the cop's dirty little secret, but, remembering Rondeau's threat toward his dad, Gavin would carry that secret to his grave.

chapter thirty-three

"I'm sorry, Toni. I'm sorry. Will you ever be able to forgive me?"

Dr. Brad Armstrong seemed more concerned about his wife's opinion of him than he did about the serious allegations being made against him, which could potentially cost him his life. He appealed to her plaintively and somewhat pathetically.

"Let's get through this first, Brad. There'll be plenty of time later to talk about forgiveness."

She was stoic, her voice calm, which was amazing in light of the ordeal confronting her. She was probably being held together with the emotional equivalent of Scotch tape, but she remained intact. Dean gave her a "hang in there" nod as she left the inter- rogation room, leaving her husband alone with him, the attorney, and Curtis.

Curtis identified everyone present for the benefit of the tape recorder, then began by telling Bradley Armstrong everything they knew about him and why they considered him a suspect in the kidnapping and murder of Janey Kemp.

"I didn't kidnap that girl."

His earnest denial didn't impress Curtis. "We'll get to that. First let's talk about the time you molested Paris Gibson." Armstrong grimaced. "I see you remember the incident," Curtis remarked. "To this day you resent Ms. Gibson, don't you?"

"She got me fired from a lucrative practice."

"Do you deny touching her inappropriately?"

He lowered his head and shook it.

"Answer audibly for the recorder, please."

"No, I don't deny it."

"Have you called her radio show recently?"

"No."

"Ever?"

"I may have."

"If I were you, I wouldn't hedge on the easy stuff, Dr. Armstrong," Curtis advised. "Have you ever called her while she's on the air? Yes or no?"

The dentist raised his head and sighed. "Yes, I called her, said something rude, and hung up."

"When was this?"

"Long time ago. Shortly after we moved to Austin and I realized she had a radio program."

"Only that once?" Dean asked.

"I swear."

"Did you know that there was some involvement between Ms. Gibson, Dr. Malloy, and a man named Jack Donner?"

Dean looked at Curtis and was on the verge of asking him where the hell that question had come from, but Armstrong answered before he had a chance. "It was on the news down in Houston."

Then Dean realized the validity of the detective's question. Valentino had said Jack's death was on their consciences, indicating that he was acquainted with their history.

"When you called her, where did you call from?"

"My house. My cell phone. I don't remember, but I certainly never called her about Janey Kemp."

Curtis had learned that Armstrong's cell and home phone records didn't list any calls to the radio station, but he'd only requested records going back several months. Armstrong could be telling the truth, or he could have used a public telephone to make the Valentino calls, or he could have an untraceable cell.

Curtis asked if he had disguised his voice when he called.

"No need. She would never have recognized my voice. We only met that . . . that once."

"Did you identify yourself to her?" Curtis asked.

"No. I just said, 'Screw you,' or something to that effect, then hung up."

"Where'd you get Valentino?"

He glanced at his lawyer, then at Dean, as though seeking an explanation.

"What?"

"Valentino," Curtis repeated.

The news stories had cited Paris Gibson's telephone warnings as a key element in the case, but the caller's name had been withheld to prevent chronic confessors from gumming up the investigation with false leads.

"You pick that name up from the silent movie actor?" Curtis asked. "And why seventy-two hours? Did you pluck that deadline from thin air? Why not forty-eight, which is closer to what it turned out to be, isn't it?"

Armstrong turned to his attorney. "What's he talking about?"

"Never mind. We'll come back to that," Curtis said. "Tell us about Janey Kemp. Where did you meet her?"

With his attorney closely monitoring every word, Armstrong admitted that he'd frequented the Sex Club website and had eventually begun joining its members at the specified meeting places. "I invented reasons to leave the house."

"You lied to your wife."

"That's not a crime," the attorney said.

"But engaging in sexual activity with minors is," Curtis fired back. "When did you first meet Janey, Dr. Armstrong?"

"I don't remember the exact date. A couple months ago."

"What were the circumstances?"

"I already knew who she was. I'd noticed her, asked around, and learned that her user name for the website was pussinboots. I'd been reading the messages she left on the boards, knew she was . . ." He stammered over his next word, then rephrased. "I knew she was sexually active and willing to do just about anything."

"In other words, she was prey to predators like you."

The lawyer ordered him not to respond.

Curtis waved a semi-apologetic dismissal of the statement. "The night you met Janey, did you have sex with her?"

"Yes."

"Janey Kemp was seventeen," the attorney stipulated.

"Barely," Curtis said.

In an anguished voice, Armstrong said, "You've got to understand, that's what these girls were there for. They came looking for it. I never had to coerce a single one of them into having sex with me. In fact, one—not Janey, another one—charged me a hundred dollars for five minutes of her time, then went right on to her next customer. She said she was working toward a Vuitton handbag."

"You have proof of this?"

"Oh, sure, she gave me a receipt," Armstrong replied sarcastically.

Curtis failed to see the humor in this and remained stone-faced. Dean believed the dentist was telling the truth about the prostitution because it coincided with what Gavin had told him.

Curtis continued the questioning. "On the night you met Janey, you had sex with her where?"

"In a motel."

"Where you were found tonight?"

He nodded. "I keep an efficiency apartment there."

"Which you rent for that purpose?"

"Don't answer," the attorney instructed.

"Did you take pictures of Janey?" Curtis asked.

"Pictures?"

"Photographs. Different in subject matter from the kind you take of your family vacations," the detective added dryly.

"Maybe. I don't remember."

Curtis narrowed his gaze on him. "Your den of iniquity is being searched even as we speak. Why don't you tell us what we might find and save us all some time here."

"I have some porno magazines. Videos. I've taken pictures of . . . of women on occasion, so maybe, yeah, there might be some pictures of Janey."

"You develop these pictures there in your makeshift darkroom?"

He looked genuinely mystified. "I don't know how to develop film."

"Then where'd you have your pictures of 'women' developed?"

"I send the film to a lab out of town."

"What lab?"

"It doesn't have a name. Just a post office box. I can give you that."

"Let me guess. This is a film-developing outfit that caters to specialized customers like you?"

Shamefaced, he nodded. "I don't use it often, but I have."

Armstrong's answers to this line of questioning were inconsistent with what Janey had told Gavin about her new boyfriend's passion for photography. Either he was telling the truth or he knew how to lie convincingly.

Curtis must have thought so, too, because for the time being he let the subject drop and asked about the last time Armstrong had seen Janey.

"It was three nights ago. I guess it was the night she disappeared."

"Where'd you see her?"

"At a spot on the shore of Lake Travis."

"You went there for the specific purpose of meeting her?"

Armstrong answered, "Yes," before his attorney could caution him not to. Too late Armstrong saw his lawyer's raised hand. "It's not a crime to make and keep a date," he said to him.

The lawyer addressed Curtis. "I'm only agreeing to let my client go into detail here because he adamantly denies anything beyond having congress with the victim, who was a consenting adult. This isn't to be considered a confession to any allegation of kidnapping or murder."

Curtis nodded and motioned for Armstrong to continue.

"Janey was waiting for me in her car."

"What time was that?" Dean asked, remembering that Gavin had said that he, too, had been in Janey's car and that she had seemed to be waiting for someone else to join her.

"I can't remember exactly," Armstrong said. "Around ten, maybe."

Curtis asked, "What did you do in her car?"

"We had sex."

"Intercourse?"

"Fellatio."

"Did you use a condom?"

"Yes."

"Then what happened?"

"I . . . I wanted to stay with her for a while longer, but she said there was something she had to do. I think she was waiting to see someone else."

"Like who?"

"Another man. She insisted I go on my way, but she promised to see me the following night, same place, same time. When I left, she was in her car, listening to the CD player. I went the next night. She wasn't there. I didn't know about her disappearance until I read about it and saw her picture in the newspaper."

"Why didn't you come forward then?" Curtis asked.

"I was scared. Wouldn't you be?"

"I don't know. Tell me. Would I?"

"I'd violated the terms of my probation. A girl I'd had sex with several times had gone missing." He raised his shoulders in a gesture of helplessness. "You do the math."

Curtis snickered. "I've done it, Dr. Armstrong. My tally says you wanted more of Janey than she was willing to give you that night. Things got rough. You tend to get rough when a woman doesn't give you what you want when you want it, isn't that right?"

"Sometimes I get angry, but I'm working through it."

"Not fast enough. In the meantime, your anger got the best of you, and before you knew it, you were choking Janey. Maybe she died right then, maybe she just became unconscious and died later.

"In any case, you panicked. You took her to that swell room you've got in that lousy motel and tried to figure out what to do with her, but in the end you rolled her body into the lake and then crawled into your hidey-hole and hoped to God you'd get away with killing her."

"No! I swear I didn't force her into doing anything, and I sure as hell didn't murder her."

The attorney was massaging his eye sockets as though wondering how in the hell he was going to construct a defense out of his client's frantic denials. Curtis looked as stern and unyielding as a cigar store Indian.

"I don't think you did it intentionally," Dean said quietly.

Armstrong turned to him with the desperate expression of a drowning man in search of a lifeline.

The role of good cop fell to him because he played it well. Let Curtis be the hard-ass. For the next several minutes, Dean would be Brad Armstrong's best friend and only source of hope. He folded his arms on the table and leaned into it.

"Did you like Janey, Brad? I assume it's okay if I call you Brad."

"Sure."

"Did you like her? As a person, I mean."

"Truthfully, not much. Don't get me wrong, she was something else." Suddenly cautious, he glanced at his attorney.

"Sexy and willing?" Dean prompted. "The kind of girl we all wanted to date in high school?"

"She was just like that. But I didn't particularly like her personality."

"Why not?"

"Like most girls with her looks, she was conceited and self-absorbed. She treated people like dirt. You either played her way or she didn't play at all."

"Did she ever turn you down?"

"Only once."

"For another guy?"

He shook his head. "She said she was PMSing and not in the mood."

Pal to pal, Dean smiled at him. "We've all been there."

Then he sat back and folded his arms across his chest, his smile reversing into a frown. "The problem is, Brad, that most guys would blow it off. Oh, there'd be some frustration and maybe some hard cussing, but eventually your average guy would go have a beer or two, watch a ball game, maybe even find a more accommodating girl. But you take rejection hard. You can't tolerate it. Which causes you to lash out, doesn't it?"

He swallowed hard and mumbled, "Sometimes."

"Like you did tonight with Melissa Hatcher."

"I haven't had time to confer with my client about Melissa Hatcher," the lawyer said. "So I can't allow him to talk about her."

"He doesn't have to say a word," Dean said. "I'm going to talk to him." Then, without waiting for the attorney's permission, he continued. "This girl advertises the merchandise. She's advertised it to me, to Sergeant Curtis here, and all the detectives in this unit. Any man would take the way she dresses as a 'come and get it.'"

"So who could blame me for—"

"Do not say a word," Brad's lawyer snapped.

Ignoring the lawyer, Dean kept his attention riveted on Armstrong. "Unfortunately for you, Brad, the state of Texas blames you. If you penetrate the sexual organ, mouth, or anus of a child, it's called 'aggravated sexual assault.' Correct?" he asked, turning to the attorney, who nodded curtly.

"How old is Melissa?" Brad asked.

"Sixteen until next February," Dean told him. "She claims you had sexual contact and intercourse."

"What if . . . what if . . . it was consensual?" Armstrong asked, seeming not to hear the admonitions of his attorney instructing him not to say anything.

"Doesn't matter," Curtis answered. "You're a convicted sex offender. Under Chapter Sixty-two that makes what you did indefensible."

Armstrong buried his head in his hands.

Dean said, "Your previous conviction for indecency with a minor was a third-degree felony. This is the big time, Brad. It's a first-degree felony."

"Not to mention capital murder," Curtis chimed in.

Without acknowledging Curtis's statement, Dean proceeded. "You've paid dearly for your inappropriate and illegal behavior. You've lost jobs, the respect of your colleagues. You're in danger of losing your family."

The man's shoulders rose and fell in a harsh sob.

"Yet in spite of the costly consequences of your unacceptable behavior, you haven't stopped it."

"I've tried," he exclaimed. "God knows, I've tried. Ask Toni. She'll tell you. I love her. I love my kids. But . . . but I can't help myself."

Dean leaned forward again. "That's precisely my point. You can't help yourself. Melissa got you so hot tonight that when she said no, you flipped out. You grabbed her, shook her, slapped her around. You didn't want to, but you couldn't control the impulse, even knowing how much you were going to regret your actions later.

"Your desire to sexually dominate this girl shot your conscience and common sense all to hell. You had to have her, simple as that. Nothing else mattered. Not the punishment you would face when caught. Not even your love for Toni and your children could stop you. It's a compulsion you haven't learned to contain. It caused you to do what you did to Melissa tonight, and what you did to Janey."

"Do not respond," the lawyer said.

Dean lowered his voice another degree and spoke to Armstrong as though they were the only two people in the room. "I have a clear picture of what happened three nights ago, Brad. Here's this sexy, desirable girl who you thought was as enamored of you as you were of her. She'd been seeing you regularly, and you thought exclusively.

"That night, she goes down on you. And it's great, but you know she's insincere. You know she's a liar and a merciless tease. You know that she's waiting for her new interest to come along and replace you.

"When you confront her about it, she tells you to get lost. You've become jealous and possessive, and she can't stand your whining any longer. Did you honestly believe that she would give up other men for *you?* she asks. You poor, delusional slob.

"You get furious. You ask yourself, where does she get off treating me like this? Calling up Paris Gibson and talking about me on the radio? Who does she think she is?"

Dean's gaze held the suspect mesmerized. "When you got into

Janey's car that night, I don't think you had already plotted her kidnapping and murder. I think you'd planned only to confront her, have it out with her, clear the air.

"And maybe if she hadn't mocked you, that's the way it would have ended. But Janey laughed in your face. She emasculated you with her ridicule, insulted you in a way you couldn't tolerate. You lost it. You wanted to punish her. And that's what you did. You devised a punishment of sexual abuse, befitting what she'd done to you. You hurt her until you decided you'd had your vengeance, to hell with the deadline you gave Paris, and then you choked her to death."

Armstrong stared at Dean in stunned horror. He looked over at Curtis, whose visage remained unmoved and unchanged. Then, folding his arms on the table, he laid his head on them. In a tormented, cracking voice, he groaned, "Oh, God. Oh, *God*."

Curtis and Dean honored the attorney's demand to have a few minutes alone with his client and left the room. Curtis was smiling and rubbing his hands together, relishing the coup de grace.

"He hasn't signed a confession yet," Dean reminded him.

"It's a matter of pen and paper. By the way, you're good."

"Thanks," Dean said absently. This had been round one of what would probably be a lengthy and exhausting interrogation, but several things about it were nagging him. "I didn't ask him specifically if he'd heard Janey on the radio talking about the jealous lover she was about to dump."

"But you alluded to it and he didn't deny it."

"He denied calling Paris about Janey."

"Before we even asked, which says 'guilty' to me," the detective argued.

"He knew about Paris's connection because it was in the news. His phone records refute the allegation that he called her."

"There are several ways he could have placed those calls without it showing up on records."

"Making weird phone calls hasn't been part of Armstrong's MO before. Why now?"

"Maybe he needed a new thrill. The Valentino phone calls spiced things up for him, and at the same time wreaked havoc on

Paris. He wanted to get his kicks and get revenge. The calls accomplished both."

That made sense, but only after you massaged it into place. "Valentino's calls have a meanness to them that I just don't see in Armstrong. He's sick, but I don't think he's evil."

Curtis frowned at him irritably. "Forget motivation for a moment and consider some facts."

"Such as?"

"His occupation. He's a dentist."

"The chemical scouring," Dean said, musing out loud. The medical examiner had been able to confirm that, like Maddie Robinson, Janey's body had been astringently washed.

"Right. It's the kind of thing a medical man would do."

"It's the kind of thing a meticulous psychopath would do, too. Someone with a compulsion for scrubbing away his guilt."

"Armstrong straddles both categories."

Dean glanced over his shoulder at the closed door of the inter-rogation room. "Janey was restrained. She was tortured. She had bite marks, for godsake."

"We'll get impressions of his bite for comparison."

"My point is, none of Armstrong's priors involved violence or even hinted at a propensity for it. He was a creep, but he wasn't a violent creep."

"What is this, Malloy?" Curtis asked crossly. "His own *wife* told us that his violent tendencies had been escalating. *You* said that was a natural progression for his particular psychosis. Are you second-guessing yourself?"

"I know what I said, and I was right."

"Okay then. He knocked Melissa Hatcher around tonight."

"There's a wide gulf between knocking a woman around and torturing one before squeezing the breath out of her."

"Not in my book. And probably not in the book of the woman being knocked around."

"Don't be obtuse, Curtis," Dean said angrily. "I'm not excus-ing either. I'm just saying—"

"Ah, shit, I know what you're saying," Curtis grumbled, then expelled his frustration on a gust of breath. After a short pause that allowed tempers to cool, he asked, "Any more misgivings?"

"The photography."

"Armstrong admitted that he might have taken some pictures of Janey."

"'Some.' 'Might have.' He talked about the photography as though it was no big deal. Janey indicated otherwise. Before we start on Armstrong again, do you mind if I get Gavin in here and ask him more about this?"

Curtis shrugged. "I'm for whatever will help nail this guy."

Dean stepped into the corridor and motioned for Gavin. He got up, leaving Melissa sitting with a couple Dean assumed were her parents.

"What's up, Dad?" he asked. "Has he confessed?"

"Not yet. In the meantime, I'd like you to talk Sergeant Curtis and me through everything Janey told you about Valentino. Any detail you can remember. All right?"

"I already have, a dozen times."

"One more time. Please."

They found Curtis pouring himself a cup of coffee. He offered them one, but they declined. Curtis took a sip from his Styrofoam cup, then said, "At the risk of beating a dead horse, even an offhanded remark Janey might have made could be important, Gavin."

"I wish I could remember something else, sir. She told me the guy was older. Older than us, I mean. That he was cool, knew how a woman liked to be treated."

"We're mainly interested in the photography," Dean told him.

"She said he was a camera freak," Gavin said. "Lights, lenses, an elaborate setup. He posed her himself. Moved her around, you know, her arms and legs. Head. Everything."

"Could she have been exaggerating to impress you? Make you think of her as a model, like in *Penthouse?*"

"It's possible," he replied. "But if she was exaggerating, she sure did her homework, because she knew a lot about it. She mentioned shutter speeds, stuff like that. Said he tinkered with gadgets to get each picture just right, and would get mad if she didn't cooperate."

"He didn't just fire off a few naughty snapshots," Dean said to Curtis. "If you study the picture that Janey gave Gavin, you can tell it was taken by an amateur trying to be artistic."

"And you don't think Armstrong is capable of that?"

"Capable," Dean said. "But if you're out cheating on your wife, who is more than likely waiting up for you, do you take that much time with photography?"

While Curtis was still mulling that over, he happened to glance beyond Dean's shoulder. "What are you doing here?"

Dean turned to see who had caused Curtis's distraction and saw Officer Griggs coming toward them. The rookie's grin dissolved under Curtis's frown and tone of stern disapproval.

"I . . . I was given the all clear, sir. Told it was okay to leave. But I was anxious to know if Armstrong had confessed, so instead—"

"You left Paris out there alone?" Dean asked.

"Well, sir, not—"

"Who told you to leave?"

"John Rondeau."

From the corner of his eye, Dean noticed Gavin's reaction to the mention of Rondeau's name. He reacted not with the expected dislike, but with alarm.

"Gavin? What is it?" His son stared back at him, whey-faced. *"Gavin?"*

"Dad . . ." The boy had to swallow hard before he could continue. "There's something I've gotta tell you."

chapter thirty-four

Through the glass-block walls, the blue-white fluorescent lighting of the radio station's lobby relieved the surrounding darkness, but only marginally. Downtown city lights were obliterated by hills. The moon was too slender to shed significant light. At this time of night, only an occasional car sped past on the narrow state highway. The nearest commercial building was a convenience store a half mile away, and it had closed at ten.

From the vantage point of the FM 101.3 building, nothing was visible except hills dotted with cedar trees, limestone boulders, and an occasional herd of beef cattle. It was an ideal spot for the transmission tower that intermittently blinked its red lights as a warning to low-flying private aircraft.

Rondeau dawdled beside his car until the taillights of Griggs's patrol car disappeared behind a hill. He frowned with contempt for the officers driving away. Sure, he had wanted them to leave. But shouldn't they have verified the order, which he told them had come straight from Curtis, rather than taking his word for it? That kind of carelessness was unacceptable. Tomorrow he would report them. It wouldn't win him their regard, but one didn't advance one's career by making friends.

He started toward the entrance, carrying with him the folder of information on Stan Crenshaw. It painted a disturbing portrait of a man whose dysfunctional family and personal insecurities had led to sexual malfeasances dating back to childhood, which were credible harbingers of Valentino's aberrations.

What offended Rondeau most, however, was the injustice it signified. Crenshaw had gotten away with his misconduct. His uncle had bought him out of every scrape. By doing so, Wilkins Crenshaw had slowly created a monster capable of kidnapping, raping, torturing, and murdering a lovely young woman.

Because of his myopic focus on Brad Armstrong, Sergeant Curtis had dismissed the juicy contents of this folder. Initially Rondeau had taken offense at the snub, but it had actually worked to his advantage. Unwittingly, Curtis had handed him a golden opportunity to become everyone's hero.

Rather than press the buzzer, he knocked on the glass door.

He didn't have to wait long before getting his first look at the singularly unimpressive and unimposing Stan Crenshaw. He appeared out of a shadowed hallway off the lobby and approached the door warily, peering through the glass that, with the darkness beyond it, Rondeau knew would be reflecting like a mirror. Crenshaw did all but cup his hands around his eyes in order to see who had knocked.

He assessed Rondeau with the condescension of the born rich, then looked beyond him toward the parking lot, where the squad car was conspicuously missing. "Where're the policemen?"

Rondeau, already tasting success, held up his badge.

"That, of course, was Johnny Mathis with his classic, "Misty." Definitely music to nuzzle by. I hope you have someone near you tonight as you listen to 101.3, classic love songs. This is Paris Gibson bringing you up to midnight with Melissa Manchester's 'I Don't Know How to Love Him.' The phone lines are open. Call me."

When the song began, she disengaged her mike. Two of her phone lines were blinking. She pressed one of the buttons, but got a dial tone. Mentally she apologized to the caller who obviously had given up on being answered.

She pressed the second blinking light. "This is Paris."

"Hello, Paris."

Her heart actually stopped before a burst of adrenaline restarted it with the hard, fast pounding of a sprinter coming off the blocks. "Who is this?"

"You know who it is." His laugh was even more frightening than his whispery voice. "Your faithful fan Valentino."

Frantically she looked over her shoulder, hoping that perhaps Stan had silently rejoined her in the studio. She would have welcomed his sneaking up on her now. But she was alone in the room. "How—"

"I know, I know, your boyfriend thinks he's nabbed his culprit. His egotistical bungling would be comical if it weren't so pathetic." He laughed again, and it caused goose bumps to break out on her arms. "I've been a bad boy, haven't I, Paris?"

Her mouth had gone dry. Her heart continued to thump against her ribs and her pulse vibrated loudly against her eardrums. She ordered herself to calm down and *think*. She must alert Dean, Sergeant Curtis, Griggs outside, someone, that they had the wrong man in custody and that Valentino was still at large. But how?

What was she thinking? She had a microphone at her fingertips! Hundreds of thousands of people were tuned in.

But even as she reached for the mike switch, she reconsidered. Should she blurt out over the airwaves that the Austin PD had blundered? What if this call turned out to be a hoax, someone playing a cruel trick on her? What if she started a public panic?

Better to keep him talking until she could figure out what to do. "On top of everything else, you're a liar, Valentino. You moved up the deadline."

"That's true. I have no honor."

"You killed Janey before giving me a chance to rescue her."

"Unfair, wasn't it? But I never claimed to be honorable, Paris."

"Then why did you call me in the first place? If you intended to kill her all along, why set up this elaborate telephone campaign?"

"To rock your world. And it worked, didn't it? You feel positively rotten over your inability to save that slut's life."

Paris refused to buy into his baiting. She'd been down that path, and Janey had died anyway. The only way she could redeem herself would be to identify this son of a bitch and see him brought to justice, and that couldn't be done by arguing with him.

She could dial Dean on her cell phone, but—damn!—it was in her office, in her handbag. Could she create a technical problem that would alert Stan? Soon the Manchester song would end. It was the last in a series. Dead air would bring Stan into the studio to see what the problem was.

While she brainstormed, Valentino rambled. "She had to die, you see, for fucking me over. She was a heartless bitch. I enjoyed watching her die slowly. I could tell when she realized that she would never get away from me. She knew she wasn't going to survive."

"That must have been a real head trip for you."

"Oh, absolutely. Although it was actually heartrending the way her eyes silently pleaded with me to spare her life."

That statement made Paris forget her recent resolve not to be riled by anything he said. "You sick bastard."

"You think I'm sick?" he asked pleasantly. "I find that strange, Paris. I tortured and killed Janey, yes, but you tortured and killed your fiancé, didn't you? Wasn't it torture for him to learn about your unfaithfulness with his best friend? Do you think of yourself as sick?"

"I didn't drive Jack's car into a bridge abutment, he did. The accident was his fault. He determined his fate, not me."

"That sounds like a rationalization," he said in the reproving tone of a priest in the confessional. "I don't see the difference between your sin and mine, except that your fiancé's torture lasted much longer and he died much more slowly. Which makes you much crueler than me, doesn't it? And that's why you must be punished.

"Would it be just to let you go on your merry way and live happily ever after with Malloy? I don't think so," he said in a nasty singsong. "That is not going to happen. You will never be together because you, Paris, are going to die. Tonight."

The line went dead. Instantly she reached for her hot-line

phone. No dial tone. Nothing. Silence. In quick succession, she tried all the phone lines, but to no avail. They were dead.

Realization crept over her like an encroaching shadow. Either he had the access and ability to disable computerized telephone equipment from off the premises or—and this is what she feared—he had simply interrupted telephone service from inside the building.

She shot from her stool. Yanking open the heavily padded door, she shouted down the dark corridor, "Stan!"

The Manchester song was winding down. Racing back to the control board, she punched her mike button. "Hello, this is Paris Gibson." Her voice sounded thin and high, not at all like her normal contralto. "This is not a—"

The sound of a high-pitched alarm interrupted her.

She swung her gaze toward the source. The sound was coming from the scanner, which recorded everything that went out over the air. You never knew it was there, really. The alarm only alerted you to an interruption in transmission.

Terror seizing her, she punched her mike button repeatedly, but, like all the others on the board, it refused to light up.

Again she lunged for the door. "Stan!" The echo of her scream seemed to chase her as she ran toward her office. Her handbag was where she'd left it on her desk, but it had been toppled onto its side. The contents had been spilled onto her desk. With shaking hands, she riffled through cosmetics, tissues, loose change, hoping to find her cell phone, but knowing it wouldn't be there.

It wasn't.

And something else was missing—her keys.

Frantically she searched through the mail scattered across her desk and even dropped to her knees and looked beneath it, but she knew that both her key ring and her phone had been taken by the same individual who had cut the phone lines and shut down transmission. All lines of communication had been severed by the man who had killed Janey and had promised to kill her.

Valentino.

Her breathing was so harsh, she couldn't hear anything else. She held it for several moments in order to listen. She crept to the open door of her office but hesitated at the threshold. The hallway, as always, was dim. Tonight the familiar darkness gave her no sense of security and comfort. It had a sinister quality, maybe because the building was as silent as a tomb.

Where was Stan? Hadn't he noticed that they weren't broadcasting? If he had checked the studio and discovered she wasn't there, why wasn't he going through the building calling for her, checking to see what had happened?

But even before her mind could completely form that question, it had arrived at the answer: Stan was unable to come and check on her.

Valentino had dispatched him, possibly even before he had called her. He could have been in the building for quite some time before she'd know of it, sealed as she'd been inside the soundproof room.

How had Valentino gotten past Griggs and Carson? Once he had, how had he opened the door to the building? A key was needed to unlock the dead bolt from either side. Had he persuaded Stan to open the door? How?

Questions for which she had no answers.

She was tempted to slam her office door, lock herself inside, and wait for help to arrive. Already, listeners all over the hill country would be wondering what had caused the station to go off the air. Dean might even know. Sergeant Curtis. Soon somebody would be rushing to her rescue.

But in the meantime, she couldn't hide herself in here. Griggs and Carson could be hurt. And Stan.

She stepped out into the hallway. Putting her back to the wall so she could see in both directions, she inched along it, toward the front of the building. As she moved along the corridor, she turned off every light switch she passed. One distinct advantage she had over Valentino was knowing the layout of the building. She was accustomed to navigating it in semidarkness.

Moving quickly, but as silently and cautiously as possible, she made her way toward the entrance. She approached each intersection of hallways with the fear of what awaited her around the corner, but when she turned the last one, the stretch of hall between her and the well-lighted lobby was clear. She raced down it and across the lobby, intent on launching herself against the door and pounding on the glass in order to get the attention of the policemen guarding her.

But the squad car wasn't there and the front door was bolted.

With a soft cry, she backed away from the door until she came up against the receptionist's desk. She rested against it to catch her breath and decide what to do.

Suddenly her ankle was grabbed. She screamed.

She looked down to see a man's hand reaching from beneath the desk. But before she could even try to work herself free of his grasp, the fingers relaxed and the hand fell lifelessly to the grimy carpet.

Stumbling over her own feet, she rounded the desk but drew up short when she saw the form lying facedown on the floor. She dropped to her knees and took the man by the shoulder, turning him over.

John Rondeau groaned. His eyelids were fluttering but remained closed. He was bleeding profusely from a wound on his head.

Gladness surged through her as she gasped his name. "John. Please, wake up. Please!" She slapped his cheek smartly, but he only groaned again, his head lolling to one side. He was unconscious.

Just beyond the reach of his outstretched hand lay an official-looking file folder. She read the name typed on the identifying tab: *Stanley Crenshaw.*

Her stomach dropped. "Oh my God."

Stan? It had been Stan all along?

But why not? she reasoned. His ineptitude could be an excellent guise. He had the time and opportunity to commit the crimes. His days were free and so were his nights before and after her program. He had just enough technical knowledge to reroute telephone calls. He was an electronics and gadget junky. Surely among all his toys was camera equipment he could easily afford. He was attractive enough to lure a thrill-seeking teenager.

And he had a lifetime's worth of anger and resentment pent

up, more than sufficient motivation to kill a woman who had spurned him. And with chilling clarity, Paris realized that just tonight she, too, had rejected him.

"Help will be here soon," she whispered to Rondeau. He didn't respond. He'd slipped deeper into unconsciousness. The policeman was out of commission and she was on her own.

But she wasn't going to wait for Valentino to find her. She was going to find him.

Quickly, she patted down Rondeau's clothing. She didn't know if computer cops were armed or not, but she hoped so. She didn't like guns, was revolted by the whole idea of guns, but she would use one if she had to in order to save her life.

She exhaled her relief when she felt a bulge beneath his jacket. She flipped it back only to discover that the holster clipped to his belt was empty.

Stan must have had the same idea. He was armed.

After murmuring another assurance to Rondeau that he would be all right—which she hoped was true—she cautiously abandoned the false security of hiding behind the desk.

As she left the lobby, she switched off the fluorescent lighting, although it occurred to her that Stan knew the building as well as she, so the darkness was no longer her exclusive advantage.

Actually, she wasn't going to hide any longer. She and Stan were in the building alone together, as they had been hundreds of nights before. She wasn't going to play a childish cat-and-mouse game with him. If she went on the offensive and confronted him, she was confident she could talk to him long enough for rescue to arrive.

The engineering room was empty, so was the men's rest room and the snack room. All the offices, including her own, were deserted. Gradually she made her way to the very back of the building, where there was a large storeroom. The door to it was closed.

The metal knob felt cold in her hand when she grasped it and pushed the door open. She was met by the dank smell of disuse and oldness. The room was cavernous, darker even than the rest of the building. The open doorway cast a wedge of light across the concrete floor, but it was so faint as to be negligible.

Paris hesitated on the threshold until her eyes could adjust to this deeper darkness. When they did she noticed the walk-in closet where Lancy/Marvin's custodial equipment and supplies were stored. The door to it was ajar. Listening intently, she was certain she heard the sound of breathing coming from inside it.

"Stan, this is silly. Come on out. Stop this craziness before anyone else is hurt, including yourself."

Gathering all her courage, she entered the storeroom. "I know you've got a gun now, but I don't believe you'll shoot me. If you had wanted to kill me, you could have on any given night."

Had the breathing inside the closet become more agitated? Or was she imagining it? Or was it an echo of her own breathing she was hearing?

"I know you're angry with me for spurning your affections, but until tonight, I didn't even know you felt that way about me. Let's talk about it."

As she tiptoed across the concrete floor, toward the closet, her ears strained to listen for the merest sound beyond the walls, indicating the arrival of help. Even now, were marksmen taking up positions? Were special tactical officers scaling the exterior walls to get onto the roof? Or had she seen too many action movies?

When she was still a few feet from the partially open closet door, she paused. "Stan?" Reaching far out in front of her, she pushed the door open all the way.

No gunshots shattered the stillness. She reminded herself of what he had done to Janey. Now that he knew he was caught, he would be desperate, conscienceless, capable of anything. The situation required training she didn't have. Dean did.

Dean. In fear and longing, her heart silently cried his name as she took the final step that placed her in the open doorway.

At the sight of Stan, she stared in bafflement.

He was breathing heavily through his nostrils because his mouth was sealed closed with duct tape that had also been used to bind his ankles and wrists. His legs were bent so that his knees were up under his chin, and he had literally been stuffed into the industrial-size stainless-steel sink.

"Stan! What . . ." She was reaching out to tear the tape off his mouth when his eyes, already wide with terror, looked beyond her and stretched even wider.

She spun around.

"Surprise!" John Rondeau said.

But it was Valentino's voice.

chapter thirty-five

"*F*uck it, fuck it," Dean repeated as he punched the rubberized digits on his cell phone.

He was steering his car with one hand and using his cell phone with the other. Several times he had redialed the hot-line number Paris had given him. She didn't answer. He dialed the radio station call-in number repeatedly, but kept getting the standard recording saying that Paris would be with him as soon as possible. He called her cell number, but got her voice mail.

"Why didn't you tell me about Rondeau?" Curtis, who was riding shotgun, was also on his cell phone. He had been put on hold, awaiting more information on John Rondeau.

"You heard it when I did."

The detective had been standing right beside him when Gavin revealed what he knew about Rondeau. It would be difficult to say who had moved first. Dean remembered shoving Curtis out of his way as he ran for the exit.

He had gained a little ground when Curtis shouted over his shoulder for units to be dispatched to the radio station. "SWAT, too! Now, now, move it!"

Dean wasn't going to hang around and see that the sergeant's orders were carried out, and apparently Curtis shared his urgency. They burst through the double doors and clambered down the staircase, taking two or three stairs at a time until they reached the garage level. Dean's car was parked the closest. The way he was pushing it now, they would beat the squad cars to the radio station.

"You failed to tell me Rondeau had accosted your kid in the bathroom."

"It was personal. I thought he was just an asshole."

"An asshole with—" Curtis broke off and listened. "Yeah, yeah," he said into the phone, "what've you got?"

While Curtis was getting the scoop on John Rondeau, Dean dialed Paris's numbers again. When he got the same result, he cursed lavishly and pressed his foot harder against the accelerator.

In what seemed like a direct correlation to his stamping on the gas pedal, the car radio went silent. Since his ears had been attuned to listen for Paris's voice, the sudden static hiss was as jarring as a blood-curdling scream.

The implication splintered his control. Viciously he punched the buttons on his radio dial. All other stations came through loud and clear. The radio wasn't malfunctioning; 101.3 had stopped transmitting.

"The station just went off the air."

Curtis, who'd been absorbed in his conversation, turned his head. "Huh?"

"She's off the air. She's stopped broadcasting."

"Jesus." Then into his cell phone Curtis said, "That'll do for now." He clicked off.

"What? Talk to me," Dean said as he took a corner practically on two wheels.

"No father in the Rondeau household. Ever. They're checking now to see if he died during John's infancy, or if there ever was a Mr. Rondeau. No significant male role model, like an uncle, scoutmaster—"

"I got it, go on."

"Mother worked to support John and his sister, older by one year."

"What have they got to say about him?"

"Nothing. Both are deceased."

Dean whipped his head toward Curtis. "He referred to them in the present tense."

"They were murdered in their home when John was fourteen. He discovered the bodies. Sister had been drowned in the bathtub. Mother had an ice pick shoved straight through her medulla while she was napping."

"Who did it?"

"Unknown. It's a cold case."

"Not anymore." Dean's fingers tensed around the steering wheel.

"We don't know that," Curtis said, reading Dean's thought. "He was interrogated, but never really considered a suspect. Mom and kids were devoted to each other. Mother worked hard to support them. Brother and sister were latch-key kids. Reliant on each other. Very close."

"I'll bet," Dean said tightly. "Real close."

"You're thinking incest?"

"Valentino's behavior is symptomatic. Why wasn't all this in Rondeau's record?"

"The facts are. APD carefully screens every applicant."

"But no one looked beyond the tragedy of his losing his whole family. Nobody was looking for incest. What happened to young John after the double murder?"

"Foster care. Lived with the same couple until he was old enough to go it alone."

"Other children in that home?"

"No."

"Luckily. Did he get along with the foster dad?"

"No record of any problems. They doted on him."

"Especially the wife."

"Don't know," Curtis said. "But they gave him a glowing review. Said he was an ideal child. Respectful. Well behaved."

"A lot of psychopaths are."

"He had an excellent academic record," Curtis continued. "No problems at school. Went to two years of college before he applied to the police academy. Wanted to become a cop—"

"Let me guess. To prevent other women from dying the way his mother and sister had."

"More or less." Curtis glanced at him. "One tiny detail . . ."

"Yeah?"

"When she died, the sister was five months pregnant."

Dean risked giving him a questioning look.

"No," Curtis said. "They checked. It wasn't Rondeau's baby."

"I could have told you it wasn't," Dean said grimly. "That's why he killed her."

Curtis's cell phone rang. "Yeah," he snapped.

Dean could see the lights on the broadcast tower. What were they, a mile away? Two? He was tailgating the SWAT van. It had caught up with them several miles back and Dean had let it pass them.

The van was speeding, but Dean willed the driver to move it even faster. They were the two lead vehicles in a motorcade that included several police units. Bringing up the rear was an ambulance. He tried not to think about that.

Curtis ended his call. "They went into Rondeau's apartment. Wasn't much of a place, but he had some fancy photographic equipment. Albums chockfull of dirty pictures. Lots of Janey. Long blond hairs visible on the bedding. He's our guy."

Dean stared straight ahead, clenching his teeth so hard it made his jaw ache.

Curtis checked the pistol he carried in a belt holster, and a second one in an ankle holster. "You got a piece?"

Dean gave him a brusque nod. "I started carrying when he started threatening Paris."

"Well enough, but listen to me. When we get there, you're gonna keep out of the way and let those guys up there do their job." He nodded toward the SWAT van. "You got it?"

"I got it. Sergeant."

The reminder of their respective ranks wasn't lost on Curtis, but he didn't back down. "You go in there half cocked, you'll do something that would fuck up our arrest and he'd walk on some legal bullshit technicality."

"I said I got it," Dean said testily.

"So you're cool?"

"I'm cool."

394 · SANDRA BROWN

Curtis slipped the pistol back into his ankle holster, muttering, "Like hell you are."

Dean said, "Right. If he's hurt Paris, I'm going to kill him."

She gaped at John Rondeau's grinning face, but her astonishment was only momentary. Then she reacted swiftly. With all her strength she pushed against his chest, but he shoved her against the metal shelving in the closet even as he fired his pistol at Stan.

The report deafened her. Or maybe it was her own scream.

Rondeau slapped her. "Shut up!" Grabbing her by the hair, he dragged her from the closet and kicked it closed with his foot. Then he pushed her with such impetus that she pitched forward onto the concrete floor.

"Hello, Paris," he said in the chilling voice she now knew well.

"Did you kill him?"

"Crenshaw? I hope so. That was the point of firing a bullet straight into his heart. What a loser. But stronger than he looks. He actually gave me this," he said, indicating the bleeding scalp wound. "He was obliging at first. Showed me how to stop transmission. At gunpoint, of course. Then he made this ridiculous but very valorous attempt to protect you by hitting me with a bottle of Snapple." He was still speaking in Valentino's voice.

"The voice . . . that's quite a trick."

"Isn't it? On the outside chance that any of my cop buddies were also Paris Gibson fans, I didn't want them to identify my voice when I called in."

"You were Valentino from the start." Her mouth was so dry, her tongue was sticking to the roof of her mouth on each word.

"Yes. That takes us back to . . . Let's see." He scratched his cheek with the barrel of his pistol. "Sometime before Maddie Robinson came along."

"So that makes two women you've killed."

He smiled indulgently. "Actually no, Paris."

"More than that?"

"Un-huh."

Keep him talking. The longer he talks, the longer you'll live.
"Why did you kill them?"

Resuming his normal voice, he said, "Because they didn't deserve to live."

"They cheated on you like Janey did."

"Janey, Maddie, my sister."

"You murdered your sister?"

"It wasn't *murder*. I meted out justice."

"I see. What happened? What did your sister do to you?"

He laughed pleasantly. "Everything. We did everything to each other. I slept between them, you see. Between her and my mother. Get the picture?" He bobbed his eyebrows up and down.

He'd wanted to shock her and he had, but she tried to keep her expression impassive. She wouldn't give him the satisfaction of seeing her revulsion.

"We kept it all in the family. Our little secret," he said in a stage whisper. "'Don't tell,' Mommy warned us. 'Because if you tell, they'll take you away and lock you up where they keep bad little boys and girls who play with each other's pee pees. Promise? Good. Now suck Mommy's titties and she'll do something extra-special nice to you.'"

Nausea rose in Paris's throat.

He continued in his blasé manner. "But then we begin to grow up. Sis gets an after-school job at a record store. She's there every afternoon instead of at home with me doing what we loved doing best. She starts staying later at the store so she can be with one of the guys who works there. She doesn't have time for me anymore.

"She's never in the mood. She says she's too tired, but it's really because she's fucking him all the time. And Mommy thinks it's grand, the way Sis has fallen in love. 'Isn't it romantic and aren't you happy for her, Johnny?'"

He lapsed into a brooding silence, then his chest heaved as though he were about to cry. "I loved them."

Taking advantage of his preoccupation, Paris glanced toward the door, gauging the distance.

His laughter brought her eyes back up to him. "Don't even

think about it, Paris. This little stroll down memory lane hasn't distracted me from what I came to do."

"If you kill me . . ."

"Oh, I am going to kill you, but it'll be blamed on Stan Crenshaw."

"He's dead."

"As a doornail. I had to kill him. See, when I got here, I found you already dead, choked to death by Crenshaw, who'd been a twisted, sick fucker from the time he was a kid. It's all there in his file, the recipe for a sexually deviant psychopath.

"Anyhow, I sized up the situation and tried to apprehend him. During the ensuing struggle, he managed to get in one good one on my noggin, which, by the way, inspired that little trick I played on you. Clever, wasn't it? You were completely taken in, weren't you?"

"Yes," she admitted.

"Sorry, but I couldn't resist. Especially the bit with your ankle," he said, chuckling. "Where was I? Oh, yes, the way I'll tell it is that I was finally able to subdue Crenshaw and was binding his ankles and hands with duct tape I found in the closet when he attempted to escape. Sadly, I had no choice but to shoot him."

"Very tidy," she said. "But not perfect. The crime scene experts will find discrepancies."

"I've got answers for any questions that could arise."

"Are you sure you've thought of everything, John?"

"I've done my research. I'm a good cop."

"Who preys on women."

"I never 'preyed' on them. My mother and sister were hardly victims. They were my coaches. Every woman I've been with since has benefited from what they taught me, and all were willing partners. I wasn't even particularly attracted to Maddie at first. But she kept after me. Then she was the one who wanted to break if off. Go figure." He shook his head with disbelief.

"And if you're referring to the girls in the Sex Club as prey, you haven't been paying attention. They're whores looking for adventure. I have no inhibitions. They love me," he whispered, waggling his tongue at her.

Again, she swallowed her nausea. "Apparently Janey didn't love you."

"Janey didn't love anybody except Janey. But she loved what I did to her. She was a heartless little bitch who used people's emotions for target practice. And you sympathized with her, Paris. You put her on the radio to complain about me. Do you know why? Because you're exactly like her.

"You play with people's emotions, too. You think you're hot shit. You've got Malloy, even Curtis, panting after you, begging for any crumb of attention you might toss them."

Suddenly he checked his wristwatch. "Speaking of Malloy, I'd better get down to business. You've been off the air for five minutes."

Five minutes? It seemed like an eternity.

"Folks are going to start noticing, and I'm sure your psychologist friend will come charging in here like the cavalry and—"

From the front of the building came what sounded like an explosion of breaking glass, followed by shouting voices and running footsteps.

Paris kicked Rondeau in the kneecap as hard as she could.

His leg buckled beneath him and he screamed in pain.

Paris scrambled to her feet and made a dash for the door.

She didn't hear the gunshot until after she felt the impact of it.

It was more forceful than she could ever have imagined. The searing pain that followed stole her breath and almost caused her to black out instantly, but adrenaline kept her running, through the door, out of his line of sight, where she collapsed.

She tried to cry out and alert the police to her location, but she was unable to utter more than a faint moan. Blackness closed in around her, until the dim corridor elongated and narrowed, like the tunnel of a nightmare.

Dean would be leading the charge. Even Rondeau had said so. She must warn him. She tried to pull herself up, but her limbs had turned to jelly and she wanted badly to throw up. She opened her mouth to call out, but her well-trained, carefully cultivated voice failed her completely.

Rondeau was coming nearer the door. She could hear his

groans of pain as he hopped across the cement floor of the storeroom. Soon he would reach the hallway. He would have the advantage over anyone coming around the blind corner at the end of it.

"Dean," she croaked. Once more she tried to stand. She made it as far as her knees, but she swayed unsteadily, then collapsed against the wall, hard. The resultant pain was like a branding iron burning through flesh, all the way to the bone. She left a blood trail on the wall as she sank to the floor.

Though her ears were ringing, she could tell that the shouting voices were coming closer. Flashlight beams crazily crisscrossed on the walls at the end of the hallway.

But hearing another sound, she turned just as Rondeau appeared in the storeroom doorway. He grunted with pain as he braced himself against the doorjamb. She took satisfaction from the odd angle at which his right leg was bent. His face was bathed in sweat and twisted into an ugly mask of rage as he glared down at her.

"You're just like them," he said. "I've got to kill you."

"*Freeze!*" The shout ricocheted off the walls like the beams of the flashlights.

But Rondeau didn't heed the warning. He raised his pistol and aimed it directly at her.

The barrage of gunfire was deafening and filled the corridor with smoke.

As she fell forward, Paris wondered vaguely if she was just losing consciousness, or dying.

chapter thirty-six

"Who actually brought him down?"

"Call it a group effort. Rondeau gave us no choice. Several of us hit him."

Paris leaned back against the hospital bed pillow, relieved by Curtis's answer to her question. She wouldn't have wanted Dean to carry the burden of taking John Rondeau's life. She learned later that he'd been the first one into the hallway, as she had known he would be. But Curtis and several SWAT officers were there, too. Any of the bullets fired at Rondeau could have been the fatal one.

This morning Curtis was looking even spiffier than usual, as though he had dressed up to pay her this visit. He was wearing a gray western-cut suit. His boots had an extra sheen. She could smell cologne. He had brought her a box of Godiva chocolates.

Yet his demeanor was all business. "Rondeau was computer savvy enough to learn how to reroute calls," he told her. "Our guys finally traced that last call to a cell phone. But he had planned on that, too. The phone was unregistered. A throwaway. That part of it was easy for him."

"He could change his voice at will, too. It was eerie."

Sometimes minutes would pass without her thinking of Rondeau and that agonizing period of time with him in the store-room. Then, without warning, a recollection would thrust itself into her consciousness and she would be forced to relive the terrifying moments.

When she described this phenomenon to Dean, he assured her that each day the recollections would become less frequent and her memory would dim a bit more. Although she would never entirely forget the experience, it would sink into her subconscious. His counsel had a footnote: He would see to it that she lived in the present, and for the future, not linger in the past.

"Rondeau wanted to move to CIB," Curtis was saying. "He had already approached me about it. Said he wanted to work in the child abuse unit."

"Where he would have unlimited access to child pornography."

Curtis nodded, his disgust plain. "He went to the radio station that night to fulfill his personal agenda, and at the same time distinguish himself as a police officer by delivering Valentino.

"With you and Crenshaw dead, he might have pulled it off. Janey's body rendered none of the perp's DNA. Apparently he'd learned about an agent that served that purpose in a homicide case in Dallas." He shook his head with chagrin. "His police work taught him well."

"About Stan, have you received any updates on his condition?" she asked.

"Elevated to fair."

Miraculously Stan had survived the gunshot to his chest and the delicate surgery that had removed the bullet. He'd had a collapsed lung and extensive tissue damage, but he would survive. When he was stable enough to be moved, Wilkins Crenshaw had flown him by private jet to Atlanta.

"I asked his uncle to call me as soon as Stan is able to talk on the phone," she said. "I want to apologize."

"I'm sure he won't hold a grudge against you. He'll be too grateful to be alive."

"Rondeau told me he had shot Stan straight through the heart."

"If that's where he was aiming, he should've spent more time at the practice range," Curtis said with a grim smile. "Lucky for you he didn't."

She'd been told that her blood loss was significant because

the bullet had entered her back just below her shoulder socket and had gone straight through. She would bear an ugly scar and her scorching tennis serve was a thing of the past, but she was alive.

If the bullet had cut a path a few inches lower, her life would have been over. Dean had advised her not to dwell on that either, although it was the common reaction of a survivor.

"Don't examine the reasons for your life being spared, Paris. To do so is futile. You could never arrive at an answer. Just be grateful you're here. I am," he'd said, his voice made husky by emotion.

Curtis brought her back to their conversation by saying that the incestuous relationships of Rondeau's boyhood had left him angry. "I don't think even he knew how angry he was," he said. "He'd learned to hide it well, but he harbored a deep-seated rage against women because of what an abusive mother had done to him."

"Dean explained it to me."

"I'm paraphrasing him," Curtis admitted. After a beat, he asked if she'd seen that morning's newspaper. "Judge Kemp is using Janey's murder as part of his campaign platform."

"That goes beyond tasteless."

"Some people," the detective snuffled with contempt.

"What's going to happen to Brad Armstrong?" she asked. "Will he go to prison?"

"He has to face the aggravated-sexual-assault charge, which carries a stiff sentence if he's convicted. But Melissa Hatcher admitted that she went with him willingly and engaged in numerous acts before she called a halt. He might plead to a lesser charge in exchange for a lighter sentence, but I predict that he'll serve time. Hopefully he'll use that time to get himself straightened out."

"I wonder if his wife will stay with him." Her eyes strayed to the floral arrangement Toni Armstrong had sent.

"Remains to be seen," Curtis said. "But if I was a gambling man, I'd say yes." They were quiet for a moment, then he slapped his thighs and, with a sigh, stood. "I should shove off and let you rest."

She laughed. "I've rested until I'm blue in the face. I can't wait to be released."

"Anxious to get back to work?"

"By next week I hope."

"Your fans will be happy. So will the hospital staff. They said every flower within a hundred-mile radius is in the main lobby downstairs."

"Dean wheeled me down there yesterday to see them. People have been exceptionally kind."

"Speaking for myself, I've missed listening to you." His entire scalp flushed a bright pink as he added, "You're a class act, Paris."

"Thank you. So are you, Sergeant Curtis."

A bit awkwardly, he reached for her right hand and gave it only one swift shake before releasing it. "I'm sure I'll be seeing you around. I mean, now that you and Malloy . . ." He let the sentence trail off.

She smiled. "Yes, I'm sure I'll be seeing you around."

Dean arrived just as she was adding the finishing touches to her makeup.

"Paris?"

"In here," she called from the small bathroom. He moved in behind her and their eyes met in the mirror above the basin. "How do I look?"

"Luscious."

She frowned dubiously at her reflection. "Hair styling isn't easy to accomplish one-handed. At least it's my left one that's out of commission."

He reached for her right hand, the back of which was bruised from the IV port that had been removed only the day before. He kissed the discolored spot. "To me you look fantastic."

"Your opinion definitely counts." She turned to face him, but when he only pecked her lips, she looked up at him with disappointment.

"I don't want to hurt you," he explained, indicating her bandaged arm and sling.

"I won't break."

With her right hand, she pulled his head down and gave him a real kiss, which he responded to in kind. They kissed with sexual passion, as well as with the desperation of knowing that they'd almost lost each other for the second time.

When they pulled apart, she said, "I received a get-well card from Liz Douglas. Very gracious of her under the circumstances."

"She's a lady. There was only one thing wrong with her. She wasn't you."

They kissed again, then, leaving his lips against hers, he whispered, "When we get home . . ."

"Um-huh?"

"Can we go straight to bed?"

"Will you do—"

"Everything. We're gonna do everything." He gave her a hard, quick kiss, then said, "Let's get out of here."

They gathered the last of her personal things and placed them in a tote bag. She put on her sunglasses. He ordered her into the hospital-mandated wheelchair and pushed her to the elevator.

As they were riding down to the ground floor, she said, "I expected Gavin to be with you."

"He sends his regards, but he left for Houston this morning to spend the weekend with Pat. He hopes to patch things up with her. Maybe even offer an olive branch to her husband."

"Good for him."

"He didn't fool me."

"You don't believe he's sincere?"

"Oh, he's sincere about setting things right with them. But he chose to go this particular weekend so we'd have time alone." As the elevator doors slid open, he leaned down and whispered directly into her ear, "I owe him."

Returning his grin, she said, "So do I."

"You are going to marry me, aren't you?"

Feigning affront, she said, "I wouldn't consent to a honeymoon otherwise."

"Gavin will be glad. He wants to make friends at his new

school, and he told me what an advantage it would be to have a stepmom who was famous and also a total fox."

"He thinks I'm a fox?"

"Cool, too. You've got his unqualified approval."

"It's nice to be wanted."

Humor aside, Dean stepped around to the front of her chair and leaned down until his face was level with hers. "I want you."

They had an audience comprised of hospital staff and visitors in the lobby. Unmindful of them, he reached for her hand again and this time pressed her palm to his lips. They exchanged a look rife with meaning and implication, then he let go of her hand and said, "Ready?"

"Ready."

"Be forewarned, Paris. You'll be running a gauntlet. There are cameras galore outside that door. Every news outlet from Dallas to Houston to El Paso has a reporter and a photographer here to cover your hospital release. You're big news."

"I know."

"And that's okay?"

"It's okay. In fact"—she removed her sunglasses and smiled up at him—"it's time I came out into the light."

Grinning, he pushed the wheelchair toward the automatic doors. They slid open and camera strobes began to flash.

Paris didn't flinch.

acknowledgments

I really hate having to ask people for help and information. An autographed copy of the book and an acknowledgment in the back of it seem insufficient thanks for all the trouble these professionals went to on my behalf.

Public Information Specialist C, Laura Albrecht of the Austin Police Department never lost patience with me, even when I continued calling her with just "one more question." She opened doors that would ordinarily have been closed. Thanks also to the detectives of the Centralized Investigative Bureau, who all too frequently go unrewarded and unrecognized for the difficult job they perform. They were cordial and informative even after I explained to them that there was a rotten cop in my story.

In my next life, I want to be a drive-time deejay like Bill Kinder of KSCS-FM. Unlike me, he gets to talk to his fans every weekday. They call in by the hundreds. What a kick! He made it look easy to do a dozen tasks at once. He never broke stride, not even to answer my questions. If I got the radio technology all wrong, it's no fault of his.

A few unfortunates work with me on a daily basis. My agent, Maria Carvainis, deserves more gratitude than I'll ever be able to express. Amie Gray's middle name should be Britannica for her diligent fact checking and her gleaning of information on the most outlandish topics. I also wish to thank Sharon Hubler for the years that she streamlined my life. Without her I would often have been at the wrong place at the wrong time, doing the wrong thing. I wish her much happiness in her new life.

And to the dear man who lives with me: Michael, my thanks and my love, always.

Sandra Brown
1 April 2003